SEDUCTION
—— and ——
SURRENDER

Two novels in one volume

SEDUCTION

—— and ——

SURRENDER

Two novels in one volume

AMANDA QUICK

WINGS BOOKS
NEW YORK

Originally published as two volumes by Bantam Books under the titles:
Seduction copyright © 1990 by Jayne A. Krentz
Surrender copyright © 1990 by Jayne A. Krentz

This 2004 edition is published by Wings Books®, an imprint of
Random House Value Publishing, a division of Random House, Inc.,
New York, by arrangement with The Bantam Dell Publishing Group,
a division of Random House, Inc.

Wings Books® and colophon are trademarks of Random House, Inc.

Random House
New York • Toronto • London • Sydney • Auckland
www.randomhouse.com

Printed and bound in the United States

Library of Congress Cataloging-in-Publication Data

Quick, Amanda.
    [Seduction]
    Seduction and Surrender : two novels in one volume / Amanda Quick.
       p. cm.
    ISBN 0-517-22353-8
    1. London (England)—Fiction. 2. Yorkshire (England)—Fiction. I. Quick,
Amanda. Surrender II. Title.

PS3561.R44S44 2004
813'.54—dc22

                                                          2003066098

10 9 8 7 6 5 4 3

Contents

SEDUCTION

ONE

Julian Richard Sinclair, Earl of Ravenwood, listened in stunned disbelief as his formal offer of marriage was rejected. On the heels of disbelief came a cold, controlled anger. *Who did the lady think she was*, he wondered. Unfortunately, he could not ask her. The lady had chosen to absent herself. Julian's generous offer was being rejected on her behalf by her obviously uncomfortable grandfather.

"Devil take it, Ravenwood, I don't like this any better than you do. Thing is, the girl's not a young chit straight out of the schoolroom," Lord Dorring explained morosely. "Used to be an amiable little thing. Always eager to please. But she's three and twenty now and during the past few years she seems to have developed a considerable will of her own. Dashed annoying at times, but there it is. Can't just order her about these days."

"I am aware of her age," Julian said dryly. "I was led to believe that because of it she would be a sensible, tractable sort of female."

"Oh, she is," Lord Dorring sputtered. "Most definitely

she is. Don't mean to imply otherwise. She's no addle-brained young twit given to hysterics or anything of that sort." His florid, bewhiskered face was flushed with evident dismay. "Normally she's very good-natured. Very amenable. A perfect model of, uh, feminine modesty and grace."

"Feminine modesty and grace," Julian repeated slowly.

Lord Dorring brightened. "Precisely, m'lord. Feminine modesty and grace. Been a great prop to her grandmother since the death of our youngest son and his wife a few years back. Sophy's parents were lost at sea the year she turned seventeen, you know. She and her sister came to live with us. I'm sure you recall." Lord Dorring cleared his throat with a cough. "Or perhaps it escaped your notice. You were somewhat occupied with, uh, other matters at the time."

Other matters being a polite euphemism for finding himself helplessly ensnared in the coils of a beautiful witch named Elizabeth, Julian reflected. "If your granddaughter is such a paragon of all the sensible virtues, Dorring, what seems to be the problem with convincing her to accept my offer?"

"My fault entirely, her grandmother assures me." Lord Dorring's bushy brows drew together in an unhappy frown. "I fear I've allowed her to read a great deal. And all the wrong sort of thing, I'm told. But one doesn't tell Sophy what to read, you know. Can't imagine how any man could accomplish that. More claret, Ravenwood?"

"Thank you. I believe I could use another glass." Julian eyed his red-faced host and forced himself to speak calmly. "I confess I do not quite understand, Dorring. What have Sophy's reading habits got to do with anything?"

"Fear I haven't always kept a close watch on what she was reading," Lord Dorring muttered, gulping his claret. "Young women pick up notions, you know, if you don't keep a watch on what they read. But after the death of her sister three years ago, I didn't want to press Sophy too hard. Her grandmother and I are quite fond of her. She really is a reasonable girl. Can't think what's gotten into her head to refuse you. I'm sure she would change her mind if she just had a little more time."

"Time?" Ravenwood's brows rose with ill-concealed sarcasm.

"You must admit you've rushed things a trifle. Even my wife says that. We tend to go about this sort of thing more slowly out here in the country. Not used to town ways, you know. And women, even sensible women, have these damn romantic notions about how a man ought to go on." Lord Dorring eyed his guest with a hopeful air. "Perhaps if you could allow her a few more days to consider your offer?"

"I would like to talk to Miss Dorring, myself," Julian said.

"Thought I explained. Not in at the moment. Gone out riding. Visits Old Bess on Wednesdays."

"I am aware of that. She was informed that I would be calling at three, I assume."

Lord Dorring coughed again to clear his throat. "I, er, believe I mentioned it. Undoubtedly slipped her mind. You know how young women are." He glanced at the clock. "Should be back by half past four."

"Unfortunately, I cannot wait." Julian set down his glass and got to his feet. "You may inform your granddaughter that I am not a patient man. I had hoped to get this marriage business settled today."

"I believe she thinks it is settled, my lord," Lord Dorring said sadly.

"You may inform her that I do not consider the matter finished. I will call again tomorrow at the same time. I would greatly appreciate it, Dorring, if you would endeavor to remind her of the appointment. I intend to speak to her personally before this is all over."

"Certainly, by all means, Ravenwood, but I should warn you it ain't always easy to predict Sophy's comings and goings. As I said, she can be a bit willful at times."

"Then I expect you to exert a bit of willpower of your own. She's your granddaughter. If she needs the reins tightened, then, by all means, tighten them."

"Good God," Dorring muttered with great feeling. "Wish it were that easy."

Julian strode toward the door of the small, faded library and stepped out into the narrow, dark hall. The butler, dressed in a manner that blended perfectly with the air of shabby gentility that characterized the rest of the aging manor house, handed him his tall, flat-crowned beaver hat and gloves.

Julian nodded brusquely and brushed past the elderly retainer. The heels of his gleaming Hessians rang hollowly on the stone floor. He was already regretting the time it had taken to dress formally for the unproductive visit.

He'd even had one of the carriages brought around for the occasion. He might as well have ridden over to Chesley Court and saved the effort of trying to add a formal touch to the call. If he'd been on horseback he could have stopped off at one of the tenants' cottages on the way home and seen to some business. That way, at least, the entire afternoon would not have been wasted.

"The Abbey," he ordered as the carriage door was opened for him. The coachman, wearing the green-and-gold Ravenwood livery, touched his hat in acknowledgment of the command.

The beautifully matched team of grays leapt forward under the light flick of the whip an instant after the door was slammed shut. It was understood that the Earl of Ravenwood was not in a mood to dawdle along country roads this afternoon.

Julian leaned back against the cushions, thrust his booted feet out in front of him, folded his arms across his chest, and concentrated on controlling his impatience. It was not an easy task.

It had never occurred to him that his offer of marriage would be rejected. Miss Sophy Dorring did not stand a chance in hell of getting a better offer, and everyone involved knew it. Certainly her grandparents were vividly aware of that blunt fact.

Lord Dorring and his wife had nearly fainted when Julian had asked for their granddaughter's hand in marriage a few days ago. As far as they were concerned, Sophy was quite past the age when it might have been possible to make such a suitable match. Julian's offer was a bolt from a truly benign providence.

Julian's mouth twisted sardonically as he considered the scene that had undoubtedly ensued when Sophy had informed her grandparents she was not interested in the marriage. Lord Dorring had obviously not known how to take charge of the situation and his lady had probably suffered a fit of the vapors. The granddaughter with the lamentable reading habits had easily emerged the victor.

The real question was why the silly chit had wanted to win the battle in the first place. By rights she should have leapt at Julian's offer along with everyone else. He was, after all, intending to install her at Ravenwood Abbey as the Countess of Ravenwood. A twenty-three-year-old country-bred miss with only passable looks and an extremely small inheritance could hardly aspire higher. Julian wondered briefly just what books Sophy had been reading and then dismissed the notion that her choice of reading material was the problem.

The problem was far more likely to be her grandfather's overly indulgent attitude toward his orphaned grandchild. Women were quick to take advantage of a weak-willed man.

Her age might also be a factor. Julian had considered her years an asset in the beginning. He'd already had one young, ungovernable wife and one was quite enough. He'd had sufficient scenes, tantrums, and hysterics from Elizabeth to last him a lifetime. He had assumed an older female would be more levelheaded and less demanding; more *grateful*, in fact.

It was not as if the girl had a great deal of choice out in the country, Julian reminded himself. She would not have all that much choice in town, for that matter. She definitely was not the type to attract the attention of the jaded males of the *ton*. Such men considered themselves connoisseurs of female flesh in much the same way they considered themselves experts on horseflesh, and they were not likely to look twice at Sophy.

She was not fashionably extreme in her coloring, being

neither strikingly dark-haired nor angelically blond. Her tawny brown curls were a pleasingly rich shade but they appeared to have a will of their own. Tendrils were always escaping from beneath her bonnets or straggling free from a painstakingly arranged coiffure.

She was no Grecian goddess, the look currently fashionable in London, but Julian admitted to himself that he had no quarrel with her slightly tilted nose, gently rounded chin, and warm smile. It would be no great task to get into bed with her frequently enough to ensure himself of an heir.

He was also willing to allow that Sophy had a fine pair of eyes. They were an interesting and unusual shade of turquoise flecked with gold. It was curious and rather satisfying to note that their owner had not the least idea of how to use them to flirt.

Instead of peeking up at a man through her lashes, Sophy had the disconcerting habit of looking straight at him. There was an open, forthright quality about her gaze that had convinced Julian that Sophy would have a great deal of difficulty pursuing the elegant art of lying. That fact suited him, too. Picking out the handful of truths buried amid Elizabeth's lies had nearly driven him insane.

Sophy was slender. The popular high-waisted gowns suited her figure but they tended to emphasize the rather small curves of her breasts. There was, however, a healthy, vibrant quality about her that Julian appreciated. He did not want a weakling. Frail women did not do well in childbirth.

Julian reviewed his mental image of the woman he intended to marry and realized that, while he had assessed her physical assets accurately, he had not, apparently, taken certain aspects of her personality into consideration. He had never guessed, for example, that beneath that sweet, demure facade, she had a streak of willful pride.

It must have been Sophy's pride that was getting in the way of a proper sense of gratitude. And her willfulness appeared more entrenched than expected. Her grandparents were obviously distraught and quite helpless against their granddaughter's unanticipated resistance. If the situation was to be salvaged, Julian decided, he would have to do it himself.

He made his decision as the carriage rocked to a halt in front of the two stately arms of the crab-pincer staircase that marked the imposing entrance to Ravenwood Abbey. He climbed out of the equipage, stalked up the stone steps, and began giving low-voiced orders as soon as the door was opened for him.

"Send a message to the stables, Jessup. I want the black saddled and ready in twenty minutes."

"Very good, my lord."

The butler turned to relay the message to a footman as Julian strode across the black-and-white marble-tiled hall and up the massive red-carpeted staircase.

Julian paid little attention to his grand surroundings. Although he had been raised there, he had cared little for Ravenwood Abbey since the early days of his marriage to Elizabeth. Once he had felt the same possessive pride toward the house as he did toward the fertile lands that surrounded it but now he only experienced a vague distaste toward his ancestral home. Every time he walked into a room he wondered if this was yet another chamber in which he had been cuckolded.

His land was quite a different matter. No woman could taint the good, rich fields of Ravenwood or his other estates. A man could count on the land. If he took care of it, he would be amply rewarded. To preserve the lands for future Earls of Ravenwood, Julian was willing to make the ultimate sacrifice: he would marry again.

He hoped the act of installing another wife there would scrub some of the lingering traces of Elizabeth out of the Abbey and most especially out of the oppressively lush, exotically sensuous bedchamber she had once made her own. Julian hated that room. He had not stepped foot in it since Elizabeth's death.

One thing was for certain, he told himself as he climbed the stairs, he would not make the same mistakes with a new bride as he had made with his first. Never again would he play the part of a fly in a spider's web.

Fifteen minutes later Julian came back down the stairs

dressed for riding. He was not surprised to find the black stallion he had named Angel ready and waiting. He had taken it for granted that the horse would be at the door when he was. Everyone in the household took care to anticipate the master of Ravenwood. No one in his right mind wanted to do anything that might invoke the devil's wrath. Julian went down the steps and vaulted into the saddle.

The groom stepped back quickly as the black tossed his head and danced for a few seconds. Powerful muscles shuddered under the glossy coat as Julian established control with a firm hand. Then he gave the signal and the animal surged forward eagerly.

It would not be hard to intercept Miss Sophy Dorring on her way home to Chesley Court, Julian decided. He knew every inch of his estate and he had a good idea of just where he would find her taking a shortcut across his land. She would undoubtedly use the path that circled the pond.

"He's like to kill himself on that horse someday," the footman remarked to the groom, who was his cousin.

The groom spit onto the cobbled surface of the court-yard. "His lordship won't make his exit from this life on a horse. Rides like the devil himself. How long's he going to stay here this time?"

"They're sayin' in the kitchens that he's here to find himself another bride. Got his eye on Lord Dorring's granddaughter. His lordship wants a quiet little country miss this time. One who won't give him any trouble."

"Can't blame him for that. I'd feel the same way if I'd been shackled to that wicked hellcat he picked last time."

"Maggie in the kitchen says that first wife of his was the witch who turned his lordship into a devil."

"Maggie's got the right of it. I tell ye, I feel sorry for Miss Dorring, though. She's a decent sort. Remember how she came by with those herbs o' hers this winter when Ma got that bad cough? Ma swears Miss Dorring saved her life."

"Miss Dorring'll be gettin' herself an Earl," the footman pointed out.

"That's as may be, but she'll pay a high price for the privilege of bein' the devil's lady."

Sophy sat on the wooden bench in front of Old Bess's cottage and carefully wrapped the last of the dried fenugreek in a small packet. She added it to the little bundle of herbs she had just finished selecting. Her supplies of such essentials as garlic, thistle, nightshade, and poppies in various forms had been growing low.

"That should do me for the next couple of months, Bess," she announced as she dusted off her hands and rose to her feet. She ignored the grass stain on the skirt of her old blue worsted riding habit.

"Ye be careful if ye need to make up a cup o' poppyhead tea for Lady Dorring's rheumatism," Bess cautioned. "The poppies came in real powerful this year."

Sophy nodded at the wrinkled old woman who had taught her so much. "I'll remember to cut back on my measurements. How is everything with you? Do you need anything?"

"Nary a thing, child, nary a thing." Bess surveyed her aging cottage and herb garden with a serene eye as she wiped her hands on her apron. "I have everythin' I need."

"You always do. You are lucky to be so content with life, Bess."

"Ye'll find contentment one o' these days, if ye truly seek it."

Sophy's smile faded. "Perhaps. But first I must seek other things."

Bess regarded her sorrowfully, her pale eyes full of understanding. "I thought ye'd gotten past yer need for vengeance, child. I thought ye'd finally left it in the past where it ought to be."

"Things have changed, Bess." Sophy started around the corner of the small, thatch-roofed cottage to where her gelding was waiting. "As it happens, I have been given a new opportunity to see that justice is done."

"If ye had any common sense, ye would take my advice and forget it, child. What's done is done. Yer sister, rest her soul, is gone. There's naught ye can do for her now. Ye have yer own life and ye must pay attention to it." Bess smiled her gap-toothed smile. "I hear there be a somewhat more pressin' matter for ye to consider these days."

Sophy glanced sharply at the elderly woman while she made a useless attempt to straighten her precariously tilted riding hat. "As usual, you manage to keep up with the village gossip. You've heard I received an offer of marriage from the devil himself?"

"The folks who call Lord Ravenwood a devil are the ones who deal in gossip. I deal only in facts. Is it true?"

"What? That the Earl is closely related to Lucifer? Yes, Bess, I am almost certain it is true. I have never before met such an arrogant man as his lordship. That sort of pride definitely belongs to the devil."

Bess shook her head impatiently. "I meant is it true he's offered for ye?"

"Yes."

"Well? When do ye be about givin' him yer answer, pray tell?"

Sophy shrugged, abandoning the effort to adjust her hat. Hats always had their way with her. "Grandfather is giving him an answer this afternoon. The Earl sent a message that he would be calling at three today to receive it."

Bess came to an abrupt halt on the stone path. Gray curls bobbed beneath her yellowed muslin cap. Her lined face crinkled in astonishment. "This afternoon? And here ye be choosin' herbs from my stock as if it were any normal day of the week? What nonsense is this, child? Ye should be at Chesley Court at this very moment and dressed in yer best clothes."

"Why? Grandfather does not need me there. He is perfectly capable of telling the devil to go to hell."

"Tellin' the devil to go to hell! Sophy, child, are ye sayin' ye told yer grandfather to turn down the Earl's offer?"

Sophy smiled grimly as she came to a halt beside the chestnut gelding. "You have it exactly right, Bess." She stuffed the little packets of herbs into the pockets of her habit.

"Nonsense," Bess exclaimed. "I can't believe Lord Dorring

is so muddle-brained as this. He knows you'll never get another offer this good if ye live to be a hundred."

"I'm not so certain of that," Sophy said dryly. "It depends, of course, on your definition of a good offer."

Bess's gaze narrowed thoughtfully. "Child, are ye doin' this because yer afraid of the Earl? Is that what's wrong? I thought ye were too sensible to believe all the stories they tell down in the village."

"I do not believe them all," Sophy said as she swung herself into the saddle. "Only about half. Does that console you, Bess?" Sophy adjusted the skirts of her habit under her legs. She rode astride, although it was not considered quite proper for a woman of her station to do so. In the country, however, people were more casual about such matters. In any event Sophy was convinced her modesty was well protected. With her habit carefully arranged this way only her tan half-boots showed beneath the skirts.

Bess caught hold of the horse's bridle and peered up at Sophy. "Here now, girl. Ye don't truly believe that tale they tell about his lordship drownin' his first wife in Ravenwood Pond, do ye?"

Sophy sighed. "No, Bess, I do not." It would have been more accurate to say she did not want to believe it.

"Thank the lord, although it be God's truth there ain't none around here who'd have blamed the man if he had killed her," Bess admitted.

"True enough, Bess."

"Then what's all this nonsense about ye refusin' his lordship's offer? I don't care for the look in yer eyes, child. I've seen it before and it don't bode well. What are ye up to now?"

"Now? Why, now I am going to ride old Dancer here back to Chesley Court and then I am going to set about storing these herbs you have so kindly given me. Grandfather's gout is acting up again and I have run out of his favorite decoction."

"Sophy, darlin', are ye truly goin' to refuse the Earl?"

"No," Sophy said honestly. "So you need not look so

horrified. In the end, if he persists, he shall have me. But it will be on my terms."

Bess's eyes widened. "Ah, now I believe I take yer meanin'. Ye've been readin' those books on the rights o' women again, haven't ye? Don't be a fool, child. Take some advice from an old woman. Don't be about playin' any of yer games with Ravenwood. He's not likely to indulge them. Ye might be able to lead Lord Dorring around by a piece of string, but the Earl's a different sort o' man, altogether."

"I agree with you on that point, Bess. The Earl is a vastly different sort of man than Grandfather. But try not to worry about me. I know what I am doing." Sophy collected the reins and gave Dancer a nudge with her heel.

"Nay, child, I'm not so sure o' that," Bess called after her. "Ye don't tease the devil and expect to come away unharmed."

"I thought you said Ravenwood was not a devil," Sophy retorted over her shoulder as Dancer broke into a lumbering trot.

She waved at Bess as the horse headed into a stand of trees. There was no need to guide Dancer back toward Chesley Court. He had made the trip so often during the past few years that he knew the route over Ravenwood lands by heart.

Sophy let the reins rest lightly on Dancer's neck as she considered the scene she would undoubtedly discover when she got back to Chesley Court.

Her grandparents would be distraught, of course. Lady Dorring had taken to her bed this morning, an array of fortifying salts and tonics arranged nearby. Lord Dorring, who had been left to face Ravenwood alone, would probably be consoling himself with a bottle of claret by now. The small house staff would be quietly morose. A suitable connection for Sophy would have been in their best interests as well as everyone else's. Without a respectable marriage settlement to fill the family coffers there was little hope of a pension for aging servants.

No one in the household could be expected to understand Sophy's staunch refusal of Ravenwood's offer. Rumors, gossip, and grim tales aside, the man was, after all, an Earl—a wealthy and powerful one at that. He owned most of the surrounding neighborhood there in Hampshire as well as two other smaller estates in neighboring counties. He also had an elegant house in London.

As far as the local people were concerned, Ravenwood ran his lands well and was fair with his tenants and servants. That was all that truly mattered in the country. Those who were dependent on the Earl and who were careful not to cross him enjoyed a comfortable living.

Ravenwood had his faults, everyone agreed, but he took care of the land and the people on it. He may have murdered his wife but he had refrained from doing anything truly heinous such as throwing away his entire inheritance in a London gaming hell.

The local people could afford to be charitable toward Ravenwood, Sophy thought. *They were not faced with the prospect of marriage to him.*

Sophy's glance was drawn, as it always was on this path, to the dark, cold waters of Ravenwood Pond as it came into sight through the trees. Here and there small crusts of ice dotted the surface of the deep pool. There was little snow left on the ground but the chill of winter was still very much in the air. Sophy shivered and Dancer nickered inquiringly.

Sophy leaned forward to pat the horse's neck reassuringly but her hand froze abruptly in midair. An icy breeze rustled the branches overhead. Sophy shivered again, but this time she knew it was not the chill of the early spring afternoon that was affecting her. She straightened in the saddle as she caught sight of the man on the midnight black stallion coming toward her through a grove of bare trees. Her pulse quickened as it always did in Ravenwood's presence.

Belatedly Sophy told herself she ought to have immediately recognized the little frisson of awareness that had gone through her a moment earlier. After all, a part of her had been in love with this man since she was eighteen.

That was the year she had first been introduced to the

Earl of Ravenwood. He, of course, probably did not even remember the occasion. He'd had eyes only for his beautiful, mesmerizing, witchy Elizabeth.

Sophy knew that her initial feelings for the wealthy Earl of Ravenwood had no doubt begun as little more than a young woman's natural infatuation with the first man who had captured her imagination. But that infatuation had not died a natural death, not even when she had accepted the obvious fact that she stood no chance of gaining his attention. Over the years infatuation had matured into something deeper and more abiding.

Sophy had been drawn to the quiet power and the innate pride and integrity she sensed in Ravenwood. In the realm of her most secret dreams she thought of him as noble in a way that had nothing to do with his inherited title.

When the dazzling Elizabeth had succeeded in turning the fascination Ravenwood felt for her into raw pain and savage rage, Sophy had wanted to offer comfort and understanding. But the Earl had been beyond either. He had sought his solace for a time on the Continent waging war under Wellington.

When he had returned, it was obvious that the Earl's emotions had long since retreated to a cold, distant place somewhere inside himself. Now any passion or warmth Ravenwood was capable of feeling appeared to be reserved for his land.

The black suited him well, Sophy decided. She had heard the stallion was called Angel, and she found herself marveling at Ravenwood's sense of irony.

Angel was a creature of darkness meant for a man who lived in shadows. The man who rode him seemed almost a part of the animal. Ravenwood was lean and powerfully built. He was endowed with unfashionably large, strong hands, hands that could easily have strangled an errant wife, just as the villagers said, Sophy reflected briefly.

He needed no padding in his coat to emphasize the breadth of his shoulders. The snug-fitting riding breeches clung to well-shaped, strongly muscled thighs.

But although he wore his clothes well, Sophy knew

there was nothing the finest tailor in London could have done to alleviate the uncompromising grimness of Raven-wood's harsh features.

His hair was as black as his stallion's silky coat and his eyes were a deep, gleaming green, a *demon* green, Sophy had sometimes thought. It was said the Earls of Ravenwood were always born with eyes to match the family emeralds.

Sophy found Ravenwood's gaze disconcerting not only because of the color of his eyes but because he had a way of looking at a person as if he were mentally putting a price on that poor unfortunate's soul. Sophy wondered what his lordship would do when he learned her price.

She reined in Dancer, pushed the plume of her riding hat out of her eyes and summoned up what she hoped was a serenely gracious smile.

"Good afternoon, my lord. What a surprise to encounter you in the middle of the woods."

The black stallion was brought to a shuddering halt a few feet away. Ravenwood sat quietly for a moment, regarding Sophy's polite little smile. He did not respond in kind.

"What, precisely, do you find surprising about this encounter, Miss Dorring? This is, after all, my land. I knew you had gone to visit Old Bess and guessed that you would be returning to Chesley Court along this route."

"How clever of you, my lord. An example of deductive logic, perhaps? I am a great admirer of that sort of reasoning."

"You were well aware that we had business to conclude today. If you are as intelligent as your grandparents appear to believe, you must also have known I wanted that business settled this afternoon. No, on the whole I cannot accept that there is any surprise in this meeting at all. In fact, I would almost be willing to wager that it was deliberately planned."

Sophy's fingers clenched on the reins as the soft words burned into her. Dancer's ears flicked in mild protest and she instantly relaxed her convulsive grip. Bess was right. Ravenwood was not a man who could be easily led about with a piece of string. Sophy knew she would have to be extraordinarily cautious.

"I was under the impression that my grandfather was conducting my business on my behalf, as is proper," Sophy said. "Did he not give you my answer to your offer?"

"He did." Ravenwood allowed his high-strung stallion to take a few prancing steps closer to Dancer. "I chose not to accept it until I discussed the matter with you, personally."

"Surely, my lord, that is not entirely correct. Or is that the manner in which such things are handled in London these days?"

"It's the manner in which I wish to handle them with you. You are not a missish little twit, Miss Dorring. Pray do not act like one. You can answer for yourself. Tell me what the problem is and I will endeavor to see if it can be resolved."

"Problem, my lord?"

His eyes took on a darker shade of green. "I would advise you not to toy with me, Miss Dorring. I am not given to indulging women who try to make a fool of me."

"I understand completely, my lord. And surely you can comprehend my reluctance to tie myself to a man who is not given to indulging women in general, much less those who try to make a fool of him."

Ravenwood's eyes narrowed. "Kindly explain yourself."

Sophy managed a faint shrug. Her hat tipped a bit farther forward under the small movement. Automatically she reached up again to push aside the bobbing plume.

"Very well, my lord, you force me to speak plainly. I do not believe you and I share a similar understanding of how a marriage between us could be made to work. I have tried to talk to you privately on the three occasions you have called at Chesley Court during the past two weeks, but you seemed totally uninterested in discussing matters with me. You treated the whole business as if you were buying a new horse for your stables. I admit I was forced to resort to drastic tactics today in order to get your attention."

Ravenwood stared at her with cold irritation. "So I was right in thinking you are not surprised to encounter me

here. Very well, you have my complete attention, Miss
Dorring. What is there you wish me to comprehend? It all
seems very straightforward to me."

"I know what you want from me," Sophy said. "It is
quite obvious. But I do not believe you have the least
notion of what I want from you. Until you do comprehend
that and agree to my wishes in the matter, there is no
possibility of our marrying."

"Perhaps we ought to take this step by step," Ravenwood
said. "What is it you think I want from you?"

"An heir and no trouble."

Ravenwood blinked with a deceptive laziness. His hard
mouth curved faintly. "Succinctly put."

"And accurate?"

"Very," he said dryly. "It is no secret that I wish to set
up my nursery. Ravenwood has been in my family's hands
for three generations. I do not intend for it to be lost in
this generation."

"In other words, you see me as a brood mare."

Saddle leather creaked as Ravenwood studied her in
ominous silence for a long moment. "I fear your grandfather was right," he finally said. "Your reading habits have
instilled a certain lack of delicacy in your manner, Miss
Dorring."

"Oh, I can be far more indelicate than that, my lord.
For instance, I understand you keep a mistress in London."

"Where the devil did you hear that? Not from Lord
Dorring, I'll wager."

"It is common talk here in the countryside."

"And you listen to the tales told by villagers who have
never been more than a few miles from their homes?" he
scoffed.

"Are the tales told by city folk any different?"

"I begin to believe you are being deliberately insulting,
Miss Dorring."

"No, my lord. Merely very cautious."

"Obstinate, not cautious. Use what little wit you have to
pay attention. If there was anything truly objectionable
about me or my behavior do you think your grandparents
would have approved my offer of marriage?"

"If the marriage settlement you are proposing is large enough, yes."

Ravenwood smiled faintly at that. "You may be correct."

Sophy hesitated. "Are you telling me the tales I have heard are all false?"

Ravenwood eyed her thoughtfully. "What else have you heard?"

Sophy had not expected this odd conversation to get so specific. "You mean besides the fact that you keep a mistress?"

"If the rest of the gossip is as silly as that bit, you should be ashamed of yourself, Miss Dorring."

"Alas, I fear I do not possess such a refined sense of shame, my lord. A regrettable failing, to be sure and one you should probably take into consideration. Gossip can be vastly entertaining, and I confess I am not above listening to it on occasion."

The Earl's mouth tightened. "A regrettable failing, indeed. What else have you heard?" he repeated.

"Well, in addition to the tidbit about your mistress, it is said you fought a duel once."

"You cannot expect me to confirm such nonsense."

"I have also heard that you banished your last wife to the country because she failed to give you an heir," Sophy continued rashly.

"I do not discuss my first wife with anyone." Ravenwood's expression was suddenly forbidding. "If we are to get on together, Miss Dorring, you would be well advised never to mention her again."

Sophy flushed. "I apologize, my lord. It is not her I am trying to discuss, rather your habit of leaving your wives in the country."

"What the devil are you talking about?"

It took more courage than Sophy had anticipated to continue on in the face of that awful tone. "I think I should make it perfectly clear that I do not intend to be left behind here at Ravenwood or one of your other estates while you spend your time in London, my lord."

He frowned. "I was under the impression you were happy here."

"It is true I enjoy rural living and in general am quite content here, but I do not want to be restricted to Ravenwood Abbey. I have spent most of my life in the country, my lord. I wish to see London again."

"Again? I was given to understand that you did not enjoy yourself during your one season in town, Miss Dorring."

Her embarrassed eyes slid away from his for a moment. "I am sure you are well aware that I was a spectacular failure when I was brought out. I did not attract a single offer that season."

"I begin to see why you failed so miserably, Miss Dorring," Ravenwood said heartlessly. "If you were as blunt with all of your admirers then as you are today with me, you undoubtedly terrified them."

"Am I succeeding in terrifying you, my lord?"

"I assure you, I am beginning to shiver in my boots."

Sophy almost smiled in spite of herself. "You hide your fear well, my lord." She saw a momentary gleam in Ravenwood's eyes and quickly squelched her wayward sense of humor.

"Let us continue this forthright conversation, Miss Dorring. I am to understand that you do not wish to spend all your time here at Ravenwood. Is there anything else on your list of demands?"

Sophy held her breath. This was the dangerous part. "I do have some other demands, my lord."

He sighed. "Let me hear them."

"You have made it clear your chief interest in this marriage is securing an heir."

"This may come as a surprise to you, Miss Dorring, but that is considered a legitimate and acceptable reason for a man to desire marriage."

"I understand," she said. "But I am not ready to be rushed into childbed, my lord."

"Not ready? I have been told you are twenty-three years old. As far as society is concerned, my dear, you are more than ready."

"I am aware that I am considered to be on the shelf, my lord. You need not point the fact out to me. But oddly enough, I do not consider myself in my dotage. And neither do you or you would not be asking me to become your wife."

Ravenwood smiled fleetingly, showing a glimpse of strong, white teeth. "I will admit that when one is thirty-four, twenty-three does not seem so very old. But you appear quite fit and healthy, Miss Dorring. I think you will withstand the rigors of childbirth very well."

"I had no idea you were such an expert."

"We stray from the subject again. Just what is it you are trying to say, Miss Dorring?"

She gathered herself. "I am saying that I will not agree to marriage with you unless you give me your word you will not force yourself upon me until I give you my permission."

She felt the heat flow into her cheeks under Ravenwood's startled gaze. Her hands trembled on Dancer's reins and the old horse moved restlessly. Another gust of wind whipped the tree branches and sliced through the fabric of Sophy's riding habit.

A cold rage leaped to life in Julian's green eyes. "I give you my word of honor, Miss Dorring, that I have never *forced* myself upon a woman in my life. But we are speaking of marriage and I cannot believe you are unaware that matrimony implies certain duties and obligations on the part of both husband and wife."

Sophy nodded quickly and her small hat tipped precariously over her eye. This time she ignored the plume. "I am also aware, my lord, that most men would not consider it wrong to insist on their rights, whether or not the women were willing. Are you one of those men?"

"You cannot expect me to enter into marriage knowing my wife was not prepared to grant me my rights as a husband," Ravenwood said between clenched teeth.

"I did not say I would never be prepared to grant you your rights. I am merely asking that I be given ample time to get to know you and to adjust to the situation."

"You are not asking, Miss Dorring, you are demanding. Is this a result of your reprehensible reading habits?"

"My grandfather warned you about those, I see."

"He did. I can guarantee that I will personally assume

the responsibility of overseeing your choice of reading material after we are wed, Miss Dorring."

"That, of course, brings me to my third demand. I must be allowed to buy and read whatever books and tracts I wish."

The black tossed his head as Ravenwood swore under his breath. The stallion steadied as his master exerted expert pressure on the reins. "Let me be quite certain I have got your demands clear," Ravenwood said in a voice that was heavily laced with sarcasm. "You will not be banished to the country, you will not share my bed until it pleases you, and you will read whatever you wish to read in spite of my advice or recommendations to the contrary."

Sophy drew a breath. "I believe that sums up my list of demands, my lord."

"You expect me to agree to such an outrageous list?"

"Highly doubtful, my lord, which is precisely why I asked my grandfather to refuse your offer this afternoon. I thought it would save us all a great deal of time."

"Forgive me, Miss Dorring, but I believe I understand perfectly why you have never married. No sane man would agree to such a ridiculous list of demands. Can it be you genuinely wish to avoid matrimony altogether?"

"I am certainly in no rush to plunge into the wedded state."

"Obviously."

"I would say we have something in common, my lord," Sophy said with great daring. "I am under the impression you wish to marry solely out of a sense of duty. Is it so very hard for you to comprehend that I might not see any great advantage in marriage, either?"

"You seem to be overlooking the advantage of my money."

Sophy glared at him. "That is, naturally, a strong inducement. It is, however, one which I can be persuaded to overlook. I may never be able to afford diamond-studded dancing slippers on the limited income left me by my father, but I shall be able to get by in reasonable comfort. And, more importantly, I will be able to spend that income exactly as I wish. If I marry, I lose that advantage."

"Why don't you simply add to your list of demands that you will not be guided by your husband in matters of economy and finance, Miss Dorring?"

"An excellent idea, my lord. I believe I will do exactly that. Thank you for pointing out the obvious solution to my dilemma."

"Unfortunately, even if you find a male who is sufficiently lacking in reason as to grant you all of your wishes, you will have no legal way of guaranteeing that your husband abides by his word after the marriage, will you?"

Sophy glanced down at her hands, knowing he was right. "No, my lord. I would be entirely dependent on my husband's sense of honor."

"Be warned, Miss Dorring," Ravenwood said with soft menace, "A man's sense of honor might be inviolate when it comes to his gaming debts or his reputation as a sportsman but it means little when it comes to dealing with a woman."

Sophy went cold. "Then I do not have much choice, do I? If that is so, I will never be able to take the risk of marriage."

"You are wrong, Miss Dorring. You have already made your choice and now you must take your chances. You have said that you would be willing to marry me if I met your demands. Very well, I will agree to your requirements."

Sophy stared at him openmouthedly. Her heart raced. "You will?"

"The bargain is made." Ravenwood's big hands shifted slightly on the stallion's reins and the horse lifted his head alertly. "We will be married as soon as possible. Your grandfather is expecting me tomorrow at three. Tell him I wish to make all the arrangements at that time. Since you and I have succeeded in arriving at a private agreement, I will expect you to have the courage to be at home tomorrow when I call."

Sophy was dumbfounded. "My lord, I do not fully comprehend you. Are you quite certain you wish to marry me on my terms?"

Ravenwood smiled unpleasantly. His emerald eyes gleamed with harsh amusement. "The real question, Sophy, is how

long you will be able to maintain your demands once you
are confronted with the reality of being my wife."

"My lord, your word of honor," Sophy said anxiously. "I
must insist upon it."

"If you were a man, I would call you out for even
questioning it. You have my word, Miss Dorring."

"Thank you, my lord. You truly do not mind that I will
spend my money as I wish?"

"Sophy, the quarterly allowance I will provide you will
be considerably larger than your entire yearly income,"
Ravenwood said bluntly. "As long as you pay your bills out
of what I allot you, I will not question your expenditures."

"Oh. I see. And . . . and my books?"

"I think I can handle whatever harebrained notions your
books put into your head. I shall undoubtedly be annoyed
from time to time but perhaps that will give us a basis for
some interesting discussions, hm? God knows most wom-
en's conversations are enough to bore a man silly."

"I shall endeavor not to bore you, my lord. But let us be
certain we understand each other perfectly. You won't try
to keep me buried in the country all year long?"

"I'll allow you to accompany me to London when it's
convenient, if that's truly what you want."

"You are too kind, my lord. And my . . . my other demand?"

"Ah, yes. My guarantee not to, er, force myself upon
you. I think we shall have to put a time limit on that one.
After all, my main goal in all this is to obtain an heir."

Sophy was instantly uneasy. "A time limit?"

"How much time do you think you will require to grow
accustomed to the sight of me?"

"Six months?" she hazarded.

"Don't be a goose, Miss Dorring. I have no intention of
waiting six months to claim my rights."

"Three months?"

He looked about to deny this counteroffer but appeared
to change his mind at the last minute. "Very well. Three
months. You see how indulgent I am?"

"I am overwhelmed by your generosity, my lord."

"And so you should be. I defy you to find another man

who would grant you such a length of time before insisting that you fulfill your wifely duties."

"You are quite right, my lord. I doubt if I could find another man who would be as agreeable as you seem inclined to be in the matter of marriage. Forgive me, but my curiosity overcomes me. Why *are* you being so agreeable?"

"Because, my dear Miss Dorring, in the end I shall have exactly what I want out of this marriage. Good day, to you. I will see you tomorrow at three."

Angel responded instantly to the sudden pressure of Ravenwood's thighs. The black swung around in a tight circle and cantered off through the trees.

Sophy sat where she was until Dancer lowered his head to sample a mouthful of grass. The horse's movement brought her back to her senses.

"Home, Dancer. I am sure my grandparents will be either in hysterics or a state of complete despair by now. The least I can do is inform them that I have salvaged the situation."

But an old adage flitted through her mind as she rode back to Chesley Court—something about those who would sit down to dine with the devil being advised to bring a long spoon.

TWO

Lady Dorring, who had taken to her bed in a fit of despondency earlier in the day, revived completely in time for dinner on hearing that her granddaughter had come to her senses.

"I cannot imagine what got into you, Sophy," Lady Dorring said as she examined the Scotch broth being presented by Hindley, the butler who doubled as a footman at meals. "To turn down the Earl was past all understanding. Thank heaven you have put it right. Allow me to tell you, young woman, we should all be extremely grateful Ravenwood is willing to be so tolerant of your outlandish behavior."

"It does give one pause, doesn't it?" Sophy murmured.

"I say," Dorring exclaimed from the head of the table. "What do you mean by that?"

"Only that I have been puzzling over why the Earl should have made an offer for my hand in the first place."

"Why in heaven's name should he not have offered for

you?" Lady Dorring demanded. "You are a fine-looking young woman from a well-bred, respectable family."

"I had my season, Grandmother, remember? I've seen how dazzling the town beauties can be and I cannot be compared to most of them. I could not compete with them five years ago and there is no reason to believe I can compete with them now. Nor do I have a sizable fortune to offer as a lure."

"Ravenwood don't need to marry for money," Lord Dorring stated bluntly. "Fact is, the marriage settlements he's suggesting are extremely generous. Extremely."

"But he could marry for land or money or beauty if he so desired," Sophy said patiently. "The question I asked myself was why was he not doing so. Why select me? An interesting puzzle."

"Sophy, please," Lady Dorring said in pained accents. "Do not ask such silly questions. You are charming and most presentable."

"Charming and most presentable describe the vast majority of the young women of the *ton*, most of whom also have the advantage of being younger than I. I knew I must have something else in my favor to warrant attracting the Earl of Ravenwood. I was interested to discover what it was. It was simple enough when I put my mind to the problem."

Lord Dorring regarded her with a genuine curiosity that was not particularly flattering. "What is it you think you have going for you, girl? I like you well enough, of course. Perfectly sound sort of granddaughter and all that, but I confess I did wonder myself why the Earl took such a fancy to you."

"Theo!"

"Sorry, my dear, sorry," Dorring apologized hastily to his incensed wife. "Just curious, you know."

"As was I," Sophy said promptly. "But I believe I have hit upon the reasoning Ravenwood is using. You see, I have three essential qualities that he feels he needs. First, I am convenient and, as Grandmother has pointed out, reasonably well-bred. He probably did not want to spend a lot of time on the matter of choosing a second wife. I have the impression he has more important things to concern him."

"Such as?" Dorring asked.

"Selecting a new mistress or a new horse or a new parcel of land. Any one of a thousand items might conceivably come before a wife in order of importance to the Earl," Sophy said.

"Sophy!"

"I fear it's true, Grandmother. Ravenwood has spent as little time as possible on making his offer. You must agree I have hardly been treated to anything even faintly resembling a courtship."

"Here, now," Lord Dorring interrupted briskly. "You can't hold it against the man that he ain't brought you any posies or love poems. Ravenwood don't strike me as the romantic type."

"I think you have the right of it, Grandfather. Ravenwood is definitely not the romantic sort. He has called here at Chesley Court only a handful of times and we've been invited to the Abbey on merely two occasions."

"I've told you, he ain't the kind to waste time on frippery matters," Lord Dorring said, obviously feeling obliged to defend another male. "He's got estates to see to and I hear he's involved in some building project in London. The man's busy."

"Just so, Grandfather." Sophy hid a smile. "But to continue, the second reason the Earl finds me so suitable is my advanced age. I do believe he feels that any woman who finds herself unmarried at this point in her life should be everlastingly grateful to the man who was kind enough to take her off the shelf. A grateful wife is, of course, a manageable wife."

"Don't think it's that so much," her grandfather said reflectively, "as it is he thinks a woman of your age is bound to be more sensible and levelheaded than some young twit with romantic notions. Said something to that effect this afternoon, I believe."

"Really, Theo." Lady Dorring glowered at her husband.

"You may be right," Sophy said to her grandfather. "Perhaps he was under the impression I would be more levelheaded than a seventeen-year-old girl who was just out of the schoolroom. Whatever the case, we may assume my age was a factor in the Earl's decision. But the last and by far the most important reason he chose me, I believe, is because I do not in any way resemble his late wife."

Lady Dorring nearly choked on the poached turbot that had just been put in front of her. "What has that to do with anything?"

"It is no secret the Earl has had his fill of beautiful women who cause him no end of trouble. We all knew Lady Ravenwood was in the habit of bringing her lovers to the Abbey. If we knew it, you can be certain his lordship did, too. No telling what went on in London."

"That's a fact," Dorring muttered. "If she was wild here in the country, she must have made Ravenwood's life pure hell in town. Heard he risked his young neck in a couple of duels over her. You can't blame him for wanting a second wife who won't go around attracting other males. No offense, Sophy, but you ain't the type to be giving him trouble in that line, and I expect he knows it."

"I wish both of you would cease this most improper conversation," Lady Dorring announced. It was clear she had little hope she would be obeyed.

"Ah, but Grandmother, Grandfather is quite right. I am perfect as the next Countess of Ravenwood. After all, I am country-bred and can be expected to be content with spending the majority of my time at Ravenwood Abbey. And I won't be trailing my paramours behind me wherever I go. I was a total failure during my one season in London and presumably would be an even greater failure if I went out into Society again. Lord Ravenwood is well aware he will not have to waste time fending off my admirers. There will not be any."

"Sophy," Lady Dorring said with fine dignity, "that is quite enough. I will tolerate no more of this ridiculous conversation. It is most unseemly."

"Yes, Grandmother. But has it escaped your notice that unseemly conversations are always the most interesting?"

"Not another word out of you, my girl. And the same goes for you, Theo."

"Yes, m'dear."

"I do not know," Lady Dorring informed them ominously,

"if your conclusions regarding Lord Ravenwood's motives are accurate or not, but I do know that on one point, he and I are agreed. You, Sophy, should be extremely grateful to the Earl."

"I did once have occasion to be grateful to his lordship," Sophy said wistfully. "That was the time he very gallantly stood up with me at one of the balls I attended during my season. I remember the event well. It was the only time I danced all evening. I doubt he even remembers. He kept looking over my shoulder the whole time to see who was dancing with his precious Elizabeth."

"Don't fret yourself about the first Lady Ravenwood. She's gone and no loss," Lord Dorring said with his usual straightforward attitude in such matters. "Take my advice, young lady. Refrain from provoking Ravenwood and you'll get on quite well with him. Don't expect more from him than is reasonable and he'll be a good husband to you. The man looks after his land and he'll look after his wife. He takes care of his own."

Her grandfather was undoubtedly right, Sophy decided later that night as she lay awake in bed. She was reasonably certain that if she refrained from provoking him excessively, Ravenwood would probably be no worse than most husbands. In any event, she was not likely to see much of him. During the course of her single season in town she had learned that husbands and wives of the *ton* tended to live separate lives.

That would be to her advantage she told herself stoutly. She had interests of her own to pursue. As Ravenwood's wife she would have time and opportunity to make her investigations on behalf of poor Amelia. One day, Sophy vowed, she would succeed in tracking down the man who had seduced and abandoned her sister.

During the past three years Sophy had managed to follow Old Bess's advice for the most part and put her sister's death behind her. Her initial rage had slowly settled into a bleak acceptance. After all, trapped in the country, there was little hope of finding and confronting the unknown man responsible.

But things would be different if she married the Earl.

Restlessly Sophy pushed back the covers and climbed out of bed. She padded barefoot across the threadbare carpet and opened the small jewelry case that sat on the dressing table. It was easy to reach inside and find the black metal ring without the aid of a candle. She had handled it often enough to recognize it by touch. Her fingers closed around it.

The ring lay cold and hard in her hand as she drew it out of the case. Against her palm she could feel the impression of the strange triangular design embossed on its surface.

Sophy hated the ring. She had found it clutched in her sister's hand the night Amelia had taken the overdose of laudanum. Sophy had known then that the black ring belonged to the man who had seduced her beautiful fair-haired sister and gotten her with child—the lover Amelia had refused to name. One of the few things Sophy had deduced for certain was that the man had been one of Lady Ravenwood's lovers.

The other thing of which Sophy was almost certain was that her sister and the unknown man had used the ruins of an old Norman castle on Ravenwood land for their secret rendezvous. Sophy had been fond of sketching the ancient pile of stone until she had found one of Amelia's handkerchiefs there. She had discovered it a few weeks after her sister's death. After that fateful day, Sophy had never returned to the scenic ruin.

What better way to find out the identity of the man who had caused Amelia to kill herself than to become the new Lady Ravenwood?

Sophy's hand clenched around the ring for a moment and then she dropped it back into the jewelry chest. It was just as well she had a rational, sensible, realistic reason for marrying the Earl of Ravenwood because her other reason for marrying him was likely to prove a wild, fruitless quest.

For she intended to try to teach the devil to love again.

Julian sprawled with negligent grace in the well-sprung traveling coach and regarded his new Countess with a critical eye. He had seen very little of Sophy during the past few weeks. He had told himself there had been no

need to make an excessive number of trips from London
to Hampshire. He had business to attend to in town. Now
he took the opportunity to scrutinize more closely the
woman he had chosen to provide him with an heir.

He regarded his bride, who had been a countess for
only a few hours with some surprise. As usual, however,
there was a certain chaotic look about her person. Several
ringlets of tawny brown hair had escaped the confines of
her new straw bonnet. A feather on the bonnet was
sticking out at an odd angle. Julian looked closer and saw
that the shaft had been broken. His gaze slipped downward and he discovered a small piece of ribbon trim on
Sophy's reticule was loose.

The hem of her traveling dress had a grass stain on it.
He thought Sophy had undoubtedly accomplished that feat
when she had bent down to receive the fistful of flowers from
a rather grubby little farm lad. Everyone in the village had
turned out to wave farewell to Sophy as she had prepared to
step into the traveling coach. Julian had not realized his wife
was such a popular figure in the local neighborhood.

He was vastly relieved his new bride had made no
complaint when he had informed her that he intended a
working honeymoon. He had recently acquired a new estate
in Norfolk and the obligatory month-long wedding trip was
the perfect opportunity to examine his newest holdings.

He was also obliged to admit Lady Dorring had done a
creditable job orchestrating the wedding. Most of the
gentry in the surrounding countryside had been invited.
Julian had not bothered to invite any of his acquaintances
from London, however. The thought of going through a
second wedding ceremony in front of the same sea of faces
that had been present as the first debacle was more than
he could stomach.

When the announcement of his forthcoming marriage
had appeared in the *Morning Post* he had been plagued
with questions, but he had handled most of the impertinent inquiries the way he usually handled such annoy-
ances: he had ignored them.

With one or two exceptions, his policy had worked. His
mouth tightened now as he recalled one of the exceptions.

A certain lady in Trevor Square had not been particularly pleased to learn of Julian's marriage. But Marianne Harwood had been too shrewd and too pragmatic to make more than a small scene. There were other fish in the sea. The earrings Julian had left behind on the occasion of that last visit had gone a long way toward soothing the ruffled features of La Belle Harwood.

"Is something wrong, my lord?" Sophy calmly broke into Julian's reverie.

Julian jerked his thoughts back to the present. "Not in the least. I was merely recalling a small business matter I had to attend to last week."

"It must have been a very unpleasant business matter. You appeared quite provoked. I thought for a moment you might have eaten a bad bit of meat pie."

Julian smiled faintly. "The incident was the sort that tends to interfere with a man's digestion but I assure you I am in excellent condition now."

"I see." Sophy stared at him with her astonishingly level gaze for a moment longer, nodded to herself and turned back to the window.

Julian scowled. "Now it's my turn to ask you if something is wrong, Sophy."

"Not in the least."

Arms folded across his chest, Julian contemplated the tassels on his polished Hessians for a few seconds before he glanced up with a quizzical gleam in his eye. "I think it would be best if we came to an understanding about one or two small matters, Madam Wife."

She glanced at him. "Yes, my lord?"

"A few weeks ago you gave me your list of demands."

She frowned. "True, my lord."

"At the time I was busy and neglected to make up a list of my own."

"I already know your demands, my lord. You want an heir and no trouble."

"I would like to take this opportunity to be a bit more precise."

"You wish to add to your list? That's hardly fair, is it?"

"I did not say I was adding to the list, merely clarifying

it." Julian paused. He saw the wariness in her turquoise eyes and smiled slightly. "Don't look so worried, my dear. The first item on my list, an heir, is plain enough. It's the second item I wish to clarify."

"No trouble. It seems simple enough."

"It will be once you understand exactly what I mean by it."

"For example?"

"For example, it will save us both a great deal of trouble if you make it a policy never to lie to me."

Her eyes widened. "I have no intention of doing any such thing, my lord."

"Excellent. Because you should know you would not be able to get away with it. There is something about your eyes, Sophy, that would betray you every time. And I would be most annoyed if I should detect a lie in your eyes. You understand me perfectly?"

"Perfectly, my lord."

"Then let us return to my earlier question. I believe I asked you if anything was wrong and you stated that there was nothing wrong. Your eyes say otherwise, my dear."

She toyed with the loose ribbon on her reticule. "Am I to have no privacy for my thoughts, my lord?"

He scowled. "Were your thoughts so very private at that moment that you felt obliged to conceal them from your husband?"

"No," she said simply. "I merely assumed you would not be pleased if I spoke them aloud so I kept them to myself."

He had set out to make a point but now Julian found himself swamped with curiosity. "I would like to hear them, if you please."

"Very well, I was engaging in a bit of deductive logic, my lord. You had just admitted that the business matters you had attended to prior to our marriage had been most provoking and I was hazarding a guess as to what sort of business matter you meant."

"And to what conclusion did your deductive logic lead you?"

"To the conclusion you had undoubtedly had some difficulty when you had informed your current mistress that you were getting married. One had hardly blame the poor woman. She has, after all, been doing all the work of a wife and now you announce you intend to give the title to another applicant for the post. A rather unskilled applicant, at that. I expect she enacted you a grand tragedy and that was what provoked you. Tell me, is she an actress or a ballet dancer?"

Julian's first impulse was an absurd desire to laugh. He quelled it instantly in the interests of husbandly discipline. "You overstep yourself, madam," he said through his teeth.

"You are the one who demanded I tell you all my private thoughts." The loose feather in her bonnet bobbed. "Will you agree now that there are times when I should be allowed some privacy?"

"You should not be speculating about such things in the first place."

"I am quite certain you are right but unfortunately I have very little control over my inner speculations."

"Perhaps you can be taught some measure of control," Julian suggested.

"I doubt it." She smiled at him suddenly and the warmth of that smile made Julian blink. "Tell me," Sophy continued impishly, "was my guess accurate?"

"The business I attended to before leaving London last week is none of your affair."

"Ah, I see the way of it now. I am to have no privacy for my speculations but you are to have all the solitude you wish for your own. That hardly seems fair, my lord. In any event, if my errant thoughts are going to upset you so much, don't you think it would be better if I kept them to myself?"

Julian leaned forward without any warning and caught her chin in his fingers. It occurred to him that her skin was very soft. "Are you teasing me, Sophy?"

She made no move to pull free of his hand. "I confess I am, my lord. You are so magnificently arrogant, you see, that the temptation is sometimes irresistible."

"I understand irresistible temptation," he told her. "I am about to be overcome by it, myself."

Julian eased over onto the seat beside her and wrapped

his hands around her small waist. He lifted her onto his thighs with one smooth motion and watched with cool satisfaction as her eyes widened in alarm.

"Ravenwood," she gasped.

"That brings me to another matter on my list of clarified demands," he murmured. "I think that when I am about to kiss you, I would like you to use my given name. You may call me Julian." He was suddenly very conscious of her firm, rounded little bottom pressing against him. The folds of her skirt clung to his breeches.

She steadied herself with her hands on his shoulders. "Need I remind you so soon that you gave me your word of honor you would not . . . would not force yourself on me?"

She was trembling. He could feel the small shivers going through her and it annoyed him. "Don't be an idiot, Sophy. I have no intention of forcing myself on you, as you call it. I am merely going to kiss you. There was nothing in our bargain about kissing."

"My lord, you promised—"

He wrapped one hand around her nape and held her carefully still while he covered her mouth with his own. Her lips parted on more words of protest just as he made contact. The result was that the kiss began on a far more intimate level than Julian had planned. He could taste the damp warmth of her instantly and it sent an unexpected flare of desire through him. The inside of her mouth was soft and wet and faintly spicy.

Sophy flinched and then moaned softly as his hands tightened on her. She started to pull away but when he refused to allow the small retreat she went quiet in his arms.

Sensing her cautious acquiescence, Julian took his time and gently deepened the kiss. *Lord, she felt good*. He had not realized she would be so sweet, so warm. There was enough feminine strength in her to make him vividly aware of his own superior strength and that realization had a startlingly arousing effect on him. He felt himself growing hard almost at once.

"Now say my name," he ordered softly against her mouth.

"Julian." The single word was shaky but audible.

He stroked his palm down her arm and nuzzled her throat. "Again."

"J—Julian. Please stop. This has gone far enough. You gave me your word."

"Am I forcing myself on you?" he asked whimsically, dropping the lightest of kisses just below her ear. His hand slid down her arm to rest intimately on the curve of her knee. Julian suddenly wanted nothing more than to ease her thighs apart and explore Sophy far more thoroughly. If the heat and honey between her legs were anything like that promised by her mouth, he would be well satisfied with his choice of wife. "Tell me, Sophy, do you call this force?"

"I don't know."

Julian laughed softly. She sounded so wretchedly unsure. "Allow me to tell you that this is not what is meant by the expression forcing myself on you."

"What is it, then?"

"I am making love to you. It's perfectly permissible between husband and wife, you know."

"You are not making love to me," she countered very seriously.

Startled, Julian raised his head to meet her eyes. "I'm not?"

"Of course not. How could you be making love to me? You do not love me."

"Call it seduction, then," he retorted. "A man has a right to seduce his own wife, surely. I gave you my word not to force myself on you but I never promised not to attempt to seduce you." *There would be no need to honor the stupid agreement*, he thought with satisfaction. She showed every sign of responding to him already.

Sophy leaned away from him, a deep anger lighting her turquoise eyes. "As far as I am concerned, seduction is but another form of forcing yourself on a woman. It is a man's way of concealing the truth of his motives."

Julian was stunned at the vehemence in her voice. "You have had experience of it, then?" he countered coldly.

"The results of a seduction are the same for a woman as the use of force, are they not?"

She scrambled awkwardly off his thighs, the wool skirts of her traveling dress twisting awkwardly around her in the process. The broken feather in her bonnet drooped further until it hung over one wary eye. She reached up and snatched it out of the way, leaving a broken feather shaft behind.

Julian shot out his hand and snagged her wrist. "Answer me, Sophy. Have you had experience of seduction?"

"It is a little late to ask me now, is it not? You ought to have made your inquiries into the matter before you offered for me."

And he knew quite suddenly that she had never lain in a man's arms. He could see the answer he wanted in her eyes. But he felt compelled to make her admit the truth. She had to learn that he would tolerate no evasions, half-truths, or any of the myriad other shapes a woman's lies could take.

"You will answer me, Sophy."

"If I do, will you answer all my questions about your past amours?"

"Of course not."

"Oh, you are so grossly unfair, my lord."

"I am your husband."

"And that gives you a right to be unfair?"

"It gives me a right and a duty to do what is best for you. Discussing my past liaisons with you would serve no good purpose and we both know it."

"I am not so certain. I think it would provide me with greater insight into your character."

He gave a crack of laughter at that. "I think you have enough insight as it is. Too much at times. Now tell me about your experience with the fine art of seduction, Sophy. Did some country squire attempt to tumble you in the woods?"

"If he had, what would you do about it?"

"See that he paid for it," Julian said simply.

Her mouth fell open. "You would conduct a duel because of a past indiscretion?"

"We stray from the topic, Sophy." His fingers closed more firmly around her wrist. He could feel the small, delicate bones there and took care not to tighten his hold too far.

Her eyes fell away from his. "You need not worry about avenging my lost honor, my lord. I assure you I have led an extremely quiet and unexciting existence. A somewhat boring existence, to be precise."

"I rather thought so." He released her hand and relaxed back against the cushion. "Now tell me why you equate seduction with force?"

"This is hardly a proper conversation for us to be conducting," she said in muffled tones.

"I have the impression you and I will have many such improper conversations. There are times, my dear, when you are a most improper young woman." He reached up and plucked the broken feather shaft from her bonnet.

She glanced at the shaft with an expression of resignation. "You should have considered my improper tendencies before you insisted on offering for me."

Julian turned the feather shaft between thumb and forefinger. "I did. I decided they were all quite manageable. Stop trying to distract me, Sophy. Tell me why you fear seduction as much as force."

"It is a private matter, my lord. I do not speak of it."

"You will speak of it to me. I am afraid I must insist, Sophy. I am your husband."

"Do stop using that fact as an excuse for indulging your curiosity," she snapped.

He slanted her a considering glance and considered the defiant tilt of her chin. "You insult me, madam."

She shifted uneasily, attempting to straighten her skirts. "You are easily insulted, my lord."

"Ah, yes, my excessive arrogance. I fear we must both learn to live with it, Sophy. Just as we must learn to live with my excessive curiosity." Julian studied the broken feather shaft and waited.

Silence descended on the swaying coach. The sound of

creaking wheels and harness leather and the steady beat of the horses' hooves suddenly became very loud.

"It was not a matter that affected me, personally," Sophy finally said in a very small voice.

"Yes?" Again Julian waited.

"It was my sister who was the victim of the seduction." Sophy stared very hard at the passing scenery. "But she had no one to avenge her."

"I understood that your sister died three years ago."

"She did."

Something about Sophy's clipped voice alerted Julian. "Are you implying that her death was the result of a seduction?"

"She found herself with child, my lord. The man who was responsible cast her aside. She could not bear the shame or the betrayal. She took a large dose of laudanum." Her fingers clenched together in her lap.

Julian sighed. "I am sorry, Sophy."

"There was no need for her to take such a course of action," Sophy whispered tightly. "Bess could have helped her."

"Old Bess? How?" Julian frowned.

"There are ways that such situations may be remedied," Sophy said. "Old Bess knows them. If only my sister had confided in me, I could have taken her to Bess. No one need ever have known."

Julian dropped the feather shaft and leaned over to capture his wife's wrist once more. This time he deliberately exerted pressure on the small bones. "What do you know of such matters?" he demanded very softly. *Elizabeth had known such things.*

Sophy blinked quickly, apparently confused by his sudden, controlled rage. "Old Bess knows much about medicinal herbs. She has taught me many things."

"She has taught you ways to rid yourself of an unwanted babe?" he demanded softly.

Sophy seemed to realize at last that she had said far too much. "She . . . she has mentioned certain herbs that a woman can use if she believes she has conceived," she admitted hesitantly. "But the herbs can be very dangerous to the mother and must be used with great skill and caution." Sophy looked down at her hands for a moment. "I am not skilled in that particular art."

"Bloody hell. You had best not be skilled in such things, Sophy. And I swear, if that old witch, Bess, is dealing in abortion, I will have her removed from my land immediately."

"Really, my lord? Are your friends in London so very pure? Have none of your amours never been obliged to resort to certain remedies because of you?"

"No, they have not," Julian rasped, thoroughly goaded now. "For your information, madam, there are techniques that may be used to prevent the problem from occurring in the first place, just as there are ways to prevent contracting certain diseases associated with . . . never mind."

"Techniques, my lord? What techniques?" Sophy's eyes lit up with obvious fascination.

"Good God, I don't believe we are discussing such matters."

"You opened the discussion, my lord. I collect you do not intend to tell me about these techniques for preventing the, er, problem."

"No, I most certainly do not."

"Ah, I see. This is yet another privileged bit of information available only to men?"

"You have no need of such information, Sophy," he said grimly. "You are not in the one business that would require that you learn such things."

"But there are women who do know such things?" she pressed.

"That is quite enough, Sophy."

"And you know such women? Would you introduce me to one of them? I should dearly love to chat with her. Perhaps she would know other such amazing things. My intellectual interests are quite far-ranging, you know. One can get only so much out of books."

He thought for an instant she was teasing him again and Julian came close to losing his temper completely. But at the last moment he realized Sophy's fascination was oddly innocent and totally genuine. He groaned and leaned back into the corner of the seat. "We will not discuss this further."

"You sound distressingly like my grandmother. Really, it is very disappointing, Julian. I had hoped that when I married I would find myself living with someone who would be a more amusing conversationalist."

"I shall endeavor to amuse you in other ways," he muttered, closing his eyes and resting his head against the cushion.

"If you are talking about seduction again, Julian, I must tell you, I do not find the topic amusing."

"Because of what happened to your sister? I can see where such a situation would have left its mark on you, Sophy. But you must learn that there is a vast difference between that which goes on between husband and wife and the sort of unpleasant seduction your sister endured."

"Really, my lord? How does a man learn to make such fine distinctions? At school? Did you learn them during your first marriage or from your experience of keeping mistresses?"

At that juncture, Julian's temper frayed to a gossamer thread. He did not move or open his eyes. He did not dare. "I have explained to you that my first marriage is not a topic for discussion. Nor is the other subject you just raised. If you are wise, you will keep that in mind, Sophy."

Something in his too-quiet words apparently made an impression on her. She said nothing more.

Julian took up the reins of his temper once again and when he knew he had himself in check he opened his eyes and regarded his new bride. "Sooner or later you must accustom yourself to me, Sophy."

"You promised me three months, my lord."

"Damn it, woman, I will not force myself upon you for the next three months. But do not expect me to make no attempt whatsoever to change your mind about lovemaking in the meantime. That is asking entirely too much and is completely outside the terms of our ridiculous agreement."

Her head snapped around. "Is this what you meant when you warned me that a man's sense of honor is unreliable when it comes to his dealings with women? Am

I to assume, my lord, that I may not rely upon your word as a gentleman?"

The insult went to the bone. "There is not a single man of my acquaintance who would risk saying such a thing to me, madam."

"Are you going to call me out?" she asked with deep interest. "I should tell you my grandfather taught me how to use his pistols. I am accounted a fair shot."

Julian wondered whether a gentleman's honor prevented him from beating his wife on her wedding day. Somehow this marriage was not getting off to the smooth, orderly start he had intended.

He looked at the bright, inquiring face opposite him and tried to think of a response to Sophy's outrageous comment. At that moment the bit of ribbon that had been dangling from her reticule fell to the floor of the carriage.

Sophy frowned and leaned forward quickly to pick it up. Julian moved simultaneously and his big hand brushed against her small one.

"Allow me," he said coolly, picking up the stray bit of ribbon and dropping it into her palm.

"Thank you," she said, slightly embarrassed. She began struggling furiously to work the ribbon back into the design on her reticule.

Julian sat back, watching in fascination as another piece of ribbon came loose. Before his eyes, the entire intricately worked pattern of ribbon trim began to unravel. In less than five minutes Sophy was sitting with a totally demolished reticule. She looked up with a bewildered gaze.

"I have never understood why this sort of thing is always happening to me," she said.

Without a word Julian took the reticule off her lap, opened it and dropped all the stray bits of ribbon inside.

As he handed the purse back to her he experienced the disquieting sensation that he had just opened Pandora's box.

THREE

Midway through the second week of her honeymoon on Julian's Norfolk estate, Sophy began to fear that she had married a man who had a serious problem with his after-dinner port.

Up until that point she had tentatively begun to enjoy her wedding trip. Eslington Park was situated against a serene backdrop of wooded knolls and lush pasture lands. The house itself was stolid and dignified in the classically inspired Palladian tradition that had been fashionable during the last century.

There was an aging, heavy feel to the interior but Sophy thought there was hope for the well-proportioned rooms with their tall windows. She looked forward to doing some redecorating.

In the meantime she had gloried in daily rides with Julian during which they explored the woods, meadows, and rich farmlands he had recently acquired. He had introduced her to his newly appointed steward, John Fleming, and seemed positively grateful when Sophy took no offense at the long hours he spent plotting the future of Eslington Park with the earnest young man.

Julian had also taken pains to introduce Sophy, as well as himself, to all the tenants on the property. He had seemed pleased when Sophy had admired sheep and assorted specimens of agricultural produce with a knowledgeable eye. *There are some advantages to being country-bred,* Sophy privately decided. At least such a woman had something intelligent to say to a husband who obviously had a love for the land.

More than once Sophy found herself wondering if Julian would ever develop a similar love for his new bride.

The tenants and neighbors had been in suspense awaiting the arrival of their new lord. But after Julian had accompanied several of the farmers into barns with total disregard for the polish on his elegant riding boots, the word went around that the new master of Eslington knew what he was about when it came to farming and sheep raising.

Sophy was readily accepted after she had cooed over a few plump babies, frowned in deep concern over a few sick ones, and held several learned discussions on the subject of the use of local herbs in home remedies. More than once Julian had been obliged to wait patiently while his wife exchanged a recipe for a cough syrup or a digestive aid with a farmer's wife.

He seemed to find it amusing to remove bits of straw from Sophy's hair after she had emerged from the close confines of a small cottage.

"You are going to make me a fine wife, Sophy," he had remarked with satisfaction during the third day of such visiting. "I chose well this time."

Sophy had hugged her pleasure at his words to herself and managed a laughing smile. "By that remark, I collect you mean I have the potential to become a good farmer's wife?"

"When all is said and done, that is precisely what I am, Sophy. A farmer." He had looked out over the landscape with the pride of a man who knows he owns everything he sees. "And a good farm wife will suit me well."

"You speak as if I will someday become this paragon,"

she had pointed out softly. "I would remind you that I am already your wife."

He had flashed her the devil's own smile. "Not yet, my sweet, but soon. Much sooner than you had planned."

The staff at Eslington Park was well trained and commendably efficient, although Sophy privately winced when servants nearly tripped over their own feet endeavoring to anticipate Julian's orders. They were obviously wary of their new master, although simultaneously proud to serve such an important man.

They had heard the rumors of his quick, ruthless temper from the coachman, groom, valet, and lady's maid who had accompanied Lord and Lady Ravenwood to Eslington, however, and were taking no chances.

All in all, the honeymoon was going quite well. The only thing that had marred her stay in Norfolk as far as Sophy was concerned was the subtle, but deliberate, pressure Julian was applying in the evenings. It was beginning to make her quite nervous.

It was obvious Julian did not intend to stay out of her bed for the next three months. He fully expected to be able to seduce her long before the stipulated time had passed.

Until the point when she had begun to notice his growing fondness for port after dinner, Sophy had been fairly certain she could handle the situation. The trick was to control her own responses to his increasingly intimate good-night kisses. If she could manage that she was quite convinced Julian would honor the letter, if not the spirit of his word. She sensed instinctively his pride would not allow him to sink to the level of using force to gain access to her bed.

But the increasing consumption of port worried her. It added a new and dangerous element to an already tense situation. She remembered all too well the night her sister Amelia had returned from one of her secret assignations and tearfully explained that a gentleman in his cups was capable of violent language and bestial behavior. Amelia's soft white arms had been marked with bruises that night. Sophy had been furious and demanded once more to know the name of Amelia's lover. Amelia had again refused to say.

"*Have you told this fine lover of yours that Dorrings have been Ravenwood neighbors for generations? If Grandfather finds out what is happening, he will go straight to Lord Ravenwood and see that a stop is put to this nonsense.*"

Amelia sniffed back more tears. "I have made certain my dear love does not know who my grandfather is for that very reason. Oh, Sophy, don't you understand? I am afraid that if my sweet love discovers I am a Dorring and thus a granddaughter of such a close neighbor of Ravenwood, he will not take the chance of meeting me again."

"*You would let your lover abuse you rather than tell him who you are?" Sophy had asked incredulously.*

"*You do not know what it is to love," Amelia had whispered and then she had sobbed herself to sleep.*

Amelia had been wrong, Sophy knew. She did know what it was to love but she was trying to deal with the dangers of the emotion in a more intelligent manner than her poor sister had done. She would not make Amelia's mistakes.

Sophy silently endured the growing anxiety over the matter of Julian's port consumption for several tense evenings before she broached the subject of his heavy drinking.

"Do you have trouble sleeping, my lord?" she finally inquired during the second week of her marriage. They were seated before the fire in the crimson drawing room. Julian had just helped himself to another large glass of port.

He regarded her with hooded eyes. "Why do you ask?"

"Forgive me, but I cannot help but notice that your taste for port is increasing in the evenings. People frequently use sherry or port or claret to aid them in getting to sleep. Are you accustomed to imbibing so much at night?"

He drummed his fingers on the arm of his chair and considered her for a long moment. "No," he finally said and drank half of his port in one gulp. "It disturbs you?"

Sophy focused her attention on her embroidery. "If you

are having trouble sleeping there are more efficacious remedies. Bess taught me many of them."

"Are you proposing to dose me with laudanum?"

"No. Laudanum is effective but I would not resort to it as a remedy for poor sleep unless other tonics had failed. If you like I can prepare a mixture of herbs for you to try. I brought my medicine chest with me."

"Thank you, Sophy. I believe I shall continue to rely on my port. I understand it and it understands me."

Sophy's brows rose inquiringly. "What is there to understand, my lord?"

"Do you wish me to be blunt, Madam Wife?"

"Of course." She was surprised at such a question. "You know I prefer free and open conversation between us. You are the one who occasionally experiences difficulty in discussing certain matters, not I."

"I give you fair warning, this is not a matter you will care to discuss."

"Nonsense. If you are having difficulty sleeping, I am certain there is a better cure than port."

"On that we agree. The question, my dear, is whether you are willing to provide the cure."

The lazy, taunting quality of his voice brought her head up swiftly. She found herself looking straight into his glittering green gaze. And suddenly she understood.

"I see," she managed to say calmly. "I had not realized our agreement would cause you such physical discomfort, my lord."

"Now that you are aware of it, would you care to consider releasing me from my bond?"

A length of embroidery floss snapped in her hand. Sophy glanced down at the dangling threads. "I thought everything was going rather well, my lord," she said distantly.

"I know you did. You have been enjoying yourself here at Eslington Park, haven't you, Sophy?"

"Very much, my lord."

"Well, so have I. In certain respects. But in other respects, I am finding this honeymoon extremely tiresome." He tossed off the remainder of the port. "Damned tiresome. The fact is, our situation is unnatural, Sophy."

She sighed with deep regret. "I suppose this means you would prefer that we cut short our honeymoon?"

The empty crystal glass snapped between his fingers. Julian swore and dusted the delicate shards from his hands. "It means," he stated grimly, "that I would like to make this a normal marriage. It is my duty as well as my pleasure to insist that we do so."

"Are you so very anxious to get on with producing your heir?"

"I am not thinking about my future heir at the moment. I am thinking about the current Earl of Ravenwood. I am also thinking about the present Countess of Ravenwood. The chief reason you are not suffering as I am, Sophy, is because you do not yet know what you are missing."

Sophy's temper flared. "You need not be so odiously condescending, my lord. I am a country girl, remember? I have been raised around animals all my life and I have been called in to help with the birthing of a babe or two in my time. I am well aware of what goes on between husband and wife and, to be truthful, I do not believe I am missing anything terribly elevating."

"It is not intended to be an intellectual exercise, madam. It is a physical pursuit."

"Like riding a horse? If you don't mind my saying so, it sounds rather less rewarding. At least when one rides a horse, one accomplishes something useful such as arriving at a given destination."

"Perhaps it is time you learned what sort of destination awaits you in the bedchamber, my dear."

Julian was on his feet, reaching for her before Sophy quite realized what was happening. He snatched her embroidery from her fingers and tossed it aside. Then his arms went around her and he dragged her close against him. She knew when she looked up into his intent face that this would not be just one more of the coaxing, persuasive good-night kisses she had been receiving lately.

Alarmed, Sophy pushed at his shoulders. "Stop it, Julian. I have told you I do not wish to be seduced."

"I'm beginning to think it's my duty to seduce you. This damned agreement of yours is too hard on me, little one. Have pity on your poor husband. I shall undoubtedly expire from sheer frustration if I am obliged to wait out the three months. Sophy, stop fighting me."

"Julian, please—"

"Hush, my sweet." His thumb moved along the edge of her soft mouth, tracing the contours. "I gave you my word I would not force you and I will keep my oath even if it kills me. But I have a right to try to change your mind and that, by God, is exactly what I intend to do. I've given you ten days to get used to the idea of being married to me. That is nine days longer than any other man would have allowed in this situation."

His mouth came down on hers with sudden, fierce demand. Sophy had been right. This was not another of the gentle assaults on her senses that she had grown to expect in the evenings. This kiss was hot and deliberately overpowering. She could feel Julian's tongue sliding boldly into her mouth. For a moment a heavy, drugging warmth surged through Sophy. Then she tasted the port on his breath and instinctively she started to struggle.

"Be still," Julian muttered, soothing her with a long, stroking movement of his big palm down her spine. "Just be still and let me kiss you. That's all I want at the moment. I intend to remove a few of your ridiculous fears."

"I am not afraid of you," she protested quickly, keenly aware of the strength in his hands. "I simply do not care to have the privacy of my bedchamber invaded yet by a man who is still very much a stranger to me."

"We are no longer strangers, Sophy. We are husband and wife and it's time we became lovers."

His mouth closed over hers again and her protests were cut off. Julian kissed her deeply, thoroughly, imprinting himself on her until Sophy was trembling with reaction. As always when he held her in his arms like this she felt breathless and strangely weak. When his hands moved lower, gripping her and forcing her up against his body, she felt the hardness in him and it made her flinch.

"Julian?" She looked up at him, wide-eyed.

"What did you expect?" He smiled wickedly. "A man is no different than any other farm animal. You claim to be an expert on the subject."

"My lord, this is hardly a matter of putting a ewe and a ram together in the same pen."

"I am glad you appreciate the difference."

He refused to let her ease away from him. Instead, he cupped her buttocks in his two large hands and urged her even closer to the bulging hardness of his thighs.

Sophy's head whirled as she felt the unmistakable shape of his swollen manhood pushing against her softness. Her skirts swirled around his leg, caught, and clung to his calves. He widened his stance and she found herself trapped between his legs.

"Sophy, little one, Sophy, my sweet, let me make love to you. It's only right." The urgent plea was punctuated with small, persuasive kisses that traced the line of her jaw and traveled down her throat to her bare shoulder.

Sophy could not respond. She felt as if she were being swept out to sea on a mighty, surging tide. She had loved Julian from afar for too long. The temptation to surrender to the sensuous warmth that he engendered in her was almost overwhelming. Unconsciously her arms went around his neck and she parted her lips invitingly. He had taught her much about kissing during the past few days.

Julian needed no second invitation. He took her lips again with a low groan of satisfaction. This time his hand moved under her breast and he cupped her gently, his thumb searching out the nipple beneath the muslin bodice.

Sophy did not hear the drawing room door open behind her but she did hear the apologetic gasp of dismay and the sound of the door closing again very quickly. Julian lifted his head to glare over the top of her curls and the spell was broken.

Sophy blushed as she realized one of the servants had witnessed the passionate kiss. She stepped back hurriedly and Julian let her go, smiling slightly at her disheveled appearance. She put her hand to her hair and found it in far worse than its usual disarray. Several curls were tumbling down around her ears and the ribbon her maid had tied so carefully before dinner had come loose. It dangled down the nape of her neck.

"I . . . Excuse me, my lord. I must go upstairs. Everything has come undone." She whirled and flew to the door.

"Sophy." There was a clink of glass on glass.

"Yes, my lord?" She paused, her hand on the doorknob, and glanced back warily.

Julian was standing by the fire, his arm resting casually along the white marble mantle. He had a fresh glass of port in his hand. Sophy was more alarmed than ever when she saw the masculine satisfaction in his eyes. His mouth was curved tenderly but the smile did little to alleviate the familiar arrogance radiating from him. He was very sure of himself now, very confident.

"Seduction is not such a fearful thing, after all, is it, my sweet? You are going to enjoy yourself and I think you have had sufficient time to realize that."

Was this what it had been like for poor Amelia? A complete devastation of the senses?

Unaware of what she was doing, Sophy touched her lower lip with the tip of her finger. "Kisses such as the ones you just gave me are your idea of seduction, my lord?"

He inclined his head, his eyes flaring with amusement. "I hope you enjoy them, Sophy, because there will be many more such kisses to come. Beginning tonight. Go on upstairs to bed, my dear. I will join you shortly. I am going to seduce you into granting me a proper wedding night. Believe me, my love, you will thank me tomorrow morning for putting an end to this entirely unnatural situation you have created. And I will take great pleasure in accepting your gratitude."

Fury surged through Sophy, mingling with the other heady emotions that were already coursing through her. She was suddenly so violently angry she could not even speak. Instead, she jerked open the heavy mahogany doors and dashed across the hall to the stairs.

She stormed into her bedchamber a few minutes later

and startled her maid who was busy turning down the bed.

"My lady! Is somethin' wrong?"

Sophy took a grip on her anger and her reeling senses. She was breathing much too quickly. "No, no, Mary. Nothing is wrong. I took the stairs too quickly, that's all. Please help me with my dress."

"Certainly, ma'am." Mary, a bright-eyed young girl in her late teens who was thrilled with her recent promotion to the status of lady's maid, came forward to assist her mistress in undressing. She handled the embroidered muslin gown with reverent care.

"I think I would like a pot of tea before bedtime, Mary. Would you please have one sent up?"

"At once, my lady."

"Oh, and Mary, have two cups put on the tray." Sophy took a deep breath. "The Earl will be joining me."

Mary's eyes widened with approval but she wisely held her tongue as she helped Sophy into a chintz dressing gown. "I'll have the tea up here straight away, ma'am. Oh, that reminds me. One of the housemaids is complainin' of her stomach. She thinks it's somethin' she ate. She was wantin' to know if I'd ask your advice."

"What? Oh, yes, of course." Sophy turned toward her chest of dried herbs and quickly filled a small packet with a selection that included powdered licorice and rhubarb. "Take these to her and tell her to mix two pinches of each into a cup of tea. That should settle her stomach. If she is not any better by morning, be sure to let me know."

"Thank you, ma'am. Alice will be ever so grateful. She suffers a lot from a nervous stomach, I hear. By the by, Allan the footman says to tell you his sore throat is much better thanks to that honey and brandy syrup you had Cook prepare for him."

"Excellent, excellent, I'm glad to hear it," Sophy said impatiently. The last thing she wanted to discuss tonight was Allan the footman's sore throat. "Now, Mary, please hurry with that tea, will you?"

"Yes, ma'am." Mary scurried out of the room.

Sophy began to pace the floor, her soft slippers making

no sound on the dark, patterned carpet. She barely noticed the bit of lace trim that had come loose from the lapel of her dressing gown and was dangling over one breast.

The overbearing, unspeakably arrogant man she had married thought he had only to touch her and she would succumb to his expertise. He would badger her and pester her and otherwise keep after her until he had his way with her. She knew that now. Bedding her was obviously a matter of masculine pride to him.

Sophy was beginning to realize she would get no peace until Julian had proven himself her master in the privacy of the bedchamber. There was little chance to work on the harmonious relationship she dreamed of while Julian was concentrating only on seducing her.

Sophy halted her pacing abruptly, wondering if the Earl of Ravenwood would be satisfied with a single night of conquest. Julian was not, after all, in love with her. At the moment apparently she constituted a challenge because she was his wife and she was refusing him the privileges he considered rightfully his. But if he thought he'd finally proven to both of them he could seduce her, perhaps he would leave her alone for a while.

Sophy went quickly to her beautifully carved medicine chest and stood looking down at the rows of tiny wooden trays and drawers. She was simmering with rage and fear and another emotion she did not want to examine too closely. There was not much time. In a few minutes Julian would come sauntering through the door that connected her bedchamber with his dressing room. And then he would take her into his arms and touch her the way he touched his little ballet dancer or actress or whatever she was.

Mary opened the door and came into the bedchamber carrying a silver tray. "Your tea, ma'am. Will there be anythin' else?"

"No, thank you, Mary. You may go." Sophy managed what she hoped was a normal smile of dismissal but Mary's eyes seemed brighter than ever as she bobbed a small curtsy and let herself out of the room. Sophy was sure she heard a muffled giggle out in the hall.

Servants seem to know everything that goes on in a large house such as this, Sophy thought resentfully. It was quite possible her maid knew perfectly well that Julian had never spent the night in his wife's bed. That thought was rather mortifying in some ways.

Fleetingly, Sophy wondered if part of Julian's irritation had to do with the fact that he knew the entire staff was speculating on why he was not visiting his new bride in her bedroom.

Sophy hardened her heart. She was not about to turn aside from her goal merely for the sake of Julian's male pride. He had more than enough of that commodity as it was. She reached into the herb chest and took a pinch of chamomile and a pinch of something far more potent. Deftly she stirred them into the pot of brewing tea.

Then she sat down to wait. She had to sit down. She was trembling so much she could not stand.

She did not have long to anticipate the inevitable. The connecting door opened softly and Sophy gave a start. Her eyes went to the doorway. Julian stood there in a black silk dressing gown that was embroidered with the Ravenwood crest. He regarded her with a quizzical little smile.

"You are entirely too nervous, little one," he said gently as he closed the door behind him. "This is what comes of putting matters off for far too long. You have built the whole business into an event of terrifying proportions. By tomorrow morning you will be able to put everything back into its proper perspective."

"I would like to beg you one last time, Julian, not to pursue this any further. I must tell you again that I feel you are breaking the spirit, if not the letter of your oath."

His smile vanished and his gaze hardened. He shoved his hands into the pockets of his gown and began to prowl slowly around her room. "We will not discuss my honor again. I assure you, it is an important matter to me and I would not do anything I felt would tarnish it."

"You have your own definition of honor, then?"

He gave her an angry glance. "I know far better how to define it than you do, Sophy."

"I lack the ability to define it properly because I am merely a woman?"

He relaxed, the faint smile edging his grim mouth again. "You are not merely a woman, my love. You are a most interesting female, believe me. I did not dream when I asked for your hand in marriage that I would be getting such a fascinating concoction. Did you know that there's a bit of lace dangling from your gown?"

Sophy glanced down uneasily and was chagrined to see the lace flopping over her breast. She made one or two fruitless efforts to push it back into place and then gave up. When she raised her head she found herself looking at Julian through a lock of hair that had slipped free of its pins. Irritably she pushed it back behind her ear. She drew herself up proudly.

"Would you care for a cup of tea, my lord?"

His smile broadened indulgently and Julian's eyes became very green. "Thank you, Sophy. After all the port I allowed myself after dinner, a cup of tea would be most welcome. I would not want to fall asleep at an awkward moment. You would be quite disappointed, I'm sure."

Arrogant man, she thought as she poured the brew with shaking fingers. He was interpreting her offer of tea as a gesture of surrender, she just knew it. A moment later when she handed him the cup he accepted it the way she imagined a battlefield commander accepted the sword of the vanquished.

"What an interesting aroma. Your own mixture, Sophy?" Julian took a sip of tea and resumed prowling her room.

"Yes." The word seemed to get caught somewhere in her throat. She watched with sick fascination as he took another sip. "Chamomile and . . . and other flowers. It has a very soothing effect on nerves that have become somewhat over agitated."

Julian nodded absently. "Excellent." He paused in front of the little rosewood desk to study the handful of books she had carefully arranged there. "Ah, the lamentable reading material of my bluestocking bride. Let me see just how regrettable your tastes really are."

He pulled first one and then another of the leather-bound volumes off the shelf. He helped himself to a second sip of tea while he studied the engraved leather bindings. "Hm. Virgil and Aristotle in translation. Admittedly a bit overpowering for the average reader but not really all that terrible. I used to read this sort of thing myself."

"I'm glad you approve, my lord," Sophy said stiffly.

He glanced at her, amused. "Do you find me condescending, Sophy?"

"Very."

"I don't mean to be, you know. I'm merely curious about you." He replaced the classics and removed another volume. "What else have we here? Wesley's *Primitive Physic*? A rather dated work, is it not?"

"Still an excellent herbal, my lord. With much detail about English herbs. Grandfather gave it to me."

"Ah, yes. Herbs." He put the book down and picked up another volume. He smiled indulgently. "Well, now, I see Lord Byron's romantic nonsense has made its way into the countryside. Did you enjoy *Childe Harold*, Sophy?"

"I found it very entertaining, my lord. What about you?"

He grinned unabashedly at the open challenge. "I'll admit I read it and I'll admit the man has a way with melodrama, but, then he comes from a long line of melodramatic fools. I fear we shall hear more from Byron's melancholy heroes."

"At least the man is not dull. I understand Lord Byron is quite the rage in London," Sophy said tentatively, wondering if she had accidentally stumbled across a point of mutual intellectual interest.

"If by that you mean the women are busy throwing themselves at him, you're right. A man could get trampled under a lot of pretty little feet if he was idiotic enough to attend a crush where Byron was also present." Julian did not sound envious in the least. It was obvious he found the Byron phenomenon amusing, nothing more. "What else have we here? Some learned text on mathematics, perhaps?"

Sophy nearly choked as she recognized the book in his hand. "Not exactly, my lord."

Julian's indulgent expression was wiped off his face in an instant as he read the title aloud. "Wollstonecraft's *A Vindication of the Rights of Women*?"

"I fear so, my lord."

His eyes were glittering as he looked up from the book in his hands. "This is the sort of thing you have been studying? This ridiculous nonsense espoused by a woman who was no better than a demirep?"

"Miss Wollstonecraft was not a . . . a demirep," Sophy flared indignantly. "She was a free thinker, an intellectual woman of great ability."

"She was a harlot. She lived openly with more than one man without benefit of marriage."

"She felt marriage was nothing but a cage for women. Once a woman marries she is at the mercy of her husband. She has no rights of her own. Miss Wollstonecraft had deep insight into the female situation and she felt something should be done about it. I happen to agree with her. You say you are curious about me, my lord. Well, you might learn something about my interests if you read that book."

"I have no intention of reading such a piece of idiocy." Julian tossed the volume carelessly aside. "And what is more, my dear, I am not going to have you poisoning your own brain with the writing of a woman who, by rights, should have been locked away in Bedlam or set up in Trevor Square as a professional courtesan."

Sophy was barely able to restrain herself from throwing her full cup of tea at him. "We had an agreement on the matter of my reading habits, my lord. Are you going to violate that, also?"

Julian gulped down the last of his tea and set the cup and saucer aside. He came toward her deliberately, his expression cold and furious. "Hurl one more accusation about my lack of honor at me, madam, and I will not answer for the consequences. I have had enough of this farce you call a honeymoon. Nothing useful is being achieved. The time has come to put matters on a normal footing. I have indulged you long enough, Sophy. From now on, you will be a proper wife in the bedchamber as well as outside it. You will accept my judgment in all areas and that includes the matter of your reading habits."

Sophy's cup and saucer clattered alarmingly as she sprang to her feet. The lock of hair she had pushed behind her ear fell free again. She took a step backward and the heel of her slipper caught on the hem of her dressing gown. There was a rending sound as the delicate fabric tore.

"Now look what you've done," she wailed as she glanced down at the drooping hem.

"I have done nothing yet." Julian stopped in front of her and surveyed her nervous, mutinous expression. His eyes softened. "Calm yourself. I have not even touched you and you already look as if you have been struggling valiantly for your sadly misplaced female honor." He raised a hand and gently caught the dangling lock of hair between his fingers. "How ever do you manage it, Sophy?" he asked softly.

"Manage what, my lord?"

"No other woman of my acquaintance goes about in such sweet disarray. There is always some bit of ribbon or lace dangling from your gowns and your hair never stays where it is meant to stay."

"You knew I did not have the trick of fashion when you made your offer, my lord," she said tightly.

"I know. I did not mean to imply any criticism. I simply wondered how you achieved the effect. You carry it off so artlessly." He released the lock of hair and slid his blunt fingers around her head, tugging more pins free as he went.

Sophy stiffened as he eased his other arm around her waist and pulled her closer. She wondered frantically how long it would take for the tea to have its inevitable effect. Julian did not seem to be at all sleepy.

"Please, Julian—"

"I am trying to do precisely that, my love," he murmured against her mouth. "I want nothing more than to please you tonight. I suggest you relax and let me show you that being a wife is not really so terrible."

"I must insist on our agreement..." She tried to argue

but she was so nervous now she could not even stand. She clutched Julian's shoulders to steady herself and wondered wildly what she would do if she had inadvertently used the wrong herbs in the tea.

"After tonight you will not mention that stupid agreement again." Julian's mouth came down heavily, his lips moving on hers in a slow, drugging fashion. His hands found the ties of her dressing gown.

Sophy jumped when the gown was slowly eased off her shoulders. She stared up into Julian's heated gaze and tried to detect some sign of cloudiness in his glittering eyes.

"Julian, could you grant me just a few more minutes? I have not finished my tea. Perhaps you would like another cup?"

"Don't sound so terribly hopeful, my sweet. You are only trying to put off the inevitable and I assure you the inevitable is going to be quite pleasant for both of us." He deliberately ran his hands down her sides to her waist and then to her hips, drawing the fabric of the fine lawn nightgown close to her figure. "Very pleasant," he whispered, his voice growing husky as he gently squeezed her buttocks.

Sophy began to burn beneath his intent gaze. The desire in him was mesmerizing. She had never had any man look at her the way Julian was looking at her now. She could feel the heat and strength in him. It made her as light-headed as if she had also drunk a cup of the herbed tea.

"Kiss me, Sophy." Julian tilted her chin with his fingers.

Obediently she lifted her head and stood on tiptoe to brush her mouth across his. *How much longer?* she wondered frantically.

"Again, Sophy."

Her fingers dug into the fabric of his dressing gown as she touched his mouth with her own once more. He was warm and hard and curiously compelling. She could have clung to him all night like this but she knew he would insist on much more than simple kisses.

"That's better, my sweet." His voice was growing thicker but whether it was from the effects of the sleeping tonic or his own desire was not clear. "As soon as you and I have reached a complete understanding, we are going to deal together very well, Sophy."

"Is this the way you deal with your mistress?" she asked daringly.

His expression hardened. "I have warned you more than once not to talk of such matters."

"You are always giving me warnings, Julian. I grow tired of them."

"Do you? Then perhaps it's time you learned I am capable of action as well as words."

He picked her up and carried her over to the turned-back bed. He released her and she dropped lightly down onto the sheets. When she scrambled to adjust herself the fine lawn gown somehow succeeded in working its way up to her thighs. She looked up and saw Julian's eyes on her breasts. She knew he could see the outline of her nipples through the soft material.

Julian shrugged out of his dressing gown, his gaze sliding along her body to her bare legs. "Such beautiful legs. I am sure the rest of you is going to prove just as lovely."

But Sophy was not listening. She was staring at his nude figure in amazement. She had never before seen a man naked, let alone fully aroused and the sight was staggering. She had thought herself mature and well informed, not an unsophisticated girl who could be easily shocked. She was, as she had so often informed Julian, a country-bred girl.

But Julian's male member seemed tremendous to Sophy's reeling senses. It thrust aggressively out of a nest of curling black hair. The skin of his flat stomach and broad, hair-covered chest was drawn tight over sleek muscles Sophy knew were quite capable of overpowering her.

In the glow of the candlelight Julian looked infinitely male and infinitely dangerous but there was a strange, compelling quality about his power that alarmed her more than anything else could have done.

"Julian, no," Sophy said quickly. "Please do not do this. You gave me your word."

The passion in his eyes flared briefly into anger but his

words began to slur. "Damn you, Sophy, I have been as patient as a man can be. Do not bring up the matter of our so-called agreement again. I am not going to violate it."

He came down onto the bed, reaching for her, his big, strong hands closing around her arm. She could see his eyes were finally beginning to glaze and Sophy felt a shock of what must have been relief when she realized he was about to sink into sleep.

"Sophy?" Her name was a drowsy question. "So soft. So sweet. You belong to me, you know." Long dark lashes slowly lowered, concealing the puzzled expression in Julian's eyes. "I will take care of you. Won't let you turn out like that bitch, Elizabeth. I'd strangle you first."

He bent his head to kiss her. Sophy stiffened but he never touched her lips. Julian groaned once and collapsed back against the pillow. His strong fingers grasped her arm a few seconds longer and then his hand fell away.

Sophy's pulse was racing with unnatural swiftness as she lay on the bed beside Julian. She did not dare to move for several minutes. Gradually her heartbeat steadied and she assured herself Julian was not going to awaken. The wine he had drunk earlier together with the herbs she had given him would ensure he slept until morning.

Sophy eased herself slowly off the bed, her gaze never leaving Julian's magnificently sprawled form. He looked very fierce and wild lying there on the white sheets.

What had she done?

Standing beside the bed, Sophy gathered her senses and tried to think rationally.

She was not certain how much Julian would remember when he awakened in the morning. If he ever realized he had been drugged his rage would be awesome and it would all be directed at her. She must contrive to make him think he had achieved his goal.

Sophy hurried over to the medicine chest. Bess had once explained that there was sometimes some bleeding after a woman made love the first time, especially if the man was careless and less than gentle. Julian might or might not be expecting to find blood on the sheets in the morning. But it would tend to confirm his belief that he had done his husbandly duty if he found some.

Sophy mixed a redish concoction using some red-leafed herbs and more of the tea. When she was done she eyed the mixture dubiously. It certainly looked the right color but it was very thin. Perhaps that would not matter once it had soaked into the sheet.

She went over to the bed again and dabbed a bit of the fake blood onto the bedding where she had lain a few minutes earlier. It was quickly absorbed, leaving a small, damp, reddish ring. Sophy wondered just how much blood a man would expect to find after he had made love to a virgin.

She frowned intently and finally decided the amount of red-brown liquid she had used was not enough to attract much notice so she added some more. Her hand shook nervously as she leaned over the bed and a large amount of the imitation blood slopped over the edge of the cup.

Startled, Sophy stepped back and more of the liquid cascaded onto the sheets. There was now a very sizable patch of wet, stained bedding. Sophy wondered if she had overdone it.

Hastily she poured the remainder of the reddish concoction into the teapot. Then she blew out the candles and slid gingerly into bed beside Julian, careful not to brush against his heavy, muscled leg.

There was no help for it. She would have to sleep on at least a portion of the wide, damp spot.

FOUR

Julian heard the bedchamber door open. Hushed feminine voices exchanged words. The door closed again and then he heard the cheerful clatter of a breakfast tray being set down on a table nearby.

He stirred slowly, feeling unusually lethargic. His mouth tasted like the inside of a horse stall. He frowned, trying to remember just how much port he had swallowed during the course of the previous evening.

It was an effort to open his eyes. When he finally did so he was totally disoriented. The walls of his room had apparently changed color overnight. He stared at the unfamiliar Chinese wallpaper for a long moment as memory slowly filtered back.

He was in Sophy's bed.

Julian eased himself up slowly onto the pillows, waiting for the rest of what should have been a very satisfying memory to emerge. Nothing came to mind except a faint, annoying headache. He scowled again and rubbed his temples.

It was not possible he could have forgotten the act of

63

making love to his new bride. The anticipation had been
responsible for keeping him in a state of aching arousal for
too long. He'd been suffering for nearly ten days awaiting
the right moment. Surely the denouement would have left
a most pleasurable recollection.

He glanced around the room and saw Sophy standing
near the wardrobe. She was wearing the same dressing
gown she had worn last night. Her back was to him and he
smiled fleetingly as he caught sight of a stray ruffle that
had been accidentally turned under around the collar.
Julian had a strong urge to go over to her and straighten
the bit of lace. Then, he decided, he would take the
dressing gown off altogether and carry her back to
bed.

He tried to remember what her small, gently curved
breasts had looked like in the candlelight but the only
image that formed was one of dark, taut nipples pushing
against the soft fabric of her lawn nightgown.

Deliberately he pressed his memory further and found
he could recall a hazy picture of his wife lying on the bed,
the nightgown drawn up above her knees. Her bare legs
had been graceful and elegant and he recalled his excitement at the thought of having those legs wrapped around
him.

He also remembered discarding his dressing gown as a
sweeping desire kindled within him. There had been
shock and uncertainty in Sophy's gaze when she had
looked at him. It had angered him. He had come down
onto the bed beside her, determined to reassure her and
make her accept him. She had been wary and nervous but
he had known that he could make her relax and enjoy his
lovemaking. She had already shown him that she responded
to him.

He had reached for her and . . .

Julian shook his head, trying to clear the cobwebs in it.
Surely he had not disgraced himself by failing to carry out
his husbandly duties. He had been consumed with the
need to make Sophy his, he would not have fallen asleep
in the middle of the procedure no matter how much port
he had downed.

Stunned by his incredible memory lapse, Julian started to push back the covers. His thigh scraped across a stiff portion of the sheet—a damp patch that had dried overnight. He smiled with relief and satisfaction as he started to glance downward. He knew what he would find and it would prove he had not humiliated himself after all.

But a moment later his sense of satisfaction gave way to appalled disbelief. The reddish brown stain on the sheet was far too wide.

Impossibly wide.

Monstrously wide.

What had he done to his gentle, delicate wife?

The only experience Julian had ever had with a virgin had been his wedding night with Elizabeth and with the bitter wisdom gained in recent years he'd had cause to question that one occasion.

But he had heard the usual male talk and he knew that in the normal course of events a woman did not bleed like a slaughtered calf. Sometimes a woman did not bleed at all.

A man would have to literally assault a woman to cause this much bleeding. He would have had to hurt her very badly to produce so much damage.

A queasy sensation gripped Julian's belly as he continued to stare down at the terrible evidence of his brutal clumsiness. His own words came back to him. *You will thank me in the morning.*

Good God, any woman who had suffered as much as Sophy obviously had would not be in any mood to thank the man who had wounded her so grievously. She must hate him this morning. Julian closed his eyes for a moment, desperately trying to remember exactly what he had done to her. No incriminating scene appeared in his beleaguered mind yet he could not deny the evidence. He opened his eyes.

"Sophy?" His voice sounded raw, even to his own ears.

Sophy jumped as if he had struck her with a whip. She whirled around to face him with an expression that made Julian grit his teeth.

"Good . . . good morning, my lord." Her eyes were very wide, filled with great feminine uneasiness.

"I have the feeling this particular morning could have been a great deal better than it is. And I am to blame." He sat up on the edge of the bed and reached for his dressing gown. He took his time getting into it, trying to think of how best to handle the situation. She would hardly be in a mood to listen to words of reassurance. God in heaven, he wished his head did not ache so.

"I believe your valet is ready with your shaving things, my lord."

He ignored that. "Are you all right?" he asked in low tones. He started to walk toward her and stopped when she immediately stepped back. She came up against the wardrobe and could retreat no further although the wish to do so was plain in her expression. She stood there, clutching an embroidered muslin petticoat and watched him anxiously.

"I am fine, my lord."

Julian sucked in his breath. "Oh, Sophy, little one, what have I done to you? Was I really such a monster last night?"

"Your shaving water will get cold, my lord."

"Sophy, I am not worried about the temperature of my shaving water. I am worried about you."

"I told you, I am fine. Please, Julian, I must dress."

He groaned and went toward her, ignoring the way she tried to edge out of reach. He caught her gently by the shoulders and looked down into her worried eyes. "We must talk."

The tip of her tongue came out and touched her lips. "Are you not satisfied, my lord? I had hoped you would be."

"Good God," he breathed, pushing her head tenderly against his shoulder. "I can just envision how desperately you hope I'm satisfied. I am certain you don't want to face the thought of another night like last night."

"No, my lord, I would prefer not to face such a night again as long as I live." Her voice was muffled against his dressing gown but he heard the fervency of her wish quite clearly.

Guilt racked him. He stroked her back soothingly. "Would it help if I swear to you on my honor that the next time will not be nearly so harsh an experience?"

"Your word of honor, my lord?"

He swore violently and pressed her face more deeply into his shoulder. He could feel the tension in her and he had not the foggiest notion of how to combat it. "I know you probably do not place much stock in my word of honor this morning, but I promise you that the next time we make love, you will not suffer."

"I would prefer not to think about the next time, Julian."

He exhaled slowly. "No, I can understand that." He felt her try to free herself, but he could not let her go just yet. He had to find a way to reassure her that he was not the monster she evidently had found him last night. "I am sorry, little one. I don't know what came over me. I know you will find this hard to comprehend, but in all truthfulness, I cannot remember precisely what happened. But you must believe, I never intended to hurt you."

She stirred against him, pushing tentatively at his shoulders. "I would rather not discuss it."

"We must, else you will make the matter out to be even worse than it already is. Sophy, look at me."

Her head came up slowly. She hesitated, slid him a quick, searching little glance and then hastily looked away. "What do you want me to do, my lord?"

His hands tightened briefly on her and he had to force himself to relax. "I would like you to say that you forgive me and that you will not hold my actions last night against me. But I suppose that is asking far too much this morning."

She bit her lip. "Is your pride satisfied, my lord?"

"Hang my pride. I am trying to find a way to apologize to you and to let you know it will never be so ... so uncomfortable for you again." Hell, *uncomfortable* was a ridiculously bland term for what she must have been feeling last night when he was rutting between her legs. "Lovemaking between a husband and wife is meant to be an enjoyable experience. It should have been a pleasure for you last night. I meant it to be pleasurable. I don't know what happened. I must have lost all sense of self-control. Damn, I must have lost my reason."

"Please, my lord, this is so terribly embarrassing. Need we discuss it?"

"You must see we cannot leave it at this."

There was a distinct pause before she asked cautiously, "Why not?"

"Sophy, be reasonable, sweetheart. We are married. We will be making love frequently. I don't want you going in fear of the experience."

"I do wish you would not call it making love when it is nothing of the kind," she snapped.

Julian closed his eyes and summoned up his patience. The very least he owed his new bride now was patience. It was, unfortunately, not one of his strong points. "Sophy, tell me one thing. Do you hate me this morning?"

She swallowed convulsively and kept her eyes on the view outside her window. "No, my lord."

"Well, that is something, at least. Not much, but something. Damn it, Sophy, what did I do to you last night? I must have thrown myself on you, but I swear I can remember nothing after getting into bed with you."

"I really cannot talk about it, my lord."

"No, I don't suppose you can." He raked his fingers through his hair. How could he expect her to give him a detailed description of his actions? He did not want to listen to the chilling tale, himself. But he desperately needed to know what he had done to her. He had to know just how much of a devil he had been. He was already starting to torture himself with vivid imaginings.

"Julian?"

"I know it is no excuse, my sweet, but I fear I drank more port last night than I realized at the time. I will never again come to your bed in such a deplorable condition. It was unpardonable. Please accept my apologies and believe that next time will be far different."

Sophy cleared her throat. "As to the matter of a next time—"

He winced. "I know you are not looking forward to it

and I give you my word I will not rush you a second time. But you must realize that eventually we will have to make love again. Sophy, this first time for you, well, it's rather like falling off a horse. If you don't remount, you might never ride again."

"I'm not certain that would be such a terrible fate," she muttered.

"*Sophy.*"

"Yes, of course. There is the little matter of your heir. Forgive me, my lord, it almost slipped my mind."

Self-loathing ripped through his gut. "I was not thinking of my heir. I was thinking of you," he ground out.

"Our agreement was for three months," she reminded him quietly. "Do you think we could return to that understanding?"

Julian cursed violently under his breath. "I don't think it would be a good idea to wait that long. Your natural uneasiness will grow to unnatural proportions if you have three whole months in which to dwell on what happened last night. Sophy, I have explained to you that the worst is over. There is no need to retreat behind that agreement you insisted upon."

"I suppose not. Especially since you have made it clear I have so few means by which to enforce the agreement." She pulled out of his arms and walked over to the window. "You were quite right, my lord, when you pointed out that a woman has very little power in a marriage. Her only hope is that she can depend upon her husband's honor as a gentleman."

Another wave of guilt rolled over him, drowning Julian for an instant. When he surfaced he longed to be able to confront the devil himself rather than Sophy. At least that way he could fight back.

The position he was in was intolerable. It was shatteringly clear that there was only one honorable way out and he had to take it even though he knew that it would ultimately make everything far more difficult for her.

"Would you be able to trust my word a second time if I agree to return to our three month arrangement?" Julian asked roughly.

She shot him a quick glance over her shoulder. "Yes, I think I could trust you this time. If, that is, you would agree not to seduce me as well as not to force me."

"I promised you seduction last night and forced myself on you, instead. Yes, I can see where you might want to expand the terms of the original agreement." Julian inclined his head formally. "Very well, Sophy. My judgment tells me it is the wrong course of action, but I cannot deny your right to insist upon it after what happened last night."

Sophy bowed her head, her fingers clenched in front of her. "Thank you, my lord."

"Do not thank me. I have a strong conviction I am making a serious mistake. Something is very wrong here." He shook his head again, trying to will forth the memories of last night. He got only a blank wall. Was he losing his mind? "You have my word I will make no attempt to seduce you for the remaining time of our agreement. It goes without saying that I will not force myself on you, either." He hesitated, wanting to reach out and hold her close again but he did not dare touch her. "Please excuse me."

He let himself out of her bedchamber feeling he could hardly sink lower in her eyes than he already had in his own.

The next two days should have been the most blissful of Sophy's life. Her honeymoon was finally turning into the dream she had once fondly conceived. Julian was kind, thoughtful, and unfailingly gentle. He treated her as if she were a rare and priceless piece of porcelain. The silent, subtle, sensual threat that had plagued her for days was finally removed.

It was not that she no longer saw desire in Julian's gaze. It was still there, but the fires were carefully banked now and she no longer feared they would rage out of control. At last she had the breathing space she had tried to negotiate before the marriage.

But instead of being able to relax and enjoy the time she had bought, Sophy was miserable. For two days she fought the misery and the guilt, trying to assure herself that she had done the right thing, the only thing she could do under the circumstances. A wife had so little power, she was obliged to use whatever means came to hand.

But her own sense of honor would not let her soothe her anxiety with such a rationale.

Sophy awoke on the third morning after her fictitious wedding night knowing she could not continue the charade another day, let alone the remainder of the three months.

She had never felt so awful in her entire life. Julian's self-chastisement was a terrible responsibility for her to bear. It was obvious he was berating himself savagely for what he thought he had done. The fact that he had done nothing at all was making Sophy feel even more guilty than he did.

She downed the tea her maid had brought, set the cup back in its saucer with a loud crash and pushed back the covers.

"My, what a lovely day, ma'am. Will you be riding after breakfast?"

"Yes, Mary, I will. Please send someone to ask Lord Ravenwood if he would care to join me, will you?"

"Oh, I don't think there will be any doubt about his lordship joinin' you," Mary said with a cheeky grin. "That man would accept an invitation to go all the way to America with you, if you asked him. The staff is enjoyin' the sight to no end, you know."

"Enjoying what sight?"

"Watchin' him fall all over himself tryin' to please you. Never seen the like. Reckon his lordship is thankin' his lucky stars he's got himself a wife who's very different from that witch he married the first time."

"Mary!"

"Sorry, ma'am. But you know as well as I do what they used to say about her back home in the village. 'Tweren't no secret. She was a wild one, she was. The brown or blue habit, my lady?"

"The new brown habit, I think, Mary. And that will be quite enough about the first Lady Ravenwood." Sophy spoke with what she hoped was a proper firmness. She did not want to hear about her predecessor today. The guilt she was suffering was causing her to wonder if, once he learned the truth, Julian would conclude she was very much like his first wife in certain scheming ways.

An hour later she found Julian waiting for her in the front hall. He looked very much at ease in his elegant riding clothes. The snug, light-colored breeches, knee-high boots, and close-fitting coat emphasized the latent power in his figure.

Julian smiled as Sophy came down the stairs. He held aloft a small basket. "I had Cook pack us a picnic lunch. Thought we could explore the old castle ruin we spotted on the hill overlooking the river. Does that appeal to you, madam?" He came forward to take her arm.

"That was very thoughtful of you, Julian," Sophy said humbly, striving to maintain a smile. His anxiousness to please her was touching and it only served to make her feel even more miserable.

"Have your maid run upstairs and fetch one of those lamentable books of yours. I can tolerate anything but the Wollstonecraft. I've picked out something from the library for myself. Who knows? If the sun stays out we may want to spend the afternoon reading under a tree somewhere along the way."

Her heart leapt for an instant. "That sounds lovely, my lord." Then reality returned. Julian would not be in any mood to sit reading with her under a tree in some leafy glade after she told him the awful truth.

He led her outside into the bright Spring sunshine. Two horses stood saddled and waiting, a blood bay gelding and Angel. Grooms stood at their heads. Julian watched Sophy's face carefully as he slid his hands around her waist and lifted her into the saddle. He looked relieved when she did not flinch at his touch.

"I'm glad you felt up to riding again today," Julian said as he vaulted into his saddle and took the reins. "I've missed our morning treks these past two days." He shot her a quick, assessing glance. "You are certain you will be, uh, comfortable?"

She blushed vividly and urged her mare into a trot.

"Most comfortable, Julian." *Until I find the courage to tell you the whole truth and then I shall feel absolutely terrible*. She wondered morosely if he would beat her.

An hour later they drew to a halt near the ruins of an old Norman castle that had once stood guard over the river. Julian dismounted and walked over to the gelding Sophy was riding. He lifted his wife gently out of the saddle. When her feet touched the ground he did not release her immediately.

"Is something wrong, my lord?"

"No." His smile was whimsical. "Not at all." He took his hand from her waist and carefully rearranged the plume that had fallen forward from the brim of her small brown velvet hat. The plume had been dangling at a typically precarious angle.

Sophy sighed. "That was one of the reasons I was such a failure during my short season in London. No matter how carefully my maid did my hair and arranged my clothing I always managed to arrive at the ball or the theater looking as if I'd just been run over by a passing carriage. I think I should like to have lived in a simpler time when people had fewer clothes to worry about."

"I would not mind living with you in such a time." Julian's grin widened as he surveyed her attire. There was laughter in his sunlit green eyes. "You would look very good running about in very few clothes, madam."

She knew she was turning pink again. Hastily she swung away from him and started toward the tumbledown pile of rocks that comprised what was left of the old castle. At any other time Sophy would have found the ruin charmingly picturesque. Today she could hardly focus on it. "A lovely view, is it not? It reminds me of that old castle on Ravenwood land. I should have brought along my sketchbook."

"I did not mean to embarrass you, Sophy," Julian said quietly as he came up behind her. "Or frighten you by reminding you of the other night. I was just trying to make a little joke." He touched her shoulder. "Forgive me for my want of delicacy."

Sophy closed her eyes. "You did not frighten me, Julian."

"Whenever you move away from me like that I worry that I've given you some new cause to fear me."

"Julian, stop it. Stop it at once. I do not fear you."

"You do not need to lie to me, little one," he assured her gently. "I am well aware that it will be a long while before I can redeem myself in your eyes."

"Oh, Julian, if you say another word of apology I think I shall scream." She stepped away from him, not daring to glance back.

"Sophy? What the devil is wrong now? I am sorry if you do not care for my apologies but I have no honorable recourse other than to try to convince you they are genuine."

It was all she could do not to burst into tears. "You don't understand," she said miserably. "The reason I do not want to hear any more apologies is because they are . . . they are entirely *unnecessary*."

There was a short pause behind her before Julian said quietly, "You are not obliged to make matters easier on me."

She gripped her riding crop in both hands. "I am not trying to make matters easier. I am trying to set you straight on a few points about which I . . . I deliberately misled you."

There was another short pause. "I don't understand. What are you trying to say, Sophy? That my lovemaking was not as bad as I know it must have been? Please don't bother. We both know the truth."

"No, Julian, you do not know the truth. Only I know the truth. I have a confession to make, my lord, and I fear you are going to be excessively angry."

"Not with you, Sophy. Never with you."

"I pray you will remember that, my lord, but common sense tells me you will not." She gathered her courage, still not daring to turn around and face him. "The reason you need not apologize for what you think you did the other night is because you did nothing."

"What?"

Sophy wiped the back of her gloved hand across her eyes. In doing so she jarred her hat and the plume bobbed forward again. "That is to say, you did not do what you think you did."

The silence behind her grew deafening before Julian spoke again. "Sophy, the blood. There was so much blood."

She hurried on quickly before her courage deserted her entirely. "On my own behalf, I should like to point out that you did try to break the spirit of our agreement as far as I am concerned. I was quite nervous and very, very angry. I hope you will take that into consideration, my lord. You, of all people, know what it is to be in the grip of a fierce temper."

"Damn it, Sophy, what the devil are you talking about?" Julian's voice was far too quiet.

"I am trying to explain, my lord, that you did not assault me the other night. You just, well, that is to say, you merely went to sleep." Sophy finally turned slowly to confront him. He stood a short distance away, his booted feet braced slightly apart, his riding crop held alongside his thigh. His emerald gaze was colder than the outer reaches of Hades.

"I went to sleep?"

Sophy nodded and stared fixedly past his shoulder. "I put some herbs in your tea. You remember I told you I had something more effective than port for inducing sleep?"

"I remember," he said with terrible softness. "But you drank the tea also."

She shook her head. "I merely pretended to drink it. You were so busy complaining about Miss Wollstonecraft's book that you did not notice what I was doing."

He stalked one step closer. The riding crop flicked restlessly against his leg. "The blood. It was all over the sheet."

"More herbs, my lord. After you fell asleep I added them to the tea to produce a reddish stain on the sheets. Only I did not know how much liquid to use, you see and I was nervous and I spilled some and thus the spot grew somewhat larger than I had intended."

"You spilled some of the tea," he repeated slowly.

"Yes, my lord."

"Enough to make me think I had torn you most savagely."

"Yes, my lord."

"You are telling me that nothing happened that night? Nothing at all?"

Some of Sophy's natural spirit revived. "Well, you did say you were going to seduce me even though I had distinctly told you I did not wish you to do so and you did come to my room over my objections and I truly did feel menaced, my lord. So it is not as if nothing *would* have happened, if you see what I mean. It is just that nothing *did* happen because I took certain steps to prevent it. You are not the only one with a temper, my lord."

"You drugged me." There was something between disbelief and rage in his voice.

"It was just a simple sleeping tonic, my lord."

The riding crop at Julian's side slashed against the leather top of his boot, cutting off her explanation. Julian's eyes burned brilliantly green. "You drugged me with one of those damn potions of yours and then you set the stage to make me think I had raped you."

There was really nothing to say in the face of that blunt statement of facts. Sophy hung her head. The plume waved in front of her eyes as she looked down at the ground. "I suppose you could view it that way, my lord. But I never meant for you to think you had . . . had hurt me. I only wanted you to think you had done what you seemed to feel was your duty. You seemed so anxious to claim your rights as a husband."

"And you assumed that if I thought I had claimed those rights, I might then leave you alone for the next few months?"

"It occurred to me that you might be satisfied for a while, my lord. I thought you might then be willing to honor the terms of our agreement."

"Sophy, if you mention that damned agreement one more time, I shall undoubtedly throttle you. At the very least, I will use my riding crop on your backside."

She drew herself up bravely. "I am prepared for violence, my lord. It is well known that you have the devil's own temper."

"Is it, indeed? Then I am surprised you would bring me

out here alone to make your grand confession. There is no one around to hear your cries for help should I decide to punish you now."

"I did not think it fair to involve the servants," she whispered.

"How very noble of you, my dear. You will forgive me if I have trouble believing that any woman capable of drugging her husband is a woman who is going to waste time worrying about what the servants might think." His eyes narrowed. "By God, what *did* they think when they changed your bedding the next morning?"

"I explained to Mary that I had spilled some tea in bed."

"In other words, I was the only one in the entire household who believed myself to be a brutal rapist? Well, that's something, at least."

"I am sorry, Julian. Truly, I am. In my own defense, I can only point out again that I really was frightened and angry. I had thought we were getting along so well, you see, getting to know one another and then there you were threatening me."

"The thought of my lovemaking scares you so much you would go to such lengths to avoid it? Damn it, Sophy, you are no green chit of a girl. You are a full-grown woman, and you know well why I married you."

"I have explained before, my lord, I am not frightened of the act itself," she said fiercely. "It is just that I want time to get to know you. I wanted time for us to learn to deal together as husband and wife. I do not wish to be turned into a brood mare for your convenience and then turned out to pasture in the country. You must admit that is all you had in mind when you married me."

"I admit nothing." He slashed the crop against his boot one more time. "As far as I am concerned, you are the one who violated the basic understandings of our marriage. My requirements were simple and few. One of them, if you will recall, was that you never lie to me."

"Julian, I did not lie to you. Perhaps I misled you, but surely you can see that I—"

"You lied to me," he cut in brutally. "And if I had not been wallowing in my own guilt these past two days I would have realized it immediately. The signs were all present. You haven't even been able to look me in the eye. If I hadn't assumed that was because you couldn't bear the sight of me, I would have understood at once that you were deceiving me."

"I am sorry, Julian."

"You are going to be a great deal sorrier, madam, before we are finished. I am not anything like your foolishly indulgent grandfather and its time you learned that fact. I thought you were intelligent enough to have realized that from the start, but apparently the lesson must be made plain."

"*Julian.*"

"Get on your horse."

Sophy hesitated. "What are you going to do, my lord?"

"When I have decided, I will tell you. In the meantime I will give you a taste of the exceedingly unpleasant experience of worrying about it."

Sophy moved slowly toward her gelding. "I know you are in a rage, Julian. And perhaps I deserve it. But I do wish you would tell me how you intend to punish me. Truthfully, I do not think I can stand the suspense."

His hands came around her waist from behind so swiftly that she started. Julian lifted her into the saddle with a barely suppressed violence. Then he stood for a moment looking up at her with cold fury in his eyes. "If you are going to play tricks on your husband, Madam Wife, you had better learn how to handle the suspense of worrying about his revenge. And I will have my revenge, Sophy. Never doubt it. I have no intention of allowing you to become the same kind of uncontrollable bitch my first wife was."

Before she could respond he had turned away and mounted his stallion. Without another word he set out at a gallop for home, leaving Sophy to follow.

She arrived a half hour behind him and discovered to her dismay that the cheerful, bustling household that had emerged during the past few days had been magically altered. Eslington Park had become a somber, forbidding place.

The butler looked at her with sad eyes as she stepped forlornly into the hall. "We were worried about you, my lady," he said gently.

"Thank you, Tyson. As you can see, I am quite all right. Where is Lord Ravenwood?"

"In the library, my lady. He has given orders he is not to be disturbed."

"I see." Sophy walked slowly toward the stairs, glancing nervously at the ominously closed library doors. She hesitated a moment. Then she picked up the skirts of her riding habit and ran up the stairs, heedless of the concerned eyes of the servants.

Julian emerged at dinner to announce his vengeance. When he sat down to the table with an implacable hardness in his eyes Sophy knew he had plotted his revenge over a bottle of claret.

A forbidding silence descended on the dining room. It seemed to Sophy that all the figures in the painted medallions set into the ceiling were staring down at her with accusing eyes.

She was trying her best to eat her fish when Julian sent the butler and the footman out of the room with a curt nod of his head. Sophy held her breath.

"I will be leaving for London in the morning," Julian said, speaking to her for the first time.

Sophy looked up, hope springing to life within her. "We're going to London, my lord?"

"No, Sophy. You are not going to London. I am. You, my dear, scheming wife, will remain here at Eslington Park. I am going to grant you your fondest wish. You may spend the remainder of your precious three months in absolute peace. I give you my solemn word I will not bother you."

It dawned on her that he was going to abandon her here in the wilds of Norfolk. Sophy swallowed in shock. "I will be all alone, my lord?"

He smiled with savage civility. "Quite alone as far as having any companions or a guilt-stricken husband to dance attendance on you. However, you will have an excellently trained staff at your disposal. Perhaps you can amuse yourself tending to their sore throats and bilious livers."

"Julian, please, I would rather you just beat me and be done with it."

"Don't tempt me," he advised dryly.

"But I do not wish to stay here by myself. Part of our agreement was that I not be banished to the country while you went to London."

"You dare mention that insane agreement to me after what you have done?"

"I am sorry if you do not like it, my lord, but you did give me your word on certain matters before our marriage. As far as I am concerned, you have come very near to breaking your oath on one point and now you are going to do so again. It is not . . . not honorable of you, my lord."

"Do not presume to lecture me on the subject of honor, Sophy. You are a woman and you know little about it," he roared.

Sophy stared at him. "I am learning quickly."

Julian swore softly and tossed aside his napkin. "Don't look at me as if you find me lacking in honor, madam. I assure you, I am not violating my oath. You will eventually get your day in London but that day will not arrive until you have learned your duty as a wife."

"My *duty*."

"At the end of your precious three months I will return here to Eslington Park and discuss the subject. I trust that by then you will have decided you can tolerate my touch. One way or another, madam, I will have what I want out of this marriage."

"An heir and no trouble."

His mouth crooked grimly. "You have already caused me a great deal of trouble, Sophy. Take what satisfaction you can from that fact because I do not intend to allow you to create any further uproar in my life."

Sophy stood forlornly amid the marble statuary in the hall the next morning, her head held at a brave angle as she watched Julian prepare for his departure. As his valet saw to the loading of his baggage into the coach his lordship took his leave of his new bride with chilling formality.

"I wish you joy of your marriage during the next two and a half months, madam."

He started to turn away and then halted with a disgusted oath as he caught sight of a dangling ribbon in her hair. He paused to retie it with a swift, impatient movement and then he was gone. The sound of his boots echoing on the marble was haunting.

Sophy endured a week of the humiliating banishment before her natural spirit revived. When it did she decided that not only had she suffered quite enough for her crime, she had also made a serious tactical error in dealing with her new husband.

The world began to seem much brighter the moment she made the decision to follow Julian to London.

If she had a few things to learn about managing a husband, then it followed that Julian had a few things to learn about managing a wife. Sophy determined to start the marriage afresh.

FIVE

Julian surveyed the solemn scene that greeted him as he walked through the door of his club. "There's enough gloom in here to suit a funeral," he remarked to his friend, Miles Thurgood. "Or a battlefield," he added after a moment's reflection.

"What did you expect?" Miles asked, his handsome young face set in the same grim lines as every other male face in the room. There was, however, an unmistakable air of ghoulish amusement in his vivid blue eyes. "It's the same at all the clubs in St. James and everywhere else in town this evening. Gloom and doom throughout the city."

"The first installment of the infamous Featherstone *Memoirs* was published today, I assume?"

"Just as the publisher promised. Right on time. Sold out within an hour, I'm told."

"Judging from the morbid look on everyone's face, I surmise the Grand Featherstone made good on her threat to name names."

"Glastonbury's and Plimpton's among others." Miles

nodded toward two men on the other side of the room. There was a bottle of port sitting on the small table between their chairs and it was obvious both middle-aged lords were sunk deep in despondency. "There'll be more in the next installment, or so we're told."

Julian's mouth thinned as he took a seat and picked up a copy of the *Gazette*. "Leave it to a woman to find a way to create more excitement than the news of the war does." He scanned the headlines, looking for the customary accounts of battle and the list of those who had fallen in the seemingly endless peninsular campaign.

Miles grinned fleetingly. "Easy for you to be so damn sanguine about the Featherstone *Memoirs*. Your new wife ain't here in town where she can get hold of the newspapers. Glastonbury and Plimpton weren't so lucky. Word has it Lady Glastonbury instructed the butler to lock poor Glastonbury out of his own house and Plimpton's lady is reported to have staged a scene that shook the rafters."

"And now both men are cowering here in their club."

"Where else can they go? This is their last refuge."

"They're a pair of fools," Julian declared, frowning as he paused to read a war dispatch.

"Fools, eh?" Miles settled back in his chair and eyed his friend with an expression of mingled laughter and respect. "I suppose you could give them sage advice on how to deal with an angry woman? Not everyone can convince his wife to rusticate in the country, Julian."

Julian refused to be drawn. He knew Miles and all his other friends were consumed with curiosity about his newly acquired bride. "Glastonbury and Plimpton should have seen to it that their wives never got their hands on a copy of the *Memoirs*."

"How were they supposed to prevent that from happening? Lady Glastonbury and Lady Plimpton probably sent footmen to wait in line along with everyone else at the publisher's office this afternoon."

"If Glastonbury and Plimpton cannot manage their wives any better than that, they both got what they deserved," Julian said heartlessly. "A man has to set down firm rules in his own home."

Miles leaned forward and lowered his voice. "Word has it both Glastonbury and Plimpton had an opportunity to save themselves but they failed to take advantage of it. The Grand Featherstone decided to make an example of them so that the next victims would be more amenable to reason."

Julian glanced up. "What the devil are you talking about?"

"Haven't you heard about the letters Charlotte is sending out to her former paramours?" drawled a soft, deep voice.

Julian's brows climbed as the newcomer sank into the chair across from him with languid ease. "What letters would those be, Daregate?"

Miles nodded. "Tell him about the letters."

Gideon Xavier Daregate, only nephew and thus heir apparent of the dissolute, profligate, and unmarried Earl of Daregate, smiled his rather cruel smile. The expression gave his aquiline features the look of a bird of prey. The silvery gray color of his cold eyes added to the impression. "Why, the little notes the Grand Featherstone is having hand carried to all potential victims. It seems that, for a price, a man can arrange to have his name left out of the *Memoirs*."

"Blackmail," Julian observed grimly.

"To be sure," Daregate murmured, looking a trifle bored.

"A man does not pay off a blackmailer. To do so only invites further demands."

"I'm certain that's what Glastonbury and Plimpton told each other," Daregate said. "In consequence, they not only find themselves featured in Charlotte's *Memoirs,* they also find themselves ill-treated in print. Apparently the Grand Featherstone was not overly impressed with their prowess in the boudoir."

Miles groaned. "The *Memoirs* are that detailed?"

"I fear so," Daregate said dryly. "They are filled with the sort of unimportant details only a woman would bother to remember. Little points of interest such as whether a man neglected to bathe and change into fresh linen before paying a call. What's the matter, Miles? You were never one of Charlotte's protectors, were you?"

"No, but Julian was for a short time." Miles grinned cheekily.

Julian winced. "God help me, that was a long time ago. I am certain Charlotte has long since forgotten me."

"I wouldn't count on it," Daregate said. "Women of that sort have long memories."

"Don't fret, Julian," Miles added helpfully, "with any luck your bride will never even hear of the *Memoirs*."

Julian grunted and went back to his newspaper. He would make damn sure of that.

"Tell us, Ravenwood," Daregate interrupted blandly, "When are you going to introduce your new Countess to Society? You know everyone is extremely curious about her. You won't be able to hide her forever."

"Between the news of Wellington's maneuvers in Spain and the Featherstone *Memoirs*, Society has more than enough to occupy its attention at the moment," Julian said quietly.

Thurgood and Daregate both opened their mouths to protest that observation but one look at their friend's cold, forbidding expression changed their minds.

"I believe I could use another bottle of claret," Daregate said politely. "I find I am a little thirsty after a full evening of hazard. Will you two join me?"

"Yes," said Julian, setting aside the newspaper. "I believe I will."

"Going to put in an appearance at Lady Eastwell's rout this evening?" Miles inquired conversationally. "Should be interesting. Gossip has it Lord Eastwell got one of Charlotte's blackmail notes today. Everyone's wondering if Lady Eastwell knows about it yet."

"I have great respect for Eastwell," Julian said. "I saw him under fire on the Continent. So did you, for that matter, Daregate. The man knows how to stand his ground against the enemy. He certainly ought to be able to deal with his wife."

Daregate grinned his humorless smile. "Come now, Ravenwood, we both know that fighting Napoléon is a picnic by the sea compared to doing battle with an enraged woman."

Miles nodded knowledgeably even though they all knew he had never been married or involved in a serious affair. "Very wise to have left your bride behind in the country, Ravenwood. Very wise, indeed. Can't get into trouble there."

Julian had been trying to convince himself of just that for the entire week he had been back in London. But tonight, as every other night since he had returned, he was not so sure he had made the right decision.

The fact was, he missed Sophy. It was regrettable, inexplicable, and damnably uncomfortable. It was also undeniable. He had been a fool to abandon her in the country. There had to have been another way to deal with her.

Unfortunately he had not been thinking clearly enough at the time to come up with an alternative.

Uneasily he considered the matter as he left his club much later that night. He bounded up into his waiting carriage and gazed broodingly out at the dark streets as his coachman snapped the whip.

It was true that his anger still flared high whenever he remembered the trick Sophy had played on him that fateful night when he had determined to claim his husbandly rights. And he reminded himself several times a day that it was crucial he teach her a lesson now, at the beginning of their marriage, while she was still relatively naive and moldable. She must not be allowed to gain the impression that she could manipulate him.

But no matter how hard he worked at reminding himself of her deviousness and the importance of nipping such behavior in the bud, he found himself remembering other things about Sophy. He missed the morning rides, the intelligent conversations about farm management, and the games of chess in the evenings.

He also missed the enticing, womanly scent of her, the way her chin tilted when she was preparing to challenge him, and the subtle, gentle innocence that glowed softly in her turquoise eyes. He also found himself recalling her happy, mischievous laughter and her concern for the health of the servants and tenants.

At various times during the past week he had even caught himself wondering just what part of Sophy's attire was askew at that particular moment. He would close his eyes briefly and envision her riding hat dangling down over her ear or imagine a torn hem on her skirt. Her maid would have her work cut out for her.

Sophy was very unlike his first wife.

Elizabeth had always been flawlessly garbed—every curl in place, every low-cut bodice cleverly arranged to display her charms to best advantage. Even in the bedchamber the first Countess of Ravenwood had maintained an air of elegant perfection. She had been a beautiful goddess of lust in her cunningly styled nightclothes, a creature designed by nature to incite passion in men and lure them to their doom. Julian felt slightly sick whenever he remembered how deeply ensnared he had been in the witch's silken web.

Determinedly he pushed aside the old memories. He had selected Sophy for his wife because of the vast difference between her and Elizabeth and he fully intended to ensure that his new bride stayed different. Whatever the cost, he would not allow his Sophy to follow the same blazing, destructive path Elizabeth had chosen.

But while he was sure of his goal, he was not quite so certain of the measures he should take to achieve that goal. Perhaps leaving Sophy behind in the country had been a mistake. It not only left her without adequate supervision, it also left him at loose ends here in town.

The carriage came to a halt in front of the imposing townhouse Julian maintained. He stared morosely at the front door and thought of the lonely bed awaiting him. If he had any sense, he would order the carriage turned around and headed toward Trevor Square. Marianne Harwood would no doubt be more than willing to receive him, even at this late hour.

But visions of the breezy, voluptuous charms of La Belle Harwood failed to entice him from his self-imposed celibacy. Within forty-eight hours after his return to London,

Julian had realized that the only woman he ached to bed was his wife.

His obsession with her was undoubtedly the direct result of denying himself what was rightfully his, he decided as he alighted from the carriage and went up the steps. He was, however, very certain of one thing: the next time he took Sophy to bed they would both remember the occasion with great clarity.

"Good evening, Guppy," Julian said as the butler opened the door. "You're up late. Thought I told you not to wait up for me."

"Good evening, my lord." Guppy cleared his throat importantly as he stood aside for his master. "Had a bit of a stir this evening. Kept the entire staff up late."

Julian, who was halfway to the library, halted and turned around, with a questioning frown. Guppy was fifty-five years old, exceedingly well trained, and not at all given to dramatics.

"A stir?"

Guppy's expression was suitably bland but his eyes were alight with subdued excitement. "The Countess of Ravenwood has arrived and taken up residence, my lord. Begging your pardon, but the staff would have been able to provide a much more comfortable welcome for Lady Ravenwood if we had been notified of her impending arrival. As it was, I fear we were taken somewhat by surprise. Not that we haven't coped, of course."

Julian froze. For an instant he could not think. *Sophy is here.* It was as if all his brooding thoughts on the way home tonight had succeeded in conjuring his new wife out of thin air. "Of course you coped, Guppy," he said mechanically. "I would expect nothing less of you and the rest of the staff. Where is Lady Ravenwood at the moment?"

"She retired a short while ago, my lord. Madam is, if I may be so bold, most gracious to staff. Mrs. Peabody showed her to the room that adjoins yours, naturally."

"Naturally." Julian forgot his intention of dosing himself with a last glass of port. The thought of Sophy upstairs in bed shook him. He strode toward the staircase. "Good night, Guppy."

"Good night, my lord." Guppy permitted himself the smallest of smiles as he turned to lock the front door.

Sophy is here. A rush of excitement filled Julian's veins. He quelled it in the next instant by reminding himself that in coming to London his new wife had openly defied him. His meek little country wife was becoming increasingly rebellious.

He stalked down the hall, torn between rage and an invidious pleasure at the thought of seeing Sophy again. The volatile combination of emotions was enough to make him light-headed. He opened the door of his bedchamber with an impatient twist of the knob and found his valet sprawled, sound asleep, in one of the red velvet armchairs.

"Hello, Knapton. Catching up on your sleep?"

"My lord." Knapton struggled awake, blinking quickly as he took in the sight of his grim-faced master standing in the doorway. "I'm sorry, my lord. Just sat down for a few minutes to wait for you. Don't know what happened. Must have dozed off."

"Never mind." Julian waved a hand in the general direction of the door. "I can get myself to bed without your assistance tonight."

"Yes, my lord. If you're quite certain you won't be needing any help, my lord." Knapton hurried toward the door.

"Knapton."

"Yes, my lord?" The valet paused in the open doorway and glanced back warily.

"I understand Lady Ravenwood arrived this evening."

Knapton's pinched face softened into an expression of pleasure. "Not more than a few hours ago, my lord. Set the whole house in an uproar for a time but everything's in order now. Lady Ravenwood has a way of managing staff, my lord."

"Lady Ravenwood has a way of managing everyone," Julian muttered under his breath as Knapton let himself out into the hall. He waited until the outer door had closed firmly behind the valet and then he stripped off his boots and evening clothes and reached for his dressing gown.

He stood for a moment after tying the silk sash, trying to think of how best to handle his defiant bride. Outrage still warred with desire in his blood. He had an overpowering urge to vent his temper on Sophy and an equally powerful need to make love to her. Maybe he should do both, he told himself.

One thing was for certain. He could not simply ignore her arrival tonight and then greet her at breakfast tomorrow morning as if her presence here was a perfectly routine matter.

Nor would he allow himself to stand here shilly-shallying another minute like a green officer facing his first battle. This was his home and he would be master in it.

Julian took a deep breath, swore softly, and strode over to the door that connected his dressing room with Sophy's bedchamber. He snatched up a candle and raised his hand to knock. But at the last instant he changed his mind. This was not a time for courtesy.

He reached for the knob, expecting to find the door locked from the other side. To his surprise, he found no resistance. The door to Sophy's darkened bedchamber opened easily.

For a moment he could not find her amid the shadows of the elegant room. Then he spotted the small, curved outline of her body in the center of the massive bed. His lower body tightened painfully. *This is my wife and she is here at last in the bedchamber where she belongs.*

Sophy stirred restlessly, hovering on the brink of an elusive dream. She came awake slowly, reorienting herself to the strange room. Then she opened her eyes and stared at the flickering flame of a candle moving silently toward her through the darkness. Panic jerked her into full alertness until, with a sigh of relief, she recognized the dark figure holding the candle. She sat straight up in bed, clutching the sheet to her throat.

"*Julian.* You gave me a start, my lord. You move like a ghost."

"Good evening, madam." The greeting was cold and emotionless. It was uttered in that very soft, very dangerous voice that always boded ill. "I trust you will forgive me for not being at home tonight when you arrived. I wasn't expecting you, you see."

"Pray do not regard it, my lord. I am well aware that my arrival is something of a surprise to you." Sophy tried her best to ignore the shiver of fear that coursed through her. She had known she must endure this confrontation from the moment she had made the decision to leave Eslington Park. She had spent hours in the swaying coach imagining just what she would say when she faced Julian's wrath.

"A surprise? That's putting it rather mildly."

"There's no need to be sarcastic, my lord. I know that you are probably somewhat angry with me."

"How perceptive of you."

Sophy swallowed bravely. This was going to be even more difficult than she had imagined. His attitude toward her had not softened much during the past week. "Perhaps it would be better if we discussed this in the morning."

"We will discuss it now. There will not be time to do so in the morning because you will be busy packing to return to Eslington Park."

"*No.* You must understand, Julian. I cannot allow you to send me away." She gripped the sheet more tightly. She had promised herself she would not plead with him. She would be calm and reasonable. He was, after all, a reasonable man. Most of the time. "I am trying to put things right between us. I have made a terrible mistake in dealing with you. I was wrong. I know that now. I have come to London because I am determined to be a proper wife to you."

"A proper wife? Sophy, I know this will amaze and astound you, but the fact is, a proper wife obeys her husband. She does not attempt to deceive him into thinking he has behaved like a monster. She does not deny him his rights in the bedchamber. She does not show up on his doorstep in town when she has been specifically ordered to stay in the country."

"Yes, well, I am perfectly aware of the fact that I have not been a very exemplary model of the sort of wife you require. But in all fairness Julian, I feel your requirements were rather stringent."

"Stringent? Madam, I required nothing more of you than a certain measure of—"

"Julian, please, I do not wish to argue with you. I am trying to make amends. We got off to a bad start in this marriage, and I admit that it is mostly my fault. It seems to me the least you can do is give me an opportunity to show you that I am willing to try to be a better wife."

There was a long silence from Julian. He stood quite still, arrogantly examining her anxious face in the candlelight. His own expression was thrown into demonic relief by the flame he held in his hand. It seemed to Sophy he had never looked more like the devil than he did at that moment.

"Let me be perfectly certain I understand you, Sophy. You say you wish to put this marriage of ours on a normal footing?"

"Yes, Julian."

"Am I to assume that you are now prepared to grant me my rights in your bed?"

She nodded quickly, her loosened hair tumbling around her shoulders. "Yes," she said again. "You see, Julian, through some deductive logic I have come to the conclusion that you were right. We may deal much more favorably together if things are normal between us."

"In other words you are trying to bribe me into allowing you to stay here in London," he summarized in a silky tone.

"No, no, you misunderstand." Alarmed by his interpretation of her actions, Sophy thrust back the covers and quickly got to her feet beside the bed. Belatedly she realized how thin the fabric of her nightgown was. She snatched up her dressing gown and held it in front of her.

Julian plucked the robe out of her hand and tossed it aside. "You won't be needing that, will you, my dear? You're a woman bent on seduction now, remember? You must learn the fine art of your new career."

Sophy stared helplessly at the dressing gown on the floor. She felt exposed and terribly vulnerable standing there in her thin lawn nightdress. Tears of frustration burned in her eyes. For an instant she was afraid she might cry. "Please, Julian," she said quietly. "Give me a chance. I will do my best to make a success of our marriage."

He raised the candle higher in order to study her face. He was silent for an excruciating length of time before he spoke again. "Do you know, my dear," he said at last, "I believe you will make me a good wife. After I have finished teaching you that I am not a puppet you can set to dancing on the end of your string."

"I never intended to treat you that way, my lord." Sophy bit her lip, stricken by the depths of his outrage. "I sincerely regret what happened at Eslington Park. You must know I have no experience in dealing with a husband. I was only trying to protect myself."

He bit off a sharp exclamation. "Be quiet, Sophy. Every time you open your mouth you manage to sound less and less like a proper wife."

Sophy ignored the advice. She was convinced her mouth was the only useful weapon in her small arsenal at that moment. Hesitantly she touched the sleeve of his silk dressing gown. "Let me stay here in town, Julian. Let me show you I am sincere about putting our marriage right. I swear to you I will work diligently at the task."

"Will you?" He regarded her with cold, glittering eyes.

Sophy felt something inside her begin to shrivel and die. She had been so certain she could convince him to give her a second chance. During the short honeymoon at Eslington Park she thought she had gotten to know this man rather well. He was not deliberately cruel or unfair in his dealings with others. She had counted on him maintaining that same code of behavior when dealing with a wife.

"Perhaps I was wrong," she said. "I had hoped you would be willing to give me the same opportunity to prove myself that you would give one of your tenants who was in arrears in regard to the rent."

For an instant he looked totally nonplussed. "You're equating yourself with one of my *tenants?*"

"I thought the analogy rather apt."

"The analogy is rather idiotic."

"Then perhaps there is no hope of putting things right between us."

"You are wrong, Sophy. I told you that I believe you will eventually make me a proper wife and I meant what I said. I intend to see to it, in fact. The only real question is how that may best be achieved. You have a great deal to learn."

So do you, Sophy thought. *And who better to teach you than your wife?* But she must remember that she had taken Julian by surprise tonight and men did not handle surprises well. Her husband needed time to accept that she was under his roof and intended to stay. "I promise you that I will not give you any trouble if you allow me to remain here in London, my lord."

"No trouble, hm?" For a brief second the candlelight revealed what might have been a gleam of amusement in Julian's cold gaze. "I cannot tell you how much that reassures me, Sophy. Get back into bed and go to sleep. I will give you my decision in the morning."

A vast sense of relief swamped her. She had won the first round. He was no longer dismissing her out of hand. Sophy smiled tremulously. "Thank you, Julian."

"Do not thank me yet, madam. We have a great deal to sort out between the two of us."

"I realize that. But we are two intelligent people who happen to be stuck with one another. We must use some common sense to learn to live tolerantly together, don't you agree?"

"Is that how you see our situation, Sophy? You consider us stuck with each other?"

"I know you would prefer that I not romanticize the matter, my lord. I am endeavoring to take a more realistic view of our marriage."

"Make the best of things, in other words?"

She brightened. "Precisely, my lord. Rather like a pair of draft horses that are obliged to work in harness together. We must share the same barn, drink from the same trough, eat from the same hay bale."

"Sophy," Julian interrupted, "Please do not draw any more farming analogies. I find they cloud my thinking."

"I would not want to do that, my lord."

"How charitable of you. I will see you in the library at eleven o'clock tomorrow morning." Julian turned and strode out of the room, taking the light with him.

Sophy was left standing alone in the darkness. But her spirits soared as she climbed back into the big bed. The first hurdle had been cleared. She sensed Julian was not entirely unwilling to have her here. If she could refrain from provoking him in the morning, she would be allowed to stay.

She had been right about his nature, Sophy told herself happily. Julian was a hard, cold man in many ways but he was an honorable one. He would deal fairly with her.

Sophy changed her mind three times about what to wear for the interview with Julian the next morning. One would have thought she was dressing for a ball instead of a discussion with her husband, she chided herself. Or perhaps a military campaign would be a more accurate analogy.

She finally chose a light yellow gown trimmed in white and asked her maid to put her hair up in a cascade of fashionable ringlets.

By the time she was satisfied with the effect she had less than five minutes to descend the staircase. She hurried along the hall and dashed down the stairs, arriving slightly breathless at the door of the library. A footman promptly opened it for her and she swept inside, a hopeful smile on her face.

Julian rose slowly from behind his desk and greeted her with a formal inclination of his head. "You need not have rushed, Sophy."

"It's quite all right," she assured him, moving forward quickly. "I did not want to keep you waiting."

"Wives are notorious for keeping their husbands waiting."

"Oh." She was not quite certain how to take the dry remark. "Well, I can always practice that particular talent another time." She glanced around and spotted a green silk chair. "This morning I am far too anxious to hear your decision regarding my future."

She stepped toward the green chair and promptly tripped. She caught herself immediately and glanced down to see what it was that had caused her to lose her footing. Julian followed her gaze.

"The ribbon of your slipper appears to have come untied," he observed politely.

Sophy flushed with embarrassment and sat down quickly. "So it has." She bent over and hastily retied the offending slipper ribbon. When she straightened she found Julian had reseated himself and was studying her with an oddly resigned expression on his face. "Is something wrong, my lord?"

"No. Everything appears to be going along in a perfectly normal fashion. Now, then, about your wish to be allowed to stay here in London."

"Yes, my lord?" She waited in an agony of anticipation to see if she had been right about his fundamental sense of fair play.

Julian hesitated, frowning thoughtfully as he leaned back in his chair to study her face. "I have decided to grant your request."

Elation bubbled up inside Sophy. She smiled very brilliantly, her relief and happiness in her eyes. "Oh, Julian, thank you. I promise you, you will not regret your decision. You are being very gracious about this and I probably do not deserve your generosity but I want to assure you I fully intend to live up to your expectations of a wife."

"That should prove interesting, if nothing else."

"Julian, please, I am very serious about this."

His rare smile flickered briefly. "I know. I can see your intentions in your eyes. And that, my dear, is why I am granting you a second chance. I've told you before, your eyes are very easy to read."

"I swear, Julian, I will become a paragon of wifehood. It is very good of you to overlook the, er, incident at Eslington Park."

"I suggest neither of us mention that debacle again."

"An excellent idea," Sophy agreed enthusiastically.

"Very well, that appears to settle the issue. We may as well start practicing this husband and wife business."

Sophy's eyes widened in alarm and her palms grew suddenly damp. She had not expected him to turn to the intimate side of their marriage with such unseemly haste. It was, after all, only eleven o'clock in the morning. "Here, my lord?" she asked weakly, glancing around at the library furnishings. "Now?"

"Most definitely here and now." Julian did not appear to notice her startled expression. He was busy scrabbling about in one of the desk drawers. "Ah, here we go." He withdrew a handful of small letters and cards and handed them to her.

"What are these?"

"Invitations. You know, receptions, parties, routs, balls. That sort of thing. They require some sort of response. I detest sorting through invitations and I have occupied my secretary with more important matters. Pick out a few events that appear interesting to you and send regrets to the others."

Sophy looked up from the sheaf of cards in her hand, feeling bewildered. "This is to be my first wifely duty, my lord?"

"Correct."

She waited a moment, wondering if it was relief or disappointment she felt. It must have been relief. "I will be happy to take care of these, Julian, but you of all people should know I have very little experience with Society."

"That, Sophy, is one of your more redeeming qualities."

"Thank you, my lord. I was sure I must possess a few somewhere."

He gave her a suspicious look but forebore to comment on that remark. "As it happens, I have a solution to the dilemma your inexperience presents. I am going to provide you with a professional guide to see you through the wilderness of the social world here."

"A guide?"

"My aunt, Lady Frances Sinclair. Feel free to call her

Fanny. Everyone else does, including the Prince. I think you'll find her interesting. Fancies herself something of a bluestocking, I believe. She and her companion are fond of conducting a small salon of intellectually minded ladies on Wednesday afternoons. She'll probably invite you to join her little club."

Sophy heard the amused condescension in his voice and smiled serenely. "Is her little club anything like a gentlemen's club in which one may drink and bet and entertain oneself until all hours?"

Julian eyed her grimly. "Definitely not."

"How disappointing. But be that as it may, I am sure I shall like your aunt."

"You'll have a chance to find out shortly." Julian glanced at the library clock. "She should be here any minute."

Sophy was stunned. "She's going to be calling this morning?"

"I'm afraid so. She sent word around an hour ago that she was to be expected. She'll undoubtedly be accompanied by her companion, Harriette Rattenbury. The two are inseparable." Julian's mouth crooked faintly. "My aunt is most anxious to meet you."

"But how did she know I was in town?"

"That's one of the things you must learn about Society, Sophy. Gossip travels on the air itself here in the city. You will do well to keep that in mind because the last thing I want to hear is gossip about my wife. Is that very clear?"

"Yes, Julian."

SIX

"I do apologize for being late but I know you will all forgive me when I tell you I have got the second installment. Here it is, fresh from the presses. I assure you I had to risk life and limb to obtain it. I haven't seen that sort of mob in the streets since the riot after the last fireworks display at Covent Garden."

Sophy and the other ten guests seated in the gold-and-white Egyptian-style drawing room turned to gaze at the young, red-haired woman who had just burst through the door. She was clutching a slender, unbound volume in her hands and her eyes were alight with excitement.

"Pray, seat yourself, Anne. You must know we are all about to expire with curiosity." Lady Frances Sinclair, perched gracefully on a gold-and-white striped settee that was adorned with small, carved sphinxes, waved her late guest to a nearby chair. "But first allow me to present my nephew's wife, Lady Ravenwood. She arrived in town a week ago and has expressed an interest in joining our little Wednesday afternoon salon. Sophy, this is Miss Anne

Silverthorne. You two will undoubtedly run into each other again this evening at the Yelverton Ball."

Sophy smiled warmly as the introductions were completed. She was thoroughly enjoying herself and had been since Fanny Sinclair and her friend Harriette Rattenbury had swept into her life the previous week.

Julian had been right about his aunt and her companion. They were obviously the greatest of friends, although to look at them, one was struck first by the differences, rather than the similarities between the two women.

Fanny Sinclair was tall, patrician featured, and had been endowed with the black hair and brilliant emerald eyes that appeared to be a trademark of the Sinclair clan. She was in her early fifties, a vivacious, charming creature who was clearly at ease amid the wealth and trappings of the *ton*.

She was also delightfully optimistic, keenly interested in everything that went on around her and remarkably free thinking. Full of witty schemes and plans, she fairly bubbled with enthusiasm for any new idea that crossed her path. The exotic Egyptian style of her townhouse suited her well. Even the odd wallpaper, which had a border of tiny mummies and sphinxes, looked appropriate as a backdrop for Lady Fanny.

As much as Sophy enjoyed the bizarre Egyptian motifs in Lady Fanny's home, she was somewhat relieved to discover that when it came to clothing fashions, Julian's aunt had an instinctive and unfailing sense of style. She had employed it often on Sophy's behalf during the past week. Sophy's wardrobe was now crammed with the latest and most flattering designs and more gowns were on order. When Sophy had been so bold as to question the excessive expenditures, Fanny had laughed gaily and waved the entire issue aside.

"Julian can afford to keep his wife in style and he shall do so if I have anything to say about it. Do not worry about the bills, my dear. Just pay them out of your allowance and request more money from Julian when you need it."

Sophy had been horrified. "I could not possibly ask him

to increase my allowance. He is already being extremely generous with me."

"Nonsense. I will tell you a secret about my nephew. He is not by nature closefisted or stingy but unfortunately he has little interest in spending money on anything except land improvement, sheep, and horses. You will have to remind him from time to time that there are certain necessities a woman needs."

Just as she would have to remind him occasionally that he had a wife, Sophy had told herself. She had not seen a great deal of her husband lately.

Harry, as Fanny's companion was called, was quite opposite in looks and manners, although she appeared to be about the same age. She was short, round, and possessed of an unflappable calm that nothing seemed to shake. Her serenity was the perfect foil for Fanny's enthusiasms. She favored imposing turbans, a monocle on a black ribbon, and the color purple, which she felt complimented her eyes. Thus far Sophy had never seen Harriette Rattenbury dressed in any other shade. The eccentricity suited her in some indefinable fashion.

Sophy had liked both women on sight and it was a fortunate circumstance because Julian had more or less abandoned her to their company. Sophy had seen very little of her husband for the past week and nothing at all of him in her bedchamber. She was not quite certain what to make of that situation but she had been too busy, thanks to Fanny and Harry, to brood over the matter.

"Now then," Fanny said as Anne began to cut open the pages of the small book, "you must not keep us in suspense any longer than is absolutely necessary, Anne. Start reading at once."

Sophy looked at her hostesses. "Are these *Memoirs* actually written by a woman of the deminonde?"

"Not just any woman of that world but *the* woman of that world," Fanny assured her with satisfaction. "It is no secret that Charlotte Featherstone has been the queen of London's courtesans for the past ten years. Men of the highest rank have fought duels for the honor of being her protector. She is retiring at the peak of her career and has decided to set Society on its ear with her *Memoirs*."

"The first installment came out a week ago and we have all been eagerly awaiting the second," one of the other ladies announced gleefully. "Anne was dispatched to fetch it for us."

"Makes an interesting change from the sort of thing we usually study and discuss on Wednesday afternoons, doesn't it?" Harriette observed blandly. "One can get a little tired of trying to muddle through those rather strange poems of Blake's and I must say there are times when it is difficult to tell the difference between Coleridge's literary visions and his opium visions."

"Let us get to the heart of the matter," Fanny declared. "Who does the Grand Featherstone name this time?"

Anne was already scanning the pages she had opened. "I see Lords Morgan and Crandon named and, oh, good heavens, there's a royal Duke here, too."

"A royal Duke? This Miss Featherstone appears to have fancy tastes," Sophy observed, intrigued.

"That she does," Jane Morland, the dark-haired, serious-eyed young woman who was sitting next to Sophy, remarked. "Just imagine, as one of the Fashionable Impures, she's met people I could never even aspire to meet. She's mingled with men from the highest levels of Society."

"She's done a fair bit more than just mingle with them, if you ask me," Harriette murmured, adjusting her monocle.

"But where did she come from? Who is she?" Sophy demanded.

"I've heard she was nothing more than the illegitimate daughter of a common streetwalker," one of the older women observed with an air of amused disgust.

"No common streetwalker could have caught the attention of all of London the way Featherstone has," Jane announced firmly. "Her admirers have included a good portion of the peers of the realm. She is obviously a cut above the ordinary."

Sophy nodded slowly. "Just think of all she must have been obliged to overcome in her life in order to have obtained her present position."

"I would imagine her present position is flat on her back," Fanny said.

"But she must have cultivated a great deal of wit and style to attract so many influential lovers," Sophy pointed out.

"I'm sure she has," Jane Morland agreed. "It is quite interesting to note how certain people possessed only of flair and intelligence seem to be able to convince others of their social superiority. Take Brummell or Byron's friend, Scrope Davies, for example."

"I would imagine Miss Featherstone must be very beautiful to have become so successful in her, uh, chosen profession," Anne said thoughtfully.

"She's not actually a great beauty," Fanny announced.

The other women all glanced at her in surprise.

Fanny smiled. "It's true. I've seen her more than once, you know. From a distance, of course. Harry and I noticed her just the other day, in fact, shopping in Bond Street, didn't we, Harry?"

"Dear me, yes. Quite a sight."

"She was seated in the most incredible yellow curricle," Fanny explained to her attentive audience. "She was wearing a deep blue gown and every finger was ablaze with diamonds. Quite a stunning picture. She's fair and she's possessed of passable looks and she certainly knows how to make the most of them, but I assure you there are many women of the *ton* who are more beautiful."

"Then why are the gentlemen of the *ton* so taken with her?" Sophy asked.

"Gentlemen are very simple-minded creatures," Harriette explained serenely as she lifted a teacup to her lips. "Easily dazzled by novelty and the expectation of romantic adventure. I imagine the Grand Featherstone has a way of leading men to expect both from her."

"It would be interesting to know her secret methods for bringing men to their knees," a middle-aged matron in dove gray silk said with a sigh.

Fanny shook her head. "Never forget that for all her flash and glitter, she is as chained in her world as we are in ours. She may be a prize for the men of the *ton* but she cannot hold their attention forever and she must know it. Furthermore, she cannot hope to marry any of her high-ranking admirers and thus move into a more secure world."

"True enough," Harriette agreed, pursing her lips. "No matter how infatuated with her he might be, no matter how many expensive necklaces he might bestow upon her, no nobleman in his right mind is going to propose marriage to a woman of the demimonde. Even if he forgot himself so far as to do so, his family would quickly quash the notion."

"You are right, Fanny," Sophy said thoughtfully. "Miss Featherstone is trapped in her world. And we are tied to ours. Still, if she managed the trick of raising herself from the gutter to the level where she apparently is today, she must be a very astute female. I believe she would make a very interesting contribution to these afternoon salons of yours, Fanny."

A ripple of shock went through the small group. But Fanny chuckled. "Very interesting, no doubt."

"Do you know something?" Sophy continued impulsively, "I believe I should like to meet her."

Every other pair of eyes in the room swung toward her in startled disbelief.

"Meet her?" Jane exclaimed, looking both scandalized and fascinated. "You would like an introduction to a woman of that sort?"

Anne Silverthorne smiled reluctantly. "It would be rather amusing, wouldn't it?"

"Hush, all three of you," one of the older woman snapped. "Introduce yourselves to a professional courtesan? Have you lost all sense of propriety? Of all the ridiculous notions."

Fanny gave Sophy an amused glance. "If Julian even suspected you of harboring such a goal, he would have you back in the country within twenty-four hours."

"Do you think Julian has ever met her?" Sophy asked.

Fanny choked on her tea and quickly set down the cup and saucer. "Excuse me," she gasped as Harriette slapped her familiarly between the shoulder blades. "I do beg your pardon."

"Are you all right, dear?" Harriette asked with mild
concern as Fanny recovered.

"Yes, yes, fine, thank you, Harry." Fanny's vivacious
smile swept the circle of anxious faces. "I am perfectly all
right now. I do beg everyone's pardon. Now then, where
were we? Oh, yes, you were about to start reading to us,
Anne. Do begin."

Anne plunged eagerly into the surprisingly lively prose
and every woman in the room listened with rapt attention.
Charlotte Featherstone's *Memoirs* were well written, entertaining, and deliciously scandalizing.

"Lord Ashford gave Featherstone a necklace worth five
thousand pounds?" a horrified member of the group
exclaimed at one point. "Just wait until his wife hears
about that. I know for a fact that Lady Ashford has been
forced to practice the most stringent economy for years.
Ashford is forever telling her he cannot afford new gowns
and jewels."

"He's telling her the truth. He probably cannot afford
them for his wife as long as he is buying them for
Charlotte Featherstone," Fanny observed.

"There's more about Ashford," Anne said with a decidedly wicked laugh. "Listen to this:"

After Lord Ashford left that evening I told my maid that
Lady Ashford should consider herself very much in my
debt. After all, if it were not for me, Ashford would
undoubtedly spend a great many more evenings at
home boring his poor wife with his lamentably un-
imaginative lovemaking. Only consider the great burden
of which I have relieved the lady.

"I would say she was well paid for her pains," Harriette
declared, pouring tea from the Georgian silver pot.

"Lady Ashford is going to be furious when she hears
about this," someone else remarked.

"And so she should be," Sophy said fiercely. "Her lord
has conducted himself most dishonorably. We may find it
amusing but when you stop to think about it, you must
realize he has publicly humiliated his wife. Think how he

would react if the situation were reversed and it was Lady Ashford who had caused this sort of talk."

"A sound point," Jane said. "I'll wager most men would call out any other man who had written such things about their wives."

Julian, for one, would be strongly inclined to spill blood over such a scandal, Sophy thought, not without some satisfaction as well as a chill of fear. His rage under such circumstances would indeed be awesome and his fierce pride would demand vengeance.

"Lady Ashford is hardly in a position to call out Charlotte Featherstone," one of the women in the group said dryly. "As it is, the poor woman will simply be forced to retreat to the country for a while until the gossip has run its course."

Another woman on the other side of the room grinned knowingly. "So Lord Ashford is a dead bore in bed, is he? How interesting."

"According to Featherstone, most men are rather boring in bed," Fanny said. "Thus far she has not had a good word to say about any of her admirers."

"Perhaps the more interesting lovers have paid the blackmail she is said to be demanding in order to be left out of the *Memoirs,*" suggested a young matron.

"Or perhaps men, in general, simply do not make interesting lovers," Harriette observed calmly. "More tea, anyone?"

The street in front of the Yelverton mansion was crowded with elegant carriages. Julian alighted from his at midnight and made his way through the crowd of lounging coachmen, grooms, and footmen to the wide steps that led to the Yelverton hall.

He was virtually under orders to appear tonight. Fanny had made it clear that this was to be Sophy's first major ball and that Julian's presence would be much appreciated. While it was true he was free to go his own way for the most part, there were certain occasions that required his presence at Sophy's side. This was one of them.

Julian, who had been getting up at an ungodly hour and

going to bed far too late for the past week in an effort to avoid unnecessary encounters with his wife, had found himself trapped when Fanny had made it plain she expected him to show up at some point tonight. He had resigned himself to a dance with his wife.

It was akin to resigning himself to torture. The few minutes on the ballroom floor with her in his arms would be more difficult for him than Sophy would ever know.

If the time spent apart from her had not been easy, this past week with Sophy living under the same roof had been hell. The night he had arrived home to find that she had come to apologize and to take up residence in town, he had been seized first with a glorious relief and then with a sense of caution.

But he had managed to convince himself she had come meekly to heel. She had clearly abandoned her outrageous demands and was prepared to assume the role of a proper wife to him. That night when he had confronted her in her bedchamber she had virtually offered herself to him.

It had taken every ounce of willpower Julian possessed to walk out of the room that night. Sophy had looked so sweet and submissive and tempting he had ached to reach out and take what was his by right. But he had been shaken by her arrival and had not fully trusted his own reactions. He had known he needed time to think.

By the following morning he had also realized that now she was with him again, he could not send her away. Nor was there any need to do so, he had told himself. After all, she had humbled her pride by coming to town and throwing herself on his mercy. It was she who had pleaded to be allowed to stay. Hadn't she apologized most sincerely for the embarrassing events at Eslington Park?

Julian had decided his pride had been salvaged and the lesson had been taught. He had made up his mind to be gracious and allow her to stay in town. The decision had not been a difficult one although he had lain awake till dawn arriving at it.

He had also determined during the course of that sleepless night that he would lay claim to his conjugal rights immediately. He had certainly been denied them

long enough. But by morning he had acknowledged it
was not that simple. Something was missing in the equation.

Not being much given to introspection or self-analysis,
he had taken most of the next morning right up until the
interview in the library to arrive at a vague notion of what
was wrong with leaping straight into bed with Sophy.

He had finally admitted to himself that he did not want
Sophy to give herself to him out of a sense of wifely duty.

It was, in fact, damned galling to think that she would
do so. He wanted her to want him. He wanted to be able
to look into those clear, honest eyes and see genuine
desire and womanly need. Above all he did not like the
notion that, no matter how willing she was to please him
now, she privately considered he had reneged on their
original bargain.

The realization had thrown him into a frustrated quandary.
It had also left him extremely short-tempered, as his
friends had been obliging enough to point out.

Daregate and Thurgood had not been stupid enough to
ask if there was trouble at home but Julian was aware they
both suspected that was the case. There had been several
hints that each was looking forward to meeting Sophy.
Tonight was the first opportunity they would have to do so
along with the rest of Society.

Julian's mood lightened a bit as he reflected that Sophy
would probably be very glad to see him by this time of the
evening. He knew she expected to be a total failure
socially, just as she had been five years ago. Having a
husband by her side this time would undoubtedly give her
some courage. Perhaps some of her gratitude would eventually lead her to see him in a more favorable light.

Julian had attended affairs at the Yelvertons before and
he knew his way around the ballroom. Rather than submit
to having himself announced by the butler, he found the
staircase that led to a balcony, which overlooked the
crowded salon.

He planted both hands against the heavily carved railing
and surveyed the throng below. The ballroom was ablaze
with lights. A band was playing in one corner and several
couples were out on the floor. Handsomely liveried footmen

laden with trays wove their way through the crush of elegantly dressed men and women. Laughter and conversation drifted upward.

Julian swept the room with his gaze, searching for Sophy. Fanny had advised him that her charge would be wearing a rose-colored gown. Sophy would undoubtedly be standing in one of the small groups of females that lined the wall near the windows.

"No, Julian, she's not over there. She's on the other side of the room. You can hardly see her because she's not very tall. When she's surrounded by a group of admiring males, as she is at the moment, she practically vanishes from sight."

Julian turned his head to see his aunt coming toward him along the corridor. Lady Fanny was smiling her familiar laughing smile and looked quite devastating in silver-and-green satin.

"Good evening, Aunt." He took her hand and raised it to his lips. "You're looking in fine form this evening. Where's Harry?"

"Cooling off with some lemonade out on the terrace. The heat was affecting her, poor dear. She will insist on wearing those heavy turbans. I was about to join her when I spotted you sneaking up here. So you came to see how your little wife was doing after all, hm?"

"I know a royal command when I hear one, madam. I'm here because you insisted. Now what's all this about Sophy disappearing from sight?"

"See for yourself." Fanny moved to the railing and proudly waved a hand to encompass the crowd below. "She has been surrounded since the moment we arrived. That was an hour ago."

Julian glanced toward the far end of the ballroom, scowling as he tried to pick out a rose silk gown from among the rainbow of beautiful gowns on the floor below. Then a man who had been standing in a knot of other males shifted position for an instant and Julian caught sight of Sophy in the middle of the group.

"What the devil is she doing down there?" Julian snapped.

"Isn't it obvious? She is well on her way to becoming a

success, Julian." Fanny smiled with satisfaction. "She is perfectly charming and has no trouble at all making conversation. So far she has prescribed a remedy for Lady Bixby's nervous stomach, a poultice for Lord Thanton's chest, and a syrup for Lady Yelverton's throat."

"None of the men standing around her at the moment appear to be seeking medical advice," Julian muttered.

"Quite right. When I left her side a short while ago she was just launching into a description of sheep-raising practices in Norfolk."

"Damn it, I taught her everything she knows about raising sheep in Norfolk. She learned it on our honeymoon."

"Well, then, you must be very pleased to know she's putting the knowledge to good use socially."

Julian's eyes narrowed as he studied the males bunched around his wife. A tall, pale-haired figure dressed in unrelieved black caught his attention. "I see Waycott has lost no time in introducing himself."

"Oh, dear. Is he in the group?" Fanny's smile slipped as she bent forward to follow his gaze. The mischief faded from her eyes. "I'm sorry, Julian. I had not realized he was here tonight. But you must know she was bound to run into him sooner or later along with a few of Elizabeth's other admirers."

"I put Sophy in your care, Fanny, because I credited you with sufficient common sense to keep her out of trouble."

"Keeping your wife out of trouble is your job, not mine," Fanny retorted with asperity. "I am her friend and adviser, nothing more."

Julian knew he was being reprimanded for his lack of attention to Sophy during the past week but he was in no mood to muster a defense. He was too concerned with the sight of the handsome blond god who was at that very moment handing a glass of lemonade to Sophy. He had seen that particular expression on Waycott's face five years ago when the Viscount had begun hovering around Elizabeth.

Julian's hand clenched at his side. With a great effort of will he forced himself to relax. Last time he had been a besotted fool who had not seen trouble coming until it was too late. This time he would move quickly and ruthlessly to head off disaster.

"Excuse me, Fanny. I do believe you are right. It is my job to protect Sophy and I had better get on with the task."

Fanny swung around, her brows knitting in a concerned expression. "Julian, be careful how you go about things. Remember that Sophy is not Elizabeth."

"Precisely. And I intend to see that she does not turn into Elizabeth." Julian was already pacing down the length of the balcony toward the small side staircase that would take him to the ballroom floor.

Once on the lower level he immediately found himself confronted with a wall of people, several of whom paused to greet him and congratulate him on his recent marriage. Julian managed to nod civilly, accepting the well-meant compliments on his Countess and ignoring the veiled curiosity that often accompanied them.

His size was in his favor. He was taller than most of the other people in the room and it was not difficult to keep the cluster of males orbiting around Sophy in sight. Within a few minutes he had made his way to where she was holding court.

He spotted the drooping flower ornament in her coiffure at the same instant that Waycott reached out to adjust it.

"If I may be allowed to pluck this rose, madam?" Waycott said with smooth gallantry as he started to pull the dangling enameled flower from Sophy's hair.

Julian shouldered his way past two young males who were watching the blond man enviously. "My privilege, Waycott." He tweaked the ornament from a curl just as Sophy looked up in surprise. Waycott's hand fell away, his pale blue eyes narrowed with silent anger.

"*Julian*." Sophy smiled up at him with genuine delight. "I was afraid you would not be able to attend this evening. Isn't it a lovely ball?"

"Lovely." Julian surveyed her deliberately, aware of a violent sense of possessiveness. Fanny had turned her out well, he realized. Sophy's dress was richly hued and perfectly cut to emphasize her slender figure. Her hair was done in an elegant series of curls piled high to show off her graceful nape.

Jewelry had been confined to a minimum he saw and it occurred to him that the Ravenwood emeralds would have looked very nice around Sophy's throat. Unfortunately, he did not have them to give to her.

"I am having the most delightful time this evening," Sophy went on cheerfully. "Everyone has been so attentive and welcoming. Have you met all my friends?" She indicated the group of hovering males with a slight nod of her head.

Julian swung a cold gaze around the small gathering and smiled laconically at each familiar face. He allowed his eyes to linger ever so briefly on Waycott's amused, assessing expression. Then he turned pointedly away from the other man. "Why, yes, Sophy, I believe I have made the acquaintance of just about everyone present. And I'm certain that by now, you've had more than enough of their company."

The unmistakable warning was not lost on any man in the surrounding circle, although Waycott seemed more amused than impressed. The others hastened to offer congratulations, however, and for a few minutes Julian was obliged to listen to a great deal of fulsome praise for his wife's charm, herbal expertise, and conversational talents.

"Has a most commendable knowledge of farming techniques, for a female," one middle-aged admirer announced. "Could talk to her for hours."

"We were just discussing sheep," a ruddy faced young man explained. "Lady Ravenwood has some interesting notions about breeding methods."

"Fascinating, I'm sure," Julian said. He inclined his head toward his wife. "I am beginning to realize I have married an expert on the subject."

"You will recall I read widely, my lord," Sophy murmured. "And lately I have taken the liberty of indulging myself in your library. You have an excellent collection of farm management books."

"I shall have to see about replacing them with something of a more elevating nature. Religious tracts, perhaps." Julian held out his hand. "In the meantime, I wonder if you can tear yourself away from such enthralling conversation long enough to favor your husband with a dance, madam?"

Sophy's eyes shimmered with laughter. "But, of course, Julian. You will forgive me, gentlemen?" she asked politely as she put her hand on her husband's arm.

"Of course," Waycott murmured. "We all understand the call of duty, do we not? Return to us when you are ready to play again, Sophy."

Julian fought back the urge to plant a fist square in the center of Waycott's too-handsome features. He knew Sophy would never forgive him for causing that sort of scene and neither would Lady Yelverton. Seething inwardly, he took the only other course open to him. He coolly ignored Waycott's jibe as he led Sophy out onto the floor.

"I get the impression you are enjoying yourself," he said as Sophy slipped easily into his arms.

"Very much. Oh, Julian, it is all so different than it was last time. Tonight everyone seems so nice. I have danced more this evening than I did during my entire season five years ago." Sophy's cheeks were flushed and her fine eyes were alight with her obvious pleasure.

"I am glad your first important event as the Countess of Ravenwood has turned out to be such a success." He put deliberate emphasis on her new title. He did not want her forgetting either her position or her obligation to that position.

Sophy's smile turned thoughtful. "I expect it's all going so well this time because I am married. I am now viewed as safe by every type of male, you see."

Startled by the observation, Julian scowled. "What the devil do you mean by that?"

"Isn't it obvious? I am no longer angling for a husband. I have already snagged him, so to speak. Thus the men feel free to flirt and pay me court because they know perfectly well they are in no danger of being obliged to make an offer. It is all a lot of harmless fun now whereas five years ago they would have been at great risk of having to declare their intentions."

Julian bit back an oath. "You are very much off the mark with that line of reasoning," he assured her through his teeth. "Don't be naive, Sophy. You are old enough to realize that your status as a married woman leaves you open to the most dishonorable sorts of approaches from men. It is precisely because you are *safe* that they can feel free to seduce you."

Her gaze grew watchful although her smile stayed in place. "Come now, Julian. You overstate the case. I am in no danger of being seduced by *any* male present as far as I can tell."

It took him a split second to realize she was lumping him in with every other man in the room. "Forgive me, madam," he said very softly, "I had not realized you were so eager to be seduced. In fact, I had quite the opposite impression. My misunderstanding, I'm sure."

"You frequently misunderstand me, my lord." She fixed her gaze on his cravat. "But as it happens, I was only teasing."

"Were you?"

"Yes, of course. Forgive me. I only meant to lighten your mood a bit. You seemed overly concerned by what is a totally nonexistent threat to my virtue. I assure you none of the men in that group made any improper advances or suggestions."

Julian sighed. "The problem, Sophy, is that I am not convinced you would recognize an improper suggestion until matters had gone too far. You may be all of twenty-three years old but you have not had much experience with Society. It is little more than a glittering hunting ground and an attractive, naive, safely married young woman such as yourself is frequently viewed as a grand prize."

She stiffened in his arms, her eyes narrowing. "Please do not be condescending, Julian. I am not that naive. I assure you I have no intention of allowing myself to be seduced by any of your friends."

"Unfortunately, my dear, that still leaves all my enemies."

SEVEN

Sophy paced her bedchamber later that night, the events of the evening spinning through her head. It had all been very exciting and wonderfully different from the way things had been five years ago when she had had her one and only fling at Society.

She was well aware that her new status as Ravenwood's wife had a lot to do with the attention she received, but she honestly felt she had held her own conversationally. At twenty-three she had far more self-confidence than she'd had at eighteen, for one thing. In addition, she had not been painfully conscious of being on display in a marriage mart the way she had been five years ago. Tonight she had been able to relax and enjoy herself. Everything had gone very well until Julian had arrived.

Initially she had been delighted to find him there, eager to have him see that she could handle herself in his world. But after the first dance it had dawned on her that Julian had not bothered to drop in at the Yelvertons' ball just to admire her newfound ability to socialize. He had come because he was worried she would get swept off her feet

by one of the predatory males who prowled the sophisticated jungle of the *ton*.

It was very depressing to realize that only Julian's
natural possessiveness had kept him by her side for the
rest of the evening.

They had arrived home an hour ago and Sophy had gone
immediately upstairs to prepare for bed. Julian had not
tried to delay her. He had bid her a formal good night and
vanished into the library. A few minutes ago Sophy had
heard his muffled footsteps in the carpeted hall outside her
room.

The glow of excitement engendered by her first major
evening in Society was fading rapidly and as far as Sophy
was concerned it was mostly Julian's fault. He had definitely done his best to dampen the buoyant pleasure she
had been experiencing.

Sophy turned at the far end of the room and paced back
toward her dressing table. She caught sight of the small
jewelry case revealed in the candlelight and stopped short
aware of a strong flicker of guilt. There was no denying
that during the hectic excitement of her first week in town
as the Countess of Ravenwood, she had temporarily put
aside her goal of vengeance for Amelia. Salvaging her
marriage had loomed as the most important matter in her
world.

It was not that she had forsaken her vow to find Amelia's
seducer, Sophy told herself, it was just that other things
had taken priority.

But as soon as she had established a proper relationship
with Julian, she would return to the project of finding the
man responsible for Amelia's death.

"I have not forgotten you, dear sister," Sophy whispered.

She was lifting the lid of the jewelry case when the door
opened behind her. She swung around with a sharp intake
of breath and saw Julian standing in the doorway that
connected their rooms. He was wearing his dressing gown
and nothing else. The jewelry case lid dropped shut with a
snap.

Julian glanced at the small case and then met Sophy's
eyes. He smiled wryly. "You need not say a word, my

dear. I got the point earlier this evening. Forgive me for failing to remember to supply you with the little trinkets you will need to dress properly here in town."

"I was not about to ask you for jewelry, my lord," Sophy said, annoyed. Honestly, the man did have a way of making the most irritating assumptions. "Was there something you wanted?"

He hesitated a moment, making no move to come farther into the room. "Yes, I believe there is," he said finally. "Sophy, I have been giving much thought to the matter of the unsettled business between us."

"Business, my lord?"

His eyes narrowed. "You would prefer me to be more blunt? Very well, I have given a great deal of consideration to the matter of consummating our marriage."

Sophy's stomach suddenly felt the way it had one day long ago when she had fallen out of a tree into a stream. "I see. I suppose it was all that talk about sheep breeding earlier at the Yelvertons' that brought the subject to mind?"

Julian stalked toward her, his hands shoved into the pockets of his dressing gown. "This has nothing to do with sheep. Tonight I realized for the first time that your lack of personal experience of the marriage bed puts you at grave risk."

Amelia blinked in amazement. "Risk, my lord?"

He nodded soberly. He picked up a crystal swan ornament from her dressing table and turned it idly in his hand. "You are too naive and far too innocent, Sophy. You do not have the sort of worldly knowledge a woman must have in order to understand the nuances and double entendres certain men employ in conversation. You are too likely to lead such men on unknowingly simply because you do not understand their true meaning."

"I think I begin to comprehend your reasoning, my lord," Sophy said. "You feel that the fact that I am not yet a proper wife in every sense of the word may be a handicap for me socially?"

"In a manner of speaking."

"What a dreadful notion. Rather like the idea of eating one's fish with the wrong fork, I imagine."

"A bit more serious than that, I assure you, Sophy. If you were unmarried your continued lack of knowledge about certain matters would be something of a safeguard. Any man who attempted to seduce you, would also know he would be expected to marry you. But as a married woman, you have no such protection. And if a certain sort of man happened to guess that you have not yet shared a bed with your husband, he would be relentless in his pursuit of you. He would see you as a very amusing conquest."

"In other words, this hypothetical male would see me as a fine prize, indeed?"

"Precisely." Julian put down the crystal swan and smiled approvingly at Sophy. "I'm glad you understand the situation."

"Oh, I do," she said, struggling to control her breathlessness. "You are telling me that you have finally decided to claim your husbandly rights."

He shrugged with apparent sangfroid. "It seems to me it would be in your best interests if I did so. For your sake, I have concluded it would be best to put matters on a normal footing."

Sophy's fingers clenched around the back of the dressing table chair. "Julian, I have made it clear that I desire to be a complete wife to you but I must request one favor before we proceed tonight."

His green eyes glittered, belying his outer calm. "What would that favor be, my dear?"

"It is that you cease explaining your logic for doing what you intend to do. Your assurance of how this is all for my own good is having the same effect on me as my special herb tea had on you at Eslington Park."

Julian stared at her, speechless for a moment. Then he stunned Sophy by giving a shout of laughter.

"In danger of going to sleep, are you?" He moved with a suddenness that took Sophy by surprise, sweeping her up into his arms and striding toward the wide bed. "I certainly cannot have that. Madam, I swear I shall do my best to engage your complete and full attention in this matter."

Sophy smiled tremulously up at him as she clung to his broad shoulders. A glorious thrill of excitement shot through her. "Believe me, my lord, you have my full attention now."

"That's just as it should be because you have certainly captured my complete concentration."

He settled her tenderly onto the bed, tugging her dressing gown from her as he did so. His sensual smile was full of masculine expectation.

As he stripped off his own dressing gown, revealing his hard, lean body in the candlelight, Sophy no longer had any doubt but that he was doing this because he felt genuine desire. Julian was fully aroused, taut, and heavy with his need. She stared at him for a long moment, a last, embarrassed flicker of uncertainty moving through her even as she felt her own body begin to respond.

"Do I frighten you, Sophy?" Julian came down onto the bed beside her, gathering her into his arms. His large hands moved over her hip, feeling the shape of her through the fabric of her nightdress. "I do not want to alarm you."

"Of course you do not frighten me. I have told you many times I am not some simple-minded chit fresh from the schoolroom." She shivered slightly as his palm warmed her hip.

"Ah, yes, I keep forgetting that my country-bred bride is well versed in matters of breeding and reproduction." He kissed her throat and smiled again when another tremor went through her. "I can see I have no reason to concern myself over the possibility of accidentally offending your delicate sensibilities."

"I believe you are teasing me, Julian."

"I believe you are right." He eased her onto her back. His fingers found the ribbons of her nightdress and he began to undo them with slow deliberation. His eyes never left her face as he freed her breasts to his touch.

"So soft and womanly you are, little one."

Sophy was mesmerized by Julian's intent gaze as he looked at her. Fascinated, she watched as the sensual laughter in his eyes converted swiftly into a dark desire.

She reached up to touch the side of his face and was surprised by his reaction to the gentle, questing caress.

He groaned thickly and his head lowered until his mouth captured hers. The kiss was hot, hungry, and demanding, revealing fully the depths of Julian's arousal. He caught her lower lip between his teeth and bit carefully. When Sophy moaned softly, he slid his tongue intimately into her mouth and simultaneously brushed his thumb across one rosy nipple.

Sophy reacted sharply to Julian's touch, covering his hand with her own as he stroked her breast. She felt her body stirring into throbbing awareness and knew she was rapidly losing control.

It was all right this time, she told herself as some small part of her called out a distant warning. Julian might not be in love with her but he was her husband. He had sworn to protect her and care for her and she trusted him to uphold his end of the marriage bargain. In return she would be a good wife, a proper wife.

It was not his fault that she was in love with him. It was not his fault that the risk she took tonight was far greater than the one he took.

"Sophy, Sophy, let yourself go. Give yourself over to me. You are so sweet. So soft." Julian broke off the passionate kiss and tugged the nightdress free. He tossed it carelessly onto the floor beside the bed, his eyes sweeping over Sophy's shadowed body. He put his hand on her bare calf and slowly stroked upward to her hip. When she trembled he leaned down to kiss her reassuringly.

The reassurance turned instantly back into demanding desire as Sophy laced her fingers in his hair and held him tightly to her. Her legs moved restlessly until he anchored one of them with one of his own. The action resulted in opening her more fully to his touch and he immediately began to explore the silken skin of her inner thigh.

Sophy's head tossed from side to side on the pillow. She heard her own small, whispering gasp of excitement as she felt Julian's fingers moving in small circles on her skin. His big hands felt so good on her body, strong and secure and knowing. She felt safe and cherished.

"Julian, *Julian*, I feel so strange."

"I know, sweetheart. Your body makes no secret of it. I'm glad. I want you to feel this way." He moved against her, letting her feel the shape of his manhood as it brushed her hip.

She flinched at the power she sensed in him but when he caught her fingers and guided them to his thrusting shaft, she did not resist. She touched him hesitantly at first, familiarizing herself with the size and shape of him.

"You see how much I want you, Sophy?" Julian's voice was husky. "But I swear I will not take you until you want me just as badly."

"How will you know when that time comes?" she asked, gazing up at him through half-closed lashes.

He smiled fleetingly and deliberately closed his palm over the soft mound between her legs. "You will tell me in your own way."

She felt the growing warmth between her thighs and moved impatiently once more, seeking an even more intimate touch. "I think that time is here," she whispered.

He slid one finger slowly into her softness. Sophy stiffened abruptly in reaction and then felt the moisture between her legs.

"Soon," Julian promised with deep satisfaction. His lips trailed over her breasts. "Very soon." He inserted his finger again and withdrew it only part way.

Hesitantly Sophy moved against his probing finger, her body instinctively tightening around it as if she would draw it deeper once more.

Julian obliged with a low exclamation of encouragement and desire. "You are so tight and warm," he muttered as his mouth closed over hers again. "And you want me. You truly want me, don't you sweetheart?" His tongue slid between her lips, imitating the provocative movements of his hand.

Sophy gasped and clutched at his shoulders, pulling him closer. When he used the pad of his thumb to tease a small, exquisitely sensitive area hidden in the dark nest of curls, she unwittingly scored his back with her nails.

"*Julian.*"

"Yes. Oh, God, *yes*."

He moved on top of her, sliding one muscular thigh between her legs to make a space for himself. Sophy opened her eyes as she felt him lower himself down along the length of her. He was heavy, overwhelmingly so. She felt deliciously crushed into the bedding. When she looked up into his stark, intent face she experienced a racing thrill that was unlike anything she had ever known.

"Raise your knees, sweetheart," he urged. "That's it, darling. Open yourself to me. Tell me you want me."

"I want you. Oh, Julian, I want you so much." She felt open and vulnerable but curiously safe. This was Julian and he would never hurt her. He began to push against her softness, moistening himself on the liquid honey that flowed from her delicate sheath. Instinctively she started to lower her legs and tighten them.

"No, darling. It will be easier this way. You must trust me now. I swear I will enter you very slowly. I will go only as far and as fast as you want me to go. You can stop me at any time."

She felt the rigid tension in his body and her palms slipped in the sweat on his back. He was lying, she thought happily. Either that or he was desperately trying to convince himself that he truly had sufficient willpower to stop on demand. Either way she sensed instinctively that he was as close to being out of control as she was.

The knowledge made her feel wonderfully wicked and womanly and strong. It was good to know she could bring her powerful, self-contained husband to such a pass. In this much, at least, they were equals.

"Do not worry, Julian. I would no more halt you now than I would try to hold back the sun," she promised breathlessly.

"I am very glad to hear that. Look at me, Sophy. I want to see your eyes when I make you my wife in every sense of the word."

She opened her eyes again and then sucked in her breath as she felt him begin to enter her. Her nails dug into him once more.

"It's all right, little one." Perspiration formed into small drops on his brow as he slowly eased forward. "It's bound to be a bit rough at first but after that we will have clear sailing."

"I do not see myself as a vessel at sea, Julian," she managed even as she wondered at the incredibly tight, stretched, full feeling he was creating within her. Her nails dug deeper.

"I think we are both at sea," he ground out as he fought to slow the penetration. *"Hold onto me, Sophy."*

She knew the frail thread of his self-control had just snapped. Even as she gloried in the knowledge he groaned heavily and surged deeply into her.

"Julian." Stunned by the swift, fiery invasion, Sophy cried out and pushed at his shoulders as if she could dislodge him.

"It's all right, love. I swear it will be all right. Don't fight me, Sophy. It will all be over soon. Try to relax." Julian dropped tiny kisses on her cheek and throat while he held himself still within her tight channel. "Give it some time, my sweet."

"Will time make you grow any smaller?" she demanded with some asperity.

He groaned and framed her dismayed face between his large palms. He looked down at her with gleaming eyes. "Time will help you adjust to me. You will learn to like this, Sophy. I know you will. You feel so wonderfully good and there is such passion in you. You must not be so impatient."

"That is easy for you to say, my lord. You have what you wanted out of all this, I assume."

"Almost all of what I wanted," he agreed with a small smile. "But it will not be perfect for me until it is perfect for you. Are you feeling any better?"

She considered the question cautiously. "Yes," she finally admitted.

"Good." He kissed her lingeringly and then he began to move slowly within her, long, slow strokes designed to ease himself carefully back and forth in the tight passage.

Sophy bit her lip and waited anxiously to see if the movement made things worse. But it did not. In truth, she did not feel so uncomfortable now, she realized. Some of the earlier excitement was returning, albeit slowly. Gradually her body adjusted to the fullness.

She was just getting to the point where she could honestly say she might be learning to enjoy the odd sensation when Julian suddenly began to move with increasing urgency.

"Julian, wait, I would have you move more slowly," she said hastily as she sensed he was abandoning himself completely to the force that drove him.

"I am sorry, Sophy. I tried. But I cannot wait any longer," he gritted his teeth and then he gave a muffled shout and flexed his hips, burying himself to the hilt.

And then Sophy felt the hot, heavy essence of him pouring into her as he went taut. Obeying an ancient instinct, she wrapped her arms and legs around him and held him close. *He is mine*, she thought with deep wonder. *In this moment and for all time, he is mine.*

"Hold me," Julian's voice was ragged. "Hold me, Sophy." Slowly the rigidity went out of him and he collapsed, heavy and damp with sweat, along the length of her.

Sophy lay still for a long time, absently smoothing Julian's sweat-streaked back with her fingertips as she gazed up at the canopy over the bed. She could not say she thought much of the final act, itself, but she had definitely enjoyed the caressing that preceded it. She also found the warm intimacy of the embrace afterward very appealing.

She sensed that Julian would never lower his guard to this extent in any other situation with her. That alone was worth putting up with the business of lovemaking.

Julian stirred reluctantly and lifted himself up on his elbows. He smiled with lazy satisfaction and chuckled when she smiled back at him. He bent his head to drop a small kiss on the tip of her nose.

"I feel like a stallion at the end of a long race. I may have won, but I am exhausted and weak. You must give me a few minutes to recover. Next time it will be better for you, sweetheart." He smoothed her hair off her forehead with a tender movement.

"A few minutes," she exclaimed, startled. "You speak as though we will do this several more times tonight."

"I rather believe we shall," Julian said with evident anticipation. His warm palm flattened possessively on her stomach. "I have been kept waiting a long time for you, Madam Wife, and I mean to make up for all the nights we have wasted."

Sophy felt the soreness between her legs and a bolt of alarm went through her. "Forgive me," she said hastily, "I want very much to be a good wife to you but I do not think I shall recover as quickly as you seem to believe you will. Would you mind very much if we did not do this again right away?"

He frowned in immediate concern. "Sophy, did I hurt you badly?"

"No, no. It's just that I have no wish to do it again quite so soon. Parts of it were . . . were quite pleasant, I assure you but if you do not mind, my lord, I would prefer to wait until another night."

He winced. "I am sorry, sweetheart. It is all my fault. I meant to go much more slowly with you." He rolled to one side and stood up beside the bed.

"Where are you going?"

"I will be back shortly," he promised.

She watched him walk through the shadows to the dresser where he poured water from the pitcher into a bowl. Then he took a towel off the stand and soaked it.

As he returned to the bed it dawned on Sophy what he intended to do. She sat up quickly, pulling the sheet to her throat. "No, Julian, please, I can manage by myself."

"You must allow me, Sophy. This is yet another of a husband's privileges." He sat down on the side of the bed and gently but firmly tugged the sheet from her reluctant grasp. "Lie down, sweetheart, and let me make you more comfortable."

"Truthfully, Julian, I would rather you did not . . ."

But there was no stopping him. He urged her down onto her back. Sophy muttered an embarrassed oath that made Julian laugh.

"There is no reason to turn reticent now, my love. It is

far too late. I have already experienced your sweet passion, remember? A few minutes ago you were warm and damp and very welcoming. You allowed me to touch you everywhere." He finished sponging her off and discarded the stained towel.

"Julian, I . . . I must ask you something," Sophy said as she quickly readjusted the sheet to preserve some semblance of modesty.

"What is it you wish to know?" He came over to the bed and calmly climbed in beside her.

"You told me there were ways of preventing this sort of thing from resulting in a babe. Did you use any of those ways tonight?"

A short, tense silence settled over the bed. Julian leaned back against the pillows, his arms folded behind his head.

"No," he finally said quite bluntly. "I did not."

"Oh." She tried to hide some of the anxiety she felt as she absorbed that information.

"You knew what I wanted out of this arrangement when you agreed to be a proper wife to me, Sophy."

"An heir and no trouble." Perhaps the illusion of intimacy a few minutes earlier had been simply that, she thought dully, an illusion. There was on denying that Julian had wanted her very much when he had come to her this evening, but she would do well not to forget that his primary goal was to get himself an heir.

Another silence gripped the shadowed bed. Then Julian asked softly, "Would it be so bad to bear me a son, Sophy?"

"What happens if I bear you a daughter, my lord?" she asked coolly, avoiding a direct answer to his question.

He smiled unexpectedly. "A daughter would do very nicely, especially if she took after her mother."

Sophy wondered how to take the compliment and decided not to question it too deeply. "But you require a son for Ravenwood."

"Then we will just have to keep trying until we get one, won't we?" Julian asked. He reached out and pulled her against his side, cradling her head on his shoulder. "But I don't think we will have too much trouble making a son. Sinclairs always produce sons and you are strong and healthy. But you did not answer my question, Sophy. Would you mind very much if it should come about that you conceived tonight?"

"It is very soon in our marriage," she pointed out hesitantly. "We both have much to learn about each other. It would seem wiser to wait." *Until you can learn to love me*, she added silently.

"I see no point in waiting. A babe would be good for you, Sophy."

"Why? Because it would make me more aware of my duties and responsibilities as your wife?" she retorted. "I assure you, I am already quite cognizant of them."

Julian sighed. "I only meant that I believe you would make a good mother. And I think a babe of your own would perhaps make you more content with your role as a wife."

Sophy groaned, angry at herself for having ruined the mood of tenderness and intimacy that Julian had offered after the lovemaking. She sought to retrieve the fragile moment with a dose of humor. Turning on her side she smiled down at him teasingly. "Tell me, Julian, are all husbands so arrogantly certain they know what is best for their wives?"

"Sophy, you wound me." He grimaced, striving to look both innocent and injured. But there was relief and a hint of laughter in his eyes. "You do think me arrogant, don't you?"

"There are times when I am unable to avoid that conclusion."

His gaze grew serious again. "I know it must seem that way to you. But in all truth, I want to be a good husband to you, Sophy."

"I know that," she murmured gently. "It is precisely because I do know it that I am so willing to tolerate your bouts of high-handedness. You see what an understanding wife you have?"

He regarded her through half-lowered lids. "A paragon of a wife."

"Never doubt it for a moment. I could give lessons."

"A notion that would send chills through the other husbands of the *ton*. I will, however, endeavor to keep your good intentions in mind when you are involved in such tricks as brewing sleeping potions and reading that damnable Wollstonecraft." He raised his head long enough to kiss Sophy soundly and then he flopped back onto the snowy pillows. "There is something else we must discuss tonight, my paragon of a wife."

"What is that?" She yawned, aware that she was growing sleepy. It was strange having him in her bed but she was discovering a certain comfort in his strength and warmth. She wondered if he would stay the night.

"You were annoyed earlier when I said that I thought we should consummate our marriage," he began slowly.

"Only because you insisted that it was for my own good."

He smiled faintly. "Yes, I can see where you get the notion that I have a tendency to be arrogant and high handed. But be that as it may, it is definitely time you knew the true risk you run when you flirt with Waycott and his like."

Sophy's sleepy good humor vanished in a heartbeat. She pushed herself up on her elbow and glared down at Julian. "I was not flirting with the Viscount."

"Yes, Sophy, you were. I will allow that you may not have realized it but I assure you, he was looking at you as if you were a gooseberry tart covered in cream. And everytime you smiled at him, he licked his chops."

"Julian, you exaggerate!"

He pulled her back down onto his shoulder. "No, Sophy, I do not. And Waycott is not the only one who was salivating around you this evening. You must be very careful of such men. Above all you must not encourage them, even unwittingly."

"Why do you fear Waycott in particular?"

"I do not fear him. But I accept the fact that he is dangerous to women and I do not want my wife courting such danger. He would seduce you in a moment if he thought it possible."

"Why me? There were a number of far more beautiful women at Lady Yelverton's ball tonight."

"He will pick you above all others if the chance comes his way because you are my wife."

"But why?"

"He bears a deep and abiding hatred for me, Sophy. Never forget that."

And suddenly everything fell into place. "Was Waycott one of Elizabeth's lovers?" she asked without pausing to think.

Julian's jaw tightened and his expression reverted to the grim, forbidding mask that had helped earn him the title of devil. "I have told you I do not discuss my first wife with anyone. Not even you, Sophy."

She started to edge out of his circling arm. "Forgive me, Julian. I forgot myself."

"Yes, you did." His arm locked around her as he felt her trying to pull away. He ignored her small struggles. "But since you are a paragon of a wife, I am sure it will not happen again, will it?"

Sophy stopped trying to escape the chain of his arm. She narrowed her gaze and studied him intently. "Are you teasing me again, Julian?"

"No, madam, I assure you, I am very serious." But he was smiling that slow, lazy smile of satisfaction that had been on his face when he had finished making love to her. "Turn your head, sweetheart. I want to examine something." He used his thumb to guide her chin until he had her face angled so that he could study her eyes in the candlelight. Then he shook his head slowly. "It is just as I feared."

"What's wrong?" she asked anxiously.

"I told myself that once I had made love to you properly, you would lose some of that clear-eyed innocence but I was wrong. Your eyes are as clear and innocent as they were before I bedded you. It is going to be very difficult to protect you from Society's predators, my dear. I can see that I have only one option."

"What option is that, my lord?" Sophy asked demurely.

"I will have to spend more of my time by your side."

Julian yawned hugely. "From now on you must give me a list of your evening engagements. I will be accompanying you whenever possible."

"Really, my lord? Are you fond of the opera?"

"I detest the opera."

Sophy grinned. "That is, indeed, a pity. Your aunt, her friend Harriette, and I plan to go to King's Theatre tomorrow evening. Will you feel obliged to join us?"

"A man does what he must," Julian said nobly.

EIGHT

"How on earth will Fanny and Harry find us in this crush?" Sophy anxiously surveyed the throng of carriages that filled the Haymarket near King's Theatre. "There must be over a thousand people here tonight."

"More like three thousand." Julian took her arm in a firm grip as he guided her into the fashionable theater. "But don't worry about Fanny and Harry. They'll have no trouble locating us."

"Why not?"

"Because the box they use is mine," Julian explained wryly as they made their way through the glittering crowd.

"Oh, I see. A convenient arrangement."

"Fanny has always thought so. It has saved her the cost of purchasing one of her own."

Sophy glanced at him. "You do not mind her using it, do you?"

Julian grinned. "No. She is one of the few members of the family I can tolerate for any length of time."

A few minutes later Julian escorted her into a plushly appointed box, well situated amid the five tiers of similar private boxes. Sophy sat down and gazed in fascination out over the great horseshoe auditorium. It was filled with bejeweled ladies and elegantly dressed men. Down in the pit, fops and dandies of all stripes were strolling about. showing off the extremes of fashion they favored. The sight of their ludicrously outrageous clothing made Sophy realize she took a secret pleasure in Julian's preference for subdued, conservatively cut garments.

It soon became apparent, however, that the real spectacle of the evening was not taking place down in the pits or on stage, but rather in the fashionable boxes.

"It's like looking at five tiers of miniature stages," Sophy exclaimed in laughing amusement. "Everyone is dressed to be on display and busy studying everyone else to see who is wearing what jewels and who is visiting whom in a box. I cannot see why you find the opera boring, Julian, with so much going on here in the audience."

Julian leaned back in his velvet chair and cocked a brow as he looked out over the auditorium. "You have a point, my dear. There is certainly more action up here than there is down on the stage."

He studied the rows of theater boxes in silence for a long moment. Sophy followed his gaze and saw it hesitate briefly on one specific box where a stunningly garbed woman held court amid several male admirers. Sophy watched her for a moment, suddenly curious about the attractive blond who seemed to be the center of much attention.

"Who is that woman, Julian?"

"Which woman?" Julian asked absently, his gaze moving on to survey the other boxes.

"The one in the third tier wearing the green gown. She must be very popular. She appears to be surrounded by men. I don't see any other women in the box."

"Ah, that woman," Julian glanced back briefly. "You need not concern yourself with her, Sophy. You are highly unlikely to meet her socially."

"One never knows, does one?"

"In this instance, I am quite certain."

"Julian, I cannot stand the mystery. Who is she?"

Julian sighed. "One of the Fashionable Impures," he explained in a tone that said he found the subject distinctly boring. "There are many here tonight. The boxes are their shop windows, so to speak."

Sophy's eyes widened. "Real ladies of the demimonde? They keep boxes here at King's Theatre?"

"As I said, the boxes make excellent show cases for their, uh, wares."

Sophy was amazed. "But it must cost a fortune to take a box for the season."

"Not quite, but it is definitely not cheap," he admitted. "I believe the demireps see it as a business investment."

Sophy leaned forward intently. "Point out some of the other Fashionable Impures, Julian. I swear, one certainly cannot tell them apart from the ladies of quality just by looking at them, can one?"

Julian gave her a short, charged glance that was half-amused and half-rueful. "An interesting observation, Sophy. And in many cases, an accurate one, I fear. But there are a few exceptions. Some women have an unmistakable air of quality and it shows regardless of how they are dressed."

Sophy was too busy studying the boxes to notice the intent look he was giving her. "Which are the exceptions? Point one or two out, will you? I would dearly love to see if I can tell a demirep from a Duchess at a glance."

"Never mind, Sophy. I have indulged your lamentable curiosity enough for one evening. I think it's time we changed the subject."

"Julian, have you ever noticed how you always change the subject just as the conversation is getting particularly interesting?"

"Do I? How ill-mannered of me."

"I do not think you are the least bit sorry about your manners. Oh, look, there's Anne Silverthorne and her grandmother." Sophy signaled her friend with her fan and Anne promptly sent back a laughing acknowledgment from a nearby box. "Can we go and visit in her box, Julian?"

"Between acts, perhaps."

"That will be fun. Anne looks lovely tonight, doesn't she? That yellow dress looks wonderful with her red hair."

"Some would say the dress is cut a bit too low for a young woman who is not married," Julian said, slanting a brief, critical glance at Anne's gown.

"If Anne waits until she is married to wear a fashionable gown, she will wait forever. She has told me she will never wed. She holds the male sex in very low esteem and the institution of marriage does not attract her at all."

Julian's mouth turned down. "I suppose you met Miss Silverthorne at my aunt's Wednesday salons?"

"Yes, as a matter of fact, I did."

"Judging by what you have just told me, I am not at all certain she is the sort of female you should be associating with, my dear."

"You are probably quite right," Sophy said cheerfully. "Anne is a terrible influence. But I fear the damage is already done. We have become close friends, you see, and one does not abandon one's friends, does one?"

"Sophy—"

"I am quite certain you would never turn your back on your friends. It would not be honorable."

Julian gave her a wary look. "Now, Sophy—"

"Do not alarm yourself, Julian. Anne is not my only friend. Jane Morland is another recent acquaintance of mine and you would no doubt approve of her. She is very serious-minded. Very much the voice of reason and restraint."

"I am relieved to hear it," Julian said. "But, Sophy, I must advise you to be as careful in choosing your female friends as you are in selecting your male ones."

"Julian, if I were as cautious in my friendships as you would have me, I would lead a very solitary existence, indeed. Either that, or I would be bored to death by some very dull creatures."

"Somehow I cannot imagine such a situation."

"Neither can I." Sophy glanced around, searching for a distraction. "I must say, Fanny and Harry are very late. I do hope they are all right."

"Now it is you who is changing the subject."

"I learned the technique from you." Sophy was about to

continue in that vein when she became aware that the striking blond courtesan in the green gown was looking straight at her across the expanse of space that separated the boxes.

For a moment Sophy simply gazed back curiously, intrigued by the other woman's forthright stare. She started to ask Julian once more what the woman's name was but a sudden loud commotion in the gallery made it clear the opera was about to begin. Sophy forgot about the woman in green and gave her attention to the stage.

The curtain behind Sophy parted during the middle of the first act and she glanced around, expecting to see Fanny and Harry bustling into the box but the visitor was Miles Thurgood. Julian casually waved him to a seat. Sophy smiled at him.

"I say, Catalani is in fine form tonight, isn't she?" Miles leaned forward to murmur in Sophy's ear. "Heard she had a flaming row with her latest paramour just before she came on stage. Word has it she dumped a chamber pot over his head. Poor fellow is due to perform in the next act. One hopes he'll be able to get cleaned up in time."

Sophy giggled, ignoring Julian's disapproving glare. "How did you hear that?" she whispered to Miles.

"Catalani's escapades behind the scenes are legendary," Miles explained with a grin.

"There is no need to regale my wife with such tales," Julian said pointedly. "Find something else to talk about if you wish to stay in this box."

"Don't pay any attention to him," Sophy admonished. "Julian is excessively straitlaced in some matters."

"Is that true, Julian?" Miles exclaimed innocently. "Do you know, now that your Countess makes the observation, I fear she may be right. I had begun to think you a bit stuffy of late. Must be the affects of marriage."

"No doubt," Julian said coldly.

"Catalani is not the only one causing talk tonight," Miles went on cheerfully. "One hears that a few more members of the *ton* have received notes from the Grand Featherstone. You've got to hand it to the woman. She's got nerve to sit here tonight surrounded by her victims."

Sophy rounded on him at once. "Charlotte Featherstone is here tonight? Where?"

"That's enough, Thurgood," Julian cut in decisively.

But Miles was nodding toward the box that held the fashionably dressed blond who had been staring at Sophy only moments earlier. "That's her right over there."

"The lady in the green gown?" Sophy peered through the gloom of the darkened theater trying to pick out the infamous courtesan.

"Damn it, Thurgood, I said that's enough," Julian snapped.

"Sorry, Ravenwood. Don't mean to say anything out of line. But everyone knows who Featherstone is. Ain't exactly a secret."

Julian's eyes were grim. "Sophy, would you like some lemonade?"

"Yes, Julian, that would be lovely."

"Excellent. I'm certain Miles would be happy to fetch you a glass, wouldn't you Thurgood?"

Miles leaped to his feet and swept Sophy a graceful bow. "It would be an honor, Lady Ravenwood. I shall return shortly." He turned to slip through the curtains at the back of the box and then paused briefly. "I beg your pardon, Lady Ravenwood," he said with a wide smile, "but the plume in your hair appears to be about to fall out. May I be allowed to adjust it for you?"

"Oh, dear." Sophy reached up to push the offending plume back into the depths of her coiffure just as Miles leaned forward helpfully.

"Go get the lemonade, Thurgood," Julian ordered, reaching for the plume, himself. "I am perfectly capable of dealing with Sophy's attire." He quickly shoved the feather back into Sophy's curls as Miles made his escape from the box.

"Really, Julian, there was no need to send him away just because he pointed out Charlotte Featherstone." Sophy gave her husband a reproving glance. "As it happens I have been most curious about the woman."

"I cannot imagine why."

"Why, because I have been reading her *Memoirs*,"

Sophy explained, leaning forward once more in an effort to get a better look at the lady in green.

"You've been reading *what?*" Julian's voice sounded half-strangled.

"We're studying the Featherstone *Memoirs* in Fanny's and Harry's Wednesday afternoon salons. Fascinating reading, I must say. Such a unique view of Society. We can hardly wait for the next installment."

"Damn it, Sophy, if I'd had any notion Fanny would be exposing you to that sort of rubbish, I would never have permitted you to visit her on Wednesdays. What the devil is the meaning of this nonsense? You're supposed to be studying literature and natural philosophy, not some harlot's gossipy scribblings."

"Calm down, Julian, I am a married woman of twenty-three, not a sixteen-year-old schoolgirl." She smiled at him. "I was right earlier. You really are most dreadfully straitlaced about some things."

His eyes narrowed as he glowered at her. "Straitlaced is a rather mild term for the way I feel about this particular subject, Sophy. You are forbidden to read any more installments of the *Memoirs*. Do you fully comprehend me?"

Some of Sophy's good humor began to slip. The last thing she wanted to do was ruin the evening with an argument but she felt she had to take a stand. Last night she had surrendered on one of the most important counts of the nuptial agreement. She would not give in on another.

"Julian," she said gently, "I must remind you that prior to our marriage we discussed the matter of my freedom to read what I choose."

"Do not throw that silly agreement in my face, Sophy. It has nothing to do with this business of the Featherstone *Memoirs*."

"It was not a silly agreement and it has everything to do with this matter. You are trying to dictate what I can and cannot read. We distinctly agreed you would not do that."

"I do not wish to argue with you about this," Julian said through clenched teeth.

"Excellent." Sophy gave him a relieved smile. "I do not wish to argue with you about it either, my lord. You see?

We can agree quite easily on some matters. It bodes well, don't you think?"

"Do not misunderstand me," Julian plowed on forcefully, "I will not debate this with you. I am telling you quite plainly that I do not want you reading any more installments of the *Memoirs*. As your husband, I expressly forbid it."

Sophy drew a deep breath knowing she must not allow him to run roughshod over her like this. "It seems to me I have already made a very large compromise regarding our wedding agreement, my lord. You cannot expect me to make another. It is not fair and I believe that, at heart, you are a fair-minded man."

"Not *fair*." Julian leaned forward and caught one of her hands. "Sophy, look at me. What happened last night does not come under the heading of compromise. You simply came to your senses and realized that particular portion of our wedding agreement was irrational and unnatural."

"Did I really? How very perceptive of me."

"This is not a matter for jest, Sophy. You were wrong to insist upon that foolish clause in the first place and ultimately you had the sense to acknowledge it. This business of reading the *Memoirs* is another matter in which you are wrong. You must allow me to guide you in this sort of thing."

She looked up at him. "Be reasonable, my lord. If I surrender on this count, too, what will you demand next? That I no longer control my inheritance?"

"The devil take your inheritance," he stormed tightly. "I do not want your money and you know it."

"So you say now. But a few weeks ago you were also saying you did not care what I chose to read. How do I know you will not also soon change your mind about my inheritance?"

"Sophy, this is outrageous. Why in the name of heaven do you want to read the *Memoirs*?"

"I find them quite fascinating, my lord. Charlotte Featherstone is a most interesting woman. Only think what she has gone through."

"She's gone through a lot of men, that's what she's gone

through and I won't have you reading the particulars about each and every one of her paramours."

"I will take care not to mention the subject again, my lord, since it obviously offends you."

"You will take care not to *read* on this subject again," he corrected ominously. Then his expression softened. "Sophy, my dear, this is not worth a quarrel between us."

"I could not agree with you more, my lord."

"What I require of you is merely some degree of rational circumspection in your reading."

"Julian, as fascinating and instructive as the subjects of animal husbandry and farming are, they do grow a bit tedious now and again. I simply must have some variety in my reading."

"Surely you do not want to lower yourself to the kind of gossip you will encounter in the *Memoirs?*"

"I did warn you the day we agreed to marry that I had a lamentable taste for entertaining gossip."

"I am not going to allow you to indulge it."

"You seem to know a great deal about the sort of gossip that is in the *Memoirs*. Are you by any chance reading them, too? Perhaps we could find a basis for a discussion."

"No, I am not reading them and I have no intention of doing so. Furthermore—"

Fanny's voice heralded them from the doorway, cutting off Julian's next words. "Sophy, Julian, good evening. Did you think we would never get here?" Fanny swept through the curtains, a vision in bronze silk. Harriette Rattenbury was right behind her, resplendent in her signature purple gown and turban.

"Good evening, everyone. So sorry for the delay." Harriette smiled cheerfully at Sophy. "My dear, you look lovely tonight. That shade of pale blue is quite becoming on you. Why the scowl? Is something wrong?"

Sophy hastily summoned up a welcoming smile and tugged her hand from Julian's grasp. "Not at all, Harry. I was worried about the two you."

"Oh, nothing to fret about," Harriette assured her, sitting down with a sigh of relief. "All my fault, I'm afraid. My rheumatism was acting up earlier this afternoon and I discovered I had run out of my special tonic. Dear Fanny insisted on sending out for more and as a consequence we were late dressing for the theater. How is the performance? Is Catalani in good form?"

"I hear she dumped a chamber pot over her lover's head just prior to the first act," Sophy said promptly.

"Then she is probably giving a rousing performance." Fanny chuckled. "It is common knowledge that she is at her best when she is quarreling with one of her paramours. Gives her work spirit and zest."

Julian eyed Sophy's outwardly composed face. "The more interesting scene is the one taking place here in this box, Aunt Fanny, and you and Harry are the cause."

"Highly unlikely," Fanny murmured. "We never get involved in scenes, do we, Harry?"

"Gracious, no. Most unseemly."

"Enough," Julian snapped. "I have just discovered that you are studying the Featherstone *Memoirs* in your Wednesday afternoon salons. What the devil happened to Shakespeare and Aristotle?"

"They're dead," Harriette pointed out.

Fanny ignored Sophy's muffled giggle and waved a hand with languid grace. "Surely, Julian, as a reasonably well-educated man, yourself, you must know how wide ranging an intelligent person's interests are. And everyone in my little club is very intelligent. There must be no fetters placed on the never-ending quest for enlightenment."

"Fanny, I am warning you, I do not want Sophy exposed to that sort of nonsense."

"It's too late," Sophy interjected. "I have already been exposed."

He turned to her with a grim look. "Then we must attempt to limit the ill effects. You will not read any more of the installments. I forbid it." He rose to his feet. "Now, if you ladies will excuse me, I believe I will go and see what is keeping Miles. I shall return shortly."

"Run along, Julian," Fanny murmured encouragingly. "We will be fine."

"No doubt," he agreed coldly. "Do try to keep Sophy

from falling out of the box in her attempt to get a closer look at Charlotte Featherstone, will you?"

He nodded once, gave Sophy a last stony-eyed glare and stalked from the box. Sophy sighed as the curtain fell into place behind him.

"He is very good with exit lines, is he not?" she noted.

"All men are good at exit lines," Harriette said as she removed her opera glass from her beaded reticule. "They use them so frequently, you know. It seems they are always walking out. Off to school, off to war, off to their clubs, or off to their mistresses."

Sophy considered that briefly. "I'd say it was not so much a case of walking out as it is of running away."

"An excellent observation," Fanny said cheerfully. "How very right you are, my dear. What we just witnessed was definitely a strategic retreat. Julian probably learned such tactics under Wellington. I see you are learning the business of being a wife very rapidly."

Sophy grimaced. "I do hope you will not pay any regard to Julian's efforts to dictate our reading selections on Wednesday afternoons."

"My dear girl, do not concern yourself with such trivia," Fanny said airily. "Of course we will not pay Julian any mind. Men are so limited in their notions of what women should do, are they not?"

"Julian is a good man, as men go, Sophy, but he does have his blind spots," Harriette said as she raised the small binoculars to her eyes and peered through them. "Of course, one can hardly blame him after what he went through with his first Countess. Then, too, I'm afraid his experiences in battle tended to reinforce a rather sober outlook on life in general. Julian has a strongly developed sense of duty, you know and . . . ah, ha. There she is."

"Who?" Sophy demanded, her mind distracted by thoughts of Elizabeth and the effects of war on a man.

"The Grand Featherstone. She is wearing green tonight, I see. And the diamond and ruby necklace Ashford gave her."

"Really? How marvelously outrageous of her to wear it after the things she wrote about him in the second installment of the *Memoirs*. Lady Ashford must be livid." Fanny promptly dug out her own opera glasses and focused quickly.

"May I borrow your opera glasses?" Sophy asked Harriette. "I did not think to purchase some."

"Certainly. We'll shop for glasses for you this week. One simply cannot come to the opera without them." Harriette smiled her serene smile. "So much to see here. One would not want to miss anything."

"Yes," Sophy agreed as she focused the small glasses on the stunning woman in green. "So much to see. You are quite right about the necklace. It is spectacular. One can understand why a wife might complain if she discovered her husband was giving his mistress such baubles."

"Especially when the wife is obliged to make do on jewelry of far less quality," Fanny said musingly, her eyes on the simple pendant that graced Sophy's throat. "I wonder why Julian has not yet given you the Ravenwood emeralds?"

"I have no need of the emeralds." Sophy, still watching Charlotte Featherstone's box, saw a familiar pale-haired man enter. She recognized Lord Waycott at once. Charlotte turned to greet him with a graceful gesture of her beringed hand. Waycott bowed over the glittering fingers with elegant aplomb.

"If you ask me," Harriette said conversationally to Fanny, "your nephew probably saw entirely too much of the Ravenwood emeralds on his first wife."

"Um, you may be right, Harry. Elizabeth caused him nothing but grief whenever she wore those emeralds. It could be that Julian does not wish to see those particular stones on any woman again. The sight would undoubtedly remind him quite painfully of Elizabeth."

Sophy wondered if that was the real reason Julian had not yet given her the Ravenwood family gems. It seemed to her there might be other, less-flattering, reasons.

It took a woman of poise, stature, and polish to wear fine jewels, especially dramatic stones such as emeralds. Julian might not think his new wife had enough presence to carry off the Ravenwood jewels. Or he might not think her pretty enough for .hem.

But last night, she reflected wistfully, for a short while in the intimacy of her bedchamber, Julian had made her feel very beautiful, indeed.

Sophy neither complained nor asked for explanations much later that evening when Julian escorted her home and then announced he was going off to spend an hour or two at one of his clubs. Julian wondered at her lack of protest as he lounged moodily in the carriage while his driver picked a way through the dark streets. Didn't Sophy care how he spent the remainder of the evening or was she just grateful he was not going to invade her bedchamber a second time?

Julian had not originally planned to go on to a club after the opera. He had fully intended to take Sophy home and then spend the rest of the night teaching her the pleasures of the marriage bed. He had passed a good portion of the day plotting exactly how he would go about the task. This time, he had vowed, he would make it right for her.

He had envisioned himself undressing her slowly, kissing every inch of her softness as he brought her to a state of perfect readiness. This time he would not lose his self-control at the last minute and plunge wildly into her. This time he would go slowly and make certain she learned that the pleasure could be shared equally between them.

Julian was well aware that he had lost his head at a critical juncture the previous evening. It was not his customary style. He had gone into Sophy's bedchamber certain that he was in control, convinced that he really was only going to make love to her for her own good.

But the real truth was that ne had wanted her so much, had been wanting her for so long, that by the time he had finally lost himself in her tight, welcoming body, he'd had no reserves of self-control on which to draw. Apparently he had used up those reserves during the previous week when he'd struggled to keep his hands off her.

The memory of his driving desire as he had finally buried himself in her silken sheath was enough to harden his body all over again. Julian shook his head, dazed at the realization of how the whole situation had escalated into something far larger and more ungovernable than he had ever anticipated. He wondered again how he had allowed himself to become so obsessed with Sophy.

There was no point attempting to analyze it, he finally decided as the carriage halted in front of his club. The important thing was to make certain the obsession did not take full control of him. He must manage it and that meant managing Sophy. He must keep a firm hand on the reins for both their sakes. His second marriage was not going to go the way of his first. Not only that, but Sophy needed his protection. She was much too naive and trusting.

But as he walked into the warm sanctuary of his club it seemed to Julian he could almost hear distant echoes of Elizabeth's mocking laughter.

"Ravenwood." Miles Thurgood looked up from where he was sitting near the fire and grinned cheerfully. "Didn't expect you to show up here tonight. Have a seat and a glass of port."

"Thank you," Julian lowered himself into a nearby chair. "Any man who has sat through an opera needs a glass of port."

"Just what I said, myself, a few minutes ago. Although I must say, tonight's spectacle was more entertaining than usual what with the Grand Featherstone putting in an appearance."

"Don't remind me."

Miles chuckled. "Watching you trying to clamp the lid on your wife's interest in the subject of Featherstone was the most amusing part of all, of course. Expect you failed miserably to distract her, eh? Women always get riveted on the one thing you wish they would ignore."

"Hardly surprising, what with you deliberately encouraging her," Julian muttered, pouring himself a glass of port.

"Be reasonable, Ravenwood. Everyone in town is talking about the *Memoirs*. You can't really expect Lady Ravenwood to ignore them."

"I can and do expect to guide my wife in her choice of literature," Julian said coldly.

"Come now, be honest," Miles urged with the familiarity of an old friend. "Your concern is not with her literary tastes, is it? You're just afraid that sooner or later she'll come across your name in those *Memoirs*."

"My involvement with Featherstone is no concern of my wife's."

"A fine sentiment and one I'm certain is echoed by every man hiding out here tonight," Miles assured him. Then his good natured expression sobered abruptly. "Speaking of those present this evening—"

Julian looked at him. "Yes?"

Miles cleared his throat and lowered his voice. "Thought you ought to know Waycott's in the gaming room."

Julian's hand tightened on his glass but his tone remained cool. "Is he? How interesting. He does not generally patronize this club."

"True. But he does have a membership, you know. Tonight, it appears, he has decided to make use of it." Miles leaned forward. "You should know he's offering to take wagers."

"Is he, indeed?"

Miles cleared his throat. "Wagers regarding you and the Ravenwood emeralds."

A cold fist clutched at Julian's insides. "What sort of wager?"

"He is betting that you will not give Sophy the Ravenwood emeralds before the year is out," Miles said. "You know what he's implying, Julian. He's as good as announcing to everyone that your new wife cannot take the place of Elizabeth in your life. If Lady Ravenwood hears about this, she will be crushed."

"Then we must endeavor to make certain she does not hear about it. I know I can depend upon you to keep silent, Thurgood."

"Yes, of course. This is hardly a quizzing matter like the business of Featherstone, but you must realize any number of people are likely to hear of it and you can't possibly keep them all quiet. Perhaps it would be simplest if you just made certain Lady Ravenwood wears the jewels soon in public. That way—" Miles broke off, alarmed, as Julian got to his feet. "What do you think you're doing?"

"I thought I would see what sort of play is going on at the tables tonight," Julian said as he walked toward the door to the gaming room.

"But you rarely play. Why should you want to go into the gaming room? *Wait!*" Miles shot to his feet and trotted after him. "Really, Julian, I think it would be much better if you did not go in there tonight."

Julian ignored him. He strolled into the crowded room and stood looking negligently around until he spotted his quarry. Waycott, who had just won at hazard, glanced around at that moment and his gaze alighted on Julian. He smiled slowly and waited.

Julian was aware that everyone else in the room was holding his breath. He knew Miles was hovering somewhere nearby and out of the corner of his eye he spotted Daregate putting down his hand of cards and getting languidly to his feet.

"Good evening, Ravenwood," Waycott said blandly as Julian came to a halt in front of him. "Enjoy the opera this evening? I saw your lovely bride there although it was difficult to spot her in the crowd. But, then, I was naturally looking for the Ravenwood emeralds."

"My wife is not the gaudy type," Julian murmured. "I think she looks best when dressed in a simple, more classic style."

"Do you indeed? And does she agree with you? Women do love their jewels. You of all men should have learned that lesson."

Julian lowered his voice but kept the edge on his words. "When it comes to the important matters, my wife defers to my wishes. She trusts my judgment not only in regard to her attire but also in regard to her acquaintances."

"Unlike your first wife, eh?" Waycott's eyes were glittering with malice. "What makes you so certain the new Lady Ravenwood will be guided by you, Ravenwood? She seems an intelligent young woman, if a little naive. I suspect she will soon begin to rely on her own judgment in both her attire and her acquaintances. And then you will be in much the same position as you were in your first marriage, won't you?"

"If I ever have cause to suspect that Sophy's notions are being shaped by someone other than myself, then I will have no option but to take steps to remedy the situation."

"What makes you believe you can remedy such a situation?" Waycott grinned lazily. "You had very little luck doing so in the past."

"There is a difference this time around," Julian said calmly.

"And what would that be?"

"This time I will know exactly where to look should any potential threat to my wife arise. I will not be slow to crush that threat."

There was a cold fever burning in Waycott's eyes now. "Should I take that as a warning?"

"I leave you to your own judgment, unsound though it is." Julian inclined his head mockingly.

Waycott's hand tightened into a clenched fist and the fever in his eyes grew hot. "Damn you, Ravenwood," he hissed very softly, "If you think you have cause to call me out, then get on with it."

"But I have no cause as of yet, do I?" Julian asked silkily.

"There is always the matter of Elizabeth," Waycott challenged tightly. His fingers flexed and unflexed nervously.

"You credit me with far too rigid a code of honor," Julian said. "I would certainly never bother to get up at dawn in order to kill a man because of Elizabeth. She was not worth that much effort."

Waycott's cheeks were stained red with his frustration and fury. "You have another wife now. Will you allow yourself to be cuckolded a second time, Ravenwood?"

"No," Julian said very quietly. "Unlike Elizabeth, Sophy is, indeed, worth the effort of killing a man and I would not hesitate to do so should it become necessary."

"You bastard. You were the one who was not worthy of Elizabeth. And do not be bothered to issue threats. We all know you will never challenge me or any other man again

because of a woman. You said so, yourself, remember?"
Waycott took a menacing step forward.

"Did I?" A surge of anticipation shot through Julian.
But before anything more could be said by either man
Daregate and Thurgood materialized at Julian's side.

"There you are, Ravenwood," Daregate said smoothly to
Julian. "Thurgood and I have been looking for you. We
mean to persuade you into giving us a hand or two of
cards. You will excuse us, Waycott?" He flashed his
slightly cruel, taunting smile.

Waycott's blond head moved in a jerky nod. He turned
on his heel and strode out of the room.

Julian watched him leave, feeling a savage disappointment. "I don't know why you bothered to interfere," he
remarked to his friends. "Sooner or later I will probably
have to kill him."

NINE

The scented letter with the elegant lilac seal arrived on the side of Sophy's tea tray the next morning. She sat up in bed, yawning and glanced curiously at the unexpected missive.

"When did this arrive, Mary?"

"One of the footmen said it was brought 'round by a lad not more than a half hour ago, my lady." Mary bustled about the room, drawing the curtains and laying out a pretty cotton morning dress that had been chosen by Fanny and Sophy a few days earlier.

Sophy sipped tea and slit the seal on the envelope. Idly she scanned the contents and then frowned as she realized they made no sense at first. There was no signature, just initials in the closing. It took her a second reading to comprehend the import of the letter.

Dear Madam:
First, allow me to begin by offering you my most sincerely felt felicitations on the occasion of your recent marriage. I have never had the honor of being introduced to

you but I feel a degree of familiarity exists between us owing to our having a certain mutual friend. I am also certain that you are a woman of sensitivity and discretion as our friend is not the sort to make the same mistake in a second marriage as he made in his first.

Having faith in your discretion, I believe that, once having read the contents of this letter, you will wish to take the simple step that will ensure that the details of my most agreeable association with our mutual friend remain private.

I am, Madam, presently engaged in the difficult task of assuring the peace and tranquillity of my old age. I do not wish to be forced to rely on charity in my later years. I am achieving my goal by means of the publication of my *Memoirs*. Perhaps you are familiar with the first installments? There will be several more published in the near future.

My aim in writing these *Memoirs* is not to humiliate or embarrass, but rather simply to raise sufficient funds to provide for an uncertain future. In that light, I am offering an opportunity to those concerned to assure themselves that specific names do not appear in print and thereby cause unpleasant gossip. This same opportunity will also afford me the funds I seek without obliging me to resort to revealing intimate details of past associations. As you can see, the proposition I will put to you presently is beneficial to all involved.

Now, then, Madam, I come to the point: If you will send the sum of two hundred pounds to me by five o'clock tomorrow afternoon you may rest assured that a number of charming letters your husband once wrote to me do not appear in my *Memoirs*.

To you such a sum of money is a mere pittance, less than the cost of a new gown. To me it is a building block in the cozy little rose-covered cottage in Bath to which I will soon retire. I look forward to hearing from you promptly.

> I remain, Madam,
> yours very truly,
> C. F.

Sophy reread the letter a third time, her hands shaking. She was dazed by the flames of rage that burst to life within her. It was not the fact that Julian might once have been intimately involved with Charlotte Featherstone that infuriated her, she realized. It was not even the threat of having that past association detailed in print, as humiliating as it would be, that left her trembling with anger.

What made Sophy lightheaded with fury was the realization that Julian had once taken the time to write love notes to a professional courtesan yet he could not be bothered to jot so much as a simple love poem to his new wife.

"Mary, put away the morning dress and get out my green riding habit."

Mary glanced at her in surprise. "You have decided to ride this mornin', ma'am?"

"Yes, I have."

"Will Lord Ravenwood be going with you?" Mary inquired as she set to work.

"No, he will not." Sophy shoved back the covers and got to her feet, still clutching Charlotte Featherstone's letter in one hand. "Anne Silverthorne and Jane Morland ride nearly every morning in the park. I believe I will join them today."

Mary nodded. "I'll send word to have a horse and a groom waitin' for you downstairs, my lady."

"Please do that, Mary."

A short while later Sophy was assisted onto a fine chestnut mare by a liveried groom who had his own pony waiting nearby. She set off at once for the park, leaving the groom to follow as best he could.

It was not difficult to find Anne and Jane who were cantering along one of the main paths. Their grooms followed at a discreet distance, chatting in low tones with each other.

Anne's froth of red curls gleamed in the morning light and her vivid eyes sparkled with welcome as she caught sight of Sophy.

"Sophy, I'm so glad you could join us this morning. We are just beginning our ride. Isn't it a beautiful day?"

"For some, perhaps," Sophy allowed ominously. "But not for others. I must talk with both of you."

Jane's perpetually serious gaze grew even darker with concern. "Is something wrong, Sophy?"

"Very wrong. I cannot even bring myself to try to explain. It is beyond anything. Never have I been so humiliated. Here. Read this." Sophy handed Charlotte's letter to Jane as the three women slowed their horses to a walk along the path.

"Good heavens," Jane breathed, looking stricken as she scanned the note. Without another word she handed the letter to Anne.

Anne perused the missive quickly and then glanced up, clearly shocked. "She is going to print the letters Ravenwood wrote to her?"

Sophy nodded, her mouth tight with anger. "So it seems. Unless, of course, I pay her two hundred pounds."

"This is outrageous," Anne declared in ringing accents.

"Only to be expected, I suppose," Jane said more prosaically. "After all, Featherstone has not hesitated to name several members of the Beau Monde in the first installments. She even mentioned a royal Duke, remember? If Ravenwood was associated with her at some time in the past, it is logical that his turn would come sooner or later."

"*How dare he.*" Sophy whispered half under her breath.

Jane gave her a sympathetic glance. "Sophy, dear, you are not that naive. It is the way of the world for most men in Society to have mistresses. At least she does not claim that Ravenwood is still an admirer. Be grateful for that much."

"*Grateful.*" Sophy could barely speak.

"You have read the first installments of the *Memoirs* along with the rest of us. You have seen the number of well-known names Featherstone was associated with at one time or another. Most of them were married during the time they were involved with Charlotte Featherstone."

"So many men leading double lives." Sophy shook her

head angrily. "And they have the gall to lecture women on honor and proper behavior. It is infuriating."

"And so grossly unfair," Anne added vehemently. "Just one more example of why I feel the married state has so little to offer an intelligent woman."

"Why did he have to write Featherstone those love letters?" Sophy asked in soft anguish.

"If he put his feelings into writing, then the entire affair must have occurred a long time ago. Only a very young man would make that mistake," Jane observed.

Ah, yes, thought Sophy. *A young man.* A young man who was still capable of strong romantic emotion. It would seem that all such sentiment had been burned out of Julian. The feelings she longed to hear him express to her he had squandered years ago on women such as Charlotte Featherstone and Elizabeth. It would seem there was nothing left for Sophy at all. Nothing.

In that moment she hated both Elizabeth and Charlotte with all the passion in her soul.

"I wonder why Featherstone did not send this note to Ravenwood?" Anne mused.

Jane's mouth curved wryly. "Probably because she knew full well Ravenwood would tell her to go to the devil. I do not see Sophy's husband paying blackmail, do you?"

"I do not know him very well," Anne admitted, "but from all accounts, no, I do not see him sending the two hundred pounds to Featherstone. Not even to spare Sophy the humiliation that is bound to follow the publication of those horrid letters."

"So," concluded Jane, "knowing she stands little chance of getting any money out of Ravenwood, Featherstone has decided to try blackmailing Sophy, instead."

"I will never pay blackmail to that woman," Sophy vowed, her hands tightening so abruptly on the reins that her mare tossed her head in startled protest.

"But what else can you do?" Anne asked gently. "Surely you do not want those letters to appear in print. Only think of the gossip that will ensue."

"It will not be that bad," Jane said soothingly. "Everyone will know the affair happened long before Ravenwood married Sophy."

"The timing of the affair will not matter," Sophy said dully. "There will be talk and we all know it. This will not be simple gossip Featherstone will be repeating. She will actually be printing letters that Julian himself wrote. Everyone will be discussing those blasted love notes. Quoting them at parties and the opera, no doubt. The entire *ton* will wonder if he has written similar letters to me and perhaps plagiarized himself in the process. I cannot bear it, I tell you."

"Sophy's right," Anne agreed. "And she is even more vulnerable because she is a new bride. People are just becoming aware of her socially. This will add a nasty edge to the talk."

There was no refuting that simple truth. All three women fell silent for a few minutes as their horses ambled along the path. Sophy's brain was churning. It was difficult to think clearly. Every time she tried to sort out her thoughts she found herself thinking of the love letters Julian had once written to another woman.

"You know, of course, exactly what would happen if this situation were reversed," Sophy finally said after a few more minutes of seething thought.

Jane frowned and Anne looked at Sophy with dawning awareness.

"Sophy, do not fret yourself about this," Jane urged. "Show the letter to Ravenwood and let him handle it."

"You've pointed out yourself that his idea of handling it would be to tell Featherstone to go to the devil. The letters would still appear in print."

"It is a most unhappy situation," Anne stated. "But I see no obvious solution."

Sophy hesitated a moment and then said quietly, "We say that because we are women and therefore accustomed to being powerless. But there is a solution if one views this in the same light as a man would view it."

Jane gave her a wary look. "What are you thinking, Sophy?"

"This," Sophy declared with a newfound sense of resolution, "is clearly a matter of honor."

Anne and Jane looked at each other and then at Sophy.

"I agree," Anne said slowly, "but I do not see how viewing it in that way changes anything."

Sophy looked at her friend. "If a man had received such a note threatening blackmail because of a past indiscretion on the part of his wife, he would not hesitate to call out the blackmailer."

"Call him out!" Jane was astounded. "But, Sophy, this is not the same sort of situation at all."

"Is it not?"

"No, it is not," Jane said quickly. "Sophy, this involves you and another female. You cannot possibly consider such a course of action."

"Why not?" Sophy demanded. "My grandfather taught me how to use a pistol and I know where I can secure a set of duelers for this event."

"Where would you get a set of pistols?" Jane asked uneasily.

"There is a fine pair in a case mounted on the wall in Julian's library."

"Dear God," Jane breathed.

Anne sucked in her breath, her expression ablaze with determination. "She is right, Jane. Why not call out Charlotte Featherstone? This is most certainly an affair of honor. If the situation was altered so that the indiscretion was Sophy's, you may be sure Ravenwood would do something quite violent."

"I would need seconds," Sophy said thoughtfully as the plan began to take shape in her head.

"I will be one of your seconds," Anne stated loyally. "As it happens, I know how to load a pistol. And Jane will also volunteer, won't you, Jane?"

Jane gave a wretched exclamation. "This is madness. You simply cannot do it, Sophy."

"Why not?"

"Well, first you would have to get Featherstone to agree to a duel. She is highly unlikely to do so."

"I am not so certain she would refuse," Sophy murmured. "She is a most unusual, adventurous woman. We have all agreed on that. She did not get where she is today by being a coward."

"But why should she risk her life in a duel?" Jane asked.

"If she is an honorable woman, she will do so."

"But that is precisely the point, Sophy. She is not an honorable woman," Jane exclaimed. "She is a woman of the demimonde, a *courtesan*, a professional prostitute."

"That does not mean she is without honor," Sophy said. "Something about the writing in her *Memoirs* leads me to believe she has a code of her own, and that she lives by it."

"Honorable people do not send blackmail threats," Jane pointed out.

"Perhaps." Sophy was quiet for a moment. "Then again, perhaps they do under certain circumstances. Featherstone no doubt feels that the men who once used her now owe her a pension for her old age. She is merely attempting to collect it."

"And according to the gossip, she is honoring her word not to name names of the people who pay the blackmail," Anne put in helpfully. "Surely that implies some sort of honorable behavior."

"Do not tell me you are actually defending her." Jane looked stunned.

"I do not care how much she collects from the others, but I will not have Julian's love letters to her appear in print," Sophy stated categorically.

"Then send her the two hundred pounds," Jane urged. "If she's so terribly honorable, she will not print the letters."

"That would not be right. It is dishonorable and cowardly to pay off a blackmailer," Sophy said. "So you see, I really have no choice but to call her out. It is exactly what a man would do in similar circumstances."

"Dear God," Jane whispered helplessly. "Your logic is beyond me. I cannot believe this is happening."

"Will both of you help me?" Sophy looked at her friends.

"You may count on me," Anne said. "And on Jane, too. She just needs time to adjust to the situation."

"Dear God," Jane said again.

"Very well," Sophy said, "the first step is to see if Featherstone will agree to meet me on a field of honor. I will send her a message today."

"As your second, I will see that it is delivered."

Jane stared at her, appalled. "Are you insane? You cannot possibly call on a woman such as Featherstone. You might be seen. It would ruin you utterly in Society. You would be forced to return to your stepfather's estate in the country. Do you want that?"

Anne paled and for an instant genuine fear appeared in her eyes. "No. I most certainly do not want that."

Sophy was alarmed at her friend's violent reaction to the thought of being sent back to the country. She frowned worriedly. "Anne, I do not want you taking any undue risks on my behalf."

Anne shook her head quickly, her cheeks returning to their normal warm color and her eyes lightening. "It's quite all right. I know exactly how this matter can be handled. I will send a boy around for your note to Featherstone and have him bring it directly to me. I will then deliver it in disguise to Featherstone and wait for a response. Do not worry, no one will recognize me. When I dress the part, I look very much like a young man. I have tried it before and enjoyed it thoroughly."

"Yes," Sophy said, thinking about it, "that should work well."

Jane's anxious glance moved from Anne to Sophy and back again. "This is madness."

"It is my only honorable option," Sophy said soberly. "We must hope Featherstone will accept the challenge."

"I, for one, will pray she refuses," Jane said tightly.

When Sophy returned from her ride a half hour later she was told Julian wished to see her in the library. Her first instinct was to send word that she was indisposed. She was not at all certain she could face her husband with any sense of composure just now. The letter of challenge to Charlotte Featherstone was waiting to be written.

But avoiding Julian would be cowardly and today, of all days, she was determined not to be a coward. She must get in practice for what lay ahead.

"Thank you, Guppy," she said to the butler. "I will go and see him at once." She spun on her booted heel and walked boldly toward the library.

Julian looked up from a journal of accounts as she swept into the room. He rose politely. "Good morning, Sophy. I see you have been riding."

"Yes, my lord. It was a fine morning for it." Her eyes went to the cased dueling pistols mounted on the wall behind Julian. They were a lethal looking pair, long, heavy-barreled weapons created by Manton, one of the most famous gunmakers in London.

Julian gave Sophy a brief, chiding smile. "If you had informed me you intended to ride today, I would have been happy to join you."

"I rode with friends."

"I see." His brows arched faintly in the characteristic way they did when he was vaguely annoyed. "Do I take that to mean you do not consider me a friend?"

Sophy looked at him and wondered if one ever risked one's life in a duel over a mere friend. "No, my lord. You are not my friend. You are my husband."

His mouth hardened. "I would be both, Sophy."

"Really, my lord?"

He sat down and slowly closed the journal. "You do not sound as if you believe such a condition possible."

"Is it, my lord?"

"I think we can manage it if we both work at it. Next time you wish to ride in the morning, you must allow me to accompany you, Sophy."

"Thank you, my lord. I will consider it. But I certainly would not wish to distract you from your work."

"I would not mind the distraction." He smiled invitingly. "We could always put the time to good use discussing farming techniques."

"I fear we have exhausted the subject of sheep breeding, my lord. Now, if you will excuse me, I must be going."

Unable to bear any more of this face-to-face confrontation, Sophy whirled and fled from the room. Plucking up the folds of her riding skirts she ran up the stairs and down the hall to the privacy of her bedchamber.

She was pacing her room, composing the note to Featherstone in her mind when Mary knocked on the door.

"Come in," Sophy said and winced when her maid walked into the room holding her jaunty green riding hat. "Oh, dear, did I lose that in the hall, Mary?"

"Lord Ravenwood told a footman you lost it but a few minutes ago in the library, ma'am. He sent it up here so's you wouldn't wonder where it was."

"I see. Thank you. Now, Mary, I need privacy. I wish to catch up on my correspondence."

"Certainly, ma'am. I'll tell the staff you don't want to be bothered for a while."

"Thank you," Sophy said again and sank down at her writing desk to pen the letter to Charlotte Featherstone.

It took several attempts to get it right but in the end Sophy was satisfied with the result.

Dear Miss C. F.:
I received your outrageous note concerning our *mutual friend* this morning. In your note you threaten to publish certain indiscreet letters unless I submit to blackmail. I will do no such thing.

I must take leave to tell you that you have committed a grave insult for which I demand satisfaction. I propose that we arrange to settle this matter at dawn tomorrow morning. You may choose the weapons, of course, but I suggest pistols as I can easily provide them.

If you are as concerned with your honor as you are with your old-age pension, you will respond in the affirmative at once.

Yours Very Truly,
S.

Sophy blotted the note very carefully and sealed it. Tears burned in her eyes. She could not get the thought of

Julian's love letters to a courtesan out of her head. *Love letters*. Sophy knew she would have sold her soul for a similar token of affection from Ravenwood.

And the man had the brazen nerve to claim he wished friendship as well as his husbandly privileges from her.

It struck Sophy as ironic that she might very possibly be risking her life tomorrow at dawn for a man who did not and probably could not love her.

Charlotte Featherstone's response to Sophy's challenge arrived later that afternoon, delivered by a ragged-looking, dirty-faced lad with red hair who came to the kitchens. The note was short and to the point. Sophy held her breath as she sat down to read it.

Madam:
Dawn tomorrow will be quite acceptable, as will pistols. I suggest Leighton Field, a short distance outside the city, as it is bound to be deserted at that hour.
Until dawn, I remain very truly yours in honor,
C. F.

Sophy's emotions were in chaos by bedtime. She was aware that Julian had been annoyed by her long silences at dinner but it had been beyond her to keep up a casual conversation. When he had retired to the library, she had excused herself and gone straight upstairs to her room.

Once inside the sanctuary of her bedchamber she read and reread Featherstone's terrifyingly brief note and wondered what she had done. But she knew there was no turning back now. Her life would be in the hands of fate tomorrow.

Sophy went through the ritual of preparing for bed but she knew she could not possibly sleep tonight. After Mary said good night, Sophy stood staring out her window and wondered if Julian would be making arrangements for her funeral within a few short hours.

Perhaps she would only be wounded, she told herself, her imagination running wild with gory scenes. Perhaps her death would be a long and lingering one from a raging fever caused by a gunshot wound.

Or perhaps it would be Charlotte Featherstone who died.

The thought of killing another human being left Sophy abruptly sick to her stomach. She swallowed heavily and wondered if her nerves would hold out until she had satisfied the requirements of honor. She dared not prepare a tonic for herself because it might slow her reactions at dawn.

Sophy tried to brace herself by deciding that with any luck at all, either she or Charlotte would merely be wounded. Or, perhaps, both she and her opponent would miss their mark and neither of them would be hurt. That would certainly make for a tidy ending to the matter.

Then again, Sophy thought morosely, it was highly unlikely things would proceed that neatly. Her life of late was not inclined to be neat.

Fear sent chills down her spine. *How did men survive this dreadful anticipation of danger and death?* she wondered, continuing to pace. They faced it not only on the eve of a duel of honor but on the battlefield and at sea. Sophy shuddered.

She wondered if Julian had ever experienced this awful waiting and then remembered the story she had heard about a duel he had once conducted over the issue of Elizabeth's honor. And there must have been moments like this also when he was forced to endure the long hours before battle. But perhaps, being a man, he had nerves that were not susceptible to this sort of anticipatory fear. Or maybe he had learned how to control it.

For the first time it occurred to Sophy that the masculine code of honor was a very hard, reckless, and demanding thing. But at least abiding by it guaranteed men the respect of their peers and if nothing else, when this was all over, Julian would be forced to respect his wife to at least some degree.

Or would he? Would a man respect a woman who had tried to abide by his own male code or would he find the whole idea laughable?

On that thought, Sophy turned away from the window. Her eyes went straight to the small jewelry case on her dressing table and she remembered the black ring.

A tremor of regret went through her. If she were to get herself killed tomorrow there would be no one left to avenge Amelia. *Which was more important,* she asked herself, *avenging Amelia or keeping Julian's love letters out of print?*

There was really no choice. For a long time now, Sophy had realized that her feelings for Julian were far stronger than her old desire to find her sister's seducer.

Was her love for Julian making her act dishonorably in regard to her sister's memory?

It was all so terribly complicated suddenly. For a moment the enormity of the crisis was overwhelming. Sophy longed to run and hide until her world had righted itself. She was so wrapped up in her thoughts that she did not hear the connecting door open behind her.

"Sophy?"

"*Julian.*" She whirled around. "I was not expecting you, my lord."

"You rarely are." He sauntered slowly into the room, his eyes watchful. "Is something wrong, my dear? You seemed upset at dinner."

"I . . . I was not feeling well."

"A headache?" he inquired dryly.

"No. My head is fine, thank you." She spoke automatically and then she realized she had spoken too quickly. She should have seized on the proffered excuse. She frowned, unable to think of a suitable substitution. Perhaps her stomach . . .

Julian smiled. "Don't bother trying to invent a useful illness on such short notice. We both know you are not very good at such things." He walked over to stand directly in front of her. "Why don't you tell me the truth? You are angry with me, aren't you?"

Sophy lifted her eyes to his, a kaleidoscope of emotions pounding through her as she considered exactly how she felt toward him tonight. Anger, love, resentment, passion, and, above all, a terrible fear that she might never see him

again, might never again lie in his arms and experience
that fragile intimacy she had first felt the other night.

"Yes, Julian. I am angry with you."

He nodded as if in complete understanding. "It is
because of that little scene at the opera, isn't it? You did
not like me forbidding you to read the *Memoirs*."

Sophy shrugged and fiddled with the lid of her jewelry
case. "We did have an agreement concerning my reading
tastes, my lord."

Julian's eyes went to the small box under her hand and
then swung to her averted face. "I seem fated to disappoint you as a husband both in bed and out."

Her head came up suddenly, her eyes widening. "Oh,
no, my lord, I never meant to imply that you were a
disappointment in . . . in bed. That is to say, what happened
the other evening was quite," she cleared her throat,
"quite bearable, even pleasant at certain points. I would
not have you think otherwise."

Julian caught her chin on the edge of his hand and held
her gaze. "I would have you find me more than merely
bearable in bed, Sophy."

And suddenly she realized he wanted to make love to
her again. That was the real purpose of his visit to her
room tonight. Her heart leapt. She would have one more
chance to hold him close and feel that joyous intimacy.

"Oh, *Julian*." Sophy gulped back a sob and threw herself into his arms. "I would like nothing more than to have
you stay with me for a while tonight."

His arms went around her immediately but there was a
note of stunned surprise as well as laughter in Julian's
voice when he spoke softly into her hair. "If this is the sort
of welcome I get when you are angry at me I can see I
shall have to work at the task of annoying you more often."

"Do not tease me tonight, Julian. Just hold me close the
way you did the last time," she mumbled against his chest.

"Your wish is my command tonight, little one." He
gently eased the dressing gown from her shoulders, pausing to kiss the hollow of her throat. "This time I will
endeavor not to disappoint you."

Sophy closed her eyes as he slowly undressed her. She

was determined to savor every moment of what could easily be their last night together. She did not even mind if the actual lovemaking was not particularly pleasant. What she sought was the unique sense of closeness that accompanied it. That closeness might be all she would ever have of Julian.

"Sophy, you are so lovely to look at and so soft to touch," Julian whispered as the last of her clothing fell into a heap at her feet. His eyes moved hungrily over her nude body and his hands followed.

Sophy shivered and swayed against him as his palms cupped her breasts. His thumbs began to glide over her nipples, gently coaxing a response. When the tender, rosy peaks began to grow taut, Julian exhaled in deep satisfaction.

His hands slid down her sides to the curve of her hips and then around behind her to cradle the firm globes of her buttocks.

Sophy's fingers tightened on his shoulders as she leaned into his strength.

"Touch me, sweetheart," Julian ordered in a husky voice. "Put your hands inside my robe and touch me."

She could not resist. Slipping her palms under the silk lapels of his dressing gown she splayed her fingers across his chest. "You are so strong," she whispered in wonder.

"You make me feel strong," Julian said, amused. "You also have the power to make me very weak."

He caught her around the waist and lifted her up so that she was looking down at him. She braced herself with her hands on his shoulders and thought she would drown in the emerald brilliance of his eyes.

His dressing gown fell open and he slowly lowered her down along the length of his body until she was once more standing on her own feet. The intimate contact sent ripples of excitement through her and left her clinging to him. She closed her eyes again as his arms swept her up into his arms.

He carried her over to the bed and settled her in the center. Then he came down beside her, his legs tangling with hers. He stroked her slowly, his hands closing around each curve, his fingers exploring every hollow.

And he talked to her—urgent, persuasive, sensual words
that enveloped her in a haze of heat and desire. Sophy
clung to each soft promise, each tender command, each
exciting description of what Julian intended to do to her
that night.

"You will tremble in my arms, sweetheart. I will make
you want me so much that you will plead with me to take
you. You will tell me of your pleasure and that will make
my pleasure complete. I want to make you happy tonight,
Sophy."

He leaned over her, his mouth heavy and demanding on
hers. Sophy reacted fiercely, eager to claim as much of his
heat and passion as she could tonight. *There might never
be another chance*, she reminded herself. She might be
lying cold and dead on the grass of Leighton Field by
sunrise. Her tongue met his, inviting him into her moist
heat. Julian meant life tonight and she clung instinctively
to life and to him.

When his hand slipped between her thighs she cried
out softly and lifted herself against his fingers.

Julian's fierce pleasure in her response was obvious but
he seemed intent on holding himself in check this time.

"Gently, little one. Give yourself to me. Put yourself in
my keeping. Open your legs a little wider, darling. There,
that's the way I want you to be for me. Sweet and moist
and eager. Trust me, darling. I will make it good this
time."

The words continued to flow around her, sweeping her
away on a tide of excitement and need that knew no
boundaries. Julian coaxed her onward, leading her toward a great unknown that loomed larger and larger on
Sophy's sensual horizon.

When he touched the tip of his tongue to her flowering
nipples Sophy thought she would come apart in a hundred
pieces. But when he moved lower and she felt first his
fingers and then his mouth on the small, exquisitely
sensitive nubbin of flesh between her legs she thought she
would fly into a million shimmering pieces.

She clutched at his head. "Julian, no, wait, please. You
should not—"

Her fingers dug into his dark hair and she cried out again. Julian cradled her hips in his big hands and ignored her struggles to dislodge him.

"Julian, no, I don't want. . . . Oh, yes, please, *yes*."

A shivering, shuddering, convulsive sense of release swept through her. In that moment she forgot everything— the impending duel, her private fears, the strangeness of such lovemaking—everything except the man who was touching her so intimately.

"Yes, sweetheart," Julian said with dark satisfaction as he moved quickly up her body. His hands speared into her hair as he bent his head to plunge his tongue between her parted lips.

She was still quivering with the aftershocks of her release when he drove himself deeply into her hot, wet tightness and surrendered to his own climax.

Incredibly, her body convulsed gently around him once more and, caught up in the throes of the unfamiliar rapture, Sophy uttered the words that were in her heart.

"I love you, Julian. I love you."

TEN

Julian sprawled heavily across the soft, slender body of his wife, conscious of being more relaxed than he could remember feeling in years. He knew he would have to move soon, if only to put out the candles. But for the moment all he wanted to do was lie there and savor the splendid satisfaction that enveloped him.

The scent of the recent lovemaking still hovered in the air filling him with a primitive satisfaction as did the echo of Sophy's words, *I love you, Julian.*

She had not been fully aware of what she was saying, he reminded himself. She was a woman discovering her own sensual potential for the first time and she had been grateful to the man who had taught her to enjoy the pleasures of sexual release. He would not read too much into words of love spoken under such circumstances, but they had sounded good, nevertheless, and a part of him had gloried in them.

He had sensed the first time he had kissed her that Sophy would learn to respond to him but he had never dreamed that her response would affect him so intensely.

He felt all-powerful, a conquering hero who had just claimed the fruits of victory and was content. But he was equally aware of a violent need to protect his sweet treasure. Sophy had finally given herself to him completely and he would take care of her.

Just as that thought flashed through his head, Sophy stirred beneath him, her lashes lifting languidly. Julian braced his weight on his elbows and looked down into her dazed and wondering gaze.

"Julian?"

He brushed his mouth across hers, reassuring her wordlessly. "That is the way it is supposed to be between a husband and his wife. And that is the way it will be between us from now on. Did you enjoy yourself, little one?"

She smiled ruefully and linked her arms around his neck. "You know very well that I did."

"I know, but I find I like to hear you say it."

"You gave me great pleasure," she whispered. The amusement faded from her eyes. "It was unlike anything I have ever known."

He kissed the tip of her nose, her cheek, the corner of her mouth. "Then we are even, you and I. You gave me the same degree of pleasure."

"Is that really true?" She searched his face intently.

"It's true." Nothing had ever been more true or certain in his life he thought.

"I am glad. Try to remember that in the future, no matter what happens, will you, Julian?"

The unexpected anxiety in her words sent a faint shaft of alarm through him. Mentally he brushed aside the uneasiness her words triggered and smiled instead. "I am hardly likely to forget it."

"I wish I could believe that." She smiled too, rather wistfully.

Julian frowned slightly, uncertain of her new mood. There was something different about Sophy tonight. He had never seen her quite like this and it began to worry him. "What troubles you, Sophy? Are you afraid that the next time you do something to annoy me I will promptly forget how good things are between us in bed? Or don't you like the fact that I can make you want me, even when you are angry at me?"

"I do not know," she said slowly. "This seduction business is very odd, is it not?"

Hearing what had just transpired between them labeled as mere seduction bothered him. For the first time he realized he did not want Sophy using that word to describe what he did to her in bed. Seduction was what had happened to her younger sister. He did not want Sophy putting his lovemaking into that category.

"Do not think of it as seduction," he ordered softly. "We made love, you and I."

"Did we?" Her eyes blazed with sudden intensity. "Do you love me, Julian?"

The uneasiness he had been feeling crystalized into anger as he finally began to perceive what she was doing. What a fool he had been. Women were so damned good at this kind of thing. Did she think that just because she had responded to him—told him she loved him—that she could now wrap him around her little finger? Julian felt the familiar trap start to close around him and instinctively prepared to fight.

He was not certain what he would have said but as he lay there on top of her, alarms sounding in his brain, Sophy smiled her strange, wistful smile and put her fingertips against her lips.

"No," she said. "You do not need to say anything. It's all right, I understand."

"Understand what? Sophy, listen to me—"

"I think it would be better if we did not discuss this further. I spoke too quickly, without thinking." Her head shifted restlessly on the pillow. "It must be very late."

He groaned but accepted the reprieve eagerly. "Yes, very late." He rolled reluctantly off of her onto his back, letting his hand slide possessively along the curve of her hip.

"Julian?"

"What is it, Sophy?"

"Should you not be going back to your own room?"

That startled him. "I had not planned on it," he said roughly.

"I'd rather you did," Sophy said very quietly.

"Why is that?" Irritation brought him up on his elbow. He had been intending to spend the night in her bed.

"You did the last time."

Only because he had known that if he had stayed with her that first time he would have made love to her a second time and she had been sore and he had not wanted her to think him a rutting bull. He had wanted to show some consideration for the discomfort she had experienced that first night. "That does not mean I intend to return to my own room every time we make love."

"Oh." In the candlelight she looked strangely disconcerted. "I would prefer some privacy tonight, Julian. Please. I must insist."

"Ah, I believe I am beginning to understand," Julian said grimly as he shoved back the covers. "You are insisting on your privacy because you did not like my lack of response to your question a moment ago. I would not let you manipulate me into giving you endless pledges of undying love so you have decided to punish me in your own womanly way."

"No, Julian, that is not true."

He paid no attention to the entreaty in her voice. Stalking across the room, he snatched up his dressing gown and went to the connecting door. Then he stopped and swung around to glower at her. "While you are lying there in your lonely bed enjoying your *privacy,* think about the pleasure we could be giving each other. There is no law that states a man and a woman can only do it once a night, my dear."

He went through the door and closed it behind himself with a loud crack that emphasized his frustration and annoyance. Damn the little chit. Who did she think she was trying to force his hand that way? And what made her think she could get away with it? He'd had experience dealing with manipulative females who had far more talent in that direction than Sophy ever would.

Sophy's paltry attempts to control him with sex made

him want to laugh. If he had not been so damnably furious with her, he would have laughed.

She was a silly, green girl in such matters even if she was twenty-three years old. Elizabeth had been older and wiser in the ways of manipulating a man when she had emerged from the schoolroom than Sophy would be when she was fifty.

Julian tossed the dressing gown across a chair and threw himself down onto the bed. Arms folded behind his head, he lay staring up at the darkened ceiling, hoping Sophy was already regretting her hasty action. If she thought she could punish him and thus bring him to heel with such simple tactics, she was sadly mistaken. He had fought far more subtle, far more strategically complex battles.

But Sophy was not Elizabeth and never would be. And Sophy had a reason to fear seduction. He also suspected that his new wife had a streak of the romantic in her soul.

Julian groaned and massaged his eyes as his temper began to cool. Perhaps he owed his wife the benefit of a doubt. It was true she had tried to coax him into vowing his love for her but it was equally true that she had a valid reason for fearing a passion that was not labeled love.

In Sophy's limited experience the only alternative to love was the sort of cruel, heartless seduction that had gotten her sister pregnant. Sophy would naturally want some assurance she was not being subjected to the latter. She would want to believe she was loved so she would not have to fear following in her sister's footsteps.

But she was a married woman sharing a bed with her lawful husband, Julian reminded himself angrily. She had no reason to fear being abandoned in her sister's condition. Hell, he wanted an heir—needed one. The last thing he was likely to do was cast her off if she got herself pregnant with his child.

Sophy had both the protection of the law and the Earl of Ravenwood's personal vow to protect and care for her. To go about in terror of her sister's fate was to indulge in a great deal of feminine nonsense and Julian decided he would not tolerate it. He must make her see there was no parallel between her sister's fate and her own.

Because he definitely did not want to spend many more nights alone in his own bed.

Julian did not know how long he lay there plotting how best to teach his wife the lesson he wanted her to learn but at some point he finally dozed off. His sleep was restless, however, and hours later the sound of Sophy's door closing softly in the hall jarred him from a light slumber.

He stirred, wondering if it was already time to rise. But when he opened one eye and glared balefully at the window he could tell it was still dark behind the curtains.

Nobody, not even Sophy, rose to ride at dawn in London. Julian turned over and told himself to go back to sleep. But some instinct kept him from dozing off again. He wondered who had opened Sophy's door at this ungodly hour.

Finally, unable to withstand the curiosity that was growing quickly within him, Julian climbed out of bed and went to the connecting door. He opened it quietly.

It took him a few seconds to realize that Sophy's bed was empty. Even as he was reaching that conclusion he heard the faint rattle of carriage wheels in the street outside the window. As he listened, the vehicle came to a halt.

A jolt of irrational but violent fear went through him.

Julian leapt for the window, tearing aside the curtains just in time to see a familiar slender figure dressed in a pair of men's breeches and a shirt jump into the closed carriage. Sophy's tawny hair was bound up in a severe coil under a veiled hat. She was carrying a wooden case in one hand. The driver, a slim, red-haired lad dressed in black, clucked to the horses and the carriage moved swiftly away down the street.

"Damn you, Sophy." Julian's fingers clenched so fiercely into the curtains that he nearly ripped them from the rod. "God damn you to hell, you bitch."

I love you. Do you love me, Julian?

Sweet, lying bitch. "You're mine," he hissed through his teeth. "You are mine and I will see you in hell before I let you go to another."

Julian dropped the curtains and raced into his own room, snatching up a shirt and pulling on a pair of breeches. He grabbed his boots and ran out into the hall. At the foot of the staircase he paused long enough to pull on the tight leather riding boots and then he started for the servants' entrance. He would have to get a horse from the stables and he would have to hurry if he was not to lose sight of the carriage.

At the last moment he swung around and dashed back toward the library. He would need a weapon. He intended to kill whoever had taken Sophy away. And after that he would consider well what to do with his lying, deceitful wife. If she thought he would tolerate from her what he had tolerated from Elizabeth she was in for a great revelation.

The pistols were gone from the wall.

Julian barely had time to register that fact when he heard the sound of a horse's hooves in the street. He ran for the front door, throwing it open just as a woman dressed in black and wearing a black veil started to alight from a tall, gray gelding. He saw that she had ridden astride, not sidesaddle.

"Oh, thank God," the woman said, clearly startled at the sight of him in the doorway. "I was afraid I would have to awaken the entire household to get to you. Much better this way. Perhaps a scandal can be avoided after all. They have gone to Leighton Field."

"Leighton Field?" That made no sense. Only cattle and duelists had any use for Leighton Field.

"Do hurry, for heaven's sake. You can take my horse. As you can see, I am not using a lady's saddle."

Julian did not hesitate. He seized the gray's bridle and vaulted into the saddle. "Who the hell are you?" he demanded of the woman in the veil. "His wife?"

"No, you do not understand, but you will soon enough. Just hurry."

"Go into the house," Julian ordered as the gray danced under him. "You can wait inside. If one of the staff finds you there, say nothing except that I have invited you to be there."

Julian put the big horse into a gallop without waiting for

a response. Why in God's name would Sophy and her lover run off to Leighton Field, Julian wondered furiously. But he soon stopped asking himself that question and began trying to figure out which male of the *ton* had sealed his own doom by taking Sophy away that morning.

Leighton Field was cold and damp in the dim, predawn light. A cluster of sullen trees, their heavy branches drooping moisture, crouched beneath a still-dark sky. Mist rose from the ground and hung, thick and gray, at knee level. Anne's small, closed carriage, the yellow curricle a short distance away, and the horses all looked as if they were floating in midair.

When Sophy stepped out into the mist, her legs disappeared beneath her into the fog. She looked at Anne, who was securing the carriage horse. The masculine disguise was astonishingly clever. If she had not known who it was, Sophy would have been certain the smudge-faced, red-haired figure was a young man.

"Sophy, are you sure you want to go through with this?" Anne asked anxiously as she came forward.

Sophy turned to gaze at the curricle stopped a few yards away. The veiled figure dressed in black had not yet alighted from the other vehicle. Charlotte Featherstone appeared to be alone. "I do not have any choice, Anne."

"I wonder where Jane is? She said that if you were determined to be a fool, she would feel obliged to witness it."

"Perhaps she changed her mind."

Anne shook her head. "Not like her."

"Well," Sophy said, straightening her shoulders, "we had best get on with it. It will be dawn soon. I understand this sort of thing is always done at dawn." She started toward the mist-bound curricle.

The lone figure in the curricle stirred as Sophy approached. Charlotte Featherstone, dressed in a handsome black riding habit, stepped down. Although the courtesan was veiled, Sophy could see her hair had been carefully coiffed for the occasion and that Charlotte was wearing a pair of dazzling pearl earrings. One glance at the other woman's

fashionable attire made Sophy feel gauche. It was obvious
the Grand Featherstone knew all there was to know about
style. She even dressed perfectly for a duel at dawn.

Anne went forward to secure the curricle horse.

"Do you know, madam," Charlotte said, lifting her veil
to smile coolly at Sophy, "I do not believe any man is
worth the discomfort of rising at such an early hour."

"Then why did you bother?" Sophy retorted. Feeling
challenged, she, too, lifted her veil.

"I am not sure," Charlotte admitted. "But it is not
because of the Earl of Ravenwood, charming though he
was to me at one time. Perhaps it is the novelty of the
whole thing."

"I can well imagine that after your rather adventurous
career, novelties are now few and far between."

Charlotte's eyes fixed steadily on Sophy's face. Her
voice lost much of its mocking quality and grew serious. "I
can assure you that having a Countess find me an opponent worthy of an honorable challenge is, indeed, a rare
event. One might say a unique event. You must realize, of
course, that no woman from your level of Society has ever
spoken to me, let alone accorded me such respect."

Sophy's head tilted slightly as she studied her opponent.
"You may be assured that I have great respect for you,
Miss Featherstone. I have read your *Memoirs* and I think I
can guess something of what it must have cost you to rise
to your present position."

"Can you really?" Charlotte murmured. "How very
imaginative of you."

Sophy flushed, momentarily embarrassed at the thought
of how naive she must seem to this sophisticated woman of
the world. "Forgive me," she apologized quietly, "I am
certain that I cannot begin to understand what you have
been through in your life. But that does not mean I cannot
respect the fact that you have made your own way in the
world and have done so on your own terms."

"I see. And because of this boundless respect you hold
for me, you propose to put a bullet through my heart this
morning?"

Sophy's mouth tightened. "I can understand why you

chose to write the *Memoirs*. I can even understand your offering past lovers the opportunity to buy their way out of print. But when you selected my husband as your next victim, you went too far. I will not have those love letters in print for all the world to see and mock."

"It would have been far simpler to pay me off, madam, than to go to all this trouble."

"I cannot do that. Paying blackmail is a wretched, dishonorable recourse. I will not stoop to it. We will settle this matter between us here this morning and that will be the end of it."

"Will it? What makes you think that, assuming I am fortunate enough to survive, I will not go ahead and print whatever I wish?"

"You have accepted my challenge. By meeting me this way, you have agreed to settle the issues between us with pistols."

"You think I will abide by that agreement? You think this will be the end of the matter, regardless of the outcome of this duel?"

"You would not have bothered to show up this morning had you not intended to end things here."

Charlotte inclined her head. "You are quite right. That is the way this silly male code of honor works, is it not? We settle everything here with pistols."

"Yes. Then it will be over."

Charlotte shook her head in wry amusement. "Poor Ravenwood. I wonder if he has any notion yet of the sort of wife he has obtained for himself. You must be coming as quite a shock to him after Elizabeth."

"We are not here to discuss my husband or his previous wife," Sophy said through her teeth. The dawn air was cold but she was suddenly aware that she was perspiring. Her nerves were stretched to the breaking point. She wanted to get this business over and done.

"No, we are here because your sense of honor demands satisfaction and because you think I share your concept of honor. An interesting proposition. I wonder, do you comprehend that this definition of honor we are employing this morning is a man's definition?"

"There does not appear to be any other definition of honor that commands respect," Sophy said.

Charlotte's eyes gleamed. "I see," she said softly. "And you would have Ravenwood's respect, if nothing else, is that it, madam?"

"I believe we have discussed this matter sufficiently," Sophy said.

"Respect is all well and good, madam," Charlotte continued thoughtfully, "but I would advise you not to waste much time in an effort to get Ravenwood to love you. Everyone knows that after his experience with Elizabeth he will never risk love again. And, in any event, I must take leave to tell you that just as no man's honor is worth rising at this hour, no man's love is worth taking any great risk over, either."

"We are not dealing with a man's honor or a man's love here," Sophy stated coldly.

"No, I can see that. The issues involved are your honor and your love." Charlotte smiled slightly. "I can accept that those are not trifling matters. They might, indeed, be worth a little blood."

"Shall we get on with it, then?" Fear surged through Sophy as she turned to Anne who was hovering nearby with the case of dueling pistols. "We are ready. There is no point waiting any longer."

Anne looked from Sophy to Charlotte. "I have made some inquiries into the business of settling arguments in this fashion. There are certain steps we must go through before I load the pistols. First, it is my duty to tell you that there is an honorable alternative to going through with the challenge. I ask that you both consider it."

Sophy frowned. "What alternative?"

"You, Lady Ravenwood, have issued the challenge. If, however, Miss Featherstone will apologize for the actions that precipitated your challenge, the matter will be at an end without a shot being fired."

Sophy blinked. "This whole thing can be ended with a simple apology?"

"I must stress that it is an honorable alternative for both of you." Anne looked at Charlotte Featherstone.

"How fascinating," Charlotte murmured. "Just think, we can both get out of this without getting any blood stains on our clothing. But I am not at all certain I feel compelled to apologize."

"It is up to you, of course," Sophy said stiffly.

"Well, it is rather early for such violent sport, don't you think? And I am a firm believer in taking the sensible course when it is available." Charlotte smiled slowly at Sophy. "You are quite certain your honor would be satisfied if I simply apologized?"

"You would have to promise to leave the love letters out of print," Sophy reminded her hurriedly. Before Charlotte could respond, hoofbeats sounded in the fog.

"It must be Jane," Anne said in a very relieved tone. "I knew she would come. We must wait for her. She is one of the seconds."

Sophy glanced around just as a big gray horse materialized out of the mist that clung to the trees. The animal thundered toward them at full gallop, looking like an apparition as it churned through the low fog. A ghost horse, Sophy thought fleetingly, and it carried the devil himself.

"Julian," she whispered.

"Somehow this does not surprise me," Charlotte remarked. "Our little drama grows more amusing by the moment."

"What's he doing with Jane's horse?" Anne demanded angrily.

The big gray was brought to a shuddering halt in front of the three women. Julian's glittering eyes went first to Sophy and then to Charlotte and Anne. He saw the box of pistols in her hand.

"What the devil is going on here?"

Sophy refused to give into a sudden, fierce desire to flee. "You are interrupting a private matter, my lord."

Julian looked at her as if she had lost her mind. He swung down from the horse and tossed the reins to Anne who automatically caught them in her free hand.

"A private matter, madam? How dare you call it such?" Julian's face was a mask of controlled fury. *"You are my wife. What the hell is this all about?"*

"Isn't it obvious, Ravenwood?" Of the three women present, it was clear only Charlotte was not feeling particularly intimidated. Her fine eyes were more cynically amused than ever. "Your wife has called me out on a point of honor." She waved a hand at the pistol case. "As you can see, we were just about to settle matters in the traditional, honorable, masculine way."

"I don't believe any of this." Julian swung around to stare at Sophy. "You called Charlotte out? You challenged her to a duel?"

Sophy nodded once, refusing to speak.

"Why, for God's sake?"

Charlotte smiled grimly. "Surely you can guess the answer to that question, Ravenwood."

Julian took a step toward her. "Bloody hell. You sent her one of your goddamned blackmail threats, didn't you?"

"I do not look upon them as blackmail threats," Charlotte said calmly. "I see them as mere business opportunities. Your wife, however, chose to view my little offer in a different light. She feels it would be dishonorable to pay me off, you see. On the other hand, she cannot bear to see your name in my memoirs. So she took what she felt was the only alternative left to an honorable woman. She challenged me to pistols for two at dawn."

"Pistols at dawn," Julian repeated as if he still could not believe the evidence of his own eyes. He took another step toward Charlotte. "Get out of here. Leave at once. Go back to town and say nothing of any of this. If I hear one word of gossip concerning this day's events I will see to it that you never get the little cottage in Bath you used to talk about. I will make certain you lose the lease on your town house. I will bring so much pressure to bear on your creditors that they will hound you out of the city. Do you understand me, Charlotte?"

"Julian, you go too far," Sophy interrupted angrily.

Charlotte drew herself up, but most of the cool mockery had disappeared from her expression. She did not look fearful, merely resigned. "I understand you, Ravenwood. You were always quite good at making yourself very clear."

"One word of any of this and I will find a way to ruin all

you have worked for, Charlotte, I swear it. You know I can do it."

"There is no need to issue threats, Ravenwood. As it happens, I have no intention of gossiping about any of this." She turned to Sophy. "It was a personal matter of honor between your wife and myself. It does not concern anyone else."

"I quite agree," Sophy said firmly.

"I would have you know, madam," Charlotte said softly, "that as far as I am concerned, it is finished, even though no pistols were fired. You need have no fear of what will appear in the *Memoirs*."

Sophy took a deep breath. "Thank you."

Charlotte smiled slightly and gave Sophy a small, graceful bow. "No, madam, it is I who should thank you. I have had a most entertaining time of it. My world is filled with men of your class who talk about honor a great deal. But their understanding of the subject is very limited. Those same men cannot be bothered to behave honorably toward a female or anyone else weaker than themselves. It is a great pleasure to meet at last someone who does comprehend the meaning of the word. It comes as no great surprise to discover that this remarkably intelligent someone is a woman. Adieu."

"Good-bye," Sophy said, returning the small bow with equal grace.

Charlotte stepped lightly into the curricle, took up the reins and gave the horse the signal. The small vehicle vanished into the mist.

Julian watched Charlotte leave and then he turned around to pin Anne with a grim glare. He took the pistol box from her hand. "Who are you, boy?"

Anne coughed and pulled her cap down lower over her eyes. She rubbed the back of her hand across her nose and snuffled. "The lady wanted a horse and carriage brought round early this mornin', sir. I borrowed my father's nag and thought I'd make a bit on the side if you know what I mean."

"I will give you a very large bit on the side if you will guarantee to keep your mouth closed about what happened here this morning. But if I hear of this I will see to it that your father loses the horse and the carriage and anything else he owns. Furthermore, he will know that it is your fault he has lost everything. Do you comprehend me, boy?"

"Uh, yes, m'lord. Very clearly m'lord."

"Very well. You will drive my wife home in the carriage. I will be right behind you. When we reach the house you will pick up a woman who will be waiting there and you will escort her wherever she wishes to go. Then you will disappear from my sight forever."

"Yes sir."

"Now, Julian," Sophy began earnestly, "there is no need to threaten everyone in sight."

Julian cut her off with a frozen look. "Not one word out of you, madam. I do not yet trust myself to be able to speak to you about this with any semblance of calm." He walked over to the carriage and opened the door. "Get in."

She got into the carriage without another word. Her veiled hat slipped down over one ear as she did so. When she was seated, Julian leaned into the carriage to adjust the hat with an annoyed movement of his hand. Then he thrust the pistol case onto Sophy's lap. Without a word he removed himself from the carriage and slammed the door.

It was undoubtedly the longest ride of her life, Sophy decided as she sat sunk in gloom in the swaying carriage. Julian was beyond outrage. He was coldly, dangerously furious. She could only hope that Anne and Jane were spared the worst of it.

The household had just begun to stir when Anne halted the carriage at the front door. Jane, still wearing her black veil, was waiting anxiously in the library when Julian strode through the door with Sophy in tow. Jane glanced quickly at her friend.

"You are all right?" she demanded in a whisper.

"I am fine, as you can see. Everyone is all right, in fact. Matters would have been even better, however, if you had not felt obliged to intervene."

"I am sorry, Sophy, but I could not allow—"

"That will be enough," Julian interrupted as Guppy,

hastily adjusting his jacket, emerged from the door behind the stairs. He looked perplexed at the sight of Sophy in breeches.

"Is all in order, my lord?"

"Certain plans that were made for this morning have been canceled unexpectedly, Guppy, but you may rest assured that I have everything under control."

"Of course, my lord," Guppy said with grand dignity.

It would be worth his job to say a word about this dawn's bizarre hall scene and Guppy knew it. It was obvious the master was in one of his dangerous, quiet rages. It was, however, equally obvious that Lord Ravenwood was in command of the situation. With a quick, worried glance at Sophy, Guppy discreetly disappeared into the kitchens.

Julian turned to confront Jane.

"I do not know who you are, madam, and I assume from your veil that you do not wish to make your identity known. But whoever you are, please be aware that I shall be eternally indebted to you. You appear to be the only one who showed any common sense in this entire affair."

"I am known for my common sense, my lord," Jane said sadly. "Indeed, I fear many of my friends find me quite dull because of it."

"If your friends had any sense, themselves, they would cherish you for that quality. Good day, madam. There is a boy with a closed carriage outside who will escort you home. Your horse is tied to the carriage. Do you wish additional company? I can send one of the footmen along with you."

"No. The carriage and lad will be sufficient." Jane glanced in confusion at Sophy who shrugged faintly. "Thank you, my lord. I do hope this is the end of the entire affair."

"You may rest assured it mostly certainly is. And I hope I can rely upon you not to breathe a word of the matter."

"You may depend upon it, my lord."

Julian walked her to the door and saw her into the small carriage. Then he stalked back up the steps and into the hall. The huge door closed very softly behind him. He stood looking at Sophy for a long moment.

Sophy held her breath, waiting for the stroke of doom.

"Go upstairs and change your clothing, madam. You have played enough at men's games today. We will discuss this matter at ten in the library."

"There is nothing to discuss, my lord," she said swiftly. "You already know everything."

Julian's emerald eyes were brilliant with his anger and another emotion that Sophy realized with a start was relief. "You are wrong, madam. There is a great deal to discuss. If you are not down here promptly at ten, I shall come to fetch you."

ELEVEN

"**P**erhaps," said Julian with an icy calm that was impressive under the circumstances, "you will be good enough to explain this entire matter from the beginning."

The words shattered the ominous silence that had gripped the library since Sophy had cautiously walked through the door a few minutes earlier. Julian had sat, unmoving, behind his massive desk, studying her with his customary inscrutable expression for a long while before choosing to begin what would no doubt be a most unpleasant interview.

Sophy took a deep breath and lifted her chin. "You already know the essentials of the situation."

"I know you must have received one of Featherstone's blackmail notes. I would very much appreciate it if you would be so good as to explain why you did not immediately turn it over to me."

"She approached me, not you, with her threat. I considered it a matter of honor to respond."

Julian's eyes narrowed. "Honor, madam?"

"If the situation were reversed, my lord, you would

184

have handled the matter as I did. You cannot deny it."

"If the situation were reversed?" he repeated blankly. "What the devil are you talking about?"

"You understand me quite well, I am certain, my lord." Sophy realized she was hovering between tears and fury. It was a volatile combination of emotions. "If some man had approached you with a threat to print the details of a...a past indiscretion of mine, you would have called him out. You know you would have done exactly what I did. You cannot deny it."

"Sophy, that's ludicrous," Julian snapped. "This is hardly the same sort of situation. Don't you dare draw any parallels between your reprehensible actions this morning and what you imagine I would have done in similar circumstances."

"Why not? Am I to be denied the chance to meet the dictates of honor just because I am a female?"

"Yes, damn it. I mean, no. By God, do not try to confuse the issue. Honor does not require from you what it would require from me in the same situation and you damn well know it."

"It seems to me only fair that I be entitled to live up to the same code as you, my lord."

"*Only fair?* Fairness has nothing to do with this."

"Am I to have no recourse in such situations, my lord?" Sophy demanded tightly. "No way to avenge myself? No way to settle a matter of honor?"

"Sophy, pay attention to me. As your husband it is my duty to avenge you, should that be required. And I am telling you here and now that it had better not ever be required. There is, however, no reversal of the situation. It is inconceivable."

"Well, you had best try to conceive of it, my lord, for that is precisely what happened. Nor were you the one called upon to deal with it. I was and I did the honorable thing. I do not see how you can fault me in this, Julian."

He stared at her, looking thoroughly taken aback for a few seconds before recovering himself. "Not fault you? Sophy, what you did today was outrageous and disgraceful.

It demonstrates a sad want of sound judgment. It was foolhardy and extremely dangerous. Not fault you? Sophy, those pistols are not toys, they are Manton's finest."

"I am well aware of that, my lord. Furthermore, I knew what I was doing with them. I told you my grandfather taught me how to use his pistols."

"You could have been killed, your little idiot." Julian shot to his feet and came around to the front of the desk. He leaned back against it, crossing one booted foot over the other. His expression was very close to savage. "Did you think about that, Sophy? Did you think about the risk you were taking? Did it cross your mind that you might well be dead by now? Or a murderess? Dueling is against the law, you know. Or was it all just a game to you?"

"I assure you, it was no game, my lord. I was—" Sophy broke off, swallowing uncomfortably as memories of the fear returned. She looked away from Julian's fierce eyes. "I was quite frightened, to be perfectly honest."

Julian swore softly. "You think you were frightened," he muttered under his breath before he said more distinctly, "What about the potential scandal, Sophy? Did you consider that?"

She kept her eyes averted. "We took steps to ensure that there would be no scandal."

"I see. And just how were you planning to explain a bullet wound, my dear? Or a dead prostitute in Leighton Field?"

"Julian, please, you've said enough."

"Enough?" Julian's voice was suddenly soft and dangerous. "Sophy, I assure you, I have hardly begun."

"Well, I do not see that I am obliged to listen to any more of your lectures on the subject." Sophy jumped to her feet, blinking back the tears that trembled on her lashes. "It is obvious you do not understand. Harry is quite right when she says that men are seriously lacking in the ability to comprehend things that are important to a woman."

"What do I fail to understand? The fact that you behaved in a shocking manner when I have specifically told you that the one thing I will not tolerate is gossip about you?"

"There will be no gossip."

"That's what you think. I did my best to threaten Featherstone this morning, but there is absolutely no guarantee she will keep her mouth shut."

"She will. She said she would."

"Damn it, Sophy, surely you are not so naive as to put any faith in the word of a professional harlot?"

"As far as I can tell, she is a woman of honor. She gave me her word there would be no mention of your name in print and she said she would not discuss the events of this morning. That is good enough for me."

"Then you are a fool. And even if Featherstone keeps quiet, what about the young boy who drove you to Leighton Field? What about the woman in the black veil? What control do you have over either of them?"

"They will not speak of this," Sophy said.

"You mean you hope they will not speak of it."

"They were my seconds. They will honor their word not to say anything about what happened this morning."

"Damn it, are you telling me that they were both friends of yours?"

"Yes, my lord."

"Including the red-haired lad? Where on earth would you meet a young man of that class and get to know him well enough to—" Julian broke off, swearing again. "I believe I perceive the truth at last. It was not a young man at all who was driving your carriage, was it, madam? Another young woman dressed in mens' clothes, I presume. Good lord. A whole generation of females is running wild."

"If women occasionally seem a bit wild, my lord, it is almost certainly because men have driven them to it. Be that as it may, I do not intend to discuss my friends' roles in all this."

"No, I don't suppose you do. They helped you arrange the meeting at Leighton Field?"

"Yes."

"Thank God one of them had the sense to come to me

this morning, although it would have been a great deal
more accommodating of her to have sent word of this
matter earlier. As it was, I barely arrived at Leighton Field
in time. What are their names, Sophy?"

Sophy's nails bit into her palms. "You must realize I
cannot tell you, my lord."

"The dictates of honor again, my dear?" His mouth
curved grimly.

"Do not laugh at me, Julian. That is the one thing I will
not tolerate from you. As you have observed, I came close
to getting killed this morning because of you. The least
you could do is refrain from finding it all laughable."

"You think I am laughing?" Julian pushed away from the
desk and stalked to the window. Bracing one hand against
the frame he turned his back to her and stared out into
the small garden. "I assure you I find absolutely nothing
in this whole mess the least amusing. I have spent the
past few hours trying to decide what to do with you,
Sophy."

"Such cogitation is probably bad for your liver, my
lord."

"Well, it hasn't done my digestion any good, I'll admit.
The only reason you are not already on your way to
Ravenwood or Eslington Park is because your sudden
absence would only create more talk. We must all act as if
nothing has happened. It is the only hope. Thus, you will
be allowed to remain here in London. However, you will
not leave this house again unless you are escorted by
either myself or my aunt. And as for your *seconds*, you are
forbidden to see them again. You obviously cannot be
trusted to choose your friends wisely."

At that final pronouncement, Sophy exploded in fury. It
was all too much. The night of passion and fearful anticipation, the meeting at dawn with Charlotte Featherstone,
Julian's arrogant indignation. It was more than Sophy
could bear. For the first time in her adult life she completely
lost her temper.

"No, damn you, Ravenwood, you go too far. You will not
tell me who I can and cannot see."

He glanced back at her over his shoulder, his gaze

sweeping over her with cold detachment. "You think not, madam?"

"I will not allow you to do so." Seething with frustration and rage, Sophy confronted him proudly. "I did not marry you in order to become your prisoner."

"Really?" he asked roughly. "Then why did you marry me, madam?"

"I married you because I love you," Sophy cried passionately. "I've loved you since I was eighteen years old, fool that I am."

"Sophy, what the hell are you saying?"

The towering rage consumed her completely. She was beyond logic or reason. "Furthermore, you cannot punish me for what occurred this morning because it was all your fault in the first place."

"My fault?" he roared, losing a good measure of his own unnatural calm.

"If you had not written those love letters to Charlotte Featherstone none of this would have happened."

"What love letters?" Julian snarled.

"The ones you wrote to her during the course of your affair with her. The ones she threatened to publish in her *Memoirs*. I could not endure it, Julian. Don't you see? I could not bear to have the whole world see the beautiful love letters you had written to your mistress when I have not received so much as a shopping list from you. You may scoff all you wish, but I, too, have my pride."

Julian was staring at her. "Is that what Featherstone threatened? To print old love letters of mine?"

"Yes, damn you. You sent love letters to a mistress and yet you cannot be bothered to give your wife the smallest token of your affection. But I suppose that is perfectly understandable when one considers the fact that you have no affection for me."

"For God's sake, Sophy, I was a very young man when I first met Charlotte Featherstone. I may or may not have scribbled a note or two to her. The truth is, I barely recall the entire affair. In any event, you would do well to keep in mind that very young men occasionally put into writing passing fancies that are far better left unwritten. Such fancies are meaningless, I assure you."

"Oh, I believe you, my lord."

"Sophy, under normal circumstances, I would never discuss a woman such as Featherstone with you. But given the bizarre situation in which we find ourselves, allow me to explain something very clearly. There is not a great degree of affection involved on either side in the sort of relationship a man has with a woman like Featherstone. It is a matter of business for the woman and convenience for the man."

"Such a relationship sounds very much like a marriage, my lord, except, of course, that a wife does not have the luxury of handling her own business affairs the way a woman of the demimonde does."

"Damn it, Sophy, there is a world of difference between your situation and Featherstone's." Julian made an obvious effort to hold onto his self-control.

"Is there, my lord? I will allow that, unless you manage to squander your fortune, I shall probably not have to worry overmuch about my pension the way Charlotte must. But other than that, I am not certain I am as well off as Charlotte."

"You've lost your senses, Sophy. You're becoming irrational."

"And you are utterly impossible, my lord." Her rage was burning itself out. Sophy was suddenly aware of being unutterably weary. "There is no dealing with such arrogance. I do not know why I bother to try."

"You find me arrogant? Believe me, Sophy, that is nothing compared to what I was this morning when I looked out your window and saw you climbing into that closed carriage."

There was a new, raw edge in his words that was alarming. Sophy was momentarily distracted by it. "I did not realize you had seen me leave the house."

"Do you know what I thought when I saw you step into that carriage?" Julian's gaze was emerald hard.

"I imagine you were concerned, my lord?"

"Goddamn it, Sophy, I thought you were leaving with your lover."

She stared at him. "Lover? What lover?"

"You may be assured that was one of the many questions I asked myself as I rode after you. I did not even know which bastard among all the bastards in London was taking you away."

"Oh, for heaven's sake, Julian, that was a perfectly stupid conclusion for you to arrive at."

"Was it?"

"It most certainly was. What on earth would I want with another man? I cannot seem to handle the one I've got." She swung around and went to the door.

"Sophy, stop right where you are. Where do you think you're going? I'm not through with you."

"But I am quite through with you, my lord. Through with being berated for trying to do the honorable thing. Through with trying to make you fall in love with me. Through with any attempt to create a marriage based on mutual respect and affection."

"Damn it, Sophy."

"Do not worry, my lord. I have learned my lesson. From now on you will have exactly the sort of marriage you desire. I will endeavor to stay out of your way. I shall occupy myself with other more important matters— matters which I should have put first right from the start."

"Will you, indeed?" he snarled. "And what about this great love you say you have for me?"

"You need not worry. I will not speak of it again. I realize to do so would only embarrass you and further humiliate me. I assure you, I have been humiliated enough by you to last me a lifetime."

Julian's expression softened slightly. "Sophy, my dear, come back here and be seated. I have much to say to you."

"I do not wish to listen to any more of your tiresome lectures. Do you know something, Julian? I find your male code of honor to be quite silly. Standing twenty paces apart in the cold air of dawn while blazing away at one another with pistols is a senseless way to resolve an argument."

"On that point, I assure you we are in complete agreement, madam."

"I doubt it. You would have gone through with it without questioning the entire process. Charlotte and I, on the other hand, discussed the subject at some length."

"You stood there talking about it?" Julian asked in amazement.

"Of course we did. We are women, my lord, and thus eminently more suited than men to an intellectual discussion of such issues. We had just been informed that an apology would resolve everything honorably and thereby make any shooting unnecessary when you had to come thundering up out of nowhere and proceed to interfere in something that was none of your business."

Julian groaned. "I do not believe this. Featherstone was going to apologize to you?"

"Yes, I believe she was. She is a woman of honor and she recognized that she owed me an apology. And I will tell you something, my lord, she was right when she said that no man was worth getting up at such an ungodly hour for the purpose of risking a bullet."

Sophy let herself out of the library and closed the door very quietly behind her. She told herself to take what satisfaction she could from having had the exit line this time. It was all she was going to get from the whole miserable affair.

Tears burned in her eyes. She dashed upstairs and headed for her room to shed them in solitude.

A long time later, she lifted her head from her folded arms, went to the basin to wash her face and then sat down at her writing table. Picking up a pen, she adjusted a sheet of paper in front of her and composed one more letter to Charlotte Featherstone.

Dear Miss C. F.:
Enclosed please find the sum of two hundred pounds. I do not send this to you because of your promise to refrain from printing certain letters; rather because I do

feel quite strongly that your many admirers owe you the same consideration they owe their wives. After all, they seem to have enjoyed the same sort of relationship with you that they have with the women they marry. Thus, they have an obligation to provide you with a pension. The enclosed draft is our mutual friend's share of the pension owed to you. I wish you good luck with your cottage in Bath.

Yours,
S.

Sophy reread the note and sealed it. She would give it to Anne to deliver. Anne seemed to know how to handle that sort of thing.

And that ended the whole fiasco, Sophy thought as she leaned back in her chair. She had told Julian the truth. She had, indeed, learned a valuable lesson this morning. There was no point trying to win her husband's respect by living up to his masculine code of honor.

And she already knew she stood little chance of winning his love.

All in all there did not seem to be much point in spending any more time working on her marriage. It was quite hopeless to try to alter the rules Julian had laid down for it. She was trapped in this velvet prison and she would have to make the best of it. From now on she would go her own way and live her own life. She and Julian would meet occasionally at routs and balls and in the bedchamber.

She would undertake to give him his heir and he, in return, would see that she was well dressed and well fed and well housed for the rest of her life. It was not a bad bargain, she reflected, just a very lonely, empty one.

It did not promise to be the kind of marriage she had longed for but at least she was finally facing reality, Sophy decided. And, she reminded herself as she got to her feet, she had other things to do here in London. She had wasted enough time trying to win Julian's love and affection. He had none to give.

And, as she had told Julian, she had another project to keep her occupied. It was past time she gave her full attention to the matter of finding her sister's seducer.

Resolved to devote herself to that task, Sophy went to the wardrobe to examine the gypsy costume she planned to wear that evening to Lady Musgrove's masquerade ball. She stood contemplating the colorful gown, scarf and mask for some time and then she glanced at her small jewelry case.

She needed a plan of action, a way to draw out those who might know something about the black ring.

Inspiration struck suddenly. What better way to start her quest for the truth than to wear the ring at a masquerade ball where her own identity was a secret? It would be interesting to see if anyone noticed the ring and commented on it. If so, she might begin to pick up a few clues about its previous owner.

But the ball was hours away and she had been up for a long time already. Sophy discovered she was physically and emotionally exhausted. She went over to the bed with the intention of taking a brief nap and was sound asleep within minutes.

Downstairs in the library Julian stood staring at the empty hearth. Sophy's remark that no man was worth the effort of rising at dawn to risk a bullet burned in his ears. He had made a similar remark after fighting his last duel over Elizabeth.

But this morning Sophy had done exactly that, Julian thought. God help him, she had done the inconceivable, for a respectable woman. She had challenged a famous courtesan to a duel and then she had risen at dawn with the intention of risking her neck over a question of honor.

And all because his wife thought herself in love with him and could not bear to see his love letters to another woman in print.

He could only be thankful Charlotte had apparently refrained from mentioning that the pearl earrings she had worn to the dawn meeting had been a gift from him years ago. He had recognized them at once. If Sophy had known about the earrings she would have been twice as incensed. The fact that Charlotte had not taunted her younger opponent with the pearls said a great deal about Featherstone's respect for the woman who had called her out.

Sophy had a right to be angry, Julian thought wearily. He had made a great deal of money available to her but he had not been very generous with her when it came to the sort of gifts a woman expected from a husband. If a courtesan deserved pearls, what did a sweet, passionate, tenderhearted, faithful wife deserve?

But he had given little thought to buying Sophy anything in the way of jewelry. He knew it was because part of him was still obsessed with recovering the emeralds. As hopeless as that now appeared, Julian still found it difficult to contemplate the thought of the Countess of Ravenwood wearing anything other than the Ravenwood family gems.

Nevertheless, there was no reason he could not buy Sophy some small, expensive trinket that would satisfy her woman's pride. He made a note to pick up something at the jeweler's that very afternoon.

Julian left the library and went slowly upstairs to his room. The relief that had soared through him when he had first realized Sophy had not left the house to go off with another man did not do much to quench the chill he felt every time he realized she might have been killed.

Julian swore softly and told himself not to think about it any more. He would only succeed in driving himself crazy.

It was obvious Sophy had meant what she said last night when she had shuddered in his arms. She really did believe herself to be in love with him.

It was understandable that Sophy might not fully comprehend her own feelings, Julian reminded himself. The difference between passion and love was not always readily discernible. He could certainly testify to that fact.

But it would certainly do no harm for Sophy to believe herself in love with him, Julian decided. He did not really mind indulging this particular romantic fantasy.

Filled with a sudden need to hear her tell him once again exactly why she had felt compelled to confront Charlotte Featherstone, Julian opened the connecting door to Sophy's bedchamber. The question died on his lips as he studied her figure on the bed.

She was curled up, sound asleep. Julian walked over and stood looking down at her for a moment. *She really is very sweet and innocent,* he thought. Looking at her now, a man would have a hard time imagining her in the sort of proud rage she had been in a short while ago.

But, then, looking at her now a man would also have trouble imagining the warm tide of womanly passion that ran through her. Sophy was proving to be a female of many interesting aspects.

Out of the corner of his eye he spotted a pile of daintily embroidered handkerchiefs wadded up on the little zebrawood writing table. It was not difficult to figure out how the little squares of fabric had come to get so sadly crumpled.

Elizabeth had always shed her tears in front of him, Julian reflected. She had been able to cry gloriously at a moment's notice. But Sophy had come up to her room to cry alone. He winced as an odd sensation very much like guilt went through him. He pushed it aside. He'd had a right to be furious with Sophy today. She could have gotten herself killed.

And then what would I have done?

She must be exhausted, Julian decided. Unwilling to wake her, he reluctantly turned around to go back to his own room. Then he spotted the wildly patterned gypsy costume hanging in the open wardrobe and remembered Sophy's plans to attend the Musgrove masquerade that evening.

Normally he had even less interest in masquerade balls than he did in the opera. He had intended to allow his aunt to escort Sophy this evening. But now it struck him that it might be wise to drop into Lady Musgrove's later tonight.

It suddenly seemed important to demonstrate to Sophy that he thought more of her than he did of his ex-mistress.

If he hurried he could get to the jeweler's and back before Sophy awoke.

"Sophy, I have been so worried. Are you all right? Did he beat you? I was certain he would not allow you out of the house for a month." Anne, wearing a red-and-white domino and a glittering silver mask that concealed the upper half of her face leaned anxiously forward to whisper to her friend.

The huge ballroom was filled with costumed men and women. Colored lanterns had been strung overhead and dozens of huge potted plants had been placed strategically about to create the effect of an indoor garden.

Sophy grimaced behind her own mask as she recognized Anne's voice. "No, of course he did not beat me and as you can see I have not been imprisoned. But he did not understand any of it, Anne."

"Not even why you did it?"

"Least of all that."

Anne nodded soberly. "I was afraid he would not. I fear Harriette is quite right when she says men do not even allow women to claim the same sense of honor they possess."

"Where is Jane?"

"She's here." Anne glanced around the crowded ballroom. "Wearing a dark blue satin domino. She's terribly afraid you will shun her forever after what she did this morning."

"Of course I will not shun her. I know she only did what she felt was best. It was all a complete disaster from the beginning."

A figure in a blue domino had materialized at Sophy's elbow. "Thank you, Sophy," Jane said humbly. "It's true that I did what I thought was best."

"You need not refine upon your point, Jane," Anne said brusquely.

Jane ignored her. "Sophy, I am so sorry but I simply could not allow you to risk getting killed over such a matter. Will you ever forgive me for my interference this morning?"

"It is over and done, Jane. Pray forget about it. As it happens, Ravenwood would undoubtedly have interrupted the duel even without your assistance. He saw me leaving the house this morning."

"He saw you? Good heavens. What must he have thought when he watched you get into the carriage?" Anne asked, sounding stricken.

Sophy shrugged. "He assumed I was running off with another man."

"That explains the look in his eyes when he opened the door to me," Jane whispered. "I knew then why he is so frequently called a devil."

"Oh, dear God," Anne said bleakly. "He must have assumed you were behaving like his first wife. Some say he killed her because of her infidelities."

"Nonsense," Sophy said. She had never completely believed that tale; never wanted to believe it, but just for a moment she did wonder to what lengths Julian might be driven if he were goaded too far. He had certainly been furious with her that morning. Anne was right, Sophy thought with a small chill. For a while there in the library, there had been a devil looking out of those green eyes.

"If you ask me, you had two close calls today," Jane said. "You not only barely missed getting hurt in a duel, but you probably came within an inch of your life when Ravenwood saw you get into the carriage."

"You may rest assured I have learned a lesson. From now on I intend to be exactly the sort of wife my husband expects. I will not interfere in his life and in return I will expect him not to interfere in mine."

Anne bit her lip thoughtfully. "I am not so certain it will work that way, Sophy."

"I will make certain it works that way," Sophy vowed. "I do have one more favor to ask you, though, Anne. Can you see to the delivery of another letter to Charlotte Featherstone?"

"Sophy, please," Jane said uneasily, "leave it alone. You've done enough in that direction."

"Do not worry, Jane. This will be the end of it. Can you do it for me, Anne?"

Anne nodded. "I can do it. What are you going to say in the letter? Wait, let me guess. You're going to send her the two hundred pounds, aren't you?"

"That is exactly what I am going to do. Julian owes it to her."

"This is beyond belief," Jane muttered.

"You may stop fretting, Jane. As I said, it is all over. I have more important matters to concern me. What is more, they are matters I should have been concerned with all along. I do not know why I let myself become distracted by marriage."

Jane's eyes gleamed with momentary amusement behind her mask. "I am sure marriage is very distracting in the beginning, Sophy. Do not chide yourself."

"Well, she's learned it's useless to try to alter the pattern of a man's behavior," Anne observed. "Having made the mistake of getting married in the first place, the best one can do is ignore one's husband as much as possible and concentrate on more interesting matters."

"You are an expert on marriage?" Jane asked.

"I have learned a lot watching Sophy. Now tell us what these more important matters are, Sophy."

Sophy hesitated, wondering how much to tell her friends about the black ring she was wearing. Before she could make up her mind a tall figure dressed in a black, hooded cape and a black mask glided up to her and bowed deeply from the waist. It was impossible to see the color of his eyes in the lantern light.

"I would like to request the honor of this dance, Lady Gypsy."

Sophy looked into shadowed eyes and felt suddenly cold. Instinctively she started to refuse and then she remembered the ring. She had to begin her search somewhere and there was no telling who might give her the clues she needed. She sketched a curtsy. "Thank you, kind sir. I would be pleased to dance with you."

The man in the black cape and mask led her out onto the floor without a word. She realized he was wearing black gloves and she did not like the feel of being close to him when he took her into his arms. He danced with

perfect grace and decorum but Sophy felt vaguely
menaced.

"Do you tell fortunes, Lady Gypsy?" the man asked in a
low, rough voice tinged with cold amusement.

"Occasionally."

"So do I. Occasionally."

That startled her. "Do you, sir? What sort of fortune do
you predict for me?"

His black gloved fingers moved over the black ring on
her hand. "A most interesting fortune, my lady. Most
interesting, indeed. But, then, that is only to be expected
from a bold young woman who would dare to wear this
ring in public."

TWELVE

Sophy froze. She would have tripped over her own feet if her partner had not tightened his grip quite painfully for an instant. "You are familiar with this ring, sir?" she asked, striving to keep her voice light.

"Yes."

"How strange. I did not know it was a common thing."

"It is most uncommon, madam. Only a few would recognize it."

"I see."

"May I ask how it came into your possession?" the hooded man asked quietly.

She had her story ready. "It is a keepsake given to me by a friend of mine before she died."

"Your friend should have warned you that the ring is very dangerous. You would be well advised to remove it and never wear it again." There was a slight pause before the stranger concluded softly, "Unless you are a very adventurous sort of female."

Sophy's heart was pounding now but she managed a seemingly careless smile beneath her half-mask. "I cannot imagine why you should be so alarmed at the sight of this ring. What is there about it that makes you think it is dangerous?"

"I am not free to tell you why it is dangerous, my lady. The wearer must discover that for herself. But I feel it my duty to warn you that it is not for the faint of heart."

"I think you tease me, sir. But truthfully I cannot believe the ring is anything more than a rather unusual piece of jewelry. In any event, I am not fainthearted."

"Then perhaps you will find a most unusual type of excitement with the ring."

Sophy shivered but kept her smile in place. At that moment she was extremely grateful to be wearing a disguise. "I am quite certain, sir, that you are deliberately taunting me because of the costume I chose to wear this evening. Do you enjoy sending chills down the spine of the poor fortune-teller whose job it is to send chills down the spines of others?"

"Do I send chills down your spine, madam?"

"A few."

"Are you enjoying them?"

"Not particularly."

"Perhaps you will learn to find pleasure in them. A certain type of female does eventually, after a bit of practice."

"Is that my fortune?" she asked, aware that her palms were growing as damp as they had that very morning when she had confronted Charlotte Featherstone.

"I do not believe I want to spoil the joy of anticipation for you by giving you a peek at your future. It will be far more interesting to let you discover the nature of your fortune in due course. Good evening, Lady Gypsy. I am certain we will meet again." The man in the black cape released her abruptly, bowed low over her ringed hand and then vanished into the crowd.

Sophy watched anxiously as he disappeared, wondering if she might be able to follow him through the throng. Perhaps she could catch him without his mask outside. Many people were leaving the ballroom in order to cool off in Lady Musgrove's lovely gardens.

Sophy picked up her skirts and started forward. She got all of ten feet before she felt a man's hand clamp firmly around her arm. Startled, she whirled around to find herself looking up at another tall man dressed very much as her previous partner had been in a black cape and mask. The only difference was that the hood of this man's cape was thrown back to reveal his midnight dark hair. He gave her a slight bow.

"Pardon me, but I seek the services of one such as yourself, Madam Gypsy. Will you be so gracious as to dance with me while you tell me my fortune? I have been somewhat unlucky at love lately and I would like to know if my luck is going to change."

Sophy glanced down at the large hand on her arm and recognized it immediately. Julian had roughened his voice and pitched it even lower than usual but she would know him anywhere. The familiar sense of awareness she always experienced when he was in the vicinity had grown stronger during the time she had been living with him.

She felt a curious sensation in her stomach as she wondered if Julian recognized her. If he did, he was certain to be angry with her for what she had done when she had awakened from her nap to find the bracelet on the pillow beside her. Warily she looked up at him.

"Do you wish your luck to change, sir?"

"Yes," Julian said as he swung her into the dance. "I believe I do want it to change."

"What . . . what sort of ill luck have you been experiencing?" she asked cautiously.

"I seem to be having great difficulty in pleasing my new bride."

"Is she very hard to please?"

"Yes, I fear so. A most demanding lady." Julian's voice seemed to roughen even further. "For example today she let me know she was annoyed with me because I had not thought to give her a token of my affection."

Sophy bit her lip and looked past Julian's shoulder. "How long have you been married, sir?"

"Several weeks."

"And in all that time you have never given her such a token?"

"I confess I did not think of doing so. Very remiss of me. However, today when my lapse was pointed out to me I took immediate steps to remedy the situation. I bought the lady a very charming bracelet and I left it on her pillow."

Sophy winced. "Was it a very expensive bracelet?"

"Very. But not expensive enough apparently to satisfy my lady." Julian's hand tightened slightly on Sophy's waist. "I found the bracelet on my own pillow this evening as I was dressing to go out. There was a note with it that said she was not amused by such a paltry trinket."

Sophy stared up at him, desperately trying to decide whether Julian was angry or simply objectively interested in her reasons for refusing the bracelet. She still could not be certain he even recognized her. "It would seem to me, sir, that you misunderstood your lady's complaint."

"Did I?" Without missing a step he adjusted the brightly patterned scarf that was starting to slide off her shoulders. "You don't think she likes jewelry?"

"I'm sure she appreciates jewelry as well as the next woman but she probably does not like the idea that you are trying to placate her with baubles."

"Placate?" He tasted the word thoughtfully. "What do you mean by that?"

Sophy cleared her throat. "Did you by any chance quarrel with your lady recently?"

"Um. Yes. She did something very foolhardy. Something that could have cost her her life. I was angry. I let her know of my anger and she chose to sulk."

"Do you not think it possible that she was hurt that you did not understand why she had done what she did?"

"She cannot expect me to condone the kind of dangerous action she took recently," Julian said evenly. "Even if she did believe it a matter of honor. I will not allow her to risk her life so foolishly."

"So you gave her a bracelet instead of the understanding she sought?"

Julian's mouth was hard beneath the edge of his mask. "Do you think that was how she viewed it?"

"I think your lady felt you were trying to pacify her after an argument in the same way you would try to buy your way back into the good graces of a mistress." Sophy held her breath, still frantically trying to decide whether or not Julian recognized her.

"An interesting theory. And a possible explanation."

"Does the technique generally work? With mistresses, I mean?"

Julian missed a step and caught himself smoothly. "Uh, yes. Generally."

"Mistresses must be very poor-spirited creatures."

"It is certainly true that my lady has nothing in common with such women. She has a full measure of pride, for example. A mistress cannot afford much pride."

"I do not believe that you are short of that commodity, yourself."

Julian's big hand flexed carefully around her fingers. "You are right."

"It would seem that you and your lady have that much in common, at least. It should provide a basis for understanding."

"Well, Madam Gypsy? Now you know my sad story. What do you think my odds are for the future?"

"If you truly want your fortune to change I think that first you must convince your lady that you respect her pride and sense of honor as much as you would that of a man."

"And how would you suggest I go about doing that?" Julian inquired.

Sophy drew in a breath. "First, you must give her something more valuable than the bracelet." Her fingers were suddenly crushed in Julian's palm.

"And what would that be, Madam Gypsy?" There was a dark, brooding menace in his voice now. "A pair of earrings, perhaps? A necklace?"

Sophy struggled and failed to release her fingers from Julian's powerful grip. "I have a strong hunch your lady would appreciate a rose you had picked by hand or a love letter or a few verses conveying some affection from you far more than she would jewelry, sir."

Julian's fingers relaxed. "Ah, you think she is a romantic at heart? I had begun to suspect that, myself."

"I think she simply knows that it is very easy for a man to clear his conscience with a gift of jewelry."

"Perhaps she will not be happy until she thinks me completely snared in the coils of love," Julian suggested coolly.

"Would that be so bad, sir?"

"It is best if she understands that I am not susceptible to that sort of emotion," Julian said gently.

"Perhaps she is learning the truth of that the hard way," Sophy said.

"Do you think so?"

"I think it very probable that she will soon prove herself intelligent enough to refrain from pining for that which is unobtainable."

"And what will she do then?"

"She will endeavor to give you the sort of marriage you wish. One in which love and mutual understanding are not important. She will stop wasting her time and energy seeking ways to make you fall in love with her. She will busy herself with other matters and live a life of her own."

Julian crushed her fingers again and his eyes glittered behind his mask. "Does that mean she will seek other conquests?"

"No, sir, it does not. Your lady is the sort to give her heart but once and if it is rejected she will not try to give it to another. She will simply pack it away in cotton wool and busy herself with other projects."

"I did not say I would reject the gift of my lady's heart. Quite the opposite. I would have her know that I would welcome such a treasure. I would take good care of her and her love."

"I see," Sophy said. "You would have her hopelessly snared in the coils of love at which you scoff but you would not take the risk, yourself. That is your way of mastering her?"

"Do not put words in my mouth, Madam Gypsy. The

lady in question is my wife," Julian stated categorically. "It would be convenient for all concerned if she also happens to love me. I merely want to assure her that her love is safe with me."

"Because you could then use that love to control her?"

"Do all fortune-tellers interpret their clients' words so broadly?"

"If you do not feel you are getting your money's worth, you need not concern yourself. I do not intend to charge you for this particular fortune."

"Thus far you have not told me my fortune. You have only tried to give me a great deal of advice," Julian said.

"It was my understanding you sought a way to change your luck."

"Why don't you simply tell me if there is any luck to be had in my future?" Julian suggested.

"Unless you are willing to change your ways I am sure you will get exactly the sort of marriage you wish, sir. Your wife will go her own way and you will go yours. You will probably see her as often as it proves necessary to ensure yourself of an heir and she will endeavor to stay out of your way the rest of the time."

"It sounds to me as if my wife intends to sulk throughout the remainder of our marriage," Julian observed dryly. "A daunting prospect." He adjusted Sophy's scarf again as it threatened to slide to the floor and then his fingertips traced the shape of the black metal ring she wore. He glanced idly down at her hand. "A most unusual piece of jewelry, Madam Gypsy. Do all fortune-tellers wear a ring such as this?"

"No. It is a keepsake." She hesitated as a jolt of fear went through her. "Do you recognize it, sir?"

"No, but it is singularly ugly. Who gave it to you?"

"It belonged to my sister," Sophy said cautiously. She told herself to be calm, Julian was only showing mild curiosity about the ring. "I wear it sometimes to remind me of her fate."

"And what was her fate?" Julian was watching her steadily now as if he could see beneath her mask.

"She was foolish enough to love a man who did not love

her in return," Sophy whispered. "Perhaps, like you, he simply was not susceptible to the emotion but he did not mind in the least that she was very susceptible. She gave her heart and it cost her her life."

"I think you draw the wrong lessons from your sister's sad story," Julian said gently.

"Well, I certainly do not intend to kill myself," Sophy retorted. "But I also do not intend to give a valuable gift to a man who is incapable of appreciating it. Excuse me, sir, I believe I see some friends of mine standing near the window. I must speak to them." Sophy made to slide away from Julian's grasp.

"What about my fortune?" Julian demanded, holding her with a grip on the ends of her scarf.

"Your fortune is in your own hands, sir." Sophy deftly slipped out from under the scarf and fled into the crowd.

Julian was left in the middle of the dance floor, the colorful silk scarf trailing from his strong fingers. He stood contemplating it for a long moment and then, with a slow smile, folded it up and tucked it into an inside cloak pocket. He knew where to find his gypsy lady later tonight.

Still smiling slightly to himself, he went outside to call for his carriage. Aunt Fanny and Harriette would see Sophy safely home as planned. Julian decided he could afford to spend an hour or so at one of his clubs before returning to the house.

He was in a much more cheerful mood than he had been earlier that day and the reason was clear. It was true Sophy was still angry with him, still feeling defiant and hurt by his failure to condone her actions that morning. But he had satisfied himself that she had been telling the truth, as usual, when she had claimed to be in love with him.

He had been almost certain of it when he'd found the bracelet flung in a heap on his pillow this afternoon. It was why he had not barged straight into her bedchamber and put the bracelet on her wrist himself. Only a woman in love would hurl such an expensive gift back in a man's face and hold out for a sonnet instead.

He was no good at sonnets, but he might try his hand at a short note to accompany the bracelet the next time he tried to give it to Sophy.

More than ever he wished he knew the fate of the emeralds. The new Countess of Ravenwood would look very good in them. He could envision her wearing the stones and nothing else.

The image danced in his mind for a moment, causing his groin to grow heavy and taut. *Later,* Julian promised himself. Later he would take his gypsy lady into his arms and touch her and kiss her until she cried out her response, until she pleaded with him for fulfillment, until she told him again of her love.

Julian discovered that now he had heard the words, he was suddenly very hungry to hear them again.

He was not overly concerned about her threat to wrap her heart in cotton wool and stow it away on the shelf. He was getting to know her and if there was one thing of which he was increasingly certain, it was that Sophy could not long ignore the tug of the tender, honest emotions that flowed so vibrantly in her veins.

Unlike Elizabeth, who was a victim of her own wild passions, Sophy was a victim of her own heart. But she was a woman and she lacked the strength necessary to protect herself from those who would abuse her nature. She needed him to take care of her.

The trick now was to make her understand that she not only needed him, she could trust him with her love.

That thought brought the image of the black metal ring to mind. Julian scowled in the darkness of the carriage. He did not like the idea that Sophy had taken to wearing the memento of her sister. Not only was it unattractive, as he had told her, but it was obvious she was using it to remind herself that it was never wise to give one's heart to a man who did not love in return.

Daregate emerged from the card room as Julian walked into his club and took a seat near a bottle of port. There was a glitter of cold amusement in Daregate's eyes when he spotted his friend. One look at his face and Julian knew word of what had happened at Leighton Field had leaked out.

"There you are, Ravenwood." Daregate clapped him on the shoulder and dropped into the nearest chair. "I was worried about you, my friend. Breaking up duels is a dangerous business. Could have gotten yourself shot. Women and pistols don't mix well, you know."

Julian fixed him with a quelling look that had predictably little effect. "How did you hear such nonsense?"

"Ah, so it is true," Daregate observed with satisfaction. "I thought it might be. Your lady is just spirited enough to do it and God knows Featherstone is eccentric enough to meet her."

Julian gave him a steady look. "I asked how you heard of it?"

Daregate poured himself a class of port. "By merest chance, I assure you. Do not worry. It is not common knowledge and will not become so."

"Featherstone?" Julian vowed he would make good on his promise to ruin her if she had, indeed, talked.

"No. You may rest assured she is saying nothing. I got it secondhand from my valet who happened to attend a boxing match this afternoon with the man who handles Featherstone's horses. He told my man he'd had to get Featherstone's rig out before dawn this morning."

"And just how did the groom figure out what was happening?"

"It seems the groom is dallying with one of Featherstone's maids who told him a certain lady of quality had taken exception to one of Featherstone's little blackmail notes. There was no name mentioned, which is why you are safe. Apparently the principals in this little matter all have some sense of discretion. But when I heard the story I guessed Sophy might have been the offended party. Can't think of any other lady with the guts to do such a thing."

Julian swore under his breath. "One word of this to anyone else and I swear I will have your head, Daregate."

"Now, Julian, don't be angry." Daregate's smile was fleeting but surprisingly genuine. "This is just servant gossip and will soon die out. As I said, there was no name mentioned. As long as none of the principals talk, you can brazen it out. If I were you, I'd be flattered. Personally, I cannot think of any other man who's wife would think enough of him to call out his mistress."

"Ex-mistress," Julian muttered. "Kindly remember that. I have spent altogether too much time explaining that fact to Sophy."

Daregate chuckled. "But did she comprehend your explanations, Ravenwood? Wives can be a little thickheaded about such things."

"How would you know? You've never bothered to marry."

"I am capable of learning by observation," Daregate said smoothly.

Julian's brows lifted. "You may have ample opportunity to put what you have learned into practice if that uncle of yours continues in his present ways. There's a good chance he'll either get himself killed by a jealous husband or else he'll drink himself to death."

"Either way, by the time his fate catches up with him there will be very little chance of salvaging the estate," Daregate said with sudden savagery. "He has gutted it and drained the blood from its carcass."

Before Julian could respond to that, Miles Thurgood strolled over to sit down nearby. It was obvious he had overheard Daregate's last words.

"If you do inherit the title, the solution is obvious," Miles said reasonably. "You will simply have to find yourself a rich heiress. Come to think of it, that redheaded friend of Sophy's is probably going to be quite wealthy when her stepfather finally has the decency to depart to the next world."

"Anne Silverthorne?" Daregate grimaced. "I'm told she has no intention of ever marrying."

"I believe Sophy felt very much the same way," Julian murmured. He thought about the young woman in boy's garb who had been handling the pistols that morning and frowned as he recalled the red hair stuffed under a cap. "In fact, I think I can assure you that they have far too much in common. Come to think of it, you would be wise to avoid her, Daregate. She would give you as much trouble as Sophy is presently giving me."

Daregate slanted him a curious look. "I will keep that in mind. If I do inherit, I will have my hands full salvaging the estate. The last thing I would need would be a wild, headstrong wife like Sophy."

"My wife is neither wild nor headstrong," Julian stated unequivocally.

Daregate gazed at him thoughtfully. "You are right. Elizabeth was wild and headstrong. Sophy is merely high-spirited. She is nothing like your first countess, is she?"

"Nothing like her at all." Julian poured himself a glass of port. "I think it's time we changed the subject."

"Agreed," Daregate said. "The prospect of having to find myself a rich, willing heiress to marry in order to save the estate is almost enough to make me wish long life and good health to my dear uncle."

"Almost," Miles repeated with amused insight, "but not quite enough. If that estate falls into your hands we all know you will do whatever you have to do in order to save it."

"Yes." Daregate tossed back his port and reached for the bottle. "It would keep me busy, wouldn't it?"

"As I said a moment ago," Julian remarked, "I think it's time to change the subject. I have a question for both of you and I do not want either it or the answer to go beyond the three of us. Is that understood?"

"Certainly," Daregate said calmly.

Miles nodded, turning serious. "Understood."

Julian looked first at one and then the other. He trusted them both. "Have you ever seen or heard of a ring of black metal embossed with a triangle and some sort of animal head?"

Daregate and Thurgood glanced at each other and then at Julian. They shook their heads.

"Don't believe so," Miles said.

"Is it important?" Daregate asked.

"Perhaps," Julian said quietly. "Then again, perhaps not. But it seems to me that I once heard rumors of such rings being used by members of a certain club."

Daregate frowned thoughtfully. "I believe I remember

those rumors too, now that you mention them. A club formed at one of the colleges, wasn't it? The young men supposedly used black rings to signal each other. It was all very secretive and I don't recall anyone ever saying what the purpose of the club was. What makes you mention it now?"

"Sophy has come into possession of such a ring. It was given to her by—" Julian broke off. He had no right to relate the full story of Sophy's sister Amelia. "By a woman friend in Hampshire. I saw it and was curious about it because the sight of it tugged at my memory."

"Probably just an old keepsake now," Miles said easily.

"It's an unpleasant looking thing," Julian said.

"If you bothered to give your wife some decent jewelry, she would not be obliged to wear old, cast-off school rings," Daregate said bluntly.

Julian scowled at him. "This from a man who may someday seriously have to contemplate marrying for money? Do not worry about Sophy's jewelry collection, Daregate. I assure you, I am quite capable of seeing my wife properly outfitted in that department."

"About time. Pity about the emeralds, though. When are you going to announce that they have disappeared forever?" Daregate asked unrepentantly.

Miles stared. "They've disappeared?"

Julian scowled. "Stolen. One of these days they will show up at a jeweler's when somebody can wait no longer to pawn them."

"If you don't make some explanation soon, people are going to begin to believe Waycott's claim that you cannot bear to see them on another woman after having first given them to Elizabeth."

Miles nodded quickly. "Have you explained to Sophy about the emeralds having disappeared? Be most unfortunate otherwise if she were to hear Waycott's remarks about you not wanting her to have them."

"If it becomes necessary, I will explain the situation to Sophy," Julian said stonily. In the meantime she could damn well learn to wear the jewelry he did choose to give her. "About the black ring," he went on softly.

"What about it?" Daregate eyed him. "Are you worried about Sophy wearing it?"

"Can't see that there's anything to worry about other than that people will think Ravenwood's being damned stingy about giving his wife jewelry," Miles said.

Julian drummed his fingers lightly on the arm of the chair. "I would like to know a bit more about this old college club. But I do not want anyone to know I am seeking answers."

Daregate leaned back in his chair and crossed his ankles. "I've got nothing better to do. I could make a few discreet inquiries for you."

Julian nodded. "I would appreciate that, Daregate. Let me know if you get wind of anything."

"I'll do that, Ravenwood. At least it will give me something interesting to do for a change. One can get very bored with gaming."

"Don't see how," Thurgood muttered. "Not as long as one wins as frequently as you do."

Much later that night Julian sent Knapton out of his bedchamber and finished his own preparations for bed. Sophy had been home for some time, according to Guppy. She would be sound asleep by now.

Shrugging into his dressing gown, Julian picked up the diamond bracelet and the other gift he had purchased late that afternoon after the bracelet had been rejected. He collected the note he had painstakingly written to accompany the presents and started toward the connecting door.

At the last moment he remembered the gypsy scarf. Smiling, he went back to the wardrobe and found the scarf in the pocket of the black cloak.

He walked into Sophy's darkened bedchamber and put the bracelet, the other package and the note and scarf down on the bedside table. Then he took off his dressing gown and climbed into bed beside his sleeping wife.

When he put his hand on her breast she turned to him, sighing softly in her sleep and snuggled close. Julian woke her slowly with long, deep kisses that drew forth the full response of her body. Everything he had learned about her on the two previous occasions when he had made love to her, he employed now. She responded as he had hoped she would. By the time her lashes fluttered open, Sophy was already clinging to his shoulders and parting her legs for him.

"Julian?"

"Who else?" he muttered huskily as he slowly sank deeply into her damp warmth. "Do you have room in your arms tonight for a man who seeks to change his luck?"

"Oh, *Julian*."

"Tell me of your love, sweetheart," he coaxed as she lifted her hips to meet his slow, careful thrust. She felt so good, he thought. So perfect, as if she had been fashioned just for him. "Tell me how much you love me, Sophy. Say the words again."

But Sophy was already convulsing gently under him and there were no coherent words to be had from her, only the soft, vibrant cries of her release.

Julian shuddered heavily, pouring himself into her, filling her, losing himself in her.

When he finally raised his head a long time later he saw that Sophy had slipped back into a deep sleep.

Another time, he promised himself as he drifted off, another time he would have the words of love from her.

THIRTEEN

When Sophy opened her eyes the next morning the first thing she saw was the scarf of her gypsy costume draped across the pillow next to her. The diamond bracelet Julian had given her yesterday was lying on top of the scarf, its rows of silver-white stones sparkling in the early light. Under both was a large package wrapped in paper. A note had been tucked between the bracelet and the scarf.

Sophy sat up slowly, her eyes never leaving the small offering on the pillow. So Julian had known who she was last night at the masquerade ball. Had he been teasing her with all that talk about wanting to become lucky at love or had he been trying to tell her something, she wondered.

She reached over and plucked the note off the pillow. Unfolding it, she quickly read the short message inside.

My Dearest Wife:
I was told last night by a reliable source that my fortune was in my own hands. But that is not altogether true.

216

Whether or not he desires it, a man's fortune as well as his honor, frequently rest in the hands of his wife. I am convinced that in my case both of these valuable possessions are safe with you. I have no talent for scribbling sonnets or poems but I would have you wear this bracelet occasionally as a token of my esteem. And, perhaps, when you have occasion to examine the other small gift, you will think of me.

Julian's initials were scrawled boldly across the bottom of the crisp page. Sophy slowly refolded the note and stared at the glittering diamond bracelet. Esteem was not exactly love but she supposed it did imply some degree of affection.

Memories of Julian's heat and strength enveloping her in the darkness last night swept through her. She told herself not to be misled by the passion he aroused in her. Passion was not love, as Amelia had discovered to her cost.

But she had more than passion from Julian, if this note was to be believed, Sophy told herself. She was unable to quell the burst of hope that welled up within her. Esteem implied respect, she decided. Julian might be angry about the incident at dawn yesterday, but perhaps he was trying to tell her he respected her in some ways.

She got out of bed and carefully placed the bracelet in her jewelry box next to Amelia's black ring. She must be realistic about her marriage, Sophy told herself firmly. Passion and esteem were all very well as far as they went but they were not enough. Julian had made it clear last night that he wanted her to trust him with her love but he had also made it clear he would never trust any woman with his own heart.

As she turned away from the jewelry case she remembered the other package on the bed. Full of curiosity, she went back across the room, picked up the heavy gift, and hefted it. It felt like a book, she decided and that thought excited her in a way the bracelet had failed to do. Eagerly she unwrapped the brown paper covering.

Joy bubbled up inside her as she read the author's name on the impressive, leather-bound volume in her hands. She could not believe it. Julian had given her a magnificent copy of Nicholas Culpeper's famous herbal, *English Physician*. She could hardly wait to show it to Old Bess. It was a complete guide to all the helpful herbs and plants that were native to England.

Sophy flew across the room to ring for Mary. When the girl knocked at the door a few minutes later she gaped to see her mistress already half-dressed.

"Here, ma'am, what's the rush? Let me help you. Oh, do be careful, ma'am or you'll split the fine seams of that dress." Mary bustled about, taking charge of the dressing process. "Is somethin' amiss?"

"No, no, Mary, nothing is amiss. Is his lordship still in the house?" Sophy leaned down to tug on her soft leather slippers.

"Yes, ma'am, I believe he's in the library. Shall I send word you wish to see him?"

"I'll tell him myself. That's fine, Mary. I'm dressed. You may go now."

Mary looked at her in shock. "Impossible. I can't let you go out o' this room with your hair down like that ma'am. It wouldn't be right. Sit still for a minute and I'll put it up for you."

Sophy surrendered, muttering impatiently as Mary put up her hair with two silver combs and several strategically placed pins. When the last curl was in place, she bounded up from the dressing table chair, grabbed the precious herbal and practically ran out the door, down the hall and down the stairs.

Arriving breathless at the library door, she knocked once and then burst into the room without waiting for a response.

"*Julian*. Thank you. Thank you so much. You are so kind. I do not know how to convey my gratitude. This is the finest gift anyone has ever given me, my lord. You are the most generous husband in England. No, the most generous husband in the whole world."

Julian slowly closed the journal he was working on

and got cautiously to his feet. His bemused eyes went first to her bare wrist and then to the book Sophy was clutching to her bosom. "I see no sign of the bracelet so I assume it is the Culpeper that is causing all this commotion?"

"Oh, yes, Julian. It is magnificent. You are magnificent. How can I ever thank you?" Impulsively Sophy darted across the room to stand on tiptoe in front of him. Still holding the book very tightly she gave her husband a quick, shy kiss and then stepped back. "Thank you, my lord. I shall treasure this book for my entire life. And I promise I will be exactly the sort of wife you want. I will not cause you any more trouble at all. Ever."

With a last brilliant smile, Sophy turned and hurried from the room, unaware of the silver comb that slipped from her hair and fell to the carpet.

Julian watched the door close behind her and then, very thoughtfully, he touched his cheek where Sophy had kissed him. It was, he realized, the first spontaneous caress she had ever given him. He walked across the room and picked up the silver comb. Smiling very slightly, he carried it back to his desk and put it down where he could see it as he worked.

The Culpeper, he decided with deep satisfaction, had obviously been a stroke of genius. He owed Fanny for the recommendation and he made a mental note to thank her. His smile broadened as he acknowledged ruefully that he could have saved the six thousand pounds he'd spent on the bracelet. Knowing Sophy, she would probably lose it the first time she wore it—if she remembered to wear it.

Sophy was in high spirits that afternoon when she sent a message to Anne and Jane that she wished to see them. They arrived around three. Anne, vibrant in a melon-colored gown, swept into the drawing room with her customary energy and enthusiasm. She was followed by a more sedately dressed Jane. Both women undid the strings of their bonnets as they seated themselves and looked at their hostess with expectation.

"Wasn't last night lovely?" Anne said cheerfully as tea was served. "I cannot tell you how much I enjoy masquerades."

"That's because you take great pleasure in fooling others," Jane observed. "Especially men. One of these days your liking for that pastime will get you into serious trouble."

"Rubbish. Pay no attention to her, Sophy. She is in one of her lecturing moods. Now, tell us why you wished to see us on such short notice. I do hope you have some excitement for us."

"Personally," Jane remarked, picking up her cup and saucer, "I would prefer a bit of peace and quiet for a while."

"As it happens, I have a very serious matter to discuss with both of you. Relax, Jane. I do not seek any further excitement. Just a few answers." Sophy picked up the muslin handkerchief in which she had wrapped the black ring. She untied the knot and let the fabric fall away to reveal the contents.

Jane leaned forward curiously. "What a strangely designed ring."

Anne reached out to touch the embossed surface. "Very odd. And very unpleasant looking. Do not tell me your husband gave you this thing? I would have thought Ravenwood had better taste than that."

"No. It belonged to my sister." Sophy stared down at the ring lying in her palm. "It was given to her by a man. It is my goal to find him. As far as I am concerned, he is guilty of murder." She told them the full story in short, crisp sentences.

When she was finished, Anne and Jane sat staring at her for a long moment. Predictably enough it was Jane who responded first.

"If what you say is true, the man who gave your sister that ring is most certainly a monster but I do not see what you can do, even if you manage to identify him. There are, unfortunately, many such monsters running around Society and they all get away with murder."

Sophy's chin lifted. "I intend to confront him with his

own evil. I want him to know that I am aware of who and what he is."

"That could be very dangerous," Jane said. "Or, at the very least, embarrassing. You can prove nothing. He will simply scoff at your accusations."

"Yes, but he will be forced to realize that the Countess of Ravenwood knows who he is," Anne said thoughtfully. "Sophy is not without some power these days. She is becoming quite popular, you know. And she has the rather sizable degree of influence that comes from being Ravenwood's wife. If she chose to exercise a measure of her power she might very well be able to ruin the owner of that ring socially. That would be a serious punishment for any man of the *ton*."

"Assuming he belongs to polite Society," Sophy amended. "I know nothing about him, except that he was most likely one of Elizabeth's lovers."

Jane sighed. "Gossip has it that is a very long list."

"It can be shortened to include only the man who wore this ring," Sophy said.

"But first we must find out something about it. How do we go about it?" Anne asked, her enthusiasm for the project obviously growing rapidly.

"Wait, both of you," Jane implored quickly. "Think before you leap into another adventure. Sophy, you have only just recently experienced Ravenwood's anger. If you ask me, you got off quite lightly. Are you really so eager to arouse his wrath all over again?"

"This has nothing to do with Ravenwood," Sophy said forcefully. Then she smiled, remembering the herbal. "Besides, he has forgiven me for what happened yesterday morning."

Jane looked at her, astonished. "Has he really? If so, then he is far more tolerant than his reputation would lead one to believe."

"My husband is not the devil everyone thinks him," Sophy said coolly. "But to return to the business of finding the owner of the ring. The fact is, I do not intend to bother Ravenwood with this. It is a task I set for myself before I ever agreed to marry him. Lately I have foolishly allowed myself to become distracted by . . . by other things. But I am finished with those unimportant matters now and I am going to get on with this."

Anne and Jane were both studying her intently.

"You are very serious about this, aren't you?" Jane finally asked.

"Finding the owner of this ring is the most important task in my life at the moment. It is a goal I have set for myself." Sophy looked at her friends. "This time I cannot take the chance that one of you might feel obliged to warn Ravenwood about what I am doing. If you feel you cannot support me fully, I ask that you leave now."

"I would not dream of leaving you to conduct such a search alone," Anne declared.

"Jane?" Sophy smiled gently. "I will understand if you feel you should not be a part of this."

Jane's mouth thinned. "You have cause to question my loyalty, Sophy. I do not blame you. But I would like to prove to you that I truly am your friend. I will help you in this."

"Good. Then it is settled." Sophy held out her hand. "Let us seal the bargain."

Solemnly they all three clasped hands in a silent pledge and then they sat back to stare at the ring.

"Where do we begin?" Anne finally asked after a moment's close thought.

"We began last night," Sophy said and told them about the man in the black hooded cape and mask.

Jane's eyes were full of shock. "He recognized the ring? Warned you about it? Dear God, Sophy, why did you not tell us?"

"I did not want to say anything until I had your solemn promise to support me in this endeavor."

"Sophy, this means there really is something mysterious to discover about this ring." Anne picked it up and examined it closely. "Are you certain your dancing partner said nothing else? Just that the wearer could count on a most unusual type of excitement?"

"Whatever that means. He said we would meet again and then he left."

"Thank heavens you were wearing a disguise," Jane said with great depth of feeling. "Now that you know there is, indeed, some mystery attached to the ring, you must not wear it in public."

Sophy frowned. "I agree I probably ought not to wear it until we learn more about it. However, if wearing it publicly is the only way to uncover the mystery, then I may have to do so."

"No," Anne said, showing unusual caution. "I agree with Jane. You must not wear it. At least not without consulting us first. Do you promise?"

Sophy hesitated, glancing from one concerned face to the other. "Very well," she agreed reluctantly. "I will talk to you two first before wearing the ring again. Now, then, we must think about this whole matter and decide just what information we have."

"The man in the black cape implied the ring was known to certain people such as himself," Anne said slowly. "Which implies a club or group of some sort."

"There is also the implication that there is more than one ring," Sophy said, trying to remember the man's exact words. "Perhaps it is the symbol of a secret society."

Jane shuddered. "I do not like the sound of this."

"But what kind of society?" Anne asked quickly, ignoring her friend's qualms. "We need to ascertain its goals before we can figure out what sort of man would wear such a ring."

"Perhaps we can learn what type of secret society would use this sort of jewelry if we can discover the meaning of the symbols embossed on the ring." Sophy turned the black band of metal between her fingers, studying the triangle and the animal head. "But how do we go about doing that?"

There was a long pause before Jane spoke up with obvious reluctance. "I can think of one place to start."

Sophy looked at her in surprise. "Where?"

"Lady Fanny's library."

* * *

Three days later Sophy flew down the stairs, her bonnet in one hand and her reticule in the other. She hurried across the hall and was almost to the door, which a footman was hastening to open, when Julian appeared in the doorway of the library. She knew at once from the cool intent expression in his eyes that he wanted to speak to her. She stifled a groan and stopped long enough to give him a bright smile.

"Good afternoon, my lord. I see you are busily at work today," she said smoothly.

Julian folded his arms and leaned one shoulder against the doorjamb. "Going out again, Sophy?"

"Yes, my lord." Sophy put the bonnet on her head and started to tie the ribbons. "As it happens, I've promised Lady Fanny and Harriette that I would visit them this afternoon."

"You've called on them every afternoon this week."

"Only the past three afternoons, my lord."

He inclined his head. "I beg your pardon. I'm sure you're right. It probably has been only the past three afternoons. I undoubtedly lost count because it seems that every time I've suggested we go riding or take in an exhibition this week you've been flying out the door."

"Life here in town is very hectic, my lord."

"Quite a change from the country, isn't it?"

Sophy eyed him warily, wondering where all this was leading. She was anxious to be on her way. The carriage was waiting. "Did you want something, my lord?"

"A little of your time, perhaps?" he suggested gently.

Sophy's fingers fumbled with the ribbons of her bonnet and the bow went askew. "I am sorry, my lord. I fear I have promised your aunt I would be there at three. She will be expecting me."

Julian glanced over his shoulder at the clock in the library. "You have a few minutes before you must rush off. Why don't you instruct your groom to walk the horse for a short while? I really would like to have your advice on a few matters."

"Advice?" That caught her attention. Julian had not

sought her advice on anything since they had left Eslington Park.

"On some business relating to Ravenwood."

"Oh." She did not know quite how to respond to that. "Will it take long, my lord?"

"No, my dear. It won't take long." He straightened and waved her gracefully through the library door. Then he glanced back at the footman. "Tell the groom that Lady Ravenwood will be out in a while."

Sophy sat down opposite Julian's desk and struggled to untie the knot she had made in her bonnet ribbons.

"Allow me, my dear." Julian shut the library door and came across the room to deal with the tangle.

"Honestly, I do not know what it is about bonnet strings," Sophy complained, flushing slightly because of Julian's nearness. "They never seem to want to go together properly."

"Don't fret about such details. This is one of those chores a husband is skilled at performing." Julian leaned over her, his big hands very deft on the offending knot. A moment later he eased the bonnet from her curls and handed it to her with a small bow.

"Thank you." Sophy sat stiffly in the chair, the bonnet on her lap. "What sort of advice did you wish from me, my lord?"

Julian went around to the other side of the desk and casually seated himself. "I have just received some reports from my steward at Ravenwood. He says the housekeeper has taken ill and may not recover."

"Poor Mrs. Boyle," Sophy said at once, thinking of the plump tyrant who had ruled the Ravenwood household for years. "Does your steward mention whether she's had Old Bess in to look at her?"

Julian glanced down at the letter in front of him. "Yes, Bess apparently went up to the house a few days ago and said the problem is with Mrs. Boyle's heart. Even if she is fortunate enough to recover, she will not be able to take up her duties again. From here on out she must lead a quiet life."

Sophy shook her head and frowned in concern. "I am so

sorry to hear that. I imagine Old Bess has instructed Mrs. Boyle in the use of foxglove tea. It is very useful in such situations, you know."

"I would not know about foxglove tea," Julian said politely, "but I do know that Mrs. Boyle's retirement leaves me—" Julian paused and then amended his words deliberately, "it leaves *us* with a problem. A new housekeeper needs to be appointed immediately."

"Definitely. Ravenwood will soon be in chaos otherwise."

Julian leaned back in his chair. "The business of hiring a housekeeper is quite important. It is also one of those things that is somewhat outside my area of expertise."

Sophy could not resist a small smile. "Good heavens, my lord. I had no idea there was anything that lay outside your area of expertise."

Julian grinned briefly. "It has been a while since you have bothered to tease me about my lamentable arrogance, Sophy. I find I almost miss your little barbs."

Her flash of amusement faded abruptly. "We have not exactly been on the sort of terms that encourage teasing, my lord."

"No, I suppose not. But I would change that."

She tilted her head. "Why?"

"Isn't it obvious?" he asked quietly. "I find that, in addition to your teasing, I rather miss the ease of the relationship we had begun to develop at Eslington Park in the days before you felt obliged to dump tea all over our bed."

Sophy felt herself turning pink. She looked down at the bonnet in her lap. "It was not such an easy relationship for me, my lord. It's true we talked more then and we discussed matters of mutual interest but I could never forget that all you really wanted from me was an heir. It put a strain on me, Julian."

"I understand that better now since I had a chat with a certain gypsy lady. She explained to me that my wife was something of a romantic by nature. I am guilty of not having taken that into account in my dealings with her and I would like to remedy the error of my ways."

Sophy's head came up quickly, her brows drawing together in annoyance. "So now you propose to indulge my so-called tendency toward romanticism? Pray do not bother, Julian. Romantic gestures are meaningless if there is no genuine feeling behind them."

"At least give me some credit for trying to please you, my dear." He smiled faintly. "You do like the Culpeper herbal, don't you?"

Guilt assailed her. "You know I am most extremely pleased with it, my lord."

"And the bracelet?" he coaxed.

"It is very pretty, my lord."

He winced. "Very pretty. I see. Well, then, I shall look forward to seeing you wear it sometime in the near future."

Sophy brightened at once, glad to be able to offer a positive response. "I expect I shall wear it this evening, my lord. I am going to a party at Lady St. John's."

"It was too much, I suppose, to hope you did not have plans for this evening?"

"Oh, I have plans for every evening this week and next. There is always so much going on here in town, isn't there?"

"Yes," Julian said grimly, "There is. You are not obliged to attend every function for which you receive an invitation, however. I should think by now you'd be happy to spend a quiet evening or two at home."

"Why on earth would I want to spend an evening here alone, my lord?" Sophy murmured tightly.

Julian folded his hands in front of him on his desk. "I was thinking of spending the evening here, myself."

Sophy forced another bright smile. He was trying to be kind, she told herself. She did not want mere kindness from him. "I see. Another romantic gesture designed to indulge my whims? That is very generous of you, but you need not bother, my lord. I am quite able to entertain myself. As I told you, now that I have been in the city a while I have a much better understanding of how husbands and wives of the *ton* are supposed to conduct their lives. And now I really must be going. Your aunt will wonder where I am."

She stood up quickly, forgetting about the bonnet on her lap. It slipped to the floor.

"Sophy, you misunderstand my intentions," Julian said as he got to his feet and strolled around the desk to pick up the bonnet. "I merely thought we might both enjoy a calm evening at home." He adjusted the bonnet on her head and tied the ribbons neatly under her chin.

She looked up at him, wishing she knew exactly what he was thinking. "Thank you for the gesture, my lord. But I would not dream of interfering in your social life. I am certain you will be quite bored if you stayed home. Good day, my lord."

"Sophy."

The command caught her just as she put her hand on the doorknob. "Yes, my lord?"

"What about the matter of hiring a new housekeeper?"

"Tell your steward to interview Molly Ashkettle. She's been on your staff for years at Ravenwood and will make a perfect replacement for poor Mrs. Boyle." Sophy rushed out the door.

Fifteen minutes later she was ushered into Lady Fanny's library. Harriette, Jane, and Anne were already there, deep into the stack of books that had been placed on the table.

"Sorry to be delayed," Sophy apologized quickly as the others looked up from their work. "My husband wanted to discuss the matter of a new housekeeper."

"How odd," Fanny said from atop a small ladder where she was rummaging around the top shelf. "Ravenwood never concerns himself with the hiring of servants. He always leaves that to his stewards or the butler. But never mind, dear, we are making great progress with your little project."

"It's true," Anne said closing one book and opening

another. "Harriette discovered a reference to the animal head on the ring a short while ago. It is a mythical creature, which appears in a very old book of natural philosophy."

"Not a very pleasant reference, I'm afraid," Harriette said, pausing to peer over the top of her spectacles. "It was associated with some sort of nasty cult in ancient times."

"I am presently going through some old books on mathematics to see if I can find out anything about the triangle," Jane said. "I have a feeling we are very close."

"So do I," Lady Fanny said as she descended from the ladder. "Although what we will have if we do find the answers is beginning to worry me a bit."

"Why do you say that?" Sophy asked, taking a seat at the table and picking up a massive tome.

Harriette looked. "Fanny was struck with a rather vague recollection last night just before bedtime."

"What sort of recollection?" Sophy demanded.

"Something to do with a secret society of rather wild young rakehells," Fanny said slowly. "I heard about it a few years ago. I never learned the particulars, but it seems to me something was said about the members using rings to identify themselves to each other. Supposedly the whole thing started at Cambridge but some of the members kept the club going after they left the classroom. At least for a time."

Sophy looked at Anne and Jane and shook her head very slightly. They had agreed not to alarm Fanny and Harriette with the real reason they wanted to learn the secret of the black ring. As far as the older women knew, Sophy was merely curious about a family heirloom that had come into her possession.

"You say this ring was left to you by your sister?" Harriette asked, turning pages slowly.

"That's right."

"Do you know where she got it?"

Sophy hesitated, trying to think of a reasonable explanation for Amelia's possession of the ring. As usual, her mind went blank when she tried to come up with a lie.

Anne rushed glibly to the rescue. "You said she had gotten it from a great aunt who passed away many years ago, didn't you, Sophy?"

"Yes," Jane put in before Sophy was obliged to respond, "I think that was what you said, Sophy."

"Yes. That's correct. A very odd sort of aunt. I do not believe I ever met her, myself," Sophy said quickly.

"Hm. Very odd, is right," Fanny mused as she plunked down two more heavy volumes and went back to the shelf for another batch. "I wonder how she came into possession of the ring."

"We'll probably never know," Anne said firmly, giving Sophy a quelling glance as Sophy began to look increasingly guilty.

Harriette turned another page in the volume she was perusing. "Have you shown the ring to Ravenwood, Sophy? Being a man, he might know more about this sort of thing than we do."

"He has seen the ring," Sophy said, happy to be able to speak the truth at last. "He did not recognize it."

"Well, then, we must persevere on our own." Fanny selected another volume off the shelf. "I do so love a puzzle, don't you, Harry?"

Harriette smiled beatifically. "Dear me, yes. Never happier than when I'm working on a puzzle."

Four days later, Sophy, poring over an ancient treatise on mathematics with Jane, discovered the origin of the peculiar triangle on the face of the ring.

"This is it," she said excitedly as the others converged around the old volume. "Look at it. The triangle is exactly like that one on the ring, including the strange loops at each corner."

"She is right," Anne said. "What does it say about the triangle?"

Sophy frowned over the Latin. "Something to do with its being useful in certain dark ceremonies for controlling the female demons who have—" She halted abruptly as she realized what she was translating. "Oh, my goodness."

"What is the matter?" Fanny leaned over her shoulder. "Ah, I see. 'A shape most useful for controlling succubi while enjoying them in a carnal manner.' How fascinating. Leave it to men to worry about a species of female demons who molest poor helpless males in their sleep."

Harriette smiled blandly. "Fascinating, indeed. Demon prostitutes who can be controlled at the same time that one enjoys their favors. You are quite right, Fanny. Definitely a fantasy creation of the male brain."

"Here is more evidence of masculine fancy," Anne announced, pointing to another picture of the mythological creature she had researched. "The beast in the triangle is said to have uncommon powers. It can, it seems, fornicate for hours without any loss of vigor."

Fanny groaned. "I think we can now say with some certainty that Sophy's heirloom ring is, indeed, a man's ring. It seems to have been expressly designed to make a male think quite highly of his own prowess in the bedchamber. Perhaps it was meant to give him good luck in that area of his life. In any event, it is definitely not the sort of jewelry Ravenwood will want his wife wearing in public."

Harriette chuckled. "If I were you, Sophy, I would not tell your husband the meaning of the designs on that ring. Put the thing away and ask Ravenwood for the family emeralds, instead."

"I am certain your advice is excellent," Sophy said quietly, thinking she would be damned before she would ask her husband for the Ravenwood emeralds. "And I do appreciate your assistance in helping me track down the details of the ring."

"Not at all," Harriette said, beaming. "It was quite a fascinating project, wasn't it, Fanny?"

"Most instructive."

"Well, we had best be on our way," Anne said, as the women began reshelving the books. "I promised Grandmother I would help her entertain some friends at cards this evening."

"And I am supposed to put in an appearance at Lady St. John's," Sophy said, dusting off her hands.

Jane eyed her friends without a word but as soon as they were all three seated in Sophy's carriage and safely out of earshot of Lady Fanny and her companion, she spoke up. "Well? Do not keep me in suspense. This is not the end of it. I know that. What will you do next, Sophy?"

Sophy stared out the window of the carriage, lost in thought for a moment. "It seems to me that we now know two things for certain about the ring. The first is that it probably belonged to a man who was part of a secret society he probably joined at Cambridge. And the second is that the society was involved in disreputable sexual practices."

"I think you are right," Anne agreed. "Your poor sister was the victim of some man who used women very badly, indeed."

"We already knew that," Jane said. "What do we do now?"

Sophy pulled her gaze away from the street scene and looked at her friends. "It seems to me there is only one person who might know the men who wear such rings."

Jane's eyes widened. "You cannot mean—"

"Of course," Anne said quickly. "Why didn't I think of it? We must contact Charlotte Featherstone at once and see what she can tell us of the ring or the man who might have worn it. Sophy, write the note this afternoon. I will deliver it in disguise at once."

"She may not choose to respond," Jane said hopefully.

"Perhaps, but it is the only recourse I have left, other than to wear the ring in public again and see who reacts to it."

"Too dangerous," Anne said at once. "Any man who recognizes the ring and sees you wearing it might think you were involved in the cult, yourself."

Sophy shuddered, remembering the man in the black hooded cape and mask. *A most unusual type of excitement.*

No, she must be very careful not to attract further attention with the ring.

Charlotte Featherstone's answer came within hours. Anne brought it to Sophy at once. Sophy tore open the envelope with a sense of mingled dread and anticipation.

From one Honorable Woman to Another:
You flatter me by requesting what you are pleased to refer to as professional information. You say in your note that you are tracing the particulars of a family heirloom and your researches have led you to believe I may be of some assistance. I am only too happy to give you what little information I have but please allow me to tell you I do not think highly of the family member who left this ring behind. Whoever he was, he must have had a nasty streak in him.

Over the years I can recall five men who wore in my presence a ring such as you describe in your note. Two are now dead and, to be frank, the world is better off without them. The remaining three are Lords Utteridge, Varley, and Ormiston. I do not know what you plan to do next, but I advise caution. I can assure you that none of the three is good company for any woman, regardless of her station in Society. I hesitate to suggest it, but perhaps you should discuss the matter, whatever it may be, with your husband before proceeding further on your own.

The letter was signed with Featherstone's beautifully scrawled C. F.

Sophy's pulse beat faster. At last she had names, she told herself. One of these three might very well be the man who was responsible for Amelia's death. "Somehow I must contrive to encounter these three men," she said evenly to Anne.

"Utteridge, Varley, and Ormiston," Anne repeated thoughtfully. "I have heard of them. They all move freely in Society, although their reputations are not the best. Using your own connections and those of my grandmother, it should not be difficult to get invitations to the parties and routs where we might expect to find these three lords."

Sophy nodded, refolding Featherstone's note. "I can see my appointment book is going to become more crowded than ever."

FOURTEEN

Waycott was making a nuisance of himself and not for the first time. Sophy was growing increasingly annoyed with him. She frowned slightly over Lord Utteridge's shoulder as he led her out onto the dance floor and saw with relief that Waycott was apparently heading out into the gardens.

It was about time he left her alone tonight, Sophy told herself. She had finally managed an introduction and a dance with the first name on her list—the once-handsome, but now dissipated-looking, Utteridge—but it had been hard work. Ever since she had arrived at the party, Waycott had been hovering, just as he had hovered on several other occasions during the past two weeks.

It had been hard enough to discover Utteridge's likely whereabouts this evening, Sophy thought, irritated—much more difficult than she and Anne and Jane had anticipated. She did not need Waycott getting in her way on top of everything else. Luckily Anne had been able to find out the pertinent information concerning the guest list at this rout at the last minute. Sophy certainly did not want to waste the time and effort that had been involved in getting herself on the same guest list.

The information available on Lord Utteridge had been minimal.

"I'm told he's run through most of his fortune at the gaming tables and has now begun to look for a rich wife," Anne had explained earlier that afternoon. "At the moment he's trying to attract the interest of Cordelia Biddle and she's scheduled to be at the Dallimores' tonight."

"Lady Fanny should be able to get me invited," Sophy had decided and that assumption had turned out to be quite correct. Lady Fanny had been a bit startled that Sophy should want to attend a function that promised to be exceedingly dull, but she had obligingly had a word with the hostess.

"It was not the least bit difficult, my dear," Fanny had said later with a knowing look in her eye. "You are considered a prize for any hostess these days."

"The power of Julian's title, I suppose," Sophy had remarked dryly, thinking that if Anne was right she would be able to use that power to ultimately punish Amelia's seducer.

"The Ravenwood title certainly helps," Harriette had agreed, looking up from her book, "but you may as well know, my girl, that it is not entirely because you're a Countess that you're fast becoming quite the thing this season."

Sophy was momentarily startled by the observation and then she grinned. "You need not go into detail, Harry. I am well aware that I owe whatever popularity I am presently enjoying to the simple fact that even the members of the *ton* suffer from the headache, digestive problems, and assorted bilious livers. I swear, whenever I attend a party I end up writing out as many medicinal recipes as an apothecary."

Harriette had exchanged a smiling glance with Fanny and gone back to her book.

But the plan had worked and Sophy had found herself cordially welcomed that evening by a delighted hostess who had never dreamed she would be lucky enough to get the new Countess of Ravenwood to her rout. After that it had been a simple matter to track down Lord Utteridge. If it were not for Waycott's persistent petitions for a dance, all would have been going quite well.

"I would venture to say that Ravenwood must be finding you quite a change from his first wife," Utteridge murmured in a syrupy voice.

Sophy, who had been waiting anxiously for just such an opening, smiled encouragingly. "Did you know her well, my lord?"

Utteridge's smile was unpleasant. "Let us say I had the pleasure of several intimate conversations with her. She was a most entrancing woman. Quite dazzling to the senses. Fascinating, mysterious, captivating. With just a smile she could leave a man bedeviled for days. She was also, I think, very dangerous."

A *succubus*. Sophy remembered the strange design on the black ring. More than one man might have felt the need to protect himself from a woman such as Elizabeth even as he willingly fell under her spell.

"Did you visit frequently with my husband and his first wife at Ravenwood?" Sophy asked as casually as possible.

Utteridge chuckled dryly. "Ravenwood seldom entertained with his wife. At least not after the first few months of their marriage. Ah, those first few months were quite amusing for the rest of us, I must say."

"Amusing?" Sophy felt a small chill.

"Yes, indeed," Utteridge said with relish. "There were scenes and public displays aplenty during that first year, which provided endless entertainment for the *ton*. But after that Ravenwood and his wife began going their separate ways. Some say he was on the point of suing for separation and divorce when Elizabeth died."

Julian must have hated those embarrassing public scenes. No wonder he was so adamant about his new wife not becoming the focus of gossip. Sophy tried to get back to her original question. "Have you ever been to Ravenwood Abbey, my lord?"

"Twice, as I recall," Utteridge said casually. "Didn't stay

long either time, although Elizabeth could be quite charm-ing. Don't care for the country, myself. A man with my constitution does not enjoy ruralizing. I'm much more comfortable in the city."

"I see." Sophy listened carefully to Utteridge's voice and the rhythms of his speech, trying to decide if he was the man in the black cape and mask who had warned her about the ring the night of the masquerade. She did not think so.

And if Utteridge spoke the truth, she did not think he could have been Amelia's seducer. Whoever that man was he had stayed at Ravenwood on more than two occasions. Amelia had gone out to meet her lover several times over a three-month period. Of course, there was always the possibility Utteridge was lying about the frequency of his visits but Sophy could not think why he should bother to do so.

This whole business of trying to track down Amelia's seducer was going to be extremely difficult, she acknowl-edged.

"Tell me, madam, do you intend to follow in your prede-cessor's footsteps? If so, I hope you will include me in your plans. I might even consider another trip into Hampshire if you were proposing to be my hostess," Utteridge said in a dangerously smooth voice.

The barely veiled insult snapped Sophy out of her reverie. She stopped in the middle of the floor, her head tilting angrily. "Exactly what are you implying, my lord?"

"Why nothing, my dear, I assure you. I was merely asking out of curiosity. You seemed interested in the activities of the previous Countess so I wondered if, perhaps, you had, um, aspirations to live the rather reck-less life she favored."

"Not at all," Sophy said tightly. "I cannot think where you could have gotten that impression."

"Calm yourself, madam. I intended no insult. I had heard a few rumors and I must admit they piqued my curiosity."

"What rumors?" Sophy demanded, suddenly anxious. If

word had gotten out about the attempted duel between herself and Charlotte Featherstone, Julian would be furious.

"Nothing important, I promise you." Utteridge smiled with cold whimsy and casually adjusted the dangling artificial flower in Sophy's hair. "Just a little chatter about the Ravenwood emeralds."

"Oh, those." Sophy hid her relief. "What about them, my lord?"

"A few people have wondered why you've never worn them in public," Utteridge said silkily, but his eyes were piercing.

"How odd," Sophy said. "Imagine anyone wasting a moment's thought on such a mundane matter. I believe the dance is finished, my lord."

"I wonder if you will excuse me, then, madam," Utteridge said with a laconic bow as the dance ended. "I believe I am engaged for the next dance."

"Of course." Sophy inclined her head aloofly and watched as Utteridge moved off through the crowd toward a young blond, blue-eyed woman dressed in pale blue silk.

"Cordelia Biddle," Waycott said, materializing just behind Sophy. "Not a brain in her head, but I'm told her inheritance more than compensates."

"I was never led to believe men particularly valued brains in a woman."

"It's true that some men have not sufficient brains themselves to appreciate such a commodity in a female." Waycott's eyes were intent on her face. "I would venture to say that Ravenwood is one of those benighted males."

"You are wrong, my lord," Sophy said bluntly.

"Then I apologize," Waycott said. "It is just that I have seen little evidence of Ravenwood's appreciation for his charming new wife and it gives a man pause."

"What, pray tell, do you expect him to do to show his appreciation?" Sophy retorted. "Sprinkle rose petals outside our front door every morning?"

"Rose petals?" Waycott's brows lifted. "I think not. Ravenwood's not the type for romantic gestures. But I would have expected him to present you with the Ravenwood emeralds by now."

"I cannot imagine why," Sophy snapped. "My coloring is all wrong for emeralds. I look infinitely better in diamonds, don't you think?" She moved her hand in a graceful gesture that drew attention to the bracelet Julian had given her. The stones glittered on her wrist.

"You are wrong, Sophy," Waycott said. "You would look lovely in emeralds. But I wonder if Ravenwood will ever trust another woman with them? Those stones must hold many painful memories for him."

"You must excuse me, my lord. I believe I see Lady Frampton over by the window. I really should see if my digestive aid helped her."

Sophy swept off, deciding she really had had enough of the Viscount. He seemed to be at nearly every social function she was attending these days.

As she moved through the crowd it occurred to her that she should not have let Utteridge go so quickly. Even if he was not the man she wanted, he apparently knew a great deal about Elizabeth's activities and was willing to talk about them. It struck her belatedly that he might be able to provide valuable information on the other two men whose names were on Charlotte's list.

Across the room Cordelia Biddle was declining another dance with Utteridge. Utteridge, in turn, appeared about to exit into the gardens. Sophy started to weave a path toward the open doors.

"Forget Utteridge," Waycott drawled from close behind Sophy. "You can do better than him. Even Elizabeth did not dally long in that direction."

Sophy's head came around very quickly, her eyes narrowing in anger. Waycott had obviously been following her. "I do not know what you are implying, my lord, nor do I wish to have you explain your meaning. But I think it would be wise of you to cease speculating on my associations."

"Why? Because you're afraid that if word gets back to Ravenwood he will drown you in that damn pond the way he did Elizabeth?"

Sophy stared at Waycott in shock for an instant before she turned her back on him and swept through the open doorway into the cool night air of the gardens.

* * *

"The next time you drag me off to a gaming hell as miserable as this place, I trust you will have the decency to see to it that I at least have a chance at winning." Julian kept his voice to a low, annoyed growl as he turned to follow Daregate away from the table.

Behind him other players stepped forward with a studied casualness that did little to conceal the feverish excitement in their eyes. Dice clicked softly and a new game of hazard was begun. Fortunes would be won and lost tonight. Estates that had been in families for generations would fall into new hands this evening because of the luck of the toss. Julian could scarcely conceal his disgust. Lands and the privileges and responsibilities that went with them were not to be risked in a stupid dice game. He did not comprehend the mind of a man who could do such a thing.

"Stop complaining," Daregate chided. "I told you it was easier to get information out of a cheerful winner than it is from a disgruntled loser. You got what you wanted, didn't you?"

"Yes, damn it, but it cost me fifteen hundred pounds."

"A pittance compared to what Crandon and Musgrove will lose tonight. The trouble with you, Ravenwood, is that you begrudge any money not spent directly on your estates."

"You know your own attitude toward gaming would alter completely tomorrow if you inherited your uncle's title and the lands that go with it. You're no more a confirmed gamester than I am." Julian signaled for his carriage as they stepped out into the chilly evening. It was nearly midnight.

"Don't be too certain of that. At the moment I am rather devoted to the gaming tables. I fear I am rather dependent on them for my income."

"It's fortunate you have a talent for dice and cards."

"One of the more useful skills I picked up at Eton," Daregate said negligently. He leapt up into the carriage as it drew to a halt in front of the two men.

Julian followed Daregate and settled on the seat across

from his friend. "Very well, it cost me enough. Let us examine precisely what I have got for my fifteen hundred pounds."

"According to Eggers, who I must tell you, is usually quite knowledgeable in matters such as this, there are at least three or four men left who still wear the black rings," Daregate said thoughtfully.

"But we only managed to get two names out of him. Utteridge and Varley." Julian reflected on the man to whom he had just lost his money. The more Eggers had won, the more he had been willing to gossip to Daregate and Julian. "I wonder if one of them was the one who gave the ring to Sophy's friend. Utteridge, I believe, spent time at the Abbey. And so did Varley, I'm almost certain." Julian's hand clenched at his side as he forced himself to recall Elizabeth's seemingly endless list of conquests.

Daregate pretended to ignore the implications and stuck to the subject at hand. "We have a starting point, at least. Either Utteridge or Varley could be the man who gave your wife's friend the ring."

"Damn. I do not like this, Daregate. One thing is for certain, Sophy must never again wear that ring. I shall have to see to it that it is destroyed immediately." And that action, he reflected with an inner wince, was going to cause more trouble between himself and Sophy. She was obviously very attached to the black ring.

"On that point, I agree wholeheartedly. She must not wear it now that we have ascertained its meaning. But she does not know just what the ring signifies, Ravenwood. To her it is merely a keepsake. Are you going to tell her the truth?"

Julian shook his head grimly. "That the original wearer belonged to a secret club whose members placed bets on who could cuckold the highest ranking members of the *ton*? Not bloody likely. She already has a sufficiently low opinion of men in general."

"Does she really?" Daregate asked with amusement. "Then you and your lady are well matched, aren't you, Ravenwood? Your opinion of women is not particularly

high. Serves you right to be married to a woman who
returns the compliment."

"Enough, Daregate. I have more important matters to
attend to tonight than sparring with a man whose opinions
on women do not differ greatly from my own. In any
event, Sophy is different from the common run of females."

Daregate looked at him, smiling slightly in the shadows.
"Yes, I know. I was beginning to wonder if you realized
that fact, yourself. Guard her well, Ravenwood. There are
wolves in our world who would take great delight in
savaging her."

"No one knows that better than I." Julian stared out the
window of the carriage. "Where do you wish to be set
down?"

Daregate shrugged. "Brook's I suppose. I am in the
mood for a little civilized drinking after that hell we just
left. Where are you going?"

"To find Sophy. She is attending Lady Dallimore's rout
tonight."

Daregate grinned. "And no doubt reigning supreme.
Your lady is quickly becoming the rage. Walk down Bond
Street or into any drawing room these days and you will
find that half the young females in the vicinity will be in a
charming state of disarray. Ribbons dangling, hats askew,
shawls trailing on the floor. It is all quite delightful but no
one can carry it off the way Sophy does."

Julian smiled to himself. "That is because she does not
have to work at it. The style comes quite naturally to her."

Fifteen minutes later Julian glided through the crush
that filled Lady Dallimore's ballroom, searching for Sophy.
Daregate was right, he realized with mild amusement.
Most of the young women in the room appeared to have
something wrong with their attire. Hair ornaments were
stuck into curls at precarious angles, ribbons trailed to the
floor, and scarves fluttered in a deceptively haphazard
manner. He almost crushed underfoot a fan that was
dangling from a long string attached to its owner's wrist.

"Hello, Ravenwood, looking for your Countess?"

Julian glanced over his shoulder and recognized a middle-
aged Baron with whom he occasionally discussed the war

news. "Evening, Tharp. As it happens, I am looking for Lady Ravenwood. Any sign of her?"

"Signs of her all over the place, my boy. Just take a look." The portly Baron waved a hand to indicate the crowded ballroom. "Impossible to make a move without stepping on a ribbon or scarf or some such frippery. Had a chat with your lady, myself, a bit earlier. Gave me a recipe for a cordial she says will relieve my digestive problems. Don't mind tellin' you, you're damn lucky to be married to that one. She'll see to it you live to a ripe old age. Probably give you a dozen sons into the bargain."

Julian's mouth tightened at that last remark. He was not at all certain Sophy would give him those sons willingly. He remembered well that she had not wanted to be rushed into childbed. "Where did you see her last, Tharp?"

"Dancing with Utteridge, I believe." Tharp's good-natured brow creased in an abrupt frown. "Come to think of it, that ain't a particularly good situation, lad. You know what Utteridge is. An out-and-out rake. If I were you, I'd put a stop to that association at once."

Julian felt a cold feeling in the region of his stomach. How in hell had Utteridge arranged to meet Sophy? More importantly, why had he done so? "I will see to the matter at once. Thank you, Tharp."

"Pleasure." The baron's expression brightened. "Thank your Countess again for that cordial recipe, will you? Anxious to give it a try. Lord knows I'm tired of subsisting on potatoes and bread. Want to be able to sink my teeth into a nice joint of beef again."

"I'll tell her." Julian shifted direction, glancing around the room for Utteridge. He did not see the man but he did catch sight of Sophy. She was just leaving to go out into the gardens. Waycott was preparing to follow a short distance behind her.

One day soon, Julian promised himself, he really would have to do something about Waycott.

The gardens were magnificent. Sophy had heard they were Lord Dallimore's pride. Under any other circumstances she would have enjoyed the sight of them by moonlight. It was obvious that much care had been given to the carefully clipped hedges, terraces, and flower beds.

But tonight the elaborately designed greenery was making her pursuit of Lord Utteridge difficult. Every time she rounded a tall hedge, she found herself in another dead end. As she got farther from the house it became increasingly more difficult to peer into the shadows. Twice she stumbled into couples who had obviously left the ballroom seeking privacy.

How far could Utteridge wander, she asked herself in gathering irritation. The gardens were not so vast that he could lose himself in them. Then she began to wonder why he had chosen to take an extended excursion in the first place.

The answer to that occurred to her almost immediately. A man of Utteridge's character would no doubt use the privacy of the gardens for an assignation. Perhaps even now some hapless young woman was listening to his smooth blandishments and thinking herself in love. If he was the man who had seduced Amelia, Sophy told herself resolutely, she would do her best to see to it that he never married Cordelia Biddle or any other innocent heiress.

She plucked up her skirts, preparing to circle a small statue of Pan prancing in the middle of a flower bed.

"It's not wise to wander around out here alone," Waycott said from the shadows. "A woman could become quite lost in these gardens."

Sophy gasped and swung around to find the viscount staring at her from a short distance away. Her initial fright gave way to anger. "Really, my lord, must you sneak up on people?"

"I am beginning to think it is the only way I will ever be able to talk to you in private." Waycott took a couple of steps forward, his pale hair was almost silver in the moonlight. The contrast with the black clothes he favored made him look vaguely unreal.

"I do not think we have anything to talk about that requires privacy," Sophy said, her fingers tightening around her fan. She did not like being alone with Waycott. Julian's warnings about him were already ringing loudly in her head.

"You are wrong, Sophy. We have much to discuss. I want you to know the truth about Ravenwood and about Elizabeth. It is past time you learned the facts."

"I already know as much as I need to know," Sophy said evenly.

Waycott shook his head, his eyes glinting in the shadows. "No one knows the full truth, least of all you. If you had known it, you would never have married him. You are too sweet and gentle to have willingly given yourself to a monster like Ravenwood."

"I must ask you to stop this at once, Lord Waycott."

"God help me, I cannot stop." Waycott's voice suddenly turned ragged. "Do you not think I would if I could? If only it were that easy. I cannot stop thinking about it. About her. About everything. It haunts me, Sophy. It eats me alive. I could have saved her but she would not let me."

For the first time Sophy began to realize that whatever Waycott's feelings had been toward Elizabeth, they had not been superficial or fleeting. The man was clearly suffering a great anguish. Her natural sympathetic instincts were instantly aroused. She took a step forward to touch his arm.

"Hush," she whispered. "You must not blame yourself. Elizabeth was very high-strung, easily overwrought. Even those of us who lived in the countryside around Ravenwood knew that much about her. Whatever happened, it is finished. You must not agitate yourself over it any longer."

"He ruined her," Waycott said, his voice a mere thread of sound. "He made her what she became. Elizabeth did not want to marry him, you know. She was forced into the alliance by her family. All her parents could think about was the Ravenwood title and fortune. They had no regard for her sensibilities. They did not begin to comprehend her delicate nature."

"Please, my lord, you must not go on like this."

"He killed her." Waycott's voice grew stronger. "In the beginning he did it slowly, through a series of little cruelties. Then he began to grow more harsh with her. She told me he beat her several times with his riding crop—beat her as if she were a horse."

Sophy shook her head quickly, thinking of how frequently she, herself, had provoked Julian's wrath. He had never once used violence to retaliate. "No, I cannot believe that."

"It's true. You did not know her in the beginning. You did not see how she changed after she married him. He was always trying to cage her spirit and drown her inner fire. She fought back the only way she could by defying him. But she grew wild in her efforts to be free."

"Some say she was more than wild," Sophy said softly. "Some say she was mad. And if it is true, it is very sad."

"He made her that way."

"No. You cannot blame her condition on Ravenwood. Madness such as that is in the blood, my lord."

"No," Waycott said again, savagely. "Her death is on Ravenwood's hands. She would be alive today if it were not for him. He deserves to pay for his crime."

"That is utter nonsense, my lord," Sophy said coldly. "Elizabeth's death was an accident. You must not make such accusations. Not to me or anyone else. You know as well as I do that such statements can cause great trouble."

Waycott shook his head as if to clear it of some thick fog. His eyes seemed to become a shade less brilliant. He ran his fingers through his pale hair. "Listen to me. I am a fool to ramble on like this in front of you."

Sophy's heart went out to him as she realized what lay behind the wild accusations. "You must have loved her very much my lord."

"Too much. More than life, itself." Waycott sounded very weary now.

"I am sorry, my lord. More sorry than I can say."

The Viscount's smile was bleak. "You are kind, Sophy. Too kind, perhaps. I begin to believe you truly do understand. I do not deserve your gentleness."

"No, Waycott, you most assuredly do not." Julian's voice sliced like a blade through the darkness as he emerged from the shadows. He reached out and removed Sophy's hand from the other man's sleeve. The diamond bracelet gleamed on her wrist as he tucked it possessively under his arm.

"Julian, please," Sophy said, alarmed by his mood.

He ignored her, his attention on the Viscount. "My wife has a weakness for those she believes to be in pain. I will not have anyone taking advantage of that weakness. Most especially not you, Waycott. Do you comprehend my meaning?"

"Completely. Good night, madam. And thank you." Waycott bowed gracefully to Sophy and strode off into the darkness of the gardens.

Sophy sighed. "Really, Julian. There was no need to cause a scene."

Julian swore under his breath as he led her swiftly back along the path toward the house. "No need to cause a scene? Sophy, you do not appear to comprehend how close you are to making me lose my temper tonight. I have made it very clear to you I do not want you seeing Waycott under any circumstances."

"He followed me out into the garden. What was I supposed to do?"

"Why the devil did you go out into the garden alone in the first place?" Julian shot back.

That brought her up short. She could not tell him about her attempt to get information from Lord Utteridge. "It was very warm inside the ballroom," she said carefully, trying to stick to the truth so that she would not humiliate herself by getting caught in an outright lie.

"You should know better than to leave the ballroom alone. Where is your common sense, Sophy?"

"I am not quite certain, my lord, but I begin to suspect that marriage might have a very wearing effect on that particular faculty."

"This is not Hampshire where you can safely go traipsing off on your own."

"Yes, Julian."

He groaned. "Whenever you use that tone I know you are finding me tiresome. Sophy, I realize that I spend a great deal of my time lecturing you, but I swear you invite every word. Why do you insist on getting yourself into these situations? Do you do it just to prove to both of us that I cannot control my own wife?"

"It is not necessary to control me, my lord," Sophy said distantly. "But I am beginning to believe you will never understand that. No doubt you feel the need to do so because of what happened with your first wife. But I can assure you, no amount of control exercised by you would have been sufficient to save her from destroying herself. She was beyond your control or anyone else's. She was, I believe, beyond human help altogether. You must not blame yourself for being unable to save her."

Julian's strong hand closed heavily over her fingers on his arm. "Damn. I have told you I do not discuss Elizabeth. I will say this much: God knows I failed to protect her from whatever it was that drove her to such wildness and perhaps you are right. Perhaps no man could have contained her kind of madness. But you may be certain I will not fail to protect you, Sophy."

"But I am not Elizabeth," Sophy snapped out, "and I promise you, I am not a candidate for Bedlam."

"I am well aware of that," Julian said soothingly. "And I thank God for it. But you do need protection, Sophy. You are too vulnerable in some ways."

"That is not true. I can take care of myself, my lord."

"If you are so damned skilled at taking care of yourself, why were you succumbing to Waycott's tragic little scene?" Julian snapped impatiently.

"He was not lying, you know. I am convinced he cared very deeply for Elizabeth. He certainly should not have fallen in love with another man's wife, but that does not alter the fact that his feelings for her were genuine."

"I will not argue the fact that he was fascinated by her. Believe me, the man was not alone in his affliction. There is no doubt, however, that his actions tonight were merely a ploy to gain your sympathy."

"What is wrong with that, pray? We all need sympathy on occasion."

"With Waycott, it would have been the first step into a treacherous sea. Given the smallest opportunity, Sophy, he will suck you under. His goal is to seduce you and throw the fact of your seduction in my face. Need I be more blatant about it than that?"

Sophy was incensed. "No, my lord, you are quite clear on the subject. But I think you may also be quite wrong about the Viscount's feelings. In any event, I give you my solemn vow I will not be seduced by him or anyone else. I have already promised you my loyalty. Why do you not trust me?"

Julian bit off a frustrated exclamation. "Sophy, I did not mean to imply you would willingly fall for his ruse."

"I believe, my lord," Sophy went on, ignoring his efforts to placate her, "that the least you can do is to give me your solemn assurance that you accept my word on the subject."

"Damn it, Sophy, I told you, I did not mean—"

"Enough." Sophy came to an abrupt halt in the middle of the path, forcing him to stop also. She looked up at him with fierce determination. "Your vow of honor that you will trust me not to get myself seduced by Waycott or anyone else. I will have your word, my lord, before I go another step with you."

"Will you, indeed?" Julian studied her moonlit face for a long moment, his own expression as remote and as unreadable as ever.

"You owe me that much, Julian. Is it really so hard to say the words? When you gave me the bracelet and Culpeper's herbal you claimed you held me in esteem. I want some proof of that esteem and I am not talking about diamonds or emeralds."

Something flickered in Julian's gaze as he lifted his hands to cup her upturned face. "You are a ferocious little thing when your sense of honor is touched on the quick."

"No more ferocious than you would be, my lord, if it was your honor that was being called into question."

His brows rose with casual menace. "Are you going to call it into question if I fail to give you the answer you want?"

"Of course not. I have no doubt but that your honor is quite untarnishable. I want assurance from you that you have the same degree of respect for mine. If esteem is all you feel for me, my lord, then, by heaven, you can give me some meaningful evidence of your regard."

He stood silent another long moment, gazing down into her eyes. "You ask a great deal, Sophy."

"No more than you ask of me."

He nodded slowly, reluctantly, conceding a major point. "Yes, you are right," he said quietly. "I do not know any other woman who would argue the issue of honor in such a fashion. In fact, I do not know any women who even concern themselves with the notion."

"Perhaps it is only that a man pays no heed to a woman's feelings on the subject except on those occasions when her loss of honor threatens to jeopardize his own."

"No more, I beg you. I surrender." Julian raised a hand to ward off further argument. "Very well, madam, you have my most solemn vow that I will put my full faith and trust in your womanly honor."

A tight knot of tension eased inside Sophy. She smiled tremulously, knowing what it had cost him to make the concession. "Thank you, Julian." Impulsively she stood on tiptoe and brushed her mouth lightly against his. "I will never betray you," she whispered earnestly.

"Then there is no reason we should not do very well together, you and I." His arms closed almost roughly around her, pulling her close against his lean, hard length. His mouth came down on hers, heavy and demanding and strangely urgent.

When Julian finally raised his head a moment later, there was a familiar look of anticipation in his eyes.

"Julian?"

"I think, my most loyal wife, that it is time we went home. I have plans for the remainder of our evening."

"Do you, indeed, my lord?"

"Most definitely." He took her arm again and led her toward the ballroom with such long strides that Sophy was obliged to skip to keep pace. "I believe we will take our leave of our hostess immediately."

But when they walked through the front door of their own house a short time later, Guppy was waiting for them with a rare expression of grave concern.

"There you are, my lord. I was just about to send a footman to find you at your club. Your aunt, Lady Sinclair, has apparently taken very ill and Miss Rattenbury has twice sent a message requesting my lady's assistance."

FIFTEEN

Julian prowled his bedchamber restlessly, aware that his inability to sleep was a direct result of the knowledge that Sophy was not next door in her own room. *Where she should be*. He ran a hand through his already tousled hair and wondered exactly when and how he had arrived at a state of affairs in which he could no longer sleep properly if Sophy was not nearby.

He dropped into the chair he had commissioned from the younger Chippendale a few years ago when both he and the cabinetmaker had been much taken with the Neoclassic style. The chair was a reflection of the idealism of his youth, Julian thought in a rare moment of insight.

During that same era, which now seemed so far in the past, he had been known to argue the Greek and Latin classics until late at night, involve himself in the radical liberal politics of the Reform Whigs and even thought it quite necessary to put bullets in the shoulders of two men who had dared to impugn Elizabeth's honor.

Much had changed in the past few years, Julian thought. He rarely had time or inclination to argue the classics these days; he'd come to the conclusion that the Whigs, even the liberal ones, were no less corrupt than the Tories; and he had long since acknowledged that the notion of Elizabeth having any honor at all was quite laughable.

Absently he smoothed his hands over the beautifully worked mahogany arms of the chair. Part of him still responded to the pure, classic motifs of the design, he realized with a sense of surprise. Just as part of him had insisted on trying a few lines of poetry to go with the diamond bracelet and the herbal he had given Sophy. The verse had been rusty and awkward.

He had not written any poetry since Cambridge and the early days with Elizabeth and in all honesty he knew he'd never had a talent for it. After one or two tries he had impatiently crumpled the paper in his fist, tossing it aside in favor of the brief note he had finally written to accompany the gifts to Sophy.

But that was not the end of it, apparently. Tonight he had received further, disquieting evidence that some of his youthful idealism still survived even though he had done everything he could to crush it beneath the weight of a cynical, realistic view of the world. He could not deny that something in him had responded to Sophy's demand for proof that he respected her sense of honor.

Julian wondered if he should have agreed to let her spend the night with Fanny and Harriette. Not that he could have influenced her decision to do so, he reflected wryly. From the moment Sophy had received Guppy's message, she had been unswervable in her determination to go immediately to Fanny's bedside.

Julian had not argued the matter. He was genuinely worried about his aunt's condition. Fanny was eccentric, unpredictable, and occasionally outrageous, but Julian realized he was quite fond of her. Since the death of his elderly parents, she had been the only member of the Ravenwood clan he genuinely cared about.

After receiving the message, Sophy had delayed only long enough to change her clothes and wake her maid. Mary had bustled about, packing a few necessities while

Sophy had collected her medicine chest and her precious copy of Culpeper's herbal.

"I am almost out of several herbs," she had fretted to Julian in the carriage that he had ordered to take her to Fanny's. "Perhaps one of the local apothecaries can provide me with some good quality chamomile and Turkish rhubarb. It is a shame that Old Bess is so far away. Her herbs are by far the most reliable."

At Fanny's they had been greeted at the door by a distraught Harriette. It was the sight of the normally placid Harriette in a state of anxiety that brought home to Julian how ill his aunt must be.

"Thank God you are here, Sophy. I have been so worried. I wanted to send for Doctor Higgs but Fanny won't hear of it. She says he is nothing but a charlatan and she will not allow him through the door of her room. I cannot blame her. The man loses more patients than he saves. But I did not know what else to do except send for you. I do hope you don't mind?"

"Of course I do not mind. I will go to her immediately, Harry." Sophy had bid Julian a hasty farewell and flown up the stairs, a footman hurrying behind her with her medicine chest.

Harriette turned back to Julian who was still standing in the hall. She looked at him anxiously. "Thank you for allowing her to come out like this at such a late hour."

"I could not have stopped her, even had I wished to do so," Julian said. "And you know I am fond of Fanny. I want her to have the best care and I rather agree with her about the doctor. The only remedies Higgs knows are bleeding and purging."

Harriette sighed. "I fear you are right. I have never had great faith in bleeding and believe me, poor Fanny does not need any further purging. She has already experienced quite enough of that sort of treatment because of this vile ailment she had contracted. Which leaves only Sophy and her herbs."

"Sophy is very good with her herbs," Julian said reassuringly. "I can personally testify to that. I have the healthiest, most robust staff in town this season."

Harriette smiled distractedly at the small attempt at humor. "Yes, I know. Our staff is getting along very well, too, thanks to her various recommendations. And my rheumatism is much more manageable since I began using Sophy's recipe for it. Whatever would we do without her now, my lord?"

The question brought Julian up short. "I don't know," he said.

Twenty minutes later Sophy had reappeared at the top of the stairs long enough to inform everyone that she believed Fanny's distress to be caused by bad fish at dinner and that it would take hours to treat her and monitor her progress. "I will definitely be staying overnight, Julian."

Knowing there was nothing else to be done, Julian had reluctantly returned home in the carriage.

The restlessness had set in almost as soon as he had dismissed Knapton and finished preparing to climb into a lonely bed.

He was wondering if he should go down to the library to find a dull book when he remembered the black ring. Between his concern over discovering Sophy in the gardens with Waycott and Fanny's illness, Julian realized he had temporarily forgotten the damned ring.

Daregate was right. It must be gotten rid of immediately. Julian determined to remove it from Sophy's small jewelry case at once. It made him uneasy even to think about it being in her possession. She was far too likely to give into the impulse to wear it again.

Julian picked up a candle and went through the connecting door. Sophy's bedchamber seemed empty and forlorn without her. The realization brought home to him just how accustomed he was now to having her in his life. Her absence from her bed was more than enough to make him curse all sellers of bad fish. If it were not for Fanny's illness, he would even now be making love to his stubborn, gentle, passionate, *honorable* wife.

Julian walked over to the dressing table and opened the lid of the jewelry case. He stood for a moment surveying Sophy's meager collection of jewelry. The only item of value in the case was the diamond bracelet he had given her. It was carefully placed in a position of honor on the red velvet lining.

She needed a pair of earrings to go with the bracelet, Julian decided.

Then his gaze fell on the black ring in the corner of the chest. It was resting on top of a small, folded slip of paper. The mere sight of the ring aroused a quiet anger in Julian. Sophy knew the ring had been given to her sister by a heartless rake who had no compunction about seducing the innocent. But even she could not know how dangerous the band of metal was or what it represented.

Julian reached into the case and picked up the ring. His fingers touched the folded paper underneath. Motivated by a new uneasiness, he picked it up also and unfolded it.

Three names were written on the paper: Utteridge, Varley, and Ormiston.

The embers of Julian's quiet anger leaped into the white hot flames of fury.

"Will she truly be all right?" Harriette stood by the side of Fanny's bed, anxiously studying her friend's pale face. After hours of spasmodic vomiting and intestinal pain, Fanny had finally fallen into an exhausted sleep.

"I believe so," Sophy said, mixing another pinch of herbs in a glass of water. "She has gotten rid of most of the noxious food that was in her stomach and as you can see, she is no longer in much pain. I will keep watch on her until morning. I am almost certain the crisis has passed but I cannot be completely sure yet."

"I will stay here with you."

"There is no need for you to do that, Harry. Pray get some sleep. You are as exhausted as Fanny is."

Harriette brushed that advice aside with a casual flick of her hand. "Nonsense. I could not possibly sleep knowing Fanny might still be in danger."

Sophy smiled in understanding. "You are a very good friend to her, Harry. Fanny is most fortunate to have you."

Harriette sat down in a bedside chair, absently adjusting her purple skirts. "No, no, Sophy. You have it backward. I am the one who is fortunate to have Fanny for my dearest friend. She is the joy of my life—the one person in the world to whom I can say anything, no matter how silly or wise. The one with whom I can share the smallest bit of gossip or the most monumental news. The one in whose presence I can cry or laugh or with whom I can occasionally indulge in a bit too much sherry."

Sophy sat down in the chair on the opposite side of the bed and studied Harriette with sudden understanding. "She is the one person on the face of the earth with whom you can be free."

Harriette smiled brilliantly for a moment. "Yes. Quite right. The one person with whom I can be free." She touched Fanny's limp hand as it lay on the embroidered counterpane.

Sophy's gaze followed the small gesture and she sensed the love implicit in it. A familiar sense of longing flared within her and she thought of her relationship with Julian. "You are very fortunate, Harry," she said softly. "I do not think there are many married people who share the bonds that you enjoy with Fanny."

"I know. It is sad but perhaps understandable. How could a man and a woman possibly understand each other the way Fanny and I do?" Harriette asked simply.

Sophy laced her fingers together in her lap. "Perhaps," she said slowly, "perhaps complete understanding is not necessary if there is genuine love and mutual respect and a willingness to be tolerant."

Harriette looked at her sharply and then asked gently. "Is that what you hope to find with Ravenwood, my dear?"

"Yes."

"I have said before, he is a good man as men go, but I do not know if he can give you what you want. Fanny and I watched helplessly at Elizabeth burned out most of the warm qualities in him that you seek to tap. Personally, I am not sure if any man is capable of giving a woman the things she truly needs."

Sophy's fingers clenched more tightly together. "He is my husband and I love him. I do not deny that he is arrogant and stubborn and exceedingly difficult at times,

but he is, as you say, a good man, an honorable man. He
takes his responsibilities seriously. I would never have
married him if I had not been certain of that much.
Indeed, at one time I thought never to marry at all."

Harriette nodded in companionable understanding.
"Marriage is a very risky venture for a woman."

"Well, I have taken the risk. Somehow or other, I hope
to find a way to make it work." Sophy smiled slightly as
she recalled the scene between herself and Julian in the
garden earlier that evening. "Just when I am convinced all
is hopeless, Julian shows me a ray of light and I regain my
enthusiasm for the venture."

Fanny stirred and opened her eyes sometime shortly
after dawn. She glanced first at Harriette who was snoring
softly in the nearest chair and smiled a weary smile of
deep affection. Then she turned her head and saw Sophy,
who was yawning hugely.

"I see I have been well attended by my guardian
angels," Fanny remarked, sounding weak but otherwise
much like her old self. "I'm afraid it has been a long night
for both of you. My apologies."

Sophy chuckled, stood up and stretched. "I collect you
are feeling much better now?"

"Infinitely better, although I vow I shall never eat cold
turbot dressing again." Fanny levered herself up against
the pillows and extended her hand to take one of Sophy's.
"I cannot thank you enough for your kindness, my dear.
Such an unpleasant sort of illness to have to deal with. I
don't know why I could not have suffered from something
more refined such as the vapors or an agitation of the
nerves."

The soft snoring from the other chair halted abruptly.
"You, my dear Fanny," Harriette announced as she came
rapidly awake, "are not likely to ever suffer from the
vapors or anything the least bit similar." She leaned forward to take her friend's hand. "How are you feeling my
dear? You gave me quite a scare. Please do not do that
again."

"I shall endeavor not to repeat the incident," Fanny
promised.

Sophy saw the undisguised emotion in the expressions of the two women and felt a sense of wonder. The affection between Fanny and Harriette was beyond that of friendship, she realized with sudden insight. She decided it was time to take her leave. She was not certain she fully understood the close association between Julian's aunt and her companion, but she was definitely certain it was time to give them both some privacy.

She rose to her feet and began repacking her medicine chest.

"Would you mind very much if I asked your butler to have your carriage brought around?" she asked Fanny.

"My dear Sophy, you must have breakfast," Harriette said immediately. "You haven't had any sleep and you simply cannot leave this house without nourishment."

Sophy looked at the tall clock in the corner and shook her head. "If I hurry, I will be able to join Julian for breakfast."

Half an hour later Sophy walked into her own bedchamber, yawned again and decided that bed was infinitely more appealing than breakfast. She had never been so exhausted in her life. She sent Mary out of the room with assurances that she did not need any assistance and sat down at the dressing table. A night spent in a chair had not done much to improve her tendency toward dishevelment, she thought critically. Her hair was a disaster.

She reached for her silver backed brush and the glint of diamonds caught her eye. She frowned, startled to discover she had left the lid of her jewelry case open. She had been in a dreadful hurry last night. She must have accidentally forgotten to close the case after removing the diamond bracelet and placing it inside.

Sophy started to shut the lid and then realized with horror that the black ring and the slip of paper containing the three names were gone.

"Looking for these, Sophy?"

At the sound of Julian's cold question, Sophy leaped to her feet and whirled around to see Ravenwood standing in the open doorway between the bedchambers. He was dressed in breeches and his favorite pair of polished Hessians and he was holding the black metal ring in one hand. In the other he held a familiar-looking slip of paper.

Sophy stared first at the ring and then into Julian's gemlike eyes. Dread assailed her. "I do not understand, my lord. Why did you take the ring from my jewelry case?" Her words sounded brave and calm but their tone did not reflect the way she was feeling. Her knees went weak as she realized the significance of Julian's having found the list of names.

"Why I took the ring is a long story. Before we go into it, perhaps you will be good enough to tell me how Fanny is doing?"

Sophy swallowed. "Much recovered, my lord."

He nodded and walked into the room to seat himself in the chair near the window. He put the ring and the piece of paper down on the table beside him. Morning light reflected dully on the black metal.

"Excellent. You are a most accomplished nurse, madam. Now that particular matter is out of the way, there is nothing to distract you from telling me precisely what you are doing with this list of names."

Sophy sank back down onto the dressing table chair and folded her hands in her lap while she tried to think how to handle this unexpected turn of events. Her mind was fogged from the long, sleepless night. "I collect you are angry with me again, my lord?"

"Again?" His brows rose in their characteristic intimidating fashion. "You are implying, I suppose, that I spend a good portion of my time with you in that mood?"

"It seems that way, my lord," Sophy said unhappily. "Whenever I think we are making progress in our association, something arises to ruin everything."

"And whose fault is that, Sophy?"

"You cannot blame it all on me," she declared, knowing she was getting near the end of her tether. It was all too much. "I doubt if you will take this into consideration, but I would like to remind you that I have had a long, trying night. I have had virtually no sleep and really am not up to an inquisition. Do you think we might postpone this until after I have had a nap?"

"No, Sophy. We are not going to postpone this discussion another minute. But if it is any consolation to you, rest assured we face each other on equal terms. I, too, did not get much sleep last night. I spent most of the time trying to envision where and how you had got hold of this list and why you connected it to the ring. What the devil do you think you're doing? How much do you know about these men and what in bloody hell did you plan to do with the information you have on them?"

Sophy eyed him warily. Something in the way he had phrased his questions made her realize he knew as much if not more about the ring and the list than she did. "I have explained to you that the ring was given to my sister."

"I know that already. And the list of names?"

Sophy chewed on her lower lip. "If I tell you about the list I fear you are going to be even more angry than you already are, my lord."

"You do not have any choice. Where did you get the list of names?"

"From Charlotte Featherstone." There was no point denying any of it now. She had never been good at lying even when she was at her best and this morning she was simply too exhausted to make the attempt. Besides, it was obvious Julian already knew too much.

"Featherstone. Damnation. I ought to have guessed. Tell me, my dear, do you expect to have any reputation left at all once it becomes known that you are socializing with a member of the demimonde or do you simply not care that the gossips will have a carnival with you once this gets out?"

Sophy looked down at her hands. "I did not speak to her directly. A friend of mine sent her the message. Miss Featherstone responded most discreetly. She really is very pleasant, Julian. I think I would probably enjoy her as a friend."

"And she would no doubt find you extremely amusing," Julian said brutally. "An endless source of entertainment for someone as jaded as herself. What was the nature of the message you sent to her?"

"I wished to know if she had ever seen a ring such as that one and if so, who had worn it." Sophy met his gaze defiantly. "You must realize, my lord, that this was all business relating to the project I told you about."

"What project was that?" he demanded.

"On top of everything else, you do not even listen to me half the time, do you? I am referring to the project I said would keep me busy and out of your way. I informed you that I intended to pursue my own interests, remember? Do you recall my telling you that I was going to be exactly the sort of wife you wanted? That I would stay out of your way and not cause you any trouble? I promised you that after you made it clear you were not interested in my love and affection."

"Damn it, Sophy, I never said that. You deliberately misunderstood me."

"No, my lord, I did not misunderstand you."

Julian stifled a muttered oath. "You are not going to distract me now, by God. We will return to that issue later. At the moment I am interested only in what you learned of the ring."

"Through some investigations I did in Lady Fanny's library, I was able to discover that the ring was most likely one worn by members of a certain type of secret society."

"What type of secret society, Sophy?"

"I have the impression you already know the answer to that, my lord. It was a society whose members very probably preyed upon women. Once I had ascertained that much, I applied to Charlotte Featherstone for information about the men who might have been a part of that club. I assumed she moved in a circle of Society that might bring her into contact with that type of man. And I was right. She knew of three who had at one time or another worn the ring in her presence."

Julian's eyes narrowed. "God save us. You are trying to track down Amelia's lover, aren't you? I should have guessed. And what in hell did you think you would do with him once you found him?"

"Ruin him socially."

Julian looked blank. "I beg your pardon?"

Sophy shifted uneasily in her chair. "He is obviously one of the hunters you warned me about, Julian. One of the male members of the *ton* who preys on young women. Such men value their social status above all else, do they not? They are nothing without it because without it they lack access to the prey they seek. I intend to deprive whoever wore that ring of his social connections, if at all possible."

"Before God, I swear your audacity leaves me breathless. You do not have an inkling of the danger, do you? Not even the smallest notion of what you are dealing with. How can you be so knowledgeable about arcane matters such as your medicinal herbs and yet be so unbelievably stupid about affairs in which your reputation and even your life may be at stake?"

"Julian, there is no risk involved, I promise you." Sophy leaned forward earnestly, hoping to reason with him. "I am going about this in a cautious manner. My plan is to arrange to meet the three men on that list and question them."

"Question them. Dear God. *Question* them."

"Very subtly, of course."

"Of course." Julian shook his head in disbelief. "Sophy, allow me to inform you that your talent for subtlety and deliberate subterfuge is akin to that of my skill for embroidery. Furthermore, the three men on that list are out-and-out bastards—rakehells of the worst sort. They cheat at cards, seduce any woman who falls into their path, and have a sense of honor that is lower than that of a mongrel dog. In fact, it would be safe to say the dog's notion of honor would be infinitely more acceptable. *And you thought to interrogate these three?*"

"I intend to use deductive logic to determine which of them is guilty."

"Any one of the three would slice you to ribbons without a moment's hesitation. He would ruin you long before you could ruin him." Julian's voice was tight with fury.

Sophy's chin came up. "I do not see how he could do that as long as I am careful."

"Lord, give me strength," Julian said through his teeth. "I am dealing with a mad woman."

What was left of Sophy's self-control snapped. She leaped to her feet, her hand sweeping out to snatch the nearest hard object. Her fingers closed around the crystal swan on her dressing table.

"Damn you, Julian, I am not a *mad woman*. Elizabeth was a mad woman but I am not. I may be silly and stupid and naive in your view, but at least I am not mad. By God, my lord, I will force you to stop confusing me with your first wife if it is the last thing I accomplish on this earth."

She hurled the ornament at him with all her strength. Julian, who had started to rise at the beginning of her tirade, barely managed to dodge the small missile. It flew past his shoulder and crashed against the wall behind him. He ignored the impact and crossed the room in three long strides.

"Have no fear, madam," he said fiercely as he swept Sophy off her feet and into his arms. "I am in no danger of confusing you with Elizabeth. It would be a complete impossibility. You are, believe me, Sophy, totally and completely unique. You are a paradox in so many ways it defies description. And you are quite right. You are not mad. I am the one who is fast becoming a candidate for Bedlam."

He strode toward the bed and dumped her unceremoniously down onto the counterpane. As she bounced there, her hair tumbling free of its moorings, he sat down on the edge of the bed and began to yank off his boots.

Sophy was incensed. "What do you think you are doing?"

"What does it look like I am doing? I am seeking the only cure I can find for my affliction." He stood up and unfastened his breeches.

She gazed at him in shock as his heavy manhood sprang free. He was already fully, magnificently erect. Belatedly she gathered her confused senses and started to wriggle off the other side of the bed.

Julian reached over quite casually and wrapped one big

hand around her wrist, effectively halting her retreat. "No, madam, you are not leaving just yet."

"You cannot mean to . . . to bed me now, Julian," Sophy said angrily. "We are in the midst of an argument."

"There is no point arguing with you further. You are beyond reason. And so am I, it seems. Therefore I think we shall try a different means of terminating this unpleasant discussion. If nothing else is achieved, I might at least obtain some temporary peace."

SIXTEEN

Sophy watched, torn between love and a seething anger, as the last of Julian's clothes hit the floor. He kept his grip on her wrist as he finished the process of undressing himself and then he tumbled her down onto her back.

Naked, he loomed over her, caging her between his strong hands. His eyes gleamed and his hard face was set in the stark lines of masculine arousal.

"I will tell you this once more and once more only," he said as he began the process of removing her clothing. "I have never mistaken you for Elizabeth. Calling you a mad woman was a figure of speech, nothing else. I meant no real insult. But it is imperative that you understand I cannot allow you to seek your own vengeance."

"You cannot stop me, my lord."

"Yes, Sophy," he muttered as he tugged her gown off, "I can and I will. Although I understand very well why you're skeptical on that point. Thus far I have given you little reason to believe me capable of fulfilling all my duties as your husband. You have cut a blazing swath through town, have you not? And poor, blundering crea-

267

ture that I am, I always seem to be following about ten paces behind, desperately trying to catch you. But this mad dashing about is at an end, my dear."

"Are you threatening me, Julian?"

"Not at all. I am merely explaining that you have finally gone too far. But you needn't worry. You have my word that I will do whatever it takes to protect you." He untied the tapes of her pleated cambric chemisette.

"I do not need your protection, my lord. I have learned my lesson well. Husbands and wives of the *ton* are supposed to go their own ways. You are not to involve yourself in my life, nor I in yours. I have told you I am willing to live by the codes of so-called polite Society."

"That is nonsense and you know it. God knows there is no way I could ignore you, even if I wished to do so." He finished removing the last of her clothing, and paused to sweep the length of her with his heated gaze. "And, my sweet Sophy, I have no wish to ignore you."

She felt the passionate hunger in him and the answering response in herself and knew that he was right. In bed, at least, neither of them could possibly ignore the other. A sudden suspicion came to her as his hand smoothed the curve of her thigh.

"You would not beat me," she said slowly.

"No?" He smiled, a brief, flashing, wickedly male smile that was as sensual as the movements of his hands on her body. "Beating you might be interesting." He gently squeezed her buttock.

Sophy felt herself warming quickly under his touch and shook her head with grave certainty. "No. You are not the type to lose control over your emotions and resort to violence against a woman. I told Lord Waycott as much when he claimed you had beaten your first wife."

Julian's captivating smile vanished. "Sophy, I do not wish to discuss either Waycott or my first wife just now." He lowered his head to close his teeth gently around one taut nipple. His fingertips brushed the tawny fleece below the gentle swell of her stomach.

"But while I am certain you would not use a crop on

me," Sophy continued breathlessly as she felt his finger part her with great care, "it occurs to me that you might not be above using other means to . . . to ensure I do your bidding."

"You may be right," Julian conceded, apparently unconcerned by her logic. He kissed her throat, the curve of her shoulder and finally her lips. He lingered over her mouth a long while until she was moaning softly and clinging to him. Then he raised his head slightly to meet her eyes. "Are you worried about the tactics I might use to convince you to follow my advice, my sweet?"

She glared up at him, struggling to think clearly while her body concentrated only on the pleasure it was receiving at his hands. "Do not think you can control me in this fashion, my lord."

"What fashion?" He slipped two fingers deeply into her and separated those two fingers very slowly, opening her completely.

Sophy gasped and felt herself tighten with excitement. "*This* fashion."

"Never. I would not presume to believe that I am such a skillful lover that I could actually convince you to abandon all your fine principles for me." He withdrew his fingers with excruciating slowness. "Ah, sweetheart. You flow like warm honey for me."

"Julian?"

"Look at me," he whispered. "Look at how hard and ready I am for you. Did you know that the mere scent of you is enough to arouse me like this? Touch me."

She sighed with longing, unable to resist his sensual plea. When her fingers curled gently around his thick shaft she felt him pulse in reaction. She nuzzled his chest. "I still do not think this is a proper way to settle our differences, my lord."

He sat up and put his hands around her waist. "No more conversation, Sophy. We will talk later." He lifted her up and held her so that she knelt, facing him. "Spread your legs and mount me, sweetheart. Ride me. I will be your stallion and you will be the one who controls the passion in both of us."

Sophy clung to his shoulders, her eyes widening as she adjusted to the new position. She braced herself as she felt his manhood brush her softness. She liked this position, she decided. It was exciting to be on top. "Yes, Julian. Oh, yes, please."

"Take as much or as little as you wish. Take it as quickly or as slowly as you wish. I am at your command."

An exuberant thrill coursed through Sophy as she realized that it was up to her to set the pace. She lowered herself carefully over his thrusting hardness, savoring the slow penetration. She heard his deep, muffled groan of desire and her hands tightened on his shoulders.

"Julian."

"You are so lovely in your passion," he whispered tightly. "Soft and flushed and so willing to give me everything." He covered her throat with damp, warm kisses as she continued to lower herself until he filled her completely.

Sophy waited a moment, letting her body accept him, feeling herself tightening around him. Then, cautiously at first, she began to move.

"Yes, my sweet lady. Oh, God, yes."

She felt Julian swelling within her, felt herself growing unbearably taut. She clutched at him, her nails raking his shoulders and her eyes closed with the delicious tension. She concentrated only on finding the perfect rhythm that would unleash the wild, soaring release. Nothing else mattered in that moment but the joy of taking her own pleasure while she pleasured Julian. She felt infinitely powerful, brimful of a woman's unique strength.

"Tell me of your love, sweetheart. Say the words." Julian's voice was soft and coaxing and urgent. "I need the words. It has been too long since you said them. You give me so much, little one, can you not give me a few simple words? I will treasure them forever."

A tight, hot tingling sensation began to uncoil within Sophy. She was beyond reason, beyond thought, beyond everything but her own emotions. The words he sought were ready on her lips.

"I love you," she whispered. "I love you with all my heart. *Julian*."

She convulsed softly around him, the small tremors of her climax rippling outward, sweeping her away on a golden tide. In the distance she heard Julian's answering growl of response, felt the sudden rigidity of the bunched muscles in his shoulders and, finally, the shattering power of his own release.

For a moment they hung suspended in a timeless realm where nothing could interfere with the pure intimacy of their union. And then, with a low, satisfied groan, Julian sprawled back onto the pillows, bringing Sophy down across his chest.

"Do not ever again think that I could possibly confuse you with Elizabeth," he said without opening his eyes. "With her there was no peace, no satisfaction and no joy to be found under any circumstances. Not even . . . never mind. It's no longer important. But believe me when I say she gave nothing of herself. She took everything and then demanded more. But you give yourself so completely, my sweet. It is a special kind of enchantment. I do not think you can even imagine how good it feels to be on the receiving end of your generosity."

It was the most he had ever said on the subject of his first wife. Sophy decided that she did not really want to hear any more. Julian was hers now. They were bound together. And if what she had begun to suspect this past week were true, she even now held a part of him within her.

Sophy stirred, crossed her arms on his chest and looked down at him. "I am sorry I threw the swan at you."

He opened one eye at that and then grinned up at her. "I am certain that in the years ahead there will be other times when you will be obliged to remind me that you do, indeed, possess a woman's temper."

Sophy widened her eyes innocently. "I would not want you to ever grow complacent, my lord."

"I am sure you will save me from such a fate." He laced his fingers through her hair and pulled her face

close to his. He took her mouth in a brief, rough kiss
and then freed her. His eyes grew serious. "Now, then,
madam, as we are both in a calmer state of mind, just as
I predicted, it is time to conclude the discussion we
began earlier."

A great deal of Sophy's languid pleasure vanished as reality
returned in a rush. "Julian, there is nothing more to be said
on the subject. I must continue with my inquiries."

"No," he said quite gently. "I cannot permit you to do
so. It is far too dangerous."

"You cannot stop me."

"I can and I will. I have made my decision. You will
return to Ravenwood tomorrow."

"*I will not go back to Ravenwood.*" Shocked and furious,
Sophy pushed herself away from him and scrambled to the
edge of the bed to retrieve her clothing. Clutching her
gown in both hands, she faced him warily. "You tried once
before to banish me to the country, my lord. It was not a
successful effort then and I warn you it will not be
successful this time." Her voice rose. "Do you think I will
surrender to your dictates just because of what transpires
between us in bed?"

"No, although it would certainly make matters easier if
you did."

The calm in his voice was far more alarming than his
earlier anger had been. It occurred to Sophy that her
husband was at his most dangerous not when he was in a
temper but when he was in this mood. She shielded
herself behind her clothing and watched him uneasily.
"My honor demands that I complete my task. I intend to
find and punish the man who caused Amelia's death. I
thought you understood and accepted my feelings regarding honor, my lord. We had an agreement."

"I do not deny your feelings on the subject but
there is a problem because your sense of honor puts
you in conflict with my own. My honor demands that I
protect you."

"I do not need your protection."

"If you believe that, then you are more hopelessly naive
than I had thought. Sophy, what you are doing is extreme-

ly dangerous and I cannot allow you to continue. That is all there is to it. You will tell your maid to begin packing at once. I will finish my business here in town and join you as soon as possible at Ravenwood Abbey. It is time we went home. I am weary of the city."

"But I have barely begun my detecting work. And I am not at all weary of the city. In fact, I am learning to enjoy town life."

Julian smiled. "That I can well believe. Your influence is showing up in all the best ballrooms and drawing rooms, madam. You have become a leader of fashion. Quite an accomplishment for a female who was a disaster during her first season."

"Julian, do not try to put me off with flattery. This is a matter of the greatest importance to me."

"I realize that. Why else would I risk making such an unpopular decision on your behalf? Believe me, I am not looking forward to having more table ornaments hurled at my head."

"I will not go back to Hampshire, my lord, and that is final." Sophy faced him with stubborn determination.

He sighed. "Then I shall undoubtedly soon be obliged to keep an appointment of my own at Leighton Field."

Sophy was dumbfounded. "What are you saying, Julian?"

"That if you stay here in town, it is only a matter of time before I will find it necessary to defend your honor in the same way you once attempted to defend mine."

She shook her head in wild denial. "No, no, that is not true. How can you suggest such a thing? I would never do anything to make it necessary for you to call out another man. I have told you that. You said you believed me."

"You do not understand. It is not your word I would doubt, Sophy. It is the insult to you that I would be obliged to avenge. And make no mistake. If I allow you to play dangerous games with men like Utteridge and Varley and Ormiston, the insults will soon be made."

"But I would not allow them to insult me. I would not put myself into such a position, Julian. I swear to you I would not."

He smiled fleetingly. "Sophy, I know you would not willingly do anything dishonorable or compromising. But these men are quite capable of manipulating events so that an innocent woman does not stand a chance. And once that had happened, I would have to demand satisfaction."

"No. Never. You must not even suggest such a possibility. I cannot bear to think of you engaging in a duel."

"The possibility already exists, Sophy. You have talked to Utteridge, have you not?"

"Yes, but I was most discreet. He could have had no notion of what I was trying to learn."

"What did you talk about?" Julian pressed quietly. "Did you mention Elizabeth by any chance?"

"Just in passing, I swear it."

"Then you will have aroused his curiosity. And that, my naive little innocent, is the first step toward disaster with a man of Utteridge's character. By the time you have finished questioning Varley and Ormiston, I will be up to my neck in dawn appointments."

Helplessly, Sophy stared at him. She recognized a trap when she saw one and this particular trap had no exit. She could not possibly allow Julian to risk his life in a duel over her honor. The very thought made her shudder with fear. "I promise you, I will be most extremely careful, my lord," she tried weakly, but she knew the argument was useless.

"There is too much risk involved. The only intelligent course of action now is to get you out of town. I want you safe in the countryside with your friends and family."

Sophy surrendered, tears burning in her eyes. "Very well, Julian. I will leave if you feel there is no other way. I would not have you risk a bullet because of my actions."

Julian's gaze softened. "Thank you, Sophy." He reached out and caught a teardrop on the end of his finger. "I know it is a great deal to ask of a woman whose notion of honor is as strong as my own. Believe me when I say I do understand your desire for vengeance."

Sophy impatiently wiped away her tears with the back of her hand. "It is just so blasted unfair. Nothing is going the way I had thought it would when I agreed to marry you. Nothing. All my plans, all my dreams, all the things I hoped for, the things we contracted for between us. All has come to naught."

Julian watched her in brooding silence for a long moment. "Are things really so bad, Sophy?"

"Yes, my lord, they are. On top of everything else, I have reason to believe I may be breeding." She did not look back at him as she fled toward the screen at the other end of the room.

"*Sophy!*" Julian surged up off the bed and went after her. "What did you just say?"

Sophy sniffed back a few more of the wretched tears as she stood on the other side of the screen and tugged on her dressing gown. "I am quite certain you heard me."

Julian swept the screen aside, ignoring it as it clattered to the carpet. His gaze riveted on her stubbornly averted face. "You are with child?"

"Quite possibly. I realized this week that it has been much too long since my last monthly flux. I will not know for certain for a while longer, but I suspect I am, indeed, carrying your babe. If so, you should be quite content, my lord. Here I am pregnant and off to the country where I cannot cause any further disturbance in your life. You will have gotten everything you wanted out of this marriage. An heir and no trouble. I trust you will be satisfied."

"Sophy, I don't know what to say." Julian raked a hand through his hair. "If what you suspect is true, then I cannot deny I am well pleased. But I had hoped . . . that is, I had thought you would perhaps—" He broke off and fumbled awkwardly for the rest of his sentence. "I would have had you happier about the whole thing," he finally managed lamely.

Sophy glared at him from under her brows, the last of her tears drying up in the face of his typical male arrogance. "You assumed, no doubt, that the prospect of impending motherhood would turn me into a sweet-tempered, contented wife? One who would be quite willing to give up all her personal aspirations in favor of devoting herself full time to running your country houses and rearing your children?"

Julian had the grace to redden. "I had hoped it would make you more content, yes. Please believe me, I would have you happy in this marriage, Sophy."

"Oh, do go away, Julian. I want a bath and a rest." Fresh tears burned in her eyes. "There is much to be done if I am to be carted off to Hampshire tomorrow."

"Sophy." Julian made no move to leave the bedchamber. He stood there watching her with an oddly helpless expression. "Sophy, please do not cry." He opened his arms.

Sophy glowered at him a moment longer through her watery eyes, hating this new lack of control over her emotions. Then, with a gulping sob she walked straight into Julian's arms. They closed tightly around her as she proceeded to dampen his bare chest with her tears.

Julian held her until the storm subsided. He did not try to cheer her or soothe her or scold her. He simply folded her tightly against his strength and kept her there until the last of the wrenching sobs had faded.

Sophy recovered herself slowly, aware of the comforting warmth of Julian's embrace. It was the first time he had ever held her other than to kiss or to make love to her, she realized, the first time he had offered her something other than passion. She did not move for a long while, savoring the feel of his big palm moving soothingly up and down her spine.

Finally, with great reluctance, she pushed herself away from him. "I beg your pardon, my lord. I do not understand myself lately. I assure you, I hardly ever cry." She did not look at him as she stepped back. Instead she busied herself groping for the handkerchief that ought to have been in the pocket of her dressing gown. When she could not locate it, she muttered a small oath.

"Is this what you are looking for?" Julian scooped up the square of embroidered cotton from where it had fallen on the carpet.

Chagrined at the thought that she could not even manage to keep a handkerchief properly placed in her pocket, Sophy snatched it from his hand. "Yes, thank you."

"Allow me to get you a fresh one." He walked over to her dressing table and found another handkerchief.

When he handed it to her with an air of grave concern she blew into it with great energy, wadded it up and shoved it into her pocket. "Thank you, my lord. Please excuse such a depressing display of emotion. I do not know what came over me. Now, I really must have my bath. If you will forgive me, I have a great many details to attend to."

"Yes, Sophy," Julian said with a sigh. "I will forgive you. I only pray that someday you will forgive me." He picked up his clothes and walked out of the room without another word.

Much later that night Julian sat alone in the library, legs outstretched before him, a bottle of claret on the table beside him. He was in a devil of a mood and he knew it. The house was quiet now for the first time in hours. Up until a short time ago it had been busy with the bustle of Sophy's travel preparations. The commotion had depressed him. It was going to be lonely here without her.

Julian helped himself to another glass of claret and wondered if Sophy was crying herself to sleep. He had felt like a brute this morning when he had told her he was sending her back to Ravenwood Abbey but he also knew he had no choice. Once he had learned what she was up to, he'd had no option but to get her out of the city. She was wading into dangerous waters and she had no knowledge of how to keep herself from drowning.

Julian swallowed a mouthful of claret and speculated on whether or not he ought to feel guilty for the way he had manipulated Sophy that morning. At the very beginning of the confrontation in her bedchamber he had quickly realized there was no way she would respond to logical arguments about her own safety. Her personal sense of honor overrode such considerations. And he could not bring himself to use physical force to get her to do the reasonable thing.

He had, therefore, fallen back on the only other approach he could think of even though he had not been at all certain it would be effective. He had used her feelings for him to maneuver her into doing as he wished.

It had been a heady shock to watch her stalwart defenses crumple so swiftly when he had warned her that her actions might force him to risk his life in a duel. She must truly be in love with him. No other emotion could be powerful enough to overcome her deep sense of honor. For his sake she had abandoned her quest for vengeance.

Julian felt at once humbled by the obvious strength of her feelings and simultaneously exultant. There was no doubt but that Sophy had given herself to him—*belonged* to him, in ways that, until now, he had never believed possible.

But even as he gloried in that realization, he was grimly aware that she was very unhappy and he was the cause. *It is just so blasted unfair. Nothing is going the way I had thought it would when I agreed to marry you.*

Now, on top of everything else, she was quite possibly pregnant. He winced as he recalled that one of the things she had asked of him was not to be rushed into childbed.

Julian sank lower in the chair and wondered if he would ever be able to redeem himself in Sophy's eyes. It seemed in that moment that he had done everything wrong, right from the beginning. *How did a man go about convincing his wife that he was worthy of her love?* he asked himself. It was a problem he had not ever imagined having to solve and after all that had passed between himself and Sophy there was every chance the tangle could never be resolved.

The door opened behind him. Julian did not glance around the wings of his chair. "Go on to bed, Guppy and send the rest of the staff to their rooms. I intend to stay in here a while and there is no point in any of you staying up. I will see to the candles."

"I have already told Guppy and the rest of the staff to

retire for the night," Sophy said, quietly closing the door.

Julian froze at the sound of her voice. Then he slowly put down his glass and got to his feet to face her. She looked very slender and fragile in a pink, high-waisted gown. It was difficult to believe she might be pregnant, Julian thought. Her hair was piled high on her head and anchored with a ribbon that was already beginning to untie itself. She smiled her gentle, beguiling smile.

"I thought you would be in bed by now," Julian said gruffly. He wondered at her mood. She was not crying, nor did she appear about to argue or scold or plead. "You need rest for your journey."

"I came to say good-bye to you, Julian." She halted in front of him, her eyes luminous.

A rush of relief went through him. Apparently she was no longer as distraught as she had been earlier. "I will be joining you soon," he promised.

"Good. I shall miss you." She traced the folds of his carefully folded cravat. "But I would not have us part with ill feelings."

"I assure you, there are no ill feelings. At least not on my part. I only want what is best for you. You must believe that, Sophy."

"I realize that. You are very thickheaded at times and stubborn and arrogant but I know you truly believe you are trying to protect me. But most importantly, I will not have you risking your life for me."

"Sophy? What are you doing?" He watched in amazement as she began untying the snowy white cravat. "Sophy, I swear to you that your going to the Abbey truly is the best possible course of action. It will not be so bad there, my dear. You will be able to see your grandparents and surely you have friends you will wish to invite for a visit."

"Yes, Julian." The cravat came free in her hands and she began unbuttoning his jacket.

"If you are indeed with child the country air will be much healthier for you than that of the city," he contin-

ued, frantically searching his mind for other good reasons
to encourage her willingness to leave.

"No doubt you are right, my lord. The air of London
seems to be constantly brown, does it not?" She started to
work on his white shirt.

"I am certain I am right." The novelty of having her
undress him was affecting his senses. He was having
trouble thinking clearly. His breeches were suddenly
uncomfortably tight over his swelling shaft.

"I find that men are always quite certain they are right.
Even when they are wrong."

"Sophy?" He swallowed heavily as her fingertips found
his bared chest. "Sophy, I know you find me arrogant on
occasion, but, I assure you—"

"Please do not say anything else, Julian. I do not want
to talk about the logic of my returning to the Abbey and I
do not want to discuss your unfortunate tendency toward
arrogance." She stood on tiptoe and offered her slightly
parted lips. "Kiss me."

"Oh, God, Sophy." He took her soft mouth hungrily,
dazed by his good fortune. Her mood seemed to have
changed completely and although he did not begin to
comprehend why, he was not about to question the turn of
events.

When she pressed herself more closely against him, he
managed to collect his senses long enough to speak once
more. "Sophy, darling, let us go upstairs. Quickly."

"Why?" She nuzzled his throat.

Julian stared down at her ruffled curls. "Why?" he
repeated. "You ask me that at this stage of events? Sophy, I
am on fire for you."

"The entire household is in bed. We are quite alone. No
one will bother us."

It finally dawned on him that she was quite prepared to
make love right there in the library. "Ah, Sophy," he
said, half-laughing, half-groaning, "you are indeed a
woman of many surprises." He pulled the ribbon from her
hair.

"I would have you remember me well while we are
parted, my lord."

"There is nothing on this earth that could ever make me forget you, my sweet wife." He picked her up and carried her over to the sofa.

He set her down on the cushion and she smiled up at him with timeless feminine promise. When she held out her arms, Julian went into them with unquestioning eagerness.

A few minutes later when he found the sofa too confining, Julian rolled off onto the carpet, taking Sophy with him. She followed happily, the curves of her bare breasts and throat blushing a delectable shade of pink. Julian lay on his back, his wife stretched out sleek and naked on top of him and made a mental note to try the entire process on the floor of the library at Ravenwood Abbey at the earliest opportunity.

SEVENTEEN

Julian had been right, Sophy thought on her third day at Ravenwood. She would never admit it to him, of course, but things really were not so bad in the country. The worst part as far as she was concerned was that he was not with her.

She'd had plenty to keep her occupied in her husband's absence, however. The interior of the magnificent country house was badly in need of attention. Julian had an excellent and willing staff, but the members of it had been functioning largely without direction since Elizabeth's death.

Sophy greeted the new housekeeper with enthusiasm, pleased to see that the steward had followed the advice to promote Mrs. Ashkettle to the post. Mrs. Ashkettle was equally pleased to see a familiar face in charge and they both threw themselves into a frenzy of supervising the cleaning, repairing, and general freshening up of the entire house.

Sophy invited her grandparents for the evening meal on

the third day and discovered the pleasure of presiding over her own table.

Her grandmother exclaimed happily over the magic Sophy had wrought during the previous three days. "An infinite improvement, my dear. The last time we were here everything seemed so dark and gloomy. Amazing what some polishing and cleaning and fresh draperies can do."

"Food ain't bad, either," Lord Dorring announced, helping himself to a second round of sausages. "You make a fine Countess, Sophy. I believe I'll have a bit more claret. Ravenwood's cellar contains some excellent stuff. When will your husband be returning?"

"Soon, I hope. He has business to finish in the city. In the meantime, it is probably just as well he is not here. The commotion in the house for the past three days would have no doubt annoyed him." Sophy smiled at the footman to signal more claret. "There are a few more rooms that still need work." Including the bedchamber that by rights belonged to the Countess of Ravenwood, she reminded herself.

It had been a surprise to find that particular room locked. Mrs. Ashkettle had rummaged through the keys that she had inherited from Mrs. Boyle and had shaken her head in bewilderment.

"None of them seem to fit, my lady. Don't understand it. Perhaps the key's been lost. Mrs. Boyle said she was always told to stay out of that room and I've followed those instructions. But now that you're here, you'll be wantin' to move into it. Don't worry, ma'am, I'll have one of the staff see to the problem right away."

But the problem had been resolved when Sophy had come across a key buried at the back of a desk drawer in the library. On a hunch she had tried her discovery on the locked door and found that it worked perfectly. She had investigated Elizabeth's old bedchamber with deep curiosity.

She had decided immediately that she would not move in until it had been completely cleaned and aired. She could not bring herself to occupy it in its present condition. It had apparently been left untouched since Elizabeth's death.

When Lord and Lady Dorring eventually took their leave after dinner, Sophy discovered she was exhausted. She went wearily up to the room she was using and allowed her maid to prepare her for bed.

"Thank you, Mary." Sophy delicately patted away a yawn. "I seem to be very tired tonight."

"Hardly surprisin' m'lady, after all the work you've been doin' around here. You ought to take it easy, if you don't mind my sayin' so. His lordship won't be pleased if he finds out you've been workin' yourself to the bone what with you carryin' the baby and all."

Sophy's eyes widened. "How did you know about the baby?"

Mary grinned unabashedly. "Ain't no secret, ma'am. I've been lookin' after you long enough now to know certain things ain't occurred on schedule. Congratulations, if I may say so. Have you told his lordship the good news yet? He'll be pleased as pie."

Sophy sighed. "Yes, Mary, he knows."

"I'll wager that's why he sent us back to the country, then. He wouldn't want you in that filthy London air while you're breedin'. His lordship's the type who looks after his female folk."

"Yes he is, isn't he? Go on to bed, Mary. I am going to read for a while."

There were few secrets in a large household and Sophy knew it. Still, she had thought to keep her precious one about the baby quiet a while longer. She was still adjusting to the idea of being pregnant with Julian's child.

"Very good, ma'am. Shall I take Cook the ointment you promised her for her hands?"

"The ointment. Oh, dear, I nearly forgot." Sophy went quickly to her medicine chest. "I must remember to visit Old Bess tomorrow and get some fresh supplies. I did not trust the freshness of the herbs the London apothecaries stocked."

"Yes, ma'am. Well, good night, then, ma'am," Mary said

as Sophy put the container of ointment into her hand. "Cook'll be grateful."

"Good night, Mary."

Sophy watched the door close behind her maid and then she wandered restlessly over to the shelf that contained her books. She really was very tired but now that she was ready for bed she did not feel like sleeping.

But she did not feel like reading, either, she discovered as she flipped idly through a few pages of Byron's latest effort, *The Giaour*. She had purchased the volume a few days before Julian had sent her into the country and she had been eager to read it. It said a great deal about her present mood that she was now unable to work up a ready interest in the poet's latest tale of adventure and intrigue in the exotic Orient.

Turning aside from her books, her eye fell on the small jewelry case on her dressing table. The black ring was no longer in it but every time she looked at the case, Sophy thought of it and fretted a little over her thwarted plans to find Amelia's seducer.

Then she touched her still-flat belly and shuddered. There was no way she could carry out her detecting project now. She could never bring herself to put Julian's life in jeopardy because of her own desire for vengeance. He was the father of her child and she was irrevocably in love with him. Even if that had not been the case, she would have had no right to let another take risks for the sake of her own personal honor.

A part of her wondered at the ease with which she had abandoned her quest. She had been distraught and furious at the time but she was not nearly so angry now. Indeed, she suspected she was experiencing a small, niggling sense of relief. There was no doubt but that other matters were taking precedence in her life again and deep inside she longed to be able to give them her full attention.

I am carrying Julian's child.

It was still difficult to believe but each day the notion became more and more real. Julian wanted this baby, she reminded herself, on a wave of hope. Perhaps it would help strengthen the bond she sometimes allowed herself to believe was growing between them.

Sophy moved around the room, still unusually restless. She eyed the bed once more, telling herself she ought to climb into it and get some sleep and then she thought of the room down the hall, the one she planned to move into as soon as possible.

On impulse Sophy picked up a candle, opened her door and went down the dark hall to the bedchamber that had once belonged to Elizabeth. She had been inside once or twice and did not find it pleasant. It was decorated with a bold sensuality that, to Sophy's taste, was unseemly.

The underlying theme of the room had obviously been heavily influenced by a taste for chinoiserie but it had gone far beyond the normal standards of the style into a realm of dark, lush, overwhelming eroticism. When Sophy had first glanced into the bedchamber she had thought it a room ruled by the night. There was a strange, unwholesome quality about the place. She and Mrs. Ashkettle had not tarried long after getting the door open.

Holding the candle in one hand, Sophy opened the door now and found that, even though she was prepared for it, the chamber affected her again in the same way it had earlier. Heavy velvet drapes kept out all light, even that of the moon.

The designs on the black-and-green lacquer furniture were probably supposed to represent exotic, iridescent dragons but the creatures looked very much like writhing snakes to Sophy. The bed was a thickly draped monstrosity with huge clawed feet and a smothering layer of pillows. Dark wallpaper covered the walls.

It was a room that a man such as Lord Byron with his penchant for sensual melodrama might have found exciting, Sophy reflected, but one in which Julian must have felt uneasy and unwelcome.

A dragon seemed to snarl in the candlelight as Sophy moved past a tall lacquer chest of drawers. Lurid, evil-looking flowers patterned a nearby table.

Sophy shuddered with distaste and tried to imagine the

room as it would be when she was finished with it. The first thing she would do was replace the furniture and the drapes. There were several pieces in storage that would go nicely in here.

Yes, Julian must have disliked this room intensely, Sophy thought. It was definitely not done in his style at all. She had learned he favored clean, elegant, classic lines.

But, then, this had not been his room, she reminded herself. It had been Elizabeth's temple of passion, the place where she had spun her silken webs and lured men into them.

Compelled by a deep, morbid curiosity, Sophy wandered about the chamber, opening drawers and wardrobe doors. There were no personal effects left. Apparently Julian had ordered the room emptied of Elizabeth's belongings before he had locked it for the last time.

It was not until she casually opened the last of a series of tiny drawers in a lacquer chest that Sophy found the small, bound volume. She stared uneasily at it for a long moment before she opened the cover and saw that it was Elizabeth's journal.

Sophy could not stop herself. Setting the candle on the table, she picked up the small book and began to read.

Two hours later she knew why Elizabeth had been near the pond on the night of her death.

"She came to you that night, did she not, Bess?" Sophy, seated on the small bench outside the old woman's thatched cottage, did not look up as she sorted through both fresh and dried herbs.

Bess heaved a deep sigh, her eyes mere slits in her wrinkled face. "So ye know, do ye? Aye, lass. She came to me, poor woman. She was beside herself that night, she was. How did ye discover that she was here?"

"I found her journal last night in her room."

"Bah. The little fool." Bess shook her head in disgust. "This business o' the ladies o' the quality scribblin' everythin' down in their little journals is dangerous. I hope ye don't go in for it."

"No." Sophy smiled. "I do not keep a diary. I sometimes make notes about my reading, but nothing more. It is all I can do to keep up with my correspondence."

"For years I've always said no good 'll ever come of teachin' so many people readin' and writin'," Bess stated. "The real important knowledge don't come out of books. Comes from payin' attention to what's around and about us and what's in here." She tapped her ample bosom in the region of her heart.

"That may be true but unfortunately not all of us have your instincts for that kind of knowledge, Bess. And many of us lack your memory. For us, being able to read and write is the only solution."

"'Tweren't no good solution for the first Countess, was it? She put her secrets down in her little book and now ye know them."

"Maybe Elizabeth wrote down her secrets because she hoped that someday someone would find them and read them," Sophy said thoughtfully. "Maybe she took a sort of pride in her wickedness."

Bess shook her head. "More'n likely the poor woman could nay help herself. Maybe the writin' was her way o' leeching some of the poison out of her blood from time to time."

"Lord knows there was a poison of some kind in her veins." Sophy remembered the entries, some jubilant, some obscene, some vindictive, and some tragic that recorded Elizabeth's affairs. "We'll never know for certain." Sophy was silent for a moment as she sealed herbs in a series of small pouches. The late afternoon sunlight felt good on her shoulders and the smells of the woods around Bess's cottage were very sweet and soothing after the air of London.

"So now ye know," Bess said, breaking the silence after a moment.

"That she came to see you because she wanted you to rid her of the babe she was carrying? Yes, I know. But the

journal ends with that entry. The pages are all blank after
that point. What happened that night, Bess?"

Bess closed her eyes and turned her face up to the
sun. "What happened was that I killed her, God save
me."

Sophy nearly dropped a handful of dried melilot flowers.
She stared at Bess in shock. "Nonsense. I do not believe
that. What are you saying?"

Bess did not open her eyes. "I did not give her what she
wanted that night. I lied and told her I did not have the
herbs that would rid her o' the babe. But the truth was, I
was afraid to give her the kind of help she demanded. I
couldn't trust her."

Sophy nodded in sudden understanding. "Your instincts
were wise, Bess. She would have had a hold over you, if
you had done what she asked. She was the kind of person
who might have used the information to threaten you
later. You would have been at her mercy. She would have
come to you again and again, not only to rid her of future
unwanted babes but to supply her with the special herbs
she used to stimulate her senses."

"Ye know about her usin' the herbs for that reason?"

"She frequently wrote in her journal after having eaten
opium. The entries are a wild jumble of meaningless
words and flights of fancy. Perhaps it was her misuse of the
poppy that made her act so strangely."

"No," Bess said quietly. "'Twas not the work of the
poppy. The poor soul had a sickness of the mind and spirit
that could not be cured. I expect she used the syrup of the
poppy and other herbs to give herself some relief from the
endless torment. I tried to tell her once that the poppy
was very useful for physical pain but not for the kind of
pain she suffered, the kind that comes from the spirit. But
she wouldn't listen."

"Why do you say you killed her, Bess?"

"I told ye. I sent her away that night without givin' her
what she wanted. She went straight to the pond and
drowned herself, poor creature."

Sophy considered that. "I doubt it," she finally said.
"She had a sickness of the spirit, I'll grant you that, but

she had been in her particular condition on at least one previous occasion and she knew how to obtain the remedy she sought. After you turned her down, she would have simply gone to another who would have helped her, even if she'd been forced to return to London."

Bess squinted at her. "She got rid of another babe?"

"Yes." Sophy touched her own stomach in an unconscious gesture of protectiveness. "She was breeding when she returned from her honeymoon with the Earl. She found someone in London who made her bleed until she lost the babe."

"I'll wager 'twas not Ravenwood's babe she was tryin' to shed the night she drowned," Bess said with a frown.

"No. It was one of her lover's." But Elizabeth had not named him, Sophy recalled. She shivered a little as she finished tying up the last of her selections. "It grows late, Bess, and if I am not deceived, a bit cool. I had best be on my way back to the Abbey."

"Ye have all the herbs and flowers ye'll be needin' for a while?"

Sophy stuffed the small packets into the pockets of her riding habit. "Yes, I think so. Next spring I believe I will put in an herb garden of my own at the Abbey. You must give me some advice when that time comes, Bess."

Bess did not move from her bench but her aged eyes were keen. "Aye, I'll help ye if I'm still around. If not ye already know more'n enough to plant yer own garden. But somethin' tells me ye'll be busy with more that gardenin' come next spring."

"I should have known you would guess."

"That ye're breedin'? 'Tis obvious enough for them that has eyes to see. Ravenwood sent ye back to the country for the sake of the babe, didn't he?"

"Partly." Sophy smiled wryly. "But mostly, I fear, he has banished me to the country because I've been a great nuisance to him in town."

Bess frowned anxiously. "What's this? Ye have been a good wife to him, haven't ye, gal?"

"Certainly. I am the best of wives. Ravenwood is

enormously fortunate to have me but I am not always sure he realizes the extent of his good luck." Sophy picked up her horse's reins.

"Bah. Ye be teasin' me agin. Go on with ye now, afore the air gives ye a chill. Be sure to eat hearty. Ye'll be needin' yer strength."

"Do not concern yourself, Bess," Sophy said as she swung up into the saddle. "My appetite is as large and as unladylike as it ever was."

She adjusted the folds of her skirt, making certain the small packets of herbs were safely stowed and then she gave her mare the signal to move off.

Behind her Bess sat on the bench, watching horse and rider until both disappeared into the trees.

The mare needed little guidance to find the shortcut back to the main house. Sophy let the animal pick her way through the woods while her own thoughts strayed once more to the reading she had done during the night.

The tale of her predecessor's downward spiral into something very close to madness had not been particularly edifying but it had certainly made compelling reading.

Sophy glanced up and saw the fateful pond as it came into sight through a stand of trees. On a whim, she halted the mare. The animal snuffled and began searching about for something to nibble while Sophy sat still and studied the scene.

As she had told Bess, she did not believe Elizabeth had taken her own life and the journal had revealed the rather interesting fact that the first Countess of Ravenwood knew how to swim. Of course, if a woman fell into a deep body of water wearing a heavy riding habit or similar attire, she might very well drown regardless of her skill in water. The enormous weight of so much water-logged fabric would be hard to handle. It could easily drag a victim under the surface.

"What am I doing pondering Elizabeth's death?" Sophy asked the mare. "It's not as if I am bored or without enough to do already at the Abbey. This is foolishness, as Julian would no doubt be the first to tell me, were he here."

The horse ignored her in favor of munching a mouthful of tall grasses. Sophy hesitated a moment longer and then slipped down out of the saddle. Reins in hand, she went to stand at the edge of the pond. There was a mystery here and she had an intuitive feeling now that it was not unrelated to the mystery of her sister's death.

Behind her the mare nickered a faint welcome to another horse. Surprised that anyone else should be riding along this portion of the Ravenwood lands, Sophy started to turn around.

She did not move quickly enough. The horse's rider had already dismounted and moved in too close. Sophy had a brief glimpse of a man in a black mask carrying a huge, black, billowing cloak. She started to scream but the folds of the cloak swept out to engulf her and then she was imprisoned in a muffling darkness.

She lost her grip on the reins, heard the mare's startled snort and then the sound of the creature's hooves striking the ground. Sophy's captor swore viciously as the horse's hoofbeats faded into the distance.

Sophy struggled frantically within the confines of the cloak but a moment later strong cords were passed around her midsection and her legs, chaining her arms and her ankles.

The wind was knocked out of her as she was thrown across the pommel of a saddle.

"Would you kill me at this late date for what happened nearly five years ago, Ravenwood?" Lord Utteridge asked with a world weary sigh of resignation. "I did not think you were so slow when it came to this sort of thing."

Julian faced him in the small alcove off Lady Salisbury's glittering ballroom. "Do not act the fool, Utteridge. I have no interest in what happened five years ago and you know it. It is the present that matters. And make no mistake: what happens in the present matters very much."

"For God's sake, man, I have done no more than dance with your new Countess. And only on one occasion, at that. We both know you cannot call me out on such a flimsy pretext. It will create scandal where there is none."

"I can understand your anxiety about even the mildest conversation with a husband, any husband. Your reputation is such that you are unlikely to be comfortable in the company of married men." Julian smiled coldly. "It will be most interesting to see how your attitude toward the sport of cuckoldry changes once you, yourself, are married. But as it happens, I seek answers from you, Utteridge, not an appointment at dawn."

Utteridge regarded him warily. "Answers about what happened five years ago? What is the point? I assure you, I lost interest in Elizabeth after you put bullets in Ormiston and Varley. I am not a complete fool."

Julian shrugged impatiently. "I do not give a bloody damn about five years ago. I have told you that. What I want is information on the rings."

Utteridge went unnaturally still and alert. "What rings?"

Julian opened his fist and revealed the embossed black ring in his palm. "Rings such as this one."

Utteridge stared at the circlet of metal. "Where the devil did you get that?"

"That need not concern you."

Utteridge's eyes lifted reluctantly from the ring to Julian's expressionless face. "It is not mine. I swear it."

"I did not think it was. But you have one like it, do you not?"

"Of course not. Why would I want such an unremarkable object?"

Julian glanced down at the ring. "It is singularly ugly, isn't it? But, then, it symbolized an ugly game. Tell me, Utteridge, do you and Varley and Ormiston still play those games?"

"By God, man, I tell you, I have not done more than exchange a few words with your wife on the dance floor. Are you hurling accusations? If so, make them plain. Do not fence with me, Ravenwood."

"No accusations. At least, not against you. Just give me answers, Utteridge, and I will leave you in peace."

"And if I do not give them to you?"

"Why, then," Julian said easily, "we must discuss that dawn appointment you mentioned a moment ago."

"You would call me out simply because you're not getting the answers you seek?" Utteridge was clearly taken aback. "Ravenwood, I tell you, I have not touched your new bride."

"I believe you. If you had, rest assured I would not be content with putting a bullet in your arm the way I did with Ormiston and Varley. You would be dead."

Utteridge stared at him. "Yes, I can see that is a very real possibility. You did not kill anyone over the issue of Elizabeth's honor but you are obviously prepared to do so on behalf of your new lady. Tell me, why do you need answers about the ring, Ravenwood?"

"Let us merely say that I have assumed the responsibility of seeing justice done on behalf of someone whose name need not concern you."

Utteridge sneered faintly. "A cuckolded friend of yours, perhaps?"

Julian shook his head. "A friend of a young woman who is now dead along with her unborn child."

Utteridge's sneer vanished. "Are we talking about murder?"

"It depends on how you look at the matter. The one on whose behalf I am acting definitely thinks the owner of this ring is a murderer."

"But did he kill this young woman you mentioned?" Utteridge persisted.

"He caused her to take her own life."

"Some stupid little chit gets herself seduced and in trouble and now you seek vengeance for her? Come now, Ravenwood. You are a man of the world. You know that sort of thing happens all the time."

"Apparently the one I represent does not view that as a sufficiently mitigating circumstance," Julian murmured. "And I am bound to take the matter as seriously as my friend does."

Utteridge frowned. "Who are you representing? The mother of the girl? A grandparent, perhaps?"

"As I said, that need not concern you. I have told you enough to assure you that I am not going to put a bullet in you, Utteridge, unless you force me to do so. You need no more information."

Utteridge grimaced. "Perhaps I owe you something after all this time. Elizabeth was a very strange woman, was she not?"

"I am not here to discuss Elizabeth."

Utteridge nodded. "As you have approached me, I believe you already know a great deal about the rings."

"I know that you and Varley and Ormiston wore them."

"There were others."

"Now dead," Ravenwood noted. "I have already traced two of them."

Utteridge slid him a thoughtful, sidelong glance. "But there is one other whom you have not named and who is not dead."

"You will give me his name."

"Why not? I owe him nothing and if I do not tell you, I am certain you will get the name from Ormiston or Varley. I will tell you what you want to know, Ravenwood, if you will assure me that will be the end of it. I have no wish to arise at dawn for any reason whatsoever. Getting up early does not suit my constitution."

"The name, Utteridge."

Half an hour later Julian leaped down from his carriage and strode up the steps of his home. His mind was full of the information he had forced out of Utteridge. When Guppy opened the door, Julian stepped into the main hall with a short nod of greeting.

"I will be spending an hour or so in the library, Guppy. Send the staff to bed."

Guppy cleared his throat. "My lord, you have a visitor. Lord Daregate arrived only a few moments ago and is waiting for you in the library."

Julian nodded and walked on into the library. Daregate was seated in a chair, reading a book he had taken from a nearby shelf. He had also helped himself to a glass of port, Julian noticed.

"It's not even midnight, Daregate. What the devil has

pried you out of your favorite gaming hell at this hour?"
Julian crossed the room and poured himself a glass of the
port.

Daregate put down the book. "I knew you planned to
make further inquiries about the ring and I thought I
would drop by and see what you have learned. You
tracked down Utteridge tonight, did you not?"

"Could not your questions have waited until a decent
hour?"

"I do not keep decent hours, Ravenwood. You know
that."

"True enough." Julian took a chair and a healthy swallow
of port. "Very well, I will endeavor to enlighten you.
There are four members of that devilish fraternity of
seducers still alive, not the two we learned about or the
three Sophy discovered."

"I see." Daregate studied the wine in his glass. "That
would make it Utteridge, Ormiston, Varley and . . . ?"

"Waycott."

Daregate's reaction was startling. His normal appearance of languid disinterest vanished and in its place was a
new, hard expression. "Good God, man, are you certain of
that?"

"As certain as I can be." Julian set down his glass with a
controlled movement that belied his inner rage. "Utteridge
gave me the information."

"Utteridge is hardly a reliable source."

"I told him I would meet him at dawn if he were
lying."

Daregate's mouth curved faintly. "Then he no doubt was
convinced to tell you the truth. Utteridge would not have
any liking for such a challenge. But, if it is true, Ravenwood,
then there is a serious problem."

"Perhaps not. It's true Waycott has been hovering around
Sophy for weeks and he did manage to convince her to feel
some sympathy for him, but I have lectured her about his
falseness."

"Sophy does not strike me as the type to be overly
impressed with one of your lectures, Ravenwood."

Julian smiled faintly, in spite of his mood. "True enough.

Women in general have a nasty habit of believing that they and they alone can see the true nature of the downtrodden and the misunderstood. They are not inclined to give a man credit for any intuitive abilities. But when I tell Sophy that Waycott was the man who seduced her friend she will turn against him completely."

"That is not what I meant by a problem," Daregate said bluntly.

Julian scowled at his friend, aware of the seriousness in Daregate's voice. "What are you talking about, then?"

"This evening I heard that Waycott left town a day ago. No one seems to know where he was headed but I think that, under the circumstances, you must consider the possibility that he went into Hampshire."

EIGHTEEN

"You went to the old witch, just as Elizabeth did, didn't you? There is only one reason a woman would seek her out." Waycott's tone was eerily conversational as he set Sophy on her feet and pulled the cloak away from her face. He watched her with an unnatural brightness in his eyes as he slowly removed his mask. "I am quite pleased, my dear. I will be able to give Ravenwood the coup de grâce when I tell him his new Countess was determined to rid herself of his heir, just as his first Countess did."

"Good evening, my lord." Sophy inclined her head graciously, just as if she were meeting him in a London drawing room. She was still bound in the cloak but she pretended to ignore that fact. She had not spent the past weeks learning to conduct herself as befit a Countess for nothing. "Imagine meeting you here. Rather an unusual location, is it not? I have always found this place very picturesque."

Sophy gazed around the small stone chamber and tried to conceal a shudder of fear. She hated this place. He had brought her to the old Norman ruin she had loved to sketch until the day she had decided it was the scene of her sister's seduction.

The ramshackle old castle, which had always looked so charmingly scenic, now appeared like something out of a nightmare to her. Late afternoon shadows were falling outside and the narrow slits of windows allowed very little light inside. The bare stones of the ceiling and walls were darkened with traces of old smoke from the massive hearth. The place was disturbingly dank and gloomy.

A fire had been laid on the hearth and there was a kettle and some provisions in a basket. The most disturbing thing of all about the room, however, was the sleeping pallet that had been arranged against one wall.

"You are familiar with my little trysting place? Excellent. You may find it very useful in the future when you begin betraying your husband on a regular basis. I am delighted I shall be the one to introduce you to the pleasures of the sport." Waycott walked over to a corner of the room and dropped the mask onto the floor. He turned to smile at Sophy from the shadows. "Elizabeth liked to come here on occasion. It made a pleasant change, she said."

A dark premonition swept over Sophy. "And was she the only one you brought here, Lord Waycott?"

Waycott glanced down at the mask on the floor and his face hardened. "Oh, no, I used it occasionally to entertain myself with a pretty little piece from the village when Elizabeth was occupied with her own strange fancies."

Rage surged through Sophy. It had a strengthening effect, she discovered. "Who was this pretty little piece you brought here, my lord? What was her name?"

"I told you, she was just a village whore. No one important. As I said, I only used her when Elizabeth was in one of her moods." Waycott looked up from his contemplation of the mask, clearly anxious for Sophy to understand. "Elizabeth's moods never lasted long, you know. But while they were upon her, she was not herself. There were . . . other men at times. I could not tolerate watching her flirt with them and then invite them to her bedchamber. Sometimes she wanted me to join them there. I could not abide that."

"So you came here. With an innocent young woman from the village." Sophy was light-headed with her anger but she struggled desperately to conceal it. Her fate, she sensed, hinged on keeping a tight rein on her emotions.

Waycott chuckled reminiscently. "She did not remain innocent for long, I assure you. I am accounted a most excellent lover, Sophy, as you will soon discover." His eyes narrowed suddenly. "But that reminds me, my dear, I must ask you how you came by the ring."

"Yes. The ring. Where and when did you lose it, my lord?"

"I am not certain." Waycott frowned. "But it is possible the village girl stole it. She always claimed she was a member of the gentry but I knew better. She was the offspring of some village merchant. Yes, I have often wondered if she stole the ring from me while I slept. She was always after me, demanding some symbol of my *love*. Stupid chit. But how did the ring get into your hands?"

"I told you the night of the masquerade ball. May I inquire how you knew I was wearing the gypsy costume?"

"What? Oh, that. It was simple enough to have one of my footmen ask one of your maids what Lady Ravenwood planned to wear that evening. It was easy to find you in the crowd. But the ring was a surprise. Now I recall you said that you had acquired it from a friend of yours." Waycott pursed his lips. "But how does it happen that a lady of your class becomes friends with a tradesman's daughter? Did she work for your family?"

"As it happens," Sophy forced herself to breathe deeply and slowly, "we knew each other rather well."

"But she did not tell you about me, did she? You showed no signs of knowing me when we met in London."

"No, she never confided the name of her lover." Sophy looked directly at him. "She is dead now, my lord. Along with your babe. She took an overdose of laudanum."

"Stupid wench." He shrugged the issue aside with an elegant movement of his shoulders. "I am afraid I shall

have to ask you to return the ring to me. It cannot be
terribly important to you."

"But it is to you?"

"I am rather fond of it." Waycott's smile was taunting.
"It symbolizes certain victories, past and present."

"I no longer have the ring," Sophy said calmly. "I gave it
to Ravenwood a few days ago."

Waycott's eyes burned for an instant. "Why the devil
did you give it to him?"

"He was curious about it." She wondered if that would
alarm Waycott.

"He can discover nothing about it. All who wear the
ring are bound to silence. Nevertheless, I intend to have it
returned to me. Soon, my dear, you will get it back from
Ravenwood."

"It is not easy to take anything away from my husband
that he does not choose to relinquish."

"You are wrong," Waycott said triumphantly. "I have
helped myself to Ravenwood's possessions before and I
will do so again."

"You are referring to Elizabeth, I suppose?"

"Elizabeth was never his. I am referring to these." He
crossed the chamber and bent over the basket on the
hearth. When he straightened he was holding a handful of
green fire. "I brought them along because I thought you
might find them interesting. Ravenwood cannot give them
to you, my dear. But I can."

"The emeralds," Sophy breathed, genuinely astounded.
She stared at the cascade of green stones and then jerked
her eyes back to Waycott's fever bright gaze. "You've had
them all along?"

"Since the night my beautiful Elizabeth died. Ravenwood
never guessed, of course. He searched the house for them
and sent word to all the jewelers in London that if anyone
came into possession of the gems, he would willingly
double the asking price. Word has it that one or two
unscrupulous merchants tried to produce copies of the
originals in order to claim the doubled price but Ravenwood
was unfortunately not deceived. A pity. That would have

been the final irony, would it not? Think of Ravenwood saddled with false stones as well as two false wives."

Sophy straightened her shoulders, unable to resist the taunt, even though she knew it would be better if she kept silent. "I am Ravenwood's true wife and I will not play him false."

"Yes, my dear, you will. And what's more, you will do so wearing these emeralds." He let the necklace stream from palm to palm. He seemed hypnotized by the shimmering green waterfall. "Elizabeth always enjoyed it that way. It gave her a special pleasure to put on the emeralds before she got into bed with me. She would make such sweet love to me while wearing these stones." Waycott looked up suddenly. "You will like doing it that way, too."

"Will I?" Sophy's palms were damp. She must not say anything more that would goad him further she told herself. She must let him think she was his helpless victim, a meek rabbit who would not give him any resistance.

"Later, Sophy," Waycott promised. "Later, I will show you how beautiful the Ravenwood emeralds look on a false Ravenwood bride. You will see how the firelight makes them glow against your skin. Elizabeth was molten gold when she wore these."

Sophy looked away from his strange eyes, concentrating on the basket of provisions. "I assume we have a long night ahead of us, my lord. Would you mind if I had something to eat and a cup of tea? I am feeling quite weak."

"But, of course, my dear." He swept a hand toward the hearth. "As you can see, I have taken pains to ensure your every comfort. I had a meal prepared for us at a nearby inn. Elizabeth and I often picnicked here before we made love. I want everything to be just as it was with her. Everything."

"I see."

Was he as mad as Elizabeth had been, she wondered. Or simply crazed with jealousy and the effects of lost love? Either way, Sophy told herself that her only hope lay in keeping Waycott calm and unalarmed.

"You are not as beautiful as she was," Waycott observed, studying her.

"No, I realize that. She was very lovely."

"But the emeralds will help you look more like her when the time comes." He dropped the jewels into the basket.

"About the food, my lord," Sophy said tentatively. "Would you mind if I prepared us a small picnic now?"

Waycott looked out through the open door. "It's getting dark, isn't it?"

"Quite dark."

"I will build us a fire." He smiled, looking pleased with himself for having come up with the idea.

"An excellent thought. It will soon be quite chilly in here. If you would remove this cloak and the ropes that bind me I would be able to prepare the meal."

"Untie you? I don't think that is such a good idea, my dear. Not yet. I believe you are still far too likely to dash out into the woods at the first opportunity and I simply cannot allow that."

"Please, my lord." Sophy lowered her eyes, doing her best to appear weary and lacking in spirit. "I want nothing more than to prepare us a cup of tea and a bit of bread and cheese."

"I think we can manage something."

Sophy tensed as Waycott came toward her. But she stood still as he untied the ropes that secured the cloak. When the last of them came free, she inhaled a deep sigh of relief but she made no sudden move.

"Thank you, my lord," she said meekly. She took a step toward the hearth, eyeing the open doorway.

"Not so fast, my dear." Waycott went down on one knee, reached beneath the hem of her heavy riding skirt and grasped her ankle. Quickly he tied one end of the rope above her half boot. Then he got to his feet, the other end of the rope dangling from his hand. "There, now I have you secured like a bitch on a lead. Go about your business, Sophy. I will enjoy having Ravenwood's woman serve me tea."

Sophy took a few tentative steps toward the hearth,

wondering if Waycott would think it a pleasant game to yank her tied foot out from under her. But he merely went over to the hearth and lit the fire. After he had a blaze going he sat down on the pallet, the end of the rope in his hand and leaned his chin on his fist.

She could feel his eyes on her as she began investigating the provisions in the basket. She held her breath as she lifted the kettle and then exhaled in relief as she discovered it was full of water.

The shadows outside the door were very heavy now. Chilled evening air flowed into the room. Sophy brushed her hands against the folds of her skirts and tried to think which pocket contained the herbs she needed. She jumped when she felt the rope twitch around her ankle.

"I believe it is time to shut the door," Waycott said as he got up from the pallet and moved across the room. "We would not want you to get cold."

"No." As the door to freedom swung shut, Sophy fought back a wave of terror. She closed her eyes and turned her face to the flames to hide her expression. This was the man who was responsible for her sister's death. She would not allow fear to incapacitate her. Her first goal was escape. Then she would find a way to exact revenge.

"Feeling faint, my dear?" Waycott sounded amused.

Sophy opened her eyes again and stared down into the flames. "A little, my lord."

"Elizabeth would not have been quivering like a rabbit. She would have found it all a wonderful game. Elizabeth loved her little games."

Sophy ignored that as she turned her back on her captor and busied herself with the small packet of tea that had been packed in the basket. She thanked heaven for the voluminous folds of her riding habit. They acted as a screen for her hands when she retrieved a small pouch of herbs from a pocket.

Panic shot through her when she glanced down and saw that she had retrieved violet leaves instead of the herbs she needed. Hurriedly she stuffed the leaves back into a pocket.

"Why did you not sell the emeralds?" she asked, trying

to distract Waycott's attention. She sat down on a stool in
front of the hearth and made a production out of adjusting
her skirts. Her fingers closed around another small packet.

"That would have been difficult to do. I told you, every
good jeweler in London was watching for the emeralds to
appear on the market. Even if I had sold them stone, by
stone, I would have been at risk. They are very uniquely
cut gems and would have been easily recognized. But in
all truth, Sophy, I had no desire to sell them."

"I understand. You liked knowing that you had stolen
them from the Earl of Ravenwood." She fumbled with the
second packet of herbs, opening it cautiously and combin-
ing the contents with the tea leaves. Then she fussed with
the kettle and teapot.

"You are very perceptive, Sophy. It is odd, but I have
often felt that you and you alone, truly understood me.
You are wasted on Ravenwood, just as Elizabeth was."

Sophy poured the boiling water into the pot and prayed
she had used a sufficient quantity of the sleeping herbs.
Then she sat tensely on the stool, waiting for the brew to
steep. The final product would be bitter, she realized. She
would have to find some way to conceal the taste.

"Do not forget the cheese and bread, Sophy," Waycott
admonished.

"Yes, of course." Sophy reached into the basket and
removed a loaf of coarse bread. Then she spotted the small
container of sugar. Her trembling fingers brushed the
glittering emeralds as she picked up the sugar. "There is
no knife for the bread, my lord."

"I am not so foolish as to put a blade in your hands,
Sophy. Tear the bread apart."

She bent her head and did as he had instructed. Then
she carefully arranged the fragments of bread and chunks
of strong cheese on a plate. When she was finished she
poured the tea into two cups. "All is ready, Lord Waycott.
Do you wish to eat by the fire?"

"Bring the food over here. I would have you serve me
the way you do your husband. Pretend we are in the
drawing room of Ravenwood Abbey. Show me what a
gracious hostess you can be."

Calling on every ounce of composure she possessed, Sophy carried the food across the room and placed the cup in his hand. "I fear I may have added a bit too much sugar to the tea. I hope it is not too sweet for your taste."

"I like my tea quite sweet." He watched her with anticipation as she put the food in front of him. "Sit down and join me, my dear. You will need your strength later. I have plans for us."

Sophy sat down slowly on the pallet, trying to keep as much distance as possible between herself and Waycott. "Tell me, Lord Waycott, are you not afraid of what Ravenwood will do when he discovers you have abused me?"

"He will do nothing. No man in his right mind would cross Ravenwood at cards or cheat him in business but everyone knows Ravenwood will never again bestir himself to risk his neck over a woman. He has made it clear he no longer thinks enough of any woman to take a bullet for her." Waycott bit off a chunk of cheese and a swallow of tea. He grimaced. "The tea is a bit strong."

Sophy closed her eyes for a moment. "I always make it that way for Ravenwood."

"Do you? Well, in that case, I will have it the same way."

"Why do you doubt that my husband would challenge you? He fought a duel over Elizabeth, did he not?"

"Two of them. Or so legend would have it. But he engaged in those appointments during the first months of his marriage when he still believed Elizabeth loved him. After the second dawn meeting he must have realized he could neither control my sweet Elizabeth's spirit nor terrorize every man in the country so he abandoned all efforts to avenge his honor where a woman is involved."

"And that is why you do not fear him. You know he will not challenge you because of me?"

Waycott took another swallow of tea, his eyes focused intently on the fire. "Why would he challenge me over the issue of your honor when he did not bother to do so over Elizabeth's?"

Sophy sensed a thread of uncertainty in Waycott's voice.

He was trying to convince himself as well as her that he had nothing to fear from Julian. "An interesting question, my lord," she said softly. "Why would he bother, indeed?"

"You are not half so beautiful as Elizabeth."

"We have already agreed upon that." Sophy watched, her stomach knotted with tension as Waycott took another sip of tea. He drank mechanically, his mind on the past.

"Nor do you have her style or charm."

"Quite true."

"He could not possibly want you as badly as he wanted Elizabeth. No, he will not bother to call me out over you." Waycott smiled slowly above the rim of his cup. "But he may very well murder you the way he murdered her. Yes, I think that is exactly what he will do when he finds out what has occurred here today."

Sophy kept silent as Waycott took the last swallow of tea. Her own cup was still full. She held it cradled in her palms and waited.

"The tea was excellent, my dear. Now I should like some of the bread and cheese. You will serve it to me."

"Yes, my lord." Sophy got to her feet.

"But first," Waycott drawled slowly, "you will undress and put the Ravenwood emeralds around your throat. That was the way Elizabeth always did it."

Sophy went very still, searching his eyes for some signs of the herb's effect. "I do not intend to undress for you, Lord Waycott."

"But you will." From out of nowhere Waycott produced a palm-size pocket pistol. "You will do exactly as I say." He smiled his too brilliant smile. "And you will do it exactly as Elizabeth did it. I will guide you every step of the way. I will show you precisely how to spread your thighs for me, madam."

"You are as mad as she was," Sophy whispered. She took a step back toward the fire. When Waycott did nothing, she took another and another.

He allowed her to retreat nearly the length of the room and then with casual brutality he yanked on the rope that bound her ankle.

Sophy gasped as she tumbled awkwardly to the hard

stone floor. She lay there for a moment, trying to steady herself and then she looked fearfully at Waycott. He was still smiling but there was a dazed quality in his eyes now.

"You must do as I say Sophy, or I will be obliged to hurt you."

She sat up cautiously. "As you hurt Elizabeth that night by the pond? Ravenwood did not kill her, did he? You killed her. Will you murder me as you did your beautiful, faithless Elizabeth?"

"What are you talking about? I did nothing to her. Ravenwood killed her. I told you that."

"No, my lord. You have tried to convince yourself all these years that Ravenwood was responsible for her death because you do not wish to admit you were the one who killed the woman you loved. But you did. You followed her the night she went to visit Old Bess. You waited by the pond for her to return. When you realized where she had gone and what she had done, you were angry with her. Angrier than you had ever been."

Waycott staggered to his feet, his handsome face contorted with violence. *"She went to the old witch to ask for a potion to get rid of the babe, just as you did today."*

"And the babe was yours, was it not?"

"Yes, it was mine. And she taunted me, saying she no more wanted my child than she had wanted Ravenwood's." Waycott took two unsteady steps toward Sophy. The pocket pistol waved erratically in his hand. "But she had always claimed she loved me. How could she wish to get rid of my babe if she loved me?"

"Elizabeth was incapable of loving anyone. She married Ravenwood to secure a good position and all the money she needed." Sophy edged away from him on her hands and knees. She dared not rise to her feet for fear Waycott would pull the rope again. "She kept you dangling on her puppet strings because you amused her. Nothing more."

"That's not true, damn you. I was the best lover she'd ever taken to her bed. She told me so." Waycott lurched to one side and stopped. He dropped the rope and rubbed his eyes with the heel of his free hand. "What's wrong with me?"

"Nothing's wrong, my lord."

"Something is wrong. I don't feel right." His hand dropped from his eyes and he tried to focus on her. "What did you do to me, you bitch?"

"Nothing, my lord."

"*You poisoned me.* You put something in my tea, didn't you? I'll kill you for this."

He lunged at Sophy who leapt to her feet and stumbled blindly out of his path. Waycott fetched up against the stone wall near the hearth. The pistol fell, unnoticed from his hand and landed with a small clinking sound in the basket that had held the food.

Waycott turned his head to locate Sophy, his eyes wild with fury and the inevitable effects of the drug.

"I'll kill you. Just as I killed Elizabeth. You deserve to die, just as she did. Oh, God, *Elizabeth.*" He leaned against the stone wall, shaking his head in a vain effort to clear it. "Elizabeth, how could you do this to me? You loved me." Waycott began to slide slowly down the wall, sobbing. "You always said you loved me."

Sophy watched with horrified fascination as Waycott cried himself into a deep slumber.

"Murderer," she breathed, her pulse leaping with rage. "You killed my sister. As surely as if you had put a gun to her head, you killed her."

Her eyes flew to the basket on the hearth. She knew how to use a pistol and Waycott deserved to die. With an anguished sob she ran to the basket and looked down. The pistol lay atop the glittering emeralds. Sophy leaned over and scooped up the small weapon.

Holding it in both hands she whirled about to point the pistol at the unconscious Waycott.

"You deserve to die," she repeated aloud and released the pistol from its half-cocked position. The trigger, which was designed to fit into a small recess for safety's sake, dropped into firing position and Sophy's finger closed hungrily around it.

She stepped closer to Waycott, her mind summoning up the image of Amelia lying on her bed, an empty bottle of laudanum on the table beside her.

"I will kill you, Waycott. This is simple justice."

For an endless moment Sophy hovered on the brink, willing herself to pull the trigger. But it was no good. She could not find the courage to do it. With a wrenching cry of despair she lowered the pistol, returning it to the half-cocked position. "Dear God, why am I so weak?"

She put the pistol back into the basket and knelt to fumble with the rope around her ankle. Her fingers shook but she managed to free herself. She could not take the emeralds or the pistol back to Ravenwood. There would be no way to explain them.

Without a backward glance she opened the door and ran out into the night. Waycott's horse nickered softly as she approached.

"Easy, my friend. I have no time to put a saddle on you," Sophy whispered as she fitted the bridle onto the gelding. "We must hurry. Everyone will be frantic at the Abbey."

She led the gelding over to a pile of rubble that had once been a fortified wall. Standing on the heap of stones, she adjusted her skirts above her knees and scrambled up onto the horse's back. The animal snorted and danced and then accepted her unfamiliar presence.

"Do not worry, friend, I know the route to the Abbey." Sophy urged the horse into a walk and then into a gentle canter.

As she rode, she tried to think. She had to have an explanation ready for the worried staff who would be waiting for her. She remembered the sound of her mare's hoofbeats disappearing into the distance when Waycott had kidnapped her. Her horse had apparently run off and would undoubtedly have gone straight home.

A riderless horse returning to Ravenwood Abbey would mean only one thing to the stable lads. They would assume Sophy had been thrown and, perhaps, injured. Search parties would have been combing the woods around the Abbey all afternoon and evening.

It was as good a story as any, Sophy decided as she guided Waycott's horse around the pond. She certainly could not tell anyone she had been kidnapped and held captive by the Viscount Waycott.

She dared not even tell Julian the full story for she knew that Waycott had been wrong when he claimed the Earl would not engage in another duel over a woman. Julian would call Waycott out if he discovered what the Viscount had done.

Damn. I should have killed Waycott myself when I had the chance. Now there is no telling what lies ahead. And I shall be forced to lie to Julian.

She was so dreadfully inept at lying, Sophy thought fearfully. But at least she would have time to prepare her tale and learn it by heart. Julian was still safely away in London.

It was not until she saw the lights of the Abbey through the trees that Sophy realized she would have to abandon Waycott's gelding. If she was going to claim she had struggled home on foot after a riding accident she could not show up on a strange horse.

Dear heaven, there was a lot to be considered once one started conjuring tales. One thing led to another.

Reluctantly, because she still had a long walk ahead of her, Sophy slid to the ground and turned the gelding loose. A slap on the rump sent it cantering off down the path.

Sophy picked up the hem of her riding habit and started walking quickly toward Ravenwood Abbey. Every step of the way she cudgeled her brain, trying to put a believable story together for the waiting servants. She must have every bit of the tale in place or she would surely trip herself up.

But as she stepped out of the woods that surrounded the great house, Sophy realized she had a much bigger task ahead of her than she had anticipated.

Light spilled from the open doors of the front hall. Footmen and stable lads scurried about readying torches and in the moonlight Sophy saw that several saddled horses were being led from the stables.

A familiar dark-haired figure in riding boots and stained breeches stood halfway up the left staircase. Julian was issuing orders in a cold, clear voice to those around him.

It was obvious he had just arrived which meant he had left London before dawn.

Sophy knew real panic in that moment. She had been finding it difficult enough to organize a story for the servants who would be bound to believe anything she told them. But she was very much afraid she was in no condition to lie convincingly to her husband.

And Julian had always claimed he would be able to tell if she tried to deceive him.

She had no choice but to make the attempt, Sophy told herself bracingly as she started forward again. She could not allow Julian to risk his life in a duel over her honor.

"There she be, my lord."

"Aye, thank the good God, 'tis safe she is."

"My lord, my lord, look, over there at the edge of the woods. It be my lady and she's safe."

The loud cries of heartfelt relief brought everyone around to the front of the house as Sophy walked out of the woods. She wondered with a sort of wretched amusement how much of the relief her staff felt was occasioned by the fact that they had been forced to explain her absence to Julian.

The Earl of Ravenwood swung his gaze instantly toward the trees and saw Sophy in the moonlight. Without a word he loped down the stone staircase and crossed the cobbled yard to catch her roughly in his arms.

"*Sophy*. By God, you have nearly killed me with worry. Where the devil have you been? Are you all right? Are you hurt? I could thrash you for terrifying me so. What happened to you?"

Even as she reminded herself of the ordeal that lay ahead of her, a tumultuous sense of relief poured through Sophy. Julian was here and she was safe. Nothing else mattered just then. Instinctively she huddled into his strong embrace, leaning her head against his shoulder. Her arms tightened convulsively around his waist. He smelled of sweat and she knew he had driven himself as hard as he must have driven Angel.

"I was so afraid, Julian."

"Not nearly so afraid as I was when I arrived a few

minutes ago to be told your horse had returned late this afternoon without you. The servants have been searching for you all evening. I was preparing to send them out again. *Where have you been?*"

"It . . . it was all my own fault, Julian. I was on my way home from Old Bess's cottage. My poor mare was startled by something in the trees and I was not paying attention. She must have tossed me off. I hit my head and quite lost my senses for some time. I do not remember much until a short time ago." Dear God, she was rambling. Talking much too fast. She had to get hold of herself.

"Does your head still pain you?" Julian thrust his fingers gently into her tousled curls, feeling for a wound or bump. "Were there any other injuries?"

Sophy realized she had lost her riding hat somewhere along the way. "Uh, no, no, Julian, I am fine. That is to say, I have a headache but nothing to worry about. And . . . and the babe is fine," she added quickly, thinking that would take his attention off her nonexistent injuries.

"Ah, yes. The babe. I am glad to hear all is well in that regard. You will not ride again during your pregnancy, Sophy." Julian stepped back, his eyes searching her face in the moonlight. "You are quite certain you are all right?"

Sophy was too relieved that he appeared to believe her to worry just then about arguing for her right to ride again. She tried a reassuring smile and was horrified when she felt her lips quiver. She blinked quickly. "I am really quite all right, my lord. But what are you doing here? I thought you would be in London for a few more days. We had no word you would be returning this soon."

Julian studied her for a long moment and then he took her hand in his and led her back toward the anxious crowd of servants. "I had a change of plans. Come along, Sophy. I will turn you over to your maid who will see to your bath and get you something to eat. When you are yourself again, we will talk."

"About what, my lord?"

"Why, about what really happened to you today, Sophy."

NINETEEN

"We were all so worried, my lady. Scared to death somethin' had happened to you. You have no idea. The stable lads were beside themselves. When your mare comes runnin' back into the yard, they started lookin' for you right off but they couldn't find no sign. Somebody went to see Old Bess and she was as worried as the rest of us when she found out you hadn't come home."

"I am sorry to have caused so much concern, Mary." Sophy was only half-listening to her maid's description of what had happened after she had failed to return that afternoon. Her mind was on the forthcoming interview with Julian. *He had not believed her.* She ought to have known he would guess immediately that she was lying about having been thrown by the mare. What was she going to tell him now, Sophy wondered frantically.

"And then the head groom, who is always one for predictin' the crack o' doom, shakes his head and says we should start draggin' the pond for your body. Lord, I about collapsed, I did, when I heard that. But all the fuss weren't nothin' compared with what happened when his lordship arrived unexpected like. Even staff who'd been here at the Abbey during the time the first Countess was here said they hadn't ever seen his lordship in such a fury. Threatened to dismiss us one and all, he did."

A knock on the door interrupted Mary's detailed account of the afternoon's events. She went to answer it and found a maid with a tea tray. "Here, I'll take that. Run along now. Her ladyship needs rest." Mary closed the door again and set the tray down on a table. "Oh, look, Cook put some cakes on the tray for you. Have one with your tea, ma'am. It'll give you some strength."

Sophy looked at the teapot and immediately felt slightly queasy. "Thank you, Mary. I'll have the tea in a bit. I am not very hungry at the moment."

"It's the blow on the head that does it," Mary said knowledgeably. "Affects the stomach, it does. But you really should have a cup of tea, at the least, ma'am."

The door opened again and Julian walked into the room without bothering to knock. He was still wearing his riding clothes and he had obviously overheard the maid's last comment. "Run along, Mary. I'll see that she drinks her tea."

Startled by his arrival, Mary dropped a quick curtsy and backed nervously toward the door. "Yes, my lord," she said as she put her hand on the doorknob. She started to leave the room and then paused to say with a small touch of defiance. "We was all very worried about madam."

"I know you were, Mary. But she is home safe and sound now and I think you will all take much better care of her in the future, will you not?"

"Oh, yes, my lord. Won't let her out of our sight."

"Excellent. You may go now, Mary."

Mary fled.

Sophy tightened her fingers in her lap as the door closed behind her maid. "You need not terrorize the staff, Julian. They all mean well and what happened this afternoon was certainly not their fault. I—" She cleared her throat. "I've ridden that path dozens of times during the past few years. There was no reason for me to have a groom along. This is the country, not the city."

"But they did not find your poor, unconscious body lying along the path that leads to Old Bess's cottage, did they?" Julian lowered himself into a chair near the window and glanced around the room. "I see you have made several changes in here and elsewhere, my dear."

The rapid change of subject was disconcerting. "I hope you don't mind, my lord," Sophy said in a stifled voice. She had a terrible premonition that he had decided on a strategy of toying with her until her nerve broke and she confessed everything.

"No, Sophy. I do not mind in the least. I have not liked this house for some time." Julian's gaze slid back to her anxious face. "Any changes in Ravenwood Abbey will be most welcome, I assure you. How are you feeling?"

"Very well, thank you." The words seemed to stick in her throat.

"I am relieved to hear it." He stretched out his booted feet and lounged back in the chair, his big hands steepled loosely in front of him. "You had us all quite worried, you know."

"I am sorry for that." Sophy took a breath and struggled to recall the small, carefully plotted details of her tale. Her theory was that if she propped up her sagging story with a large number of specifics, she might still salvage it. "I think it was a small animal that startled my mare. A squirrel, perhaps. Normally there would have been no problem. As you know, I am a reasonably skilled rider."

"I have often admired your riding skills," Julian agreed blandly.

Sophy felt herself flushing. "Yes, well, as it happened, I had just been returning from Old Bess's and I had purchased a large quantity of herbs from her and I had the packets arranged in my skirts. I was busy adjusting them, the packets, that is, as we went along because I was afraid some of the herbs might slip out enroute, you see."

"I see."

Sophy stared at him for a few seconds, feeling mesmerized by the steady, waiting expression in his eyes. He appeared so serene and patient but she knew it was a hunter's patience she saw in him. The knowledge rattled her. "And . . . and I am afraid my attention was not on my riding as it should have been. I was fumbling with a packet of . . . of dried rhubarb, I believe it was, when the mare shied. I never quite got my balance after that."

"That was the point at which you fell to the ground and struck your head?"

They had not found her lying unconscious along the path, Sophy reminded herself. "Not quite, my lord. I started to slip from the saddle at that point but, uh, I believe the mare carried me for some distance into the woods before I finally lost my seat altogether."

"Would it make this any easier for you if I told you I have just now returned from a ride along the path to Old Bess's cottage?"

Sophy eyed him uneasily. "You have, my lord?"

"Yes, Sophy," he said very gently. "I have. I took a torch with me and in the vicinity of the pond I discovered some rather interesting tracks. There appears to have been another horse and rider on that same path today."

Sophy leaped to her feet. "Oh, Julian, pray do not ask me any more questions tonight. I cannot talk right now. I am far too distraught. I was wrong when I said I felt well. The truth is I feel absolutely wretched."

"But not, I think, because of a blow on the head." Julian's voice was even softer and more reassuring than it had been a moment ago. "Perhaps you are making yourself ill with worry, my dear. You have my word that there is no necessity to do that."

Sophy did not understand or trust the tenderness she heard in his words. "I do not take your meaning, my lord."

"Why don't you come over here and sit with me for a moment while you calm yourself." He held out his hand.

Sophy glanced longingly at the offered hand and then at his face. She steeled herself against the lure he was offering. She must be strong. "There . . . there is no room on the chair for me, Julian."

"I will make room. Come here, Sophy. The situation is not nearly so bleak nor as complicated as you appear to think."

She told herself it would be a major error to go to him.

She would lose whatever strength of will she possessed if she allowed him to cosset her just now. But she ached to feel his arms around her again and in the end his outstretched hand was too much to resist in her tired, weakened condition.

"I should probably lie down for a while," she said as she took a step toward Julian.

"You will rest soon, little one, I promise you."

He continued to wait with that subtle air of limitless patience as she took a second and then a third step toward him.

"Julian, I should not do this," she breathed softly as his fingers closed over her hand, engulfing it.

"I am your husband, sweetheart." He tugged her down onto his lap and cradled her against his shoulder. "Who else can you talk to about what really happened today, if not me?"

At that she lost most of what was left of her fortitude. She had been through too much today. The kidnapping, the threat of rape, her narrow escape, the moment when she had held the pocket pistol in her hand and found herself unable to shoot Waycott—all conspired to weaken her.

If Julian had shouted at her or if he had been cold with rage, she might have been able to resist, but his soothing, tender tone was irresistible. She turned her face into the hollow of his shoulder and closed her eyes. His arms tightened comfortingly around her and his broad shoulders promised protection as nothing else could.

"Julian, I love you," she said into his shirt.

"I know, sweetheart. I know. So you will tell me the truth now, hm?"

"I cannot do that," she said starkly.

He did not argue the point. He just sat there stroking the curve of her back with his big, strong hands. There was silence in the room until Sophy, succumbing to the temptation once more, began to relax against him.

"Do you trust me, Sophy?"

"Yes, Julian."

"Then why will you not tell me the truth about what happened today?"

She heaved a sigh. "I am afraid, my lord."

"Of me?"

"No."

"I am pleased to hear that, at least." He paused for a moment and then said thoughtfully, "Some wives in your situation might have reason to fear their husbands."

"They must be wives whose husbands do not hold them in high esteem," Sophy said instantly. "Sad, unfortunate wives who do not enjoy either the respect or the trust of their husbands. I pity them."

Julian gave a muffled exclamation that sounded like something between a groan and a chuckle. He retied a velvet ribbon that had come undone on Sophy's dressing gown. "You, of course, are excluded from that group of females, my dear. You enjoy my esteem, my respect, and my trust, do you not?"

"So you have said, my lord." Wistfully, Sophy wondered what it would be like to have Julian's love added to the list.

"Then you are right not to fear me for, knowing you, I know very well that you did nothing wrong today. You would never betray me, would you, Sophy?"

Her fingers clenched around a handful of his shirt. "Never, Julian. Never in this life or any other. I am very glad you realize that."

"I do, my sweet." He fell silent again for another long moment and once more Sophy relaxed under the soothing stroke of his hand. "Unfortunately, I find that, although I trust you completely, my curiosity is not assuaged. I really must know what happened to you today. You must make allowances for the fact that I am your husband, Sophy. The title causes me to feel somewhat protective."

"Please, Julian, do not force me to tell you. I am all right, I promise you."

"It is not my intention to force you to do anything. We will play a guessing game, instead."

Sophy stiffened against him. "I do not want to play any games."

He paid no attention to the small protest. "You say you do not wish to tell me the full story because you are afraid. Yet you also claim you are not afraid of me. Therefore, we can safely conclude that you are afraid of someone else. Do you not trust me to be able to protect you, my dear?"

"It is not that, Julian." Sophy lifted her head quickly, anxious that he not doubt her faith in his ability to defend her. "I know you would go to any length to protect me."

"You are right," Julian said simply. "You are very important to me, Sophy."

"I understand, Julian." She touched her stomach fleetingly. "You are no doubt concerned because of your future heir. But you need not worry about the babe, truly—"

Julian's emerald eyes flickered for the first time with a show of real anger. It was gone almost at once. He cradled her face between his palms. "Let us have this clear, Sophy. You are important to me because you are *Sophy,* my dear, unconventional, honorable, loving wife—not because of the child you carry."

"Oh." She could not tear her eyes away from his brilliant gaze. This was as close as he had ever come to telling her he loved her. It might be as close as he ever got. "Thank you, Julian."

"Do not thank me. It is I who owe you thanks." He covered her mouth with his and kissed her with slow thoroughness. When he finally raised his head, there was a familiar gleam in his eyes. His mouth curved faintly. "You are a powerful distraction, my dear, but I think that this time I will endeavor to resist. At least for a while longer."

"But, Julian—"

"Now, we will finish our guessing game. You are afraid of whoever was on the path by the pond this afternoon. You do not seem to fear for your own safety, so we must conclude that you fear for mine."

"Julian, please, I beg of you—"

"If you fear for my safety, yet you will not give me a fair warning of the danger, it follows that you do not fear a direct attack on my person. You would not conceal that important information from me, would you?"

"No, my lord." She knew now it was hopeless to keep the truth to herself. The hunter was closing in on his prey.

"We are left with only one other possibility," Julian said with inevitable logic. "If you are afraid for me but you do not fear I will be attacked, then it must be that you are afraid that I will challenge this mysterious, unknown third party to a duel."

Sophy straightened in his lap, grasped two fistfulls of his shirt and narrowed her eyes. "Julian, you must give me your word of honor that you will not do that. You must promise me for the sake of our unborn child. I will not have you risking your life. Do you hear me?"

"It is Waycott, is it not?"

Sophy's eyes widened. "How did you know?"

"It was not terribly difficult to guess. What happened on the path this afternoon, Sophy?"

She stared up at him in helpless frustration. The gentle, reassuring expression in Julian's eyes was vanishing as though it had never existed. In its place was the cold, prowling look of the predator. He had won the immediate battle and now he was preparing his strategy for the one that lay ahead.

"*I will not let you call him out, Julian*. You will not risk a bullet from Waycott, do you understand?"

"What happened on the path today?"

Sophy could have wept. "Julian, please—"

"What happened today, Sophy?"

He had not raised his voice but she knew immediately his patience was exhausted. He would have his answer. Sophy pushed herself up off his lap. He allowed her to get to her feet but his eyes never left her averted face.

Slowly she walked across the room to the window and stood staring out into the night. In short, concise sentences she told him the entire tale.

"He killed them, Julian," she concluded, her hands knotted in front of her. "He killed them both. He drowned Elizabeth because she had finally goaded him too far by taunting him with her plan to rid herself of his babe. He killed my sister by treating her as though she were nothing more important than a casual plaything."

"I knew about your sister. I put the pieces of that puzzle together myself before I left London. And I have always had my suspicions about what happened to Elizabeth that night. I wondered if one of her lovers had finally been pushed too far."

Sophy leaned her forehead against the cool glass pane. "God help me, I could not bring myself to pull the trigger when I had the chance. I am such a coward."

"No, Sophy, you are no coward." Julian moved to stand directly behind her. "You are the bravest woman I have ever met and I would trust you with my life as well as my honor. You must know you did the honorable thing this evening. One does not shoot an unconscious man in cold blood, no matter what he has done."

Sophy turned slowly to look up at him with a sense of uncertainty. "But if I had shot him when I had the chance it would all be over by now. I would not have to worry about you."

"You would have had to live with the knowledge that you had killed a man and I would not wish that fate on you, sweetheart, no matter how much Waycott deserved to die."

Sophy experienced a twinge of impatience. "Julian, I must tell you that I am not so much concerned with whether or not I behaved honorably as I am with the fact that I did not settle the matter once and for all. I am afraid that when it comes to this sort of thing, I have a very practical streak in me. The man is a murderer and he is still free."

"Not for much longer."

Alarm flared within her. "Julian, please, you must promise me you will not challenge him. You could be killed, even if Waycott fought a fair duel which is highly unlikely."

Julian smiled. "As I understand it, he is in no condition to fight at all at the moment. You said he was unconscious, did you not? I can well believe he will remain so for some time. I, myself, have had extensive experience with your special tea brews, if you recall."

"Do not tease me, Julian."

He caught her wrists and brought her hands to his

chest. "I am not teasing you, sweetheart. I am just exceedingly grateful you are alive and unhurt. You will never know what it did to me tonight to arrive here and find that you were missing."

She refused to be comforted because she knew what lay ahead. "What will you do, Julian?"

"That depends. How long do you estimate Waycott will be asleep?"

Sophy frowned. "Another three or four hours, perhaps."

"Excellent. I will deal with him later, then." He began untying the ribbons of her dressing gown. "In the meantime I can spend some time reassuring myself that you are, indeed, unhurt."

Sophy looked up at him very earnestly as the gown fell away from her. "Julian, I must have your word of honor that you will not challenge Waycott."

"Do not worry about it, my dear." He kissed the curve of her throat.

"Your word, Julian. You will give it to me." There was nothing more she wanted at the moment than to be in Julian's arms but this was far more important. She stood stiff and unyielding, ignoring the warm, inviting touch of his mouth on her skin.

"Do not concern yourself with what happens to Waycott. I will deal with everything. He will never come near you again."

"Damn you, Julian, *I will have your promise not to call him out*. Your safety is far more important to me than your stupid, male sense of honor. I have told you what I think of dueling. It settles nothing and can easily get you killed into the bargain. You will not challenge Waycott, do you hear me? Give me your word, Julian."

He stopped kissing the hollow of her shoulder and slowly raised his head to look down at her. He was scowling for the first time. "I am not a bad shot, Sophy."

"I do not care how accurate your aim is, I will not have you take such a risk and that is final."

His brows rose slightly. "It is?"

"Yes, damn you. I will not take the chance of losing you in a silly duel with a man who will most likely cheat. I feel about this precisely the way you felt the morning you interrupted my appointment with Charlotte Featherstone. I will not stand for it."

"I do not believe I have ever heard you so adamant, my dear," Julian said dryly.

"Your word, Julian. Give it to me."

He sighed in capitulation. "Very well. If it means so much to you, you have my solemn vow not to challenge Waycott to a duel with pistols."

Sophy closed her eyes in overwhelming relief. "Thank you, Julian."

"Now may I be allowed to make love to my wife?"

She gave him a misty smile. "Yes, my lord."

Julian roused himself an hour later and propped himself on his elbow to look down into Sophy's worried eyes. The glow she always wore after his lovemaking was already wearing off to be replaced again by concern. It was rather reassuring to know that his safety meant so much to her.

"You will be careful, Julian?"

"Very careful."

"Perhaps you should take some of the stable lads with you."

"No, this is between Waycott and myself. I will handle this alone."

"But what will you do?" she demanded fretfully.

"Force him to leave the country. I believe I shall suggest that he emigrate to America."

"But how can you make him go?"

Julian leaned over her, his hands on either side of her shoulders. "Stop asking so many questions, my love. I do not have time to answer them now. I will give you a full accounting when I return. I swear it." He brushed his mouth against hers. "Get some rest."

"That is a ridiculous instruction. I will not be able to sleep a wink until you return."

"Then read a good book."

"Wollstonecraft," she threatened. "I shall study *A Vindication on the Rights of Women* until you return."

"That knowledge will indeed force me to hurry back to

your side," Julian said, getting to his feet. "I cannot have you any more thoroughly corrupted by that nonsense about the rights of women than you already are."

She sat up and reached for his hand. "Julian, I am frightened."

"I know the feeling. I felt the same way when I arrived here this evening and found you missing." He gently freed his hand and began to dress. "But in this case, you need have no fear. You have my promise I will not propose a duel to Waycott, remember?"

"Yes, but—" She broke off, nibbling her lower lip in concern. "But I do not like this, Julian."

"It will all be over soon." He fastened his breeches and sat down in the chair to tug on his boots. "I will be home before dawn unless you have made Waycott so groggy with your special tea that he cannot understand simple English."

"I did not give him as much as I gave you," she said uneasily. "I was afraid he would notice the odd taste."

"How unfortunate. I would have preferred Waycott suffer the same appalling headache I was forced to endure."

"You had been drinking that night, Julian," she explained seriously. "It changed the effects of the herbs. Waycott had only the tea. He will awake fairly clearheaded."

"I will remember that." Julian finished putting on his boots. He strode to the door and paused to glance back at her. A surge of raw possessiveness went through him. It was followed by a shocking tenderness. She was everything to him, he realized. Nothing in the world was more important than his sweet Sophy.

"Did you forgot something, Julian?" she asked from the shadows of the bed.

"Only a minor detail," he said quietly. His hand fell away from the doorknob and he went back to the bed. He leaned down and kissed her soft mouth once more. "I love you."

He saw her eyes widen in astonishment but he knew he could not afford the time it would take to listen to her demands for details and explanations. He went back across the room and opened the door.

"Julian, wait—"

"I will be back as soon as possible, sweetheart. Then we will talk."

"No, wait, there is something else I must tell you. The emeralds."

"What about them?"

"I almost forgot. Waycott has them. He stole them the night he killed Elizabeth. They are in the basket on the hearth, right under his pistol."

"How very interesting. I must remember to bring them back with me," Julian said and went out into the hall.

The old Norman ruin was an eerie, uninviting jumble of stones and deep shadows in the moonlight. For the first time in years Julian experienced the same response to it that he had often had as a boy—it was a place where one could easily learn to believe in ghosts. The thought of Sophy being held captive within the dark confines of this place added fuel to the white hot fires of his anger.

He had managed to keep Sophy from seeing the depths of his fury because he had known it would alarm her. But it had taken every ounce of his self-control to keep his rage from showing.

One thing was certain: Waycott would pay for what he had tried to do to Sophy.

There was no sign of activity around the ruin as far as Julian could see. He walked the black into the nearest stand of trees, dismounted and draped the reins around a convenient limb. Then he made his way through the fragments of the ancient stone walls to the one room that was still standing. There was no glow of light from the narrow openings high up on the wall. The fire Sophy had said was burning on the hearth must have sunk into embers by now.

Julian had great faith in Sophy's skill with herbs but he decided not to take chances. He entered the chamber where she had been held with great caution. Nothing and no one stirred from within. He stood in the open doorway, letting his eyes adjust to the darkness. And then he spotted Waycott's sprawled body near the wall by the hearth.

Sophy was right. Things would be a great deal simpler if
someone put a pistol to the Viscount's head and pulled the
trigger. But there were some things a gentleman did not
do. Julian shook his head in resignation and went over to
the hearth to stoke up the fire.

When he was finished, he pulled up the stool and sat
down. Idly he glanced into the basket and saw the emeralds pooled at the bottom beneath the pocket pistol. With
a sense of satisfaction, he picked up the necklace and
watched the stones glitter in the firelight. The Ravenwood
emeralds were going to look very good on the new Countess of Ravenwood.

Twenty minutes later the Viscount stirred and groaned.
Julian watched, unmoving, as Waycott slowly recovered
his senses. He continued to wait while Waycott blinked
and then frowned at the fire, waited as the man sat up and
put a hand to his temple, waited until the Viscount finally
began to realize there was someone else in the room.

"That's right, Waycott, Sophy is safe and now you must
deal with me." Julian casually let the emeralds cascade
from one palm to the other and back again. "I suppose it
was inevitable that at some point you would finally go too
far. You are a man obsessed, are you not?"

Waycott inched backward until he was sitting propped
against the wall. He leaned his fair head against the damp
stones and stared at Julian through lids narrowed with
hatred. "So dear little Sophy ran straight to you, did she?
And you believed every word she said, I suppose. I may
be obsessed, Ravenwood, but you are a fool."

Julian glanced down at the glittering emeralds. "You are
partially correct, Waycott. I was a fool once, a long time
ago. I did not recognize a witch in a silk ball gown. But
those days are over. In some ways, I almost pity you. The
rest of us managed to extricate ourselves from Elizabeth's
spell years ago. You alone remained ensnared."

"*Because I alone loved her.* The rest of you only wanted
to use her. You wanted to steal her innocence and beauty
and thereby tarnish it forever. I wanted to protect her."

"As I said, you are as obsessed as you ever were. If you
had been content to suffer alone, I would have continued

to ignore you. Unfortunately, you chose to try to use Sophy as a means of avenging yourself against me. That I cannot overlook or ignore. I warned you, Waycott. Now you will pay for involving Sophy and we will put an end to this whole business."

Waycott laughed crudely. "What did your sweet little Sophy tell about what happened here today? Did she tell you I found her on the path by the pond? Did she tell you that she was on her way back from the same abortionist Elizabeth had consulted? Your dear, sweet, innocent Sophy is already scheming to rid herself of your heir, Ravenwood. She doesn't want to bear your brat any more than Elizabeth did."

For an instant, Sophy's words flashed in Julian's head and a lingering sense of guilt shot through him. *I do not wish to be rushed into childbed.*

Julian shook his head and smiled grimly at Waycott. "You are as clever as any footpad when it comes to sinking a knife into a man's back but in this case your aim is off. You see, Waycott, Sophy and I have gotten to know each other very well. She is an honorable woman. We have made a bargain, she and I, and while I regret to say I have not always upheld my end of the arrangement, she has always been true to her side. I know she went to see Old Bess for a fresh supply of herbs, not to seek an abortion."

"You are indeed a fool, Ravenwood, if you believe that. Did Sophy also lie to you about what happened over there on that pallet? Did she tell you how easily she pulled up her skirts and spread her thighs for me? She's not particularly skilled yet, but I expect she'll improve with practice."

Julian's fury momentarily slipped its leash. He dropped the emeralds to the floor and came up off the stool in one smooth, swift movement. He took two strides across the chamber and caught Waycott by the front of the shirt. Then he hauled the Viscount to his feet and slammed a fist into the handsome face. Something broke in the region of Waycott's nose and blood spurted. Julian hit him again.

"You son of a bitch, you don't want to admit you married a whore, do you?" Waycott slid sideways out of reach along the wall and wiped the back of his hand against his bleeding nose. "But you did, you rotten bastard. I wonder how long it will be until you realize it."

"Sophy would never dishonor herself or me. I know she did not allow you to touch her."

"Is that why you reacted so quickly when I told you what happened between Sophy and me?" Waycott taunted.

Julian damped down his rage. "It is useless trying to talk to you, Waycott. When it comes to this, you are truly beyond reason. I suppose I should pity you, but I fear I cannot allow even a madman to insult my wife."

Waycott eyed him uneasily. "You will never call me out. We both know that."

"Unfortunately, you are right," Julian agreed, thinking of the vow he had made to Sophy. He had broken, or at least bent, far too many promises to her already. He would not break another even though he longed for nothing more than to be free to put a bullet into Waycott. He walked over to the hearth and stood staring down into the flames.

"I knew it," Waycott gloated. "I told her you would never again risk your neck over a woman. You have lost your taste for vengeance. You will not challenge me."

"No, Waycott, I will not call you out." Julian clasped his hands behind his back and turned his head to smile at the other man with cool anticipation. "Not for the reasons you assume but for other, private reasons. Rest assured, however, that decision will not prevent me from accepting a challenge from you."

Waycott looked baffled. "What the devil are you talking about?"

"I will not call you out, Waycott. I am bound by a certain vow in that regard. But I think we can arrange matters so that you will finally feel obliged to call me out. And when you do, I can promise you, I will be most eager to meet you. I have already chosen my seconds. You remember Daregate, don't you? And Thurgood? They will be only too happy to assist me and to ensure that matters are conducted with utmost fairness. Daregate, you know, is very good at spotting a cheat. I can even supply the pistols. I await your earliest convenience."

Waycott's mouth fell open. Then the expression of shock

was replaced with a sneer. "Why should I call you out? It is not my wife who has betrayed me."

"This is not a matter of a wife's betrayal. There has been no betrayal. Do not waste any more breath trying to convince me that I have been cuckolded, because I know the truth. The sleeping potion in your tea and that rope on the floor that you used to tether Sophy are evidence enough. But as it happens I believed her before I saw the evidence. I already know my wife to be a woman of honor."

"A woman of honor? Honor is a meaningless term to a female."

"To a woman such as Elizabeth, yes. But not to a woman like Sophy. We will not discuss the subject of honor again, however. There is no point because you, yourself, do not have any comprehension of the matter. Now, back to the issue at hand."

"Are you calling my honor into question?" Waycott snarled.

"Certainly. And what is more, I will continue to call your so-called honor into question in the most public sort of way until you finally issue a challenge or emigrate to America. Those are the two choices you face, Waycott."

"You cannot force me to do either."

"If you think not, you have a surprise in store. I will, indeed, force you to make your choice. I will hound you until you do so. You see, I intend to make life intolerable for you here in England, Waycott. I will be like a wolf nipping at your heels until I draw blood."

Waycott was very pale in the firelight. "You are bluffing."

"Shall I tell you how it will be? Listen well, Waycott and hear your fate. No matter what you do or where you go in England, I or an agent of mine will be behind you. If you see a horse at Tattersall's you wish to purchase, I will outbid you and see that the animal goes to another. If you try to buy a new pair of boots at Hoby's, or order a coat from Weston's, I will inform the proprietors that they will not have any future business from me if they continue to serve you."

"You cannot do that," Waycott hissed.

"And that is only the beginning," Julian continued relentlessly. "I shall let all the owners of the various parcels of land that surround your estate in Suffolk know that I am willing to buy them out. In time, Waycott, your lands will be surrounded by properties owned by me. Furthermore, I shall make certain that your reputation suffers so that no reputable club will have you and no respectable hostess will want you under her roof."

"It will never work."

"Yes it will, Waycott. I have the money, land, and a sufficiently powerful title to ensure that my plan will work. What's more, I will have Sophy on my side. Her name is golden in London these days, Waycott. When she turns against you, the entire social world will turn against you."

"No." Waycott shook his head furiously, his eyes wild. "She will never do so. I did not hurt her. She will understand why I did what I did. She is sympathetic to me."

"Not any longer."

"Because I brought her here? But I can explain that to her."

"You will never have the chance. Even if I allowed you to get close enough to plead with her, which I have no intention of doing, you would find no sympathy or leniency from that quarter. You see, Waycott, you sealed your own doom before you even met Sophy."

"What in God's name are you talking about now?"

"Remember that young woman whom you seduced here three years ago and whom you later abandoned when she got pregnant? The one who took your devilish ring? The one you told Sophy was unimportant? The one you called the village whore?"

"What about her?" Waycott screamed.

"She was Sophy's sister."

Waycott's expression went blank with shock. "Oh, my God."

"Exactly," Julian said quietly. "You begin to perceive the depths of your problem. I see no point in my staying here any longer. Consider your two choices carefully, Waycott.

If I were you, I'd choose America. I've heard from those who patronize Manton that you are not a good marksman."

Julian turned his back on Waycott, picked up the emeralds and walked out the door. He had untied the black's reins before he heard the muffled shot from within the old castle.

He had been wrong. Waycott had had three choices, not two. It was obvious the Viscount had found the pocket pistol in the basket and taken the third way out.

Julian put one foot in the stirrup and then reluctantly decided to go back into the ominously silent ruin. The scene that awaited him would be unpleasant, to say the least, but given Waycott's general ineptitude it would be best to make certain the Viscount had not made a muddle of the whole thing

TWENTY

It seemed to Sophy that she had been sitting huddled in a chair for hours before she finally heard Julian's booted footsteps in the hall. With a soft cry of relief, she leaped to her feet and flew to the door.

One anxious glance at her husband's harsh, weary face told her that something very grim had occurred. The half-empty bottle of claret and the glass that he had obviously stopped to pick up in the library confirmed the impression.

"Are you all right, Julian?"

"Yes."

He walked into the room, closed the door behind him and set the claret on the dressing table. Without another word he reached out to pull Sophy into his arms. They stood together in silence for a long while before either spoke.

"What happened?" Sophy finally asked.

"Waycott is dead."

She could not deny the sense of relief that went through her at that news. She tilted her head back to meet his eyes. "You killed him?"

"A matter of opinion, I imagine. Some would certainly say I was responsible. However, I did not actually pull the trigger. He performed that task himself."

Sophy closed her eyes. "He took his own life. Just as Amelia did."

"Perhaps there is some justice in the ending."

"Sit down, Julian. I will pour you some claret."

He did not argue. Sprawling in a chair near the window he watched with brooding eyes as Sophy poured the wine and carried it over to him.

"Thank you," he said as he took the glass from her. His eyes met hers. "You have a way of giving me what I want when I need it." He took a large mouthful of wine and swallowed it. "Are you all right? Has the news about Waycott unsettled you?"

"No." Sophy shook her head and sat down near Julian. "God forgive me, but I am glad it is over, even if it means another death. He would not go to America?"

"I do not believe he was rational enough to think clearly on the subject. I told him I would hound him, make his life a torment, until he left England and then I told him the young village girl he had seduced was your sister. Then I walked out the door. He found the pistol and used it on himself just as I was mounting my horse. I went back to see if he had managed to properly finish the business." Julian took another sip of wine. "He had."

"How terrible for you."

He looked at her. "No, Sophy. The terrible part was walking into that hellish little chamber and seeing the rope he had tied around your ankle and the pallet where he intended to rape you."

She shivered and hugged herself tightly. "Please, do not remind me."

"Like you, I am glad it's over. Even if today's events had not occurred, I would have had to stop Waycott eventually. The bastard was getting worse, not better in his obsession with the past."

Sophy frowned thoughtfully. "Perhaps his condition took a turn for the worse because you decided to marry again. Some part of him could not bear to believe you could find any woman worthy of putting in Elizabeth's place. He wanted you to be as true to her memory as he was."

"Bloody hell. The man was mad."

"Yes." Sophy was silent for a moment. "What will happen now?"

"His body will be found in a day or two and it will be obvious that Lord Waycott took his own life. The matter will end there."

"As it should." Sophy touched his arm and smiled tentatively. "Thank you, Julian."

"For what? Not protecting you with sufficient care to ensure that this day's events never happened? You managed your own escape, if you will recall. The last thing I deserve from you is your thanks, madam."

"I will not have you blame yourself, my lord," she said fiercely. "What happened today could not have been predicted by any of us. The important thing is that it is over. I am thanking you because I appreciate how hard it must have been for you to resist calling out Lord Waycott. I know you, Julian. Your sense of honor would have demanded a duel. It must have been very difficult for you to abide by your vow to me."

Julian shifted slightly in the chair. "Sophy, I think it would be best if we changed the subject."

"But I want you to know how grateful I am that you kept your promise to me. I hope you realize I could not allow you to take such a risk, Julian. I love you too much to let you do it."

"Sophy—"

"And I could not bear for our babe not to know his father."

Julian put down his wineglass and reached over to capture Sophy's hand in his. "I, too, am very curious to meet our son or daughter. I meant what I said when I walked out the door earlier tonight. I love you, Sophy. And I would have you remember that no matter what happens, no matter how often I fail to live up to your ideal of a perfect husband, I will always love you."

She smiled quietly and squeezed his large hand. "I know."

Julian's brows rose with a familiar arrogance but there

was a gleam of loving amusement in his eyes. "You do? How so?"

"Well, let us say that I have had some time to think while I waited for you to return tonight. It occurred to me, rather belatedly, that any man who believed my outlandish tale of what had really happened this afternoon, the kidnapping and the drugged tea and all the rest, must be a man who was at least a little bit in love."

"Not a little bit in love." Julian raised her palm to his lips and kissed it. His eyes were emerald green when they met hers. "A great deal in love. Head over heels, overwhelmingly and completely in love. I only regret that it took me so long to realize it."

"You always were inclined to be stubborn and thick-headed."

Julian grinned briefly and tugged her down across his thighs. "And you, my sweet wife, have the same tendencies. Luckily we understand each other." He kissed her deeply and then raised his head to search her eyes. "I am sorry about some things, Sophy. I have not always treated you as well as I ought to have done. I have ridden roughshod over most of our wedding agreements because I was convinced I knew what was best for you and for our marriage. And there will undoubtedly be times in the future when I will act as I believe best, even when that does not accord with what you believe to be best."

She laced her fingers through the dark depths of his hair. "As I said, stubborn and thickheaded."

"About the babe, sweetheart."

"The babe is fine, my lord." The memory of Waycott's accusations returned. "You must know I did not go to Old Bess for a potion to get rid of your child."

"I realize that; you would not do such a thing. But the fact remains that I had no right to get you with child so quickly. I could have prevented it."

"Someday, my lord," Sophy said with a teasing smile, "you must tell me exactly how one does prevent such an occurrence. Anne Silverthorne told me about a certain type of pouch made of sheep gut that is tied on the male member with little red strings. Do you know of such things?"

Julian groaned in despair. "How the hell would Anne Silverthorne know of such matters? Good lord, Sophy, you have been keeping very bad company in London. It is fortunate I got you away from the city before you were corrupted further by my aunt's acquaintances."

"Quite true, my lord. And as it happens, I am content to learn all I need to know about corruption at your hands." Sophy touched Julian's big hands with loving fingers and then bent her head to kiss his wrist. When she looked up, she saw his love for her in his eyes.

"I have said all along," Julian remarked softly, "that you and I would deal very well together."

"You were apparently right yet again, my lord."

He got to his feet and pulled her up to stand in front of him. "I am almost always right," he said as he brushed his mouth against hers. "And on those occasions when I am not, I shall have you to put me right. Now I find that it is almost dawn, my love and I have need of your softness and your heat. You are a tonic for me. I have discovered that when I am in your arms, I can forget everything else but you. Let us go to bed."

"I would like that very much, Julian."

He undressed her slowly, with infinite care, his muscular hands gliding over every inch of her soft, fair skin. He bent his head to kiss the budding peaks of her breasts and his fingers found the flowing warmth between her legs.

And when he was very certain she was on fire for him, Julian carried her over to the bed, laid her down upon it, and made love to her until they both could put the memory of the day's events far behind them.

A long time later Julian rolled reluctantly to one side, cradling Sophy in one arm. He yawned mightily and said, "The emeralds."

"What about them?" Sophy snuggled close. "You found them in the basket, I presume?"

"I found them. And you will wear them on the next occasion that warrants such finery. I cannot wait to see you in them."

Sophy stilled. "I do not think I want to wear them, Julian. I do not like them. They won't become me."

"Don't be a goose, Sophy. You will look magnificent in them."

"They should be worn by a taller woman. A blond, perhaps. In any event, knowing me, the clasp will probably come undone and I shall lose them. Things are always coming undone on my person, my lord. You know that."

Julian grinned in the darkness. "It is one of your charms. But have no fear, I shall always be nearby to retrieve any lost items, including the emeralds."

"Julian, I truly do not want to wear the emeralds," Sophy said insistently.

"Why?"

She was silent for a long moment. "I cannot explain."

"It is because in your mind you associate them with Elizabeth, do you not?" he asked gently.

She sighed softly. "Yes."

"Sophy, the Ravenwood emeralds have nothing to do with Elizabeth. Those stones have been in my family for three generations and they will remain in the family as long as there are Ravenwood wives to wear them. Elizabeth may have toyed with them for a short while, but they never belonged to her in any real sense. Do you understand.

"No."

"You are being stubborn, Sophy."

"It is one of my charms."

"You will wear the emeralds," Julian vowed softly as he pulled her across his chest.

"Never."

"I can see," Julian said, his green eyes gleaming behind his lashes, "that I must find a way to convince you to change your mind."

"There is no way you can do that," Sophy said with great determination.

"Ah, sweetheart. Why do you persist in underestimating me?" He used his hands to frame her face for his kiss and a moment later, Sophy softened eagerly against his hard length.

* * *

In spring of the following year the Earl and Countess of Ravenwood gave a house party to celebrate the recent birth of a healthy son. Everyone who was invited to the country, came, including a few, such as Lord Daregate, who normally could not be persuaded away from London during the season.

During a quiet moment in the Ravenwood gardens, Daregate grinned knowingly at Julian. "I always said Sophy would look good in the emeralds. She was quite beautiful in them tonight at dinner."

"I shall convey your compliments to her," Julian said, smiling to himself with satisfaction. "She fretted about wearing them. I had to work long and hard to convince her to do so."

"I wonder why you had to go to all that effort," Daregate mused. "Most women would have been willing to kill to wear those stones."

"She associated them too much with Elizabeth."

"Yes, I can see where that might have bothered a sensitive creature like Sophy. How did you convince her otherwise?"

"An intelligent husband eventually learns the sort of reasoning that works with a woman. It's taken me some time, but I am getting the hang of it," Julian said complacently. "In this instance I finally hit upon the brilliant notion of pointing out that the Ravenwood emeralds went very nicely with my eyes."

Daregate stared at him for an instant and then gave a crack of laughter. "Brilliant, indeed. Sophy would be unable to resist such logic. As it happens, they are a nice match for your son's eyes, too. The Ravenwood emeralds breed true, it seems." Daregate paused to examine a small garden set apart from the rest of the lush greenery. "What have we here?"

Julian glanced down at his feet. "Sophy's herb garden. She had it put in this spring and already the local villagers have begun asking for cuttings, recipes, and concoctions. I spend a small fortune in herbals these days. I believe Sophy is getting ready to write one of her own. I find I am married to a busy woman."

"I am in favor of keeping women busy, myself," Daregate said dryly. "I believe work keeps them out of trouble."

"That is amusing, considering the fact that most of the work you do is at a hazard table."

"Not for much longer, I believe," Daregate announced calmly. "Word has it my dear cousin's constitution is failing rapidly. He has taken to his bed and found religion."

"A sure sign of an impending demise. May we then anticipate your own nuptials shortly?"

"First," said Daregate with a glance back toward the main house, "I must find a suitable heiress. There is very little money left in the estate."

Julian followed his friend's gaze and saw a flash of red hair through the open windows. "Sophy tells me that Anne Silverthorne's stepfather recently departed for the hereafter. Miss Silverthorne has inherited everything."

"So I am told."

Julian chuckled. "Good luck, my friend. I fear you will have your hands full with that lady. She is, after all, a close friend of my wife's and you know what I went through with Sophy."

"You appear to have survived," Daregate observed cheerfully.

"Barely." Julian grinned and clapped Daregate on the shoulder. "Come inside and I will pour you some of the best brandy you have ever had."

"French?"

"Naturally. I bought a shipment of it from our friendly local smuggler two months ago. Sophy lectured me severely for days about the risk."

"Judging by her actions toward you now, she appears to have forgiven you."

"I have learned how to deal with my wife, Daregate."

"What, pray tell, is the secret of marital bliss?" Daregate inquired, his eyes straying once more toward the window where Anne Silverthorne stood.

"That, my friend, you must discover for yourself. I fear there is no easy path to domestic harmony. But the effort is worthwhile with the right female."

Much later that night, Julian sprawled alongside Sophy.

His body was still damp from the recent lovemaking and he could feel satisfaction flowing through him like a powerful drug.

"Daregate asked me for the secret of domestic happiness earlier this evening," Julian murmured, cradling Sophy close.

"Really?" She traced a design on his bare chest. "What did you tell him?"

"That he would have to discover it for himself, the hard way, just as I did." Julian turned on his side and smoothed Sophy's hair off her cheek. He smiled down at her, loving everything about her. "Thank you for consenting to wear the emeralds at last. Did it bother you to have them around your throat tonight?"

Sophy shook her head slowly. "No. I did not wish to wear them at first but then I realized you were right. The stones match your eyes perfectly. When I finally got used to the idea I knew that I would think only of you whenever I wore them."

"That is how it should be." He kissed her slowly, lingeringly, savoring the unlimited happiness that filled him. His hand was gliding up Sophy's leg when he heard the small, demanding cry from the next room.

"Your son is hungry, my lord."

Julian groaned. "He has an infallible sense of timing, has he not?"

"He is as demanding as his father."

"Very well, madam. Let Nurse sleep. I shall fetch the next Earl of Ravenwood for you. Pacify him quickly and then we will get back to more important business."

He was getting used to this business of being a father, Julian thought as he went into the small nursery that had been set up next door to the master bedchamber. In fact, he was getting quite good at the whole business.

His son stopped crying as soon as he felt his father's strong hands lifting and holding him. The green-eyed, dark-haired babe gurgled happily and when Julian placed the infant at Sophy's breast, the Ravenwood heir settled down to suckle cheerfully.

Julian sat on the edge of the bed and watched his wife

and son in the shadows. The sight of them together filled him with a contentment and a possessive satisfaction that was akin to the feeling he experienced when he made love to Sophy.

"Sophy, tell me again that at last you have gotten everything you wanted out of this marriage," Julian demanded softly.

"Everything and more, Julian." Her smile was very brilliant in the darkness. "Everything and more."

SURRENDER

Prologue

The hall clock struck midnight. It was a death knell.
The beautiful, old-fashioned, terrifyingly heavy
dress that did not fit her properly because it had been
made for another woman, hampered her frantic flight
down the corridor. The fine wool fabric tangled itself
around her legs, threatening to trip her with every
desperate step. She pulled the skirts higher, higher,
almost to her knees, and risked a glance back over her
shoulder.

He was closing on her, running her down the way a
hound, maddened with blood lust, runs a deer to earth.
His once demonically handsome face, the face that had
lured an innocent, trusting woman first into marriage
and then to her doom, was now a mask of fear and
murderous, burning rage. With wild eyes that bulged
from his head and hair that stood on end, he stalked
her. The knife in his hand would soon be at her throat.

"Demon bitch." His shout of rage echoed down the
upstairs hall. The light of a flickering taper glinted on
the evil-looking blade he clutched. "You are dead. Why
cannot you leave me in peace? I swear I will send you

347

back to hell where you belong. And this time I will make certain the deed is done right. Hear me, you accursed specter. *This time I will make certain.*"

She wanted to scream and could not. All she could do was run for her life.

"I will watch your blood flow through my fingers until you are drained," he cried out behind her, much closer. "This time you will stay dead, demon bitch. You have caused me trouble enough."

She was at the top of the stairs now, gasping for breath. Fear clawed at her insides. Holding the thick skirts even higher, she started down the staircase, one hand on the banister to keep herself from falling. It would be a bitter irony to die of a broken neck rather than a slashed throat.

He was so close, so very close. She knew there was every chance she would not make it back to safety. This time she had gone too far, taken one risk too many. She had played the part of a ghost and now she was very likely to become one. He would be on top of her before she reached the bottom step.

She had finally gotten the proof she had sought. In his rage he had confessed. If she lived, she would have justice for her poor mother. But it was fast becoming apparent that her quest would cost her her life.

Soon she would feel his hands on her, grabbing at her in a dreadful parody of the sexual embrace he had threatened her with when she was younger. Then she would feel the knife.

The knife.

Dear God, the knife.

She was halfway down the stairs when her pursuer's hideous scream rent the shadows.

She looked back in horror and realized that for the rest of her life, midnight would never be quite the same again. For her, midnight would mean nightmare.

1

Victoria Claire Huntington knew when she was being stalked. She had not reached the advanced age of twenty-four without learning to recognize the sophisticated fortune hunters of the ton. Heiresses were, after all, fair game.

The fact that she was still single and mistress of her own sizable inheritance was proof of her skill at evading the slick, deceitful opportunists who thrived in her world. Victoria had determined long ago never to fall victim to their attractive, superficial charms.

But Lucas Mallory Colebrook, the new Earl of Stonevale, was different. He might very well be an opportunist, but there was definitely nothing slick or superficial about him. Amid the brightly plumed birds of the ton, this man was a hawk.

Victoria was beginning to wonder if the very qualities that should have warned her off, the underlying strength and the implacable will she sensed in Stonevale, were exactly what had drawn her to him. There was no denying she had been fascinated by the man since they had been introduced less than an hour ago. The attrac-

tion she felt was deeply disturbing. In fact, it was quite
dangerous.

"I believe I have won again, my lord." Victoria lowered her elegantly gloved hand and fanned her cards
out across the green baize table. She smiled her most
dazzling smile at her opponent.

"Congratulations, Miss Huntington. Your luck is certainly running strong this evening." Stonevale, whose
gray eyes made Victoria think of ghosts hovering in the
dead of night, did not look in the least dismayed at his
loss. He appeared, in fact, quietly satisfied, as if a
carefully devised plan had just come to fruition. There
was a sense of cool anticipation about him.

"Yes, my luck has been amazingly strong tonight, has
it not?" Victoria murmured. "One might almost suspect
it had some assistance."

"I refuse to contemplate such a possibility. I cannot
allow you to impugn your own honor, Miss Huntington."

"Very gallant of you, my lord. But it was not *my*
honor which concerned me. I assure you I am well
aware that I was not cheating." Victoria held her breath,
knowing she had stepped out onto very thin ice with
that remark. She had practically accused the earl of
playing with marked cards in order to ensure her win.

Stonevale's eyes met and held hers across the table.
His expression was unnervingly calm. Frighteningly calm,
Victoria thought with a small shiver. There should have
been some flicker of emotion in that cool, gray gaze.
But she could read nothing in his face except a certain
watchfulness.

"Would you care to clarify that remark, Miss Huntington?"

Victoria quickly decided to step back onto more solid
ground. "Pray, pay me no heed, my lord. It is simply
that I am as astounded as you should be at my luck with
cards this evening. I am only an indifferent player at
best. You, on the other hand, have a reputation as a
skilled gamester, or so I have been told."

"You flatter me, Miss Huntington."

"I don't believe so," Victoria said. "I have heard tales
of the ability you display at the tables of White's and

Brooks's as well as at certain other clubs here in town
that are of a, shall we say, less reputable nature."

"Greatly embroidered tales, I imagine. But you make
me curious. As we have only just met, where did you
hear such stories?"

She could hardly admit she had asked her friend
Annabella Lyndwood about him the moment he entered the ballroom two hours before. "I am certain you
are aware of how such rumors fly, my lord."

"Indeed. But a woman of your obvious intelligence
should know better than to listen to gossip." With a
smooth, effortless motion Stonevale gathered up the
cards into a neat stack. He rested his graceful, long-
fingered hand on top of the deck and smiled coolly at
Victoria. "Now, Miss Huntington, have you given any
thought to collecting your winnings?"

Victoria watched him warily, unable to repress the
excitement that was bubbling within her. If she had any
sense, she would end this here and now, she told
herself. But tonight it was difficult to think with the sort
of cold, clear logic she usually employed in such circumstances. She had never met anyone quite like
Stonevale.

The hum of conversation and laughter in Lady
Atherton's card room receded, and the music from the
ballroom seemed faint and distant now. The Athertons'
huge London house was filled with well-dressed members of the ton as well as countless servants, but Victoria suddenly felt as if she were completely alone with
the earl.

"My winnings," Victoria repeated slowly, trying to
school her thoughts. "Yes, I shall have to do something
about them, won't I?"

"I believe the wager was for a favor, was it not? As
the winner, you are entitled to request one of me. I am
at your service."

"As it happens, sir, I do not need any favors from you
at the moment."

"Are you quite certain of that?"

She was startled by the knowing expression in the

earl's eyes. This was a man who always knew more than he ought. "Quite."

"I fear I must contradict you, Miss Huntington. I believe you do need a favor of me. I am given to understand that you will require an escort later this evening when you and Miss Lyndwood have your little adventure at the fair."

Victoria went very still. "What do you know of that?"

Stonevale gently riffled the cards with one long finger. "Lyndwood and I are friends. Belong to the same clubs. Play cards together occasionally. You know how it is."

"Lord Lyndwood? Annabella's brother? You've been talking to him?"

"Yes."

Victoria was incensed. "He promised to be our escort this evening and he gave us his word he would keep quiet on the matter. How dare he discuss this business with his cronies? This is too much by half. And men have the nerve to accuse women of gossiping. What an outrage."

"You must not be so hard on the man, Miss Huntington."

"What did Lyndwood do? Make a general announcement at one of his clubs that he would be taking his sister and her friend to the fair?"

"It was not a general announcement, I assure you. He was most discreet. After all, his sister is involved, is she not? If you must know the truth, I believe Lyndwood confided in me because he was feeling the strain of the situation."

"Strain? What strain? There is absolutely nothing about any of this that should make him anxious. He is simply going to escort Annabella and me to the park where the fair is being held. What could be simpler?" she snapped.

"As I understand it, you and his sister applied a certain degree of pressure on Lyndwood to get him to agree to your plans. The poor boy is still green enough to be manipulated by such feminine tactics. Fortunately, he is also wise enough to regret his weakness and smart enough to seek assistance."

"Poor boy, indeed. What nonsense. You make it sound as though Annabella and I coerced Bertie into this."

"Didn't you?" Stonevale shot back.

"Of course not. We merely impressed upon him that we have every intention of going to the fair tonight and he insisted on accompanying us. Very gallant of him. Or so we thought."

"You left him little choice as a gentleman. He could hardly agree to let you go on your own and you knew it. It was blackmail. Furthermore, I suspect it was largely your idea, Miss Huntington."

"*Blackmail.*" Victoria was now furious. "I resent that accusation, my lord."

"Why? It is little more than the truth. Do you think Lyndwood would have willingly consented to escort you and his sister to such a disreputable event unless you threatened to go on your own? Miss Lyndwood's mama would have a fit of the vapors if she got word of this little escapade tonight, and so, I imagine, would your aunt."

"I assure you, Aunt Cleo is far too sturdy to indulge in a fit of the vapors," Victoria declared loyally. But she knew Stonevale was perfectly correct about Annabella's mama. Lady Lyndwood would indeed have hysterics if she discovered her daughter's plans for this evening. Proper young ladies of the ton did not go to the fairgrounds at night.

"Your aunt may be a sturdy character. I will take your word for it, as I have not yet had the honor of meeting Lady Nettleship. But I sincerely doubt she would approve of your plans for this evening," Stonevale said.

"I shall throttle Lord Lyndwood when I see him. He is no gentleman to have betrayed a confidence in this manner."

"It was not entirely his fault he confided in me. I spent enough years as an officer to know when a young

man is agitated about something. It was not that difficult to press him for the details."

Victoria narrowed her eyes. "Why?"

"Let us say I had a great curiosity about the matter.
When Lyndwood discovered I was only too happy to
come to his assistance tonight, he confessed all and
pleaded for a companion."

"You have not answered my question. Why was your
curiosity so great?"

"My reasons are not particularly important," Stonevale's long fingers rippled easily through the deck of
cards again. "It seems to me we have a more immediate
problem."

"I see no problem." Other than getting rid of you,
Victoria added silently. Her first instincts had been
correct. She should have run when she had the chance.
But it was beginning to appear as though she'd never
had the opportunity in the first place. Everything suddenly seemed to be proceeding according to some master plan that had been set in motion and over which she
had less and less control.

"We should go over the details of the evening's adventure, don't you think?"

"The details have already been taken care of, thank
you." Victoria did not like the feeling of not being in
charge.

"Please understand. Perhaps it is the ex-soldier in me
or perhaps it is mere curiosity, but I like to know
exactly what is involved in a venture before it begins.
Would you be so good as to outline the schedule of
events more clearly for me?" Stonevale asked innocently.

"I do not see why I should. I did not invite you
along."

"I merely wish to be of assistance, Miss Huntington.
Not only is Lyndwood grateful for my help tonight, but
you, yourself, might also find it very convenient to have
an extra escort on hand. The mob can become very
boisterous and rowdy at night."

"I'm not in the least concerned with the rowdy crowds.
That is part of what will make the entire venture
exciting."

"Then I'm sure you will at least be grateful for my continued silence on the matter should I happen to be introduced to your aunt this evening."

Victoria studied him mutely for a short, taut moment. "It would seem that Lord Lyndwood is not the only one in danger of being blackmailed. It appears I am also slated to become a victim."

"You wound me, Miss Huntington."

"Not fatally, unfortunately, else I would be rid of my problem, wouldn't I?"

"I urge you to look upon me as a solution rather than a problem." Stonevale smiled his slow smile. It did not affect the ghosts in his eyes. "I ask only to serve you in the capacity of escort this evening when you venture out into the dangerous streets of the city. I am most anxious to discharge my gaming debt."

"And if I decline to collect my winnings by accepting your escort, you will tell my aunt what is planned, is that it?"

Stonevale sighed. "It would be most unpleasant for all concerned if Miss Lyndwood's mama or your aunt discovered your scheme for tonight, but one can never tell what topics of conversation will arise in the course of an evening, can one?"

Victoria snapped her closed fan against the table. "I knew it. This *is* blackmail."

"A nasty word for it, but, yes, I suppose in a manner of speaking, it is blackmail."

Fortune hunter. That was the only explanation. She had never before encountered one quite so bold and aggressive. The type generally tended to be extremely well mannered and gracious, at least initially. But Victoria trusted her instincts. She locked eyes with Stonevale for an instant, fascinated by the waiting, expectant gleam in his hard, gray gaze. When she started to rise from the card table, the earl got to his feet to assist her.

"I shall look forward to seeing you later this evening," he murmured in her ear as she rose.

"If you are fishing for a fortune, my lord," Victoria drawled, "cast your lures elsewhere. You are wasting your time with me. I will grant that your technique is a novel one, but I do not find it at all attractive. I assure you, I have resisted far more agreeable bait."

"So I have been told."

He paced beside her as they moved into the glittering, crowded ballroom. Victoria became aware again, as she had earlier, of Stonevale's curiously balanced, but uneven stride. The elegant black evening clothes, finely tied cravat, close-fitting breeches, and polished boots did not disguise the limp that marred the movement of his left leg.

"What, precisely, have you been told, my lord?" Victoria demanded.

He shrugged. "It is said you have little interest in marriage, Miss Huntington."

"Your sources are wrong." She smiled thinly. "I do not have even a little interest in the married state. I have absolutely *no* interest in it, whatsoever."

Stonevale slanted her a considering glance. "A pity. Perhaps if you had a husband and a family to occupy your time in the evenings, you would not be obliged to amuse yourself with risky adventures such as the one you have planned for tonight."

Victoria's smile widened. "I am certain that the sort of adventure I have planned for this evening will be vastly more entertaining than the evening duties of a wife."

"What makes you so certain of that?"

"Personal history, my lord. My mother was married for her fortune and it destroyed her. My dear aunt was also married for her money. Fortunately for her my uncle had the grace to die early on in a hunting accident. But since I cannot count on similar good fortune, I have chosen not to take the risk of marriage."

"You do not fear that you might be missing an important part of a woman's life?" he ventured.

"Not in the least. I have seen nothing of marriage to recommend it." Victoria opened her gilded fan to conceal a shudder. Memories of her stepfather's casual little cruelties and drunken acts of violence toward her mother were never far below the surface. Even the bright lights of the ballroom could not entirely banish them.

She fanned herself languidly once or twice, hoping Stonevale would gain the impression that she was acutely bored with the direction of the conversation. "Now, if you will excuse me, my lord, I see a friend I must speak to."

He followed her glance. "Ah, yes, the intrepid Annabella Lyndwood. She is no doubt anxious to discuss the evening's plans, too. It appears, since you are determined not to be cooperative, that I shall be left to discover the details on my own. But never fear, I am very good at games of strategy." Stonevale inclined his head briefly over Victoria's hand. "Until later, Miss Huntington."

"I shall pray you find something more entertaining to do with your time tonight than to accompany us."

"Not likely." The earl's faint smile flared into a brief, wicked grin that momentarily displayed his strong white teeth.

Victoria turned away from him with an elegant swirl of her golden yellow silk skirts, refusing to give the man the satisfaction of a backward glance. This man was not only potentially dangerous, he was insufferable.

Victoria stifled a small groan as she swept through the crowd. She ought to have known better than to have allowed the earl to entice her into the card room tonight. It was, after all, not quite the thing for a lady to play cards with a man at an affair such as this. But she'd always had a hard time resisting adventure and the damnable man had seemed to sense that almost at once. *Sensed it and used the weakness.* She must remember that.

It was not as if she'd had any warning. Stonevale had, after all, been properly introduced to her by Jessica Atherton, no less.

Everyone knew Lady Atherton was entirely above reproach, a paragon, in fact. Slender, dark-haired, and blue-eyed, the viscountess was not only young, delicate, and quite lovely, she was also becomingly modest, unfailingly gracious, eminently respectable, and a stickler for the proprieties. In other words, she would certainly never have introduced a known rake or fortune hunter to one of her guests.

"Vicky, I've been looking everywhere for you." Annabella Lyndwood hurried over to her friend's side.

She flicked open her fan and proceeded to use it to shield her lips as she spoke in a whisper. "Were you actually playing cards with Stonevale? How very naughty of you. Who won?"

Victoria sighed. "I did, for all the good it did me."

"Did he tell you Bertie has invited him to accompany us tonight? I was furious about that, but Bertie insists we should have another man along for protection."

"So I was given to understand."

"Oh, dear, you are angry. I am so sorry, truly I am, Vicky, but there was no help for it. Bertie promised he would say nothing about our plans, but apparently Stonevale tricked him into revealing all."

"Yes, I can see how that might happen. Probably poured hock down Bertie's throat until the truth emerged. It is certainly a pity your brother could not keep his mouth shut, but don't fret, Bella. I am determined we shall enjoy ourselves regardless."

Annabella's sky blue eyes gleamed in obvious relief. Her fair curls bounced enticingly as she nodded her head and smiled. Annabella Lyndwood was held by certain high sticklers to be just the slightest bit too well rounded for fashion. But that tendency toward a full figure had certainly not put off her many suitors. She had recently turned twenty-one and had confided to Victoria that she would undoubtedly be obliged to accept one of the several offers she had received this Season. Annabella had gotten a late start in the marriage mart because of the untimely death of her father, but she had proven enormously popular when she had finally made her appearance in London.

"What do you know of him, Bella?" Victoria asked quietly.

"Who? Stonevale? Not much, to be perfectly truthful. Bertie says he's respected in the clubs. He just recently acceded to the title, I believe. The previous earl was a distant relative of some sort. An uncle or something. Bertie mentioned estates in Yorkshire."

"Did Bertie have anything else to say about him?"

"Let me think. According to Bertie, the family line

has almost died out. It came close to dying out entirely,
I gather, when Lucas Colebrook was badly wounded on
the Peninsula a year or so ago."

Victoria felt her stomach tighten in an odd manner.
"The limp?"

"Yes. It was the end of his career in the military,
apparently. Still, that career would have ended regardless once he inherited. His first duty is to his title and
estates now, of course."

"Of course." Victoria did not want to ask the next
question, but she could not resist. "How did it happen?"

"The injury to his leg? I don't know the details.
Bertie says Stonevale never talks about it. But according to my brother, Wellington, himself, mentioned the
earl in several of the dispatches. The story is that during the battle in which he was wounded, Stonevale
managed to stay in the saddle and lead his men on to
take their objective before he collapsed and was left for
dead on the field."

Left for dead. Victoria felt sick. She pushed the
queasy sensation aside, reminding herself that Lucas
Colebrook was not the sort of man for whom she could
afford pity. Furthermore, she seriously doubted that he
would welcome it. Unless, of course, he could figure
out some way to use it to his advantage.

It occurred to her to wonder if Stonevale had suggested the card game earlier so that he would not be
obliged to endure a set of country dances. The limp
probably kept him off the floor.

"What do you think of him, Vicky? I have seen the
Perfect Miss Pilkington eyeing him all evening and so
have several other ladies in the room. Not to mention
their mamas. Nothing like a little fresh blood on the
scene to whet the appetite, is there?" Annabella teased
lightly.

"What a perfectly disgusting image." But Victoria
laughed in spite of herself. "I wonder if Stonevale knows
he's being looked over like a prize stallion?"

"I don't know, but thus far you are the only one he is
looking over in return. No one could help but notice
that it was you he coaxed into the card room."

"I suppose he's hanging out for a fortune," Victoria said.

"Really, Vicky, you always believe men are after your inheritance. You are positively single-minded to the point of idiocy on the subject. Is it not possible that some of your admirers are seriously interested in you, not your money?"

"Bella, I'm nearly twenty-five years old. We are both aware that men of the ton do not make offers to women of my advanced years unless they are lured by practical reasons. My fortune is a very practical reason."

"You speak as if you are on the shelf, and that is simply not true."

"Of course it's true, and to be honest, I prefer it that way," Victoria said evenly.

Annabella shook her head. "But, why?"

"It makes everything so much simpler," Victoria explained vaguely, unconsciously scanning the crowd in search of Stonevale. She spotted him at last talking to his hostess near the door that opened onto the vast Atherton gardens. She studied the intimate manner in which he stood towering over the angelic Lady Atherton, who was a vision in pink.

"If it makes you feel any better, Bertie has said absolutely nothing to imply that Stonevale is a fortune hunter," Annabella said. "Quite the contrary. It's rumored the old earl was an eccentric who hoarded his wealth until the day he died. Now it all belongs to our new earl. And you know Bertie. He would not dream of inviting anyone to accompany us tonight unless he approved of him."

That much was true, Victoria conceded. Lord Lyndwood, only two years older than his sister, took the duties of his recently inherited title quite seriously. He was highly protective of his flirtatious, exuberant sibling and he was always pleasant to Victoria. He would not expose either woman to a man whose background or reputation was questionable. Perhaps Annabella was right, Victoria thought, perhaps she was a bit overanxious on the subject of wily fortune hunters.

Then she recalled Stonevale's eyes. Even if he were

not a fortune hunter, he was still more dangerous than any man she had ever met with the possible exception of her stepfather.

Victoria sucked in her breath at the thought and then discarded it angrily. No, she told herself with sudden fierceness, regardless of how dangerous Stonevale might be in his own right, she would not put him into the same category as the brutal man who had married her mother. Something deep within her was very certain the two men were not of the same mold.

"Well, congratulations, Victoria, my dear. I see you have captured the attention of our new earl. Stonevale is an interesting specimen, is he not?"

Startled out of her thoughts by the familiar, throaty voice, Victoria glanced to her left and saw Isabel Rycott standing nearby. She forced herself to smile. The truth was, she did not particularly care for the woman, but she did feel a trace of envy when she was around her.

Isabel Rycott always reminded Victoria of an exotic jewel. She was in her early thirties and had about her an air of lush, feminine mystery that seemed to attract men the way honey enticed bees. The sense of exoticism was enhanced by Isabel's catlike grace, her sleek black hair, and faintly slanted eyes. She was one of a handful of other women in the room besides Victoria who had defied the current style by wearing a strong color rather than demure white or pastel tonight. Her riveting deep emerald green gown shimmered brilliantly in the light of the ballroom.

But it was not Isabel's unusual looks that made Victoria regard her with a certain wistful envy. It was the freedom conferred upon her by her age and her status as a widow that Victoria secretly admired. A woman in Lady Rycott's position was far less subject to the close scrutiny of the ton than Victoria was. Lady Rycott was even free to indulge in discreet affairs.

Victoria had never met a man with whom she had wanted to have an affair, but she would have liked very much to have had the freedom to do so if she chose.

"Good evening, Lady Rycott." Victoria looked down

at the woman who stood several inches shorter than she. "Are you acquainted with the earl?"

Isabel shook her exquisitely shaped head. "We have not yet been introduced, unfortunately. He has only recently entered Society, although I hear he has been active at the gaming tables in the clubs for some time now."

"I heard the same thing," Annabella said. "Bertie says the man is an excellent gamester. Very coolheaded."

"Really?" Isabel glanced across the room to where the earl was still standing with Lady Atherton. "He's not at all in the way of being handsome, is he? Still, there is something quite intriguing about him."

Handsome? Victoria could have laughed aloud at the notion of using such an insipid word to describe Stonevale. No, he was not handsome. His face was strong, harsh even, with a sharp blade of a nose, an aggressive jaw, and an unrelenting awareness in those gray eyes. His hair was the color of a moonless night sky, shot with silver at the temples, but none of it added up to handsome. When one looked at Stonevale, one saw quiet, controlled, masculine power, not a fine dandy.

"You must admit," Annabella said, "that he certainly wears his clothes well."

"Yes," Isabel agreed softly. "He wears his clothes exceedingly well."

Victoria did not like the assessing look Isabel was employing as she surveyed the earl, but there was no denying that Stonevale was one of those rare men who was not dominated by the elegant tailoring that was so fashionable. His powerful shoulders, flat waist, and strongly molded thighs needed no padding or camouflage.

"Perhaps he will turn out to be rather amusing," Isabel said.

"Yes, indeed," Annabella agreed cheerfully.

Victoria glanced again at the tall, dark figure beside Lady Atherton. "Amusing may not be quite the right word." Dangerous was the right word.

But Victoria was suddenly willing to experiment with this dash of danger; the social whirl of the ton, which lately she depended upon more and more to fill up the long hours of the night, was no longer enough. She needed something else to help her hold the restless nightmares at bay.

The Earl of Stonevale might be just the tonic for which she had been searching.

"Dearest Lucas, what did you think of her? Will she do?" Lady Atherton gazed up at Stonevale with an anxious expression in her beautiful, gentle eyes.

"I think she will do nicely, Jessica." Lucas sipped champagne from the glass in his hand, his eyes moving across the crowd.

"I know she is a bit old."

"I, myself, am a bit old," he pointed out dryly.

"Nonsense. Thirty-four is an excellent age for a man intent on marriage. Edward was thirty-three when I married him."

"Yes, he was, wasn't he?"

Jessica Atherton's eyes were instantly filled with a heart-wrenching contrition. "Lucas, I am so sorry. How clumsy of me. You must know I did not mean to hurt you."

"I'll survive." Lucas finally spotted Victoria in the crowd. He kept his gaze on the tall figure of his quarry as she stepped out onto the dance floor with a plump, elderly baron. Victoria obviously enjoyed dancing, although she appeared to restrict her partners to very young, socially awkward males or those much older than herself. She probably viewed such men as harmless.

He regretted he did not dare risk asking her out onto the floor. It would be interesting to see if she followed him there as easily as she had followed him into the card room. But he was not certain how well she would tolerate the lack of grace in his damned left leg, and at this juncture he could not take any chances.

He sensed no streak of cruelty in her, though. She definitely had a temper, but he knew she would not stoop to insults or cutting remarks about his limp. Nevertheless she might very well trod quite forcefully on his toes if he managed to goad her as he had in the card room. The image made Lucas smile.

"It was quite outrageous of her to accompany you into the card room, of course," Lady Atherton said. "But, then, I fear that is our Miss Huntington. She does have a tendency to come very close to the edge of what is considered proper. But under a husband's guidance, I am certain that regrettable element of her nature could be controlled."

"An interesting notion."

"And she does have a noticeable predilection for that rather overbright shade of yellow," Lady Atherton added.

"It's clear Miss Huntington has a mind and a will of her own. But I must allow that the yellow looks attractive on her. Not many women could wear it successfully."

Lucas studied Victoria's tall, willowy figure in the high-waisted gown. The yellow silk was a ray of honey-eyed sunlight in the crowded room. It gleamed with a warm richness amid the array of classical white and watery pastels.

The only real problem with the gown as far as he was concerned was that the bodice was cut far too low. It revealed entirely too much of the gentle, high slopes of Victoria's breasts. Lucas had an almost irresistible urge to borrow some matron's shawl and wrap it firmly around Victoria's upper torso. Such an impulse was so out of character for him that he was momentarily astonished.

"I fear she has a reputation for being something of an Original. Her aunt's doing, no doubt. Cleo Nettleship is most unusual in her own right," Lady Atherton said.

"I would much prefer a lady who is out of the common run. Makes for more interesting conversation, wouldn't you say? One way or another, I suspect I shall have to endure a good many conversations with the woman I eventually marry. No getting around it."

Jessica sighed softly. " 'Tis unfortunate, but there simply is not a large selection of heiresses around this Season. But, then, there rarely is. However, there is still Miss Pilkington. You really should meet her before you make up your mind, Lucas. I vow she is a very admirable female. Always perfectly correct in her behavior, whereas, I fear, Miss Huntington has a certain tendency to be somewhat headstrong."

"Never mind Miss Pilkington. I'm quite content with Miss Huntington."

"If only she weren't very nearly five and twenty. Miss Pilkington is only nineteen. Younger women tend to be more amenable to a husband's influence, Lucas."

"Jessica, please believe me when I tell you Miss Huntington's age is not a problem."

"You are quite certain?" Lady Atherton eyed him uneasily.

"I would far rather deal with a woman of a certain age who knows what she's about than a young chit straight out of the schoolroom. And I would have to say that Miss Huntington does, indeed, know what she is about."

"You mean because she has managed to stay single so long? You are probably right. She's made it very clear she has no interest whatsoever in turning over her inheritance to a husband. Everyone but the most desperate of fortune hunters has quite given up on her."

Stonevale flashed a crooked smile. "Which narrows the field for me."

"Don't misunderstand me. She is an engaging creature, rather refreshing in some ways, like her aunt. Victoria does have her share of admirers. But they all seem to be relegated to the status of friends."

"In other words, they have all learned their places and they stay in them."

"If they overstep themselves, she drops them immediately. Miss Huntington is known for being kind for the most part, always has a smile and a charming word. Quite willing to dance with the less attractive men in the room. But she is very firm with all of the gallants who hang around her," Jessica added.

That did not surprise him. Miss Huntington would not have remained her own mistress this long unless she had learned the trick of manipulating the males in her orbit. He was going to find himself walking a very narrow line during this courtship.

"She is well educated, I take it?" Lucas asked.

"Some would say extraordinarily so. I've heard that

Lady Nettleship assumed most of the responsibility for educating her niece and one can certainly see the results. Miss Huntington would undoubtedly have come to grief in Society long ago were it not for the fact that her aunt's position is unassailable."

"What happened to Miss Huntington's parents?"

Lady Atherton hesitated, then spoke evenly. "Dead. All of them. Quite sad, really. But the Lord giveth and the Lord taketh away."

"He certainly does."

Lady Atherton cast him an uncertain glance and then cleared her throat. "Yes, well, the father died when Miss Huntington was a small child and her mother soon remarried. But Caroline Huntington was killed in a riding accident a little over eighteen months ago. Then Miss Huntington's stepfather, Samuel Whitlock, died less than two months after his wife. A terrible accident on a flight of stairs, I am given to understand. Broke his neck."

"A strange list of tragedies, but it does have the net effect of leaving Miss Huntington free of parents who might feel obliged to inquire deeply into my finances. The useful rumor of my uncle's hoarded wealth would not hold up under close scrutiny."

Jessica pursed her lips in disapproval. "I fear there's no getting around the fact that Miss Huntington spent the minimal amount of time in mourning after her stepfather's death. She made it quite clear she mourned only her mother, and even that ended as soon as it was seemly to do so."

"You reassure me, Jessica. The last thing I want is a woman who enjoys such entertainments as extended mournings. Life can be very short and it's a shame to waste it in a lot of useless grieving for what one cannot have, don't you think?"

"But one must learn to endure the tragedies thrust upon us. Such things build character. And one must also be conscious of the proprieties," Jessica admonished, looking faintly hurt. "In any event, Lady Nettleship, the aunt, is an excellent female with fine connections, but there is no denying she is a trifle odd in some ways.

I fear she has allowed her niece to run a bit wild. Do you think you can tolerate Miss Huntington's rather unusual manners?"

"I think I can manage Miss Huntington very well, Jessica." Lucas took another swallow of champagne, his attention on Victoria, who was still dancing with her middle-aged baron.

She was not what he had expected, Lucas reflected with a curious sense of relief. He had been prepared to do his duty to his name, his title, and the many people for whom he was now responsible, but he had not expected to be able to enjoy himself in the process.

Definitely not what he had expected.

For one thing, he had not anticipated this near-violent rush of physical attraction. Jessica had informed him that Victoria Huntington was presentable enough, but that was as far as the description had gone.

She was taller than he had been led to believe, much taller than the majority of the women around her. But Lucas was a tall man and it was good to find a woman who's head would rest nicely on his shoulder instead of somewhere down around the middle of his chest.

Not what he had expected.

And she moved with a long, graceful stride that had not a trace of the customary mincing quality women so often affected. She also danced well, he realized, not without a small pang of annoyance. He knew he could not even compete with the middle-aged baron when it came to partnering her.

Lucas watched as Victoria's baron guided her effortlessly under a glittering chandelier. The massed lights revealed the golden highlights in her rich, tawny brown hair. She wore the thick stuff cut entirely too short for Lucas's taste. But the short, artfully careless style did reveal the delicate, enticing line of her nape and framed her fine amber eyes. The lady definitely knew what she was about when it came to fashion.

Not what he had expected.

Jessica had warned him that although there was nothing truly objectionable about Miss Huntington's features, she was not an outstanding beauty. Studying the lively, animated quality of Victoria's face from a distance, Lucas supposed Jessica was correct in one sense. But he decided that the warm golden eyes, so full of challenge, the arrogant yet feminine nose, and that flashing smile went together very nicely. There was a fascinating, vivid element about Victoria that caught and held the eye. It hinted at an underlying passion that was just waiting to be set free by the right man.

Lucas took another glance at the smile Victoria was giving her baron and decided he would very much like to taste Victoria's mouth. Soon.

"Lucas, dearest?"

Reluctantly Lucas turned away from the sight of his heiress. *His heiress*, he thought, amused as he ran the phrase through his mind again.

"Yes, Jessica?" He looked inquiringly down at the beautiful woman he had once loved and lost due to the lack of a title and a fortune.

"Will she do, Lucas? Truly? It is not too late to meet Miss Pilkington, you know."

Lucas reflected on how Jessica, bowing to the dictates of her family, had married another man to secure both a title and a fortune. At the time he had not really comprehended or forgiven her. Now, having acquired the title but still lacking the fortune he desperately needed, Lucas finally understood the position Jessica had been in four years earlier.

He knew now that marriage was not a matter of emotion; it was a matter of duty. Duty was something Lucas understood very well.

"Well, Lucas?" Jessica prompted again, beautiful eyes full of grave concern. "Can you bring yourself to marry her? For the sake of Stonevale?"

"Yes," Lucas said. "Miss Huntington will do very well."

2

"Is my aunt at home, Rathbone?" Victoria inquired as she hurried into the front hall of the town house. Carriage wheels clattered on the street outside as Annabella and her elderly aunt, who had accompanied Victoria to the ball, took their leave.

Victoria was rather glad to be out of the close confines of the vehicle. Annabella's aunt, who had acted as a chaperon for the younger women, had felt obliged to read her charges a lengthy lecture on the subject of the rather doubtful propriety of females playing cards with men at fashionable parties.

Victoria hated lectures of that sort.

Rathbone, a massive, distinguished-looking man with thinning gray hair and a nose that would have graced any duke, solemnly indicated the closed door of the library. "I believe Lady Nettleship is engaged with several members of her Society for the Investigation of Natural History and Horticulture."

"Excellent. Pray, do not look so glum, Rathbone. All is not lost. Apparently they have not yet managed to set fire to the library."

369

"Only a matter of time," Rathbone muttered.

Victoria grinned as she sailed past him, stripping off her gloves as she went toward the library door. "Come now, Rathbone. You have been in the service of my aunt ever since I first came to visit as a small child, and never once has she burned the place down around our ears."

"Begging your pardon, Miss Huntington, but there was that time you and she conducted the experiments with the gunpowder," Rathbone felt obliged to point out.

"What? You mean to tell me you still recall our pitiful little attempt to manufacture our own fireworks? What a long memory you have, Rathbone."

"Some moments in our lives are indelibly etched in our recollections, as sharp today as on the day they occurred. I, personally, shall never forget the look on the first footman's face when the explosion occurred. We thought for one horrifying instant that you had been killed."

"But, as it turned out, I was only slightly stunned. It was the fact that I was covered in ashes that gave everyone pause," Victoria noted.

"You did look as gray as death, if you don't mind my saying so, Miss Huntington."

"Yes, it was a rather spectacular effect, was it not? Ah, well, one cannot reflect too much on past glories. There are far too many new and intriguing wonders of the natural world waiting to be explored. Let us see what my aunt is up to this evening."

Rathbone watched a footman open the door of the library, his expression making it clear he was prepared for virtually any sight which might await.

But as it happened, there was nothing at all to be seen immediately. The library was in utter darkness. Even the fire on the hearth had been extinguished. Victoria stepped cautiously inside, trying in vain to peer through the deep gloom. From the depths of the room she heard the sound of a handle being cranked.

"Aunt Cleo?"

The response was a brilliant arc of dazzling white

light. It blazed forth from the center of the darkness, casting the group of people gathered into a small circle inside the room into stark relief for one flaring instant. The small crowd gasped in amazement.

A second later the giant spark vanished and a resounding cheer went up.

Victoria smiled toward the open door where Rathbone and the footman stood. "Nothing to worry about tonight," she assured them. "The members of the society are merely playing with Lord Potbury's new electricity machine."

"Vastly reassuring, Miss Huntington." Rathbone answered dryly.

"Oh, Vicky, dear, you're home," a voice sang out of the gloom. "Did you enjoy yourself at the Athertons' rout? Do come in. We're right in the middle of the most fascinating series of demonstrations."

"So it would seem. I regret I missed some of them. You know how much I enjoy electricity experiments."

"Yes, I know, dear." The shaft of light from the open door revealed Victoria's aunt Cleo as she came forward to greet her niece. Lady Nettleship was almost as tall as Victoria. She was in her early fifties and her tawny hair was elegantly streaked with silver. She had lively eyes and the same vivid, animated quality in her features which had historically characterized the women in Victoria's family.

That quality lent an impression of beauty, even to a woman of Aunt Cleo's years, where an objective eye could discover little true perfection. Cleo was dressed in the height of fashion, as always. Her gown of ripe peach was styled to reveal her still-slender figure.

"Rathbone, do close the door," Lady Nettleship said briskly. "The effect of the machine is far more impressive in darkness."

"With pleasure, madam." Rathbone nodded to the footman, who shut the door in obvious relief, and the library was once more plunged into thick darkness.

"Come in, come in," Cleo said, taking her niece's arm and guiding her through the gloom to where the small group still clustered around the electricity machine. "You know everyone, here, do you not?"

"I believe so," Victoria said, relying on her memory of the brief glimpse of faces she'd had a moment earlier. A murmur of greetings rumbled from the shadows. Visitors to Lady Nettleship's house were accustomed to such inconveniences as being introduced in the middle of a Stygian darkness.

" 'Evening, Miss Huntington."

"Your servant, Miss Huntington. Looking lovely tonight. Quite lovely."

"Pleasure, Miss Huntington. You're just in time for the next experiment."

Victoria recognized these three masculine voices at once. Lords Potbury, Grimshaw, and Tottingham comprised her aunt's faithful circle of admirers. They varied in age from fifty in Lord Potbury's case to Lord Tottingham's nearly seventy years. Grimshaw, Victoria knew, was somewhere in his early sixties.

The three had danced attendance on her aunt for longer than Victoria could remember. She did not know if they had initially been as interested in scientific explorations as their lady was, but over the years they had certainly developed a similar passion for experimentation and collection.

"Please, do carry on with your demonstrations," Victoria urged. "I can only stay for one or two and then I must be off to bed. Lady Atherton's rout was really quite exhausting."

"Of course, of course," Cleo said, patting her arm. "Potbury, why don't you let Grimshaw work the crank this time?"

"Don't mind if I do," Potbury said. "Bit tiring, I must say. Here you go, Grimshaw. Put some push into it."

Grimshaw muttered a response and a moment later the sound of the hand crank rumbled forth once more. Cloth rubbed rapidly against a long glass cylinder until a sizable charge built up. Everyone waited expectantly, and in due course another searing flash of light crackled and danced in the shadows. Gasps of satisfaction and delight again filled the room.

"Heard there's been some efforts to reanimate a couple of corpses with electricity," Potbury announced to the small group.

"How fascinating," Cleo said, clearly enchanted with the notion. "What was the outcome?"

"Got a few twitches and such from the arms and legs but nothing permanent. Tried it myself with a frog. Easy enough to get a few jerks out of the limbs but still stone dead when all was said and done. Don't think there'll be much gained from that line of inquiry."

"Where did the experimenters obtain the corpses?" Victoria asked, unable to stifle her morbid curiosity.

"From the hangman's noose," Grimshaw said. "Where else? A respectable experimenter can't exactly go about robbing graves, y'know."

"If the corpses were those of villains, then it's just as well they stayed dead, I suppose," Lady Nettleship stated. "No point spending all that time and energy hanging thieves and cutthroats only to have them spring up again good as new a day or two later because someone wanted to experiment with electricity."

"No." Victoria felt a little queasy at the thought of such a possibility. Such things were disturbingly close to the contents of her dreams lately. "I quite agree with you, Aunt Cleo. No point getting rid of villains if one cannot count on them staying dead."

"Speaking of the difficulty of obtaining corpses for experimentation, I must say some people are certainly making a nice livelihood robbing graves." The darkened room did not conceal the shudder in Lady Finch's words. "I heard the resurrectionists struck again the other night at a little churchyard on the outskirts of town. Took two bodies that had just been buried that morning."

"Well? What do you expect?" Potbury asked in prosaic tones. "Doctors at Edinburgh and Glasgow Schools of Surgery have got to have something to cut up. Can't expect to train good surgeons without something to practice on. The resurrectionists may be illegal but they are filling a need."

"Excuse me," Victoria whispered to her aunt as the

conversation about the traffic in dead bodies threatened to grab everyone's attention. "I believe I will go on to bed."

"Sleep well, my dear." Cleo patted her hand affectionately. "Remind me in the morning to show you the wonderful collection of beetles Lady Woodbury brought by. Found them all on her last trip to Sussex. She's very kindly agreed to let us study them for a few days."

"I shall look forward to seeing them," Victoria said, not without genuine enthusiasm. An interesting collection of insects was almost as intriguing as a new exotic plant from China or America. "But now, I really must be off to bed."

"Good night, dear. Mustn't exhaust yourself, you know. Perhaps you've been going it a bit strong lately. Just as well you're in before dawn for once."

"Yes. Perhaps it is." Victoria let herself out of the darkened library, blinking a few times in the glare of the brightly lit hall before she started up the red-carpeted stairs. As she reached the landing, her gathering sense of excitement was almost overpowering.

"You may go, Nan," she informed her young maid as she entered her airy, yellow, gold, and white bedroom.

"But your lovely gown, ma'am. You'll need help getting it off."

Victoria smiled in resignation, knowing she would only create questions where there were none if she refused assistance. But she dismissed the abigail as soon as possible and then turned back to the depths of her wardrobe.

From beneath a pile of shawls she pulled a pair of men's breeches and from under a stack of blankets she removed some boots. She found the jacket where she had stored it inside her large, wooden chest and set to work.

Within a short while Victoria was standing in front of her dressing glass examining her appearance with a critical eye. She had been quietly gathering the masculine clothing for weeks, and this was the first time she had tried on the entire outfit.

The breeches fit a bit too snugly, tending to outline

the flare of her hips and the feminine shape of her calves, but there was no help for it. With any luck the tails of her dark blue coat and the night itself would hide the most obvious hints of femininity. At least her breasts, being rather on the small side, were easily concealed beneath the finely pleated shirt and yellow waistcoat.

When Victoria set the beaver hat at a rakish angle on her short hair, she was pleased with the overall effect. She was certain that, at least at night, she could safely pass as a young dandy. After all, people saw only what they expected to see.

Anticipation welled up deep inside her and she realized she wasn't as excited about the forthcoming expedition to the fair as she was anxious about seeing Stonevale again.

It was true, as Annabella had said, Stonevale must be a gentleman or Lady Atherton and Bertie Lyndwood would not count him among their acquaintances. But a woman, especially an heiress, could not depend upon any man's sense of gentlemanly honor. She had learned that lesson well from her stepfather. Still, Victoria knew she would be safe enough tonight so long as she stayed in control of the situation.

She relaxed, allowing herself a small, assured smile. She'd had a great deal of experience controlling situations that involved men.

Victoria crossed the deep blue carpet to the yellow velvet armchair near the window and settled in it. In a little while it would be safe to leave the house.

Tonight there would be no time to worry about the creeping restlessness that frequently threatened her in the long, dark hours of the night; no time to dwell on that sense of something dangerous left unfinished; no time to fret about bizarre notions such as the possibility of bringing the dead back to life with electricity.

Best of all, it was nearly midnight already. With any luck she would be awake most of the night, so there would be less time for the nerve-shattering dreams that increasingly invaded her nights as of late. She had come to fear those nightmares. A small shiver went through her even now as she pushed the memory of the last one to the farthest corner of her mind. She could still see the knife in his hand.

No, there would be little opportunity for those nightmares to strike tonight. With any luck she would not be home before dawn. She could deal with the daylight hours. It was the darkness she had learned to fear.

Victoria gazed out into the shadowed garden and wondered what Stonevale would think when he saw her dressed as a man.

The cheerful anticipation of his stunned expression was enough to banish the small, tattered remnant of horror that still hovered at the edge of her mind.

Lucas leaned forward on the carriage seat and scowled out into the shadows of the dark street. He was not in a good mood. "I don't care for this nonsense. Why are we not fetching Miss Huntington from her front steps?"

"I've told you," Annabella Lyndwood protested. "Her aunt is a very understanding person, but Victoria is afraid that even she would have a few doubts about our plans for this evening."

"I'm glad somebody besides myself has the sense to have doubts," Lucas growled. He turned toward the other man in the carriage. "Lyndwood, I think we should have a few contingency arrangements made in case we become separated in the crowd this evening."

"Excellent idea," Lyndwood agreed with alacrity. He was clearly relieved to have Lucas along. "Perhaps we ought to arrange for the carriage to wait at a specific location somewhat removed from the activity?"

Lucas nodded, thinking swiftly. "It will be difficult to maneuver the carriage near the park. At this time of night the crowds will be large and unpredictable. Tell your coachman that if he does not find us waiting for him at the same place where he sets us down, he should drive two streets over from the grounds and wait there near a small tavern called the Hound's Tooth."

Lyndwood nodded, his handsome, concerned features in deep shadow. "I know the place and so does my coachman, I'll wager. Don't mind telling you again I appreciate your joining us tonight, Stonevale. When the ladies take a notion to have an adventure, ain't much a man can do to stop them, is there?"

"That remains to be seen," Stonevale said.

Annabella, dressed in a stylish blue walking dress with a matching blue pelisse, giggled. "If you believe you can stop Victoria from doing anything she pleases, you have a surprise in store for you, my lord."

"Miss Huntington gets up to these tricks frequently, I take it?"

Annabella chuckled again. "Victoria is never dull, I assure you, but this is a first for her, I believe. She told me she has been planning this for some time."

"It would seem Miss Huntington has gone ungoverned by a husband for far too long," Lucas observed, and glowered at Annabella as the giggles turned into outright laughter. "I have said something amusing?"

"Miss Huntington intends to go the entirety of her life without such governance," Annabella informed him.

"I understand she fears being married for her fortune," Lucas said carefully. He wanted information but he did not want to raise too many questions about his motives.

"She fears marriage altogether," Annabella replied, her laughter fading. "She has seen nothing but very sad examples of the wedded state in her own family. And of course the business of being constantly pursued for her inheritance for so many years has only inclined her more than ever away from any desire for matrimony. Sometimes, I confess I wonder if she isn't right in her thinking. What good is marriage for a woman?"

"Damme, Bella," her brother broke in sharply. "What a mutton-headed thing to say. Don't go taking any foolish notions into your brain about following Miss Huntington's example in life. Mama would have hysterics. To be perfectly truthful, as charming as Victoria is, if her aunt wasn't such a good friend of Mama's, I should think twice about allowing you to go about with her. Only look at the situation I am in tonight because of that woman's influence on you. The sooner you are married, the better. Thank God, Barton has almost come up to scratch."

Annabella smiled demurely in the darkness. "I know

you cannot wait to rid yourself of the responsibility of supervising my behavior, but I fear you must contain your enthusiasm for a while longer, Bertie. Upon due reflection I have decided to have you refuse Lord Barton's offer, if and when it comes."

"Upon due reflection probably means you discussed the matter with Miss Huntington," Lyndwood said morosely.

"I do recall a conversation on the subject," Annabella said. "She was kind enough to give me her opinion as to the sort of husband Lord Barton would make."

Lucas broke in on the fraternal wrangling, his interest sharpened by Annabella's last remark. "How was Miss Huntington able to form an opinion about Barton?"

"Oh, I believe he pursued her quite industriously for several months last year. During that time she had an opportunity to learn a great deal about him."

"Did she?" Lucas was aware of the chill in his own words. "Just what did she learn?"

"A number of small items such as the fact that Barton has apparently fathered a babe or two on his mistress, that he has been known to get so deeply into his cups that he has had to be carried into his house by his coachman, and that he has a passion for gaming hells," Annabella answered.

"Here now," Lyndwood muttered, "can't hold a few insignificant peccadilloes against a man."

"Really?" inquired a familiar, husky female voice from the open window of the carriage. "Would Viscount Barton be equally prepared to overlook a similar list of *insignificant peccadilloes* in his prospective wife?"

Lucas turned his head sharply toward the carriage window, aware that the mere sound of Victoria's voice had immediately reactivated the desire he had first experienced in Jessica Atherton's card room. He concealed his eagerness with the cold control he had learned years ago, prepared to greet his heiress with proper formality.

But instead of a striking woman in an elegant gown and bonnet, he found himself staring at a figure dressed to the nines in men's clothes. Laughing eyes met his through the shadows, challenging him.

"Good God," he said through his teeth, "this is insanity."

"No, my lord, this is amusing."

Lucas recovered himself as he heard the groom start to clamber down from the driver's seat. He shoved open the door before the man could arrive to open it properly, and reached out and caught hold of Victoria's wrist before she realized his intent. He had been expecting a lady with a taste for some mild adventure, not this outrageous creature.

"Get in here, you little baggage, before someone recognizes you."

His urgency brought Victoria through the door far more quickly than she intended. She gasped as she landed heavily on the seat beside Lucas and grabbed her beaver-trimmed hat to keep it in place. He saw she was clutching an expensive-looking inlaid walking stick in her hand.

"Thank you, my lord," she said with heavy sarcasm.

Lucas ignored her. "Let's get out of here, Lyndwood."

Lyndwood obliged by tapping his stick against the roof of the carriage. "To the park, if you please," he called out.

Annabella smiled at Victoria as the carriage clattered into motion. "You look very well turned out this evening, Vicky. Do I detect Brummell's influence in your choice of blue? He is particularly fond of the color, I'm told. But you have always preferred yellow."

"I decided a yellow coat might be a bit too striking for the occasion," Victoria conceded.

"So you limited yourself to a yellow waistcoat. I congratulate you on your sense of restraint. And, pray tell, who tied your cravat? I warrant I haven't seen such a clever design in ages."

"Like it, do you?" Victoria fingered the carefully arranged neckcloth. "Invented this particular fold myself. Call it the *Victoire*."

Annabella gave a peal of laughter. "Vicky, I swear you sound just like one of the dandies on Bond Street. You've got the whole tone exactly right. Just the proper sense of affected boredom. I declare you could trod the boards and make your living as an actress."

"Why, thank you, Bella. That is high praise indeed."

Lucas lounged back in the seat and surveyed the striking figure beside him with a critical eye. His initial shock was giving way to annoyance and a certain uneasiness that was new to him. It was clear Victoria Huntington was fond of mischief, and this brand of mischief could land her in serious trouble.

"Do you go about like this often, Miss Huntington?" Lucas was aware he had automatically used the tone of voice that in the past he had reserved for young officers under his command who had landed themselves in trouble. He could not help himself. He was irritated.

"This is my first experiment with men's clothes, sir. But to be truthful, I shall probably be strongly tempted to try it again in the future. I find that the masculine attire affords me far more freedom than I have when I wear women's clothes," Victoria admitted.

"It certainly affords you a far greater opportunity for bringing down a wave of humiliation and social disaster on your lovely head, Miss Huntington. If it got out that you have a taste for running around London at night dressed as a man, your reputation would be in shreds within twenty-four hours."

Victoria wrapped her fingers even more firmly around the handle of her walking stick. "What an odd thing for you to say, sir. Do you know, your attitude quite takes me by surprise. I would have thought you less of a prig. I suppose the card game at the ball misled me. Don't you have any taste for adventure? No, I suppose you don't. You are, after all, a good friend of Lady Atherton's are you not?"

The woman was deliberately baiting him. Lucas wished very strongly that they were alone in the carriage. "I do not know what you are implying, Miss Huntington, but I assure you, Lady Atherton is above reproach."

"Well, yes, that is just the point. Everyone knows Jessica Atherton would never in a million years allow herself to be found in this carriage on her way to the fair tonight," Victoria declared.

Annabella giggled again. "That is certainly the truth."

"Are you implying Lady Atherton is a prig?" Lucas demanded.

Victoria shrugged, the movement surprisingly sensual in the well-cut jacket. "I mean no offense, my lord. Just that she isn't the sort of female who enjoys adventure. One naturally has to assume that her friends are equally limited in their choice of entertainment and equally disapproving of those who have broader tastes."

"And you are a woman who enjoys adventure?" Stonevale baited.

"Oh, yes, my lord. I enjoy it very much."

"Even though it carries with it the risk of ruining yourself in Society?"

"There would be no real adventure if there were no real risk, would there, my lord? I would have thought a successful gamester such as yourself would understand that."

Her words made him more uneasy than ever. "You may be right, Miss Huntington. But I have always preferred risks in which the odds were at least somewhat in my favor."

"How very dull your life must be, sir."

Lucas instinctively started to react to the goading remark but caught himself in time. His self-control reasserted itself, along with his sense of reason. The last thing he could afford now was to have his quarry declare him a priggish bore. His instincts told him Victoria would respond to a challenge or even an all-out battle of wills, but she would ignore him entirely if he managed to bore her.

A priggish bore. Good God. The thought of that label stuck on him was enough to make him laugh. It was certainly not the usual description applied to his character. But around Miss Huntington, Lucas discovered, he was rapidly developing a most uncharacteristic regard for the proprieties. He was still in shock from the sight of her in men's clothes.

Victoria was no longer paying any attention to him, however. She was smiling at Annabella. "So you decided to turn down Barton's offer, did you? I am happy to hear it. The man would have made you a perfectly horrid husband."

"I am convinced you are right," Annabella shuddered delicately. "I might have been able to overlook Barton's interest in hazard but just imagine marrying a man who has actually fathered two bastards on some poor woman to whom he will not give his name."

"It certainly casts a nasty reflection on his honor," Victoria agreed grimly.

Lucas studied her profile in the dim light. "Just how did you come to discover the business of Barton's illegitimate offspring? I cannot believe that gossip reached your ears on the dance floor of a hostess such as Lady Atherton."

"No, it did not, as a matter of fact. I hired a runner to discover what he could about Barton and he was the one who turned up the news of the two children and the mistress."

Lucas felt a chill clutch his insides. "You hired a Bow Street runner?"

"I thought it the most efficient approach to the problem."

"It was a brilliant approach," Annabella declared.

Lyndwood groaned. "Good Lord, if Mama only knew. Poor Barton. D'ya know, I think he rather cared for you, Bella."

"I doubt that," Victoria said briskly. "His family has told him they expect him to marry and he is simply in the process of casting about for a wife who will suit his father. He tried me last year until I managed to make him see I would not do at all and then he moved on to try his luck with the Perfect Miss Pilkington. Evidently she, too, had the good sense to see that he was the lowest sort of fortune hunter. Then he spotted Bella, here, and decided to have a go at her. Nothing more to it than that."

"The Perfect Miss Pilkington?" Lucas glanced from one woman to the other. "Why do you call Miss Pilkington perfect?"

"Because she is," Annabella explained reasonably.

"Never puts a foot wrong. A model of feminine perfection. A paragon, in fact."

"You will understand about Miss Pilkington, my lord," Victoria said, "when we tell you that she is a protégée of Lady Atherton's."

"I see." No wonder Jessica had wanted to introduce him to the other heiress. It was a good bet that if he had decided to pursue Miss Pilkington, he would not now be sitting in a carriage with a young lady dressed outrageously in masculine attire. Lucas wondered for half a second if he had made a serious mistake earlier in the evening. And then he decided that whatever the risks, the night was going to be infinitely more interesting with Miss Huntington.

"I thought you would, my lord," Victoria said.

"Well, one thing is certain," Lucas pointed out dryly, "because of your interference, Miss Lyndwood will never have a chance to find out precisely how Barton does feel about her, will she? And Barton, himself, will never know he was done in by a paid runner and a certain Miss Huntington. The man will never even have a chance to defend himself."

"Could he defend himself?" Victoria retorted, her eyes clashing with his in the shadows. This time there was no mischief or humor in her steady, challenging gaze. "Are you saying that what the runner discovered was untrue?"

Lucas held his ground, speaking evenly. "I am saying that it was none of your business to interfere in the matter. There might very well be mitigating circumstances."

"Hah. I doubt that very much," Victoria said.

"So do I," chimed in Annabella. "Just imagine that poor woman tucked away with Barton's children."

Lyndwood bestirred himself on the other side of the coach. "Neither of you two ladies ought to know a deuced thing about any of Barton's offspring who happen to have been born on the wrong side of the blanket. T'ain't right for you even to be discussing such matters, is it, Stonevale?"

"Such conversation is certainly not the mark of well-bred ladies of the ton," Lucas muttered, grimly aware he sounded exactly like the boring prig Victoria had insinuated he was.

Victoria's smile was triumphant. "Lord Stonevale, allow me to point out that if you find my conversation too offensive for your delicate sensibilities, there is an easy remedy for you. Simply open the carriage door and depart."

Lucas realized in that moment that Victoria Huntington had the power to slice through his iron-willed self-control as no one else had been able to do in years. Furthermore, she accomplished the trick quite effortlessly. This lady was dangerous. He was going to have to work hard at staying in command of the situation.

Lucas cleared his throat. "My sensibilities will survive your indelicate manners, Miss Huntington. And I could not possibly exit now. My honor still requires that I pay my gaming debts."

"Hah. This is no honorable gaming debt, sir. This is blackmail, pure and simple."

"I assure you," Stonevale returned, "I am fast discovering that blackmail is neither pure nor simple, not with you cast in the role of the victim."

Her eyes gleamed with mischief at that sally and Lucas felt his whole body react with sharp desire. He folded his arms across his chest and leaned back against the cushions, his gaze holding hers in the shadows. In that moment he wanted nothing more than to be alone with this bewitching creature. He longed to pull her down onto the carriage seat and show her the extent of the risks she was running when she challenged him so openly.

For an instant a charged silence hung between them. When Victoria finally blinked and allowed her gaze to slide away from his own, he knew she had discerned his thoughts.

But Lucas's small sense of victory was short-lived. It was dawning on him rapidly that this courtship he had embarked upon was going to be even more hazardous than he had first thought. With Jessica Atherton's help and his own skill at getting by on his wits and his ability

at the card table, he had hoped to conceal the true state
of his finances from Society long enough to achieve his
objective. He had made his plans with his usual care.

But if his intended bride took a notion to hire a
runner to look into his affairs, it was all too likely the
full truth would come out. The rumor of his nonexistent
inheritance would not hold up for long. It was becoming clear that the task of stalking this particular heiress
would be the most exacting hunting he had ever done.
One wrong move, one miscalculation on his part, and
he would lose the game.

"How long do you intend to spend on your adventure
this evening, Miss Huntington?" Lucas kept his tone
detached.

"Is time a problem for you? Do you have another
engagement planned?" she asked far too sweetly.

He knew intuitively that she was fishing to find out if
he had a mistress expecting him later. "No, I do not.
Lyndwood and I must secure arrangements to have all
of us taken up by his carriage at a specific location, and
to do that efficiently in the crowd, we need to decide
upon a definite departure time."

"Oh. Yes, I can see that. I would suggest two hours
would be ample time to enjoy the fair."

Annabella sighed. "I am afraid I cannot stay out that
long, Vicky. Mama will be coming home from the
Milricks' soirée in another two hours and she will expect me to be in by then."

Lucas hid his relief. "An hour then?"

"An hour's long enough for me," Bertie Lyndwood
said quickly.

"That's probably all the time I should allow," Annabella
said with regret.

"Oh, very well." Victoria sounded mildly irritated
but resigned. "An hour it is. We shall have to hurry,
though, if we are to see everything."

Lucas said nothing, but privately he considered that
the next hour was undoubtedly going to be one of the
longest of his life.

Half an hour later he was confirmed in his belief. The
huge park was ablaze with lanterns that illuminated a

seemingly unlimited array of stalls selling meat pies and ale, booths featuring acrobats and rope dancers, and packed tents featuring puppet shows and games.

The crowd was a mix of the high and the low. Servants who had snuck out of their masters' houses, shopkeepers and their wives, apprentices and shopgirls, dandies out for a lark, a few daring members of the nobility, prostitutes, pimps, pickpockets, young boys from flash houses, military men and dockworkers all rubbed elbows together as they sought the after-dark thrills of the fair.

"My lord," Victoria murmured as they stopped to buy a custard tart, "I know you are concerned about calling attention to my disguise."

"Concerned is quite an understatement, Miss Huntington. Those damned breeches fit you like a second skin," Lucas muttered, eyeing the smooth line of her hips.

"I shall be happy to give you the name of my tailor. In the meantime, perhaps it would be best if you released my arm. A certain man across the way is staring."

"Bloody hell." Lucas dropped her arm as if he had been burned. He felt himself turning a dull red as he realized what a stranger would think to see him holding another gentleman's arm the way a man holds the arm of a woman. "This silly getup of yours is bound to cause trouble."

"No one will think twice about it unless they see you treating me as though I were a female." Victoria took an enthusiastic bite of her tart.

"It isn't just the way I treat you, it's the way you look in those breeches."

Victoria fingered her collar. "I thought the coat hid my figure rather well."

"I have news for you. It doesn't."

"You're determined to be difficult tonight, aren't you, my lord? Kindly remember that it was you who insisted on inviting yourself along on this venture. I am merely the innocent victim of your blackmail scheme."

Lucas grinned ruefully. "Innocent victim, Miss Huntington? Somehow I feel that description could never be applied to you. Whatever else you are, you will never be anyone's innocent victim."

Victoria surveyed him, considering his words for a moment. "I should probably take offense at that but I am having far too much fun. Oh, look, the acrobats are starting another performance. Let's go watch them."

Lucas glanced around. "I don't see Lyndwood and his sister."

"Bertie wanted more beer. They'll be back in a moment. Stop fretting, sir."

"I am not fretting, Miss Huntington, I am trying to exercise a measure of prudence. No one else on the scene appears inclined to do so."

"That's because there's little sport to be had in exercising prudence. Come, let's hurry or we won't be able to see the acrobats."

A short while later Lucas had just begun to relax and even convince himself they might all survive the hour at the fair unscathed when disaster broke out with no warning.

It might have been the particularly extravagant fireworks display which started the small fire. Or perhaps it was the fight that occurred between two prostitutes who were demanding payment for their favors from a soldier. Or it could simply have been the normal propensity of any large London crowd to turn itself into a mob on the slightest pretext.

Whatever the reason, the conversion of the throng of cheerful fair-goers into a wild, unruly human wave bent on causing trouble happened in less than a moment. Fireworks burst overhead, people screamed, curses filled the air.

Horses reared and plunged. A gang of boys took advantage of the opportunity to steal a tray of pies, causing the pie seller to run after them, hurling insults into the evening air. There were more screams and another flash of fireworks. Flames leapt up as a nearby booth caught fire and then all was chaos; dangerous, terrifying chaos; a chaos in which people would be trampled, assaulted, and robbed. Some might even be killed.

Lucas reacted automatically the instant he felt the mood of the crowd shift. For the second time that night he clamped his fingers in a viselike grip around Victoria's fine-boned wrist.

"This way," he ordered, pitching his voice to be heard above the din. "Follow me."

"What about Annabella and Bertie?" Victoria cried.

"They're on their own, the same as we are."

Victoria did not attempt to argue further, for which Lucas was profoundly grateful. Apparently the lady was capable of displaying some common sense when it was called for.

Chaining her to his side with his grip on her wrist, Lucas hauled her through the melee toward the uncertain safety of the narrow alleys and streets that bordered the park.

He had known from the start the lady was going to be nothing but trouble.

3

The danger, which had coalesced out of thin air, left Victoria stunned. In that moment the only promise of safety in the entire world lay in the iron grip on her wrist. She followed Lucas blindly, relying instinctively on his strength and the savage manner in which he wielded his stick to forge a way for them through the crowd.

Victoria felt a hand claw at her coat and realized someone was trying to pick her pocket. Another hand tried to grab the inlaid walking stick she carried. Without thinking, she lashed out with the stout length of wood, slashing at the grasping hands.

There was a scream from one of her assailants which brought Lucas's head around briefly. With one quick glance he saw that the would-be thieves had already released their intended victim.

"Good girl." He immediately turned his attention back to forging ahead through the mob.

He did not try to work his way back against the driving force of the crowd. Instead, Victoria realized, he chose to ride the human flow, as if guiding a boat through a strong current. He kept maneuvering steadily toward the edge of the wild, churning river, his pace controlled and strong in spite of his limp. He did not break out into a mad dash and thereby jeopardize his balance and hers. It was obvious he had long since learned to compensate for the weakness in his left leg.

Lucas's cool self-mastery amid the chaos made it clear to Victoria that he was one of those rare men who did not become rattled under pressure. She felt safe with him, even though the mob roiled around her like a violent sea.

As they reached the fringes of the mass of shouting, staggering, shoving humanity, the crowd thinned. Lucas made a calculated bid to escape it altogether; he had apparently been watching for his chance. In what seemed like an instant, he yanked Victoria into a tunnel of darkness between two buildings.

Victoria stumbled after him into the relative safety of the pitch black alley. Her boots skidded on slime and she caught her breath against the terrible stench that welled up from the confines of the narrow stone walls.

She thought the danger was over until she heard the crude drunken shouts from the alley entrance.

" 'Ere now, mate. Bring that light in 'ere. I saw 'em go inter this little 'ole, I tell ye. Two of 'um. Rich coves, by the look of 'em."

"Damn." Lucas swore with deadly softness. "Get behind me and stay down, Victoria."

Not waiting for her to obey, Lucas flung Victoria behind him with such force that she fetched up against the brick wall of the alley. She caught her balance and glanced anxiously toward the entrance just as a lantern appeared. In its pale light she saw the faces of two young ruffians armed with knives. They spotted their quarry and moved forward expectantly.

"What'er ye waitin' for, Long Tom?" the second man asked his pal in an urgent tone. " 'Urry up and spice the swells. There be plenty o' work out 'ere for the likes o' us tonight."

Stonevale stood his ground, shielding Victoria. As

she watched she saw him remove a small, shiny object from his greatcoat pocket.

"Bloody 'ell. 'E's got a pop," the first man cursed as the lamplight fell on the pistol lodged in Stonevale's hand.

"An excellent observation, gentlemen." Stonevale sounded faintly bored. "Which of you would like to test the accuracy of my aim?"

The first young man into the alley slithered to a halt and his companion piled into him. They both toppled into the muck. The lantern fell to the ground, glass shattering in a shower of small sparks. The weak flame continued to flicker a moment longer, casting strange, menacing shadows over the tense scene.

"Bloody damn 'ell," the first man said again, clearly frustrated. "Ye try to make a decent livin' and look at what 'appens." He found his balance and scrambled back toward the alley entrance.

The other would-be footpad needed no further encouragement. There was a clatter of boots on stone, muffled curses, and a few seconds later Victoria and Lucas had the alley to themselves.

But Lucas wasted no time. His long fingers clamped around Victoria's wrist once more and he hauled her through the dark alley into the next street.

The mob had not yet spilled over in this direction, and they were met with blessed silence. Victoria tried to slow her step in order to catch her breath but Stonevale refused to stop, and she stumbled obediently after him, panting.

"Lucas, I must say, that was very well done of you back there in the alley."

Lucas tightened his grip on her wrist. "It would have been entirely unnecessary if you had not taken it into your head to attend the fair tonight."

"Really, Lucas, must you—"

"We can only hope Lyndwood's coachman followed orders," Lucas interrupted as he continued pulling Victoria along at a rapid pace.

"I'm worried about Annabella and Bertie," Victoria got out between sharp, strained breaths.

"Yes. So you should be."

Victoria winced, aware he had no compunction about pointing out her guilt in the matter. The worst of it was he was right; this had all been her idea.

Mercifully, Stonevale said no more as he guided her around the corner and into the street where the coachman had been told to wait in case of emergency. Victoria saw the familiar lines of the Lyndwood coach pulled up in front of the tavern and she heaved a sigh of relief when she spotted two people inside.

"They're here, Lucas. They're safe." Victoria flushed as she realized she had unthinkingly been using Stonevale's given name since the excitement started.

"Yes. It appears we are to be favored with some luck tonight, after all." He said nothing else as they neared the carriage.

"Good God, we were worried about you," Lyndwood said, pushing open the carriage door. "Thought for certain you'd been run down by the mob. Hurry. We don't want to hang out in this street for long. No telling when the crowd might take a notion to come this way."

"Rest assured, Lyndwood, I have no intention of dawdling." Lucas tossed Victoria up into the carriage and followed quickly, slamming the door behind him.

The carriage took off at once and none too soon. In the distance the shouts of the mob filled the night air.

Victoria looked anxiously at Annabella. "Are you all right, Bella?"

Annabella clasped her friend's hand. "I'm fine. Bertie and I were on the fringes of the crowd when the trouble broke out. We managed to get out of the way almost at once. But I was so worried about you two. You were right in the heart of the throng, were you not?"

"It was a near thing," Victoria said. A wave of euphoria was washing over her now, rapidly replacing the tension that had gripped her a moment earlier. "We were accosted in an alley by two men intent on robbing us. But Stonevale produced a pistol and stopped them instantly. He was magnificent."

"Good heavens," Annabella whispered, shocked.

"Damme, Stonevale." Lyndwood frowned with obvious concern. "A near thing, is right. Neither of you was hurt, I take it?"

"We are both perfectly fit, Lyndwood, as you can see." Lucas dismissed the inquiry with a deceptively neutral tone. "Although Miss Huntington's disguise appears to have suffered somewhat."

Victoria belatedly checked her hair and realized something was amiss. "Oh, dear, I've lost my hat."

"You are extremely lucky not to have lost more than a hat, Miss Huntington." Again Stonevale's voice seemed far too calm.

Victoria slanted a sidelong glance at his hard profile and realized that Lucas was in a blazing fury. For the first time since the riot had erupted around her, she felt a trickle of genuine fear.

Lucas glanced out at the empty side street as the carriage drew to a halt. "You intend to be set down here, Miss Huntington? We are nowhere near your front door."

"It will do," she said calmly, collecting her handsome walking stick.

"And how do you intend to get into the house if not through the front door?" Stonevale asked, annoyed.

"I shall go over the garden wall and back through the conservatory, the same way I left earlier. Don't worry, my lord, I know my way." Victoria was already stepping down from the carriage as the door was opened. She hoped he wouldn't feel obliged to follow.

"Good night, Vicky," Annabella called softly. "It turned out to be a most interesting adventure, did it not?"

"It certainly did," Victoria replied.

Lucas followed Victoria through the carriage door. "Wait here, Lyndwood," he instructed over his shoulder. "I shall return as soon as I have escorted our reckless little dandy back over the garden wall."

Victoria turned toward him in alarm. "There is no need to see me home, my lord. I assure you, I am perfectly capable of finding my own way."

"I wouldn't hear of it, Miss Huntington." He must have spotted the new uneasiness in her because he smiled knowingly. "Excellent," he murmured, grasping her arm and propelling her into the shadows. "I see you understand me well enough now to realize that I am not in a good temper. It is always best not to argue with me when I am in this mood."

"My lord," she began, her chin lifting imperiously, "if you think to hold me accountable for what happened this evening, you can think again."

"But I do hold you accountable, Miss Huntington." He glanced up at the high stone wall covered with thick ivy. "How do we get inside the garden?"

She tried to retrieve her arm. When he took no notice of her small struggle, she gave up and nodded toward the far end of the walk. "There is a way over there."

He hauled her along in the indicated direction until she pointed out the heavy vines which concealed a few chinks in the bricks. Without a word, Victoria wedged the toe of her boot into the first opening and grabbed a vine.

Beneath her, Lucas shook his head in grim disapproval as he watched her climb the garden wall. Victoria felt awkard and clumsy under his close scrutiny. She had not as yet had much practice scaling garden walls. She could only hope the fitful moonlight hid the shape of her snugly clad derriere as she went over the top.

Behind her, Lucas grabbed a trailing bit of ivy, found the chink in the wall with the toe of his boot, and followed.

On the other side of the wall, Victoria dropped lightly to the ground and looked up to see that Lucas was almost on top of her. She stepped back quickly as he dropped down in front of her. She noticed he took most of his weight on his strong right leg and did not stumble as he caught his balance.

"My lord," she hissed, "you should be getting back to the carriage. The Lyndwoods will be waiting."

"I have one or two things to say to you first." He stood in the midst of the fragrant, deeply shadowed garden, a tall, lean, menacing figure as dark and dangerous as the night.

Victoria summoned up her courage. "I must tell you, Stonevale, that I have no wish to endure a lecture for what happened this evening. I am already quite aware that none of us would have been in jeopardy if I had not insisted upon going to the fair."

"In that, Miss Huntington, you are correct."

The total lack of emotion in his voice was far more unnerving than a scolding would have been. But Victoria suddenly remembered the way he had defended her in the alley. Impulsively she touched his sleeve.

"I know I am deeply indebted to you, my lord, but I must tell you quite truthfully that up until the moment the crowd turned violent, I was having a fine time. I cannot remember when I have enjoyed an outing more." She took a deep breath when there was no response and rushed on. "I would also have you know, my lord, that I thought you were quite wonderful. Very cool under fire, as they say. You got us free of the mob and I assure you I shall never forget the way you handled those two footpads in the alley. For that, my thanks."

"Your thanks," he repeated in a considering tone. "I am not certain that is sufficient reward under the circumstances."

Victoria looked up at him, suddenly aware that Aunt Cleo's botanical garden was a very dark and lonely place at this hour of the night. She wondered for one awful moment if Stonevale was going to lose his grip on the reins of his temper, and then she started wondering what she should do if he did. Belatedly she took a step back.

"My lord?"

"No," he said, as if having reached a conclusion. "Your paltry thanks are not enough for what I have been through and what I undoubtedly have yet to endure."

Without any warning Lucas's hands closed around her shoulders, and in one smooth, swift motion he backed her up against the garden wall.

Before Victoria could react, Lucas moved in close, so close that the hard, unforgiving length of his body pressed against her much softer frame.

Lucas's booted foot slid between her legs. Victoria froze for an instant, held still by the shock of his muscled thigh alongside her own leg. Her eyes widened in the moonlight as she looked up into Stonevale's starkly etched face.

"You are a hotheaded, reckless hoyden; a little shrew who is badly in need of taming before she lands in serious trouble. If I had any sense, I would end this here and now," Lucas rasped.

Victoria licked her dry lips. "End what, my lord?"

"This." His mouth came down on hers with a fierce, plundering heat that made her fully aware, at last, of the true extent of his dangerous mood.

She had been prepared for his anger but nothing could have readied her for the masculine arousal that poured over her in a searing conflagration.

Stonevale wanted her.

Victoria was momentarily stunned by the sensual assault. She had been kissed a few times by daring or desperate suitors and once or twice because her own curiosity had gotten the better of her. But she had never known anything like the rough, deep, demanding kiss that held her now.

She trembled and her fingers clenched around Lucas's upper arms. He responded with a husky groan and then he was crushing her into the ivy, his thigh forcing her legs further apart. Victoria felt the small jabs of the vines and inhaled the fragrance of crumpled leaves and the musky scent of Lucas's body. Her head spun as if she were being whirled about on a dance floor.

When she felt Lucas's tongue slide along her lower lip, she opened her mouth for him in the same instinctive, unquestioning manner in which she had earlier followed him to safety.

She flinched when his hands circled her waist, but she did not struggle as she knew she should, not even when she felt his thumbs glide up to rest just under the weight of her small breasts.

"My lord," she managed in a ragged voice as he freed her mouth to catch the lobe of her ear between his teeth. "My lord, I don't know . . . that is, you ought not to be doing this."

"I want you to have good cause to remember me, Victoria," Lucas whispered.

Victoria swallowed hard, trying to collect herself. "I assure you, I am not likely to forget you."

"Excellent."

His teeth grazed her tender earlobe, causing no real pain but leaving her with a disquieting sensation of vulnerability. The odd caress left Victoria feeling shaken to the depths of her being. Her insides turned warm and her pulse quickened.

Without stopping to think, she moved her hands up to twine her arms around Lucas's neck. She liked the scent of him, she realized. She also liked the feel of his strong shoulders under her hands. She was acutely aware of the heavy, masculine bulge outlined by his tight breeches.

"This," Lucas whispered, "is going to prove a most interesting association." The anger seemed to evaporate from him in that moment, leaving only the desire—his eyes alive and glittering with it.

"Do you think so?" Victoria was feeling very daring now as she looked up at him. The recent rush of euphoric relief engendered by the close brush with danger was meshing with another kind of thrill, a new and unfamiliar thrill, a thrill of deep sensuality. She felt oddly weak and realized she was clinging to Lucas.

"You don't realize it yet, but you have handed me the keys to the citadel. I know your secrets now, and I give you fair warning, I will use them to court you."

"*Court me?*" Victoria woke from her dazed, sensual reverie.

"I mean to court you, woo you, seduce you. I will make you mine, Victoria. Only the bravest, most determined of suitors would endure what I shall be obliged to endure in order to win you, but in the end I will have you." His smile was slow, dangerous, and infinitely compelling in the moonlight.

"What makes you think I will ever surrender to you, my lord?"

"You will surrender to me because you will not be able to help yourself. You will never find another man who is willing to give you what you want," Lucas told her. "When all is said and done, you won't be able to resist me. Now that I know what you desire, I have you in the palm of my hand."

"What is it you think I want, my lord?"

"Adventure." He kissed the tip of her nose. "Excitement." He kissed her eyelids. "And a companion to share it all with you. The fair tonight was a tame event compared to the sights I can show you. I can take you places where no lady would ever dare allow herself to be seen. I can show you the side of life no respectable woman of the ton ever knows."

"The risks," she heard herself whisper.

It was as though he read her mind. "You can explore that other world with me and no one will ever be the wiser. You would not want to jeopardize your aunt's position or your own in Society by getting caught."

It dawned on her slowly just what he was offering. The bait he dangled was irresistible and he obviously knew it. "But, Lucas, if anyone ever found out, it would be disastrous."

"What we choose to do in the dark hours between midnight and dawn will be a secret only you and I will share. I'm offering you a bargain, Victoria; one I do not think you can ignore. I mean to satisfy your curiosity concerning the wilder side of life."

"You must spell out the agreement more clearly than that, my lord. What precisely would you have of me in return?"

Lucas shrugged. "Very little. A lady by day, a companion in adventure by night."

"I am not so foolish as to believe it will truly be that simple. You say you would court me, woo me, but I will tell you clearly once more that I do not intend to marry."

"Very well, we will not talk of marriage," he said soothingly. "I, as do you, seek a companion for my nights. I am at your service. We will spend those nights as you wish. All I ask is that you save your adventures for our nights together."

"You are quite certain that is all you will require of me in exchange for your midnight protection and escort?"

"That is all I ask at the moment. The rest is in the hands of fate. We will play games together, Victoria. Dangerous games. Games unlike any you have ever played."

She looked up at him, fascinated by the hooded assurance of his eyes, mesmerized by the dark promise of his words. Victoria knew then she should flee, but she could no more have run from the lure he was dangling than she could have flown to the moon.

She was still aware of the edge of his hand under her breasts and she suddenly ached to know how it would feel if he moved his long fingers upward and touched her nipples. She shivered.

Again Lucas seemed to read her mind. He moved his hands slowly upward until he was cupping her breasts. She could feel the heat of his palms through her waistcoat and shirt, and, biting back a small cry, she clutched him.

Before she could summon the strength to protest, Lucas's hands had slipped downward again to clasp her waist. She was left feeling breathless, filled with an urgency, a longing for more of the forbidden touch.

"Well, Victoria? Is it agreed? Will you play the lady by day and my companion in adventure at night? Will there be other evenings such as the one we just spent together?"

"I thought you did not approve of the sort of thing we did tonight."

"I will admit I was astonished initially at your boldness and daring, but I have since recovered myself and it has occurred to me that nights spent with you will be far more amusing than any I might spend at my clubs or in the company of the boring young ladies on the marriage mart," Lucas assured her.

She hesitated, but she could feel herself slipping over the edge of a very high cliff. "It must be our secret," she cautioned. "No one must ever know. If my aunt discovered what I was doing, she would be beside herself with worry. Nor could I allow her to be publicly humiliated by my actions. She has been too good to me and I owe her more than I can ever repay."

"Your secrets will be safe with me. You have my word," Lucas agreed.

She believed him then. Victoria knew without any need for proof that this man's word was his bond. He would not gossip in the clubs or the drawing rooms. He would not treat her with anything more than proper courtesy at the routs and soirées where they would meet socially. "Oh, Lucas, I would so love to explore the night with you."

He brushed his mouth against hers. "Say yes, Victoria. Say you will take what I am offering."

"I must think about it. This is such an important decision. I must have time to reflect properly on it."

"May I call upon you and your aunt tomorrow? You can give me your final decision then."

She drew a deep breath, knowing this was the start of it. "You do not waste any time, my lord."

"I have never been the type to waste time."

"Very well. You may call upon us." She tightened her arms briefly around his neck, already knowing what her final answer would be. Then she released him, feeling abruptly nervous and even a little shy. She glanced up at the darkened windows of the house. "I must go in. And you must hurry back to the Lyndwoods' carriage. They will be wondering what has happened to you."

"I will simply tell them there was some difficulty getting over the garden wall," he said casually.

He bowed gracefully over her hand. When he raised his head, the moonlight revealed his faint, slashing smile. And then he turned, strode to the wall, and unerringly found the hidden toeholds. In another moment he had vanished into the night. Victoria hesitated a moment longer, wondering just what she had done, and then she let herself into the dark conservatory.

Some time later she lay awake thinking there had been far too much satisfaction and triumph in Stonevale's parting smile.

I mean to court you, woo you, seduce you.

She would have to tread warily, Victoria told herself, but she could deal with her midnight lord. She would learn to handle him because she had no choice; she could not resist what he was offering. She needed what he was offering.

For the first time in many months, Victoria enjoyed an untroubled sleep.

Ten minutes after making his exit from the garden, Lucas alighted from the Lyndwoods' carriage, said his good nights, and stalked up the front steps of the town house he had recently inherited. His butler, who, along with the rest of the small staff had been engaged for Lucas by Jessica Atherton, opened the door.

"Send everyone to bed, Griggs. I have some matters to attend to in the library," Lucas ordered.

"Very good, my lord."

Lucas walked into the library, which contained the few good pieces of furniture that were left in the house, and poured himself a liberal measure of port. His damned leg was aching again. All that idiotic running about at the fair followed by climbing that damned garden wall had set it off.

He swore silently and took a long swallow of the port, knowing from past experience it would ease the dull throb in his upper thigh.

It was not just his leg that ached. Another part of him was left throbbing as a result of the garden meeting with Victoria. He could still feel the softness of her as he crushed her up against the garden wall. The sweet, spicy scent of her still lingered in his head, mingling with the fragrance of the rich port.

His eyes fell on the portrait that hung over the mantel. Slowly Lucas made his way across the faded carpet to stand in front of the unsmiling face of his uncle.

Maitland Colebrook, the previous Earl of Stonevale, had not had much to smile about in his last years. Plagued by ill health and depressed spirits, he suffered from an abiding resentment against everything and everyone. Maitland's unpredictable temper had often flared into uncontrolled violence, a violence that was frequently loosed on whoever happened to be in the vicinity, leaving Stonevale always wanting of servants.

In his younger days Maitland Colebrook had been

given to debauchery, drink, and gaming on a wild scale. He had disappeared from Society after going through the bulk of his inheritance, an inheritance which had already been thinned out by his father.

He had become an eccentric recluse, cutting off all communication not only with his London acquaintances, but with his relatives. He had retired to the country to drain what little was left from his estates. He had never married, and when the end had come several months ago, he had grudgingly summoned his heir, a nephew he barely knew.

Lucas remembered the interview well. The gloomy master bedroom with its decaying draperies and shabby furnishings looked pleasant compared to Maitland Colebrook, who, withered and pasty-faced, was propped up in the ancient oak bed, a bottle of port and a bottle of laudanum at his side.

"It's all yours, nephew, every last cursed inch of Stonevale. If you have any sense, you'll walk away and let it rot into the ground. No good has ever come of these lands," he wheezed, wrapping his bony fingers around a dingy blanket and glaring coldly at Lucas.

"Probably because no one in recent history has bothered to put any time and money into them," Lucas had pointed bitterly. Any fool could see that Stonevale had potential. The land was good; it could be made productive again.

Money was the key to reviving Stonevale; money and a lord who cared about his people and estates.

"No point pouring money into Stonevale. Place is cursed, I tell you. Ask anyone around here. Been that way for generations. Bad soil, lazy farmers, undependable water supply. Not a damn thing that's worth saving. Should have sold the whole bloody place. Don't know why I didn't," the old man continued, his voice dry and raspy.

At that point the dying earl had leaned over to yank open a drawer in the night table. His shaking fingers had fumbled around inside for a moment, then closed over an object he could retrieve by the touch. Then he had hurled the thing at Lucas, who had automatically reached out to catch it.

When he opened his fingers, Lucas found himself staring down at a circular amber pendant dangling from a thin chain. There were two figures carved on the pendant rendered in such a finely crafted manner that they appeared to be two miniature humans frozen for all time in the translucent yellow-gold stone. The images were clearly of a knight and his lady.

"What is this, sir?" Lucas demanded, his fingers again closing tightly around the pendant.

"Damned if I know. A gift from my father just before he died. Claimed he'd found it in the old maze in the center of the south garden. Local folks think it represents the legend."

Lucas studied the stone. "What legend?"

Maitland turned purple with sudden fury. "The legend that makes this godforsaken estate so useless, the one responsible for ruining my life, for denying me a son of my own. The legend of the Amber Knight and his lady."

"What is the truth behind the legend?"

"Go ask one of the old witches in the village if you want to know the tale. I've got better things to do than tell you stories."

And with that, Maitland had lapsed into a fit of coughing. Lucas had quickly poured a glass of port and offered it to the pale, thin lips. His uncle had taken a long swallow and quietened.

"It's no good, you know," Maitland Colebrook continued. "None of it. Never was; never will be. Bad luck, the whole wretched place. Take my advice and let it go, boy. Don't try to save it."

Lucas looked down at the amber pendant, possessiveness and sudden resolve flaring in him. "Do you know, Uncle, I believe I will ignore your advice. I am going to save Stonevale."

Maitland Colebrook looked up at him with bloodshot, weary eyes. "And just where do you think you'll get the blunt? I've heard you've some skill at the gaming tables, but you cannot win enough to supply yourself with the sort of steady income you would need to save this estate. I know. I tried that in my younger days."

"Then I'll have to find another way to get the money, won't I?"

"Only other way is to snare yourself an heiress, and that's easier said than done. No decent woman of the ton who has money of her own will look twice at a penniless earl. Her family will be able to do better by her than you."

Lucas met his uncle's glare. "Perhaps I should look a little lower than the ton."

"You'd be wasting your time. Hell, I know the talk in the clubs. There's always a lot of speculation about offering one's title in exchange for some merchant's daughter who comes equipped with an inheritance. But fact is, it don't work that way very often. Money marries money and that's as true among the Cits as it is in the ton."

His uncle's words rang again in Lucas's head tonight as he stood gazing up at the dour portrait of Maitland Colebrook. He smiled grimly and raised his glass in a small toast.

"You were wrong, Uncle. I've found my heiress and I've set my snares well tonight. She's going to lead me a damned merry dance but in the end she will be mine."

And that end could not come fast enough to suit him, Lucas decided as he tossed down the rest of his port. He wanted Victoria's fortune, but he had learned tonight that he also wanted Victoria.

Lucas set down his glass, aware of the amber pendant warm against his chest. He had worn it around his neck, concealed under his clothing, since the night Maitland Colebrook had tossed it at him.

As Lucas stood alone in the library contemplating his future it occurred to him that the rich, tawny glow of the amber was an exact match for the color of Victoria's eyes.

4

Lucas walked up the steps of Lady Nettleship's town house with a sense of keen anticipation mixed with icy determination. He was in a mood not unlike the one that came over him when he sat down to a gaming table. Everything in him was focused now on winning, and Lucas knew he was very good at winning.

He had learned long ago that for a man who must live by his wits, there was no substitute for careful planning and strategy. He knew the value of a cool head and the ability to push aside all emotion in the midst of battle or a card game. Cold-blooded logic was the key to survival and Lucas knew it.

He was well aware that the reason he was able to survive and even flourish at the tables of the clubs and gaming hells of London was simply that he never allowed his emotions to interfere with his play. Unlike the wildly impulsive young bucks, the flamboyant, drunken lords, or the foolish dandies who loved to throw their money away in melodramatic style, Lucas never allowed himself to act out of either exuberance, false pride, or desperation.

405

When one's luck was running poorly, one simply quit the table and waited for another time and place. Lucas had always found another time and place.

But as successful as he was at the gaming tables, his uncle had been right; there was little chance of winning enough blunt to save Stonevale. Lucas knew he could waste a lifetime attempting to accomplish that feat. The lands and people of Stonevale could not wait that long.

It did not, however, take a lifetime's winnings to keep up appearances here in London. If a man was very clever and watched his expenditures, he could survive from one night's winnings until the next. Polite Society might speculate upon, but it never openly inquired into, a man's financial situation as long as he had the appearance of wealth. Having the title and access to Jessica Atherton's social connections also helped.

Lucas glanced over his shoulder at the expensive black curricle and the beautifully matched grays he had driven here this morning. His tiger was at the horses' heads, calming the high-spirited creatures and preparing to walk them until the master had finished his morning call.

The entire rig had cost far more than Lucas had wanted to spend, but he had reluctantly laid out the necessary just as he had done at his tailor's. When a man went hunting for an heiress, he had to camouflage himself well; especially when said heiress was given to hiring Bow Street runners.

Lady Nettleship's front door opened just as Lucas was mentally running through the day's strategy one last time. Lucas handed the butler his card.

"The Earl of Stonevale to see Lady Nettleship and her niece."

The butler peered down a very long nose. "I will see if Lady Nettleship is receiving this morning."

For one grim moment Lucas wondered what he would do if Victoria had changed her mind about allowing him to pay a call this morning. It was entirely possible that in the clear light of day she had sensed danger.

He should have resisted the hot urge that had driven him to kiss her last night. He had never intended to do so, not this early in the game. But for a short, perilous time there in the dark garden he had broken his own cardinal rule and allowed his emotions to dominate his actions. Lucas vowed he would be more cautious in the future.

The butler returned, and a moment later Lucas experienced relief which melted into triumph when he was shown into the stately drawing room. With the discipline of long practice, he made certain neither emotion was visible in his expression, but reminded himself that the first hurdle was behind him; he had been admitted into the home of his quarry.

An instant later his triumph turned to irritation when he did not immediately spot Victoria in the sunny room. He realized he had not expected her to lose her nerve this morning. But the lady who had followed him fearlessly into that alley last night had apparently had a few second thoughts about meeting him in the light of day. Lucas forced himself to give his full attention to the striking middle-aged woman seated on the elegant sofa.

"Your servant, Lady Nettleship," he murmured as he bowed over the beringed hand. "I see now that Victoria's fine eyes are a family trademark."

"Very charming, my lord. Do sit down. We've been expecting you. Victoria, do put down those beetles, my dear, and come greet your guest." Victoria's aunt turned her head slightly in the direction of her niece and smiled.

Satisfaction soared in him. The little baggage had not changed her mind after all. Lucas straightened with a smile and turned to see Victoria standing quietly near the window at the far end of the room. No wonder he hadn't spotted her at once. She was dressed in a yellow and white dress that tended to blend with the gold drapery behind her.

Her very motionlessness told him that she had deliberately chosen her position so that she would be able to study him unobserved for a few minutes as he entered the room. Lucas's brows rose faintly in amused acknowledgment of her tactics. There was no substitute for getting a close look at one's opponent before facing him. It was clear he was not the only one who knew something about strategy.

"Good morning, Miss Huntington. For a moment I feared you had discovered you had a conflicting social engagement today."

She came forward smoothly, her soft slippers making no noise on the carpet. She was carrying a flat box in her hands and her eyes were alight with mischief. "How could you possibly think I would forget your visit to us this morning, my lord?"

"One can never be completely certain of a lady's memory." Lucas inclined his head over the hand she gracefully extended. Her fingers felt cold and he knew then that she was not as composed as she appeared. This pleased him.

"I assure you my memory is excellent."

"Unfortunately for a man, it is not always a lady's memory that fails. Sometimes she simply changes her mind," Lucas said.

Victoria tilted her head and studied him. "Not without good cause. Please sit down, as my aunt suggested. Are you at all interested in beetles?"

"Beetles?" For the first time Lucas glanced into the box and found himself viewing an array of dead insects pinned inside. They were carefully arranged in rows according to size, with the largest, a true monster, at one end. "To be perfectly truthful, Miss Huntington, I have never paid much heed to beetles."

"Oh, but these are very excellent beetles, are they not, Aunt Cleo?"

"A fine collection," Lady Nettleship agreed enthusiastically. "Lady Woodbury, a member of our little society, collected them."

"Fascinating." Lucas sat down slowly, his eyes on Victoria as she took a place on the sofa next to her aunt. "One wonders how Lady Woodbury managed to kill so many large insects."

"In the usual manner, I presume," Cleo said. "Pinched them under the wings or used camphor or a length of wire."

"Do you collect insects, Miss Huntington?" Lucas asked.

"No, I fear I have not the stomach for it." She glanced down into the box. "The poor things do not always die quickly, you know."

He watched her profile. "The will to survive can be amazingly strong."

"Yes." She put the lid on the box of beetles.

"I fear my niece is a bit too softhearted for certain areas of intellectual inquiry," Cleo said with smile.

"I will admit I prefer botany and horticulture to the study of insects."

"Your interests appear to be quite varied, Miss Huntington," Lucas observed.

"Did you think them limited?" She glanced at him through her lashes, her eyes gleaming with a mocking innocence.

Lucas recognized a trap when he saw one. "Not at all. In the course of our brief association it has become quite clear to me that you are a woman with a most unusual mind."

Cleo glanced at him with interest. "Are you a student of horticulture and botany, sir?"

"As you may have heard, I have only recently acceded to my title. I find that coming into my inheritance has greatly expanded my range of interests. It seems to me that I shall need to learn something about horticulture and similar subjects if I am to implement improvements on my estate," Lucas said.

Cleo looked pleased. "Excellent. Then you will no doubt be interested in Victoria's watercolors and her drawings of plants."

Victoria turned a bright shade of pink, which amazed Lucas. "Aunt Cleo, I'm sure his lordship would not be in the least interested in my dabbles."

"I assure you, I would be most interested," Lucas said quickly. Anything that could make Victoria blush was bound to be fascinating.

"She has a wonderful ability." Lady Nettleship said as she jumped to her feet and went to a nearby table to fetch a sketchbook. "Take a look at these."

"Aunt Cleo, really . . ."

"Now, no false modesty, Vicky. Your work is lovely and so wonderfully true to life. I have been telling you for ages that you should get some of it published. Here you are, my lord. What do you think of these?" Cleo thrust the book into Lucas's hands with an air of expectant triumph.

Aware that Victoria was watching him in a resigned silence, Lucas took his time examining the sketchbook. He opened it expecting to find the usual assortment of amateurish artwork a man associated with females. It was considered quite fashionable for young ladies to learn to sketch and paint flowers.

But Lucas was startled at the clarity and liveliness of Victoria's work. Her plants bloomed on the pages of the sketchbook, glowing with exuberant energy. They were not just artistically beautiful, they were precise in every detail.

Lucas was fascinated as page after page full of roses, irises, poppies, and lilies came to life in front of him. Each one was labeled in a fine hand with its formal, botanical name: *Rosa provincialis, Passiflora alata, Cyclamen linearifolium.*

He looked up to find Victoria still watching him with an oddly anxious expression. He realized then that her art was a vulnerable subject for her. He closed the sketchbook. "These are excellent, Miss Huntington, as I'm sure you've been told. Even to my untrained eye these sketches and watercolors are beautiful."

"Thank you." She smiled suddenly, very brilliantly, as if he had just told her that she, not her art, was beautiful. Her amber eyes were almost gold. "You're very kind."

"I am rarely kind, Miss Huntington," he told her quietly. "I am merely telling you the truth. I will admit, however, that I don't recognize all of these plants. Where did you get your subjects?"

"From the conservatory," Cleo explained. "Together, Victoria and I have established what I like to believe is a most creditable botanical garden. Nothing on the scale of Kew, of course, but we're rather proud of it.

Would you care to view the conservatory? Victoria would be happy to give you a short tour."

Lucas nodded. "I should very much like to see it."

Victoria rose gracefully. "This way, my lord."

"Run along, then," Cleo said. "Perhaps you will join us for a dish of tea when you have finished viewing the plants, my lord?"

"Thank you." Lucas smiled to himself as he followed Victoria out into the hall and down a short passageway that led to the back of the house. Matters were going well, he decided as she led him into a large glass gallery filled with plants and the rich, humid scent of soil. Already he was alone with his quarry.

He looked around and realized that today he would be doing his hunting in a real jungle. He examined the view through the glass. Beyond the conservatory windows was a large, charming garden with a familiar-looking brick wall covered in ivy.

"I wondered what the garden looked like by day," Lucas remarked.

Victoria's brows snapped together in an admonishing frown. "Hush, my lord. Someone might overhear you."

"Not likely. We appear to have the place to ourselves." He examined the lush greenery and the array of exotic blooms that filled the glass room. "You and your aunt are, indeed, interested in horticulture, aren't you? This is amazing."

"My aunt had the conservatory built some years ago," Victoria said as she started down one green-shrouded aisle. "She has friends who travel all over the world and send us cuttings and small plants. Recently Sir Percy Hickinbottom, one of her many admirers, sent a new variety of rose he discovered on an expedition in China. He named it Cleo's Blush China in her honor. Wasn't that sweet? Last month he sent the most beautiful chrysanthemum plant. We are quite hopeful it will survive. Are you at all familiar with chrysanthemums, my lord?"

"No, but I do know what it means when a person suddenly becomes excessively chatty. Relax, Victoria. There is no need to be so anxious."

"I am not at all anxious." Her chin lifted proudly as she paused beside a large tray of strange, lumpish-looking plants that were covered in thorns. "Do you care for cacti?"

Lucas glanced down curiously at the assortment of spiny plants that were unlike anything he had ever seen. Experimentally he touched one of the thorns and discovered it was needle sharp. He glanced up and met Victoria's gaze.

"I am always interested in an adversary's defenses,' Lucas said.

"Is that because it is your instinct to find a way past those defenses?"

"Only when the prize promises to be worth the battle." He was going to enjoy fencing with her, Lucas thought. She was no coward.

"How can you estimate the value of the prize in advance of the battle?"

It had not been a mistake after all to kiss her last night, Lucas decided. He knew from the way she was watching him that she had been thinking a great deal about the embrace they had shared. "Sometimes one is allowed a small sample of the goods. The bit I was allowed to taste last night was very promising."

"I see. And do you go around sampling a great many potential prizes before you determine which ones you will pursue?" She glared at him.

His mouth quirked as he saw the hauteur flash in her eyes. "One must have some basis for comparison."

The hauteur changed almost imperceptibly into disgust. She turned away and started down the aisle again. "I rather suspected that might be the case."

Lucas was suddenly annoyed. She had started this. He reached out and clamped a hand around her wrist, drawing her to a sudden halt. She swung around to fix him with a defiant gaze.

"What is it, Victoria? You don't like the fact that there have been other prizes in my life? They have not been very important."

"I do not like the fact that you may have been very

indiscriminate in selecting and pursuing those prizes, nor the fact that you have been casual about the matter."

"I assure you, I have never been indiscriminate and rarely casual. In truth, there have not been all that many prizes. I have spent most of my life in the army, and one does not keep expensive mistresses on an officer's pay." He deliberately exerted enough pressure on her wrist to draw her closer. "What about you? You fence very skillfully. Is it because you have had a great deal of experience at this game?"

"I have had a great deal of practice at playing the role of cactus, my lord."

"And tell me," Lucas said smiling, "has anyone ever gotten past the spines?"

"That is none of your affair, is it?"

He saw the bright warmth in her cheeks but her eyes never wavered. "Forgive me. I cannot help but entertain a certain curiosity under the circumstances. After all, I fully intend to get past the thorns and claim the treasure for myself. I told you that much last night."

"You are not subtle, are you, Stonevale?" she said.

"I am when subtlety is required, but I think I can be completely honest about my intentions in this case. You're not a silly young girl straight out of the schoolroom. I do not think you are the type to be easily frightened by an honest man's intentions."

Victoria straightened and peered at him. "Speaking of honesty, just what are your intentions, my lord? You were not quite clear on that subject last night. I must know."

"I thought I had made myself very plain. You must be aware by now that I want you. I will do what I must to claim you."

"Last night—" she began urgently, and then broke off, hunting for the right words. "Last night I warned you not to think in terms of marriage."

"I heard your warning. You issued it several times in a variety of ways, as I recall."

"You do understand, then, that I am not playing a game when it comes to that subject? I have no interest in marriage."

"I understand." Lucas smiled faintly at the earnest expression in her eyes. She might not think she was playing a game, but that fact would not save her from losing it. "You do want to play other games, though, do you not, Victoria? Midnight games?"

She was silent for a moment, but Lucas noticed that her fingers trembled ever so slightly as she reached up absently to touch a broad leaf that draped over her shoulder. "You were right last night, my lord. I would dearly love a companion to share my evening adventures. Someone I can trust to keep his silence, someone who can take me into the sort of places I cannot go alone or even with friends such as Annabella Lyndwood and her brother. I admit that what you offered in the garden last night is very tempting. What worries me most is that you seem to be aware of just how tempting I find it."

"You hesitate because you are not certain you can take what I offer and get away without paying for it. Is that the problem, Victoria?"

She nodded, her mouth curving wryly. "You are quite correct, my lord. You have gone straight to the heart of the matter. I am not at all certain you will remain satisfied with whatever payment I choose to bestow."

Lucas drew a long breath and folded his arms across his chest. "The problem, it would seem, is mine. As long as I am satisfied with the bargain, why should you worry?"

"Because, quite frankly, my lord, I do not see you remaining content with a few stolen kisses taken in the garden, and I promise you that is all you will get from me by way of payment. There. Have I made myself perfectly clear?"

"Perfectly."

She waited for him to argue, and when he politely examined the unusual cacti instead, she lost a measure of her self-control, just as Lucas had known she would. The lady was swimming far out of her depth and she did not yet realize it.

"There will be no talk of marriage?" she demanded.

"None." He tested the spine of another of the curious cactus plants and found it as sharp as the first. "But I feel compelled to warn you that my guarantee not to speak of marriage does not mean I will not do my best to lure you into my arms. You are right, Victoria. I would like more than a few stolen kisses from you."

"You are far too bold, my lord."

"I see no need to dance around the truth. You know what I want in exchange for my companionship at midnight."

"Then the price is too high. I will never pay it," she said.

"I said you would know the price I seek, I did not say I will force you to pay it." He looked at her, enjoying the storm of emotion and curiosity that lit her eyes. "You need have no fear of me, Victoria. You have my word of honor I will not force your surrender."

"Pray, do not use that word again," she said through her teeth.

Lucas shrugged. "Surrender? Very well. Use whatever word you wish to describe my goal, but do not deceive yourself about the nature of that goal."

Her mouth pursed with strong disapproval. "Your *goal*, my lord, is a most dishonorable one."

"You leave me little choice. You have forbidden me to speak of a more honorable one."

"It seems to me you agreed very quickly not to speak of it," she pointed out tartly. She toyed thoughtfully with the leaf that hung over her shoulder. "One would almost think, my lord, that you are not interested in marriage, after all."

"Not every man is, Victoria. Why should a sane man rush to sacrifice his freedom if he can claim the woman he wants without giving her his name?" he pointed out dryly.

"Assuming he can claim her without doing so."

Lucas grinned. "It happens all the time. Surely you have been out in the world long enough to know that, Victoria."

"I know it." She sighed, sounding exasperated. "Don't misunderstand me. I am well aware that most men do not go into marriage out of a feeling of love. They generally go into it out of necessity, either to ensure themselves of an heir or to get their hands on a fortune or both."

"I have always found love to be a very vague and totally insufficient reason for doing much of anything."

She studied him through narrowed lashes. "You sound very cynical, my lord, but I suppose that is only to be expected from a man who is proposing to try for what is nothing more than a sordid, scandalous affair."

Lucas shook his head ruefully. "I fear you are confused, Victoria. You forbid me to talk of the honorable estate of marriage and then in the same breath accuse me of being cynical when I speak of having an affair with you."

Victoria bit off what sounded like a very unladylike oath. "You are right," she conceded. "It's this business of being an heiress that confuses matters. Annabella tells me I am extremely skittish on the subject; too wary by half."

Lucas smiled gently, taking pity on her obvious dilemma. "Always looking for danger in the nearest hedge?"

"I suppose so," Victoria said.

"Not a bad policy, all things considered."

"It has certainly been a very practical policy for me," Victoria acknowledged.

"Because it has seen you safely into spinsterhood?"

"Beast." But her mouth curved back into an amused smile. "You are quite right, however. I am a spinster and glad of it. Furthermore I intend to keep things that way."

Lucas's attention wandered from the cacti to a spectacular yellow-gold bloom he did not recognize. The flower, touched here and there with deep purple, flared like a crown from the green stalk that held it. He moved toward it, drawn by the shade of gold which reminded him of Victoria's eyes. He cupped the regal bloom in one hand and studied it. "After what happened between us in the garden last night, you will never convince me that you intend to live your entire life without exploring your own passions, Victoria You are too much like this flower, lush and sweet and full of passionate promise."

She grinned. "Really, my lord, you needn't get carried away by a flower. I understand your background is in the military world, not the literary one."

"Sometimes a man can learn more of life when he is surrounded by death than he can from all the poetry of the ancients. Even if you did manage to ignore your womanly passions for the rest of your days, I doubt that you could ignore your own intellectual curiosity."

"*Curiosity*. You think you can talk me into an illicit affair by appealing to my intellectual curiosity? How very original."

"It makes perfect sense to me. Any woman who can work up an admiration for beetles and cacti must certainly entertain a few scientific questions concerning her own physical nature." He inclined his head in a small, elegant bow. "I offer myself to you in the interest of intellectual inquiry, Miss Huntington. I'm hoping you will not be able to refuse."

Outraged, Victoria stared at him for a few tense seconds and then the mirth appeared in her eyes. In a moment she was laughing so hard she had to grab a post for support.

Lucas watched her, his hand still cupping the yellow-gold bloom. He was fascinated by her wholehearted amusement. She did not giggle in that annoying way young woman so often did, as if trying to imitate tinkling bells and rippling brooks. Victoria's laughter was full of life and warmth. It made him want to pull her into his arms and kiss her until he converted the humor in her into the passion he had tasted last night.

He could do it, Lucas thought. He knew from the way she had responded in the garden that he could make her feel desire. And he would use that knowledge, along with her quest for adventure, to seduce her. In the end she would be powerless to resist him. As he had told her in the garden, she would not easily find another man who could offer the bait he was holding out.

And once he had her locked safely in his arms, it

would be only a short step to marriage. Victoria might speak daringly of engaging in an illicit liaison, but he knew that she would find it difficult to actually conduct an affair that threatened her aunt's as well as her own position in Society. She was, after all, a young woman of excellent breeding and she knew both the rules and the risks that governed the world in which she lived.

Society required that young women of her background save their illicit affairs until after they were wed and had given their husbands an heir. After that, many wives felt free to pursue their own romantic interests so long as they were discreet. Their husbands, who generally kept mistresses before and after marriage, did the same, not always so discreetly.

But as Lucas watched Victoria's laughter fade slowly back into a glowing smile, it struck him quite forcefully that he did not intend to let his unsuspecting future bride trod the usual social path from altar to marriage bed to a string of discreet affairs.

He had always known that he would never be one of those men who overlooked his wife's infidelities. It was not in his nature to share the woman he considered his own. But the possessiveness he felt was far beyond what he had expected to feel toward the woman who would one day bear his name.

Once she was his, Lucas decided, Victoria would remain his and his alone. Social conventions be hanged. He was not going to share this half-wild, unpredictable creature with any man.

"My lord, you are impossible. Utterly impossible." Victoria wiped the moisture from her eyes and shook her head, still grinning. "Imagine offering yourself in the spirit of intellectual inquiry. How very altruistic. How very noble. You are far too generous."

"I shall do what it takes to win you."

"And just how am I to be won, my lord?"

"With adventure and excitement and passion. I will give you all of those things, Victoria."

She looked at him, her decision in her eyes. "I will pick and choose among them, taking only as much of any of them as I wish and paying for them as I wish."

He inclined his head in acquiescence, quietly satisfied with the victory. "That is your prerogative."

She hesitated and then impulsively took one step forward, reaching out to touch his sleeve. "Lucas, do you mean it when you say you want me, just *me*, not my money?"

He lifted a hand to stroke the fine line of her jaw. "I want you."

"I cannot promise you anything," she said with grave honesty. "I enjoyed your kisses last night, but that is as far as it should go and we both know it."

He covered her fingers as they lay on his sleeve. "I understand. Don't concern yourself with promises now. Together we will find out just how far this liaison of ours will go."

She did not move for a moment. She just stood there gazing up at him with a barely suppressed longing that made him want to pull her into his arms. It was not the promise of either passion or reckless excitement he saw in her beautiful amber eyes now, but something else, something sweet and vulnerable, an altogether heart-wrenching look of hopeful expectation.

"If you're very sure this is what you want, if you're sure this will be enough," Victoria said, "then I accept your offer to be my midnight companion."

Lucas exhaled deeply. "Then the bargain is sealed." He leaned down and brushed his mouth lightly across hers. She trembled at the touch and Lucas wanted simultaneously to soothe her and pull her down onto the tile floor and make passionate love to her. Before he could deal with the conflicting emotions, she was slipping out of reach and thrusting a small piece of paper into his hand.

"What's this?" he asked, frowning at the elegant writing on the paper. "A gaming hell? A brothel? A race meeting? A gentlemen's club?"

"Those are the first items on my list," she informed him.

"What list?" Then it hit him. He had seriously underestimated his opponent, a mistake he rarely made. "Bloody hell. You expect me to take you to a gaming hell and a brothel? Good God, Vicky, be reasonable. A nighttime visit to a fair or the dark walks of Vauxhall Gardens is one thing. It is quite another matter to sneak you into a brothel or take you to a gaming hell. You cannot be serious."

"You are wrong, my lord. I am very serious," Victoria said, unyielding.

He looked at her and saw that she was. "Damn it, Vicky. This wasn't quite what I had in mind."

Victoria dismissed the protest. "Thursday night would be an excellent time for our next adventure. I will no doubt see you at the Kinsleys' ball earlier in the evening and we can make our final plans. In the meantime—"

Cleo Nettleship's voice broke into Victoria's instructions. "Vicky, dear, are you still out there? Don't get too carried away or you will bore Lord Stonevale. Not everyone enjoys an extended tour of the conservatory, you know."

Lucas turned to see Lady Nettleship standing in the doorway, beaming at him. "I assure you, madam, I have never been less bored in my life."

"One rarely is around Victoria."

Lucas glanced at Victoria's satisfied expression and then he looked once more at the yellow-gold bloom he had been examining earlier. "Before we leave the conservatory, Miss Huntington, I would appreciate it if you would tell me the name of this strange plant."

"*Strelitzia reginae.* Everyone was thrilled when the first one flowered at Kew. Aunt Cleo and I were very fortunate to have this one bloom, too. Magnificent, isn't it?" Victoria said excitedly.

Lucas looked at her. She was glowing with life in her yellow-gold gown. Her amber eyes were brilliant. "Yes," he said. "Magnificent."

5

One week later Victoria put on her new yellow-trimmed brown riding habit, adjusted the dashing little military-style hat with its yellow feather at a rakish angle over one eye, and called for her favorite horse and groom. It was five o'clock and nearly everyone would be riding in the park.

Everyone today had better include the Earl of Stonevale. Last night, during the five minutes she'd had with him at the Bannerbrook rout, Victoria had given him very strict instructions to put in an appearance. She had a few things to say to him.

The problem in dealing with Lucas, Victoria had discovered, was that although he appeared unfailingly obedient when it came to receiving her instructions, he had a nasty habit of carrying them out in his own way. Enough was enough.

Cleo was crossing the hall into the library when Victoria came down the stairs. She peered at her niece in mild astonishment. "Going riding this afternoon, my dear?"

"Yes, I am. I feel in need of a little exercise." Victoria

paused briefly to kiss Cleo's cheek before hurrying toward the door. "Don't worry, I shall be home in plenty of time to dress for Grimshaw's little lecture on recent agricultural improvements in Yorkshire."

"Excellent." Cleo smiled benignly. "I am quite looking forward to it and so is Lucas."

Victoria halted on the threshold and whirled around. "I beg your pardon?"

"I merely said I was quite looking forward to Grimshaw's lecture."

"You said Lucas was looking forward to it."

"Oh, yes, I did, didn't I? And so he is. Told me so himself. Well, it's only natural he'd be interested, isn't it? His estates are, after all, somewhere in Yorkshire, I believe. I invited him on Wednesday when I was showing him my new dahlia plants. I must say the earl seems to be developing more than a passing interest in horticulture and related matters," Cleo remarked.

Yes, the earl did seem to be developing more than a passing interest in the subject, Victoria thought grimly, adjusting her small hat with a quick yank. Lately, in fact, his interest in matters of horticulture and agriculture had begun to border on the keen. She was beginning to feel she was running a poor second to such fascinating topics as methods of manuring and crop rotation.

For a man who only a week ago had seemed bent on seduction, he had certainly veered off course recently. Victoria did not know whether to be incensed or relieved.

A few minutes later she entered the park at a brisk trot, her groom following discreetly behind her on a pony. The public trails were thronged with elegantly attired riders, curricles, and small, open carriages. At this time of day the social world went into the park to see and be seen, not to actually ride for pleasure or exercise. That sort of riding was done in the early-morning hours.

Victoria automatically smiled and greeted her myriad acquaintances while keeping an eagle eye out for Lucas. She was beginning to think he had deliberately avoided the meeting altogether and was wondering what his excuse would be, when he materialized at her elbow on a spectacular chestnut. For a moment she forgot her annoyance.

"What an excellent animal, Lucas. He's beautiful."

Lucas smiled faintly. "Thank you. I'm rather fond of old George, myself. We've been through a lot together, haven't we, George?"

Victoria wrinkled her nose. "Did you name him after the king?"

"No. I named him George because George seemed a simple enough name for me to remember."

"No one's likely to forget a horse like that, regardless of his name. Have you any colts by him?" Victoria asked.

"Not yet, but George has big plans for the future."

At this, she grinned. "I see. You expect him to sire a dynasty?"

"Why not? The male of the species has certain obligations when he bears the sort of bloodlines old George here bears. We men do what we must, don't we, old boy?" He patted the stallion's neck and the horse ducked his head and blew through his nose.

Victoria's grin faded. She was sorry she had raised the topic of dynasty founding. Lucas occasionally made an oblique reference to the little matter of his future obligations to his name and title and she had discovered she preferred to avoid the subject. The idea of the present Earl of Stonevale someday taking a wife and getting himself an heir was becoming strangely unpalatable.

"Well, he's a lovely animal, but that is not what I wish to discuss with you, Lucas," she said quickly.

"I regret to hear that. I enjoy talking about horses." Lucas nodded politely toward a middle-aged man and woman in a handsome carriage. They smiled back and glanced pointedly at Victoria.

Victoria summoned up a regal smile for Lord Foxton and his lady and urged her horse to a slightly faster pace. Lucas and George promptly fell behind. She glanced back over her shoulder and scowled.

"Really, Lucas, do stop dawdling. I told you I specifically wish to speak to you today."

"Then don't rush ahead without warning like that."

"I was trying to avoid having to speak to Lady Foxton. She was giving me a very knowing look. And she's not the first to do so. That's one of the things I wanted to discuss with you, Lucas. People are starting to notice our, uh, association."

"What did you expect? You know as well as I do that if two people dance more than twice together at a ball, someone will wonder if there's a marriage offer brewing," Lucas said.

"But we do not dance together."

"Details. We've been paired off at a few routs and that's enough." He tipped his hat to another elderly lady, who smiled archly.

"Never mind that. It can't be helped. I specifically asked to speak to you today because I was afraid I would not get another chance tonight to speak to you privately and I have a few matters I want to clarify."

"I was afraid of that."

"There's no need to adopt the attitude of a martyr. You agreed to our adventuring. In fact, you insisted on accompanying me on our midnight tours. This bargain between us was made at your instigation, Lucas," Victoria said.

Lucas narrowed his eyes. "I sense a complaint about my performance to date. I'm crushed. Haven't you enjoyed yourself on the two occasions I risked life and limb to climb your garden wall?"

"Don't look at me like that. You know very well I found those two occasions this past week quite interesting. But they weren't what I expected, Lucas."

"What did you expect to find when you went spying on a man's world?"

Victoria chewed her lower lip thoughtfully. "I'm not sure, precisely. More adventure, I think. More excitement."

"Didn't you get adventure and excitement enough on Wednesday night?"

"The late-night supper at the restaurant was amusing, I'll admit. At least I found it so until those two young men got sick all over the skirts of their little opera dancers." Recalling the scene she had witnessed and how it had completely put her off her own food, Victoria made a face.

"I hate to disillusion you, Vicky, but the unfortunate truth is men don't do very edifying things when they get together late at night and start drinking. How about the excursion to Vauxhall? You liked that, didn't you?"

"For heaven's sake, Lucas, you cannot fob me off with trips to Vauxhall. Much too tame. Too respectable. I could have gone there with Annabella or any of my other female acquaintances and no one would have thought it amiss."

"Be fair. Dressed as a man, you saw a whole different side to the place."

"You are missing my point, Lucas," Victoria said firmly. "Deliberately, I think."

"What is your point?"

"My point is that thus far you have not taken me to any of the places on my list."

"Ah, yes, the famous list. I was afraid this conference today was going to focus on that damned list."

"You promised, Lucas. You said you would take me wherever I wanted to go. Instead, you've been deliberately trying to give me a disgust with the whole notion of adventuring, haven't you? Don't think I can't see right through your plan. You've been hoping that such revolting incidents as that business of witnessing those young men drinking until they became ill and viewing that boxing match at Vauxhall will put me off the entire scheme," Victoria accused.

"I was only trying to show you what you were getting into without putting you at undue risk in the process. You know you did not care for all the blood at the boxing match."

"Ah-hah, I knew it. You are trying to fob me off with mild adventures. Well, it won't work," Victoria declared. "I demand that you live up to your part of this bargain. Tomorrow night I insist we go to a brothel or a gaming hell." She brightened, considering the prospect. "I think I should prefer the latter. Yes, let us go to a real gaming hell."

"You won't like it, Vicky."

"That is for me to judge. Now, do we have an agreement or must I find someone else to take me?"

Lucas smiled and inclined his head to yet another curious middle-aged woman passing in a carriage. Outwardly, he was the picture of polite gallantry, but his voice, when he responded to Victoria's threat, was suddenly ice cold.

"Do not issue an ultimatum you cannot possibly carry out, Vicky."

Victoria was learning that when he used that particular tone, it was best to back off and find another path to her goal. It irked her that the man tended to turn utterly implacable when she pushed too hard, but he did have a point. Where was she going to find another companion who would show her the night?

There was, too, another aspect to the situation. She was becoming increasingly enthralled by the farewell kisses Lucas gave her before he departed from her garden after an adventure. There had been two more such embraces since the night they had gone to the fair and Victoria was already anticipating the next occasion when he would take her in his arms.

"Lucas, you seem to be overlooking the fact that I am in charge of this adventuring project. Must I remind you that I am the one who makes the decisions? Now, as to our next venture . . . Oh damn." Victoria broke off with a somewhat forced smile as a familiar couple in a curricle pulled abreast of her horse. She looked across into Isabel Rycott's amused eyes.

Isabel glittered like the small, perfect jewel she was in a rich shade of ruby. Seated next to her, holding the reins, was her current escort, Richard Edgeworth. Victoria had been introduced to him the previous evening and had not been much impressed. In fact, she wondered what Isabel, who could have her pick of men, saw in him.

On the surface there was certainly nothing wrong with the man. Edgeworth was fair-haired and handsome by most standards. He was in his early thirties, but Victoria did not think his looks would last into his forties. There was an unpleasant hint of sullen discontent in his eyes, as if Edgeworth had always felt himself victimized by life. There was, too, a curiously weak, dissolute quality about his mouth that implied a certain lack of inner strength.

Victoria wondered briefly if she was being too hard on the man. She was, after all, starting to use Lucas as her standard of comparison.

"Good afternoon, Vicky, dear," Isabel said. "So nice to see you again."

"Your servant, Miss Huntington," Edgeworth murmured. His gaze slid toward Lucas and away again. "Stonevale."

"Edgeworth."

Sensing the coldness between the two men, Victoria glanced at Lucas's enigmatic face but could read nothing of his thoughts. She turned quickly back to Isabel Rycott. "What a stunning hat, Lady Rycott. You must give me the name of your milliner."

"I will be happy to do so. She has a shop in Oxford Street. Perhaps we'll have a moment to chat tonight at Lady Atherton's small party?"

"I'm afraid I won't be there," Victoria said, remembering that she had declined the invitation earlier in the week. She wondered if Lucas had accepted. "I have other plans. Perhaps another time."

"Perhaps." Lady Rycott shot Lucas a mysterious smile and signaled to her companion that she wished to move on down the path. To this, Edgeworth gave the reins a small snap, his fine gray gloves giving the gesture an elegant touch.

"You don't care for Lady Rycott, do you?" Lucas observed casually as their carriage moved out of hearing range.

"And I got the impression you're not a particular friend of Mr. Edgeworth's," Victoria said.

"A small matter of a gaming debt, I'm afraid."

Victoria slid him a sidelong glance. "You played cards with him?"

"Only once. The man cheats."

Victoria was horrified. "Edgeworth is a cheat? How astonishing. Why is he still allowed to play in the clubs?"

Lucas watched the carriage roll out of sight behind a crop of trees. "Because he's never been caught. He is quite good at it."

"What happened the night you played with him?" Victoria asked, her interest piqued.

Lucas grinned briefly. "Halfway through the game, after losing rather heavily, I somehow managed to drop the entire deck of cards on the floor. Naturally a new pack had to be fetched immediately."

"An unmarked deck. How very clever of you." Victoria was delighted. "And Edgeworth started losing?"

"Yes. Heavily."

"Excellent. You see, Lucas, that is just the sort of excitement I wish to witness firsthand."

"There wasn't much to see. A few cards on the floor. A few glares from Edgeworth. Me mentally on my knees thanking the powers that be that I'd figured out what the devil was going on before I played too deep."

"There you go, trying to discourage me from exactly the sort of adventure I am anxious to experience." She frowned. "Was that card game the only time you and Edgeworth have encountered each other?"

"What makes you ask that?"

"I don't know. Something about the way the two of you reacted to each other a moment ago. I almost had the impression you had known each other for some time. Never mind. To get back to my original subject—"

"Why don't you like Isabel Rycott?"

Victoria's jaw tightened. "Is it that obvious?"

Lucas nodded to another couple on the path. "Only to someone who knows you well. And I am getting to know you very well, my dear."

"I have no real reason to dislike her. She was introduced to me a few weeks ago and immediately claimed a past acquaintanceship with my mother and stepfather," Victoria explained cautiously.

"Your stepfather was a man named Samuel Whitlock?"

"Yes."

"You have never spoken much of your family, other than your aunt Cleo," Lucas pointed out.

"It is not a subject I care to discuss. How did you know my stepfather's name, Lucas?"

"I believe Jessica Atherton mentioned it."

"Yes, of course." Her voice turned brittle.

"Now what's amiss?" Lucas asked gently.

"Nothing."

"Vicky, I'm your friend, remember? One of these days I intend to be your lover. You can talk to me."

She looked around sharply, aware of the heat rising in her cheeks. "Really, Lucas, what a thing to say in public. And neither of us is at all certain about the course of our future relationship. Kindly do not go about presuming too much."

"You don't like the idea that I discussed you with Lady Atherton, do you?"

"No, I do not."

"You don't much care for her, either?" Lucas asked.

"I do not dislike Jessica Atherton. I have explained once before that she and I do not have a lot in common, but I have nothing against her. Who can have anything against a paragon?" Victoria paused. "How long have you known her, Lucas?"

"Jessica Atherton? Several years. I was acquainted with her before her marriage to Atherton."

There was more to it than that, Victoria decided, listening to the clipped note in his words. She did not know how to ask for further details, however, so she changed the subject.

"I cannot imagine what Lady Rycott sees in Edgeworth," Victoria observed. "She probably does not know about his card-playing habits."

"Probably not."

"It is certainly convenient being a widow, is it not?" Victoria mused.

That got Lucas's attention. "What the devil are you on about now?"

"Do you realize that as a widow in command of her own financial affairs, Lady Rycott has considerably more freedom to go about with an escort of her choice than I do?"

"I had not given the matter much thought," Lucas muttered repressively.

"I have. Considerable thought. As a woman who has never been married, I am far more restricted than Lady Rycott. I must always be conscious of what people will say. I am still at an age when I must have a care for my reputation. But Isabel Rycott can ride in an open carriage with Edgeworth and dance with him tonight and let him take her home after the Athertons' party, and no one will pay any heed. It's not fair, Lucas. Not fair at all."

"Pray don't take a notion to marry me and then murder me in my bed so that you may enjoy the freedoms of wealthy widowhood."

Victoria laughed softly. "I would not think of it. Even the prospect of being a free and wealthy widow is not enough of an inducement to lure me into marriage."

Lucas eyed her thoughtfully. "If our interview is finished, we had best part. We've been riding together for some distance and we certainly wouldn't want anyone to speculate unduly on our association."

"No, you are quite right." But for a moment Victoria longed to have the freedom Isabel Rycott did. She was not in the least anxious to say good-bye. "One moment, Lucas. About our next adventure. I really must insist on something a little more exciting than Vauxhall or another restaurant. I shall be waiting in my aunt's garden tomorrow night after the Chillingsworth party and I shall be expecting to be taken to a gaming hell at the very least."

Stonevale's brows rose at her tone of authority. "Your wish is my command, Vicky. But in the meantime, I shall look forward to seeing you this evening when I attend Grimshaw's lecture."

Victoria grinned. "Are you really interested in agricultural improvements in Yorkshire?"

"Is that so amusing?"

She shrugged her shoulders. "No. I suppose not."

Lucas tipped his hat to her. "Be warned, Vicky. You still don't know everything there is to know about me.

Good afternoon." Before she could respond, he had turned George's head and was cantering down the path. Victoria stared after him until Annabella Lyndwood called to her from a short distance away. Shaking off an odd emotion she could not identify, Victoria went to greet her friend.

The night after Grimshaw's lecture Victoria slipped cautiously through the darkened town house and out into the conservatory. Pale moonlight pierced the windows, turning the array of exotic plants into a strange and forbidding world.

Victoria was growing accustomed to the eerie jungle that was the conservatory at night. She hurried down one aisle and let herself out into the garden. The night air was chilled and the grass was damp beneath her booted feet. She hesitated, searching the shadows for Lucas. As usual, she did not spot him until he moved.

Lucas stepped away from the shelter of the wall, a dark and forbidding figure dressed chiefly in black. His Hessians gleamed faintly in the moonlight. His face was in shadow. Victoria caught her breath at the sight of him and anticipation rushed through her veins, leaving her trembling with excitement.

Lucas held out his hand. Smiling in welcome, she put her fingers trustingly into his. As she did so, Lucas tipped up her chin with his other hand and kissed her; a quick, hard, possessive kiss. It was just the sort of kiss she knew she ought to protest but which instead always left her hungering for more. These stolen moments of fleeting, sultry passion were creating a sense of strong frustration within her.

"The carriage I hired for the evening is waiting around the corner," Lucas said as he dropped lightly down beside her on the street side of the wall. "Hurry. I don't want anyone to see us near your aunt's garden."

"You worry too much, Lucas." Nevertheless, she made haste to where the dark carriage was waiting and quickly leapt inside.

Lucas was right behind her, taking his weight, as usual, on his right leg as he came through the door. In the dim moonlight she saw him wince as he took the seat across from her. His hand went to his thigh and absently rubbed it.

"Does your leg hurt?" Victoria asked, concerned.

"Let's just say that I am aware of it occasionally."

"And this is one of those occasions?"

"Yes. Don't fret about it, Vicky."

She bit her lip. "I heard from a friend that you were wounded on the Peninsula. Is it true?"

His eyes met hers in the shadows. "I feel much toward that subject the way you do toward your stepfather."

"Meaning you don't discuss it?" she said.

"Precisely."

"Dear God, Lucas, it must have been terrible for you."

"I said I do not discuss it." He stopped massaging his leg. "Now do me a favor and pay attention. You are going to get your heart's wish this evening. We're going to a certain establishment that can only be classified as a gaming hell. I do not dare try to get you into one of my clubs. There's too much chance someone would recognize you, even in your disguise. In any event, I would certainly be obliged to explain you and I can't."

A thrill shot through her. "A gaming hell. Lucas, this is wonderful. How exciting. I cannot wait."

Lucas sighed. "I wish I could share your enthusiasm. Vicky, these places are run with only one object in mind and that is to separate the client from his blunt. To that end there is a great deal of drinking and wenching."

"Will it be dangerous?" she demanded, growing more excited by the minute.

Lucas gave her a disapproving look. "Things do not often turn violent inside the establishment, largely because it would be bad for business, but there are occasionally problems when one leaves."

"What are you talking about?"

"It is not unknown for someone who has suffered heavy losses to attempt to recover them with the aid of a knife or pistol. It is also not uncommon for the management to employ a certain type of debt collector who meets one outside in an alley," he explained.

Victoria's eyes widened. "Oh."

"What I am trying to say is that we must take care. I must have your word that you will do exactly as I instruct at all times. We will take absolutely no chances," Lucas ordered.

"Lucas, you are far too anxious about all this. Try to relax and calm yourself. I assure you, I will behave sensibly." She smiled brilliantly.

Lucas studied her smile for a moment and groaned. "Something tells me I am going to regret this night."

"Nonsense. We'll have a marvelous time."

"One of these days, Vicky, we really must discuss my end of this bargain."

She stilled, suddenly very alert. "You said you would be content with whatever I chose to pay."

It was Lucas's turn to smile. Victoria shivered and turned her attention to the view outside the carriage. The streets may have been dark, but they certainly were not empty. They were filled with an endless line of carriages carrying the members of the ton to and from their interminable round of parties. The streets would be busy until dawn when the elegant vehicles would be replaced by farmers' carts and milk wagons.

Twenty minutes later Victoria felt the rented carriage draw to a halt. She peered out excitedly and saw a dingy, unpromising establishment with a broken sign hanging over its front door. She glanced at the faded lettering on the swinging sign.

"The Green Pig?"

"The name does not exactly whet one's enthusiasm, does it?"

"Do not sound so hopeful. I am not about to change my mind at this juncture."

"Somehow I didn't think you would. Well, onward then, if you're determined to go through with this."

If the outside of the Green Pig could be described as dingy, the inside could only be called sordid. Everything appeared to have been decorated in red at one time, but the red velvet drapes and carpets had turned dark and sooty and indelibly stained from years of rough wear and tear. The roaring blaze on the hearth cast an evil light over the entire scene, making the interior glow like the hell it was called.

Victoria stared about in amazement as she followed Lucas toward the bar. She had never seen anything like this in her life. The shadowy room teemed with men from every walk of life, all intent on the next roll of the dice or turn of the card. Dandies and coachmen and professional boxers rubbed shoulders as they crowded around the tables. The tinkle of dice and the accompanying shouts of triumph or groans of despair created a continuous din. Tension, nervous excitement, and male sweat thickened the air, especially around the green baize tables where players stood three and four deep. Barmaids circulated through the throng, using ale and overflowing bosoms to coax reluctant players back into a game.

Lucas thrust a tankard into Victoria's hand. "Camouflage," he muttered. "It will look odd if you are not drinking. But have a care. The Pig is notorious for the strength of its ale."

"Do not fret, Lucas. I shall not get so foxed that you will be obliged to carry me out of here," Victoria assured him.

"Good God, I should hope not."

Victoria took in the scene around her as she stood sipping at the contents of the tankard. Her eye was caught by a rather depressed-looking man being led upstairs by a sympathetic serving girl. When he returned a short time later, the gamester appeared eager to return to the fray, all signs of depression vanquished.

Victoria was fascinated. "This is amazing, Lucas. Quite unique. Totally different from anything I have ever witnessed before."

Lucas eyed the crowd. "I am not so certain of that. It bears a certain striking resemblance to that crush at the Bannerbrooks the other night, don't you think?"

Victoria nearly choked on her laughter and a sip of ale. "If Lady Bannerbrook overheard that remark, I swear it would be weeks before you received another invitation from her."

"If Lady Bannerbrook knew where you were tonight, you would wait until the crack of doom for another invitation from her. What's more, you wouldn't get one from anyone else in Society, either."

"Now, do not try to terrorize me or depress me, Lucas, I am having a wonderful time. This is much better than the restaurant and a thousand times better than Vauxhall. Tell me, why on earth do those men keep trotting upstairs with the barmaids?"

Lucas glanced briefly toward the narrow staircase at the far end of the room. "Those are losers who are being consoled and encouraged to try their luck again."

"Consoled?"

"There are several small bedrooms upstairs, Vicky."

She blinked, aware of the heat rising in her cheeks. "I see." She turned to peer more closely at the newest couple on the stairs. The man was staggering drunkenly and had to be supported by his companion. Victoria frowned. "I do hope you have never had occasion to climb those stairs, Lucas."

His teeth flashed in a rare, quick grin around the rim of his tankard. "Never, I give you my word. I told you once I have always been extremely discriminating in certain matters. In any event, the stairs are primarily for losers."

"And you always win," Victoria concluded with a sense of satisfaction. "Really, Lucas, I cannot wait to throw the dice. My aunt and I taught ourselves how to play hazard when we were investigating a certain area of mathematics that relates to chance. Quite a fascinating game. Did you know that it is far easier to throw some numbers than others?"

"I am aware of that." Lucas's tone was exceedingly dry.

"Oh, yes, of course you would be aware of such things, wouldn't you? Well, then, let us find ourselves a table."

"Control your enthusiasm, my dear. You do not want

to throw the dice here. There isn't an honest pair in the house."

"Nonsense. You are merely saying that to put me off. I came here to have fun and I intend to play. I am quite a skilled gamester, if you will recall."

"Victoria, you are not quite as skilled in such matters as you believe."

Her eyes widened innocently. "But I must be very good at gaming because I won the night we played cards."

"Victoria . . ."

"The only other possible explanation for your losses that evening is that you did not play fair. But I hesitate to insult you by making such an odious accusation."

"Wise girl," Lucas said coolly.

"If I did insult you, would you call me out?" Victoria asked.

"Hardly. I have a great dislike for pistols at dawn or any other time."

"An odd thing for an ex-soldier to say."

"The only reasonable thing for an ex-soldier to say if you ask me."

"You carry a pistol," Victoria pointed out softly.

He shrugged. "This is London and you will insist on dragging me out into the streets at night. I don't have much choice."

Victoria took another sip of ale and then, feeling deliciously bold, she leaned closer. "Did you cheat that night we played cards, Lucas? I have been dying of curiosity ever since."

"It does not signify."

"Hah. If you are going to be that way, I shall find another fashion in which to amuse myself." Victoria started toward the nearest table.

"Victoria, wait. . . ."

But Victoria was already making a place for herself near the action. Half-crushed by the press of hot, sweaty masculine bodies, she leaned forward to peer at the play. She was aware of Lucas moving into a position behind her but she paid no heed. The dice were already being handed to her. They clicked in her palm as she shook them and then hurled them lightly down onto the green baize.

"The young nob's got 'imself a main o' seven," someone called. Instantly bets were placed on Victoria's next roll.

Victoria felt a thrill go through her. Seven was an excellent number for a main, she recalled. She could almost ignore the smell of the male bodies that crushed her now. Knowing Lucas was at her back gave her a heady sense of invulnerability. She was quite safe and having a wonderful time. She rolled the dice again.

"Eleven, by God," a man yelled gleefully. "The cull's nicked it." Shouts of triumph went up around the table.

Under cover of the din, Victoria turned to whisper to Lucas. "Nicked it? What's that mean? I thought I'd won."

"You did win. That's what 'nicked it' means. Collect your stakes, Vicky. You've had enough play," Lucas announced.

"But I am winning. I cannot possibly leave now."

A swaying, red-faced man in a threadbare coat and a dirty cravat overheard Victoria's remark. He rounded on Lucas, eyes glaring. "Here now, the boy's got a right to play. You can't be draggin' him off."

"The man is perfectly correct, Lucas. I have a right to play."

Lucas ignored the man and leaned closer to Victoria. He was clearly annoyed now. "Vicky, the management will let you win for a while until you're hooked and then you'll start losing. Heavily. Trust me, I know what I'm talking about."

"Well, I shall just play as long as I am winning," she assured him cheerfully, and turned back to the table. She thought she heard Lucas swear softly and succinctly as she returned to the fray, but the shouts of her enthusiastic fellow players drowned out the words.

Ten minutes later her excellent luck turned with a vengeance, just as Lucas had predicted. Victoria watched in shock as she lost all her accumulated winnings in one throw of the dice. Angrily she turned to whisper again to Lucas.

"Did you see that? How could that happen? I was winning, Lucas. I cannot believe my luck would suddenly alter in such a fashion."

Lucas led her away from the table. "That's the thing about luck, especially in a place such as this. I did warn you."

"You needn't look so smug, you know. I *was* winning. Furthermore, I . . ."

But Lucas was no longer paying any attention to her. His gaze, which had been unobtrusively scanning the room, stopped abruptly on a group of card players in the corner. "Damn it to hell."

"What's wrong?" Victoria glanced at the card table.

"I chose this place because I was fairly certain we would not run into any of your acquaintances here, but it appears I was wrong. We must leave at once."

"Lucas, do stop fretting so. No one will recognize me. One sees only what one expects to see and no one I know will expect to see me here dressed as a man," Victoria argued.

"I am taking no chances. Come along, Vicky." Lucas started toward the door.

Reluctantly she followed, casting one last, annoyed glance at the card table. "Good grief, that's Ferdie Merivale, isn't it?"

"None other."

"He appears quite drunk, Lucas. Look at him, he's barely able to sit in his chair and yet he is trying to play cards," Victoria noted, concerned.

"So he is. With Duddingstone, no less. Which means that Merivale will no doubt part with a large portion of the fortune he recently inherited. Stop dawdling, Vicky."

"What do you know of this Duddingstone?"

"He's an excellent player, a brilliant cheat, and completely without conscience. He's not above taking advantage of a young fool like Merivale. Does it quite regularly, in fact."

Victoria halted abruptly. "Then we must do something."

"I am trying to do something. I am trying to get you out of here before Ferdie Merivale recognizes you."

"He is in no shape to recognize me or anyone else.

Lucas, we cannot leave him in Duddingstone's clutches.
I am friends with Ferdie's sister, Lucinda. I simply
cannot stand by and let poor Ferdie be fleeced by a
notorious player. He's a nice boy."

"We are not going to stand by and watch. We are
going to leave at once."

"No, Lucas. I must insist we do something."

Lucas turned around and glowered at her. "What,
exactly, do you suggest we do?"

Victoria considered the problem. "You will simply
have to interrupt the play and persuade Ferdie to leave."

"My God. You don't ask much, do you? What if
Ferdie doesn't wish to leave?"

"You must make him do so."

"Impossible. That will cause a scene and that is the
last thing we can afford."

"Do not worry about me, Lucas. I shall wait here
near the door. Ferdie will never see me. All you have
to do is fetch him out of here and put him in a carriage
and send him home."

"You are the one I intend to put into a carriage and
send home," Lucas said through gritted teeth. "I knew
this was going to be a mistake. I should never have
allowed you to talk me into bringing you here."

"Hurry, Lucas. They are about to begin another round
of play. You must rescue Ferdie."

"Now listen to me, Victoria. . . ."

"I am not leaving here until you have rescued poor
Ferdie. He's a very sweet boy and he does not deserve
to get chewed to pieces by this Duddingstone person.
Go on. Save him." She gave Lucas a slight push in the
direction of the card table. "I promise to stay out of
sight."

Lucas swore softly, but like any good soldier, he
appeared to recognize defeat when he saw it. Without a
word he turned on his heel and started back into the
crowd.

Victoria could see very little of what was happening,
but a few minutes later Ferdie Merivale emerged from
the throng, Lucas directly behind him. Victoria noticed
that one of Ferdie's arms appeared to be twisted at an

odd angle behind his back. The young man did not look happy as he preceded Lucas out into the street.

Victoria caught Lucas's commanding glance and followed the two men at a discreet distance. Outside she could clearly hear Ferdie Merivale complaining loudly in a slurred voice.

"Damme, Stonevale, you can't do this. My luck was about to turn. Just a few more hands and I'd have had the man."

"A few more hands and you would be obliged to leave town tomorrow to rusticate indefinitely in the country. You would not care for that, Merivale. You are a city creature. How much had you already lost to Duddingstone?"

Ferdie muttered something indistinct and Lucas shook his head grimly. "I know you don't much appreciate this at the moment, Merivale, and I am not particularly enjoying myself, either, but neither of us has much choice. Perhaps tomorrow you will be grateful." Lucas signaled a passing coach.

"Bloody damn, Stonevale, I don't want rescuing. I can handle the play," Ferdie wailed drunkenly.

"Do us both a favor. Next time you decide to throw away your inheritance, do it someplace where I am not likely to witness it. You have been a greater nuisance than you know tonight." Lucas tossed the young man into the coach and gave instructions to the driver.

The coach rattled off down the street and Lucas stepped back. He turned to look at Victoria.

"Satisfied?"

"That was very well done of you, my lord." Laughing with relief and pride in his rescue efforts, Victoria stepped off the sidewalk to join him. "I swear, you have my undying gratitude even if you do not have Ferdie's."

She saw him open his mouth to say something in response, saw the startling change in his expression as his eyes went to a point behind her, and then she heard the clatter of horses' hooves on stone and the rattle of carriage wheels.

The wheels sounded much too close. Victoria turned

around to see just how close and saw a black carriage drawn by two black horses bearing down upon her.

At that moment the safety of the walkway seemed miles away, and the scream that began in her throat disappeared into the pounding hooves and the screeching wheels of a carriage.

Then something heavy struck her, carrying her back out of the path of the hurtling carriage. She sprawled under Lucas's full weight as hooves and wheels went past scant inches from her booted foot.

6

"Some drunken idiot showing off his lamentable driving skills, no doubt," Victoria said from the opposite side of the carriage.

"No doubt."

She tried to see Lucas's expression in the shadows. She was still somewhat shaken from the near miss, but mostly she was bubbling over with the excitement of the entire affair. Her main concern now was for her companion.

Lucas had uttered barely a word since he had helped her up from the pavement and tossed her into a carriage. She could feel the angry tension in him. He was absently rubbing his leg and she wondered if he had hurt it rescuing her.

"You were very quick, Lucas. I vow I would have been run down if you had not moved so fast."

Nothing.

"Does your leg pain you very much?"

"I'll survive."

Victoria sighed. "It is all my fault, isn't it? If I had not

442

insisted on going to that gaming hell tonight, you would not have hurt your leg."

"That is certainly one way of looking at the incident," Lucas said.

"I'm so sorry, Lucas."

"Sorry?"

"Well, not about going to the Green Pig, precisely," she admitted candidly. "For I did have a marvelous time. But I am terribly sorry you got hurt." Impulsively she slipped across the short distance between them and sat down next to him. "Here, let me massage it for you. I am quite good with horses, you know."

"Is that a recommendation?"

She smiled, relieved to hear the unwilling humor in the question. "Of course. One needs to learn how to soothe a spirited animal after a bruising ride."

"You're the one who probably got bruised. You were on the bottom. You are certain you're not hurt?"

"Oh, I am quite all right. One of the useful things about men's clothing is that it provides much more protection for the body than an evening gown. If only you had not twisted your leg when you threw yourself toward me the way you did."

As she talked she put her hands on his thigh and probed experimentally. She was instantly aware of the strong sinew and muscle under her fingers. The snug-fitting breeches hid nothing of his natural contours. It was almost like touching his bare skin, she thought as she cautiously began to knead his leg.

Lucas made no move to stop her. He simply sat there looking down at her as she worked over him. Victoria concentrated fiercely, anxious to bring him some relief from his obvious discomfort.

There was very little give in him, she thought, squeezing the solid muscle. Hard as stone.

"I really do appreciate what you did for Ferdie Merivale." Victoria found herself speaking quickly in an effort to fill what seemed to her a highly charged silence. Her fingers dug deeper into his thigh.

"I'm glad you do because I doubt that Merivale does."

Lucas sucked in his breath. "Easy, if you please, Vicky. That is my injured leg, you know."

"Oh, yes, of course." She lightened her touch, glancing up to see his expression. "Is that better?"

"Much better." He was silent for a moment longer and then he said, "You do have excellent hands. I envy your horses."

This time when she looked up into his shadowed face, she realized he was smiling slightly, a piercingly sensual smile that sent a rush of heated awareness through her. She could feel the tension in his leg changing in some indefinable fashion and she found herself running her palm along the inside of his thigh.

He lifted a hand and drew his slightly rough fingertip slowly down the line of her throat to the nape of her neck. Victoria held her breath, sensing he was going to kiss her. She'd learned to recognize that glittering gaze. She'd seen it on the occasions when she'd stood with him in her aunt's garden after an evening's escapade. The anticipation alone was enough to set fire to her senses.

"Lucas?"

"Tell me, Vicky, do you like my good-night kisses?"

"I . . ." The words seemed to get caught in her throat. "Yes. Yes, I do."

"One of the things I like about you, my dear, is that you can be so delightfully honest at the most interesting times." He threaded his fingers through her hair and then his hand tightened on the back of her head, urging her close. "I wonder if you have any idea of how it affects me."

She went to him willingly, tumbling across his lap as the coach swayed and jounced. With a soft little sigh of pleasure she wrapped her arms around his neck and lifted her face for his kiss. There was no doubt about it, she thought, her appetite for this sort of thing had been well and truly whetted by those previous kisses in the garden.

Lucas's mouth came down on hers, his tongue sliding along the edge of her lower lip, seeking admittance.

Eager now for the heat and excitement she always

found in his good-night embraces, Victoria nestled closer. His arms were strong and hard around her, and when his hand moved to the buttons of her waistcoat, she made no move to resist.

All the pent-up excitement of the evening was flowing through her and this was the most thrilling moment of all. Victoria barely felt her cravat being loosened, but when his fingertips glided down her throat, she tightened her arms around his neck.

Lucas laughed softly against her mouth as his fingers went lower to part her waistcoat and shirt. "There is something rather strange about unfastening men's clothes on you, sweetheart."

Victoria could not respond because he was suddenly cupping her bare breast in his hand. She gasped instead and went taut. Then, instead of protesting, as she knew she ought, Victoria turned her hot face into his shoulder and clutched him tightly.

"Do you like the feel of my hand on you, Vicky?"

She nodded jerkily. "*Yes.*" She could feel her nipple tighten under the touch of his thumb.

"So honest. Can you feel what you're doing to me?"

She could. He was growing hard beneath her buttocks. His thighs parted slightly, making her even more aware of the solid shape of his manhood beneath the tight breeches.

"Lucas, your poor leg."

"I assure you it is not paining me in the least right now."

"We must stop."

"Do you really want me to stop touching you?" Lucas whispered.

"Please don't ask me such a question." Breathlessly she dug her fingers into the muscles of his shoulders and strained against his hand. She was growing hotter and she could feel a warm dampness between her legs.

As if he, too, knew about the moist heat between her thighs, Lucas moved his hands down to the fastenings of her breeches. Victoria completely lost her voice just when she knew she should be raising it to its loudest level in a fierce demand for him to halt. Instead she was suddenly fascinated with the masculine scent of his body and the sensual tension in him. Her fingers clenched and unclenched on his shoulders.

"You are damp and ready for me, aren't you?" Lucas slid his hand inside the open breeches and found her secret warmth. "Your body is already preparing its welcome."

"*Lucas.*"

"Do not be embarrassed, my sweet. I am glad to know you want me as much as I want you. When the time comes, we are going to deal very well with each other."

Dazed, she managed to lift her head long enough to look up at him. "When the time comes?"

"Not tonight. I would much prefer a bed instead of a carriage seat for our first time together. And I want all the time in the world, not the few minutes we have left before we reach your home."

"Lucas, we must stop. We must." He had never touched her like this and she did not know how to handle her own emotions. A delicious sense of eagerness was gripping her.

"Are you sure you want to stop, little one? You feel so good, darling." His mouth was on hers again and then on her throat as his fingers slipped lower, parting soft petals to seek out the tiny bud of desire. "So damned good. And you want me. Say it, Vicky. Give me the words at least."

Victoria sucked in her breath as the wondrous sensations made her tremble in need. She wanted to tell him again that he must cease touching her so intimately, but she knew she could not. Not yet, at any rate. She wanted more of this exotic feeling and she sensed that only Lucas could provide her with what she desired.

"The words, sweetheart. Is that so much to ask?" His voice was gentle, coaxing, intimate. "All I'm asking is for you to tell me what you are feeling. Does this feel good?"

"Yes, oh, Lucas, *yes.*" She squeezed her eyes shut so she would not have to meet the gleaming satisfaction she knew she would find in his intent gaze. She twisted helplessly against his probing hand.

"Keep talking to me, sweetheart. Keep telling me how you feel when I touch you like this." He slid one finger gently into her warmth.

She cried out and muffled the sound against the fabric of his jacket.

"And this . . ."

She flinched and suddenly she could not get enough of his long, sensitive fingers. She lifted her hips, silently pleading for more but not knowing what it was she sought. "Lucas, do that again. Please touch me again."

"Like this, my sweet?" His fingers worked magic in the hot, damp area between her legs. "God, you are beautiful, Vicky. You respond to me as though you had been made for me."

"Please." She could barely speak as she arched her hips and writhed again beneath his touch. "I don't know . . . I can't . . . *Please.*"

"Yes. I know. I will. Just give yourself up to it, darling. Do you want me?" he asked again.

"Oh, yes, yes, *yes.*" And then she was beyond thought, beyond speech. Something tight and vibrant that lay coiled within her suddenly released itself without warning, reverberating through her body until she was shivering. The small convulsions made her tremble from head to toe, but she was not cold, nor did she know any fear. She had never felt so joyously alive in her life.

And then she collapsed in an exhausted little heap against Lucas's hard chest.

"So beautiful. Such a sweet, hot passion." Lucas dropped light, reassuring kisses all over her face and throat as he withdrew his hand from between her thighs and hastily refastened her breeches. "I will go out of my mind waiting for you. But I do not think you will make me wait too long, will you, sweetheart? You would not be so cruel."

Victoria hesitated until she could breathe normally before lifting her head away from his shoulder. The

carriage was already slowing. She looked up at him, still
dazed. He was smiling faintly, a warm, knowing expression in his eyes.

"That was . . ." She licked her lips and tried again.
"That was very strange."

"Think of it as an experiment in natural history."

"An experiment?" In spite of her odd mood, the
laughter welled up inside her, revitalizing her and flushing away some of the sensual lethargy that had held her
in thrall. "You are utterly impossible, my lord."

"Not at all." His smile was gentle, but there was a
disturbing heat in his eyes. "The things I want to do
with you are all quite possible. Some may be improb-
able, but not impossible."

She was staring wordlessly into his eyes when she
suddenly became aware that the carriage had stopped.
She gave herself a small shake and her fingers flew to
her untied cravat. "Good heavens, we're here. I must
get out or the coachman will think we've fallen asleep."

She scrambled about the carriage, collecting her walking stick and coat. As she pushed open the door she
realized that Lucas was moving far more cautiously than
usual. She frowned at him as she jumped down. "Are
you all right?"

"No."

"Oh, dear, your leg."

"It is not my leg that is bothering me." He stepped
down beside her and adjusted his coat with great care.

"Then what is it, Lucas?" Victoria prodded.

"Nothing you can do anything about tonight, but rest
assured I will look forward to you resolving the problem
in the near future." He rapped on the side of the
coachman's seat with his stick. "Be so good as to wait a
few minutes. I shall return shortly."

The coachman tipped his hat with a bored air and
reached for the flask he kept under his box.

"But Lucas, what is it? What is the matter?" Victoria
asked again as they hurried around the corner and
through an alley to the garden wall.

"Think back on all your studies of natural history,

particularly the details of reproduction among the male of the species and I'm sure the answer will come to you."

"Oh dear." She swallowed, aware that her face was burning. She was not precisely certain what he meant, but she was at last getting an inkling of the probable source of his discomfort. "Heavens. I had no idea. Are you, uh, very uncomfortable, my lord?"

"Don't look so contrite," he said with a quick, fleeting grin. "I am well pleased with the results of the experiment. They were worth any minor discomfort I am now experiencing." He gave her an assist up the garden wall. "And I did offer myself in the spirit of intellectual inquiry, did I not?"

"I do wish you would stop talking about the whole thing as an experiment." Victoria dropped down into the fragrant, shadowed garden and stood back as he lowered himself down beside her.

"I think it will be easier for you to think of it that way for a while." He kissed her nose and stood back. "Good night, Victoria. Sleep well."

She stood watching for a moment as he vanished back over the wall and then, reluctantly, she turned toward the conservatory door. She abruptly longed for the privacy of her room so that she could think about what was happening between her and Lucas.

The feelings he was arousing in her were startling in their intensity and a little frightening. For a few minutes there in the coach she knew she had surrendered a large measure of her self-control to him. She had put herself literally in his hands and he had shown her the power of her own body.

She frowned in thought as she approached the conservatory door. She must not let matters get out of control. She had to be careful. But Lucas was so different from any other man she had ever met. It was becoming increasingly difficult to think logically about him. More and more she was reacting on the basis of emotion, and that, she knew, was dangerous.

Damn it, she thought resentfully, it simply was not

fair that a widow such as Isabel Rycott was free to
indulge in a discreet romantic liaison while a dedicated
spinster was not granted the same privilege. At least
not a spinster who was only twenty-four. Perhaps in
another ten years she would be able to behave as she
wished, but who wanted to wait ten years to discover
the mysteries Lucas was now revealing to her?

And who knew where Lucas would be ten years from
now, Victoria thought in sullen disgust. He would undoubtedly be off in the country, attending to his estates, a wife, and several children.

It simply was not fair.

Victoria knew now that if she was ever going to
experiment with this particular aspect of natural history, she wanted that experiment to take place with
Lucas. Perhaps she should do as he said and regard this
entire matter from a scientific point of view.

She was mulling over the pros and cons of that angle
when she spotted the white silk neck scarf fluttering
from the handle of the conservatory door.

One of the servants must have left it here when he or
she went into the garden to collect herbs for supper,
she thought. But surely she would have noticed it earlier when she had left the house to meet Lucas.

Curious, she lifted the scarf away from the handle.
She felt the monogram beneath her fingers but could
not read it in the pale moonlight.

Victoria hurried indoors, paused in the conservatory
to listen for any sound, and then decided her aunt had
probably not yet returned from the Crandalls' ball. The
Crandalls' affairs were famous for lasting until dawn.

Victoria went upstairs and into her room and immediately lit a candle. Then she held the end of the scarf
near the glow of light and deciphered the monogram. It
was in the shape of an elaborately worked "W."

Victoria's fingers shook as she carefully folded the
scarf. She had seen similar monograms before. They
had been embroidered on the handkerchiefs and neck-
cloths of her dead stepfather, Samuel Whitlock.

The morning light poured through the conservatory

windows, illuminating the spectacular spray of *Plumeria rubra* that Victoria was endeavoring to capture with her watercolors. She frowned at the emerging flower portrait on her easel, knowing her attention was not completely on her work and wondering if she should simply abandon the project. Normally when she was engaged in her sketching or painting, her concentration was complete.

But this morning her thoughts churned, writhed, and danced with memories of her passion in Lucas's arms the previous night. She had been unable to get the images out of her head although she had spent several fitful hours trying to calm herself. She knew she would turn herself into a candidate for Bedlam if she did not sort out her confusion and make some decisions.

"There you are, Vicky, dear. I have been looking for you." Cleo Nettleship rounded the corner of the aisle of plants and headed toward her niece. She was wearing a delightful morning dress of pale coral. "Such a lovely day, is it not? I should have known I'd find you out here." She paused briefly, her attention caught by a small plant on a tray. "Good heavens, did you notice the new American iris we got from Chester last month? It's blooming beautifully. How exciting. I must remember to tell Lucas."

Victoria gave a small start and a drop of pink splashed on the page. "Damn."

"I beg your pardon, dear?"

"Nothing, Aunt Cleo. I just had a small accident with my paint. Do you think Lucas will be interested in the iris?"

"Certainly. Haven't you noticed how enamored he has become of horticulture? He is learning everything he can about such matters in preparation for taking over his estates. But he is particularly fascinated with the new species of plants that are arriving in this country from America. I imagine that at the rate he's going, his gardens at Stonevale will one day be a great attraction," Cleo said.

Victoria concentrated on putting a faint shadow on the pink blossom. "He does seem to have developed a strong interest in the subject, doesn't he? Does that strike you as odd, Aunt Cleo? The man has been a soldier most of his adult life."

"I don't find it in the least odd. Only think of Plimpton and Burney. Two ex–military men who have settled down on their estates and produced magnificent results both in their gardens and in their crop production. Perhaps there is something in the business of gardening and horticulture that appeals to men who have witnessed a great deal of violence and bloodshed."

Victoria recalled Lucas's refusal to discuss the circum-stances surrounding the injury of his leg. "I wonder if you might be right about that, Aunt Cleo."

"Speaking of Lucas, dear." Cleo paused again to examine another plant that was putting forth shoots.

Victoria caught the slight change in her aunt's inflection and braced herself. Cleo rarely lectured, but when she did, Victoria had learned to pay attention. For all her scattered scientific interests and her unending social life, Cleo Nettleship was a wise and intelligent woman.

"What about him, Aunt Cleo?"

"I hesitate to say too much, Vicky, dear. You are, after all, a grown woman and you have always given every indication of knowing precisely what you are about. But I must confess I have never known you to spend quite so much time in the company of any one man. Nor have I heard you mention a particular male acquaintance quite as frequently as you seem to mention Stonevale. And one cannot help but notice lately that he seems to be underfoot a great deal of the time."

Victoria's fingers tightened around her brush. "I thought you liked Lucas."

"I do. Very much. That is not the point, Vicky, and I think you know it." Her aunt spoke gently as she poked a finger into a bedding tray to check for moisture.

"If Lucas seems to be underfoot much of the time, I expect it is because you are constantly inviting him to attend lectures and demonstrations you think will interest him," Victoria declared defensively.

"True, I have extended a number of invitations and he has always accepted." Cleo looked thoughtful. "But it is not just at our natural history and horticulture meetings that he appears, is it? Lately he seems to have put in an appearance at nearly every soirée you have attended."

Victoria swallowed uneasily. "He is a friend of Lady Atherton's. She has introduced him into her circle."

Cleo nodded again. "Very true. And Lady Atherton's circle of acquaintances does include us, does it not? But all the same, I think perhaps you should consider exactly what it is you wish to have happen next, Vicky."

Victoria set down her brush and looked at her aunt. "Why don't you come out and tell me what it is that's worrying you, Aunt Cleo?"

"I am not worried so much, dear, as concerned that you understand your position vis-à-vis the earl. You have always insisted you do not wish to marry."

Victoria stiffened. "That has always been true and still is."

Cleo's face softened as she regarded her niece's stubborn expression. "Then, Vicky, you have a certain obligation, one might even say your female honor requires that you do not give false hope to your male acquaintances. Do you comprehend what I am trying to say?"

Victoria stared at her aunt in outraged astonishment. "You think I have been leading the earl on? Allowing him to believe an offer of marriage might someday be welcome?"

"Not for a moment do I think you have done such a thing deliberately," Cleo said hastily. "But lately, my dear, I have begun to wonder if Stonevale might interpret some of your interest in him as a signal that you might be willing to entertain an offer. He could hardly be blamed if he had."

Victoria bristled. "And what about your interest in him? How is he supposed to interpret all your various invitations, Aunt Cleo?"

"It is not at all the same thing, dear. If he is misinterpreting my invitations, it is only because you always choose to attend the same lectures and demonstrations he chooses to attend," she explained evenly.

"There is hardly anything to remark upon in that. I have always attended the most interesting of the lectures and talks given by your friends."

"I cannot help but note, dear, that until recently you rarely attended the talks on crop rotation, orchard management, and viticulture," Cleo pointed out dryly. "Your interests have always focused more on animals, electricity, and exotic plants."

Victoria felt her face growing very warm. "I assure you, Aunt Cleo, Stonevale is very well aware of my opinions on marriage. I am certain he would not misinterpret our friendship."

"What about you, Vicky?" Cleo came closer and smiled down at her niece. "Is there any possibility you may not be quite so certain of your own feelings on the subject of marriage as you once were?"

"Believe me, my opinions on marriage have not changed in the least," Victoria said with absolute conviction.

"Forgive me for asking, my dear, but is it possible that you are toying with the notion of another sort of liaison with Stonevale?"

Victoria's eyes collided with her aunt's. "You think I am contemplating a . . . an affair with Lucas?"

Cleo held her niece's gaze and spoke very firmly. "I am not blind, Vicky. Nor am I lacking in intelligence. Furthermore, I am a woman who has been out in the world for a good many years. I have seen the way you look at Stonevale when you don't think he is aware of your regard. Add to that his obvious interest in you and the fact that you are a normal, healthy young female who does not wish the chains of marriage, and I fear we must conclude you are treading on treacherous ground. I would be extremely remiss in my duty as your aunt if I did not warn you."

Victoria's hand clenched into a small fist in her lap. She stared blankly at the half-finished flower in front of her. "I appreciate your concern, Aunt Cleo."

"No, you don't, you resent it, and I cannot entirely blame you for that. But we must face facts and it is not only your own reputation you must consider here. Stonevale's is in jeopardy as well," Cleo said.

Victoria's head snapped up. "Stonevale's reputation?"

"You know very well, my dear, that a man of his position has an obligation to his name and title. Someday he must marry a socially acceptable woman from a good family. He cannot afford to be known as a seducer of respectable, innocent young females. Such a reputation would immediately ruin his chances for a proper marriage and cast him out of Society. Nor would he wish for such a nasty reputation. He is a decent man, Vicky."

"It is all so very unfair."

"What is unfair? That your status as a young, unmarried woman of good breeding makes it completely impossible for you to even consider a romantic liaison with Stonevale? Yes, it is most unfair. But Society is very strict about such matters and you must heed most of the unwritten laws if you wish to survive in our world. You flout enough of the rules as it is. Be patient. And as you grow older you will be able to get away with disregarding more and more of them."

"I am four and twenty. Quite on the shelf and you know it, Aunt Cleo."

Cleo smiled and shook her head. "You know as well as I do that is not completely true. Society still views you as eligible and the size of your inheritance guarantees that you will remain so for a few more years. You must be careful."

"If I were widowed like Isabel Rycott, I would be free," Victoria muttered tightly.

Cleo grinned, breaking the tension. "Are you by any chance contemplating marriage to the earl and then doing him in so that you can gain the freedom Isabel Rycott enjoys?"

Victoria's answering grin was reluctant. "Stonevale asked me very particularly not to consider that course of action."

Cleo stared at her in astonishment and then burst into a gale of delighted laughter. "I am pleased to learn that Stonevale is every bit as quick and intelligent as I had thought. Obviously the two of you have arrived at some sort of mutual understanding. You do not need my advice, after all, Vicky. Please forgive my intrusion into your affairs."

Victoria relaxed slightly. "I appreciate your concern, truly I do. And I will treat what you have said with the utmost consideration."

"Do that. Society will tolerate a great deal but there are limits, as we both know, especially for females. I should hate to see you ruined socially at such an early age, my dear. You take far too much pleasure in your friends to risk losing them," Cleo warned gently.

"That is certainly true enough." A small jolt of alarm went through Victoria. She would be heartbroken if she thought she could never entertain Annabella or some of her other friends again.

Cleo nodded in satisfaction. "Precisely, my dear. Now, if you will recall, we are engaged to talk to our man of affairs this morning. Something to do with that ship we invested in last year. Apparently it has returned safely with a lovely cargo from China. We are several thousand pounds richer as of this morning. Isn't that nice?"

Victoria was immediately distracted. She loved the more exciting sort of business ventures such as investing in shipping. A bit of risk always added an element of interest to the deal.

"Marvelous!" Victoria exclaimed. "We must thank Mr. Beckford for recommending that particular ship to us. Oh, Aunt Cleo, wait, there is something I wanted to ask you about." Victoria reached under her chair and picked up the monogrammed silk scarf she had found on the conservatory door the previous night. "Do you recognize this?"

Cleo examined the monogram with a slight frown and handed it back to her niece. "No. It's obviously not one of mine. Wherever did you find it?"

"In the garden. I asked the servants if one of them

knew anything about it and they all said they did not recognize it. Perhaps it belongs to one of the members of your natural history society?" Victoria said, running her finger over the elegantly woven "W."

"Hmmm. Perhaps. It is a man's scarf. Let me think. Who do we know who has a name beginning with 'W'? There's Wibberly and Wilkins for starters. I must remember to ask both of them the next time I see them if either lost this. Is that all, Vicky?"

"Yes, Aunt Cleo. That is all I wanted to ask. Let's go talk to Mr. Beckford about our latest business success. Perhaps he will have something else to recommend."

7

Victoria hated to admit it but the notion of going to a brothel had been a serious mistake.

She clutched her glass of champagne and sat tensely in the shadows, partially concealed by a garishly gilded screen. There were several such discreetly shadowed areas around this room and the adjoining one. All the lamps had been turned very low. Drunken giggles and other sounds of a very unsettling nature emanated from behind most of the screens. Victoria shuddered to think of what was going on upstairs.

It was very late, well after three in the morning. Lucas had dictated the time of their arrival. He had said he wanted to take no chance of running into anyone who might be sober enough to recognize Victoria. He had also specified this particular house because it catered to those who favored some modicum of privacy. Hence the screens and subdued lighting.

Everyone around her except Lucas appeared to be staggeringly drunk. Some men, snoring heavily, lay sprawled on pink velvet sofas. The room was too loud, too hot, and choked with smoke from rich cigars. There

458

was another sort of smoke coming from two or three odd pipes scattered here and there around the pink and gold chamber.

Victoria was beginning to feel a little sick. A moment earlier she had watched Lucas casually wave off two young women whose gowns were cut so low as to reveal the tops of their rouged nipples.

"We just came to observe the activities tonight," he'd explained smoothly when one of the women had protested being sent away.

"But it's ever so much more fun to join in the play," the other cooed. Her eyes had moved over Lucas in a glance that made Victoria want to dump the contents of a chamber pot on her head.

"What about the young gennelman?" the first woman asked with a beckoning smile aimed at Victoria. "Wouldn't you like to come upstairs with me? My, you're a pretty boy. I have a lovely-looking glass on the wall o' my room. You can watch *everything* in it. And you should see my collection of rods and whips. Every bit as fine as the ones they use on young lordlings in school."

Victoria had shaken her head quickly and edged a bit deeper into the shadows. Lucas had shot her a sardonic glance and sipped his champagne, offering little help. She could almost hear him saying "I told you so."

In addition to acknowledging that the brothel idea was a bad one, she was also fast arriving at the conclusion that men's clothing was not always very comfortable. Her flawlessly tied cravat was much too high and much too tight around her throat tonight, for example. The top folds were halfway up her ears and covered her chin. She was practically drowning in the thing and it was all Lucas's fault. He had retied it for her in the carriage because he'd claimed he wanted her features better concealed.

He had also insisted she keep her hat on and pulled down low over her eyes until she'd found a secluded spot to sit. As a further precaution, Lucas had deliberately chosen a house that was not patronized by the males of the ton. He had wanted to take as few risks as possible.

Her stomach grew more queasy. She *had* to get out of here. She did not think she could take much more of the appalling display.

She was about to lean forward and inform Lucas that she was bored and quite ready to leave when a cheer went up at the far end of the shadowed, crowded chamber. Then a sudden hush fell over the throng of drunken men and provocatively dressed women.

The middle-aged mistress of the brothel, dressed in a billowing, low-cut gown, walked into the center of the garishly decorated room. The bawd's face was a mask of white face powder and rouge in the style that had been popular several years earlier. Her dress was made of expensive pink velvet that matched the chairs, but it lacked the elegance of simplicity which was the hallmark of fashion in polite circles. The gown was as cheap looking and overblown as the woman herself.

"Gather 'round, all you fine gentlemen who are so anxious to prove your mettle this evening. The house invites you to inspect the lovely bit of goods we have on offer tonight. Guaranteed as clean and virgin as the day she was brought into this world. Fresh from the country and not yet thirteen years of age, I present our newest recruit to our noble profession, little Miss Molly."

Victoria stared past the edge of the screen in horror as a dazed-looking young girl dressed in a thin white shift was pushed into the center of the room. Molly gazed around at the leering men and laughing women and hugged herself tightly. The laughter increased.

Molly's frightened gaze moved from one face to another until her eyes somehow collided with Victoria's. The girl did not look away. Victoria clutched the arm of the chair as the sick feeling in her stomach grew more intense.

"Now, then, let us begin the bidding. Sweet young things such as our Molly do not come cheap," the madam said.

"I think it's time we left," Lucas muttered as voices rose loudly in the room. He flicked one last, disgusted glance at the brothel owner and started to get to his feet.

"No." Victoria shook her head, unable to look away from the terrified Molly. "No, Lucas, we cannot leave. Not yet."

"Damn it, Vicky, you don't want to see this."

"They are bidding on her, Lucas. As if she were a cow or a horse."

"And the winner will take her upstairs and introduce her to her new profession," Lucas concluded roughly. "Perhaps he won't even bother with privacy. Perhaps he will do the business right here in front of an audience. Surely you do not wish to witness such a thing."

"Of course not. Lucas, we must save her."

Lucas stared at her in amazement as he sank slowly back into his chair. "Save her? How do you propose we do that? It is a common enough occurrence here in town. The young women from the country step off the hay wagons straight into the arms of ruthless old abbesses such as this one. The girls are doomed and there is nothing that can be done."

"Well, there is certainly something that can be done about this one," Victoria stated. "I shall buy her."

Lucas sucked in his breath. "You don't know what you're doing, Vicky."

But Victoria was already watching the bidding frenzy. She had the advantage of knowing she was undoubtedly wealthier than anyone else in the room and she intended to use that fact.

"Thirty pounds," a man on the other side of the room shouted.

The brothel mistress regarded him with acute scorn. "For a certified virgin, sir? Come now, you cannot expect me to listen to such a ridiculous offer. Let us hear from some more noble sports."

"Who's to say she's still virgin?" hooted another. "I'll risk fifty pounds and no more."

"Interestin'," the bawd approved, "but not nearly good enough. Come now, I expected better from this crowd. You spend more on a horse."

"You can ride a horse longer than you can a virgin," someone called out, snickering.

"Nonsense. Our Molly will give you a fine ride, won't

you, Molly, dear?" The madam stroked Molly's blond hair in a mockingly affectionate gesture. The girl shuddered.

"Not pretty enough to go for more than eighty pounds. And I'll want my money back if you've lied about her condition."

Molly started to weep and the laughter in the room grew even more raucous. Victoria looked straight at the girl, willing her to stay strong as she bided her time.

The bidding crept higher but not at a very great rate after the initial rush. The miserliness of the bids verified what Victoria had already concluded. Not everyone in the room was convinced that poor Molly was worth a huge sum nor were there any men of great wealth here tonight. Men of vast wealth preferred to keep fashionable mistresses and only ventured into brothels such as this one for casual entertainment.

Victoria waited a few more minutes until the bidding stopped at ninety pounds. Then she casually raised her hand from behind the screen. "Three hundred pounds."

Lucas groaned.

The middle-aged woman turned a beaming countenance toward the shadowed screen. "Why, sir, you have excellent taste, whoever you be. Excellent, indeed. I do believe little Molly is yours to do with as you please this evening." She patted the young girl's hand. "What a lucky girl you are, my dear. Such a nice, discreet gentleman he is. Run along now and mind you don't make a fuss or it'll be the worse for you."

"You do not have three hundred pounds on you," Lucas reminded Victoria between set teeth. "You can hardly give the old bawd your personal marker, can you? She'll realize who you are."

Victoria blinked. "You are quite right. Very well, you will have to pay the woman. Say it is on my behalf as I am rather shy. Hurry, Lucas."

"Bloody, hell," Lucas murmured as he got slowly to his feet. "Don't think I won't collect from you for this."

"I assure you, I'm good for the blunt," Victoria said sharply.

He stood up and strode toward the bawd, ignoring

the shouts and ribald comments. When he reached the center of the room, he gave Molly a small push toward the screen where Victoria hovered. "Go on, girl. Move."

Molly looked up at him in terror and then responded automatically to the tone of command. She made her way through the laughing crowd to where Victoria waited.

"Hush, now, and all will be well," Victoria murmured as she took the girl's shaking hand and led her toward the door, cramming her hat down low over her eyes as she tugged the girl out into the hall.

Molly was too frightened to even protest. Perhaps being led out into the night appeared a better alternative to being taken up the stairs. The girl staggered a bit and Victoria realized she had undoubtedly been given several glasses of wine or perhaps an opium concoction to keep her dazed.

"Well, well, and just where d'ye think ye be goin' with the new piece? Ye ain't allowed t' take the merchandise off the premises." A very big, coarse-faced man loomed in Victoria's path. He was supposed to be the brothel's butler, but Victoria could see he had another job as well.

"My walking stick, if you please," she said imperiously.

"I just told ye, ye cannot be takin' the girl off the premises," the man boomed.

"I'm not going to take her off the premises," Victoria said in an utterly bored tone. She remembered what one of the prostitutes had said about rods and whips. "But I do have certain tastes I like to indulge. And I have found that my walking stick makes a very fine rod for my purposes. It has just the right heft and balance, if you take my meaning."

Little Molly stifled a scream but the big man looked somewhat mollified. It was obvious he was accustomed to such bizarre things.

"So that's the way of it, is it?" He leered at Molly. "Yer in for a fine time tonight, Molly, my girl."

Victoria waited tensely, glancing back over her shoulder once more for Lucas. He was still nowhere in sight. When the butler appeared with her walking stick, she decided she had to act on her own and find a way to the door directly behind the big man.

"Now, I believe I would prefer the comfort of my own carriage for what I have in mind," she said coolly. She started forward, yanking Molly with her.

The man narrowed his eyes and crossed his beefy arms across his chest. "I told ye, ye ain't takin' the little piece off the premises."

Victoria did the only thing she could think of. She lunged forward suddenly, ramming the end of the walking stick straight at the large man's crotch.

The butler shrieked and fell back, cursing and clutching himself. Victoria raced for the door, hauling Molly along in her wake.

"Hell," said Lucas from somewhere behind her. "I should have guessed something like this would happen."

There was a roar from the butler and then a solid, sickening thud. Victoria looked back from the doorway and saw the big man sprawled on the floor and Lucas calmly reaching for his coat and gloves.

"Go on," he ordered. "Get into the carriage."

In all the commotion Molly had clung to Victoria, and now pale and nervous, she began to babble in fear.

Victoria patted her shoulder as she steered her out into the night. "Do be quiet, dear. No one's going to hurt you."

The dozing coachman who had driven Lucas and Victoria to the brothel flapped the reins on the horses' rumps and moved the vehicle into position when he saw his customers emerge. He leered at poor Molly as Victoria thrust her up into the cab.

"I want t' go home," Molly wailed as Victoria climbed in behind her. The girl threw herself, sobbing, against Victoria's shoulder. "Please sir, just let me go home to Lower Burryton. My ma will be ever so scared. I should never 'ave left but I was told there were plenty o' good jobs 'ere in Town and my family needs the money so."

"Hush, hush, 'tis all right. You will go home, I promise." Victoria was still comforting the sobbing girl when

Lucas emerged through the carriage door. He eyed the crying Molly.

"Well, she's yours now, what do you propose to do with her?" Lucas asked as he signaled the coachman to pull away. "You can hardly take her to your aunt's house. You cannot possibly explain her presence. Everyone will know what you've been up to tonight."

"Once again you have the right of it, Lucas. How very perceptive of you. She cannot go home with me, so we must send her home with you. Your housekeeper can see to her welfare tonight and get her on the northbound stage in the morning."

"Bloody hell," said Lucas. But he looked resigned to the inevitable.

Silence, broken only by Molly's sobs, reigned for a few minutes.

"Had enough of brothels?" Lucas finally inquired calmly.

Victoria shuddered. "Quite enough. I never want to see such a place again as long as I live. It was sickening, Lucas. That those poor women should be reduced to being forced to survive by selling themselves to those awful men goes against all decent sensibility."

"Allowing you to witness such a scene goes against all decent sensibility, too," said Lucas. "I have only myself to blame for having indulged you in such a foolish fashion. I begin to think our night games have gone far enough."

Victoria was suddenly alarmed by his unexpectedly grim tone. "Surely you do not mean to put a halt to our adventures."

Lucas glanced meaningfully at the still-sobbing Molly. "We had best discuss this at another time."

"But, Lucas . . ."

"By the bye, you owe me three hundred pounds." Lucas leaned his head back against the seat cushions and closed his eyes. "Plus whatever it costs to get her out of town tomorrow morning."

Victoria sniffed. "Really, Lucas. If you're going to be that way about it, I shall see that you are repaid immediately."

"There is no great rush, Vicky. I can wait to collect."

She bit her lip. "But you do intend to collect?"

Lucas opened his eyes and looked at Victoria. "Oh yes, my dear," he said, "you may be certain of that."

Lucas plucked a glass of champagne off a passing tray and turned to greet Jessica Atherton, who was making her way determinedly toward him through the glittering crowd. She looked as lovely as always in her ball gown of blush rose, and her hair was fashionably ornamented with two combs studded with rubies.

But the expression on Jessica's face was that of a woman on a holy mission. It occurred to Lucas that more and more he was beginning to notice a certain pinched look about the woman he had once loved and lost.

What he had once interpreted as an expression of becoming modesty now seemed to border on perpetual disapproval. And there was something about her eyes that bothered him, something eternally distant and sadly aloof, as if she had looked out at the world and found that it did not live up to her high standards and never would.

Lucas contemplated his problem with the look in Jessica's eyes for the three or four minutes it took her to reach him. Just as she arrived at his side he finally realized exactly what it was about her that bothered him now. There was no fire in her, he thought suddenly, only the uncomfortable chill of angelic righteousness and a touch of female martyrdom. Thank God he did not have to look forward to getting into bed beside this untouchable, ethereal creature tonight or any other night.

It occurred to Lucas that during the brief time he had been engaged in the unconventional wooing of Victoria Huntington, he had become addicted to fire.

"Dearest Lucas, I have been anxiously waiting for you to arrive." Jessica smiled achingly up at him as if she had been afraid he had dropped off the earth sometime during the past few days. "Is everything going well with you?"

"Very well, thank you, Jessica." Lucas took the smallest of sips from his champagne and scanned the crowd for Victoria.

Jessica lowered her voice in a melodramatic fashion. "I have been extremely concerned to know if our plans were proceeding smoothly. There has been some gossip, nothing substantial, you understand."

Lucas did not like the way she said *our plans*, as if Jessica were somehow intimately involved in this courtship. But he could hardly deny that she had set the entire business in motion. If it had not been for Jessica, he might never have met Victoria. "What sort of gossip are you talking about Jessica?"

"Simply that you are seen frequently with Miss Huntington at parties and soirées and that you have ridden together more than once in the park. It is one thing to attend lectures and such events with her in the company of her aunt, but quite another to meet Miss Huntington in the park. I must ask if all this is leading up to our desired goal, Lucas."

Lucas set his back teeth at the way Jessica had used the word "our" again. "Kindly refrain from worrying about me. I am quite satisfied with the status of my association with Miss Huntington."

"Really, Lucas, you needn't act so churlish. I am only concerned for your success in this important matter of marrying an heiress. I know it is required of you and I am doing my best to assist you. There is still Miss Pilkington, you know."

Lucas stifled an oath and tried to appear properly grateful. "Thank you, Jessica. I appreciate your efforts. You have been most helpful."

She was somewhat mollified. "It is the least I could do in view of our past connection. I do hope you realize that I shall always think fondly of you, Lucas."

Fondness was about the limit of whatever affection Jessica Atherton would ever feel for anyone, Lucas decided. *No heat in her at all.*

He smiled to himself as he finally caught sight of Victoria on the far side of the room. She was in animated conversation with her friend Annabella Lyndwood.

When Victoria fell in love, she was going to burn like wildfire, he decided.

As if she sensed his gaze on her, Victoria looked up and saw him. She said something to Annabella and started through the crowd.

Lucas studied her as she moved toward him. Her height as well as the egg-yolk yellow silk gown made it easy to follow her progress. She looked vivid, regal, and almost unbearably provocative tonight. The gown was cut much too low again, of course. All her gowns seemed to be cut too low. This one made him long to grab her, take her out into the gardens, and pull the small bodice straight down to her waist. Her breasts were a constant source of delight to him; high, softly curved, and perfectly suited to the palm of his hand.

As she moved toward him, pausing politely to chat with friends en route, he remembered the hot, slick feel of her on his fingers the other night in the carriage. His body tightened just at the thought. Capturing his heiress was proving to be a very taxing business.

He was getting damned tired of denying himself what lately he had sensed Victoria was more and more eager to offer.

But with this particular female, strategy was everything and Lucas had plotted very carefully even as she had shivered in his arms with her first feminine climax. Forcing himself to think in strategic terms had been the only way to keep a tight rein on his own raging desire. Lucas did not think he could endure too many such "experiments," however.

He grinned a little when he saw Victoria pause in the crowd to cast a critical, assessing eye on Jessica Atherton. Then he watched her paste a very engaging smile on her lips and continue forward. Beside him, Jessica continued talking in confidential tones.

"You know, Lucas, I have had a few second thoughts about Victoria's suitability. It is true that her social connections are excellent and she does have a sizable inheritance, but I am not at all certain you would find her easy to manage."

"Don't fret, Jessica. I believe I can manage Miss

Huntington." Lucas inclined his head toward Victoria as she closed the distance between them and continued smoothly, "Good evening, Miss Huntington. What a coincidence running into you here at the Ridleys'. Is your aunt with you?" Beside him, he felt Jessica stiffen and close her mouth instantly.

"Yes, of course," said Victoria. "I left her talking to Lady Ridley. Good evening, Jessica. What a charming gown. I trust you are well?"

Jessica turned around quickly and smiled with a determined graciousness. "Very well, thank you, and yourself?"

"I have been slightly indisposed for the past day or two," Victoria said with a warning glint in her eye as she slid a quick glance at Lucas.

"I am so sorry to hear that," Jessica said.

"Oh, 'tis nothing significant, mind you, merely a small problem with my digestion. I fear my appetite is often affected by my mood and I confess I have been in a rather ill humor lately. Do you have the same reaction to ill humors, Jessica?"

"As a matter of fact, I do. It is not at all uncommon for me to lose my appetite completely when I am in distress. I am often a victim of the headache, too," Jessica agreed.

"Precisely. You are always so understanding, Jessica. So perceptive. Unlike some people." Victoria smiled pointedly at Lucas.

Lucas managed to pretend he noticed nothing amiss. "I hope you are feeling better, Miss Huntington."

"Oh, I will feel infinitely better just as soon as I have occasion to settle a small matter that has been plaguing me recently."

"I know what you mean," Jessica put in helpfully. "One's digestion is often improved when one's peace of mind is restored."

"How very true." Victoria's smile would have outshone the sun. She aimed it straight at Lucas. "Lord Stonevale, I was wondering if I might have a word with you?"

"I am at your service, of course, Miss Huntington."

But he made no move to escort her out of Jessica's hearing. Instead he placidly took another minuscule sip of champagne. "What is it you wished to speak to me about?"

Victoria cleared her throat meaningfully and glanced at Jessica. "A small matter, my lord. It concerns a forthcoming lecture. You know how interested you are in lectures."

"It depends. Is this lecture of a scientific nature?"

"Definitely. I believe it might be described as a matter of *intellectual inquiry.*"

"Then I am naturally interested to learn more." He drew his watch from his pocket. "Unfortunately, however, I have promised to meet a friend at my club and I fear I am late. Please tell your aunt that I am always happy to receive invitations to her society's lectures and shall look forward to this one, whatever it is. If you will excuse me, Miss Huntington? Lady Atherton?"

Lucas inclined his head politely to both women and made his escape from the ballroom.

This was not his first such escape in the past few days. Lucas grinned as he hailed a carriage. He had been studiously avoiding Victoria's increasingly pointed attempts to speak to him in private.

Strategy.

He was certain he knew what the topic of discussion would be when he finally allowed his heiress to pin him down.

He was almost positive that what Victoria was working herself up for was a request for more of the sort of *intellectual inquiry* that he had introduced her to that night in the carriage after the visit to the Green Pig.

Lucas cautioned himself for the thousandth time that he must not give in easily. After all, he thought wryly as the carriage halted at the steps of his St. James Street club, he wanted the lady to continue to respect him in the morning.

But there was another, far more serious consideration. Vicky was his responsibility. As her future lord and husband, it was his duty to protect her. Once he had made love to her, a new risk arose. There was every possibility she would get pregnant.

He supposed he should look upon that possibility as another useful tactic. Perhaps, back at the beginning of this strange courtship he might have done so. Now, however, it occurred to Lucas that he would far rather have Vicky come to him of her own free will. He wanted her to want him, he realized. He wanted her to want him enough to take the risk of surrendering completely. He wanted her to marry him because she loved him, not because she had to.

Lucas shook his head ruefully. Something about the wooing of Victoria Huntington was threatening to turn his clear-headed, cool-thinking soldier's brain into romantic mush.

The club's gaming room was far different in outer appearances than the gaming hell where Lucas had taken Victoria. Here, only gentlemen of respectable birth and reputation were allowed. The atmosphere around the green baize tables was far more subdued and aristocratic in tone. But the stakes were higher here in St. James than in the stews, and the potential for disaster enormous.

The potential for profit was correspondingly higher, too, however, and since the games were far more likely to be honest in this environment, such clubs were where Lucas habitually came to make his living.

"I say, Stonevale, been wanting to speak to you." Ferdie Merivale got to his feet and hastened forward as he saw Lucas walk into the room.

Lucas picked up a bottle of claret and poured himself a glass. He cocked a brow at the young man and wondered if he was about to be called out for his rescue efforts at the Green Pig. Then he thought of how he would explain such a situation to the lady who had gotten him into the mess in the first place. *Oh, by the bye, Vicky, the young pup you insisted I rescue has decided to try to kill me tomorrow morning.*

At least Molly the farm girl was safely out of town and not likely to come back anytime soon.

"What is it, Merivale?"

Ferdie flushed and ran a finger under the extremely

high fold of his neckcloth. But his gaze was determined and direct. "I wished to thank you, my lord."

Lucas narrowed his eyes in muted surprise. "Do you, indeed? For what?"

"For your interference the other night," Merivale plowed on gamely. "Don't believe I was properly appreciative at the time. Had a few glasses of claret before I got into the game, you know."

"Glasses or bottles?"

"Bottles," Ferdie admitted ruefully. "At any rate, I had no way of knowing what sort of reputation Duddingstone had. I've since learned that respectable men don't sit down to cards with him."

"*Intelligent* men don't sit down to cards with him," Lucas corrected. "I am glad you realize what he is. I will not bore you with a lecture on your responsibility to your name and estates, but I would urge you to think twice about risking more than you can afford to lose in a card game with anyone, respectable or otherwise."

Merivale grinned. "Are you quite certain you're not going to bore me with a lecture? Completely unnecessary, you know. I swear I have had three or four from my mother."

Lucas grinned. "Sorry. I fear I spent too long in the army. One gets accustomed to issuing warnings to green officers. And spare me your thanks, Merivale. To tell you the truth, I had no real intention of rescuing you that evening. I had other things on my mind at the time."

"Then why did you bother, sir?" Merivale asked.

"My, uh, companion took pity on you and suggested I do something. I obliged. That was all there was to it."

"I do not believe that for a moment, sir. You were kind enough to get me out of a situation in which I could have lost a great deal and I want you to know I am in your debt." Ferdie Merivale bowed slightly and went back to join his friends at the bar.

Lucas shook his head in silent amazement. Victoria had been correct. Ferdie Merivale wasn't such a bad lot after all. If he continued to grow up at this pace, the young man might very well become a credit to his title and his family.

None of that, however, made up for the fact that because he had been occupied with stuffing Merivale into a carriage, Victoria had nearly been run down. Every time he recalled the terrible scene, Lucas's insides went cold.

Deliberately he shook off the chill. He had business to do tonight. He picked up the claret bottle and went across the room to see who was playing cards. He needed to augment his financial reserves. It cost a staggering amount to move in Victoria's social circles.

The one truly irksome thing about this courtship was that the money he was spending on the social trappings he needed for camouflage was money that could not be sunk into the hungry lands of Stonevale.

Lucas consoled himself with the knowledge that one sometimes had to take risks in order to secure a greater profit.

He soon found what he was looking for—a game of whist where the play would be deep enough to suit his current financial needs. He was invited to sit down at once. Lucas did so, putting the bottle on the table.

In reality, he would actually drink very little this evening. He had learned long ago that a clear head gave him a distinct advantage in a game where his opponents usually preferred to fortify themselves with endless bottles of claret and port. The bottle of claret sitting at his elbow was simply more camouflage.

A long time later, after nearly four hours of steady play, Lucas finally decided he had enough to placate his tailor and his bootmaker as well as sufficient to keep his small staff satisfied for a few more weeks. He excused himself from the game and went to collect his hat and coat.

He realized he was tired. The intensity and concentration he brought to his card playing often left him feeling exhausted. But he knew it was precisely that intensity and concentration that helped him win on a reliable basis.

It was the fashion among the men of the ton to play wildly and without much thought or analysis. Gaming was just one more way of displaying one's wealth and style, a method of enhancing one's sense of power and masculinity and impressing one's companions with one's sangfroid.

Huge losses were handled with casual disdain as if money meant nothing. But it was no secret that some men went home and put a pistol to their own heads after a disastrous night at the tables.

Lucas much preferred winning and he took great care to do so. Indeed, a man who was good at strategy could prosper at the gaming tables.

He was halfway to the door when he spotted Edgeworth watching him from the hearth. The other man's sullen dislike was palpable, but Lucas was not particularly concerned. The feeling was mutual. He had not minded in the least relieving Edgeworth of a sizable sum a fortnight ago. Lucas also had no intention of ever getting into another game with the man.

"Good evening, Stonevale. Enjoying your outrageous little heiress?" Edgeworth spoke just loudly enough to catch Lucas's attention. "A very interesting young lady, is she not?"

Lucas contemplated Edgeworth's taunting expression and wondered if he could simply ignore the man. Probably not. Young Merivale and his friend had overheard the remark. They were already turning their heads to see how Lucas would respond.

"I do not discuss respectable women with your sort, Edgeworth," Lucas said mildly. "Now that I think of it, I do not believe I would discuss women of any kind with you."

" 'Tis said the lady in question has no intention of ever marrying," Edgeworth continued, ignoring the clear warning in Lucas's voice. "Since matrimony is not a possibility, may we assume you have other goals in mind for Miss Huntington? After all, the two of you are seen together so frequently one cannot help but speculate on the nature of your association."

This was what came of having a reputation for being slow to anger, Lucas thought ruefully. The fact that he had made no accusation against Edgeworth the night of their infamous card game had obviously emboldened the man.

Meditatively Lucas sipped the claret, aware of his audience. Merivale and his companion were frowning now, waiting to see how Lucas would handle what bordered on a thinly veiled insult to Victoria's virtue.

"One would be wise to resist the temptation to speculate too much on Miss Huntington's social activities," Lucas said. "Unless, of course, one is prepared to present oneself at dawn in Clery Field accompanied by a pair of seconds."

The small tableau of Edgeworth, Merivale, and Merivale's friend went abruptly still.

Edgeworth eyed Lucas through narrowed lids. "Just what is that supposed to mean, Stonevale?"

Lucas smiled his thinnest, coldest smile. "Precisely what it sounds like. I am, as you well know, prepared to let a little matter such as cheating at cards go unremarked. I am not, however, quite so sanguine when a slur is cast on an innocent young woman's name. I leave the decision up to you, Edgeworth."

Edgeworth straightened away from the mantel, his face turning an angry shade of red. "Damn you, Stonevale. God damn you to hell, you bastard. Do you think your luck will hold out forever?" He turned on his heel and walked swiftly out of the room.

Merivale and his companion watched with open mouths as Edgeworth departed. Lucas swallowed a far larger amount of claret than he'd had all evening. He considered himself fortunate that Edgeworth did not care to play any game in which the deck was not marked.

"Good God," Ferdie Merivale said, mopping his brow with a linen handkerchief. "Thought for a moment there I was going to get my first invitation to act as a second. I must say, you handled him very well, sir. Certainly cannot have Miss Huntington's name bandied about in such a manner."

"I should say not," Merivale's companion put in. "Miss Huntington is a very decent sort of female. Danced with me at my first ball when I was damn sure I would make a complete ass of myself on the floor. After a couple of dances with her, I felt much more confident, and after being seen with her, I had no trouble getting other dances, I can tell you."

"She was extremely good to my sister," Merivale

added. "Poor Lucinda was stricken with the most awful case of shyness when she made her debut a year ago. Frozen with fear, you might say. But Miss Huntington took her under her wing and showed her how to go on in Society. Mama was excessively grateful, I can tell you. As a friend of Miss Huntington's, Lucinda soon got some excellent invitations."

"Edgeworth backed right down, didn't he?" the other young man observed eagerly. "But, then, lately I have heard rumors the man don't much care for a fair game of any kind."

"I believe, sir," Merivale said slowly, "that Edgeworth is a bit annoyed with you because of that little scene at the card table a while back. Everyone knows you're much too good a player to drop an entire deck on the floor by accident. After you called for a new deck and began to win, people started wondering at Edgeworth's incredible luck in the past. He's finding it harder and harder to get into a game these days. Wouldn't be surprised if there's some talk of kicking him out of his clubs soon."

"Interesting." Lucas nodded briefly at the two young men. "If you will excuse me, I must be going."

A moment later Lucas walked down the front steps of the club and hailed the nearest carriage. Inside, he sprawled back against the seat and exhaled deeply. He needed to think.

Idly he rubbed his jaw and stared out into the night. This game he was playing with Victoria was getting increasingly risky. Aside from the very real physical dangers of their midnight adventures, there was now a genuine risk to her reputation. Killing Edgeworth in a duel would not be enough to silence the gossip, once it had started.

He could not allow Victoria to get hurt, Lucas told himself grimly. The thing had reached a very serious stage. They were courting an increasing risk of discovery with every midnight outing, and every time they were seen together at parties or in the park, tongues wagged.

Lucas knew Victoria well enough now to realize that even if he refused to escort her on any more midnight adventures, she would probably find some way of going about on her own. She had grown extremely confident in her flimsy masculine disguise.

There was another possibility, too, Lucas reflected. If he stopped providing escort, she might very well find another man who would. And that was the most intolerable thought.

Lucas absently massaged his leg while he examined his own logic. It was clear that the dangerous courtship had to end and soon. The only solution was to marry Victoria as quickly as possible.

His nerves would not tolerate too much more of this wild, reckless, midnight wooing.

Two days later Lucas folded his arms across his chest and sent an amused scowl at Victoria, who was shifting restlessly again in the neighboring seat. She pretended not to notice his admonishing look as she readjusted her skirts.

Next to Victoria sat Cleo Nettleship, paying rapt attention to the speaker, a certain Sir Elihu Winthrop, who was delivering a stimulating lecture entitled "An Enumeration of the Principles of the Cultivation of Buckwheat."

Lucas, at least, was finding the subject stimulating. He was already making plans to put some of Stonevale's fields into buckwheat. The stuff made excellent fodder for cattle and sheep and, according to Winthrop, was frequently consumed by humans over on the continent. Of course, everyone knew that people on the continent would eat virtually anything. Still, there were periodic shortages of wheat throughout England and buckwheat might provide a good emergency grain for his people.

Victoria began to tap her foot impatiently. Lucas knew he should probably not be too hard on her. She obviously had other things on her mind this afternoon and he was quite certain he knew what was making her so fidgety.

Lucas hid a quick smile of satisfaction. He had absolutely no intention of making it easy on the lady. Now that he had her hooked, she was going to have to work a little more at getting herself landed.

For a moment he allowed himself a few glittering

memories of her sweet passion and then, when he realized what it was doing to the region of his groin, he gave his full attention back to the speaker. Winthrop was now deep into a discussion of various methods of manuring buckwheat.

"Most educational," Lady Nettleship declared at the end of the lecture. "Although I confess I have a much stronger interest in lectures on exotic plants. Still, one should certainly be aware of the newest techniques employed in domestic agriculture. Did you enjoy it, Lucas?"

"Very much. Thank you again for letting me know the lecture was going to be held today."

"Anytime, anytime. Are you ready to leave, Victoria?"

"Yes, Aunt Cleo. Quite ready." Victoria was on her feet, collecting her bonnet and reticule.

"Well, we mustn't rush out of here. I see one or two people I should speak to first." Cleo glanced around the room with enthusiasm. "I will be right back."

Victoria shot Lucas a meaningful look from beneath her lashes as they started toward the doors of the lecture hall. He looked down at her, enjoying the sight of her in a charming little yellow spencer jacket worn over a white muslin walking dress. She looked very lovely, he thought with a sense of possessive pride. He ushered her politely toward the exit, nodding at several of the society's members with whom he was becoming friends.

The departure from the hall took some time as several people stopped to talk. Lucas could feel Victoria simmering with impatience beside him.

"Is something wrong?" he finally inquired quite casually as they stood in the entryway waiting for Lady Nettleship.

"No, but Lucas, I must talk to you."

"Then something *is* wrong?"

"Nothing is wrong. I simply wish to speak to you in private and I have not had an opportunity to do so since the night we—" She broke off, turning pink. Then she gamely cleared her throat and finished the sentence, "Since the night we went to the Green Pig."

"Speaking of which, I ran into Ferdie Merivale the

other evening at my club. You will be happy to know he was not nearly as annoyed with me as I had expected. Even thanked me for rescuing him. It seems he's come to his senses and feels he had a rather close call."

Victoria's eyes brightened for a moment. "I'm so glad. I have always liked Ferdie and his sister."

"Too bad I cannot tell him he owes the lesson to you, not me. I'd have left him to his fate, I'm afraid."

"Only because you were so concerned with protecting me," Victoria said with a touching loyalty. "Otherwise, I am certain you would have done something on your own for the boy. And you were very helpful with little Molly, too."

Lucas smiled wryly. "Will you be at the Foxtons' tonight?"

"Yes, but you know how difficult it is to find any privacy at a crush like that. Lucas, why do you not ride in the park tomorrow afternoon? I shall arrange to be there, also."

"As much as I would wish to do so, I'm afraid I have another engagement."

Victoria's face fell. "You do? Are you very sure you cannot make it? Even for a few minutes around five?"

He took pity on her. The poor woman was obviously so far out of her depth now that she could not possibly swim to shore by herself. Lucas contemplated just how he would save her. "I dislike riding in the park in the afternoons, Vicky. Too crowded."

"Yes, I know, but I simply must speak to you. If you won't join me in the park, you must come to the garden tonight. We can talk there." Victoria lowered her voice. "This is very important, Lucas."

"I fear I had not planned on one of our little adventures tonight. These things do take planning, you know."

"Damn it, Lucas," she hissed softly, "I am not planning an adventure. But I do want to see you. I would greatly appreciate it if you could fit me into your busy schedule."

Lucas looked at her in mild surprise. "You sound upset, Miss Huntington."

Victoria fidgeted. "I am upset, Lord Stonevale. You are being exceedingly difficult."

"I am only thinking of your reputation, Victoria. We must be very, very careful these days," Lucas warned, glancing about to prove his point.

"Hang my reputation. I must talk to you."

He was startled and rather warmed by her insistence. She was obviously at the end of her tether. Lord knew he was more than ready for the next phase of this business, himself. It was time to end her frustration and his own.

"Very well," Lucas said, as if considering the matter carefully, "I will check my engagement book and see if I can spare a few minutes with you in your garden later this evening around midnight. Will that suffice?"

"You are far too kind, my lord."

He winced as the knife edge of her tongue took a slice out of his hide. "Not at all."

"I begin to believe you are toying with me, Lucas."

His brows rose. He must never forget the woman was extremely astute. "I will do my best to be in your garden tonight at the usual time. Now, if you will excuse me for a moment, I see Tottingham over in the corner. He promised to loan me his copy of White's *Natural History and Antiquities of Selborne*. I have been wanting to read it since he mentioned it to me."

"You need not bother Tottingham with your request, my lord," Victoria said icily. "If you manage to keep your appointment with me tonight, I will allow you to borrow my copy."

He grinned. "Victoria, my sweet, are you by any chance trying to bribe me?"

She turned an even brighter shade of pink and whirled around to go in search of her aunt.

8

Lucas saw her waiting for him in the shadows of a tree as he came over the garden wall. She was an elegant ghost hooded and cloaked in a maroon velvet cape lined with yellow satin. The same cape she had worn earlier that evening to the Foxtons' ball.

He eased himself carefully to the ground, catching his weight on his right foot and using his left primarily for balance. But even taking care, the short drop sent a sharp twinge through his bad leg. He had no business climbing garden walls.

Lucas straightened, idly massaging the old wound, and wondered how he had come to find himself dancing on the end of Victoria's string for so long. He had let the lady run him in circles.

It was high time to take her to bed and make her his own. He would have much preferred to marry her first, but barring that possibility, he would take what he could get. Just the thought of being able to spend a comfortable night in a bed with Victoria instead of racketing around in hired carriages and flirting with disaster was enough to make his leg feel better and assured himself that bed was bound to lead to marriage.

"Lucas?" Her voice was the softest of whispers as she came forward through the damp grass. She lifted her cloaked face and looked up at him with a sweet, vulnerable expression that wrenched his heart.

He groaned and thrust his hands under the hood to frame her face. Without a word he lowered his head to drink hungrily of her mouth. When he finally released her, his whole body was tight with desire.

"Damn, but it was hard to watch you dance with one man after another tonight at the Foxtons'," he muttered against her throat.

"Lucas, please, you must not kiss me like that tonight. There is no time. My aunt will be home shortly. I told her I had the headache when I left the Foxtons. She will probably go straight to my room to check on me when she comes home."

"What is it that was so important we are once again risking your reputation, Vicky?"

She clutched the velvet cloak more tightly around her, meeting his eyes bravely in the flickering moonlight. "I thought this would be easy to say, but I am discovering it is not easy at all."

He wanted to fold her close against his chest and assure her she did not have to say anything, but he resisted the temptation. She must take this step herself. *Strategy*, he reminded himself bleakly.

Strategy and a desperate wish not to be blamed later for having seduced her. Far better for both of them that she engineer her own fall into bed with him.

"I am listening, my sweet."

She lifted her chin determinedly. "I have done a great deal of thinking lately, my lord."

"Not always a good thing. I have found that sometimes too much thinking can disturb one's peace of mind."

"Well, mine is already disturbed." She stepped away from him and turned to pace back and forth in the wet grass. She seemed unaware of the way the toes of her satin evening slippers were growing damp. "I have gone through this problem many times in my own mind. For reasons I am certain you will understand, it is a subject that is almost impossible to discuss openly with anyone else, even my aunt."

"I understand," he said gravely. "There are some things we cannot discuss, even with those who are close to us."

"Yes, precisely." She turned and paced in the opposite direction. "I believe I have told you that I do not wish to marry."

"On several occasions."

"Lately I have discovered, however, that I am not entirely opposed to a . . . a romantic liaison with a man."

"I see."

"I am glad, because this is very hard to put into words." She swung around and stalked back the way she had come. "Do you, uh, recall what happened the other night in the carriage after we left the Green Pig?"

"Very clearly."

She ducked her head deeper inside the hood. "I was astonished to learn that the connection between a man and a woman can be quite so . . . so intense."

He hid his amusement. "I am pleased you found the experience pleasant."

"*Pleasant.*" She halted and spun to face him, her eyes huge in the pale light. "It was vastly more than pleasant, my lord. It was rather unnerving in some respects but very, very exciting. Quite astonishingly delightful, in fact."

Her delicious honesty on the subject entranced him. "You flatter me."

"Not at all." She resumed her pacing. "Lucas, I have given this much thought and I have decided I wish to repeat the experience. In fact, I have decided I would like to discover the full range of that particular sort of experience. As a matter of intellectual inquiry, you understand."

"Intellectual inquiry," he repeated slowly. "Rather like collecting beetles, I imagine."

"I suppose one could say that."

"Will you put me on display in a box when you've finished your inquiries?"

Victoria scowled at him from inside her cloak. "Lucas, don't you dare tease me. I am perfectly serious about this."

"Yes, I can see that."

"To be quite blunt, I would like to establish a romantic connection with you of the sort Isabel Rycott enjoys with her friend Edgeworth."

"Good God, I sincerely hope not."

Victoria stopped and turned toward him with a shocked, embarrassed expression. "You do not want me?"

Instantly he realized how she had interpreted his words. He moved forward and pulled her roughly into his arms, covering her mouth with his own in a kiss of such fierce possession that she trembled in response. When he finally released her, he captured her face between his hands and looked down at her, knowing the full force of his need was probably blazing in his eyes.

"I want you more than I have ever wanted anything else on the face of this earth. Don't ever forget that, Victoria. No matter what happens, promise me you will never forget that."

She circled his wrists with her fingers, smiling tremulously. "And I want you, Lucas. I have never known anything like this need I feel for you. Please, will you make love to me?"

"*Vicky.* Oh, Vicky, my sweet, wayward, passionate hoyden." He crushed her against his length, light-headed with a strange combination of passion, tenderness, and relief. "I will make love to you until you go up in flames and then I will join you and we will burn together."

"That does not sound particularly comfortable, my lord," she remarked, her voice muffled against his coat.

He grinned. "Wait until you try it."

She laughed softly and her arms went around his waist. She hugged him tightly. "Lucas, I am so excited."

"So am I," he whispered, and then added deliberately, "It is almost as if you had just agreed to marry me."

She went rigid. "Lucas . . ."

"Almost, but not quite. Calm yourself, Vicky. I don't mean to frighten you, but you cannot help but know by now that I would not be averse to something more than a romantic connection with you. Would you care to discuss marriage rather than a romantic liaison?" He held his breath, praying she would say yes and everything would suddenly become very simple.

"Thank you, Lucas. That is very nice of you, you know. Entirely unnecessary, but very nice. I do appreciate the offer, because you certainly were not obliged to make it," she said, beaming.

"But the answer is no?"

"You know it is, but thank you again for asking." She raised her head to brush her mouth lightly against his own. Then she smiled brilliantly up at him. "Now, let us get on to making our plans."

Her rather casual dismissal of his proposal irritated Lucas. The little baggage thought she could have it all without paying the price. Perhaps it was time to gently point out that this was not going to be quite as simple and straightforward as she had anticipated.

"Very well. When?"

She blinked. "When what, my lord?"

"When shall we arrange our first meeting as lovers? And how? Have you given any thought to that? It needs some consideration. Also, there is the matter of where, isn't there? We cannot just hire a carriage to drive us around London for several hours while we make love on the cushions. Most uncomfortable and I don't want the coachman making a guess about what is going on inside," he explained roughly.

Her expression moved from startled to appalled. "I thought . . . I thought you would take care of those little matters. That is, I assumed you knew how to make the arrangements for this sort of thing, Lucas."

"Not likely. I've never formed a romantic connection of such an intimate nature with a young lady of your sort before in my life. It generally is not done, Victoria. At least, not by men who consider themselves gentlemen. You put me in something of an awkward situation, you see."

She groaned. "Aunt Cleo warned me that it is not only my own reputation I am toying with, but yours also."

"Did she really?" Lucas was not particularly surprised to hear that Lady Nettleship had guessed in which direction the wind was blowing. He wondered what Cleo's real views on the matter were. "Lady Nettleship is a very perceptive woman. She obviously does not like the notion of you playing ducks and drakes with your reputation."

"Or yours. Lucas, I understand this is not easy for you and there certainly are dangers involved. I am not so blind that I do not comprehend that."

"That speaks well for your intelligence, Vicky."

She bit her lip and slanted him a sidelong glance. "I suppose it really is not fair of me to ask you to do this."

"As you said, one cannot deny there are risks involved."

She sighed, a very tragic-sounding sort of sigh. "You are quite right. I have no business jeopardizing your reputation as well as my own, do I? Perhaps we should simply forget it."

"My offer presents a possible alternative," he began cautiously.

She patted his arm affectionately as if he were a well-meaning puppy. "Your offer of marriage was very sweet, Lucas. But I fear the only real alternative for me is to wait a few more years until I am well and truly established as a spinster. Perhaps then no one will care too much if I choose to follow in Lady Rycott's footsteps. Do forgive me, Lucas. I am sorry I ever brought up the subject."

Alarm swept through him as he realized she was already backing away from the affair. What's more she was considering spinsterhood rather than marriage as the only alternative. If he let her go completely, he might never get her back. Even worse, she might find another man who would not have any hesitation at all in letting her take all the risks she wished.

Lucas reached out a little roughly and caught her chin between thumb and forefinger. "Victoria, if a romantic liaison is truly what you want, then it will be my privilege to give it to you."

Her sudden smile was much too luminous and her eyes glowed with what looked suspiciously like feminine triumph. "In the spirit of intellectual inquiry, my lord?"

Somewhere inside Lucas a warning bell belatedly clanged. He studied Victoria's delighted, cheerfully smug expression and a nasty notion was born in him that he'd just been well and truly outmaneuvered.

"I have always been a great believer in the benefits of intellectual inquiry," he said grimly.

"Oh, Lucas, how can I ever thank you?" She threw her arms around his neck and hugged him fiercely. "You are always so good to me."

Swearing silently, he succumbed to the allure of her obvious delight. He was beginning to realize that it would always be difficult to refuse Victoria whatever she happened to want. He would do well in the future to remember his weakness in that regard.

Reluctantly Lucas pulled her arms from around his neck, kissing her reassuringly on the tip of her nose. "Then 'tis settled. Now, my sweet, you had better get back into the house. I think I hear a carriage coming down the street."

"Oh, dear, that must be Aunt Cleo. I must go." She turned swiftly, the cloak whirling around her sadly dampened slippers. Then she swung back with a quick frown of concern. "Do be careful of your leg when you go back over the wall, Lucas. I worry about all this climbing about. It cannot be good for you."

"I'm inclined to agree." The damned leg was already aching from his first assault on the wall this evening. Now he must repeat the process. "I look forward to the night when this wall climbing is no longer necessary. Good night, Vicky."

"About our plans for our first, uh, liaison . . ." She glanced anxiously toward the conservatory door as she, too, heard the carriage in the street.

"Don't fret, Vicky. I will arrange everything."

"You will?"

He paused, straddling the garden wall, and looked down into her upturned face. He bit back an oath. "Yes, Vicky, I will. That's my job, is it not?"

"You will let me know just as soon as you have got the details worked out?" she called out hopefully.

"Believe me, my dear, you will be the first to know." He cleared the wall and dropped down into the alley. His thigh protested strongly and his limp was more pronounced than usual as he made his way back toward the street where he had left the carriage. One way or another he definitely had to put a stop to this wall climbing.

Lucas checked the street and saw no one. He crossed it and started around the corner. He very nearly walked straight into the man holding the knife.

The footpad appeared equally surprised at the suddenness of the encounter. He had obviously been lounging in the shadows, waiting for his quarry, and had not heard Lucas approach. But he reacted immediately, lunging forward with the blade held low.

Lucas was already diving to the side, cursing as he felt his bad leg give away. He landed hard on the knee of his injured leg and forced himself to ignore the pain while he reached up and grabbed for his attacker's knife arm.

The man yelled in rage and surprise as Lucas rolled onto his back and tugged hard. The assailant slammed into the brick wall of the darkened house on the corner and the knife clattered to the paving stones.

Lucas kept rolling, moving up onto his knees. Then he staggered to his feet, bracing himself with one hand against the brick wall. Raw agony tore through his left leg.

The footpad was already thudding away into the darkness, footsteps echoing harshly in the night. He did not stop to retrieve his knife.

"'Ere, now," the coachman yelled, pounding up the street as he belatedly realized his passenger was in trouble. "What's goin' on? What 'appened, m'lord? Are ye hurt?"

"No." Lucas glanced down at his expensive Weston

jacket and swore again. He had just paid a fortune for the damn thing and now he would have to purchase a new one.

"Some footpad lookin' to prig a gennelman's purse," the coachman declared, reaching down to scoop up the knife. "Wicked-lookin' thing. The cove meant business, didn't 'e?"

"Yes," said Lucas. "But I am not certain just what sort of business he had in mind."

"Streets ain't safe for man nor beast," the coachman remarked. "You 'andled him right proper m'lord. Saw the way you sent 'im flyin'. Learn that sort of thing at Gentleman Jackson's academy, did ye?"

"No. I learned that sort of thing the hard way." Lucas started toward the coach and sucked in his breath as his left leg nearly collapsed again. He summoned up a vision of the bottle of port waiting in his library. "Let's be off, if you don't mind. It is not my intention to amuse myself standing around the streets at this hour."

"Certainly, sir. But I'd just like to say I never met a member o' the fancy could 'andle 'imself as well as you just did in a street fight. Most of the nabobs I run across would o' ended up with their gullets slit."

Victoria stepped back into her room and closed the door quietly behind her. Then she shut her eyes and leaned back against the wooden panels. Her heart was racing and she felt as though her legs were going to melt.

She had done it.

It had taken more raw courage than she had dreamed it would, more than she had even believed she possessed, but she had done it. She was going to have an affair with Lucas Mallory Colebrook, the Earl of Stonevale.

Her hands were trembling as she came away from the door and walked a little unsteadily across the room to stare out of the window into the darkness.

Now that she had accomplished her goal after days of agonizing over the matter, she discovered she was weak with reaction. There were so many dangers, both for herself and for Lucas.

But the chance to discover passion in Lucas's arms was worth any risk.

Such an admirable man. He was not a silly, foppish dandy or a callous rakehell. He cared about her reputation yet he accepted her desire to avoid marriage. He was not after her fortune, it seemed, only her.

"Dear God, listen to me. I sound as if I am in love with the man." Victoria caught her breath as the realization momentarily swamped her. "I *am* in love with him."

She hugged herself with the wonder of this latest adventure. To be in love and yet to be free. What more could a woman ask?

She stood at the window for a long time, trying to see the future in the darkness. But everything seemed cloudy and without solid form. After a long while, she went to bed.

At dawn she came awake suddenly, sitting bolt upright against the pillows.

Demon bitch. I will send you back to hell.

The knife.

Dear God, the knife.

She did not remember much about the nightmare that had jolted her from sleep, but she did not need to recall the details. She'd had similar dreams often enough during the past few months and they always ended the same way, leaving her restless and disturbed, filling her with a sense of dark, brooding menace that could not be logically explained away.

At least she had not cried out this time, she thought in relief. Occasionally she screamed in the middle of the terrible dreams and poor Nan would come running to check on her.

Victoria got out of bed. She knew from experience that daylight would banish the disquieting sensation. In the meantime there was not much point in trying to go back to sleep.

She reached for her wrapper. It was a clear day and soon the morning light would be streaming into the conservatory. A perfect day for painting. When all else failed, she could frequently find peace of mind by losing herself in her art.

Dressing quickly, she hurried downstairs. The household was just beginning to stir. She could hear cook clattering the pans in the kitchen.

Her easel, paintbox, and sketchbooks were just where she had left them. Victoria stood looking around the lush conservatory for a moment and then her eyes fell on the glorious blooms of *Strelitzia reginae*.

In the morning sunlight the flower was a wonderful cross between gold and yellow, a fabulous shade of amber touched with highlights of royal blue.

She quickly set about shifting all her equipment to a new vantage point where she would have a clear view of *Strelitzia*. She remembered how Lucas had admired it that first day in the conservatory.

She was going to paint it for him, she decided on a sudden impulse. He had appeared genuinely pleased by her botanical watercolors and sketches and there was no doubt about his new enthusiasm for horticulture. Perhaps he would like *Strelitzia reginae* as a memento of their first night together as lovers. It would be her gift to him on that memorable night.

Almost like a wedding gift, came the unbidden thought. She banished it quickly and sat down to go to work.

She saw the snuffbox inside her paintbox the moment she raised the lid.

For a few seconds she simply stared at it, astonished, and wondered why anyone would deposit a perfectly good snuffbox in her paintbox. It was as odd to find such an object here as it had been to discover the monogrammed scarf on the conservatory door a few nights earlier.

With a small, niggling sense of dread, Victoria picked up the tiny snuffbox and examined it carefully. It was a nicely worked box but not particularly distinguished except for the letter "W" engraved on the inside of the lid.

For a minute she was short of breath. She reminded herself violently that she did not believe in ghosts. But the thought that someone might be playing a macabre game with her was even more chilling than the prospect of a phantom.

And even more impossible, she told herself, taking several deep breaths to calm her nerves. She had to be sensible. This could not be her stepfather's snuffbox any more than the scarf could possibly have belonged to him.

This was all some sort of bizarre coincidence. One of her aunt's numerous acquaintances had been on a visit to the conservatory and had left the scarf and snuffbox behind. The scarf had been found immediately but the snuffbox had been set down and forgotten only to be discovered much later. By her.

It was the only possible explanation because no one, *no one* except herself knew what had really happened on that dreadful night when her stepfather had died at the foot of a flight of stairs.

Four days later Victoria looked around the Middleships' glittering ballroom at the sea of fashionably dressed guests and realized she was as nervous and excited as a bride at her own wedding party. *This was the night.*

As this was as close as she ever intended to get to a genuine wedding celebration, she had best enjoy it, she decided.

Three days ago Lucas had calmly told her that he had made all the arrangements for their first night together. The plans were contingent on Lady Nettleship accepting a long-standing invitation to a weekend house party in the country, he had warned. But that had been no problem. This morning Cleo had set off cheerfully for the nearby country home of one of her dearest friends.

"You are quite certain you do not mind staying here alone for one evening?" Aunt Cleo had demanded for the third time as she tied her bonnet and prepared to follow several bags into her traveling coach.

"Hardly alone, Aunt Cleo. I have all the servants including Nan. I shall do very well. You will recall that I am invited to the Middleships' ball tonight and their soirées never end before dawn. I shan't be home until sunrise and you will be back in the afternoon."

"Well, you are nearly twenty-five. I daresay no one can remark upon you staying here in your own home for one night without having me, and you will be accompanied by Lady Lyndwood and her daughter when you attend the ball, so all is well. Take care, Vicky." Cleo had given her a good-bye peck on the cheek before settling into the coach for the trip.

Victoria had waved from the steps and then felt her stomach do a series of strange little flips as anticipation set in with a vengeance.

This was the night. There was no turning back now. This was what she wanted; Lucas was the man she wanted. She was on the brink of a romantic liaison with the man she loved. The dazzling prospect of this sort of intellectual inquiry was enough to take away her breath.

The time had come. Victoria began to edge through the crowd, making her way unobtrusively toward the door. Lucas would be waiting.

"Off so soon, Victoria?" Isabel Rycott seemed to materialize out of nowhere.

"I fear I have a number of engagements this evening," Victoria said politely. "I promised a friend I would drop in at the Bridgewaters' for a while and then I have to go on to yet another rout after that."

Isabel tapped Victoria's gloved wrist admonishingly with her fan and smiled her mysterious smile. "I understand completely, my dear. You will slip from one party to another until you happen across your earl, will you not?"

Victoria flushed. "I have no idea what you are talking about, Lady Rycott."

Isabel laughed softly but with a strange touch of bitterness. "Don't be embarrassed, my dear. It is not so very unique to find oneself attracted to an interesting man. It is part of the female condition. But a wise woman takes care to remain in command of her emotions and the situation at all times. She is careful to choose men who are not particularly strong, men who can be easily managed."

"Really, Lady Rycott, I must be off."

"Yes, of course. But do keep my words in mind. As Samuel's and Caroline's friend, I want only the best for you." Isabel's eyes glittered with sudden harshness. "And you needn't act so superior, damn you."

Victoria was shocked. "I assure you, it is not my intention to offend you in any way."

Isabel's mouth twisted in a smile that was not in the least charming or even particularly mysterious. "Yes. You are noted for your kindness, are you not? But I know what you think of my friend Edgeworth. I saw it in your eyes the day we met in the park. You find him sadly lacking when you compare him to your precious earl."

Victoria started. "I never said—"

"You did not have to say anything. I saw it in your eyes. Such arrogance. You think I have landed the spavined, broken-down pony while you have got the fine-blooded stallion. But you will be sorry for your choice," Isabel hissed.

"Please, Lady Rycott, do not upset yourself."

"I am not in the least upset. I will tell you something, my dear. I will take an Edgeworth over a man like Stonevale any day, and if you were smart you would do the same. Your failure to do so will probably be your downfall."

Victoria was nonplussed by the bizarre conversation. She wondered how many glasses of wine Lady Rycott had consumed. The gem-hard glitter in Isabel's beautiful eyes was almost frightening. "Please excuse me, Lady Rycott." She made to move away, but Isabel's fingers reached out to grip her bare arm.

"You think you have chosen the more exciting, more interesting man, but you are a fool. The plain truth is that men are of little use to a woman if they cannot be manipulated. Don't you understand? We are trapped by Society into being dependent on men for so much. Our only defense is to be stronger than they are in all the ways that count. When a strong woman allies herself with a weak, manageable man, she can have everything she wants. *Everything*."

"Lady Rycott, you are hurting my arm."

Isabel glanced down at her own fingers, registering surprise. She instantly removed her hand from Victoria's arm, quickly regaining total control of herself. "Never mind. It is undoubtedly too late for you anyway. But you should have been shrewd enough to know by now that a strong man is very dangerous. If you'd had any sense, Vicky, you would have picked an Edgeworth, not a Stonevale."

Isabel turned away and disappeared into the crowd, but not before Victoria thought she glimpsed the brightness of tears in her exotic eyes.

Victoria stood staring after the other woman for a moment, utterly at a loss. Her happy anticipation was briefly dimmed by the startling encounter. But by the time she had collected her cloak and pulled the hood up over her head to conceal her features, she was back in the grip of excitement. She hurried down the steps of the town house.

The closed carriage was waiting for her, just as Lucas had promised. The coachman sat on the box, heavily shrouded in his top hat and enveloping cape. She shot him a quick, laughing glance and then allowed one of the Middleships' footmen to assist her into the carriage.

A few minutes later the vehicle was making excellent progress through the streets of London, and within a short while they had reached the quieter, outlying areas of the city. The noise of passing traffic faded and the buildings grew more sparse. Moonlit meadows, fields, and farms came into view.

Then, without any warning, the carriage came to a halt in an inn yard. Victoria's mouth went dry. The time had come and she was suddenly awash in a sea of contradictory emotions. Anticipation and excitement and longing did battle with anxiety, uncertainty, and a few second thoughts. She was forced to wonder once more if she was doing the right thing.

But she was four and twenty, she reminded herself, not a silly little seventeen-year-old chit fresh out of the schoolroom. She knew her own mind and she had already made her decision. She would not back out now.

She glanced out at the courtyard, listening to her "coachman" give directions to the young boy who came out of the inn to assist with the horses. No matter what sort of orders he was issuing, Lucas always sounded so very much in command.

A moment later the carriage door opened and Lucas stood looking at her. He had removed the hat and coachman's cape. Without a word he held out his hand.

"Are you very certain this is what you want, Victoria?" he asked quietly.

"Yes, Lucas. I want this night with you more than I have ever wanted anything in my life."

His smile was enigmatic but tender. "Then you shall have it. Come with me."

A short time later Victoria found herself sitting in front of a pleasant fire in a comfortable upstairs room, sipping tea the landlord's wife had brought her on a tray. There was a decanter of sherry next to the teapot. The good woman had addressed her as "my lady" and Victoria knew it was because Lucas had informed the innkeeper that she was his wife. No one had thought to question two obvious members of the Quality who claimed such a relationship.

"I've told the innkeeper that you are weary and we plan to rest for a few hours, but that we are in a hurry and must be on our way before dawn," Lucas announced as he walked into the room and shut the door behind him. "That will give me time to get you safely back to the last party on your list of invitations tonight before most of the guests have taken their leave. You will be able to go home with Annabella Lyndwood and her mother, just as you had planned. No one will be the wiser."

"Except, perhaps, myself?" Victoria smiled tremulously over the rim of her cup.

Lucas's eyes gentled as he looked down at her. "I think both of us are going to learn a great deal tonight." He walked over to the chair that stood across from hers near the hearth. His eyes were gleaming as he sat down and poured two glasses of sherry. "Here's to intellectual inquiry, Vicky."

She put down her teacup and took one of the sherry glasses from his hand, aware that her fingers were trembling slightly. "To intellectual inquiry," she murmured, lifting her glass in a small toast.

Lucas raised his glass in an answering salute, his eyes

never leaving hers. They finished the sherry in a charged silence and then Lucas removed the glass from Victoria's fingers and set it down alongside his.

Victoria remembered her gift and stood up abruptly. She hurried to where she had hung her cloak and reticule.

"Vicky? What's wrong?" Lucas called after her.

"Nothing is wrong. I have something for you. A small present." She turned back toward him, clutching the little parcel in both hands. It suddenly seemed like a rather paltry gift. "It is not much, really. I thought, *hoped* you might like it." She smiled wistfully. "It seemed like the sort of night one might want to remember with a gift."

He stood up slowly. "It is exactly that sort of night. I only wish I had a gift for you. My lamentable military mind, I fear. I was so concerned with the practical aspects of this evening that I failed to think about other, perhaps more important matters." He came toward her and took the parcel out of her hands. Then he led her back to her seat by the fire and sat down to open his present.

Victoria sat tensely as Lucas reverently removed the paper wrapping and stared thoughtfully down at *Strelitzia reginae*. She realized she was in an agony of suspense. It really was not much of a present, she thought. Just a painting of a flower.

But when Lucas looked up again, revealing a rare, intense emotion in his eyes, she took a deep breath and relaxed slightly. He was pleased.

"Thank you, Vicky. It is beautiful and I will hang it where I shall be able to look at it daily. And whenever I do look at it, I will remember this night."

"I am glad you like it. Not every man would care for a picture of a flower, you know."

"Just as well. I'd as soon you didn't go around giving any other man your paintings under similar circumstances." He reached out and took her hand.

"Lucas?"

"Your fingers are cold," he observed, cradling her palm. He turned her hand in his and bent his head to kiss her bare wrist. Her fingers curled. "You are very tense."

"I am nervous, if you must have the plain truth," she admitted.

"Would it make you feel any better to know that I, too, am anxious about what lies ahead?"

"That I refuse to believe, my lord."

"Then you sadly overestimate my fortitude. I want you very much, Vicky, but I do not want to hurt you or frighten you or somehow spoil the magic with clumsiness or a lack of self-control," Lucas said quietly.

Victoria looked up at him in surprise and was suddenly overwhelmed with a need to reassure him. "I should have realized this would be as awkward for you as it is for me. We are very much alike in many ways, are we not?"

Lucas nodded. "I like to think so."

"You are doing this because I asked it of you. I have forced you to go against your own code of honor."

He smiled faintly and his hand tightened around her fingers. "Do not credit me with too many fine scruples and sensibilities, Vicky. You cannot know how much I have wanted to hold you naked in my arms and feel you shiver when I enter you, how much I have longed to have you cling to me and draw me deep inside you. I am here tonight because you have made it clear that this is the only way I will ever learn how hot you will burn and I cannot live the rest of my life without discovering the answer to that question."

Victoria stared at him, unable to look away from the intensity of his gaze. She felt the heat of the flames on her skin, but it was nothing compared to the warmth that was pooling within her. She knew her fingers were trembling within his.

"Lucas, I have something to tell you."

"What is that, my sweet?" His voice was indulgent as his fingers trailed along the inside of her arm.

"I . . . I think I have fallen in love with you," she blurted.

"Only think?" He glanced up, eyes gleaming.

"Oh, *Lucas*."

He tugged her gently out of her chair and down onto his thighs, where he held her tightly against his chest. He speared his fingers through her curls, gripped her head, and kissed her.

Victoria thought she would drown under the impact of his mouth. At the touch of his tongue against her lips all her qualms and fears vanished as if he had waved a magic wand. Of course he wanted her. There could be no doubt of that. And she wanted him. Dear God, how she wanted him.

The next few minutes were a haze of small movements and tender, stroking caresses that somehow combined to remove Victoria's gown and petticoats along with most of her remaining inhibitions. It occurred to her that she ought to be feeling at least somewhat embarrassed. But all she could really feel was her own stirring passion and a sense of wonder that this man should want her so much that he would risk his reputation to please her.

"You are very good to me." She touched his cheek with gentle fingers. "You give me so much. All those nights of adventure and now this very special night."

"Just remember that from now on all your adventures must be with me." His hand stroked her slowly from breast to thigh until she moaned against his shirt. The heat in his eyes sent flames through her.

He set her on her feet and then led her over to the bed. When they reached it, she snuggled under the covers, watching in fascination as he doused the candles. When only the flames of the small fire lit the room, Lucas sat down on the edge of the bed, putting a considerable dent into it. A moment later one highly polished Hessian hit the floor. The second soon followed.

Victoria unconsciously clenched the sheet in her hands as she watched Lucas undress. The firelight turned his skin to bronze and underscored the smoothly muscled contours of his broad shoulders. His belly was hard and flat. Something gleamed in the mat of dark curls on his chest and Victoria looked more closely.

"What is that pendant, Lucas? Is it made of gold?"

He touched it absently. "Amber. There's a small carving on it. It's been in the family for years, I was told."

"And you wear it always?"

He shrugged. "I have worn it constantly since it was given to me by my uncle." Lucas smiled. "I like to think it brings me good luck, and it must work, otherwise I would not be here with you." His fingers suddenly tightened around it. "But I think it would suit you better than it does me."

He removed the chain from around his neck and moved closer.

"No, Lucas, I could not possibly take your pendant. It is a family heirloom. You cannot give it away."

"I can do anything I want with it." He placed it carefully around her throat and nodded in satisfaction. The amber glowed like honey-colored fire against her skin. The small figures of the knight and his lady were visible in all their exquisite detail. "It looks right on you. I want you to have it, Vicky. 'Tis a symbol of what we will share between us tonight. As long as you wear it, I will know you care for me and that you *think* you might be in love with me."

She answered his gentle, sensually teasing smile with one of her own. "In that case, I will never have cause to remove it. I cannot imagine not feeling about you the way I do now."

"Remember that, hmmm?" He brushed his knuckles lightly across her cheek before reaching down to open his breeches.

He stepped out of the remainder of his clothes, revealing a hard, aroused male body. But Victoria noticed nothing else about him in that moment except the wide, ragged scar on his thigh.

"Dear God," she whispered.

"Does it bother you?" He stood waiting, his breeches still in his hands, his eyes unreadable.

She reached out to touch the ruined flesh with gentle, soothing fingers. "Bother me? Of course it does not bother me. Not in the way you mean." She looked up at him, stricken. "But how it must have hurt you. I cannot bear the thought that you suffered such agony, that you came so close to death."

"Hush, Vicky. Do not fret about it. It was a long time

ago and I assure you right now it is not bothering me in the slightest. I have far more important things on my mind and none of them have anything to do with death. They are all matters of life." He caught her fingers in his hand and kissed them. "Do you know I didn't think it would upset you too much. There are women who would have recoiled in shock and revulsion. But somehow I rather thought you would not be put off by it. You are a most unusual woman, Victoria."

"Not really, but I—" She broke off as she finally noticed the rest of him. "Oh, my." Victoria gazed at him, mesmerized. He was hard and swollen in a state of full arousal and his masculinity appeared overwhelming to her inexperienced eyes.

"Well, at least your mind is off that damned scar," Lucas observed with wry humor as he tossed his breeches over a chair.

"You are very . . ." Her tongue seemed to grow awkward in her mouth. She moistened her lips and tried again. "You are quite magnificent, my lord. Rather large, in fact. Bigger than I had imagined." She felt herself turning red as he quirked a brow. "Not that I was quite certain just what you would look like, but I am . . . that is, the plain fact is that I was not expecting quite so much of you."

Lucas muttered an exclamation that was half laugh and half groan as he came down beside her and slid under the covers. "Vicky, my darling, you say the most delightfully honest things at the most amazing times. God, but you are sweet. I wonder how I waited this long to have you near me like this."

He pulled her close, his hand closing around her bare buttocks to urge her against his strong thighs. He used his foot to gently pry apart her legs and she suddenly realized she had been clamping them together. Fully intending to force herself to relax, she wound up squeezing her knees even more tightly shut.

Lucas's smile was deeply sensual. "I must tell you, sweetheart, that this particular aspect of our intellectual inquiry cannot proceed much farther if you keep your knees locked together."

The comment broke through her nervousness and elicited a small gurgle of laughter from her. Victoria put her arms around his neck and smiled up at him. "Is that right, my lord? I would never have guessed. I shall rely upon you to keep me informed of the small details of this experiment."

"Very well, here is one small detail that most certainly must not be overlooked." He bent his head and sipped one nipple carefully between his strong, white teeth.

"*Lucas.*" Victoria gasped and closed her eyes at the thrill that shot through her. Instinctively she arched herself so that he could take her more completely into his mouth.

Lucas obliged her, and when she was dazed with the sensations pouring through her, Victoria felt his leg slide effortlessly between her thighs. This time she offered no resistance at all, opening herself completely to his touch.

"So soft. So sweet and soft and welcoming." Lucas's voice was husky with his passion. His long, elegant fingers moved over her, exploring, searching, setting her on fire, just as he had promised.

As she adjusted to the exquisite delights unfolding in and around her, Victoria slowly grew more bold. When she stroked his shoulders and then traced the line of his spine down to his hips, Lucas encouraged her with dark, heated words.

"You feel so good, Vicky. Your touch is like none I have ever known."

He brushed himself lightly against her thigh, letting her feel the fullness of his manhood but not forcing her to accept him yet.

Without stopping to think, Victoria reached down to glide her fingertips across the broad tip of his engorged shaft. She gasped a little and drew back when she encountered a bead of moisture.

"Please," Lucas rasped against her breast. "Do it again." He thrust himself back into her palm, asking silently for another caress.

This time Victoria stroked him tentatively with quivering fingers and was delighted with his deep groan of response. She discovered she loved knowing she had such an effect on him.

Slowly he moved on top of her, settling himself between her legs. She felt his hands under her knees, raising them until she was completely open to him. Then he lowered his mouth and kissed her.

"Lift yourself," he urged.

She drew a deep breath and did so cautiously. He was ready and waiting for her. She retreated instantly as she felt him start to enter her. He was very large and solid, she realized. There was no give to him at all. She lifted her lashes and looked up into his stark face.

"I am not at all certain this is going to work," Victoria said tightly.

"It will work. Do not be in such a rush, darling. We have hours yet." He kissed her throat and nibbled tenderly at her ear. "Although I am quite certain I won't be able to wait hours to show you that we will fit together very well indeed. If I did hold off that long, I would be headed for Bedlam in the morning, a ruined man."

She started to laugh nervously at the image, but just as the giggle emerged he slid his palm down over her belly and carefully sought the blossoming petals between her legs with one long finger. Victoria's small giggle turned into a breathless gasp.

Then he was doing the things he had done to her that night in the carriage, the things that would soon make her shiver and cry out against his shoulder. The fabulous spiral of excitement twisted and condensed within her and turned her into a wild, writhing creature of light and energy.

As the storm within her threatened to break, Victoria clutched tightly at Lucas, digging her nails into his shoulders and lifting her hips impulsively against his hand. Her pleas began as small, frantic, cajoling cries of delight and finally were transformed into fierce little feminine demands for release.

"Do you want me now, sweetheart?" Lucas parted her with his fingers and let her feel the broad head of his shaft once more.

This time she did not retreat. "*Yes.* Oh, dear God, yes, my love."

He groaned, his whole body taut with the effort he was exerting to retain his self-control. Slowly he started to sink into her.

Victoria flinched, unprepared for the full force of his intrusion. Much of the dazzling excitement she had been feeling vanished as the pressure built. But she refused to stop now. She had come this far and it was clear that Lucas was at the end of his tether. She could not deny him the same release he had once given so generously to her. She tightened her grip on his arm and braced herself.

"Take it easy, darling, this is not supposed to be an act of martyrdom," Lucas whispered.

"I'm sorry. Please, Lucas, go ahead. I will be all right."

"I want you to be more than all right." His mouth fastened on hers and he withdrew himself from her. He reached down to insert his hand once more between their bodies.

He teased her with his fingers, sliding first one and then another just inside her, stretching her gently, drawing forth the sweet, hot honey. Soon she was once more swept back into the grip of sensual excitement.

This time he waited until she went coiled and taut beneath him, waited until her head tipped back over his arm, waited until she cried out, waited until she began to convulse gently and clutched at him so passionately she left small marks in his skin.

Then and only then did Lucas thrust fully into her in one long, relentless stroke that filled her completely.

He was drinking the last of her soft cries of mingled release and erotic surprise when his own shuddering climax broke over him.

9

Victoria came slowly awake as she realized that the unending pounding she was hearing was the sound of someone knocking forcefully on her door. But that made no sense. Nan would not dream of knocking so impolitely and no one else in the household except her aunt would feel free to barge in on her so early in the morning like this.

But this was not a normal morning. This was the morning after . . .

Victoria's eyes flew open as the full realization of what was happening and where she was struck her. Relief rushed through her as she realized it was still dark outside. She and Lucas were safe. They had time to get back to the ball before dawn. Then she realized she was alone in the bed.

She sat up suddenly, clutching the sheet to her throat, and saw that Lucas was hastily pulling on his breeches near the foot of the bed. He swore softly, grabbed his shirt, and stalked barefoot to the door.

"Lucas, no, *wait*, I have a dreadful feeling you should not open that door."

505

But it was too late. Lucas had already yanked open
the door and was starting to growl ferociously at whoever stood on the other side.

"What the hell is the meaning of this interruption?
My wife and I are trying to sleep." There was a shattering pause and then Lucas continued with awful gravity,
"I beg your pardon, Lady Nettleship. I certainly did
not mean to yell at you. Forgive me. To be perfectly
honest, you are the last person I expected to see tonight."

"Yes," Cleo Nettleship said in frozen accents, "I can
understand that."

Victoria closed her eyes and lowered her forehead
down onto her updrawn knees as the enormity of the
disaster struck her.

"If you will give me a few minutes to dress, I will join
you downstairs. Under the circumstances you will probably desire a few explanations."

"You are quite correct, sir. But you will answer my
first question before I go downstairs. Is my niece all
right?"

"Victoria is quite all right, madam. I give you my
word."

"Do not be long. It is not yet dawn, but there is very
little time to spare. There are decisions that have to be
made and acted upon at once, as I am sure you are well
aware."

"I understand. I will join you in a few minutes. We
will talk while Victoria gets dressed."

Lucas closed the door quietly and turned slowly
toward the bed. His face was an unreadable mask in the
dim glow of the smoldering fire. "I am sorry, Vicky. As
you can see, we have something of a problem."

"Dear heaven, what are we going to do?" She could
not seem to get her thoughts in order. It was as if she
were swimming in a sea of chaos.

"We will do what must be done, of course." He sat
down on the chair and swiftly pulled on his boots. Then
he finished dressing with the quick, efficient movements of a military man.

Victoria looked blankly at Lucas. "I do not understand. Why is my aunt here? How could she possibly

know about us and this inn? I did not know myself where you would be taking me until we got here. Lucas, none of this makes any sense."

He walked over to the bed and stood looking down at her, his expression grim. "I have no idea what your aunt is doing here or how she found out about us tonight. I assure you, I fully intend to discover the answers. But it makes no real difference now, Vicky. Surely you can see that? We both knew from the outset that there were certain risks involved in this sort of entanglement. We have been caught and there is no way to go back to the beginning. We must deal with the situation as it stands."

She hugged her knees and looked up at him, her eyes wide with uncertainty and a dawning fear. "You sound so very military about all this. And you look like a soldier getting ready for battle. You frighten me, Lucas."

His eyes softened for a moment as he leaned over and caught her face between his rough hands. "This is not how I would have chosen to have had things turn out between us. But now that the dice have fallen this way, all I can do is ask you to put your trust in me. I will take care of you, Victoria. I swear it on my honor."

Before she could think of a reply to that, he was gone, out the door and down the stairs to meet her aunt. Victoria sat perfectly still for a few minutes and then, very slowly, she pushed back the covers and got out of bed.

As she stood up she was chagrined to discover she was sore in places she had never been sore before in her life. She would have given a great deal to have been allowed to relax in a hot bath. But that was impossible.

She felt the unfamiliar weight of the pendant around her throat and reached up to touch the amber figures as if they were a talisman.

Memories of the night sleeted through her mind like silver rain as she made her way to where her clothes waited on a chair. She struggled into her petticoats and gown without nearly as much dexterity as Lucas had

demonstrated pulling on his own clothing. She had
never before tried to get into a ball gown without the
assistance of a maid. It was not easy.

Later, enveloped in her cloak, Victoria drew a deep,
steadying breath and went out the door and down the
stairs. A concerned-looking innkeeper, who appeared to
have been recently rousted from his sleep, showed her
to a private parlor.

Victoria stepped through the door, instantly aware of
the quiet tension in the room. Lucas stood near the
hearth, one arm resting on the mantel, his booted foot
propped on a log. Lady Nettleship was seated in a chair
at the table. They both looked toward the door as
Victoria came into the room.

"Perhaps I have been shown to the wrong parlor,"
she said wryly. "I seem to have walked in on a funeral."

"I pray you will not consider it such when all is said
and done," Aunt Cleo remarked. "Sit down, Victoria."

It had been a long time since her aunt had used that
tone. Victoria sat. Her gaze flew to Lucas but she could
read nothing in his eyes. There was about him that air
of implacable determination which she saw rarely but
which never failed to make her feel uneasy.

"Now, then," Cleo said as if calling to order a meeting of her Society for the Investigation of Natural History and Horticulture, "Lucas and I have already
discussed what must be done. He is quite prepared to
do the proper thing, and you, I trust, are also willing to
pay the price of your indiscretion. A marriage by special license can be arranged first thing in the morning. I
will attend as a witness so that everyone will know it
has my sanction."

Marriage. Victoria's hands clenched together in her
lap. All the while she had been struggling into her
clothing upstairs she had refused to think about what
might happen next. Frantically she tried to calm herself
and think rationally.

"There is no need for any of us to overreact," she said
cautiously. "I am sorry you had to discover us, Aunt
Cleo, but surely if you are the only one who knows
about what happened tonight, it can all be hushed up?"

"I did not raise you to be a fool, Vicky. The very fact that I did discover you and Lucas here together means that someone else knows. How do you think I found out?"

Victoria closed her eyes briefly. "Yes, of course. How stupid of me. Forgive me, Aunt Cleo, but how did you find out?"

"A messenger was sent to my friends' house in the country, where I had just finished dinner," Cleo said coldly. "The note was unsigned and merely stated that I would be interested to know that my niece was here at this inn with a man whom I knew to be a friend. I came at once, naturally."

"Naturally." Victoria looked across the room at Lucas. *Marriage,* she repeated silently; marriage to the man she loved. It was not what she would have chosen at the outset, but it did not seem so bad now that she considered it.

Indeed there were certain definite advantages. They would no longer have to conceal their relationship from Society. They could go about freely together in each other's company. They could sleep together every night. No, marriage did not sound so very terrible anymore. "It would take some time to procure a special license," she said.

Lucas met her gaze. "I have one in my pocket. I have been carrying it around for several days."

Her eyes widened in astonishment. "You have? But why on earth would you have one with you?"

"For just such an emergency as this, of course. Why do you think? The risk of discovery has been with us from the moment we met and there were other risks as well. In the event the inevitable happened, I wanted to be prepared to limit the damage as much as possible." He smiled fleetingly. "I learned long ago that it is always wise to have a position to which one can fall back and regroup."

"The military mind at work." Victoria shook her head in unwilling admiration for his strategic planning. "Everyone seems to have considered the potential for disaster except me."

Cleo gave her an oddly pitying glance. "I must confess, Victoria, I am astonished to see that you have precipitated yourself into this sort of situation. It is true you have often flirted with the outrageous in many ways, but you have always been quite cautious in your dealings with men. How on earth could you have let yourself—" She broke off abruptly, glancing at Lucas. "Never mind. I think I know the answer to that. In any event there is no point looking back. We must go forward."

"We cannot move in any direction," Lucas pointed out quietly, "until Victoria has made her decision. She is not a child. She cannot be forced into marriage. I have already offered for her and I would be honored if she will give me her hand in marriage, but I will not coerce her into it."

"Well, Victoria?" Cleo regarded her solemnly. "Lucas is obviously willing to do what must be done. What about you?"

Victoria looked at Lucas, love and longing and guilt and uncertainty twisting themselves into a tight knot in the pit of her stomach. This was all her fault and she knew it. Lucas was in this situation only because he had tried to please her in spite of his better judgment.

It was not only her own honor and her aunt's position in Society she had jeopardized, but Lucas's honor and position as well.

"I am entirely to blame for all that has happened," Victoria said, looking down at her clenched hands. "If Lord Stonevale will do me the great honor of accepting my hand in marriage, then I will give it to him."

There was a taut silence following her words. When Victoria looked up again, she was aware that her aunt had relaxed somewhat, but she only had eyes for Lucas, who was watching her with unwavering intensity.

Without a word he left the hearth and came toward her. He pulled her gently to her feet. "You honor me. Thank you, Vicky. I give you my word I will try to make you happy."

She smiled slowly, a great deal of tension dissolving inside her at the touch of his hands. She loved him and he obviously cared deeply for her. "I have always considered marriage a fate worse than death, but I believe that with you I shall view it in an entirely different light, my lord."

Lucas grinned, his eyes lighting with satisfaction. He dropped a quick, possessive, little kiss on the tip of her nose and turned to face Cleo. "Very well, madam, the worst is over. The lady is resigned to her fate. Now we must move swiftly and carefully."

Cleo arched her brows. "Somehow I have already gained the impression that you will see to it we all do precisely that, Stonevale. I leave everything to you."

Several hours later Victoria conceded with amusement that her aunt's prediction had been absolutely correct. Matters had moved with blinding speed since she and Lucas had been married early that morning. Her aunt's household was in a frenzy as Victoria's bags were packed in preparation for the hurried departure for Stonevale. Lucas had decreed and Aunt Cleo had quickly agreed that leaving for the country was the best move at this point for all concerned.

"We shall tell everyone that because of your advanced years, neither of you wished for a formal wedding," Cleo had explained to Victoria as she outlined Lucas's plans. Lucas himself was nowhere around. Directly after the short ceremony he had excused himself to go home to his own town house to prepare for the departure.

Victoria had wrinkled her nose at the phrase "advanced years" but she could not quarrel with the reasoning. It was a slim excuse for such a hasty marriage, but it was all they had. There would be plenty of talk as it was.

"We shall also put it about that Lucas has received word that there are matters requiring his immediate attention at Stonevale. The two of you will leave town this afternoon and spend your honeymoon on his estates while he sees to his lands. With any luck, you will both be out of town by the time anyone thinks to start asking questions. When you return in a few weeks, it will all be a fait accompli, long past the interesting-gossip stage," Cleo explained.

Victoria had inclined her head in demure agreement. The more she grew accustomed to the idea of being married to Lucas Mallory Colebrook, the less burdening and more appealing it all became. As she watched her baggage fill the hall she began to think of the whole thing as a grand adventure, one that would prove even more exciting than her midnight escapades.

Rathbone's announcement an hour later of Lady Jessica Atherton's presence on the doorstep came as a shock.

"She rarely calls on us. She must have gotten word of the wedding. But how could she possibly know about it already?" Victoria demanded of her aunt in dismay.

Cleo exhaled in disgust. "You surely do not need to be told that gossip flows through London like the Thames. It was only a matter of time before Jessica Atherton found out along with everyone else. But I had rather hoped for a bit more time than this. Come, Victoria, it cannot be all that bad. After all, if she were going to cut us dead because of this, she would not be paying a social call, now, would she?" Cleo turned her head toward the drawing-room door.

Jessica Atherton glided swiftly into the room, a vision in pale lavendar, smiling her gracious, condescending smile. She went straight to Cleo and took both the other woman's hands in a gesture of deepest sympathy and understanding.

"Cleo, dear, I was so sorry to hear of this rather hasty business. I knew how you would be feeling, so I came as soon as I heard."

"Very kind of you, Jessica. Pray sit down." Cleo waved her to a nearby chair and slid a chiding glance at Victoria, who was rolling her eyes toward the ceiling. "Just how did you come to hear of Victoria's recent marriage?"

"Why, the news is all over Town, of course." Jessica smiled pityingly at Victoria. "You have always been so impetuous, Vicky. It would have been far wiser to do things in a more proper fashion, but there is no denying this is an excellent match for both you and Lucas and I want you to know you have my heartfelt congratulations."

Victoria forced a grudging smile of gratitude. The problem with dealing with Jessica was that one always had the impression one should be grateful. It was very wearing. "Thank you, Jessica."

Jessica settled deeper into the cushions of her chair. "You are quite welcome. Do try not to worry much about the gossip. There is bound to be some, of course, but it will fade with time. As you can see I have already taken steps to help squelch it by paying this call today. Few will disapprove openly when they learn that I have been here to call upon you and lend countenance to the match."

Cleo's brows rose. "You are quite right, Jessica. How very considerate of you to act so swiftly on Victoria's behalf."

"As you know, Lucas is an old friend of mine and I can do no less than make his bride feel welcome." Jessica reached out and patted one of Victoria's hands.

"My aunt is right," Victoria managed. "You are most thoughtful, Jessica."

Jessica's smile took on the aura of a benign saint's. "Do you know, Lady Nettleship, I have often heard about your impressive conservatory. I wonder if Victoria might take a moment to show it to me since I am here."

"But, of course. Show her the conservatory, Vicky," Cleo said quickly, obviously relieved to get out of the duty of playing hostess. "I am sure Jessica will enjoy the new roses from China."

Victoria got to her feet, trying to hide her reluctance. But as she led Jessica Atherton down the hall toward the conservatory, she chided herself for being churlish. Jessica was going out of her way to do a favor for Lucas and herself. The least she could do was act properly grateful to the woman.

"What a perfectly charming collection of plants," Jessica said as she was shown into the glass-walled room. "Quite delightful."

She started down one aisle, pausing to examine several small items along the way. Victoria followed, offering desultory comments on the various species of roses and irises that passed beneath Jessica's graciously approving gaze.

But as they made their way to the far end of the room, Victoria became aware that Jessica was paying less and less attention to the plants she was admiring. In fact, by the time they reached the end of the aisle, Jessica's expression had changed considerably.

Victoria stifled a groan of dismay as it dawned on her that Jessica had asked for the tour because she wanted to have a few words in private.

Jessica halted abruptly near a blood red parrot tulip. She seemed to gather herself. When she spoke, it was in a soft, urgent little voice. "You will be a good wife to him, will you not, Vicky?" Jessica did not meet Victoria's eyes, pretending to study the tulip instead. "He deserves a good wife."

Victoria's first response to the impertinent, highly personal question was anger. She quelled it. Jessica meant well and it was clear she cared about Lucas's happiness. "I assure you I shall do my best, Jessica."

"Yes, I am sure you will try. It is just that you are hardly his type, are you? I knew it from the beginning, but he kept insisting you would do."

"What type did you think he preferred, Jessica?"

Jessica's eyes squeezed shut for a moment. "A woman who will make him an admirable hostess and see to the management of his home in a proper fashion. A woman who will give him an heir and ensure that his children are raised to take their positions in Society. A well-behaved woman who knows her duty and fulfills it without complaint. A woman who will endeavor to make his life comfortable in every way. One who will not plague him with silly demands nor give him any trouble or cause for embarrassment. Lucas is a very proud man, you know."

Victoria made another bid for her patience. "I assure you again I will do my best. In any event, he seems quite satisfied with the bargain."

"Yes, he has made his decision. Lucas is a man who

knows his own mind and acts accordingly. He is aware
of the responsibilities his title has brought him. He told
me this marriage would suit him well and I pray he is
right."

"Lucas has already spoken to you of our marriage,
Jessica?" Victoria was suddenly paying complete attention to her maddening visitor.

"Naturally. Lucas felt he could confide in me right
from the start. We have, as I explained, known each
other for several years. We understand each other."
Jessica's fingers trailed gracefully along a long leaf. "Dear
Lucas. I know I hurt him dreadfully when I was forced
to refuse his offer of marriage four years ago. But when
he found himself in the same position a few months
ago, he finally understood why I had done what I did.
He felt he could come to me for help."

Victoria swallowed thickly. "I had not realized. . . ."

"Lucas comprehends the notion of duty better than
most men and he knows now that I only did what was
necessary when I accepted Lord Atherton's offer instead of his. Marriage is a matter of duty and practical-
ity, is it not? One does what one must."

Victoria grew cold. "I was not aware that you and
Lucas knew each other quite so well," she finally
managed.

"Very well, indeed." A glimmer of moisture appeared
at the edge of Jessica's dark lashes and splashed down
onto the rose petal where it glistened like a drop of
dew. "You cannot imagine how hard it was for me when
he sought me out after all this time to tell me he had
inherited his uncle's title and would be needing a suitable wife."

Victoria stared at Jessica's lovely profile and watched
another teardrop fall to the petals of the rose. "A suitable wife," she heard herself echo, sounding stupid,
even to her own ears.

"He asked me to introduce him into the sort of social
circles where he could meet the sort of woman he
needed."

"How did Lucas describe this woman he sought?"
Victoria asked, her mouth going dry.

"Well, his first requirement, of course, was that she be an heiress."

"An heiress." Victoria felt dazed.

"As I am certain you must realize by now, the business about his uncle having died with a fortune hidden under the bed is all rubbish. I put the story about myself so that people would not suspect the true state of Lucas's financial affairs."

Victoria stiffened. "Yes, of course. How very clever of you."

"I did my best," Jessica said with tragic pride. "I could not refuse to help him, not after all we had once meant to each other. But there have been times when I confess it was difficult watching him court you."

"I can imagine." Victoria wanted to pick up the nearest flowerpot and hurl it through one of the glass walls of the conservatory.

"When I got word this morning that you and Lucas had been married so precipitously, I told myself it was best this way. I know Lucas needs this marriage if he is to salvage his estates, and it would be easier on him, as well as me, to get the business done as quickly as possible."

"What about me, Jessica? Or did you consider me at all when you arranged to introduce me to Lucas?"

Jessica turned to her then, briefly considering her words. "You? What have you to complain of? You were in danger of spending the rest of your life on the shelf. Instead you are now a countess. You are married to Lucas. What more could you want?"

"To have been allowed to have spent the rest of my life on the shelf, perhaps?" Victoria's hands tightened into small fists at her sides. "Believe what you wish when you say you were only doing a favor for Lucas but do not lie to yourself about what you have done to me. I assure you, I am not at all grateful for your interference. *How could you have done such a cruel, heartless thing to me?*"

Without waiting for an answer, Victoria whirled on her heel and started down the aisle toward the door.

"Vicky, wait, please wait. You must not be angry. I

thought you understood. You are an intelligent woman. Indeed, you are known for your quick mind. I thought that at your age you would surely realize that your inheritance was your chief attraction. I mean, why else would a man want to offer for a woman who is inclined to such outrageous behavior, such an ungoverned female who has no—" Jessica broke off, looking haunted. "That is to say, I assumed you were as satisfied with the bargain as Lucas is. You have got yourself an earl, after all."

Victoria halted and spun around. "And Lucas has my money. You are quite right, Jessica. It is a bargain we have both made and now we must live with it. But you have done your part. You need not concern yourself further in our lives."

Jessica's eyes widened and more tears glistened and pearled on her lashes. "I am sorry if you are not content. But you are a woman and you must know it is not our lot to be content. Only a schoolgirl expects to marry for love. We all do what we must. If you cannot bring yourself to feel any real affection for Lucas, only think how hard this is on him. This is going to be just as difficult for him as it is for you. After all, he must have an heir from you."

"Thank you for reminding me of my wifely duty."

"Dear heaven, you truly are angry. You do not comprehend at all. I believed you did. Victoria, please, I am sorry. You cannot know how sorry." Jessica dissolved completely into tears, groping frantically for a handkerchief.

Victoria hesitated, torn between fury and a reluctant sympathy she did not want to feel. Jessica's tears were real.

Then, annoyed with herself but unable to ignore the sobbing woman, she went forward and hesitantly touched Jessica's arm.

"You must not do this to yourself, Jessica. You will make yourself ill. Pull yourself together. What is done is done. I do not hold you responsible. I made my own decisions at every point along the way. I have no one but myself to blame for what has happened."

Jessica gulped back her sobs and clutched helplessly at Victoria, who found herself patting her awkwardly.

"Please, I beg you, Vicky, do not hold any of this against Lucas. He only did what he had to do for the sake of his title."

Victoria tried to think of a response that would not further alarm the weeping woman. But there was nothing to be said. The truth was she wanted to do a great deal of damage to the Earl of Stonevale. Even as the images formed in her head, she heard his voice in the hall.

"Vicky? Whr way. Your aunt says you have not yet changed into your traveling dress." His boots rang on the tile of the conservatory as he stepped into the room, looking for her. He glanced briefly around, frowning impatiently, and then his eyes collided with hers over Jessica's heaving shoulders.

Victoria watched dispassionately as Lucas registered just who it was who was crying her heart out in his wife's arms.

"Lady Atherton has come to give us her good wishes, my lord. Was that not kind of her under the circumstances? I understand that you and she are extremely close friends of very long standing and that she has been of great assistance in securing an heiress for you. It appears the rumors of your uncle's hoarded wealth were quite unfounded. Now, if you will excuse me, I believe I shall leave the two of you alone together to make your good-byes. I certainly would not wish to intrude."

Realization dawned in Lucas's gaze. He did not move. "Damn it to hell, Vicky," he said very softly.

She smiled grimly. "My sentiments precisely."

She freed herself from Jessica's grasp and stepped around her, heading toward the door. When she reached the point in the aisle where Lucas blocked her path, she looked up at him and said nothing.

"We will talk later," he promised through his teeth.

"There does not appear to be a great deal left to say. If you will excuse me, my lord?"

He moved reluctantly out of her way, his eyes gleaming with frustrated anger. "Do not be long in dressing for the trip, Vicky. I want to get started as soon as possible. We have a long drive ahead of us."

She did not bother to respond to that. It took all her concentration simply to get through the door without hurling some of the cacti at his head.

Victoria was trembling with fury and raw pain by the time she reached her bedchamber. She walked into the room to discover an excited Nan fussing with several last-minute items.

"Oh, there you are, ma'am. I've almost finished. Albert says the last of the bags is going into the coach now and the horses are ready. You must hurry and change. I hear his lordship just arrived and is impatient to be on his way."

"There is no rush, Nan. I will not be going anywhere today. Please be so good as to leave me in peace until I send for you."

Nan's mouth fell open in shock. "What are you saying, ma'am? His lordship has already given strict instructions that we are not to delay. He will be furious if he hears we're dawdling up here."

"Please go, Nan."

Nan bit her lip. She had rarely seen her mistress in this mood and it was obvious she was not at all certain what to do. She opted to retreat for the moment. "Would a dish o' tea help, ma'am? If yer not feelin' well, I'm sure his lordship would understand a short wait for tea."

"I do not want tea, only some peace."

"Dear me, there will be the devil to pay for this bit o' nonsense," Nan mumbled as she went to the door. "Men don't take kindly to delays when they're waitin' to set off on a trip, especially not them that's used to givin' orders to fightin' men in the field. Accustomed to havin' people jump when they say jump, that type is."

Victoria watched the door close behind her muttering maid and then she went slowly over to the window. Jessica Atherton's elegant carriage was waiting on the street below. As Victoria watched she saw Lucas escort his former love down the steps and put her into the vehicle. He ordered the coachman to be off, turned, and stalked grimly back up the steps into the house.

A moment later she was not surprised to hear hurried footsteps in the hall outside her room and the inevitable knock on her door.

"His lordship wishes to talk to you, my lady." Nan's voice was muffled by the closed door. "He says 'tis terribly urgent."

Victoria crossed the room and opened the door. "Tell his lordship I am indisposed."

"Oh, please, ma'am, don't make me tell him that. He is not in a good temper just now, truly he isn't."

"To hell with his temper." Victoria closed the door in Nan's shocked face. Then she went back to her post by the window to idly watch the last of her luggage loaded into the traveling coach Cleo had insisted on loaning the newly married couple.

The next knock on the door was, predictably enough, Aunt Cleo's. "Vicky, dear, open up at once. What is this nonsense? Your husband wishes to be off without delay. Ex—military men are not very good about unnecessary delays."

Victoria sighed and crossed the room again to open the door. "Tell my husband that he is free to leave anytime he chooses. Tell him not to wait upon me as I shall not be coming with him."

Cleo eyed her severely. "So that's the way of it, is it?" She walked into the room and closed the door. "I thought there was something distinctly odd about Lady Atherton's visit this morning. What in the world did she say to upset you so?"

"Did you know that Lucas once asked her to marry him?"

"No, but I hardly see that it matters. Lucas is thirty-four years old. Stands to reason you aren't the first woman he's asked to marry him. Is that what has upset you? Come now, Vicky, you are far too intelligent to fly up into the boughs over a minor fiddle like that. Whatever happened between those two occurred years ago," Cleo said.

"She was unable to accept his offer of marriage because he did not have either a title or sufficient financial resources to suit her or her family."

"Well, that is her problem, is it not? Lucas has his title now. I fail to see how all this affects you, Vicky."

"Lucas inherited the title," Victoria said coolly. "But there was apparently very little money to go with it. Jessica explained that his lordship came to the conclusion he would be obliged to marry an heiress for the sake of his damned title and he asked his dear friend Lady Atherton to arrange an introduction to a suitable female. Would you care to hazard a guess as to just which female of your acquaintance was thus honored?"

Cleo's brows climbed in their characteristic gesture. "I'd sooner hazard a guess as to just which female of my acquaintance obligingly made herself a bed and now complains because she must sleep in it. If she has half the common sense I trust she has, she will attend to the business of making that bed a comfortable one for both herself and her husband."

Victoria blinked at the unexpected lack of support. She crossed her arms under her breasts and stared at her aunt. "You do not seem unduly shocked by all this."

"Forgive me. I have already had to deal with the shock of finding you in that inn last night. One shock at a time is sufficient at my age."

Victoria felt herself turning an angry red. She looked away. "Yes, of course. I am sorry for that. Far more sorry now than I was when you first discovered us, I assure you."

Cleo's face softened. "Vicky dear, I fear you are letting yourself be unnecessarily upset. I am not surprised to hear that Lucas is not as well off as you had assumed. He told me the truth this morning while we waited for you to dress at the inn."

"He told you he was marrying me for my money?"

"He told me he had asked to be introduced to you because he was, to be blunt, hanging out for an heiress. But he said that he was marrying you because he had become quite fond of you and decided you would make him a very suitable wife in every respect."

"*Fond* of me. How very gracious of him," Victoria said.

"Victoria, I shall be quite blunt with you. I knew from the first that you were probably bound to get into trouble with Stonevale. There is something between the two of you that fairly crackles in the air when you are in the same room together. But I rather liked him and I decided that if you were to risk everything for a man, it might as well be with him."

"I am so glad you approve, Aunt Cleo."

"There is no need to take that tone with me. You are the one who brought yourself to this pass."

Victoria looked down at the pattern of the carpet and then raised her eyes to meet her aunt's sympathetic, but unyielding gaze. "You are right, as usual. Now I must decide how to proceed."

Aunt Cleo softened her tone. "The first thing you must do is change into your traveling clothes. Lucas is determined to be on his way this afternoon and I must say I think he is absolutely correct. The sooner you are out of town, the better."

"I have no intention of going anywhere with Stonevale."

"Vicky, you are being unreasonable. You have no choice but to go with him."

Before Cleo could say more, there was a desperate pounding on the door. Nan's voice came clearly through the wood. "Forgive me, ma'am, but his lordship says to tell you that if yer not so obligin' as to come downstairs immediately, he'll be obliged to come up here and fetch you down."

Lucas would do it, too. Victoria did not fool herself on that score. There was no point in delaying the inevitable interview. She stepped past her aunt and then, her hand on the doorknob, she turned and looked at Cleo. "I have certainly got myself a most charming and gallant husband, have I not? What bride could ask for more?"

10

He was waiting for her in the library, standing near the window that looked out onto the garden where he had so often waited for her at midnight. Victoria walked into the room and heard the door close very softly behind her. A respectful hush seemed to have fallen over the household, as if everyone was holding his or her breath.

The entire staff, including her maid and Rathbone, was moving with great caution, she noticed. Lucas had only been her husband for a few hours and he was technically a guest under her aunt's roof, but he had clearly established himself as a figure of authority. No one wanted to risk his temper. That was left for Victoria to brave.

"You sent for me, my lord?" she asked, taking refuge in an icy, correct politeness.

He watched her come part way into the room and halt. His expression was starkly controlled. "You have not changed into your traveling dress."

It took more courage than she had expected to face him and tell him her decision. "For the very good reason that I will not be joining you. I wish you a good journey, my lord." She swung around on her heel and started for the door.

"If you walk out on me now, Vicky, you will regret it more than you can possibly imagine."

The deadly soft tone stopped her as nothing else would have. She turned back to face him. "I beg your pardon. Did you have something else you wished to say to me?"

"A great deal. But the time grows late and I would rather have this conversation in the coach than here in your aunt's library. For now, however, I will only say that I apologize for Lady Atherton's emotional outburst. I assure you, I had no idea she would fall apart in such an unfortunate manner."

"Yes, her timing was rather poor, was it not? When had you planned to tell me the truth, yourself?"

"What truth would you have me tell you? That I once asked Jessica to marry me? That is old news, Vicky, and need not concern us."

"Damn you," she hissed. "You know very well which truth interests me now. You deliberately set out to form a connection with me because I am an heiress. Do you have the gall to deny it?"

Lucas held her cold glare. "No. You guessed as much at the time, if you will recall. I seem to have a very clear memory of your warning me off. But you wanted what I offered, regardless, didn't you? You played a risky game and you lost, but it was your choice to play. Did you not once inform me that there was no real risk without real danger?"

"Must you throw my stupidity in my face like this?"

"Why not? It is little more than you expect from me, is it not? I am nothing but a heartless fortune hunter who has snagged himself an heiress."

She felt as if she had been punched in the stomach. "And now you expect me to accept my humiliation without protest?"

He crossed the room in a few short strides and gripped her upper arms. His eyes were blazing. "I expect you to show some trust in me, damn you. For the past few weeks you've been willing enough to trust me with your safety and your honor. Now that you are my wife, I expect no less."

"Trust you? After what you have done to me?"

"What have I done that is so wicked? I did not set us up to be discovered last night. I told you the entire plan was dangerous, but you had to have your night of *intellectual inquiry* at all costs, remember?"

"Don't you dare mock me, Lucas."

"I am not mocking you. I am reminding you of how you tried to justify your desire to let me make love to you. You wanted what happened last night as much as I did. Hell, you even told me you loved me."

Victoria shook her head, her eyes moist. "I told you I *thought* I loved you. I was obviously mistaken."

"You gave me the painting of *Strelitzia reginae* and then you gave yourself to me without any reservations. I believed you did love me, madam. When your aunt knocked on the door, my first instinct was to protect you. What would you have had me do? Refuse to offer marriage?"

"Pray do not twist my words. You saw the opening you had been waiting for and you took it. Do not bother to deny it."

"I will not deny that I wanted to marry you. I would not have risked your honor or my own last night if I had not been certain that sooner or later we would be married. It was unfortunate that your aunt discovered us and precipitated this chain of events, but the end result was inevitable."

"There was nothing inevitable about it," she stormed.

"Vicky, be reasonable. You must see that we could not have carried on as we had been for much longer. Things were getting shaky enough even before we went off together last night. People were starting to talk and you were doing nothing to stem the gossip. We were taking dangerous risks to indulge your midnight whims. Sooner or later we would have been discovered, and once that happened neither of us would have had a choice. There was also the possibility you'd get pregnant, did you think of that?"

"Why could you not have told the whole truth before

any of it started?" She could hear her voice climbing toward the hysterical shriek of an enraged fishwife. Frantically she fought to control herself.

"To be perfectly blunt, I told you nothing because I was out to win you and I was afraid that if I went into a great deal of detail about my personal financial circumstances, you wouldn't give me a chance. You were so adamant about not getting married, so skittish on the subject of fortune hunters, that I had no choice but to woo you in the only way you allowed. You will never know how hard the past few weeks have been on me, Vicky. The least you could do is show some consideration and kindness."

She was incredulous. "Kindness? How dare you attempt to make me feel sorry for you now?"

"Why not? You are quite prepared to be kind to everyone else, up to and including Lady Atherton. I saw the way you were trying to offer her some comfort as she wept all over your shoulder in the conservatory." Lucas released her abruptly and ran his fingers through his hair. "Why shouldn't I try to gain a little kindness for myself? After all, I am your husband and God knows that role is not going to be an easy one."

"What have you got to offer in return?"

He took a deep breath. "I will do my damnedest to be a good husband to you. You have my word on it."

"And just how do you interpret the notion of being a good husband to me?" She rubbed her hands over her forearms where his fingers had gripped her tightly enough to leave red marks. "Obviously you will not have to provide financial support. I am the one supplying the capital in this marriage, according to your former love. You do bring me a title. I'll grant you that much, but I have never been overly concerned with titles."

Lucas's mouth tightened. "I also brought you the adventure you had been seeking."

"You mean you tricked me with adventure."

"Vicky, listen to me. . . ."

"There is one thing I must know, Lucas. Do you intend to begin a romantic liaison with Lady Atherton now that you have taken care of the business of getting married?"

"God, no. 'Tis plain you don't think much of my integrity at the moment, but if you knew Jessica as well as you think you do, you would realize the whole idea of a romantic liaison with her is out of the question."

Victoria winced. "Forgive me. Of course it is. Lady Atherton is a paragon of all that is proper. She would not dream of getting involved in an illicit affair with you."

"Quite right."

"She is such a noble creature. She had no qualms at all, apparently, about following the dictates of duty rather than her heart four years ago when she accepted Lord Atherton's offer instead of yours."

"She did what she was obligated to do," Lucas said impatiently.

"How dreadfully understanding you are about the entire matter," Vicky said.

"Four years is a long time," Lucas said with a shrug. "And to tell you the truth, I am greatly relieved now not to be married to Jessica. Lately I have come to realize it would have been a bad match."

Victoria gave him a sidelong glance. "Why do you say that? She seems so very perfect for you. She is obviously the sort who would be a dutiful wife, being, as we have just noted, a paragon of female behavior."

"Sheathe your claws, Vicky." Lucas's mouth quirked faintly. "The fact is, I find her rather dull. I have discovered recently that I prefer a more adventurous sort of female. And after last night, I would have to say that I also prefer a more passionate sort."

"Really?" Victoria's chin rose. "You speak from experience, I presume? You have had an opportunity to compare my performance in bed with that of Lady Atherton's?"

Lucas's smile broadened into a wicked grin. "Don't be a goose, Vicky. Even in your wildest flights of imagination, can you possibly envisage Jessica sneaking off to an inn with me or any other man? I assure you, she was just as prim and proper four years ago as she is today.

She would never have risked her reputation for a man or a night of the sort of intellectual inquiry we shared at that inn."

Victoria sighed. "Unlike me."

"Yes. Unlike you. Completely unlike you. In fact, I have never met a woman who is anything like you. You are quite unique, Vicky. Which is why I am not always certain just how to handle you, I suppose. But I assure you, I fully intend to do my best. Now, we have wasted far too much time on this pointless discussion. Go upstairs and change at once." He glanced at the clock. "You have fifteen minutes."

"For the last time, my lord, I am not going anywhere with you."

She jumped slightly when he moved without any warning, covering the short distance between them with his distinctive, oddly balanced stride. He caught her chin on the edge of his hand and forced her to look up at him. When she did, she froze. The full, unleashed force of his will glittered in his eyes.

Victoria suddenly understood why men had followed Lucas into battle and why everyone else in the household was walking about with such extreme care.

"Victoria," he said, "it occurs to me that you do not fully comprehend just how serious I am about leaving in fifteen minutes. That is no doubt my fault. Until now I have been so indulgent of your headstrong ways, so willing to ignore my own better judgment in an effort to please you, that you are obviously under the impression you can disregard a direct order from me. I assure you, that is not the case."

"I do not take orders from you or any other man."

"You do now, Vicky. For better or worse, you have a husband and he means to leave London in"—he paused to glance at the tall clock—"thirteen minutes. If you are not dressed for traveling when he is ready to go, he will personally put you into the coach in whatever garment you happen to have on at the time. Is that very clear, madam?"

Victoria sucked in her breath, realizing he would do exactly as he said. "You appear to hold the whip hand, my lord," she drawled in a scathing tone. "And like most men, you do not hesitate to use it."

"I assure you, I would never use a whip on you, Vicky, and you know it. Now stop trying my patience. You have less than twelve minutes left."

Victoria turned and fled.

The journey into the distant wilds of Yorkshire was the longest Victoria had ever endured in her life. She saw very little of her husband along the way. Lucas spent most of his time outside the coach, choosing to ride his stallion, George, alongside the vehicle, rather than deal with Victoria's temper. At night she and Nan shared a room at the inns where they stopped and Lucas took a separate room for himself and his valet. Meals were a series of chillingly polite affairs.

By the time they reached Stonevale, Victoria's mood had not improved one bit and she suspected Lucas's hadn't either, although he seemed content to ignore her as long as she gave him no trouble.

Her first view of the lands surrounding her new home was not inspiring. It did not take even her extensive background in horticulture and botany to detect that this summer's crops would be mediocre at best. There was a generally depressed atmosphere about everything she saw, from the farmers' run-down cottages to the gaunt animals standing listlessly in the fields.

The lack of goods in the village shop windows emphasized the economic gloom that hung over the area like a dark cloud. Victoria frowned at the sight of several children playing in the dirt. Their clothing was as bad as any street urchin's in London.

"This is inexcusable," she muttered to Nan. "These lands have been allowed to wither and die."

"I reckon his lordship has a sizable job ahead o' him," Nan offered cautiously. She was well aware of her mistress's feelings about the earl. "He'll earn his fancy title, he will, if he manages to put some life back into this place."

"Yes, he certainly will," Victoria agreed grimly. And he'll need my money to do it, she added silently. For the first time she began to realize the magnitude of the responsibility Lucas had faced when he had inherited Stonevale. Everyone living in and around the estate depended on the general prosperity and leadership of the great house that dominated the economy. Victoria was well aware that the fortunes and futures of the local tenants and villagers were closely tied to Stonevale.

If she had been handed the task of salvaging these lands, would she have been above marrying for money? She wondered. Probably not. As Lady Atherton had said, damn her, one did what one must.

That acknowledgment did not make Victoria feel any more charitable toward Lucas, however. She might be able to understand his need to marry an heiress; she would never forgive him for choosing her and tricking her into this marriage. Surely he could have found a willing sacrifice if he had been willing to search for one among the ladies of the ton. There were those who would have traded a fortune for a landed title.

"It's a lovely house, ain't it, ma'am?" Nan said, leaning eagerly out of the coach window to catch the first glimpse of the great house of Stonevale. "Pity the grounds and garden are so shabby. Not like Lady Nettleship's country place at all."

Victoria found herself leaning forward for a look, although she had vowed she would adopt an air of disdainful aloofness about everything concerning Lucas's home.

Her maid was right. Stonevale was a magnificent house. The stone facade was imposing and well proportioned. The wide front steps descended to a cobbled courtyard and a huge curving drive. A large fountain and pool decorated the middle of the curve. But the pool was full of rubble instead of water. The fountain was silent.

There was the same air of depression and hopelessness about the house as there was about the village and surrounding fields. Victoria stared at her new home with a sense of dismay as the coach halted. It was all a far cry from the luxurious, comfortable, well-gardened world she had known with her aunt.

Lucas turned his mount over to a groom and came forward to escort Victoria up the steps and into the house.

"As you can see," he said quietly, "there is much to be done."

"That is certainly an accurate observation, my lord." She was feeling somewhat dazed.

"I would like us to share the task together, Vicky. We both have a stake in Stonevale. It is your home now as well as mine. It will be our children's home."

She flinched at that, recalling more of Jessica Atherton's words. *If you cannot bring yourself to have any real affection for Lucas, only think how hard this is on him. He must have an heir from you.*

Victoria composed her features immediately, but she knew Lucas had seen her brief expression of anger because his own face hardened. "I will introduce you to the staff, although as yet there is not much of it. The butler's name is Griggs. He's from my London staff. The housekeeper is Mrs. Sneath. She's from the village."

Exhausted from the long trip, depressed by what she had seen of Stonevale, and too proud to give an inch in response to Lucas's small overtures, Victoria picked up her skirts and climbed the stairs to her new bedchamber.

Dinner that night was not an impressive affair. Griggs apologized for the poor quality of the wine and the lack of footmen to serve. The food was limited, both in quality and selection. The surroundings were even less prepossessing than the food. The carpet was threadbare, the furniture scarred and unpolished, the silver tarnished. The chandelier overhead had obviously not been cleaned in years.

But it was the grim silence at the table that really got to Victoria. She was not a creature of long silences and she had almost reached the end of her ability to maintain one. It annoyed her now that Lucas seemed oblivious to her efforts.

"Well, my lord," she began after fortifying herself with a large sip of wine. "Where do you propose to begin spending my money? On the gardens, perhaps?

Or the tenants' farms? Or maybe you would like to refurnish the house itself? It certainly needs it."

Lucas swirled the wine in his glass and regarded her for a moment. "Where would you like to start, Vicky?"

"Why would my feelings on the subject matter to you? Salvaging Stonevale is your project, not mine." She smiled a cold, brittle smile. "And now that you have my money, I am certain you will think of lots of ways to spend it. My stepfather certainly had no problem spending my mother's money on his horses and his women."

"It occurs to me, madam, that you are in this fix in the first place because you lacked a suitable challenge in your life."

She glared at him. "What is that supposed to mean?"

"You are a woman of intelligence and energy who happened to have access to a great deal of money. You used that money to buy your independence and finance your social life, but you did not use it to do anything else particularly useful."

That stung. "I have always given large sums to charities."

"Which demanded very little of your time or skills. Furthermore, you had neither a husband nor a family to absorb your considerable energies. Other than your interest in botanical painting and the occasional scientific lecture, you did not devise anything else of a serious nature to occupy your time and ability. Your only outlet for action was your social life. So you got bored and started looking for adventure. And that, my dear, is what got you into trouble."

Victoria was incensed. "I was not bored with town life, sir, I assure you."

"No? I rather think it was boredom that led you to dream up your midnight escapades."

She paled. "That is not true. You know nothing of why I sought my midnight adventures and I would appreciate it if you refrained from making silly conjectures."

He shook his head thoughtfully. "No, I believe I am correct in my logic. You were initially attracted to me solely because I was willing to give you the adventure you wanted. If you dislike the notion of being married for your money, how do you think I felt knowing that my primary appeal for you was that I could offer you some fleeting excitement? You were perfectly willing to use me for your own ends, were you not?"

"That is not true," she retorted before stopping to think.

"No? Are you admitting your feelings for me went deeper than a frivolous desire to use me to provide you with the adventure you wanted?"

Victoria scowled at him. "Yes, I mean no. Damn it, Lucas, you are twisting my words."

"Either way, you are here now, madam, and there is no going back. You were aware of the risks and you chose to run them. The first rule of gaming, my sweet, is learning how to pay up without whimpering when you lose. If you play, you pay," Lucas said.

"I am not whimpering. I am furious. There is a vast difference."

Lucas leaned back and folded his arms. "You are sulking, Vicky. It is nothing more than that. Having never dealt with you in this mood, I will admit I'm curious to see how long it will last. I had hoped you would be through the worst of it by the time we got here, but it appears I was wrong."

"Yes, it certainly does appear that you were wrong." She was vibrating with the force of her anger. The injustice of his accusations was intolerable. "Completely wrong."

"You should be grateful to me, Vicky. I am offering you a way to avoid future disasters of the sort that led you into this situation. I am pleased to be able to give you a project that will in turn give you something important to do both with your time and your money." Lucas looked at her. "Help me restore Stonevale and its lands."

"How kind of you to refer to it as *my* money."

"Vicky, I want you to be a part of this place. I want you to share it with me. I admit that I can do nothing without access to your inheritance, but I do not intend to spend your money without consulting you. I am more than happy to involve you in every detail. You have a good mind and a vast store of knowledge, thanks to the way you have been raised. You can be a tremendous influence on what happens here at Stonevale. All I ask is that you work with me instead of amusing yourself with a fit of the sulks."

"What you offer is certainly very exciting to say the least," she said in silky tones. "If you are so eager to include me in every little decision, then perhaps you would like to consider giving me a written wedding contract? One in which you guarantee not to touch a penny of my money without my consent?"

His mouth curved ruefully. "I am not a complete fool, madam. It would be the height of idiocy for me to have such a contract drawn up while you are in your present mood. Perhaps we can discuss the matter again when you have decided you are ready to be a true and loving wife to me."

"Hah. You would never give me such a contract and we both know it."

"Even if I did, it would carry little real weight under the law, Vicky. We are husband and wife. That relationship will always give me certain rights."

"It is the principle of the thing."

Lucas smiled briefly. "The hell it is. If I were to give you such a contract right now, you would use it to get even with me for this marriage. Admit it, Vicky. You are not accustomed to being outmaneuvered and all you can think of at the moment is revenge."

"At least the notion of revenge has the undeniable advantage of providing me with something useful to occupy my time and energy, does it not?" She smiled coldly and rose to her feet. "Now, if you will excuse me, my lord, I fear I am not yet done feeling sorry for myself. I believe I shall retire to my bedchamber and sulk for a while."

Griggs scrambled to open the door for her as she swept out of the dining room.

Lucas watched his wife's magnificent exit through hooded eyes and then signaled the butler for the port he had brought with him from London. His leg ached from the long days of riding it had recently endured.

For a considerable length of time Lucas sipped the port and contemplated which he would rather do: strangle Jessica Atherton or turn Victoria over his knee.

On the whole, turning his wife over his knee sounded far and away the more interesting option. He would give a lot right now for another glimpse of her enticingly curved backside.

Lucas slowly and deliberately worked his way through the bottle of port in splendid solitude. The wine was useful for something besides dulling the ache in his thigh. It also took some of the edge off his frustrated desire. Since that hot, sweet night of illicit passion at the inn, he had been plagued with memories that pushed his normally ironclad self-control to the limits.

He could not believe that Victoria was not haunted by the same memories. She had been so responsive, so magnificent in her passion, so welcoming and trusting. Damn it, he thought, she had even told him she thought she was in love with him, and he was quite certain she had never said as much to any other man.

And he knew for a fact that she had never given herself to anyone else. The joy of watching her sensual discovery had been the most erotic experience he had ever known.

The painting of *Strelitzia reginae* was already hanging on the wall upstairs near his dressing table, where he would be able to see it every morning. Lucas had directed that it be among the first of his personal items that were unpacked. He wondered if Victoria had any idea how much the small gift had meant to him.

Probably not. She was not thinking of anything else at the moment except her savaged pride.

He had been startled to find himself so deeply touched by *Strelitzia*. Perhaps it was because it was the first gift any woman had ever given him since his mother had died. He refused to count the keepsake locket with a wisp of dark hair in it that Jessica Atherton had given him four years ago.

She had pressed it into his palm even as she had

tearfully rejected his offer of marriage and explained where her duty lay. He had tossed the locket into a ditch one night on the eve of a battle.

Lucas finished the last of the port and contemplated the empty bottle. Then he contemplated the notion of the empty bed that awaited him.

If matters had not exploded in his face the way they had, he would be back in his London town house preparing to climb a certain garden wall tonight. His reckless, passionate midnight companion would be waiting eagerly for the night's adventure.

But things had changed. He was married to the little baggage now and somehow he had to find a way to deal with her. He refused to spend the rest of his days with a sulking wife and he was even more certain he was not going to spend his nights alone in his own bedchamber.

It was so damn easy for Victoria to be kind to everyone else, Lucas thought in annoyance as he got to his feet. Why could she not spare a little kindness for her husband? Surely she must realize he had not had a lot of choice in his actions lately.

A man in his position had no option but to secure an heiress in any manner he could. Victoria was old enough to understand the realities of marriage. In any event, the deed was done and there was nothing for it but for Victoria to accept the situation with good grace. This sulking business would have to stop. He would not tolerate her ill humor much longer.

Nor would he tolerate a lonely bed for long. He was a married man now and that gave him certain rights and privileges.

With a hardening sense of determination, Lucas stalked out of the dining room and up the staircase. He would make one more effort to talk to Victoria tonight, and if she still refused to listen to him, he swore he would find another way to take the edge off her temper.

His valet, Ormsby, was busy in the master bedchamber, still unpacking. He glanced up with surprise as Lucas entered the room.

"Good evening, sir. Did you wish to retire early tonight?"

"Yes, as a matter of fact, I do. Tell Griggs to send the staff to bed, too. It has been a long trip for everyone."

Ormsby nodded. "Will you be needing anything for your leg, sir? It generally bothers you after long hours in the saddle."

"I have just finished a bottle of port. That should take care of it."

"Very good, sir." Ormsby moved about with soothing efficiency. "Nan told me that Lady Stonevale has also retired for the evening. If this is any indication, it appears we shall all be keeping rather different hours here in the country than we did in Town."

"Just as well. I much prefer country life to the demands of the city." Lucas absently rubbed his bad leg. He was not going to miss climbing that damned garden wall one bit. Nor was he going to miss the nerve-racking business of constantly worrying about protecting his companion's identity and safety while she flitted blithely through the gaming hells, brothels, and back streets of London.

Ormsby took his leave a few minutes later. Lucas waited until the sound of his footsteps had receded before he picked up a candle and went to the connecting door. There was no sound from Victoria's room. She was probably already in bed; perhaps asleep.

He quietly opened the door, telling himself he had every right to walk into his wife's bedchamber. The knob twisted easily in his hand. He wondered if Victoria had tried to lock it against him. He had taken possession of the key earlier just in case.

Her bedroom was shrouded in darkness except for the pale light coming in through the window. Victoria apparently liked to sleep with the drapes open, he noted. A rather unusual quirk.

With the aid of the candle and the moonlight, Lucas could make out the slender shape of his wife as she lay huddled under the covers. His belly tightened.

Unfortunately the candlelight also revealed a little too much of the faded drapes, dirty carpet, and worn furnishings that decorated the bedchamber. Lucas felt a sharp twinge that could have been embarrassment. The new home he had provided for Victoria was definitely not up to her usual standards.

He walked over to the bed, wondering how to announce himself and tell her he had come to claim his right as a husband.

On the way up the stairs he had composed a rather lengthy speech about wifely duties and husbandly rights, but now it all sounded unconvincing. What was he going to do if she simply did not want him anymore, he wondered bleakly?

But even as the cold thought formed in his head the candlelight fell on the warm pool of golden amber that nestled between her breasts.

She was still wearing the pendant.

Relief flooded through Lucas. All was not lost after all, he thought jubilantly.

Even as that realization flared like fire through his veins, Victoria stirred restlessly on the pillow. Her lashes fluttered briefly, and then, without any warning, she opened her eyes, looked straight up at him, and screamed.

"Dear God, no, *no*. Stay away from me."

Lucas stared in shock as Victoria sat bolt upright in bed. She held out a hand as if trying to ward him off. He had been wrong. She could not bear the thought of him coming to her bed. His insides clenched in a sickening fashion.

"Vicky, for God's sake . . ."

"The knife. Merciful heavens the *knife*." She was staring at the candle in horror. "No, please, *no*."

Lucas finally understood that she was still half-asleep. He had evidently awakened her in the middle of a nightmare and she was trapped in the remnants of the dream.

He moved quickly, putting the candle down on the nearest table and grasping Victoria by the shoulders. She opened her mouth to scream again, her eyes focused on something only she could see.

Lucas shook her. "Victoria, stop it."

When there was no sign of any response in her eyes, he did what he had occasionally had to do when con-

fronted by a soldier who had slipped over the edge of
sanity into battle-front hysteria. He drew back one hand,
and with cool calculation, he slapped Victoria quite
hard.

That stopped her. She gasped, blinked in confusion,
and finally focused on his face.

"Lucas," she breathed. "Dear heaven, 'tis you." She
gave a small cry of overwhelming relief and threw herself into his arms. She clutched him as if he were an
angel sent to rescue her from the pits of hell.

There were hurried footsteps in the hall and then
anxious knocking on Victoria's door. "Ma'am? My lady?
'Tis me, Nan. Be everythin' all right?"

Lucas reluctantly disengaged himself from Victoria's
clinging grasp. She whimpered softly in protest and he
soothed her with a touch.

"Hush, darling. I have to go reassure your maid. I
will be right back."

He went to the door and opened it to find Nan
hovering nervously in the hall.

"I was on the stairs, startin' for my bed, when I heard
her ladyship scream." Nan looked up at him, her eyes
faintly suspicious in the glow of the candle she held. "Is
all well?"

"She is fine, Nan. It was my fault. I awakened her in
the middle of a bad dream."

"Oh, I wondered if that might be it." Nan's eyes lost
their trace of accusation. "Poor thing. She's been havin'
some trouble with bad dreams for the past few months.
I think it is one o' the reasons she's taken such a likin'
for the parties and nightlife o' London this Season.
Keeps her busy till dawn. But looks like she'll be sufferin'
with those plaguey dreams again now that we're all
keepin' country hours. Mayhap I should sleep a little
closer to her."

"You needn't worry about her, Nan. She's got a husband now, remember? I will take good care of her. I am
much closer than you are."

Nan flushed and nodded quickly. "Yes, sir. Well, I'll
be off, then." She bobbed a quick curtsy and hurried
back down the hall.

Lucas closed the door and turned back to the bed. Victoria was watching him from the shadows, her arms wrapped around her updrawn knees. Her eyes were huge in the dim light.

"My apologies, Vicky. I did not mean to startle you awake so abruptly," Lucas said.

"What were you doing sneaking about in my room in the first place?" she asked tartly.

He sighed, aware that the few moments of vulnerability had already passed. "I know this will come as something of a shock, Vicky, but you have a husband now and husbands have a right to sneak around their wives' bedchambers." He crossed the room and sat down on the side of the bed, ignoring her hostile gaze. "Your maid says you suffer from bad dreams frequently of late. Is there a particular reason, do you think?"

"No."

"I only ask because I, too, have had the occasional unpleasant dream," he said softly.

"I imagine everyone does from time to time."

"Yes, but my dream is a very specific one and it is always the same. Is yours?"

She hesitated. "Yes." Then, probably in an effort to change the focus of the conversation, she asked quickly, "What do you dream of, my lord?"

"Of being trapped beneath a dead horse in the middle of a field of dead and dying men." Lucas drew a deep breath and looked at the flickering candle. "Some of those men took a very long time to die. Every time I have the dream I have to listen to them in their agony. And I have to live through the torment of wondering whether or not I shall also die, wondering whether one of the human vermin who come out to loot the dead after a battle will simply slit my throat for me and end the matter once and for all."

Her small, anguished gasp and the fleeting touch of her fingers on the sleeve of his dressing gown brought his eyes back to her face.

"How terrible," Victoria whispered. "Dear God, Lucas, how ghastly. Your dream is even worse than mine."

"Of what do you dream, Vicky?"

Her fingers clenched around the sheet and she looked down. "In my dream I am always standing at the top of a staircase. A . . . a man is coming toward me. He holds a candle in one hand and a dagger in the other."

Lucas waited, sensing there was more. Something about the way she had hesitated over the phrase "a man" gave him the impression her nightmare figure had a face she recognized. But it was obvious she did not intend to add to the description of the dream and he was unwilling to jeopardize their new intimacy by prodding her for details.

In fact, Lucas decided, he had already gotten closer to her tonight than he had at any time since the fateful night he had made love to her. If he was wise, he would not push too far, too fast.

Strategy, he reminded himself. In the long run, a man always got farther with strategy than he did with force.

He suppressed a groan and got to his feet. "Are you all right now?"

She nodded quickly, not quite meeting his eyes. "Yes, thank you. I shall be fine."

"Then I will say good night. Call me if you need me, Vicky."

Forcing himself to walk back to his own chamber was one of the hardest things Lucas had done of late.

11

The following afternoon Victoria sought relief from
the tension of the ever-so-civilized, now-silent battle
raging between herself and Lucas by fleeing into the
nearby woods with her sketchbook.

She walked for some time before coming to a halt.
Eventually she chose a comfortable spot on a hill beneath some trees where she could sit gazing out over
the uninspiring view of the depressed farming commu-
nity. From here she could see the cottages that needed
patching, the rutted lanes that needed repair, and the
nearly empty fields. Lucas was out there somewhere in
one of those fields, she knew. He'd made plans to ride
out on an inspection tour with his steward this afternoon.

There was certainly much to be done here, Victoria
was forced to acknowledge. Whatever else one could
say about her husband, at least he apparently intended
to put her money to good use. There was no evidence
yet that he was going to pour it into wine, women, and
song.

But, then, Lucas was not a frivolous man, in spite of
his reputation as an accomplished gamester.

Frowning at her uneasy, chaotic thoughts, she bent her attention to the small plants and grasses around her. With a practiced eye she picked out several familiar species. But then she spotted a rather unusual cluster of mushrooms and her interest was immediately piqued in spite of her mood. She opened her sketchbook.

This was what she needed, she thought. She wanted the temporary peace of mind her sketching and painting could bring her.

Victoria spent a long time detailing the delicate mushrooms, losing herself in her work. Time passed quickly and the pressures of her new marriage faded, at least for the moment.

When she was finished with the mushrooms, she went on to draw several interesting dead leaves that had fallen nearby in a graceful heap. After the leaves she discovered a quite fascinating puffball. Puffballs always presented a serious challenge. It was difficult to get just the right airy appearance without sacrificing the tiny details. Botanical drawing was an exhilarating combination of art and science. Victoria loved it.

Two hours later she finally closed the sketchbook and leaned back against the tree trunk. She discovered she was feeling much better. Calmer and more steadied. The warm afternoon sun felt good and somehow the fields and farms below did not look quite so bleak. There was hope for Stonevale, she thought suddenly. Lucas would be able to salvage these lands. If any man could do it, Lucas could.

With her money, of course.

But even that thought was not as irritating as it had been earlier. An insidious notion occurred to her. Perhaps Lucas had had a point last night at dinner. What had she ever done that was so terribly useful with her money in the past?

Nevertheless, it *was* her money. Victoria scowled at that notion and got to her feet, brushing leaves from her walking dress. She must remember that she was the innocent victim in this situation.

*   *   *

Three days later Victoria made her first trip into the village. She had wanted to ride on horseback, the better to explore her new home, but Lucas had put his foot down immediately.

"I will not have the new Countess of Stonevale make her first public appearance on horseback. A certain amount of propriety is demanded in this instance, madam. You will go in a carriage together with a maid and a groom or you will not go at all," he stated.

As her relationship with Lucas could only be described as precariously balanced at best, Victoria had decided not to argue the point.

In choosing that course of action, she realized she was fast becoming as prudent as the rest of the household. She was learning that it was decidedly easier on both herself and the staff of Stonevale if she refrained from challenging her husband at each and every turn.

It irked her to think she might be surrendering some small stretch of ground to him. But the truth was, it was difficult to maintain her bristling defenses twenty-four hours a day. She was accustomed to being happy with Lucas, not at war with him.

And there were definitely a few distinct benefits to maintaining some semblance of peace in the household, she grudgingly admitted to herself. There was no denying that in response to her newfound discretion, Lucas, in turn, refrained from letting everyone feel the chill of his shockingly cold temper. The man had an air of absolute authority about him, which, when he chose to exercise it, got attention in a hurry.

His capacity for leadership and command was, Victoria had decided, in part a product of his military background. But she also suspected that a good portion of it came very naturally to Lucas. He was a born leader.

And the arrogance of a natural leader was no doubt bred in the bone. Without such arrogance and the accompanying leadership characteristics, Lucas would not have had a chance of salvaging Stonevale and the land around it.

Victoria reflected on that unpalatable notion as the

carriage jolted uncomfortably over the bad road into the village.

She had to admit that she had caught an occasional glimpse of the hard steel core of Lucas's character before her marriage. Indeed, it was probably part of what had drawn her to him. But the truth was, she had rarely been forced to confront that steel directly. Lucas had, after all, been deliberately wooing her. Naturally he had hidden the more unpleasant elements of his nature from her.

"You cannot really be meanin' to shop in this drab place, ma'am," Nan said as the carriage entered the main street of the village. "Hardly the likes o' Bond Street or Oxford Street, is it?"

"No, it certainly isn't. But we aren't here to find a ball gown. My goal is just to have a look around and perhaps meet some of the people with whom Stonevale does business on a daily basis. This is our new home, Nan. We must meet our neighbors."

"If you say so, ma'am." Nan did not look convinced of the wisdom of the idea.

Victoria smiled faintly and decided to make the appeal on a more practical basis. "You have seen the conditions at Stonevale. The house is in a terrible state. Utterly deplorable. His lordship is too busy with his farmers to worry about the running of the household, and being a military man, I doubt he would know how to run it, even if he tried."

"That be true enough, I reckon. Runnin' a household the size o' Stonevale is a lady's job, beggin' your pardon, ma'am."

"Unfortunately, I fear you are correct, Nan. And I appear to be the lady who is stuck with the task. As long as we must live there, we might as well make the place habitable. And if we are going to spend money to make it comfortable, we may as well spend as much as possible here in the village. These people rely on Stonevale for their incomes."

Nan brightened somewhat at this bit of logic. "I see your point, ma'am."

People came out of the shops and the small, decrepit

taverns to watch as the Stonevale carriage made its way sedately down the rutted street. Victoria smiled and waved.

There were one or two tentative waves in response, but the general lack of enthusiasm for the new mistress of Stonevale was rather daunting. Victoria wondered if it was her, personally, they found unappealing, or if their attitude was simply an extension of the local feeling toward Stonevale in general. She could not blame the villagers for being less than optimistic about their futures, given the obvious neglect they had endured from the past master of the great house.

These poor people, she thought, nibbling on her lower lip. They had suffered a great deal. This was a place where money could accomplish much.

In the middle of the village, Victoria spotted a tiny dry-goods shop. "I think here would be an excellent place to begin our shopping."

Nan managed to keep her mouth shut, although her opinion of the place was plain.

Victoria was smiling in amusement at her maid's superior attitude when she stepped down from the carriage with the aid of her footman.

The warmth of a bright spring sun fell on her full force, highlighting the deep amber yellow shade of her gown and glinting off her honey-colored hair. The amber feather in her tiny, yellow hat bobbed in the small breeze and the amber pendant she wore around her throat caught the sunlight and glowed with a life of its own. Everyone on the street stared as if momentarily transfixed.

Then a little girl, who had been watching from behind the safety of her mother's skirts, suddenly crowed in delight and ran out into the street, making a beeline for Victoria.

"Amber Lady, Amber Lady," the child shouted merrily as she raced forward on bare feet. "Pretty Amber Lady. You came back. My granny always said you would. She said you'd have hair the color of gold and honey all mixed up and you'd be wearin' a golden dress."

"Here now," Nan snapped not unkindly as she moved

to intercept the youngster. "We don't want to get mud all over her ladyship, now, do we? Shoo, child. Go on back to your ma."

The girl ignored her, darting swiftly around the obstacle to grab hold of Victoria's yellow skirts with grubby fingers.

"Hello," Victoria said with a welcoming smile. "What would your name be?"

"Lucy 'awkins," the child said proudly, looking up at her with eyes full of wonder. "And that's my ma. And over there's my big sis."

The woman Lucy had pointed out as her mother was already hurrying forward with a horrified grimace on her worn-looking face. She could not have been more than five years older than Victoria, but she appeared to be at least twenty years her senior.

"I'm so sorry, mum. She's just a child. She didn't mean nothin'. Don't know her manners around her betters. She ain't seen that many of 'em. Betters, I mean."

"It is quite all right. She's done no harm."

"She ain't?" The woman's face held an expression of honest bewilderment. "She dirtied your dress, mum," she pointed out in case Victoria had failed to notice the muddy fingerprints on the fine amber muslin.

Victoria did not bother to glance down at the stains. "I appreciate her warm welcome. Lucy is the first person from the village whom I have had a chance to meet, except for our housekeeper, Mrs. Sneath. Speaking of which, is there any chance your older daughter or one of her friends might be interested in a job in the kitchens? We are in desperate need of staff. I cannot imagine how Stonevale has managed to function at all with so few people working there."

"A job?" The woman's face went blank in open astonishment. "A real job at the big house, yer ladyship? Why, we'd be ever so grateful. My husband ain't worked in ages and neither 'as a lot o' other men around here."

"It is Lord Stonevale and myself who will be grateful, I assure you." Victoria glanced around the ring of curious faces that was starting to gather near the carriage.

"In fact, we shall be needing a number of people. If anyone is interested in working in the gardens or the stables or the kitchens, please present yourselves tomorrow morning. You shall be taken on immediately. Now, if you will excuse me, I thought I would do a little shopping in your charming village."

When Victoria started forward with Nan at her heels, the crowd parted magically. She could still hear Lucy's squeals about the Amber Lady as she stepped over the threshold of the small shop.

Two hours later Victoria sailed into Stonevale's main hall. "Do you by any chance know the whereabouts of his lordship, Griggs? I must see him at once."

"I believe he is in the library with Mr. Satherwaite, madam. His lordship expressly requested that he not be disturbed while he was in conference with his new steward."

"I am certain he will make an exception in my case and I am particularly delighted to catch him with Satherwaite. Very convenient." Victoria smiled and started briskly for the closed door of the library, stripping off one of her fine kid gloves as she went forward.

Griggs sprang for the door. "Forgive me, madam, but his lordship was most particular about his request."

"Don't fret, Griggs. I shall deal with him."

"Begging your pardon, madam, but I have been privileged to be in his lordship's employ for several months now and I pride myself on having learned his preferences. I can assure you he has a strong preference for being obeyed."

Victoria smiled grimly. "Believe me, I understand better than most that Stonevale has a few difficult quirks in his nature. Be so good as to open the door, Griggs. Rest assured I shall take full responsibility for any mayhem which may ensue."

Looking doubtful, but unwilling to contradict his mistress, Griggs opened the door with an expression of deep foreboding.

"Thank you, Griggs." Victoria peeled off her second glove as she went into the room. She saw Lucas glance up, scowling. But the scowl changed to an expression of surprise as he saw who it was who had interrupted him.

"Good afternoon, madam." Lucas rose politely to his feet. "I thought you had gone into the village."

"I did. Now I am returned, as you can plainly see. How fortunate to find you together with your steward." She smiled at Mr. Satherwaite, an earnest-looking young man seated on the other side of Stonevale's desk. The steward dropped the journal he had been holding and sprang to his feet, bowing deeply.

"Your servant, your ladyship."

Lucas eyed Victoria somewhat cautiously. "How can I be of service, my dear?"

"I just wanted to apprise you of a few minor details. I have let it be known in the village that we will be taking on staff. Those who are interested, which I gather will be a sizable number, have been instructed to present themselves in the morning. Mr. Satherwaite can handle them, I am certain. I will be consulting with Griggs and Mrs. Sneath as to the exact number of people we shall require in the house proper. Since I am certain you are busy enough with the tenants' problems, I shall also attend to the staffing of the gardens."

"I see," Lucas said.

"In addition, I should mention that I have made a number of purchases in the village. The tradesmen will be delivering most of them tomorrow morning. Please arrange to have their bills paid at once. It is quite obvious they cannot afford to wait upon our convenience, as is customary."

"Anything else, madam?" Lucas asked dryly.

"Yes, I met the vicar's wife, Mrs. Worth, while I was in the village and have invited her and her husband to tea tomorrow afternoon. We will be discussing the various charity needs of the village. Kindly arrange your schedule so that you may join us."

Lucas inclined his head in grave acknowledgment of the command. "I will consult my schedule to see if I am free. Will that be all?"

"Not quite. We really must do something about that terrible road into the village. Most uncomfortable."

Lucas nodded. "I shall put it on my list of items needing repair."

"Do that, my lord. I think that will be all for now." Victoria smiled warmly again at Mr. Satherwaite, who was looking dumbfounded, turned on her heel, and headed for the door. She paused on the threshold and glanced back over her shoulder at Lucas. "There was one other thing, my lord."

"Somehow I am not surprised," Lucas said. "Pray, continue. You have my full attention, madam."

"What is this nonsense about an Amber Lady?"

Lucas's eyes flicked briefly to the pendant she wore. "Where did you hear the phrase?"

"One of the children in the village called me by that odd title. I simply wondered if you were familiar with it. Apparently it is some sort of local legend."

Lucas glanced at Satherwaite. "I will tell you what little I know of the story later."

Victoria shrugged. "As you wish, my lord." She swept back out of the library and Griggs hastily closed the door behind her. The butler regarded her with an air of acute concern.

"Have no fear, Griggs," Victoria said, grinning with unabashed triumph at her small, successful assault on the sanctity of the library. "My lord has teeth but it takes considerably more than a minor interruption from his wife to make him bite."

"I shall remember that, madam."

In the library Lucas sat down again and reached for the next aging ledger. He realized Satherwaite was watching him with an expression of deep curiosity.

"My wife, as you can see, will be taking an active interest in the estate," Lucas remarked.

"Yes, my lord. She appears to have a rather keen interest in local matters."

Lucas smiled complacently. "Lady Stonevale is a woman of great energy and enthusiasm. She has been needing an interesting challenge to occupy her full attention."

"Shopping in our poor village was certainly an act of gracious mercy on her part. I cannot imagine a lady of her excellent taste finding anything she truly desired in the local shops."

"I believe the point was to do something for the local economy," Lucas mused. "And I am grateful to her. It will take both of us to save Stonevale. As I said, we are facing a challenge."

Satherwaite looked at the stack of journals and ledgers that stood on the desk. "No offense, sir, but rescuing these lands presents enough of a challenge to occupy a regiment." He looked back at his employer with a hint of the sort of hero worship a young man often feels for an older male who has seen combat. "Of course, you have had some experience with military matters, sir."

"Just between you and me, Satherwaite, I don't mind telling you that I find the challenge of making this land productive again infinitely more appealing than the business of war."

Satherwaite, who clearly did not see how anything could be more exciting than the business of war, wisely kept his mouth shut and opened the journal in front of him.

Later that evening Lucas leaned back in his chair, stretched his feet out toward the fire, and indulged himself in the purely masculine pleasure of watching his wife pour after-dinner tea in the drawing room.

It was a small thing, this matter of pouring the tea, but it seemed to symbolize so much. He was not so foolish as to think Victoria had surrendered to the inevitable yet, but he saw the distinctly wifely act as a definite step in that direction.

He suddenly realized that in common with most of his sex, he was not given to a great deal of idle reflection on all the small routines that turned a household into a home. At least, he had not been particularly conscious of them until recently when, having gotten himself a wife, he had discovered he had not automatically gotten all the little niceties that were supposed to come along with one.

For the past three days he had been living in a state of armed truce, a truce that was only an inch away from open warfare. Nothing in the household had been seen to beyond such minimal matters as producing meals and emptying chamber pots. Griggs had been getting desperate. Mrs. Sneath had threatened to quit because of overwork.

But as of the moment of Victoria's return from the village, things had begun to change. Lucas realized he thirsted mightily for each small sip of the honey of domestic harmony. Having his tea poured for him by Victoria was one such golden drop. It was the first he'd tasted since he'd taken his wedding vows.

"About the legend of the Amber Lady, my lord," Victoria said coolly as she handed him his cup and saucer. "I would like to hear the details now, if you please."

"I confess I do not know all of the tale." Lucas stirred his tea, trying to think of ways to stretch out the conversation. Victoria was in the habit of rushing off to bed early lately. "My uncle mentioned the matter shortly before he died. It was in conjunction with the pendant he gave me." He frowned, wishing he had not called her attention to the amber around her throat. Victoria appeared totally oblivious of the fact that she wore it twenty-four hours a day. "I asked for the story, but you must realize my uncle was a bitter, ill-tempered man. To top it off, when I saw him, he was on his deathbed and not particularly inclined to humor me or anyone else."

"What did he tell you?"

"Just that the pendant had been handed down through the family for several generations. It apparently belonged to the first lord of Stonevale. My uncle said I might get more information from the villagers. I asked Mrs. Sneath about it. As you know, she was about the only member of the staff left when the old bastard died. He had turned off everyone else."

"Go on, what did Mrs. Sneath say?"

Lucas looked at her and saw the bright curiosity shining in her beautiful eyes. "Having met Mrs. Sneath, you must know she is not the talkative sort. But she did tell me that the villagers tell an old children's story

about the first lord of Stonevale and his lady. The man
had been dubbed the Amber Knight because of the
colors he wore into battle."

"So he was a warrior, too," Victoria murmured, staring into the fire.

"Most men who acquired estates the size of Stonevale
were," Lucas pointed out dryly.

"They called his wife the Amber Lady?"

Lucas nodded. "According to the legend, the lord
and his lady were very much in love and devoted to the
land and the people on it. Stonevale grew prosperous
under their guidance. Several generations of happily
married men succeeded the first and the lands flour-
ished. People began to say that the well-being of the
estate and its surrounding lands was contingent on the
happiness of the lord and lady who lived in the great
house."

Victoria frowned. "A rather precarious thing on which
to hang the welfare of this entire region."

"It is just a superstition, Vicky."

"I know, but—"

Lucas interrupted her swiftly. "According to Mrs.
Sneath, it became a saying in the village that the Earls
of Stonevale must marry for love or the lands would
suffer. Given the wealth of the estate, it was very
convenient for each succeeding earl to make a love
match rather than a business match."

"Very convenient. There was no need to marry for
money until the present generation, I take it?"

Lucas hurried on, anxious to skirt the quicksand he
sensed waiting for him in that direction. "At any rate,
three generations back, the Earl of Stonevale fell in
love with a young woman who, it seemed, had already
given her heart to another." Lucas paused. "Not only
her heart, but everything else, apparently. Her family
rushed her into the marriage knowing she was carrying
another man's babe, the child of a penniless second son
who left for America when he found out she had married the Earl of Stonevale."

"That poor girl. How sad for her to be forced to
marry a man she did not love. But her family was not

about to lose the opportunity of having their daughter become a countess, I suppose," Victoria murmured with a touch of bitterness.

"Probably not," Lucas agreed. "But as long as you are overflowing with sympathy for the young lady, you might spare some for my ancestor who found himself tied to a woman who was not exactly a virgin on her wedding night."

Victoria's gaze turned even more frosty. "So? I did not come to this marriage a virgin, either, if you will recall.

"It is hardly the same thing, given the fact that I was the one and only man you slept with before the wedding. In any event," Lucas added, feeling a little dangerous now himself, "we haven't even had a *wedding* night, so your point is irrelevant, to say the least."

"Do you know, Lucas, I do not see why your ancestor or you or any other man has any right to expect his wife to be a virgin. You men certainly do not bother to remain in a chaste state until your wedding nights."

"There is the little matter of attempting to ensure one's children are one's own."

Victoria shrugged. "Aunt Cleo one told me that women have been inventing ways to feign virginity for as long as men have been so arrogant as to insist upon it. Even if one is certain one's wife is a virgin at marriage, that still does not ensure her children are not the footman's by-blows, does it?"

"Victoria . . ."

"No, it would seem to me, my lord, that the only way a man can be relatively certain his children are his own is if he truly trusts his wife and knows he can believe her when she tells him they are his."

"I trust you, Victoria," Lucas said softly.

"Well, as you said, 'tis all irrelevant as far as we are concerned, is it not?"

"Not entirely," he muttered. "Victoria, could we please get on with the legend?"

She blinked and occupied herself with the teapot. "Yes, of course. Kindly continue with the story, my lord."

Lucas took a swallow of tea, wondering how in hell he had allowed the conversation to get so wildly off track. "The earl had his suspicions, but no proof, and since he was very much in love with his new wife, he decided to believe what he wanted to believe. That worked until the babe was born dead. His lady was so grief-stricken that she lost her wits. She confessed all, blamed her unhappiness on her husband for having made it impossible to marry her true love, and claimed she was now so miserable she wanted to die. Then she promptly did precisely that."

Victoria's eyes flew to his, deep suspicion in her amber gaze. "How?"

"Pray do not look at me like that. He didn't kill her, you know. She simply never recovered from childbirth. Mrs. Sneath says the legend has it that she willed herself to die and the fever obligingly took her."

"What a tragic story. What did the earl do?"

"He grew bitter and cynical toward all women. There was pressure from the family to produce an heir, so he eventually remarried. But this time not for love. It was strictly a business decision on his part and he and his second wife hardly formed what could be called a happily married couple. In fact, after the required heir was born, the earl and his wife spent very little time together and none at all at Stonevale, apparently."

"Was that when the lands began to go into a decline?"

Lucas nodded. "Yes, according to the tale and to the old ledgers and records. I went through several of them today just out of curiosity and I must admit one can trace the gradual decline of the estate to that disastrous marriage three generations ago."

"Truly?"

"Yes, truly. The next earl, my uncle's father, was not only a cold and bitter man, he was also a rake and a poor gamester. He started the tradition of the Earls of Stonevale spending more time at the gaming tables and less on their lands. He, too, eventually married, but not for love. Once my uncle was born, his father and mother went their separate ways," Lucas said.

"And the lands continued to decline. Hardly surprising, given the lack of interest on the part of the masters. What about your uncle?"

"Maitland Colebrook never even bothered to marry for the sake of the title or anything else, let alone love. He concentrated instead on going through what was left of the family fortune. He bled the estate dry and then retired to the country to rail against his ill fate."

"So that is how the villagers explain their present impoverished situation." Victoria stared thoughtfully into the fire again. "Interesting."

Lucas studied her averted profile, wondering what she would do if he pulled her into his lap and kissed her. Would she melt for him the way she always had in the past or would she use her nails on his eyes and cut him to shreds with her tongue? One thing was for certain, when he eventually got around to taking her into his arms, it would be a real adventure for all concerned.

"The most interesting part is that business of the Hawkins child in the village calling you the Amber Lady," Lucas said quietly.

"Why is that? She had obviously been told the tale, and when she saw me dressed in that particular shade of yellow, she jumped to a child's conclusion."

Lucas watched the firelight bring out the amber and gold in Victoria's tawny brown hair. "I am not so certain she jumped to the wrong conclusion. There is something rather amberish about you, you know. Your eyes, your hair, the colors you choose to wear."

She glared at him. "For heaven's sake, Lucas, do not talk such nonsense."

He held out his cup for more tea. "It is little wonder the child would like to believe you are the Amber Lady. I have not yet told you the last bit of the legend."

She glanced at him warily as she poured tea into his cup. "How does the tale conclude?"

" 'Tis said that one day the Amber Knight and his lady will return to the great house and the lands of Stonevale will once more prosper along with their love."

"What a tidy ending," Victoria said scornfully. "But if the luck of the region depends upon the lord and lady marrying for love, then it is obvious everyone around here will have to wait for another chance at bettering their fortunes. The newest Earl of Stonevale married for money, not love."

"Damn it, Vicky. . . ."

She was already on her feet. "If you will excuse me, my lord, I will bid you good night. I grow weary."

Lucas swore again as he got to his feet. He waited until the door had closed behind her before he put down his teacup and, with cold deliberation, went across the room to pick up the brandy decanter.

Idly he massaged his aching leg. It was going to be a long night.

Three hours later as Lucas lay awake in bed listening to the soft sounds in the room next door, he wondered if he was being a fool to continue to restrain himself. Maybe this waiting game was not such wise strategy after all.

He heard another whisper of movement from the next chamber. It sounded as if Victoria had gotten out of bed. It was obvious she was not yet asleep. Perhaps she was afraid to go to sleep too early for fear of inducing another nightmare.

There was nothing like the sort of passion they could experience together to ward off bad dreams, Lucas told himself. As a concerned husband he owed her what comfort and reassurance he could give her, even if he had to force it on her.

Resolutely he pushed back the covers and reached for his dressing gown. This had gone far enough. One way or the other they had to form a normal marital relationship and it was rapidly becoming clear that his self-imposed restraint was having no effect whatsoever on her recalcitrance.

In other words, he thought ruefully, she was hardly begging for his lovemaking.

He heard the outer door to her bedchamber open and close just as he lifted his hand to knock on the connecting door. Quietly he twisted the knob and stepped into his wife's empty room.

Fury and panic seized him. Surely she was not idiotic enough to run off in the middle of the night. Then he recalled that Victoria was very much accustomed to running about in the dead of night. He had even taught her something about how it was done.

Lucas put down his candle and hastily pulled on breeches, boots, and a shirt. A few minutes later he was moving swiftly down the hall. His instincts told him she would leave via the kitchen door. It was the way he would have gone if he had been trying to sneak out of the house. He hurried after her.

A few minutes later he emerged from the house. He saw Victoria almost at once. She was standing quietly in the dilapidated, sadly overgrown kitchen garden. She was wearing her long, hooded, amber-colored cloak to ward off the chill and she was bathed in moonlight. Memories of all those other nights when he had rendez-voused with her in her aunt's garden swept over him, leaving him filled with a hunger that was sharpened to the point of pain.

This was his wife and he wanted her.

Lucas stepped slowly out into the shadows, making no sound. But she sensed his presence and turned toward him. He sucked in his breath.

"I have missed our midnight meetings in the garden," he said softly.

"You wooed me most cleverly when you promised me adventure in the middle of the night, did you not? I succumbed to that lure as I would have succumbed to no other."

His stomach clenched at the soft bitterness in her voice. "Were you going to seek an adventure on your own tonight, Vicky? I doubt there are any gaming hells or brothels or inns filled with young lordlings and their opera dancers in the village." He walked toward her until he was standing only a short distance away.

"I merely wanted to walk," she said quietly.

"Will you allow me to accompany you?"

"Have I any choice in the matter?"

"No." As if he would allow her to wander around out

here alone at night, Lucas thought. "Where were you planning to walk?"

"I am not certain. I had not really thought about it."

He considered quickly, trying to remember what he had seen during the past few days as he had ridden over his lands. "There is an empty cottage not far from here. I believe it belonged to the gamekeeper back in the days when Stonevale had a gamekeeper. Why don't we walk there and back?"

"All right." She fell silent.

"It is a lovely night, is it not?"

"I find it rather chilly," she told him distantly.

"Yes," Lucas agreed thinking swiftly. There was some old firewood stacked outside the cottage, he recalled. Too bad he had not ordered the place cleaned yesterday when he'd examined it. He stumbled slightly over a nonexistent stone and stifled a small groan.

"What is the matter with you?" Victoria asked, frowning in annoyance.

"Nothing important. My leg is acting up a bit tonight." He tried to sound stoic and brave.

"Really, Lucas, I should think you would have learned by now not to go about in the cold night air when it is paining you."

"You are undoubtedly correct about that, madam. But you seem to favor running about at night and that leaves me with little choice but to accompany you."

"You should have gone after an heiress who is not fond of this sort of sport," she told him. "The Perfect Miss Pilkington would have done nicely for you."

"Do you think so? I admit she was on Jessica Atherton's list, but somehow I could not seem to work up much enthusiasm. There was something a bit boring about the prospect of being married to Miss Pilkington. As you and Annabella said, she was a bit too much like Lady Atherton."

Victoria retreated deeper into the hood of her cloak until her voice was muffled. "You are right on that account. If you think Lady Atherton has grown somewhat dull over the years, you should see Miss Pilkington. Do not mistake me. She is very nice but she's only nineteen and she told me herself, she believes she may have a religious calling."

"I see. We would not have suited each other at all. I cannot imagine taking her to a gaming hell. Nor can I envision her using a walking stick on a brothel butler."

"On the other hand, she probably wouldn't have given you any trouble. I am certain she would have made a most dutiful wife. Speaking of duty . . ."

He sighed. "Yes?"

"Lady Atherton did warn me that I must be prepared to do mine and provide you with an heir."

"I wouldn't mind throttling Lady Atherton."

"She was only trying to help. After all, you did ask her to assist you in finding an heiress."

"You need not remind me."

"Lucas?" Victoria asked shyly.

"Hmmm?"

"Lady Atherton pointed out that if I thought doing my duty was going to be difficult for me, I should only consider how very hard it was going to be on you to have to pretend some degree of affection in the marital bed."

"God damn it to hell and back." Lucas came to a halt and swung her around to face him. He glared down at her incredulously. "You cannot tell me you believed her? After that night we spent together at the inn?"

She faced him staunchly, her eyes glittering within the shadow of the cloak. "I have learned from both my mother and my aunt that men do not seem to have any great degree of difficulty pretending that sort of physical affection when it suits them."

"Men are not the only ones who can manage the trick," Lucas muttered, and then added ruthlessly, "Some would say I have good cause to question the depths of your feelings that night."

Anger flashed in her gaze. "How dare you question my feelings that night? I was painfully honest with you about the depth of my emotions, as I recall."

He shrugged. "If your feelings ran as deep as you imply, I doubt you could have buried them so quickly afterward."

"I buried them quickly because I felt ill-used. Damn you, I had no choice but to suppress my foolish affection. I feel nothing but humiliation whenever I recall my actions that cursed night."

"I must say you have done an excellent job of suppressing your feelings. One would never guess you ever held me in anything but complete dislike."

"Yes, well, that is certainly—" She broke off as he stumbled and winced. "What's wrong now?" she demanded impatiently.

"I told you, my leg is troubling me somewhat this evening."

"There are times, Lucas, when you display very little common sense." She took his arm to steady him. "I suppose we ought to return to the house before you take a bad fall."

"I don't believe I can make it that far. The cottage is closer. If I could just rest inside it for a while, I am certain I will be all right."

"Very well," she muttered irritably. "Here, you had better let me assist you."

"Thank you, Vicky. You are very kind." Leaning rather heavily on her, Lucas allowed himself to be assisted into the dark confines of the small gamekeeper's cottage.

12

Strategy.

    Lucas settled himself on the floor of the cottage, his arm propped on one up-drawn knee, his sore leg stretched out straight. He watched cheerfully as Victoria busied herself building a fire. She had refused to allow him to carry the wood, insisting he rest, instead.

"This is a pleasant little place, is it not?" she asked, glancing about as the fire she had just built blazed into existence and revealed the interior of the cottage. "It looks like someone has lived here fairly recently. The chimney is clear and the floor is not nearly as dusty as one would expect."

"I wouldn't be surprised if some evicted tenant took up residence here until we arrived. My uncle was extremely prone to evictions."

"A nasty man."

"Bear in mind that I descend from a slightly different branch of the family," he pointed out.

Instead of smiling, she took that very seriously. "We are certainly not responsible for the actions of other members of our family. Here, let me rub your leg for you."

Lucas did not protest. His mind was on fire with images of what had happened the first time she had rubbed his throbbing leg. "Thank you. I would appreciate it."

She folded her cloak on the floor and knelt on it. Keeping her eyes focused on his leg, she went to work, massaging gently. Lucas groaned at the first touch of her hands.

"Am I hurting you?"

"No. That feels wonderful." He closed his eyes and leaned his head back against the wall. "You can have no idea."

"It must have been terrible."

Lucas opened his eyes and studied his wife. "What must have been terrible?"

"That day when you were wounded."

"I will admit it was not the highlight of my life. A little higher, please. Yes. Right there. Thank you." Her hand was mere inches from his groin. He wondered how she could be unaware of the rapidly growing bulge in his snug breeches. "That fire feels good."

"Lucas?" There was a short, poignant pause.

Lucas saw the intent look on Victoria's face. "Yes?"

"Did you love her very much?"

He closed his eyes again as he struggled to follow her train of thought. "Who?"

"Lady Atherton, of course."

"Oh, her. Well, I must have thought I did at the time, else why would I have bothered to ask her to marry me?"

"Why, indeed?" Victoria muttered.

"But looking back on it, I find it hard to believe I was that much of an idiot."

"She still loves you."

"She loves the idea of suffering from a star-crossed love and the feeling of being a gallant martyr to duty far more than she'll ever love any man. I do not envy Lord Atherton one bit." Atherton's bed must be a very cold one, Lucas thought.

"Forgive me, my lord," Victoria said wryly, "but that is a remarkably perceptive comment for a man."

He opened one eye. "You think women are the only ones who can make remarkably perceptive comments?"

"Well, no, but . . ."

He closed his eye. "Some of us males are capable of learning from our mistakes and of gaining a measure of perception in the process."

"Is that right?"

Lucas inhaled sharply. "Ah, Vicky, could you possibly go a bit easier on that portion of my leg? Perhaps if you moved your hands a bit higher?"

"Like this?" She slid her fingers up his thigh a few more inches.

Lucas did not trust himself to speak. Her touch was now so intimate he was afraid he would lose his self-control entirely in another moment or two.

"Lucas, are you all right?" Victoria began to sound genuinely worried.

"After that night we spent together at the inn, you should know what your touch does to me, my sweet."

Her hands stilled instantly on his thigh. "Do you want me to stop?" she asked hesitantly.

"Never. Not in a million years. A man could die happy under such torture."

"Lucas, are you by any chance trying to get me to . . . to seduce you?"

He opened his eyes and looked straight at her. "I would sell my soul to get you to seduce me."

She blinked at his bluntness. Then her eyes filled with longing. "I do not think the price would be quite so high, my lord."

He touched her face and then let his fingers slide along the chain of the pendant. "Thank God for your honesty in matters of intellectual inquiry."

"Oh, *Lucas*." With a small cry she threw herself against his chest and nestled there, her arms wrapping around his waist. "I have thought about that night so often. I was so happy with you for those few hours."

"Only your pride is keeping you from being happy in that way again." He stroked her arm, enjoying the weight of her against his chest. "Is your pride worth all this disharmony between us? We are bound together for life now, Vicky. Do you intend to put us both through hell every night?"

She kept her head tucked against his shoulder so that she did not have to look at him. "When you put it like that, it does not make much sense, does it? Aunt Cleo said that I had made my bed and now must lie in it. She said it was up to me to make that bed as comfortable as possible."

"Much as I appreciate your aunt's sentiments, I'd just as soon not have a martyr in my bed. I narrowly escaped that fate once before, as you will recall," Lucas said.

Her shoulders shook with soft, nervous laughter. "Yes, I do recall. Very well, Lucas, I shall view my decision to carry out my responsibilities as your wife as a matter of logic and common sense, not a matter of duty. There is, as you say, no point in putting us both through hell."

"Give me the logical bluestocking rather than the pious martyr any day." Lucas tipped up her chin and kissed her. "At least when the bluestocking talks herself into succumbing to passion, she doesn't have to pretend she cannot enjoy it." His mouth moved slowly on hers.

Victoria seemed to hesitate briefly, as if silently running through her logic one more time to be certain this was the right solution to the problem she had set herself. Then, with a tiny gasp, she responded with the sweet, hot fervor that Lucas always found so enthralling.

Her hands tightened around his back and she parted her lips for him. Lucas let his tongue plunge into her mouth in anticipation of the way he would soon be surging into her body. She pressed herself against him. He could feel her breasts beneath the bodice of her dress and his entire body throbbed with impatience.

"Sweetheart, I have waited so long for our wedding night." He tore his mouth from hers and reached for the amber cloak on which she had been kneeling. He tossed it out deftly with one hand so that it formed a blanket for her to lie on.

"It will get dirty." Her protest was automatic, but without any real heat.

"You have others." He fumbled with her gown, a

part of him appalled by his haste and the unaccustomed clumsiness that accompanied it. So much for strategy. Another part of him was running wild and free now that the torment of waiting was nearly over.

That first time he had prepared himself to hold back until he was certain she was as eager as he was. He had been so intent on not hurting her or alarming her, so intent on pleasing her. But this time he could think only of possessing her once more. He had to reassure himself that she was his again.

This time he could not contain himself.

Victoria looked startled by his urgency, but she went willingly over onto her back as he eased her down onto the cloak. He gave up fighting with her clothes and contented himself with pushing her skirts up to her waist. Then he looked up quickly to see if she was offended by the lack of gallantry. When he saw her luminous smile and the reflected heat of the fire in her eyes, he went to work on his own clothing.

"Damn."

"What is it?" she asked softly.

"Nothing. Merely my own clumsiness." He finally managed to get the breeches open. He decided he could not take the time to remove them or his boots. His need was raging through him.

And then he was falling on her in a white-hot fever. He put his hands on her thighs and she opened them for him, offering herself. He moved between her legs, feeling the moist heat of her as he pushed against her softness. He took one of her nipples into his mouth and bit down with exquisite care as he surged into her tight, hot channel.

She cried out and clung to him. He could feel the initial resistance of her body as he pushed steadily deeper. He reminded himself that this was all still very new to her.

"Lift yourself, sweetheart. Open yourself for me." He slid one hand down under her to cup her lush buttocks and urged her upward so that he could sink himself even deeper into her clinging warmth.

"*Lucas.*"

"Am I hurting you?" His voice was husky, even to his own ears.

"No, not precisely. But the feeling is indescribable. Oh, Lucas."

"I know, I know, darling, I know." He sank himself slowly to the hilt. He felt her thighs shiver as they closed around him and the knowledge that she had willingly made herself so vulnerable to him nearly undid him. "Wrap your legs around my waist. That's it. *Yes.*"

With a soft exclamation, she gave herself to him just as she had that first night. She was clinging to him, whispering his name, pleading with him for the release he promised.

Glittering shards of sensation flickered through his senses. Lucas was aware of the heat of the fire, the alluring scent of Victoria's aroused body, the silky strength of her soft thighs as they tightened around him.

He opened his eyes and saw that hers were tightly closed. She was breathing quickly, her throat arched back over his arm. She was in the grip of her passion and the sight was devastating to his senses. He was utterly fascinated. He moved slowly, deliberately, within her, letting her pull him back every time he had retreated to the entrance of her tight little channel.

"*Lucas.*"

"Yes." He eased back into her again, glorying in her hot, clinging warmth. He was sweating now, his whole body surging toward release. Then he felt the sudden tension in Victoria and knew she was close to her own climax.

He moved his hand on her buttocks, letting one finger glide intimately along the dark cleft to the point where their bodies were joined.

Victoria's eyes flew open and her lips parted on a soft, startled, purely feminine shriek.

"Lucas? Dear heaven, *Lucas.*"

And then she was convulsing gently around him, drawing him even more deeply into her. Lucas heard his own triumphant shout fill the small room as his release swept over him.

Several minutes passed before he felt like stirring. When he did, it was only to roll onto his side and gather Victoria close against him. The fire was still blazing merrily, casting cheerful, dancing shadows on the walls. Lucas felt his wife's leg slide lazily along his as she allowed herself to be cuddled.

"You must admit there are some benefits to marriage, madam. At least this time we do not have to concern ourselves with being discovered and threatened with social ruin." Lucas yawned mightily, aware of a singular contentment. "But do you think that perhaps next time we might try it in the comfort of your bed or mine? That mattress at the inn was lumpy and this floor is damned hard."

"We are having an adventure. Don't you think it might be a bit ordinary to use one of our own beds, sir?"

"This is what I get for marrying a woman with a taste for excitement. She only wants to make love in unusual locations and under novel circumstances." Lucas ruffled her short curls affectionately. "Fear not, madam, your husband will do his best to keep you amused and entertained in your own bed."

"It sounds like a great deal of work on your part," she said.

"Believe me, it will be infinitely easier to dream up interesting things to do with you in the comfort of your bedchamber than it is to chase after you at midnight, wondering what mischief you're up to."

She did not respond to that. Instead she wriggled a bit, quite delightfully, in fact. She made no move to free herself from his arms but her silence continued for some time. Lucas began to worry.

"Lucas?"

"Yes, my sweet?"

"Do you swear to me that you did not arrange for my aunt to discover us that first time at the inn?"

Anger snapped to life within him, driving out much of the contentment he had been enjoying. He pushed himself up on one elbow and scowled down at her. "Damn it, Vicky, I set out to seduce you, not humiliate you. How can you think I would deliberately do such a thing?"

"You said, yourself, you were determined to marry an heiress."

"I was determined to marry *you*," he corrected roughly, "not just any heiress. Furthermore, to be perfectly blunt about it, my dear, I had no need to resort to extreme measures such as arranging for your aunt to discover us in compromising circumstances."

Her brows came together in a swift frown. "What do you mean by that?"

"Only that I was doing a creditable job of seducing you into marriage just fine on my own. I did not require anyone else's assistance. At the rate we were going, it would have been only a matter of time before you talked yourself into marrying me."

"Why, you arrogant beast." She tried to push herself away from him and sit up.

Lucas grinned and threw one leg over her bare thighs. He rolled back on top of her, pinning her wrists to the floor on either side of her head. "'Tis true and you know it, sweetheart. Admit it. Admit you could not possibly have conducted the sort of torrid love affair you wished for unless we got married. It would have proved impossible."

She glared up at him, struggling futilely. "It would have been possible. It merely required planning."

"I assure you, when it comes to planning and strategy, I am very, very good and even I could not have kept you content or safe for long. Hell, I could not even manage it that one time we tried to seclude ourselves at the inn. And it would have been impossible for you to steal away from a soirée to run off to an inn in a strange coach every time you wanted to make love. Sooner or later someone would have been bound to notice."

"I would have been most discreet," Victoria insisted.

"Is that right? And what would we have done when the Season was over and there were very few large parties from which you could disappear without being noticed?"

She bit her lip in annoyance. "I would have thought of something."

"No, love. We were headed for trouble right from the start."

"And you knew it."

"Of course I knew it. As you are far from being an idiot, you would soon have come to your senses and realized it also. At that point I am convinced you would have started to think seriously about marrying me." He smiled deliberately. "To be perfectly truthful, given your appetite for *intellectual inquiry*, I do not believe I would have had to wait too long."

She went still and looked up at him through her lashes. "You were so sure of me you took to carrying a special license in your pocket."

"I wanted to be prepared. We were playing with fire, love."

Victoria closed her eyes to his satisfied grin. "And I got burned."

"Are the flames so bad?" he asked softly, brushing his mouth across hers. His body reacted immediately and he groaned.

"I have given the situation much thought during the past few days," she said, her expression very serious now. "If the world were a different place, I would never have chosen marriage."

Her insistence on that point began to annoy him. He scowled. "If the world were a different place, I would not have been obliged to capture an heiress."

"True. Lucas, as I said, I have given this much thought. We both did what was required of us by our sense of honor and now we have been forced to seal a bargain. This is something of a business arrangement. I have decided to think of our marriage in that light. I see us as two business associates who have invested in the same enterprise."

Lucas frowned. "I do not like all this talk of going into trade."

She shook her head restlessly. "Think of it how you will; the point is, we are investing together in a future, and as long as we can find a way to work comfortably together, I begin to believe we can be reasonably content together."

"Reasonably content," he echoed, thinking seriously of putting her over his knee. "Is that how you felt a few minutes ago when you were shivering in my arms? Reasonably content?"

The flush on her face was more than just the effect of the fire's warmth. "Really, Lucas. A gentleman would not ask such an intimate question."

"How would you know? You haven't been with any other gentlemen in such circumstances."

"I can hazard a guess," she retorted. "Besides, that is not the issue."

"And what is the issue? You mean to think of our marriage as a partnership? An investment? A business arrangement in which the associates happen to sleep together?" His eyes caught hers in a burning gaze.

"But is that not precisely what it is? Isn't that what you wanted?"

"No, damn it. 'Tis not at all what I wanted."

"I see. Perhaps you do not care for the notion of me being an equal partner? Perhaps you just wanted my money and would prefer I stay out of the matter entirely, except insofar as I am needed to provide your heir."

"Vicky, Vicky, calm yourself. You are twisting my words and getting everything wrong."

"I am trying to do as everyone says I must. I am attempting to find a sensible, intelligent way to deal with this matter. I thought you would be pleased that I am finally being so reasonable about everything."

Lucas fought to quell his outrage. "I don't want a business associate, I want a wife."

"What is the difference, other than the fact that as your wife I shall share your bed occasionally?"

"It will be more than occasionally and the difference is that you love me, madam. You said so yourself."

Her eyes widened. "I did not."

"Yes, you did. That first night at the inn. I heard you."

"I only said I *thought* I was in love with you. In any case, all that is naturally changed by what happened."

"The devil it is." His fingers tightened on her wrists.

"Vicky, stop talking all this nonsense about a business arrangement. We are man and wife."

"Are you saying there is more to our relationship than a bargain?"

"Of course there is."

Her eyes narrowed. "Are you claiming to be in love with me, then, my lord?"

"You would not believe me if I told you I was." He released her and sat up, adjusting his clothing.

"Who knows? Why don't you try it and see?"

He looked at her and did not quite know what to make of the look in her eyes. But she was challenging him, of that much he was certain. "What do you want from me, Vicky?"

"What I imagine every new bride wishes to hear," she said coolly. "A declaration of undying love and a promise of eternal devotion. But I am not likely to get it, am I?"

"Bloody hell." He stood up, sensing the treacherous sand beneath his feet. Women were the very devil with words and a woman like this one would know how to take full advantage of any leverage he gave her. He'd already had ample proof of how skillfully she could maneuver him into going against his own better judgment. Just the memory of those dreadful nights climbing Lady Nettleship's garden wall was enough to start his leg aching again. "You tease me at your peril, madam."

"Does that mean you cannot give me what I want?"

"I do not trust your mood, Vicky, nor whatever is behind your request. I believe you are looking for a way to manipulate me. If I gave you a declaration of undying love and eternal devotion, you would hurl it in my face every time I refused to indulge one of your whims. You would say I had lied about loving you."

"Does that mean you do not love me?"

"It means it was a goddamned mistake to indulge you so much initially in London. You have come to expect that with very little effort you can keep me on a leash," he said through his teeth.

"I see." She got slowly to her feet and concentrated on arranging her clothing.

Lucas stared at her slender, rigidly held back, feeling hunted. A few minutes ago they had been sharing a passion unlike any he had ever known. Now the fragile relationship seemed to have been shattered by mere words. For the life of him he could not figure out where everything had gone wrong.

"Vicky, don't do this to yourself." He turned her around and pulled her into his arms. He thought he heard a small sniff and he immediately felt helpless. He did not like the feeling at all. "You are no green girl, damn it."

She hesitated and then nodded reluctantly against his shoulder, her face buried in his shirt. "You are right. I am behaving like a silly little chit straight out of the schoolroom who cannot face the world as it is." She pulled back and looked up at him with renewed determination. "As I said, Lucas, I do believe this marriage can work if we both agree to act logically and reasonably. I vow I will uphold my end of this bargain."

He looked down into eyes that still shimmered with tears and he did not know what to say. He realized he wanted to hear the sweet, tentative words of love he had heard from her that first night, but he sensed that now was not the time to demand them.

"Vicky?"

"Yes, my lord?"

"Thank you for making up your mind to make the best of this marriage," he heard himself say gently. "I am grateful."

"You are welcome, my lord."

He grimaced a little at the excruciating formality of her tone but managed a reassuring smile. As he stood looking down at her the amber pendant glowed in the firelight and Lucas relaxed slightly.

It would be all right, he decided. She would find the words again in her own good time. "Do not tie yourself in knots trying to dissect your feelings, Vicky. Or mine." He touched the gold chain of the pendant and smiled. "Everything will come right in time. Let's go home."

She nodded in swift agreement and stood back as he shook out her cloak. The garment was dusty but otherwise unharmed. He put it around her, thinking that even though she was tall for a woman, she was still considerably smaller than he was. He was aware again of a fierce need to protect her and keep her safe.

"Lucas," she said thoughtfully as he put out the fire, "if you did not arrange for us to be discovered that night at the inn, who did?"

He shrugged. "Who knows?"

"Lady Atherton, perhaps? In her never-ending zeal to assist you in your quest for an heiress?"

He grinned, relieved to hear the returning edge of impudence in her voice. " 'Tis possible, I suppose. Does it matter? What's done is done." He took her arm and led her toward the door.

"You are quite right," she said slowly. "What's done is done. But there were one or two rather odd things that happened to me recently in Town and combined with the mystery of wondering who had been spying on us, I began to think."

"About what?"

"Never mind. 'Tis just my imagination."

Lucas went cold. He dragged her to an abrupt halt just outside the cottage. "Victoria, what in hell are you talking about? What odd things happened?"

"Really, Lucas, it was nothing, I'm sure."

"I would like an answer, madam."

"Do you know, Lucas, when you talk in that particular tone, there is a strong tendency for everyone in the vicinity to jump through the nearest hoop. Did you learn that in the army?"

He prayed silently for patience. "Enough, Victoria. Tell me what made you ask me about who might have spied on us. Tell me now, wife, or we will stand here until you do."

"It occurs to me that on the two occasions when we have conducted our *intellectual inquiries*, you have not been particularly affectionate afterward. The first time I will grant there was the extenuating circumstance of my aunt's presence. But this time there is no excuse. Is it this way with all men?"

"You cannot resist goading me, can you? One of

these days you really will push too far. Answer me or we are likely to discover that this is the day."

Victoria shrugged. "Very well, but it really does not amount to much. It is just that on two occasions in Town I came across objects that did not belong to me. They were both marked with a 'W.' One was a scarf that had been left on the conservatory door. I found it that night we went to the gaming hell."

"The night you were nearly run down by that carriage." Lucas frowned. "What was the other object?"

"A snuffbox, of all things. I found it in my paintbox."

"And no one ever claimed either object?"

"No." She shook her head and resumed walking back toward the house.

He fell into step beside her, trying to think. "When did you find the snuffbox?"

She muttered a response that he did not quite catch.

He flicked an impatient glance at her averted face. "What was that?"

"I said I found it the morning after our last, fateful interview in my aunt's garden. You may recall the evening, my lord. It was the night I asked you to arrange for us to, uh . . ."

"Oh, yes. That night. Fateful, indeed." He turned her words over in his mind, looking for a pattern that was not there. " 'Tis strange."

"Why do you say that?"

"I was attacked by a footpad that night on my way back to the carriage," he explained briefly. "I wondered at the time if the man might have been deliberately waiting for me, but I dismissed it as unlikely."

Victoria whirled around, her eyes wide with shock. "You were attacked? By a footpad? Why didn't you tell me? For heaven's sake, Lucas, you should have said something."

"Such as?" Her renewed concern for his safety pleased and reassured him.

"Do not be flippant. This is a very serious matter. You could have been hurt. Did he take your money or your watch?"

"No, he did not."

"No, of course not," she agreed quickly. "You would have been much too quick for him."

"You flatter me. I fear the simple truth is that I was lucky." He took her arm again and resumed guiding her back to the house. "The footpad was of no particular consequence, unless one considers the damage done to my coat. But it is a rather interesting coincidence."

"What is? And how can you say the attack on you was of no consequence? It seems to me it could have had very alarming consequences."

"Yes, but the interesting part is the coincidence of each of us having a rather narrow escape just before you discovered those objects with 'W' inscribed on them."

She was stunned into a rare silence. Lucas could almost hear her mind working feverishly. "What do you make of such coincidences?"

"To be honest, I do not know what to make of them. There probably isn't anything at all to be made of them. I will admit it had occurred to me that the footpad might have been hired by Edgeworth."

"Edgeworth. Oh, yes, him. Because of his embarrassing loss at cards? Do you think he would have stooped to that sort of vengeance just because he lost money to you?"

Lucas reflected on his last conversation with Edgeworth. "There was a bit more bad blood between us than just the gaming-table scene. But even if he resorted to such tactics, it still fails to explain the object you discovered in the conservatory."

She frowned. "No. Nor does it tie in with the carriage incident, although I suppose that if that had been a deliberate attack also, we might have been wrong in thinking I was the intended victim."

"You think I was the target?" He was surprised by her insight and took a minute to think about it. "I'm not sure. 'Tis possible. We were not standing very far apart on the street when it happened."

"Edgeworth again?"

Lucas chewed on that. On the night of the carriage incident he and Edgeworth had not yet had their confrontation over Vicky's honor. But there was still the

matter of the gaming loss and Edgeworth might have
begun to realize his reputation was declining in the clubs.
And, of course, there was always that bit of bad business
in the past that would forever stand between them.

"Possible," Lucas said finally.

"But what could either of those attacks have to do
with my discovering the scarf and the snuffbox?"

"Do you know anyone whose name begins with a 'W'?"

"*No*. I mean, yes, of course. Several people. As I
said, none of them had lost either item."

She rushed on, telling him about all the people whose
name began with "W" and how her aunt had talked to
them all about the missing items, but Lucas was not
listening.

His attention had been caught and held by the strange
note in her voice when she had first answered the
direct question. Once before quite recently he had
heard that hesitation, detected that slight distance, as if
she did not want to get too close to the question. He
reflected for another instant and then he had it. He had
heard it the night she described her nightmare.

". . . and she also checked with Lady Wibberly, who
takes an inordinate amount of snuff. Lord Wilkins, too,
I believe. He wears scarves. And then we asked
Waterson, but to no avail."

"Vicky."

"One can never be certain Lord Waterson remembers things all that well, however. It is entirely possible
he lost both items and doesn't recall it. Always has his
mind on higher things like meteorology, you know. He
has built the most impressive instrument for measuring
rainfall."

"Victoria."

"As I said, what with my aunt's long list of acquaintances, it is possible we missed someone."

"Vicky, darling, please hush for a minute. I want to
ask you a very particular question and I would be very
grateful if you gave me a direct answer." He stopped,
obliging her to halt also. Then he turned her toward
him and caught hold of her shoulders.

"Yes, Lucas?"

"Vicky, is there someone whose name begins with 'W' whom you do not like? Someone who frightens you or whom you feel you cannot trust? Someone who, perhaps, makes you exceedingly anxious?"

"No," she said instantly.

He smiled slightly at the obvious lie. "Try again with your answer, my sweet. And don't be afraid to tell me the truth. I'm your midnight companion in adventure, remember? You can tell me things you would tell no one else."

"Lucas, please, do not press me like this."

He urged her close, pushing her face into his shirt. Her amber cloak swirled around his legs. "Tell me, Vicky."

Her shoulders were stiff, her body unyielding. "You do not understand."

"Try me."

"Lucas, he's *dead*."

Lucas frowned into her soft hair, hearing the desperation in that simple statement. He flipped through the information Jessica Atherton had given him before he began to stalk his heiress. It took him less than a couple of seconds to hit upon a name: Samuel Whitlock. "Are we, by any chance," he asked gently, "talking about your stepfather?"

She jerked her head back, making a visible effort to pull herself together. "I told you it was impossible. He is dead and buried."

"But you did not like him very much, did you?"

Her eyes glittered in the moonlight. "I hated him for what he did to my mother and for what he would have done to me if he'd gotten the chance. My mother saved me from that lecherous bastard by sending me to live with my aunt for most of my life. But she could not save herself. In the end, he killed her."

13

You believe your stepfather killed your mother?"
Lucas's voice sounded amazingly calm, Victoria
thought. It was the sort of voice in which he might have
asked if she would care for a glass of sherry before
dinner. As he spoke he draped an arm around her
shoulder and resumed walking toward the house.

"Yes. Yes, I do, although I have never said as much
to anyone except my aunt." Victoria felt the heavy
weight around her shoulders and was oddly reassured.
He was so very strong, she thought fleetingly. Comfortingly so.

She was not certain why Lucas's arm around her had
such a soothing effect, but she didn't question it just
then. She was too busy reminding herself to be very
careful about what she said next. She had already blurted
out a great deal more than she had ever intended.

"What does your aunt think?"

Victoria clutched at the edges of her cloak. "That 'tis
very possible. She knows the sort of man he was. A
cruel drunkard who lacked any shred of decency. She
did point out that if he murdered her, it would be

579

interesting to know why Samuel Whitlock waited so many years to do it. Why did he not simply get it over and done soon after he married my mother and had access to her fortune?"

"There may have been no real reason to kill her in the early years," Lucas said reflectively, as though working out a curious puzzle in his mind. "After all, as you said, he did have access to her money. Why should he risk hanging for murder?"

Victoria sighed. "That was Aunt Cleo's point. My mother not only sent me to live with my aunt, she frequently came to stay with us for weeks, sometimes months at a time. After she realized what sort of man she had married, she spent as little time with him as possible. When he got drunk he got violent."

"In other words, in addition to turning her money over to him, she obligingly stayed out of his way. So why kill her after all those years?" Lucas asked.

"Perhaps he simply got tired of her," Victoria said tightly. "Perhaps he got especially angry at her one day and lost his temper. He had a terrifying temper. When he lost it, he lost his self-control completely. He was like a madman." Unlike Lucas, she thought fleetingly, who was always controlled, even when he was angry.

"Your mother died in a riding accident, I believe?"

"Yes. Near his house in the country. She had gone there to entertain his friends that weekend. She had been staying with Aunt Cleo and me for several weeks prior to that, as usual, but Whitlock ordered her to return for a few days to do her duty as a wife, as he put it. My mother was very beautiful, very charming. An excellent hostess, in fact, and Whitlock often used her to impress his friends," Victoria explained.

"A riding accident sounds more like a planned murder, not one done in the heat of anger."

Victoria shrugged. "You may be right. I only know he did it."

"How do you know that?"

Because he told me so, himself, she thought wildly. *He told me even as he plunged forward to his death at the foot of those stairs.*

But she could hardly tell Lucas why she was so certain of her stepfather's guilt. Lucas was entirely too shrewd. Once he had that bit of information, he would probe for more and she had already learned she had a bad habit of becoming altogether too trusting and vulnerable in his arms.

Besides, she reminded herself grimly, while Lucas was a very unusual man in some respects, he was not likely to be so tolerant and understanding as to welcome the news that he was married to a murderess.

"I have no real proof, of course," Victoria said cautiously. "But in my heart I am certain of his guilt."

He let that go. "Riding accidents happen all the time, Vicky."

"My mother was an excellent rider." Victoria hoped this would close the matter, but Lucas, in his inimitable fashion, pushed on.

"Did you confront Whitlock?"

This was getting too close to dangerous territory. "He knew I had no proof. He laughed at me."

Lucas's hand tightened around her shoulders. "What did you do then?"

"There was nothing I could do. He died less than two months later and Aunt Cleo and I decided it was rough justice."

"He was found at the foot of a staircase, I believe?"

She glanced up quickly. "Where did you hear that?"

Lucas's mouth curved wryly. "Jessica Atherton."

"You certainly obtained a great deal of information from Lady Atherton."

"Let us not start that quarrel again. Did your stepfather die that way?"

"Yes." Victoria picked her words carefully. "He had apparently been drinking very heavily that night, which was not unusual for him. He tripped and fell at the top of a long flight of stairs. That was the end of the matter."

"Not quite."

She started. "What do you mean by that?"

"Merely that you are still upset by the sight of his initial embroidered on someone else's scarf or engraved on a strange snuffbox. What's the matter, Vicky? Are you beginning to wonder if there really are such things as ghosts? Did you think Whitlock had come back to haunt you?"

"*Do not say that.*" She got control of herself instantly. "Of course I don't believe in ghosts. What bothered me about the scarf and the snuffbox was that it appeared both had been left where I was the most likely one to find each."

"The location of the scarf is particularly interesting, isn't it? It implies someone knew you would be coming back into the house late via the conservatory door."

"Yes, that is exactly it, Lucas. Looking back on it, it makes one wonder if someone was spying on us the whole time. That same someone apparently was watching so closely that he or she saw me leave the party that night and get into the carriage you had hired," Victoria concluded.

"And followed us to the inn? 'Tis possible."

"It could have been Jessica Atherton."

Lucas's tone lightened. "I cannot envision Lady Atherton climbing the garden wall at midnight."

"You have a point. So that means the scarf and snuffbox were left by someone else. Unless . . ."

"Unless what?"

Victoria was struck by an idea. "Do you suppose she hired a Bow Street runner to follow us around?"

"You, of all people, my dear, would know how easy that is to do."

There was an acute silence following that remark, a silence during which it occurred to Victoria that if she'd been thinking clearly, instead of following her heart, she might have had the good sense to hire a runner herself to obtain some information on the mysterious Lord Stonevale.

"I wondered, myself, how long it would take you to get around to doing just that," Lucas said.

She frowned, afraid he had read her mind. "Doing what?"

His teeth flashed in a wicked grin. "Hiring a runner to have me investigated. It was one of the reasons I wanted to get the courtship over and done as quickly as possible."

"You are perfectly despicable, Stonevale."

"I am also perfectly content with our bargain, madam." He paused outside the kitchen door to brush his mouth lightly over hers. His eyes gleamed. "And while I would not have wanted you put in the awkward position you were in that night at the inn, I cannot say I am particularly sorry things happened the way they did. All in all, considering the risks we were running, we got off lightly."

"I do not see how we could have gotten off much worse."

"Then you lack imagination, madam. I used to lie awake nights thinking about all that could go wrong during our midnight jaunts." He tipped up her chin. "Are you really so unhappy with me, Vicky?"

She wanted to rail at him for not loving her as she loved him. She wanted to accuse him of having manipulated her into this marriage where her emotions threatened to tear her apart while his seemed under perfect control. She longed to bring him to a more forceful realization of his overwhelming guilt, to make him grovel for her forgiveness and proclaim his undying love and devotion.

In short, Victoria realized, she wanted some vengeance for the situation in which she found herself. However, she was realistic enough to know she would probably never get it.

But she had learned her lesson well, Victoria vowed silently. She would keep the secrets of her heart, just as she had learned to keep other, darker secrets. If the Earl of Stonevale was content with his marriage, she would strive to be satisfied also. But she would not give him any more than what he had set out to trap—an heiress who was obliged to accept the fact that she had been married for her money with relatively good grace.

"I believe," Victoria said carefully, "that as husbands go, you are probably not such a bad one."

"You damn me with faint praise, madam," he complained softly. "Surely you can do better than that?"

She licked her lower lip as she looked up at him. He

was a menacing figure by moonlight. Large and powerful, he loomed over her. The stark lines of his face were
etched with palest silver and deepest shadow. His eyes
glittered with a sensual threat that made her recently
sated senses flicker back to life. She ought to be afraid
of him, she told herself. Instead, she always felt ridiculously safe in his presence. Damn the man.

Her instinct was to throw her arms around him and
confess her love. But her sense of self-protection and
her pride stepped in to cut off such a rash and useless
course of action. She would not make herself totally
vulnerable to Lucas ever again the way she had that
fateful night at the inn.

"I believe, my lord, that I have already explained to
you I will do my best to live up to my part of our
bargain."

Lucas shook his head ruefully and kissed the tip of
her nose. "So proud. And so determined not to give an
inch more than you must. How can you be so cruel,
Vicky?"

"I hardly think 'tis being cruel to say I am willing to
accept the situation in which I find myself. What more
can you rightfully demand of me, Lucas?"

"Everything."

"You sound as if you talk of my complete surrender,
my lord."

"Perhaps I do."

"For that I vow you will have to wait until the world
allows women to wear breeches in public," she shot
back tartly. "In other words, forever."

"Perhaps not quite so long. But we will come back to
the matter later. For now I will be content with the
progress we have made tonight." He took her hand and
led her into the dark, slumbering house.

The vicar and his wife were nervous. It was painfully
obvious they were not accustomed to taking tea in the
great house of Stonevale. Victoria decided that if she
were to hazard a guess, she would say they had never
before been invited into the house for any reason at all,
let alone a consultation about the charity needs of the

district. That irritated her. It was further proof that the previous earl had not cared about the people who lived on and near his lands.

"I cannot tell you how very happy we are to have you and your lovely lady installed here at the house, Lord Stonevale." The Reverend Worth, a ruddy-faced, solidly built man in his fifties, spoke very earnestly.

"Yes, indeed. We're delighted to welcome you," Mrs. Worth, a sweet-faced little wren of a woman who sat stiffly next to her husband, said tremulously. The teacup in her small hand trembled as she took a very tiny sip. Every now and then she would steal a quick, timid glance around the drawing room, as if she could not quite believe she was inside the great house.

"Thank you," Victoria said gently, smiling at the uneasy woman. "It was very kind of you to arrange to be here on such short notice."

"Not at all, not at all," the woman sputtered, and nearly spilled her tea. "We are ever so grateful for your interest in local matters."

The vicar made a valiant effort to meet his host's eyes in a man-to-man look. "Hope you don't mind my saying so, sir, but your family's lands have been neglected entirely too long. I am delighted to say that I have already heard talk in the village of the improvements you have begun. 'Tis a great relief."

"I am glad you are pleased, Reverend Worth. I couldn't agree with you more about the status of the estate and the surrounding countryside." Lucas put down his cup with a distinct snap that made Victoria hide a quick grin. Her husband was concealing his impatience well, but she knew for a fact that he would have much preferred to have been allowed to escape this particular social function.

He was, he had told her in no uncertain terms that morning, a busy man and he did not have time to waste taking tea with the vicar. Victoria had informed him that he was not going to be let off the hook and in the end she had won, much to the interested surprise of one or two of the new servants who had happened to overhear the discussion in the hall. It was not going unnoticed that the new Earl of Stonevale had a decided tendency to indulge his bride.

"There is a great deal to be done," Worth noted. "The situation around here was getting desperate."

"Your ladyship has made a wonderful impression on the local people," Mrs. Worth said shyly. "When I went to visit Betsy Hawkins this morning to take her a petticoat for her daughter, she told me quite proudly she wouldn't be needing any more charity. Her daughter had a job up here in the kitchens, she said, and her husband was going to start work in the stables. She was so happy, madam. You cannot imagine. That poor lady has had a hard time of it, as have many others."

"We are grateful to have so many willing workers. We shall need a great many people to get this place in shape," Victoria said, meaning every word. It had been a harrowing chore getting the drawing room in even halfway decent condition for today's visit. She'd started the new staff cleaning it at dawn that morning.

"Well, I don't mind telling you that thanks to a poacher's ghost story, you are off to a fine start as far as folks around here are concerned." The vicar chuckled and then caught himself as his wife threw him a horrified look. He hastily picked up his teacup and cleared his throat. "Beg pardon."

But Lucas was not to be sidetracked. "What ghost story and what poacher, Reverend?"

The vicar's initial uneasiness became visibly more noticeable. It was clear he felt he had already said too much. He coughed slightly. "I fear, sir, that a few of the local men are not above poaching in the woods, especially when times are hard, as they have been lately. Lord knows it's sometimes worth life and limb to do it, what with the mantraps the previous earl set."

"You needn't worry, vicar. Having served in the army and thus been obliged to live off the land occasionally myself, I assure you I am inclined to ignore a little poaching. I have already made arrangements to destroy what mantraps the hunters have not already discovered."

The vicar's smile broke like sunshine on a cloudy

day. "I am extremely happy to hear that. Your uncle, as
you must know, had an entirely different attitude."

"Now about this particular poacher's ghost story,"
Lucas prodded quietly.

The vicar exchanged a quick glance with his wife
and then sighed heavily. "Yes, well, it was just an
amusing tale I happened to overhear this morning. You
know how country folk talk. It seems a certain intrepid
hunter was taking a shortcut home last night when he
caught a glimpse of the Amber Knight and his lady. You
have heard the legend, of course?"

"I am aware of it."

Victoria leaned forward intently. "The Amber Knight
and his lady were seen in the district?"

The vicar's wife laughed nervously. "Right here on
the grounds of the estate, if you please. At least, according to the way the tale was being told this morning.
It seems the knight and his lady were spotted walking
home through the gardens sometime after midnight. Is
that not a delightful notion?"

"Fascinating," Victoria said as the truth began to
crystallize in her head. She pictured how she and Lucas
might have appeared to a startled poacher in the dead
of night, her amber cloak swirling around her. "Walking home through the gardens, you say?" She felt Lucas's quelling glance but chose to ignore him. This was
far too amusing. "What would they have been doing
running around at that time of night, do you suppose?"

Lucas cleared his throat. "Would you pour me another cup of tea, my dear? I seem to find myself rather
thirsty."

"Yes, of course." Victoria laughed at him with her
eyes as she dutifully poured the tea. He gave her a
severe glare in return, which only inspired her to fresh
mischief. "You were saying, Mrs. Worth?"

"Was I? About what they might have been doing
running around at midnight? Oh, dear." The good woman's smile was tentative. "Well, they are ghosts, you
know. I suppose that is the only time they are allowed
to run around. And according to legend, the pair was
very much prone to midnight trysts. It seems the two

had a habit of riding the lands at night and returning to the house shortly before dawn."

The vicar cleared his throat. "That's quite enough speculation about ghosts, my dear. You'll have Lord Stonevale and his lady thinking we deal in nothing but village gossip."

"Never," declared Victoria. "I find it all most interesting, don't you, Stonevale?"

"I find it all a lot of nonsense," Lucas said repressively.

"You must understand," the vicar's wife said hurriedly, "the villagers were thrilled to hear the story. They want to believe it because they want to believe that things really have begun to change for the better around here. According to the legend, Stonevale will prosper again only when the Amber Knight and his lady return. I pray you won't begrudge the people their small tale of hope, my lord."

"Yes." Victoria smiled sweetly at her husband. "Pray, don't be a killjoy, Stonevale."

The vicar and his wife stared in shock at Victoria. Lucas merely gave his wife another quelling glance and drank his tea.

The vicar, apparently sensing that he and his wife had accidentally stumbled into a mild bit of marital teasing, turned a bit ruddier and plowed forth gamely with a change of topic. "Far rather see a couple of harmless ghosts than that highwayman who's been plaguing the district for the past couple of months."

"Highwayman?" Victoria's attention was instantly riveted in a new direction. "What is this about a highwayman? Have you been robbed, Reverend?"

"Not I. And not any of the villagers that I know of. Daresay, none of them would be worth the fellow's time. But there have been reports of a couple of coaches stopped. The villain's a bit inept, I fear. On one occasion the driver of the coach pulled a pistol and sent the highwayman fleeing for the bushes. The second time the passengers fobbed him off with a few coins and a worthless ring."

"Highwaymen usually have a lair in the locality where

they conduct business," Lucas observed thoughtfully. "Do you think this man might be a local resident?"

The vicar shook his head a bit too quickly, looking more uneasy than ever. "I daresay not. Probably just someone riding through. I wouldn't be surprised if the fellow has quit the district by now. In his profession 'tis probably wise to keep shifting business locations." Satisfied that he had salvaged the social situation, the vicar fell back on a safe subject. "I say, Stonevale. Don't mean to be impertinent, but have you given much thought to the sort of crops you'll want to plant? I've lived around here for a number of years now and I have some notion of what does well in this soil."

Mrs. Worth was instantly alarmed. "Really, dear, I am certain his lordship will ask for advice if he requires it."

"Of course, of course." The vicar flushed a dark red. "Sorry about that. Horticulture is a hobby of mine. I fancy myself something of a student of the subject."

Lucas's head came up alertly. "Do you indeed, sir?"

The vicar coughed slightly again, but this time he looked a little more sure of himself. "Pleased to say I've had one or two papers published in the *Botanical Progress*. Working on a book on flower gardening at the moment."

"What do you know about buckwheat?" Lucas asked bluntly, all traces of restlessness vanishing instantly.

"Fine animal fodder. Good for your poorest soil, of course, but I'm more in favor of oats, wheat, and corn where possible."

"I have heard buckwheat can be eaten by humans in times of wheat shortages."

"Only by those who live on the continent. Doubt you'd get an Englishman to eat it unless he was frightfully hungry."

"I see your point. I have also become quite interested in marl as opposed to manure of late," Lucas said. "What is your opinion?"

"As it happens, I have done a bit of investigation on the subject," the vicar said, glowing with enthusiasm. "Tried marl out on my wife's rosebushes. Also peat,

ground bone, and fish. Kept a detailed log. Would you
care to hear the results?"

"I certainly would." Lucas stood up. "Why don't we
go to the library where I have some maps of the estate
we can look at?" He turned belatedly to Victoria. "You
will excuse us, my dear?"

"Of course."

"Come along, vicar, I have several questions to put
to you. Now, about manure. I must admit it has the
advantage of being readily available."

"True. And when one does run short, one can always
have it brought in from London. Several thousand horses
stabled in London, you know. Something has to be
done with all that manure. Have you by any chance
read Humphrey Davy's *Elements of Agricultural Chemistry?*"

"No," said Lucas. "But I did get hold of a copy of
Marshall's *The Rural Economy of Yorkshire.* Marshall is
very fond of marl."

"It has its merits, I'll grant you. I shall loan you my
copy of Davy's *Elements,* if you like. The man takes a
very scientific approach to the subject of manuring. I
believe you will find it most interesting."

"I would appreciate that very much," Lucas said.

The two men moved out of the room, talking intently.

Victoria looked at her guest. "More tea, Mrs. Worth?"

"Thank you, my lady." She gave her hostess an apologetic look. "Please forgive my husband. I fear he is
quite impassioned in his studies of horticulture and
agriculture."

Victoria grinned. "Believe me, he is in good company. My husband's interest has grown just as strong of
late. You may have noticed."

Mrs. Worth relaxed. Her small chuckle was delightful. "I did. Imagine discussing manure in a drawing
room. But, then, that is life in the country."

"It is not altogether different from life at my aunt's
home in London. My aunt is very much interested in
matters of intellectual inquiry and I fear I have followed
in her footsteps. I quite enjoy such discussions."

The vicar's wife beamed enthusiastically. "Perhaps

you and Lord Stonevale would be interested in attending some of the meetings of our local Society for the Investigation of Curious Matters. We meet every week on Monday afternoons in our home. Quite a large crowd attends, I am pleased to say." The good lady suddenly flushed and began to stammer. "Of course our meetings would probably not be of great interest to you. I am certain you are already far ahead of us since you have had the advantages of being in Town."

"Not at all. The prospect of attending your next meeting sounds quite delightful. I shall look forward to it."

Mrs. Worth's smile returned in full force. "How kind of you. I cannot wait to tell my friends."

"You say you grow roses, Mrs. Worth?"

Mrs. Worth began to beam, and said shyly. "They are my passion, I fear."

"I would dearly love to discuss some plans for the gardens here at Stonevale. I cannot live without a proper garden and Lucas is far too busy with farming problems to help me. Would you care to examine the grounds with me?"

"I should be delighted."

"Excellent. And while we're about it, we can get on with our discussion of the most pressing charity needs in the area. In all truth, I am far more anxious to get started on that project than I am the gardens."

The vicar's wife smiled with genuine approval. "It is easy to see why the villagers are so eager to believe their Amber Lady has returned."

Victoria laughed. "You refer to my preference for a certain shade in clothing, I imagine. Pure coincidence, I assure you." She glanced down at her yellow and white afternoon dress with a wry smile.

Mrs. Worth was startled and then embarrassed that her hostess would think she had made such a personal remark. "Oh, no, madam, I was not referring to your lovely dress, although I will allow the color is stunning on you and does create a sort of amber effect. No, I was referring to the legend. It holds that the knight's lady was very kind and gentle."

Victoria wrinkled her nose and grinned. "Then it

cannot have been referring to me. I am certainly no paragon. Just ask my husband."

A week later Victoria sat in front of her dressing-table mirror while Nan finished preparing her for bed. Her maid was handing her a dressing gown when the connecting door between Lucas's room and her own was opened after a perfunctory knock. Lucas sauntered in with a proprietary air that Victoria was learning to expect from him. She glared at him in the mirror and nodded to her maid, who bobbed a small curtsy to Lucas.

"You may go now, Nan. Thank you."

"Yes, ma'am. Shall I have a tea tray sent up?"

Victoria met Lucas's sinfully amused eyes in the mirror and shook her head. "No, thank you, Nan. I will not be wanting any tea tonight."

"Very well, ma'am. Good night to you and yer lordship." She made her way quickly to the door.

Lucas waited until the door had closed behind the maid and then he moved with lazy menace to stand directly behind Victoria. He leaned forward and planted both hands on her dressing table, effectively caging her. His eyes continued to hold hers in the mirror.

Victoria could not repress a small thrill of anticipation. The man had a devastating effect on her senses. And she was learning the power she held over his physical reaction to her. She wondered if it would always be like this between them.

"I saw that a letter arrived from your aunt today." Lucas bent his head to kiss her nape. "What does Lady Nettleship have to say?"

"That it appears as though we are all going to brush through the scandal relatively unscathed." Victoria smiled ruefully, remembering the contents of her aunt's letter. "Thanks to Jessica Atherton, who has put it about that our hasty marriage is the great romance of the Season."

"Good old Jessica." Lucas ran his tongue along the sensitive rim of her ear.

Victoria shuddered. "I swear, Lucas, I do not like being indebted to that woman."

"Nor do I, but as a soldier I long ago learned to accept help from whatever quarter made it available."

"Obviously, or we would not now be in our present position."

"Shrew. You cannot resist such remarks, can you?"

"It is very difficult," Victoria admitted. Her blood was already heating just from the expression in his eyes and his closeness. It struck her that even if someone waved a magic wand and dissolved the marriage tomorrow, she would never be truly free of this man.

"Any other news from your aunt?"

Victoria saw the flicker of intensity in his eyes and knew it had nothing to do with the sensual assault he was launching against her. "Do you mean has she discovered any other objects marked with a 'W'? The answer is no. She also states she still has not found anyone claiming to have lost either the scarf or the snuffbox."

"Does she mention Edgeworth by any chance?"

"No."

"Just as well. Tell me, Vicky, what sort of letter did you write back to your aunt?" Lucas asked.

"I told her about my plans for the gardens and invited her to visit at her earliest convenience. I also mentioned how you and the vicar have discovered a mutual interest in farming techniques, horticulture, and manure. That was about all, I believe. Oh, and I asked her to send me some plant cuttings and seeds."

"What? No discussion of how you have nobly accepted your unhappy fate and have vowed to be a dutiful wife?" He kissed her neck. "No talk of how you have come to recognize that your womanly honor demands you submit yourself to your husband, even though the marital act is, naturally, quite repellent under the circumstances?" He nibbled on her earlobe. "No mention of how bravely you endure the performance of your duties in the marriage bed?" He kissed the curve of her shoulder. "No pathetic little commentary on how you have been made to pay the price of your folly and what a lesson this has all been to you?"

She shot to her feet and whirled around, pummeling

him unmercifully in the ribs. "Stonevale, you are a miserable, teasing beast of a husband and you deserve to rot."

"My leg, my leg. Cease and desist at once, madam, or you'll ruin me for life." Lucas retreated toward the bed, his laughter filling the bedroom.

"To hell with your leg." She continued her attack, closing in on him, forcing him back until he toppled onto the bed. Then she jumped on top of him, straddling him triumphantly. Lucas held up his hands in surrender.

"I beg for mercy, my lady. Would you continue to beat on a helpless man who is already down?"

"You may be down but you are far from helpless, Stonevale. You still have the use of your mouth and it seems to me that is what got you into trouble in the first place tonight. You could not resist taunting me in a most villainous fashion, could you?"

His smile was slow and filled with sensual promise. "Allow me to put my mouth to better use, madam."

He reached up with one hand and splayed his strong fingers around the back of her head. Then he dragged her face down to his and captured her lips with his own.

With a soft sigh Victoria gave herself up to the magic of her husband's embrace.

14

Lucas knew he had only himself to blame when the gossamer web of domestic harmony he was just starting to weave was ripped to shreds on the following Monday morning.

He should have seen it coming, he told himself. He should have been prepared. He, who always prided himself on his sense of strategy and planning, had been caught off guard, and there was no excuse.

But his wife's timing was as good as that of any field marshal who has studied the opponent well.

She breezed into the library, waving the newest letter from her aunt, just at the very moment Lucas was going through a detailed summary of her investments for the past three years.

"There you are, Lucas, I have been looking for you. No, do not bother to get up. I just wanted to tell you I shall be writing a fairly large draft on my account to cover an investment I plan to make soon. I assumed you would want to take it into consideration when you plan your own expenditures this month."

Lucas sat down again and looked up, his mind still

reeling from the shock of what he had learned recently about Victoria's investment habits. She smiled brightly at him from the other side of the massive desk, looking as elegant and vibrant as ever in a sun yellow morning gown.

"How large a sum will you be needing and what sort of investment are you considering?" he asked cautiously.

"Oh, I should think a few thousand pounds will be enough to get me into this particular investment."

"A few *thousand?*"

"Perhaps ten or fifteen." She glanced down at the letter in her hand. "Aunt Cleo says the group will be investing in some new collieries in Lancashire."

"Ten or fifteen thousand pounds? For a coal production project in Lancashire?" Lucas was stunned. "You cannot possibly mean to do anything so foolish. I cannot allow you to do it."

It was when he saw the light of battle flare in her beautiful eyes that Lucas knew he had just made a serious, tactical mistake.

"Our man of affairs, Mr. Beckford, has recently recommended the project very strongly," Victoria said. "Aunt Cleo writes that she intends to invest, herself."

"Your aunt is free to do as she chooses, but I cannot allow you to pour that amount of money into a coal pit in Lancashire. One can go through a fortune very quickly investing in collieries."

"I have a fortune, Lucas, remember?" she asked far too sweetly. "You married me for it."

Lucas tried to forge a path out of the mire in which he found himself. "Your inheritance is sizable, my dear, but it is not inexhaustible. Far from it. You are intelligent enough to realize that. You do not have enough money to warrant taking risks of ten or fifteen thousand pounds. Sums of that size should be put into acquiring land, not digging expensive pits in the ground."

"But I already own some properties in London from which I receive a very nice income. And," she added, with a challenging smile, "I am now a partner with you in owning a good-sized chunk of Yorkshire. I do not wish to acquire any more land, Lucas."

Lucas returned to the accounting summary and said, very matter-of-factly, "Then you can put the money into the improvements we will be needing here at Stonevale."

"You are busy enough as it is spending a great deal of my money on such improvements. This colliery project is a personal investment I wish to make on my own behalf."

"Vicky, trust me on this matter. Collieries are risky investments, especially when they are being run by others. If you are seriously interested in mining, we can think about having an engineer survey Stonevale. There is coal in Yorkshire as well as other minerals and there may be some worth going after on the estate. But I cannot allow you to throw your money into a distant project over which we will have no management control."

Victoria marched to the library desk and threw the letter down. "You are going to forbid me the right to spend my money as I wish?"

Lucas prayed for divine guidance but there was none forthcoming. He would have to deal with the devilish question on his own and he already knew he was damned either way.

He tried to choose his next words with care. "You have come to me with a large income that must be protected for the sake of our children and our grandchildren and their children. As your husband it is my duty to guide you in your investments."

"I thought so," Victoria announced grimly. "This is how it always starts, I imagine. One's husband begins by telling his wife that she is incompetent to manage her own affairs and that she must allow him to do it for her. From there he moves to take complete control, allowing her no say whatsoever in how her money is spent."

That angered him. Lucas gestured impatiently at the account book lying open on the desk. "To be perfectly blunt, my dear, I am not certain you should be making all your own decisions. You seem to have a tendency to take great risks in your financial affairs. You have been in deep water more than once."

"I have always come about," she shot back. "As you can plainly see if you look at my current income."

"Yes, thanks to your properties in Town. You see, Vicky? It is the investments in land that are most reliable. They are what shelter an inheritance such as yours. You have no business taking risks in the funds or in shipping and distant mining projects."

"No business taking risks? That is ludicrous coming from you. Before you married me, your entire income came from taking risks. What can be more risky than the battlefield or the gaming tables?"

The fact that she had a point only served to annoy him further. "Damn it, Vicky, I had no choice in how I made my money. I did what I had to do. But matters have changed. We both have a responsibility to manage Stonevale and the income you brought to this marriage as wisely as possible. Your days of taking huge risks with your capital are over."

She stepped forward and planted both hands on his desk. Her eyes shimmered with fury. "Say it in plain language, Stonevale. I want us both to hear you say it."

"I do not know how much plainer I can make it."

"Tell me very clearly that you are forbidding me to spend my money in any way I wish. Let us have the words plain between us."

His own temper leapt to match hers. "You are deliberately trying to set a trap for me, Vicky. You want me to choose between saying the words that will give you complete freedom and the ones that will damn me as just another tyrannical husband like the man who married your mother. Do you think you can manipulate me so easily, madam?"

"I am not trying to manipulate you. It is just the reverse. You are trying to manipulate me." Victoria's tone was unwavering under his severe gaze.

"I am trying to protect you from your own reckless nature."

"Reckless? You call me reckless? You, who made your living first as a soldier and then as a gamester? Hah. That is an excuse and well you know it. You want complete control of my money and you are telling me you will no longer allow me any say in how I spend it. What's next, Lucas? Will you force me to accept a small quarterly allowance? Will I be obliged to buy all my clothes and paints and books and the occasional horse out of whatever you choose to allow me by way of an income?"

That did it. He lost what was left of his temper. "Why not? If you are going to play the role of a frivolous, spendthrift woman who doesn't give a thought to economy, I shall have no choice but to treat you as such. But we both know you are too smart to act that way just to spite me."

"Are you forbidding me the free use of my money?"

"I am forbidding you to risk a vast sum on a project you know nothing about except that your aunt's man of affairs recommends it."

"I have made a great deal of money from some of Mr. Beckford's recommendations."

"You have also lost money on some of them. I have seen the evidence in your accounts. Mr. Beckford has been far from infallible," Lucas said, flipping recklessly through Victoria's business ledger.

"One must expect to take a few losses when one is playing for important stakes."

"There are many men far wealthier than you who have brought their families to ruin with that attitude."

"Say it, damn you. Say the words, Lucas. Tell me to my face I no longer have any control over my inheritance."

Lucas gave up trying to salvage the situation. "Vicky, I thought I had made it clear that just because I choose to indulge you in some of your wilder notions, it does not mean I will allow you to manipulate me whenever you wish. One way or another you will learn that."

"Say it, Lucas." Her eyes continued to challenge him boldly and her smile was deliberately taunting.

Lucas swore very softly. "Very well, madam, since you are obviously determined to force this issue into a full-scale battle, I will give you what you seem to be looking for, namely an opponent. You are hereby forbidden to invest in the colliery project. I shall instruct your bankers that you are to be given a small quarterly allowance and nothing more unless I personally authorize it."

She stared at him in stunned amazement, clearly shocked by the extent of his retaliation. "I do not believe this. You cannot possibly mean what you say. To forbid me to invest in the coal-mining project is one thing, but to forbid me any use of my money at all is . . . is unbelievable."

Lucas leaned back in his chair and studied her dispassionately. She really did look taken aback. This was obviously not the outcome she had expected when she had begun the skirmish.

"I can understand your surprise," he said gently. "I am quite certain that when you walked in here a few minutes ago, you were fairly sure you would walk out the victor. You are too shrewd to have launched the assault without first being convinced you stood a good chance of winning. But you underestimated me, my dear, and I fear you will persist in losing these skirmishes if you do not stop doing that. A good field marshal never makes the mistake of underestimating her opponent."

"You speak as if we are on a battlefield."

Lucas nodded bleakly. "I fear that is precisely the situation you have created."

"And to think I actually thought you were going to make a tolerable husband after all." She whirled around and flew to the door. Not pausing to give him a chance to get there ahead of her, she yanked it open.

"Where do you think you are going, Vicky?"

"Out." Her smile could have separated him from his skin.

"Vicky, if you think you can fly off in a tantrum and go looking for some mischief, you are sadly mistaken."

"Have no fear, my lord, I shall be in quite unexceptional company. I am attending a meeting at the vicar's. I'll wager that even you, with your newfound proper, conservative airs and priggish ways, cannot find anything to say against my spending the afternoon in such a gathering."

"What sort of society is holding this meeting?"

"One devoted to the investigation of curious matters," she retorted loftily.

"I might be able to find time to accompany you," he began carefully.

"Good gracious, Lucas, that is quite impossible. I am certain you are far too busy to join me. You have so many thoughtful, important decisions to make right here." She went out the door, slamming it pointedly behind her.

Lucas winced as the lamps shivered under the impact. He sat in silence for a moment and then got deliberately to his feet to cross the room and pour himself a glass of brandy.

He stood at the window to drink it and told himself morosely that it was going to be a long campaign. He had sadly deluded himself when he had decided the difficult part would be over once he got her to marry him. It was obvious the truly hard work came after the wedding.

Good God. Had he really turned a touch priggish under the weight of his newfound responsibilities? He wondered.

Victoria was still fuming by the time she reached the comfortable home of the vicar and his wife. But she managed a charming smile as she was shown into a pleasant, sunny room full of various members of the local gentry and their ladies. The welcome was gratifyingly warm and her ill humor faded quickly.

"Welcome to our little society meeting, Lady Stonevale. We have all been concentrating our attentions of late on trying to prepare an improved remedy for gout and rheumatic pains," Mrs. Worth explained after the introductions had been made. She waved to a table full of small glasses. Each contained a liquid. "Medicinal herbs and plants are a great interest for most of us. Sir Alfred, here, for example, is quite hopeful of claiming the Society of Arts' prize for discovering a means of increasing opium-poppy production in England. He has obtained a very high-quality product, indeed."

"How exciting," Victoria said. "You should feel quite proud of yourself, Sir Alfred."

Sir Alfred blushed modestly.

"And Dr. Thornby over there has been experimenting with various tinctures and decoctions that combine alcohol and other ingredients such as liquorice, rhubarb, and camomile."

It was Dr. Thornby's turn to be flushed with pride.

"Fascinating," Victoria murmured, examining the various glasses. "My aunt and I have attended many medical lectures on such matters. Have you had much success?"

"As you know," Dr. Thornby began with barely contained enthusiasm, "the combination of alcohol and opium in laudanum is quite effective for pain relief but tends to make the sufferer extremely drowsy. This is fine for certain ailments but not for more chronic problems such as gout or rheumatic pains or certain, ahem, women's ailments. Something is needed for these which brings relief but does not induce sleep."

"You want a pain-relieving concoction that will allow the sufferer to go about his daily routine," Victoria said with a quick nod of understanding. "Very important research. Very important, indeed."

"The farmers and laborers in my area of the country have achieved some success on their own through trial and error," remarked a plump gentleman in the corner. "They've developed some excellent remedies."

"The problem," said another, "is lack of standardization and analysis. Every family has its own remedies of course, but each recipe has been handed down for generations and is the result of tradition and folklore rather than proper scientific principles and study. Every housewife has her particular recipe for cough syrup, for example, but no two mixtures are quite the same."

"Obviously there are several aspects of the problem to be studied," Victoria noted.

"Quite true." Dr. Thornby approached the table. "But there is only one scientific approach to the problem.

We must conduct an experiment and take careful notes. Each of these glasses contains a particular remedy. Our goal today is to see which of them creates an immediately soothing effect without bringing on sleep."

"What about the actual relief of pain?" Victoria asked with deep interest. "How will you measure that? I am not, myself, suffering even a headache at the moment."

"We will have to do that in a second phase of the experiment," the vicar conceded. "Difficult to find five or ten people all having an attack of the gout or a headache at the same time, I'm afraid."

"As it happens," Mrs. Worth said helpfully, "I have a touch of rheumatic pain this afternoon."

"And my gout's been flaring up," another member of the group offered.

"I have been suffering from toothache all day," declared an elderly gentleman.

"I do believe I have a headache," Lady Alice volunteered.

The vicar brightened, as did Dr. Thornby and Sir Alfred.

"Excellent, excellent. We may be able to accomplish both phases of the experiment today." Sir Alfred's glance was both shy and distinctly hopeful as he looked at Victoria. "Understand you have an interest in this sort of thing, Lady Stonevale. Would you care to join us in our testing or would you prefer to observe?"

"Heavens, it is always far more interesting to participate in an experiment than to merely observe it. I should greatly enjoy helping you test your concoctions. It should prove most enlightening."

Sir Alfred was much flattered, as was everyone else in the room. Dr. Thornby stepped forward to take charge again. "Now then, I shall put the notebook here on the table and each of us must write a clear, concise description of our sensations as we proceed from glass to glass. I propose we each start with straight brandy first and record our reactions to it before we move on to the various tonic mixtures."

"Yes, of course," the vicar exclaimed. "We need to

be able to judge the differences between the pure spirits and the spirits infused with other ingredients. Very clever of you, Thornby."

Victoria frowned consideringly as a thought struck her. "Might it not be best if at least one of us stayed with the pure spirits for the entire experiment? That way the reactions of those using the various concoctions can be judged against the use of spirits alone at every point."

There were several immediate nods of approval.

"Brilliant idea, your ladyship," Sir Alfred said. "You are obviously quite conversant with such scientific investigation techniques."

"I have had some experience," Victoria admitted modestly. "As it was my idea and as I have no particular physical complaint to alleviate this afternoon, I shall volunteer to stick with the spirits alone."

"Very helpful of you, Lady Stonevale. Very helpful, indeed," Dr. Thornby said. "Let us begin." He graciously extended a glass of brandy to Victoria.

Lucas was appalled at the sight that greeted him that afternoon when he returned from a visit to one of his tenants. A very unsteady Victoria was being assisted up the front steps by her maid and two very concerned footmen. Lucas threw his horse's reins at the groom and hurried forward.

"My God, what is the matter here? Are you ill, Vicky?" He peered at her with deep concern.

"Oh, hello, Lucas." She turned a beatific smile upon him and nearly lost her balance in the process. "Did you enjoy being a cautious, conservative prig all day? I have spent my time this afternoon in a far more useful fashion. I have been conducting a little . . ." She paused to burp discreetly. "A little experiment."

A spicy cloud of brandy fumes wafted past Lucas's nose. He glared at the anxious maid as the truth dawned on him. "I will take care of her ladyship," he announced in a voice laced with steel.

"Yes, my lord. I'll run have cook prepare some nice tea for her ladyship."

"Don't bother," Lucas growled as he caught Victoria around the waist.

He got her past the anxious gazes of the butler, two more footmen, and a couple of housemaids, and finally, he got her up the stairs and into bed. As she sprawled gracefully back on her pillows, Victoria smiled once more and regarded him with a dreamy gaze.

"Lucas, dear, you really must learn not to look so frightfully menacing. You do have a nasty habit of glaring, you know."

"What the devil have you been drinking?"

She frowned. "Let me see. Brandy, for the most part, I believe. Did I explain about the experiment?"

"Not precisely, but we can go into the details later."

"Oh, dear, does that mean another lecture?"

"Yes, I am afraid it does, Vicky," Lucas said grimly. "I will tolerate a great deal from you, my dear, but I will not have you coming home foxed in the middle of the afternoon, and that is final."

"I believe you will have to read me the lecture later, Lucas. I do not feel very well at the moment." Victoria turned on her side and grabbed wildly for the chamber pot under the bed.

Lucas sighed and held her head. She was right. The lecture would have to wait.

As it turned out, the lecture was put off until the following morning. Victoria tried to avoid it entirely by waking late and announcing she would take tea in her room. But a maid arrived shortly after nine with a request from Lucas that his wife attend him in his library at ten.

Victoria briefly considered the odds of getting out of the nasty business altogether by claiming to be still indisposed from the effects of the scientific experiment, but the pragmatic side of her nature interfered.

May as well get the thing over and done, she told herself as she got slowly out of bed. She scowled as a faint headache flared behind her eyes. At least her stomach was stable again. When her maid appeared with tea, Victoria drank the entire pot and felt somewhat better.

She chose the brightest yellow and white morning gown in her wardrobe and dressed as carefully as if she were going out for a formal visit before she headed reluctantly downstairs.

Lucas rose from behind his wide desk, scanning her face carefully as she entered the room.

"Please sit down, Vicky. I must admit you are looking none the worse for wear. I congratulate you on your excellent constitution. I know several men who would be in a much less viable condition after the sort of 'experiment' you engaged in yesterday afternoon."

"Scientific progress exacts a certain toll," Victoria said with dignity as she sat down. "I am proud that I have made some small contribution to the welfare of mankind."

"A contribution to the welfare of mankind?" Lucas's mouth twitched. "Is that what you call it? You came home thoroughly cup-shot in the middle of the day and you tell me it was all in the name of intellectual inquiry?"

"I have done far more risky things in the name of intellectual inquiry," Victoria retorted meaningfully. "Only consider the fact that I am married to a man who will not even let me spend my own money as I see fit. And all because I fell victim to the dangers of another sort of experiment."

His mouth hardened into a grim line. "Do not try to deflect me by hurling old accusations. It is your behavior yesterday that is under consideration here. What, precisely, were you doing at the vicar's?"

"Sampling medicinal drafts in order to log their various effects," Victoria informed him, her chin at a haughty angle. Just let him dare to find fault with such a pure, scientific investigation, she thought wrathfully.

"And those medicinal drafts were all based on brandy?"

"No, of course not. Some of the herbs were dissolved in ale and not a few were infused with sherry and claret. We were not certain which spirits mixed best with the herbs, you see."

"Good Lord. How many glasses of this experiment did you drink?"

Victoria massaged her temples. The headache was getting worse. "I do not remember precisely, but I am sure it is all carefully recorded in Dr. Thornby's book of experiments."

"The vicar and his wife were involved in this?"

"Well, actually, I fear Mrs. Worth dozed off quite early on," Victoria said placatingly. "And the vicar had a rather large dose of one of the concoctions and went into a corner to sit facing the wall for the duration of the experiment."

"I dread to ask what concoctions you swallowed."

Victoria brightened. "Oh, I stuck with pure spirits the entire time, Lucas. Mine was the standard by which the effects of the other mixtures were judged. It was a very important part of the experiment."

Lucas swore softly and fell silent. The ticking of the tall clock grew very loud in the room. Victoria began to get restless.

"I fear I shall have to lay down yet another rule for you, madam," Lucas said at last.

"I was afraid of that." She wanted to fight back but her head was hurting too much. She could not seem to generate any enthusiasm for the conflict. She just wanted to retreat to her bed and lie down.

Lucas ignored her morose expression, but his voice was surprisingly gentle when he explained the new rule. "Henceforth, you will not engage in any further scientific experiments without my approval. Is that quite clear?"

"As usual, you have made yourself excruciatingly clear, my lord." Victoria rose, her head high. "Marriage is a rather dull business for a female, is it not? No adventuring, no intellectual inquiry, no freedom to spend one's money as one sees fit. I wonder how women survive it for a lifetime without expiring from sheer boredom."

She got up and went out the door.

Lucas lay in bed that night and watched the moon

through his window. There had been no sound from
Victoria's room since something large and heavy had
been dragged in front of the connecting door an hour
ago.

He had listened to her barricade herself in her bedchamber with some annoyance. He did not like the idea
of her pushing heavy objects around unaided. At the
very least, she should have asked a servant to do the
job. But she had no doubt been too embarrassed to
have a footman or her maid participate in the small act
of defiance.

On the other hand, the show of spirit was a good
sign, he told himself. She was obviously feeling much
better than she had that morning. Things were getting
back to normal.

Normal, that is, if life with Vicky could ever be
termed such.

Lucas shoved aside the covers and got to his feet.

The strategist in him knew that there had been no
way to avoid the recent confrontations. Some battles
were unavoidable, and when those arose, a man could
do nothing except hunker down and fight.

Victoria had still not fully accepted the marriage. She
was an independent, headstrong creature who had been
allowed free rein for too long. Her own intelligence, her
gentle instincts, and her desire not to jeopardize
her aunt's position in Society had acted as controls
until he had come along.

But now Lucas knew she saw him as the one who
stood in her way, the one who threatened her independence. She was torn between her feelings for him and
her anger at being trapped in the marriage.

Lucas remembered all the males who had danced
attendance on her in London, and groaned. She was
accustomed to keeping men in their place, accustomed
to being the one in command.

But he sensed, even if she did not, that one of the
reasons she had been initially fascinated with him was
the very fact that she could not be quite certain of her
ability to control him. She was a strong woman who
needed a man who was even stronger.

Having found him, she could not resist testing him.

He was sorry open warfare had broken out. But Lucas knew that now that the battle lines had been drawn, he could not give in and allow Victoria her own way or there would be hell to pay in the future.

Life had changed drastically for both of them. He had to make her understand that. They had future generations to think about now, not just their own lives. An estate such as Stonevale was meant to be held in trust for one's descendants. It was an investment in the future, not just the present.

Those descendants would carry Victoria's blood as well as his own, Lucas told himself. She had as large a stake in this land as he did. Neither of them could continue to go on in the rather reckless fashion they had indulged before the marriage.

Good God. He really was starting to sound quite priggish.

For all either of them knew, the next generation of Colebrooks might be on its way. The image of Victoria growing round and ripe with his babe sent a savage thrill of satisfaction through him.

Lucas scowled again, thinking of how she had pushed a very heavy object in front of her door. He could not allow her to do that sort of thing, not now when she might be pregnant. She belonged to him and he would take care of her whether she liked it or not.

But first he had to find a way to breach her bristling defenses. Lucas thought of the cacti in Lady Nettleship's garden and smiled. Then he went to the wardrobe and took out a shirt and a pair of breeches.

Victoria saw him the moment he appeared on the ledge outside her window, a dark, dangerous, masculine shape against the silvered night. This was no nightmare image. This was Lucas. She knew now she had been waiting for him.

It was inconceivable that he would let a little thing like her dressing table lodged against the connecting door stop him. She sat up and hugged her knees as the dark figure on the ledge opened her window and stepped into her bedchamber. He was fully dressed.

"Ah, so it was the dressing table," Lucas remarked calmly, glancing toward the connecting door. "You really should not be moving heavy objects about like that, my dear. Next time ask for assistance."

"Will there be a next time?" she asked softly, aware of the challenge that hung between them.

"Probably." He paced forward to stand at the foot of her bed. "I fear we are destined to quarrel occasionally, my sweet. Given your reckless ways and my lamentably dull, plodding ones, it is inevitable."

"Dull and plodding is not how I would describe you, Lucas. I think the terms 'arrogant, domineering, and stubborn' suit you far better."

"And priggish?"

"I regret to say it, but yes, priggish is beginning to suit you nicely."

He wrapped a hand around the bedpost and smiled ruefully. " 'Tis a relief, of course, to know you do not think so badly of me, after all."

She tensed. "Lucas, if you believe for one moment that you can sneak in here in the dead of night and claim your husbandly privileges, you are wrong. If you try to get into this bed, I will scream the house down."

"I doubt that. You would not want to humiliate either me or yourself in front of the servants. In any event you sadly misjudge me, madam, if you think I would be so foolish as to deal with your temper in such a fashion. But, then, I have warned you before that you have a habit of underestimating me."

She eyed him warily. "What do you plan to do?"

He glanced away from her, looking back over his shoulder to where the open curtains rippled in the night air. "The night beckons, madam, and you have always been one to answer the summons. Have you ever gone riding at midnight?"

She stared at him. "Are you serious?"

"Never more so."

"You would take me riding at this hour?"

"Yes."

"This is a trick, is it not? You are trying to disarm me, trying to make me forget my anger at your high-handedness."

"Yes."

"You do not even deny it?"

He shrugged eloquently. "Why should I? 'Tis the truth."

"Then I should refuse your offer."

His wicked grin flashed in the shadows. "The question is not should you, but can you?"

He knew her far too well, she realized. She chewed thoughtfully on her lip. Going with him was no capitulation. She would merely be taking advantage of a glorious opportunity for adventure. *Riding in the moonlight*. It sounded wonderful. Besides, although her headache had disappeared several hours earlier, she had been unable to get to sleep.

"You will get the wrong notion if I choose to accompany you," she said.

"Will I?"

She nodded grimly. "You will think I have forgiven you for your recent treatment of me."

"I am not so foolish as to think you would forgive me so easily."

"Good. Because I will not."

"I understand," he said gravely.

"You are not to view it as some sort of surrender."

"You make yourself quite clear," Lucas assured her.

Victoria hesitated a second longer and then leapt out of bed and dashed to the closet to find the breeches she had worn on their midnight adventures in London.

"Turn around," she ordered as she tugged off her nightclothes.

"Why? I have seen you naked several times now." He lounged against the bedpost, arms folded across his chest. "And I have been curious to see how you go about getting into a pair of men's breeches."

She glared at him and carried her clothing across the

room to where the privacy screen stood. "You are no gentleman, Lucas," she announced as she went behind the screen and began struggling into the breeches.

"You would be bored by a gentleman. Admit it, Vicky."

"I admit nothing."

Ten minutes later, wearing an amber scarf around her throat and a hooded cloak over her breeches and shirt, Victoria stood outside the stables with a bridle in her hand and watched as Lucas quickly saddled her mare and a sleepy-looking George.

"I only hope I do not live to regret this," Lucas said as he handed her up onto her mount.

"It is too late for second thoughts." She picked up her reins, enjoying the rare freedom of riding astride. "And I like you best when you are going against your better judgment, Lucas. Let us be off."

"Slowly," he called after her as he swung up into the saddle. "It is the middle of the night, Vicky. Have a care where you guide your mare. Stick to the lane."

"But I would like to ride through the woods," she protested.

"I cannot be certain all the mantraps have been removed yet," he told her. "So we will stay on the road."

She was feeling too exhilarated to argue further. Just being out on horseback in the moonlight was ample adventure for now. She turned her horse toward the main drive and George fell good-naturedly into step beside her mare.

There was silence for several minutes as they walked the horses beneath the canopy of trees that lined the approach to Stonevale. Lucas spoke eventually.

"I have been talking to the vicar about planting some more trees. Oak or elm, perhaps. The timber would be an excellent investment for our children or our grandchildren."

"Lucas, I do not wish to speak about investments of any kind tonight," Victoria said rather forcefully.

"What about the future? Would you like to talk about that?"

Her hands tightened on the reins. "Not particularly."

His voice gentled. "Has it occurred to you that you might even now be carrying my babe?"

"It is not something I want to think about."

"Do you find the subject so terrifying, then? I am surprised at you, Vicky. You are no coward, of that I am certain."

"Did you bring me out here to discuss your heir, my lord? Because, if so, we may as well turn back now."

He was silent for a moment. "Do you hate me so much that you do not even want to bear my child?"

"*I do not hate you*," she stormed, feeling pressed. "That is not the point."

"I am greatly relieved to hear that."

Victoria sighed. "I simply do not want to talk about your heir tonight or any other night until we have settled this matter that stands between us."

"The only thing that stands between us is your pride and your fear of losing your independence. Does it make you feel any better to know that you are not the only one who is no longer free?"

She slid him a sidelong glance. "You are referring to yourself, sir?"

"Yes."

"You seem free enough to me."

"Look around you, Vicky. I lost whatever freedom I enjoyed the day I inherited Stonevale. I am tied to this land and my responsibilities to our descendants for the rest of my life."

"And you are a man who will always fulfill your responsibilities, regardless of what comes." She studied the road between her mare's ears, thinking about her own words.

"I will do my best, Vicky, even when some of those responsibilities are not to your liking. But I would have you remember, even in the midst of our battles, that what I do, I do because I truly think it is best for us and for our future. I do not set myself against you lightly." He smiled. "Believe me, it requires far too much effort to do battle with you for me to waste my time and energy on minor skirmishes. I much prefer to indulge you whenever possible."

She was indignant. "Indulge me? You think you indulge me? You have a vastly overrated opinion of your own actions, my lord."

He motioned toward their midnight surroundings. "Look around you, my dear. What other man of your acquaintance would drag himself out of a warm bed at this hour merely to entertain you?"

She felt a grin tug at her mouth. There was something about being out with Lucas at this hour of night that always had a euphoric effect on her senses. At the moment she could no longer even summon up the hot anger she had nursed all day. "Well, as to that, my lord, I am not precisely certain just what other men of my acquaintance would humor me so. I have not had a chance to do a proper survey, you see. Perhaps if I started asking about, I would turn up one or two other noble types who would indulge me in this minor fashion."

"If I catch you doing such a survey, I will see to it that you do not sit a horse comfortably for a week."

Her amusement faded at once. "So much for your indulgence, my lord."

"I have limits, madam. And I fear you must learn to tolerate them."

"I have a dressing table I can continue to push in front of my door every night," Victoria warned.

Lucas smiled confidently. "The ledge that leads from my window to yours is wide enough to provide a safe path, even on moonless nights. But I warn you, madam, if you oblige me to use it in foul weather, I cannot guarantee to be in a particularly indulgent mood by the time I arrive at your window."

"But you will, nevertheless, arrive at my window?"

"You may count on that, my sweet. It is as certain as sunrise."

Victoria risked another sidelong glance and saw that he was watching her with eyes that reflected the moonlight. Her whole body responded to the irresistible power he held over her. He wanted her and he made no effort to hide it. It gave her a sense of her own power and it also made her light-headed with excitement.

At that moment her horse nickered softly.

"Lucas, I . . ."

"Hush." He reined in his horse and reached across to halt her mare. His sensual flirtation had turned to acute alertness.

Instinctively she kept her voice low. "What is it?"

"It seems we are not alone out here," he said. "Hurry. Into the trees."

She did not argue. Obediently she followed his stallion into the woods at the side of the road. They sat watching the moonlit lane from the shelter of the trees.

"Who are we hiding from?" she asked very softly.

"I'm not yet certain, but I can think of only one other person who might have business at midnight on this road."

"The highwayman." Victoria was suddenly breathless. "He has not left the district, after all. Lucas, how exciting. I have never seen a real highwayman."

"For which you should be very grateful, madam. I suppose I have no one but myself to blame for the fact that you might see one now."

Victoria heard the clip-clop of a horse's hooves in the distance. A moment later a dark figure riding what appeared to be a bulky-looking plow horse rounded the bend. The highwayman was dressed in a somewhat tattered-looking black cape. He had a scarf across the lower portion of his face.

As he came down the lane Victoria saw that he was impatiently kicking his horse's rounded sides. The rider's urgent voice carried clearly on the night air.

"Hurry it up, ye good-fer-nothin' nag. Do ye think we've got all night? That carriage will be here any minute now. Move, damn your fat sides."

The horse continued to plod stolidly along until the rider turned it and guided it into the woods on the opposite side of the road.

Victoria realized that she and Lucas were trapped on this side of the road. They could not move out onto the lane until the highwayman, or whoever he was, chose to leave the vicinity. Beside her, she thought she heard the softest of disgusted oaths from Lucas. But before she could catch his attention to see how he intended to get them out of this fix, the rattle of coach wheels shattered the stillness.

It seemed they were to be a witness to the local highwayman's latest piece of business.

A few seconds later the coach, a staid old vehicle pulled by an equally elderly team, rounded the bend in the lane and rumbled forward at a stately pace.

The highwayman urged his horse out of the trees and into the middle of the road. He brandished a large pistol.

"Halt," he yelled loudly. "Stand and deliver."

There was a startled cry from the coachman, who immediately began sawing on the reins to pull the slowly cantering horses to a halt.

"Here now," the coachman called uneasily. "What's all this?"

"Ye heard me, man. Tell your passengers to stand and deliver or it'll be the worse for all o' ye."

Lucas sighed. "Well, we cannot have this sort of nonsense going on around here. Stay right where you are, Vicky. Do not come out of these trees until I call you out. Understood?"

She realized he intended to halt the robbery. "I can help you."

"You will do no such thing. Do not move from this spot. That's an order, Vicky."

Without waiting for her response, he removed a pistol from his pocket and rode out onto the lane behind the highwayman.

15

"That'll be enough of that now. Hand over the pistol before someone gets hurt, lad."

Lucas's voice was the amazingly calm and overwhelmingly commanding one he used only rarely but always to great effect. It was definitely a tone that compelled instant obedience. Victoria was impressed in spite of herself.

The highwayman whipped around in his saddle. "What the devil . . . ? Damme, who are you? This is my coach. Go find yerself another one. I got no intention o' sharin' it with the likes o' ye."

"You misunderstand, lad. I don't want the coach. I'm in another line of work myself. Now hand over the pistol."

"Who be ye?" There was a quaver in the highwayman's voice now. "Who be ye, mister? Ye cannot be the ghost they been sayin' 'as come back. Ye cannot be."

"The pistol, if you please." Lucas sharpened his tone just slightly and the pistol was instantly dropped into his outstretched palm. "Wise lad. Now let us see to the passengers."

At that instant the coachman, no doubt under the impression he was suddenly facing two highwaymen instead of one, saw his chance and leapt from his box, sprinting for the bushes.

A piercing scream rose from the inside of the coach as one of the passengers apparently looked out the window and realized the coachman was abandoning his charges.

The team of horses started violently at the shriek of dismay and leapt forward, reins flapping wildly.

"Bloody hell." Lucas made a futile grab for one of the horses as the coach surged past him.

In that instant the highwayman saw his opportunity and drove his heels violently into his plump mount. The animal bolted in fright and broke into a heavy canter down the road in the opposite direction in which the coach was going.

Another scream soared through the open window of the coach. Victoria saw Lucas turn his horse to chase after the coach and she wasted no more time. The vehicle was much closer to her than it was to Lucas now and the highwayman was clearly bent on escape.

She urged her mare quickly out onto the road. "I've got it, Lucas. Don't let him get away." She cantered her mare up alongside one of the elderly coach horses and reached down for the reins. The animal began to slow immediately as if vastly relieved to be back under human control.

"For God's sake be careful," Lucas yelled. But it was obvious the coach had already come to a safe halt. He spun his horse around in the other direction and went after the lumbering plow horse.

Victoria patted the sweating neck of the coach horse and glanced back in time to see that it was going to be no contest between Lucas's blooded stallion and the farm horse. The highwayman did not stand a chance.

She collected the reins of the coach horses and pulled the hood of her cloak back up over her head so that her face was in deep shadow. "It is all right," she called to the missing coachman. "You can come out now. You are in no danger. Take charge of your team, if you please, my good man."

An elderly, diminutive woman wearing a turban stuck her head out the coach window. "Good heavens, you're a female, ain't you? Whatever is the world coming to allowing women to run around in the middle of the night in breeches? You should be ashamed of yourself, young woman."

Victoria grinned. "Yes, ma'am," she said in her demurest accents. "My husband holds much the same opinion as yourself."

"And just where is your husband, pray tell?"

Victoria nodded down the road to where Lucas was leading a dejected-looking highwayman back toward the coach. "That's him there, ma'am. He's caught your highwayman for you."

"Heavens, I don't want him." The woman leaned back into the coach and spoke to her companion, who appeared to be having a quiet fit of hysterics. "Martha, do stop that infernal noise and call John Coachman. I believe he ran off into the woods. One simply cannot rely upon staff these days."

"I be right here, ma'am," the coachman called, emerging hastily from the brush. "I was just waitin' me chance to get the bleeder." He glanced suspiciously at Victoria, who tossed him the reins. "You sure you ain't about to rob us?"

"No, I am not about to rob you."

"For pity's sake, does she look like a highwayman?" The elderly woman leaned her head back out the window and glowered at her coachman as he took control of the team. "She's a female dressed in men's breeches and she ought to be thoroughly ashamed of herself. Imagine a woman of decent breeding running around like that on horseback in the middle of the night. If her husband had any sense, he'd beat her."

Lucas rode up with his captive in tow in time to hear that last remark. "I promise you, madam, I will take your advice under consideration."

The woman switched her attention immediately to him. "You being her husband, I take it? What in heaven's name do you think you're doing letting her run about like this?"

Lucas smiled. "Trying to keep up with her, and I assure you, it is not easy. Are you and your companion all right?"

"Quite all right, thank you very much. We are late coming back from the home of friends. A mistake I shall not make again. What are you going to do with him?" She nodded toward the drooping highwayman, who was still wearing his scarf as a mask.

"Well, as to that," Lucas began thoughtfully, "I suppose I ought to turn him over to the proper authorities."

There was a whimper of protest from the highwayman, but that was all.

"Yes, yes, the proper authorities," the woman said briskly. "Do that. And when you've finished with that business, I suggest you do something about your wife. A woman who's allowed to run around in the middle of the night wearing breeches will come to a bad end, I can tell you that. Now, enough of this foolishness. Home, John."

"Yes, yer ladyship." The coachman heaved himself back up onto his box and flicked the reins. The coach lumbered forward and was soon out of sight around the next bend in the lane.

Victoria examined the highwayman. It did not take sophisticated powers of deduction to determine that the horse, at least, was probably from a nearby farm. "Surely a professional highwayman should invest in a faster animal. Who are you, lad? Are you from these parts?"

There was another whimper from the highwayman, who cast a frantic eye toward Lucas, as if he sought help from that quarter.

"Answer the lady," Lucas ordered softly.

The young man reluctantly reached up and pulled down his scarf. Victoria realized with a pang that he could not have been more than fifteen at the most. He stared first at Lucas and then at Victoria with a frightened expression. "Name's Billy."

"Billy what?" Lucas prodded patiently.

"Billy Simms."

"Well, Billy, I am afraid you are in a great deal of trouble," Lucas remarked, dropping his pistol back into his pocket. "The Earl of Stonevale does not approve of highwaymen operating in this district."

"Ye think I give a bloody damn what his 'igh-and-mighty lordship approves of?" Billy burst out. "I wouldn't be operatin' as a bleedin' 'ighwayman at all if the last earl 'adn't thrown Ma and me and my sis out of our 'ome. What was I supposed to do after Pa got taken off with the fever? We're livin' wi' me aunt and her family and there ain't enough room nor food to go 'round. Am I s'posed to watch all my womenfolk starve? Not bloody likely. I did what I 'ad to do usin' the pistol my pa left me. That's all."

Lucas regarded him in measured silence for a long moment. "You have a point, Billy. In your shoes I'd probably have done the same."

Billy eyed him in some confusion. "Ye look like gentry to me. Ye certain ye would have taken to the roads like this?"

"As you say, Billy, a man does what he has to do. But be that as it may, from what I hear, things have changed in these parts. There is a new earl in charge of Stonevale now."

"He won't be no better 'n the last one, ye mark my words. The bleedin' Quality's all the same. Out to suck the last drop 'o blood from people like me and mine. Ma says the new folks up at the great house are different and I heard what they're sayin' in the village about the ghosts reappearin', but I don't believe none of it."

"Is that right?" Lucas's horse tossed its head and he absently patted George's neck. "You thought I was a ghost at first, didn't you?"

Billy shot him a sullen look. "Ye took me by surprise, that's all. Ain't no such thing as ghosts." But he was staring at the amber scarf draped around Victoria's throat. The color had been clearly discernible earlier in the light from the coach.

"I'm sure you're right, Billy. But all that is beside the point. We have something of a problem here."

Billy wiped his nose with the back of his hand. "What problem?"

"Why, the problem of what to do with you, of course."

"Why don't ye just shoot me with yer bloody damn pistol and be done with it?"

"That's a possibility, naturally. And not an uncommon ending for a highwayman. What do you think, madam?" Lucas glanced at Victoria.

"I think," Victoria said softly, "that Billy should present himself at the stables of the Earl of Stonevale tomorrow morning and inform the head groom that he is to be hired. In the meantime I think he should go home and put his mother's mind at ease. She is undoubtedly extremely worried about him."

Billy looked up sharply. "What makes ye think I could get a job at the big 'ouse?"

"Rest assured, Billy," Lucas said calmly, "there will be a job waiting for you. One with more of a future than this one. It won't provide quite as much excitement as being a highwayman, but we have agreed a man does what he must. You've got womenfolk to see to and you cannot afford to be in a profession that's likely to get you killed this week or next."

The boy eyed Lucas suspiciously. "Is this a game yer playin' with me?"

Victoria smiled in the shadows of her hood. " 'Tis no game, Billy. Go home to your mother and in the morning report to the head groom. The wages may not be as high as what you can make out here on the road, but at least they'll be steady. And that's what your family needs. What have you got to lose? If things don't work out, you can always go back into this line of work."

Billy stared at her for a long moment, trying to peer beneath the hood of her cloak. Finally he shook his head in awe. "Yer them, ain't ye? The two o' ye be the ghosts. The Amber Knight and his lady. Look at that scarf yer wearin'. It's true what they been sayin' in the village. Ye come back after all this time t' ride the lands o' Stonevale at midnight."

"Go home, Billy. I think we have all had enough excitement for tonight," Lucas said.

"Aye, sir. Ye don't have to tell me twice. I ain't accustomed to makin' conversation with a couple o' ghosts." Billy tugged at the reins of his sturdy mount and kicked the beast into what must have been a bone-shaking trot.

Victoria watched as the boy vanished around the bend in the road. Then she threw back the hood of her cloak and laughed softly. "I must admit, my lord, that I always have an interesting time of it when you and I go adventuring at midnight."

Lucas muttered an oath. "Never a dull moment, is there?"

"Never. What shall we do next?"

"We could follow the suggestion made by that lady in the coach. I could take you home and beat you for being so brazen as to run around in the middle of the night in a pair of men's breeches. But it probably wouldn't do much good."

"Not a bit of good," Victoria agreed cheerfully. "In any event, tonight's adventure was all your idea in the first place, so it would hardly be fair of you to beat me."

"Ah, but you don't think me a fair man, do you, Vicky? You think I am high-handed and domineering and quite utterly ruthless, not to mention priggish."

She lowered her lashes. "Lucas, I . . ."

"Never mind, Vicky. It is past time we headed home. You've had your adventure for tonight."

He turned George's head back in the direction from which they had ridden earlier and Victoria had no choice but to follow.

Half an hour later she was safely back in her own bed and she was very much alone in it. But she was far from asleep.

She turned on her side and plumped a pillow, trying to get Lucas's words out of her head. *You think I am high-handed and domineering and quite utterly ruthless.*

And so he was, she assured herself for the hundredth time. Surely she did not need any more proof of that after their confrontation earlier in the day. She had known that sooner or later he would show his true colors and behave like any other so-called gentleman behaved after he married and took control of his wife's money.

But she also knew perfectly well that any other so-called gentleman of her acquaintance would have turned poor Billy over to the authorities and seen the youngster hung without a qualm. Either that or the gentleman would have shot the boy down on the road and thought himself a hero in doing so.

Yet from the moment she had realized they were dealing with a young local lad, she'd never had any doubts about how Lucas would handle the situation. She had known he would neither shoot the boy nor send him to the gallows.

The truth was, her husband was not at all like most of the gentlemen of her acquaintance and she had known that from the start. That was how she had gotten into this situation.

That did not mean, however, that Lucas was not excessively arrogant, high-handed, and domineering at times.

She turned over on her other side and gazed at the closed door that connected their rooms. The dressing table was still in front of it. Lucas had gone straight back to his own bedchamber after seeing her to her door.

Victoria had been anticipating that he would come to her bed after their night of adventure. The fact that he had not disturbed her.

She wondered if she'd gone too far by barricading her door against him. Perhaps she had dealt his pride an overly severe blow with that bit of defiance. He was her husband, after all. He did have rights.

Nor could she deny that as his wife, she had her obligations.

They were supposed to be partners in this marriage, just as they had been partners in sharing the night's adventure.

And right now she wanted to be with him.

Victoria gave up the useless attempt to get to sleep and slid out from under the covers. Her nightgown floated around her ankles as she went over to the dressing table that blocked the door. She listened intently for sounds from the next room that might indicate Lucas was having trouble sleeping, too, but she heard nothing.

The urge to open the connecting door very quietly and peek into his room to see if he was sound asleep was overpowering. But the barricade was something of a nuisance. She could move it back into its proper position, but in doing so she would surely wake Lucas.

She glanced at the window and smiled. If the Earl of Stonevale could get from one room to another using the window ledge, then so could she.

Victoria went over to the window, opened it, and looked down. From here the ground seemed very far away and the ledge that led to Lucas's window did not look nearly as wide as she had thought it would. Still, he had managed to walk it even with his bad leg.

Victoria took a deep breath and stepped out onto the ledge. The chilled air caught at her thin muslin gown and she shivered.

Clutching at the cold stone of the wall, she edged slowly toward the other window. It was not going to be quite as easy as she had thought. She was discovering the hard way that she did not have a head for heights. Every time she looked down she got dizzy.

Halfway between the two windows Victoria came to a complete halt. She knew she could not go on. Lucas had made this ledge-walking business sound like a stroll in the park. She did not know how he had managed it, but she was forced to admit defeat.

It was when she tried to retreat back along the ledge that she realized she had a major problem on her hands. Going back was not going to be any simpler than going forward.

This was ridiculous. She was appalled at her inability to move. Shivering with cold, pressed rigidly back against the stone wall, Victoria closed her eyes and tried to think. She certainly could not stand out here all night. She opened her eyes and realized that Lucas's window was open.

"Lucas? Lucas, can you hear me?"

There was no immediate response and her heart sank. The thought of having to scream ignominiously for help until one of the servants heard her was too mortifying to even contemplate.

"*Lucas*," she called, a bit more loudly this time. "Lucas, are you in there? Damn you, Stonevale, this is all your fault. Wake up and do something."

"Hell and damnation," Lucas said, appearing abruptly at the window. "I should have guessed you'd try something like this. What the devil do you think you're doing?"

Relief poured through her. "I just came out for a stroll," she muttered. "It would seem I have a slight problem with heights."

"Don't move. I'll come and fetch you."

"I'm not going anywhere." She watched as he put one bare leg over the windowsill and stepped out onto the ledge. "Good heavens, my lord, you're naked."

"Sorry to offend your delicate sensibilities. Would you prefer I went back inside and dressed first?"

"*No*. No, don't you dare. Get me off this horrible ledge before you do anything else."

"Yes, my lady. At your service, my lady. So glad to be of some assistance, my lady. Keep your voice down, my lady, or the servants will really have something to talk about in the morning."

She relaxed a little as his strong fingers closed around her wrist. "How on earth did you manage this earlier when you came to my bedchamber?"

"Be assured I didn't use this route because I enjoy running about on ledges. I used it because you'd shoved that damned dressing table in front of the door, remember? I take it the barricade is still in place and that's why you're out here?"

"I fear that is precisely the case." She followed him gratefully back to his open window. A moment later she was standing safely inside his bedchamber. She gave a sigh of relief and brushed off her hands. "Thank you very much, Lucas. I do not mind telling you, I was a trifle uneasy out there."

"And I don't mind telling you that I was a trifle

horrified to see you out there." His hands closed around her shoulders in a fierce grip. "I am, naturally, extremely gratified by your enthusiasm for my bed, but the next time you want to join me in it, try knocking."

She scowled at him. "You are assuming a great deal, my lord."

"Am I? Are you telling me you were out on that ledge because you were bored and couldn't think of anything else to do for the rest of the night except stroll from window to window?"

It was no good. She could not possibly deny that she had been attempting to get to his bedchamber. "Do not tease me, Lucas. This is humiliating enough as it is."

His smile was slow and deeply sensual. "What is so humiliating about admitting you enjoy what we find together in the marriage bed, sweetheart?"

" 'Tis not that. It is just that I have been furious with you all day and now you are no doubt jumping to the conclusion that I am here because I wanted you to make love to me."

"Isn't that precisely why you're here?"

"Yes, it is. But it doesn't mean that I have changed my mind about anything else, and of course you are bound to think that I have. Or worse, you will conclude that you can always bring me to heel by taking me for a midnight adventure. It is not that way at all."

He laughed softly. "There is nothing in any of this to shame you, Vicky. But if it will make you feel any less humiliated, I promise not to conclude that your presence here means I am permanently forgiven. Will that do? Tomorrow we can go right back to the battle lines you drew today, if that is what you truly wish."

"Lucas, you are incorrigible. You know very well that things will be different between us in the morning. How can I possibly continue to give you the cold shoulder tomorrow after you have made love to me tonight?"

"I don't know," he said, scooping her up and settling her into his bed. "How can you?"

She looked up at him through her lashes as he came down beside her. "Maybe I should be the one applying for a job in your stables instead of Billy Simms. That way, I could supplement the allowance you intend to grant me."

He kissed her throat. "Did you risk life and limb on that damned ledge just so you could continue our argument or did you come here so that I could make love to you?"

Victoria relaxed and put her arms around his neck. "I came here so that you could fulfill your husbandly duties and make love to me."

"I rather thought so." His hand closed over her breast and his mouth closed over her lips.

Sometime later Victoria stirred sleepily in the huge bed. She opened her eyes to see Lucas at the window. He had one foot out on the ledge. "Where in heaven's name are you going?"

"To shove that dressing table away from your door. Do you want your maid to know you felt obliged to barricade yourself in your room tonight?"

"No, of course, not. But be careful, Lucas."

"I'll be right back."

He vanished into the night and a couple of minutes later Victoria heard the heavy dressing table being shifted back into its proper position. The connecting door opened and Lucas sauntered back into his own room, dusting off his hands. Victoria glowered at him.

"Now what have I done?" he demanded as he slid back into bed beside her.

"I don't see how you can be so casual about wandering around naked."

"Who will see? Except you, of course." He grinned, throwing one leg over hers. "And you are every bit as naked as I am."

"Never mind." She paused. "Lucas, I have something to say to you."

"What would that be, my sweet?"

Victoria studied Lucas for a moment, choosing her words. "About our argument."

"Which one?"

"The one about my money."

"Can this discussion not wait until breakfast? I'm exhausted. Running about on horseback in the middle of the night, rescuing ladies from window ledges, and shoving heavy furniture around takes its toll on a man of my years."

"This is important, Lucas."

"Very well, then, say it so that we can both get some sleep."

"I just wanted to say that I am sorry, or at least somewhat sorry for most of the nasty things I said to you during the course of our discussion about money," Victoria said very gravely.

"*Most* of the nasty things? Not all of them?"

"No, not all of them, because I do not feel that I was entirely in the wrong. Nevertheless, I shouldn't have implied that you are like every other husband who takes control of his wife's money. The truth is, you are quite different from any other man I have ever met."

He touched the amber pendant where it lay nestled between her breasts. "And you, madam, are quite different from any other woman I have ever met. Since you have apologized for *most* of the nasty things you said, I suppose the least I can do is revoke my threat to put you on a limited quarterly allowance."

"Well, I should think so. Really, Lucas, you can have had no notion of how arrogant you sounded when you made that horrid threat."

He laughed and pulled her down across his chest. "I don't think you have any notion of how arrogant you sound when you set out to make me jump fences to suit your whims."

"I do no such thing."

"Don't you?" His thumbs traced the line of her cheekbones. "You are constantly testing me, Vicky, constantly pushing and probing to see how far I will let you go before I pull in the reins. And when I do reach my limits and refuse to indulge you in some manner, you retaliate by accusing me of being a typical, untrustworthy, domineering male who's only after his wife's money."

She realized he was perfectly serious. "Lucas, that is not true."

"I think it is true, sweetheart. And to be quite honest, I don't entirely blame you. You have good cause to be cautious about placing your trust in me. But I do not like it when you try to manipulate me."

She went still. "Is that how you see my behavior? As an attempt to manage you?"

"I think it is your way of proving to yourself that you are not at my mercy, that you can control me and therefore the situation in which you find yourself. It is a perfectly natural response on your part, but it does make for some awkward moments between us."

"It seems to me that you have tried to manipulate and control me right from the start," Victoria said quietly. "You even told me you were doing it that first night in my aunt's garden when you said I would be unable to resist you because you would give me what no other man ever had."

"So I did."

"Well? Aren't you going to apologize for that?"

"There's not much point, is there? I don't regret it." He eased her mouth down to his. "I would have done whatever I had to do in order to get you."

A small chill went through Victoria. Lucas had meant to get himself an heiress at whatever cost. There had been no love involved in the bargain, at least not on his side. He had been quite ruthless, right from the start. She had to keep reminding herself of that fact, especially when she lay in his arms. It was so easy to pretend that all was well between them at times like this, so easy to pretend that he was not plotting her surrender.

"Isabel Rycott once told me that weak men are more useful to a woman than strong ones because they are easier to control," Victoria mused against his lips.

"Look at me, my sweet. I am utterly at your mercy. A helpless slave to your wicked, carnal desires. How much more useful can a man be?"

"There is that. I must admit, you are not the least bit stingy when it comes to this area of our marriage." Victoria parted her lips and drew her tongue along the edge of his hard mouth.

Lucas groaned and set about proving just how willing he was to serve his lady in this area of their marriage.

Victoria awoke once more shortly after dawn, aware that Lucas was shifting about restlessly in his sleep. She put her hand on the ragged scar on his thigh and began to massage the taut muscles. He relaxed almost at once and fell back into a calm slumber.

She lay awake beside him for a few minutes, thinking that she had not been troubled with nightmares since her first night here at Stonevale. But the faint, nagging sense of unease had not completely vanished. Victoria could not completely escape the feeling that something dark and menacing was slowly closing in on her.

She cuddled closer to Lucas's hard, warm body and his arm went around her. She reached up and absently touched the amber pendant at her throat as she often did these days. A moment later she relaxed and fell asleep.

16

"You won't believe this, ma'am, but they're sayin' the ghosts were seen again last night. Fair gives one the shivers, don't it? Except that nobody around here seems to mind havin' these two particular ghosts runnin' about. But I reckon that's how country folk are. Peculiar." Nan finished fastening the bodice of Victoria's yellow-printed muslin gown and reached for the silver hairbrush.

Victoria watched her maid in the mirror. "Is this the Amber Knight and his lady you are talking about, Nan?"

"Yes, ma'am. So they be sayin' in the kitchens, at any rate."

"Are they saying precisely where the ghosts were seen?" Victoria asked carefully just as the connecting door opened and Lucas walked into her bedchamber. She was relieved to note he was fully dressed and even more pleased to see that he did not appear to be favoring his bad leg unduly.

" 'Mornin', your lordship." Nan dropped a quick curtsy and went back to work brushing Victoria's short curls into fashionable, casual disarray.

"Good morning," Lucas said easily. He met Victoria's

gaze in the mirror and smiled with lazy satisfaction. "Finish your tale, Nan. Where were the ghosts seen?"

Nan's eyes brightened. "Ridin' down one of the lanes, just as bold as you please. Can you imagine? What would a couple of self-respectin' ghosts be doing riding horseback in the middle of the night, I ask you? The tales some people come up with."

"I agree with you," Lucas remarked, his eyes gleaming as they continued to hold Victoria's in the mirror. "I cannot for the life of me imagine why a couple of intelligent ghosts would be out riding at that hour. Who saw them?"

"Well, as to that, I am not sure exactly, sir. I had the story from one of the kitchen girls who had it from a new stable lad. He just started work this mornin'. Don't know where he got it," Nan said.

"Probably made the whole thing up," Victoria said. "That will be all for now, Nan. Thank you."

"Yes, m'lady." Nan bobbed another curtsy and left the room.

Lucas grinned as the door closed behind the maid. "Ten to one Billy Simms has put a nice twist on the events of last night."

"No doubt." Victoria laughed. "It is getting to be a great joke, is it not, Lucas?"

"I fear it will not be quite so amusing when someone finally realizes that the ghosts are merely the current Earl of Stonevale and his hoyden of a countess. But we shall face that problem when it arises. Are you ready to go down to breakfast?"

"Yes, indeed. In fact, I find myself with an excellent appetite this morning."

"I cannot imagine why," Lucas murmured as he opened the door for her.

Victoria stepped forward and looped her arm into his. "Nothing like a little exercise to work up an appetite, is there? What are your plans for the day, my lord?"

"I am going to meet with the vicar to go over some ideas I have been studying for the new irrigation system. And your plans, my dear?"

She smiled serenely as they started down the stairs.

"Oh, I thought I would spend the morning going over the interest rates offered by certain moneylenders I may need to consult in the event I should ever happen to find myself placed on a strict allowance."

"Save your energy, madam. The day I allow you to go to a moneylender will be the day I have truly abandoned the fight and raised the white flag of defeat."

"An interesting notion. Somehow I cannot quite imagine you admitting defeat in anything, Stonevale."

"You are getting to know me well, Vicky."

The three letters arrived just as they were finishing breakfast. Victoria recognized her aunt's seal on one of them and Annabella Lyndwood's on the another. She tore Annabella's note open first.

My Dearest Vicky,

What a fine stir you have caused. Everyone is having a wonderful time discussing what is being termed the Great Romance of the Year. Lady Hesterly's daughter even went so far as to suggest that Byron scribble a verse or two to celebrate the event. That notion, of course, is reported to have sent Caro Lamb flying up into the boughs. It is well known she does not like being cast into the shade by someone more outrageously romantic than herself.

Be that as it may, the rest of the gossip pales in comparison to talk of your marriage. Do hurry back, Vicky. I assure you that you will be heralded as a mythic goddess of love straight out of a classic tale of romance. And I must say, life has become rather boring without you. The only recent excitement is that I have succeeded in persuading Bertie to definitely refuse Viscount Barton's offer. He is presently moping (Lord Barton, that is, not Bertie) but shows every sign of perking up and turning his attentions elsewhere.

Affectionately yours,
Annabella

"So much for poor Barton," Lucas muttered. "Foiled by females."

"So much, indeed," Victoria agreed with relish. She opened her aunt's note next and scanned the contents quickly before giving a small shriek of dismay. "Dear heaven, of all the wretched luck."

Lucas looked up from the newspaper that had arrived with the letters. "What's wrong?"

"Everything. This is terrible. A disaster."

Lucas folded the newspaper and put it down beside his plate. "Has something happened to your aunt? Is she ill?"

"No, no, no, it is nothing like that. The disaster has happened to us. Oh, Lucas, what on earth are we to do? How do we get out of this horrible situation? This is intolerable."

"Perhaps I could be of greater assistance if you would give me a few more details concerning this intolerable, horrible disaster."

Victoria glanced up, her brows snapping together in a severe frown. "This is not funny, Lucas. Aunt Cleo writes that Jessica Atherton called upon her and suggested that it would be wise for you and me to put in an appearance in London before the Season ends. Lady Atherton has very kindly stated that she will honor us with a reception."

Lucas looked thoughtful. Then he shrugged. "Perhaps she's right. It might not be a bad idea. It would serve to enforce the notion that ours is a love match."

Victoria was appalled. "Lucas, are you listening? It is none other than Jessica Atherton who is proposing to give us this reception."

"Who better? As we both know, her position in Society is unassailable."

Outraged, Victoria stared at him. "Have you lost your senses? Do you honestly believe I will allow Jessica Atherton to assist us in this manner? Not in a million years. *I will not be indebted to that woman again.*"

There was a beat of silence from Lucas's end of the

table. "Again?" he echoed at last. "Are you by any chance implying you already feel indebted to her for having performed the introduction that led to our marriage?"

"Don't you dare tease me, Lucas. I am not at all in a mood to be teased. This is awful. What on earth shall I say to Aunt Cleo? How will we get out of this?"

"My advice," he said as he rose to his feet, "is that we do not try. Your aunt is quite right. It would be a wise move to make an appearance in the ballroom of a hostess such as Jessica Atherton before the Season is over. It would set the seal of approval on your marriage as far as Society is concerned."

Victoria could not believe her ears. "Never. I absolutely refuse. This is one issue on which neither you nor my aunt can make me change my mind. I have had more than enough of Jessica Atherton and her *generous, kind* assistance. I do not care if I never see the woman again as long as I live. I will not go to London if it means having to attend a ball in our honor given by her. It is unthinkable."

Lucas walked to her chair, leaned down, and kissed the top of her curls. "My dear, you are overreacting. The whole notion of letting Jessica give us a reception seems quite reasonable to me."

"It is the most unreasonable thing I have ever heard."

"We will discuss it later when you've had a chance to calm down. Now I must be off. The vicar is due to arrive shortly."

"I will not be budged on this, Lucas. I warn you." She glared at his back as he exited the breakfast room, and then, when she had finished fuming, Victoria reached for the third and last letter. She examined it curiously but failed to recognize either the handwriting or the seal.

Impatiently she opened it. A pamphlet, a newspaper clipping, and a short note fell out of the envelope. The note was unsigned and it was extremely brief.

Madam: Given your interest in matters of intellectual inquiry, the enclosed

should intrigue you greatly. It appears
the dead do not always remain so.

The note was signed with a single initial: a "W."

With a sense of dawning dread, Victoria picked up
the pamphlet and read the title: "On Certain Curious
Investigations into the Matter of Using Electricity to
Reanimate the Dead."

The newspaper article was a detailed account of how
a coffin which had recently been exhumed had been
opened and found to be empty. The theft of the de-
ceased was presumed to be the work of a ring of body
snatchers who were in the business of supplying the
medical schools with corpses. There was, however, some
speculation that a certain group of experimenters had
purchased the body for their experiments with electricity. The authorities were concerned.

For the first time in her life that she could remember, Victoria felt faint. She nodded sharply to the footman to indicate she wanted more coffee and watched
numbly as he poured it into her cup. The dark brew
seemed to fall from spout to cup in slow motion.

Very carefully, because she did not quite trust the
steadiness of her fingers, she picked up the delicate
china teacup and swallowed most of the contents in one
gulp. The light-headed sensation passed.

When she thought she could manage the act without
collapsing, Victoria got to her feet, collected the envel-
lopes and their contents, and went upstairs to her room.

Lucas was aware of being in an excellent mood as he
made his way across the hall and into the library. He
looked about him with satisfaction.

Stonevale was a far different place than it had been
when he had inherited it. Fine woodwork gleamed
once more under new layers of polish. Faded draperies
had been repaired or replaced. The old carpets had
been cleaned to reveal their subtle, beautiful patterns,
and the windows sparkled in the morning sun.

The house was fully staffed now and the domestic
routines were already well established. The footmen

wore their new livery with obvious pride and the food served at table was fresh and properly prepared.

Through the library window Lucas could see the progress the gardeners were making under Victoria's direction. The small conservatory she had ordered would soon be finished. Several trays of unusual plants were on their way from London.

Lucas knew that all the progress that had been made in and around the house itself was the direct result of Victoria's time and attention. Her money alone would not have achieved the miracle of turning Stonevale into a home. That feat required a woman's touch.

She had brought something infinitely more valuable than her inheritance to this marriage, Lucas acknowledged. She had brought herself with all her natural enthusiasm, intelligence, and generous nature. The staff and tenants adored her. The villagers were proud that she found their shops worth her patronage. The fact that the tradesmen's bills were always paid promptly did not go unnoticed, either. The quality of merchandise available in the village was already markedly improved.

He had chosen well, Lucas told himself as he studied the garden through the window. He had almost everything he could want in a wife, an intelligent lady for his days and a passionate creature of fire and spirit to warm his bed at night. What more could any man ask?

But the raw fact of the matter was that he was oddly unsatisfied. He had discovered of late that there were a few other things he wanted from Victoria. He found himself longing for the sweet, tremulous words of love she had withheld from him since the day of their marriage and he wanted her full and complete trust.

He probably did not deserve either her love or her trust, but lately he had come to realize he would not be able to rest until he had both. He did not care for her businesslike approach to her fate. This marriage was not just another financial investment for her, by God. He would not allow her to go on treating it that way much longer.

He glanced at the painting of *Strelitzia reginae* that

he'd brought downstairs earlier and propped on his desk. Every time he looked at it he remembered Victoria's glowing expression that night at the inn.

I think I have fallen in love with you, Lucas.

The door of the library opened just as Lucas was adjusting the position of the painting so that it would be visible from the chair on the opposite side of the desk. Reverend Worth was ushered into the room. He beamed at his host and brandished a magazine. "Latest issue of *Agricultural Review*," he announced. "Thought you might like to see it."

"Very much. Thank you, sir. Please sit down."

"My, there will certainly be a lovely prospect from these windows when Lady Stonevale finishes with the gardens." The vicar peered out at the ongoing work as he took one of the mahogany armchairs. "Your wife is a fine woman, sir, if you don't mind my saying so. A man could not ask for a better helpmate."

"I was just thinking something along those lines myself."

"You realize, of course, that in the village they've started calling her their Amber Lady on a regular basis?"

Lucas grinned. "I won't worry until the tenants start calling me their Amber Knight. I would not want them to think their landlord is a ghost. They might get the notion they can delay the payment of their rents until the afterlife."

"Rest assured," the vicar told him with a chuckle, "that they view you as altogether real and quite solid. Definitely not a ghost. You are a natural leader, Stonevale, as I'm sure you're well aware. And leadership is precisely what this land and the people on it have needed for some time. Which reminds me."

"Yes?"

The vicar arched his brows knowingly. "Word in the village has it the Amber Knight and his lady were running about again late last night."

"Is that so?"

"Seems a certain lad of the village reported seeing them. Personally I questioned what this particular lad was doing out at midnight himself, although I believe I can hazard a guess. In any event, apparently his meeting with the knight and the lady changed the lad's mind about pursuing an extremely dangerous career as a highwayman. The boy has chosen to go to work in your stables, instead."

"A much safer, if less exciting job."

"Yes, indeed." The vicar smiled. "The lad is basically a good boy, and as he has the responsibility of caring for his mother and sister, I am particularly pleased that the knight did not deem it his duty to see the young man shot down on the road or hung."

Lucas shrugged. "Perhaps the knight has already seen far too many young men die senseless deaths. I imagine even a ghost can get a bellyful of that sort of thing. Now, then, vicar, I must ask you what progress you are making on your gardening book."

The vicar gazed at him with piercing understanding for a second and then blinked and smiled genially. "Kind of you to inquire. I am working on the chapter dealing with roses." He glanced at the picture propped on the desk. "I must say, that's a wonderful rendering of *Strelitzia reginae*. Quite perfect in every detail and it seems to have a life of its own. Magnificent. How did you come by it, if I may ask?"

"It was a gift."

"Was it, indeed? I am still looking for someone to do the colored plates for my book, you know."

"Yes, I believe you mentioned you were inquiring for a skilled watercolorist who also knew something of botany."

The vicar continued to examine Victoria's painting. "Whoever did this would be perfect. You do not happen to know the artist by any chance, do you?"

"In point of fact," Lucas said smoothly, "I do."

"Excellent, excellent. Any possibility you might arrange for me to contact him?"

"The artist is a woman, and yes, I think I can arrange for you to talk to her."

"I would be most extremely grateful," the vicar said happily. "Most extremely."

"My pleasure," Lucas said. "I will make certain you

meet her. Now, then, I want to ask your opinion on putting in an irrigation system for the farms that border the woods." Lucas spread a map out on the desk and indicated a section of land.

"Yes, indeed. Got to do something to increase productivity in that area, don't you? Let's see what you have in mind." The vicar leaned forward to examine the map and then glanced up one last time. "Don't mean to press you, Stonevale, but do you have any idea of how soon I might get in touch with the watercolorist you mentioned?"

"Soon," Lucas promised. "Very soon."

Two hours later Lucas saw his visitor out the door and then he headed for the stairs carrying his precious picture of *Strelitzia reginae*. He was feeling quite pleased with himself. The correct word might have been "smug," he admitted as he reached the landing and started down the hall toward his room.

Finding just the right gift for a wife who had brought considerably more money than her husband into the marriage was not the easiest task in the world. A man could hardly use the lady's own inheritance to buy her a diamond necklace.

Lucas rehung his picture with careful precision, stepped back to admire his handiwork, and then went over to the connecting door and knocked. When there was no answer from within, he frowned and tried again. He was certain Griggs had said Victoria was in her bedchamber.

"Vicky?"

When there was still no response, he turned the knob and opened the door to glance into the room. He saw her at once seated near the window with the three letters that had arrived at breakfast on the little rosewood secretary in front of her. She turned her head as he walked into the room. Her smile was wan.

"I am sorry, Lucas, but I am not feeling all that well. I came up here to rest."

An odd tension hummed through him. It was not unlike the sort of feeling he had known on the battlefield before the first shot was fired. "You were feeling well enough at breakfast."

"That was before I opened the post."

He relaxed somewhat. "I take it you are still annoyed at being obliged to accept Jessica's invitation?"

"Jessica Atherton is no longer of much consequence one way or the other."

"I am relieved to hear it." He went into the room and sat down across from her. He thrust his legs out in front of him, absently massaging his thigh. "What is it, Vicky? I have seen you in a variety of moods, but never one quite like this. I swear, madam, you leave me panting for breath trying to keep pace with you."

"I have never been in quite this position before and I admit I do not know how to deal with it. But 'tis certain something must be done or I shall go out of my mind."

"You are really not feeling well?" He grinned. "Mayhap you are breeding, after all, madam. Have you thought of that?"

"To be truthful, Lucas, being with child would be simpler than this business."

She was not carrying his babe after all. Disappointment shot through him. "I am sorry to hear that. Perhaps you had better tell me just what is troubling you, my dear."

She looked down at the papers on her little desk. When she glanced up again, her amber eyes were startling in their intensity.

"Lucas, do you believe it is possible to reanimate the dead through the use of electricity machines?"

"Reanimate the dead? Nonsense. I fear you have been playing too much lately at being a ghost, Vicky. I have never heard a single reliable instance in which such an experiment has been successful."

"But we do not know of all the experiments that have been done, do we? People all over England are playing with electricity these days."

Lucas looked doubtful. "I am certain that any successful experiment in reanimation would have been in all the journals and newspapers."

"Perhaps not, if someone paid the experimenter to keep quiet about the results."

He began to realize just how frightened she was and a cold anger swept through him. Without asking any more questions, he reached over and picked up the sheaf of papers lying on her desk. He immediately tossed aside Annabella and Lady Nettleship's notes. A glance at the pamphlet and clipping was sufficient to show that they were concerned with missing bodies and attempts at reanimation.

"Interesting, but I see no reports of successful attempts. Where did you get these?" He indicated the pamphlet and clipping.

"They were sent to me. They were in the third envelope that I opened at breakfast. Along with this." Victoria handed him a short note.

Lucas scanned it quickly and had to force himself to keep his rage under tight rein. " 'Madam: given your interest in intellectual inquiry the enclosed should intrigue you greatly. It appears the dead do not always remain so. Signed "W." ' " He tossed the note down on the table with a savage little flick of his hand. "Goddamned bastard."

"Lucas it is him, it is this 'W' again, the one who left the scarf and the snuffbox." Victoria was struggling for her self-control.

Lucas recognized the symptoms of shock and fear. He made a deliberate effort to keep his voice calm, much as he would have if he were dealing with a brave but frightened young officer on the eve of combat. "Calm yourself, Vicky. This has gone quite far enough. I will take steps to find out who is behind this and I will put a halt to it."

Her beautiful mouth trembled. "I know who is behind it. Samuel Whitlock. The man who killed my mother. He has come back, Lucas. Somehow he has returned from the dead and he is going to kill me or else drive me to my death the same way I—" She broke off and covered her face in her hands. "Oh, my God. *Oh, my God.*"

Lucas got up and reached down to pull her into his arms. She stood in the circle of his sheltering embrace, shaking. Although his hands moved gently, soothingly on her slender back, his rage was so cold now it could have frozen the marrow in his bones.

The shudders eventually ceased racking Victoria's body and she slowly disengaged herself from his grasp and went to her dressing table for a handkerchief.

"You must think I'm a witless little fool to believe in such things as reanimation of the dead," she whispered, keeping her back to him as she dried her eyes.

"I think," said Lucas, "that you have been very frightened and that someone has deliberately set out to accomplish that goal." He watched her face in the dressing-table mirror. "Who would do such a thing, Vicky?"

"I just told you. Samuel Whitlock."

"No, my dear, not Samuel Whitlock. He's dead. You have been so terrified by the signature on that note that you have not been thinking logically."

"It has to be him." She whirled around. "Don't you see, Lucas? He is not dead. Either he did not really die that night at the bottom of the stairs or else he has been brought back to life by someone with an electricity machine. One way or another he has come back and he is after me. Whitlock is the only one who could possibly have any reason for carrying out this horrible revenge."

Lucas studied her. "That brings up an interesting point. Just what is his reason for wanting revenge against you?"

Victoria's eyes clouded with an infinite sadness. "Lucas, I cannot tell you. If I did, you would be filled with such disgust for me that you would not be able to tolerate the sight of me."

In spite of himself, he felt his mouth twitch in a small grin. "Having led up to the grand revelation with a remark such as that, you most certainly will have to tell me the whole truth now. If you don't, I shall expire of curiosity."

"This is no joke. Lucas, you have no idea of what I have done."

He walked over to her and drew her tense body back against his chest. "I assure you that it is very unlikely you could tell me anything about yourself that would make me unable to tolerate the sight of you. I doubt there is anything to which you could confess that could compare with some of the small slices of hell I have seen on a battlefield. Tell me everything, my sweet."

"Very well, Lucas." Her voice was tragic. "But never say I did not warn you."

"I will never say it."

"I killed him." She went perfectly still in his arms, obviously bracing herself for his shock and disgust. "I murdered Samuel Whitlock."

"Hmmm," Lucas murmured. "I did rather wonder about that."

She jerked her head back to stare up at him. "You did? But what made you think such a thing? I have kept the secret to myself all these months. Even my aunt has no notion of what I did."

"It was nothing specific that you said or did. Just a few simple things that made me mildly curious."

"What simple things, for heaven's sake?"

"Well, there was the timing of Whitlock's death so soon after your mother's, and the fact that you were convinced he had killed her and would never hang for it. In addition to those two points, I have had occasion to get to know you rather well. Not as well as I would like, I will admit, but well enough to predict with some certainty that you would not let your mother's murder go unavenged."

There was a distinct pause and then Victoria spoke in a very small voice. "You do not sound particularly upset about this, my lord."

Lucas considered her words. "The only thing that upsets me is the thought of the risks you must have taken to get the job done."

She sighed. "I did not actually set out to kill him, you know. All I wanted from him was a confession. But I will admit I was not sorry when I realized he was dead. In fact, I experienced the most amazing sense of relief."

"I hate to be indelicate, but you did actually witness his death?"

Victoria buried her face in Lucas's chest. "Oh, yes. I witnessed it. And almost witnessed my own in the process."

"Good God. What happened?"

" 'Tis a long story. Are you quite certain you want to hear it?"

"I assure you I am prepared to listen all day and all night, if necessary." He eased her down into her armchair and resumed the seat across from her. "Talk, Vicky. Tell me everything."

She was twisting the handkerchief in her lap, but she met his eyes unflinchingly. "You must understand that my stepfather drank heavily. Sometimes he turned violent. His habits were no secret and I decided to make use of his weakness."

"Strategy," Lucas said approvingly.

She frowned. "Yes, well, I could not think of anything else, you see. I knew the house well because I had lived there for a few years before my mother sent me to my aunt's. It was a huge, old place with hidden passages and long halls with unexpected openings into certain rooms. I used that information to haunt my stepfather."

"You *haunted* him?"

She blew her nose. "Yes."

"Amazing."

"Really, Lucas, I'm sure you should not be looking quite so fascinated by all this. 'Tis rather reprehensible when you think about it."

"Let's just say I find it intellectually interesting. What's wrong with that? Surely no worse than trying to reanimate dead bodies. Pray, continue, sweetheart."

"I arranged to stay with friends who happened to live in a neighboring house for a week. Everyone knew I did not feel comfortable around my stepfather and these people had been friends of my mother's, so they were sympathetic to me. Several times during that week I slipped out of the house in the middle of the night and walked through the woods to my stepfather's house. I wore the dress in which my mother had been married and I began haunting Samuel Whitlock."

"You hoped that in his drunken stupors he would think he was seeing the ghost of his dead wife?"

Victoria nodded. "At first he thought he was having

nightmares. Then he began talking to me. It was eerie, Lucas. He ordered me to go away and leave him in peace. Then he told me about how he had never wanted to marry in the first place but he had to have the money and why could I not understand that? He pleaded with me to leave him alone. Finally, one night his nerve broke entirely. He came after me with a knife, saying he would kill me again and this time he would make certain of the job."

Lucas shut his eyes for a second, trying not to think of how close she had come to her own death. "That is when he had his accident on the stairs?"

"Yes. I was fleeing from him down the hall. I started down the stairs. He was directly behind me, holding the knife high in his hand and screaming about how he was going to kill me. He lost his footing about a third of the way down and fell all the way to the bottom."

"The servants," Lucas murmured. "Where were they?"

"There were only two in the house, an elderly couple with rooms far removed at the back. They were in the habit of retiring early and staying out of their master's way until morning. The screaming they may have heard that night was certainly not the first time they had heard such noises in that house. They had learned to mind their own business."

"I see. Did you check to see if your stepfather was truly dead?"

"No. I was so frightened that I ran. Perhaps the fall didn't kill him." She looked at the newspaper clippings. "Lucas, I do not know what to believe. Do you think he might have merely engineered his burial to haunt me as I once haunted him?"

"It is a possibility."

Victoria chewed her lip. "What has he been doing all these months if he is still alive?"

"Hiding, perhaps? Waiting to see if you would go to the authorities with your report?"

"He was dead. I know he was dead. I killed him," she said.

"You did not murder him, Vicky. You tried in a very clever fashion to extract a confession and you got it. In the process, you almost got yourself killed, and that is all there is to the matter," Lucas said very firmly. "As to whether or not he is actually dead, that remains to be seen. This business with the pamphlet and the note certainly indicate there are some loose ends that need tying up."

"Such as who sent me this note and the pamphlet and clipping."

"Yes," Lucas agreed. "That is one of several questions I think we should get answered as soon as possible. There is also the little matter of that carriage that nearly ran you down and the footpad who assaulted me the night before you found the snuffbox."

"Lucas, this is making my head spin. I cannot go on like this. I must have answers."

"I could not agree more wholeheartedly. As I said, there are several questions that now must be answered as quickly as possible. I think the best place to begin is in Town, where this all started." He smiled. "Now we have an excellent reason to go to London in addition to the invitation to Lady Atherton's ball, don't we?"

Victoria gave a weak laugh. "Lucas, I swear you are impossible. Even at a time like this, you are still plotting to get me to do precisely as you wish."

"Strategy, my dear. I'm known for it. Now, while this will no doubt seem anticlimactic, I have a small surprise for you. Remember that picture of *Strelitzia reginae?*"

"Yes, of course. What about it?"

Lucas flashed her an easy grin. "The vicar would like half a dozen more watercolors on similar subjects for his book on flower gardening."

The expression of shock on Victoria's face was extremely gratifying, Lucas thought.

17

Naturally Lucas had taken her horrendous revelation as calmly as if she had merely told him what Cook was preparing for dinner. What had she expected? Victoria was still asking herself that question a few days later as she stood with Annabella and Aunt Cleo in the shop of a fashionable London modiste.

Had she actually assumed, even for a moment, that he would have reacted as one would have expected any normal husband to react to such shocking news?

If there was one thing she had learned about Lucas by now, it was that he wad definitely not an ordinary sort of husband. While he was occasionally arrogant, high-handed, stubborn, and yes, a bit stuffy in certain matters, he was never at a loss.

And he always took care of his own. His dedication to his lands and the people of Stonevale proved that.

Still, even knowing what she did about him, she had not expected quite such a placid, pragmatic reaction. She was still a bit awed by his cool acceptance of her rather sordid past. Of course, she was dealing with a man who had once taken her to a gaming hell and a brothel, Victoria reminded herself, a man who took her riding at midnight.

"Is this not a lovely bit of silk, dear? Just your color, too." Aunt Cleo indicated a bolt of amber yellow stuff. "It would make a very nice evening gown."

"Oh, yes, Vicky. Absolutely perfect for Jessica Atherton's ball," Annabella declared. "You must be completely stunning for that great event, and your aunt is correct: the color is just right."

"Very pretty." Victoria reached out to finger the beautiful fabric.

"What do you think of the muslin, Vicky?" Aunt Cleo glanced at her inquiringly.

"Quite nice." Victoria forced herself to pay closer attention to the business at hand. The muslin was a deep yellow. She liked it at once.

"But not for Lady Atherton's ball," Annabella insisted.

"Perhaps a walking dress trimmed in aqua, then?" Victoria suggested, unwilling to let the fine muslin go.

The modiste, a tiny woman with a thick French accent, nodded emphatically. "Most charming, my lady."

"Very well, a ball gown in the silk and a walking dress in the yellow muslin," Victoria said decisively. "Now, as to the gown, I will want it in the height of fashion, do you understand?"

"It must be absolutely riveting," Annabella declared. "Perhaps something along the lines of this one." She indicated a fashion plate she had noticed earlier.

"A lovely gown, madam," the modiste assured her.

Aunt Cleo frowned as she peered down at the plate Annabella had pointed out. It showed a drawing of a woman in a dress that displayed a great deal of bosom. "Do you think Lucas will like that one, Vicky, dear? You know what he said last night at dinner. He distinctly mentioned that he did not want you getting anything with an extremely low neckline."

"Lucas is fond of saying things like that," Victoria explained. "But he really does not know all that much about fashion. This gown is for Lady Atherton's party, and Annabella is quite right: it simply must be as dramatic as possible."

"Yes, well, I shall leave you to explain it to Lucas," Cleo remarked. "He is your husband, after all."

Annabella giggled. "I am certain that by this time Vicky has molded her lord into an agreeable sort of husband who does not give his wife any trouble."

Victoria smiled serenely and decided it was not absolutely necessary to admit that there were still some rough edges on Lucas that needed a great deal more polishing before he would be molded into a perfectly agreeable husband. "He will be quite content with this gown."

"I swear, Vicky, you are an inspiration to us all," Annabella said in admiring tones.

Cleo Nettleship's brows rose. "Or an extremely dangerous example. Very well, then, let us be off. We have several more appointments to keep today."

A short time later Victoria followed her aunt and Annabella out onto Bond Street. The exclusive shopping district was crowded, as usual. Fashionable carriages, well-dressed women, and outrageously garbed dandies littered the landscape.

Aunt Cleo's carriage was waiting at the curb, but as they started toward it another carriage pulled up behind it and the groom jumped down to assist his passenger.

Isabel Rycott stepped out. She was dressed in a deep green that set off her eyes. A small, feathered hat was perched jauntily on her sleek, dark hair.

"Good morning, Lady Nettleship. So nice to see you."

"Isabel." Cleo inclined her head politely.

"And the radiant bride." Isabel smiled her mysterious smile as she turned to Victoria. "What a commotion you caused when you married Lord Stonevale. Quite romantic, I'm sure, although one wonders what your dear parents would have said about such a hasty marriage."

"As they are no longer around, it hardly signifies, does it?" Victoria remarked.

"Perhaps you are right. I had heard that you and your husband were back in Town. Lady Atherton is having a reception for you, is she not?"

"That is correct," Victoria said. "I hope you have been keeping well, Lady Rycott." She forced a smile.

"Very well, thank you."

"And your friend, Edgeworth? Is he in good health?"

Isabel's smile tightened fractionally. "I have not seen much of Edgeworth recently. I assume he is fine. Tell me, Vicky, dear, will we be seeing you tonight at the Foxtons'?"

It was Cleo who responded. "We are thinking of dropping in for a short time, although we will not be able to stay long. Vicky and Stonevale are in Town for only a few days and they have received scores of invitations. Impossible to accept them all, you know."

"I can imagine," Isabel murmured. "Now that Lady Atherton has given her opinion that it is the wedding of the Season, more than one hostess is anxious to have the famous couple grace her ballroom. Good day to you both. I trust I will see you this evening, and if not, then perhaps at the Atherton reception."

Victoria watched Isabel enter the modiste's shop and then she stepped up into the carriage, following her aunt and Annabella. "Really, that woman can be so damnably annoying. I cannot put my finger on it, but I know I shall never like her."

"Who? Isabel Rycott? I know what you mean. There is something about the woman that grates," Annabella agreed.

"Not on men," Cleo observed dryly.

Victoria grimaced and glanced back at the shop as the carriage pulled away from the curb. "Interesting what she said about Edgeworth, is it not?"

"He was not her first paramour and doubtless will not be her last," Cleo said. "Isabel always has a man or two trailing after her."

Annabella frowned thoughtfully. "Come to think of it, one does not see Edgeworth about much these days at all, not with Isabel Rycott or anyone else."

"Really?" Victoria could not wait to mention that little tidbit to Lucas.

As it happened, she did not get a chance to talk to her husband until she came down the stairs of his town house that evening. She had dressed with care for her first night out in London as a married woman. The yellow and cream gown fell in a graceful, slender line to her ankles. She had chosen to wear no jewelry except the amber pendant and a tortoiseshell comb in her hair.

Lucas was standing in the hall, waiting for her. He was dressed in starkly elegant black and white. His dark hair gleamed in the light of the chandelier. Victoria looked down at him from the third step and wondered if he would ever truly love her as she loved him. Perhaps the best she could hope for was his affection, companionship, and the protection he offered everyone toward whom he felt responsible.

She could hardly complain if that was all she ever received from him, Victoria told herself. It was a great deal more than many women were fortunate enough to obtain from husbands, especially those who had been married for their money.

Lucas bowed gallantly over her hand as she came down the last two steps. "You look lovely, madam. I consider myself the luckiest of men tonight."

She smiled. "I am feeling rather lucky myself, sir."

"Shall we go out and perform for the crowds?" he asked dryly as he led her out the door.

"That is exactly what it feels like, does it not? I would much rather go for a midnight ride with you, Lucas."

"Personally, I am looking forward to a relatively quiet evening of being squeezed and trampled and bored in a series of overheated ballrooms. It sounds positively restful compared to the adventures we always seem to encounter when you drag me out after midnight."

Victoria flashed him a berating look as he handed her up into the carriage. "Really, Lucas, the way you complain, one would almost think you did not thoroughly enjoy yourself on our midnight adventures. Now, then, I have been waiting all day for a chance to speak to you about Edgeworth."

"What about him?" Lucas asked as he sat down across from her.

"I ran into Isabel Rycott today on Bond Street and she made it clear she is no longer seeing him. In fact, I got the impression from what my aunt and Annabella said that he is no longer circulating much in the higher levels of the ton."

"Perhaps he has suffered some more losses at the gaming tables," Lucas offered mildly.

"Lucas, you suggested once or twice that he might have been involved in either the carriage incident or the footpad attack. Have you given any more thought as to whether he might have been the one who sent the pamphlet and note to me?"

"I have thought about it." Lucas studied the street outside the carriage window. "I do not doubt for a moment that he would not be at all concerned if I suffered an unfortunate accident. But I cannot see that it makes much sense to bother you. Not unless he was paving the way for a blackmail attempt."

"But there has been no demand for payment," Victoria said.

"I know. As I said, it makes no sense. Not yet, at any rate. Nevertheless, I intend to start my inquiries with Edgeworth. 'Tis as good a place as any."

"Shall we hire ourselves a runner?" Victoria asked, growing excited by the prospect. "The one I employed to track down information on Lord Barton was excellent."

Lucas met her eyes. "I would rather not get involved in hiring a runner if I can avoid it."

"Why not?"

"Because in doing so, I would run the risk of bringing up awkward questions about your stepfather's death, and those, in turn, might lead to awkward questions about you."

"Oh." Victoria sat back in her seat. "Yes, I see the problem. You are very clever, Lucas. Always thinking ahead."

"One tries."

"How will you go about tracking down Edgeworth?" Victoria asked.

"I shall start by making a few inquiries at my clubs. Someone is certain to know something about a man who gambles as much as Edgeworth does."

"An excellent notion."

"I am glad you approve. Because it means that you will be obliged to go straight home to bed after we have put in a few appearances this evening."

"What?" Her eyes darkened. "You cannot mean that."

"I fear so, madam. I cannot possibly sneak you into my clubs. We both know that. And since I do not want you running about at night without me, that leaves us with no option except to see you safely tucked up in bed at home."

"While you are out gathering information?" Victoria was incensed. "That is not fair, Lucas."

"It is not a question of fairness. It is a question of your safety. I will not risk any more runaway carriages, footpads, or ghosts who leave behind items marked with a 'W.' "

"But, Lucas, I will stay in Aunt Cleo's company or Annabella's. I will not be alone," Victoria insisted.

"Not good enough, Vicky. One cannot expect your aunt or Annabella to be on guard for a runaway carriage or a footpad, especially since they do not know they should be on guard for such things in the first place. No, I want to know you are safe at home while I am at my clubs."

Victoria's temper sparked as she sensed his implacability. "You cannot shut me out of this investigation. I will not allow you to do so. We agreed that the chief reason we would come back to London was to pursue this matter. This is my affair."

"I am not shutting you out. I'm simply ensuring that I know exactly where you are at a time when I cannot be with you. The danger lies here in London, Vicky. All the incidents occurred here. So while we are in Town, I want you under either my direct observation or lock and key," Lucas declared, his tone as definite as his words.

Victoria bristled. "Lucas, I must tell you that while you have made a tolerable husband in some respects, I do not like it at all when you assume the attitude of a superior officer and start giving orders to me. I am not under your command. I am your partner, remember? We are in business together."

"Above all, you are my wife, and as your husband I have certain responsibilities toward you. I am sorry if I offend you with the occasional command. I fear old habits are sometimes hard to break."

Victoria gave him a withering look. "Do not blame your old military habits. That is nothing but an excuse, my lord, and you are well aware of it."

"Well, then, to be perfectly truthful, Vicky, I must admit there are times when nothing else except a direct order will suffice in dealing with you. Tonight is one of those times. Now stop looking at me as though you would like to strangle me and try to look like a loving bride. I believe we have arrived at the Foxtons'."

"Lucas, I warn you I will not tolerate being treated like a witless child."

"I would not dream of doing so." He glanced out the window as the carriage drew to a halt. "It looks as if we have helped Lady Foxton draw a sizable crowd tonight. She will undoubtedly be feeling suitably grateful. Ready, my dear?"

"Damn it, Lucas, you are not going to get away with acting like this." She glared at him as he stepped out of the carriage and reached back to take her hand. "Just because you can seduce me virtually anytime you please does not mean I have become a weak-willed, fluff-brained female whom you can order about as it suits you."

His hand tightened roughly around her fingers and sudden laughter filled his eyes. "I do not believe I heard that properly. Would you care to repeat that, madam?"

"You heard me. Oh, look, there's Annabella and Bertie, now." She summoned up a brilliant smile. "I cannot wait to talk to them." Victoria rushed off, dragging Lucas along with her into the throng of people clustered on the front steps of the Foxtons' town house.

His wife's sense of timing was, as always, devastating. Lucas grinned ruefully to himself as he got out of the carriage in front of one of his clubs. Her admission that he had the power to seduce her at will was enough to

make him want to carry her straight back home and
take her to bed.

Instead he had been obliged to escort her into the
Foxtons' ballroom, where he had been forced to spend
his time fending off a lot of Victoria's old admirers.
Every last one of them had felt it necessary to profess
heartfelt anguish at the news that she had accepted
another's hand in marriage. Victoria had enjoyed herself immensely and had flirted so outrageously that
Lucas was determined to exact retribution when he
returned home.

Just what form his retribution would take was a matter to which he intended to give considerable attention.
But in the meantime there were other matters that
needed his full concentration.

The first person Lucas saw when he walked into the
club was Ferdie Merivale. The young man smiled in
welcome.

"Congratulations on your marriage, Stonevale. Cannot say I was terribly surprised. Wish you the best and
all that. You are a lucky man. Lovely lady, your new
countess."

"Thank you, Merivale." Lucas poured himself a glass
of claret.

"Come to play a few hands of cards?" Merivale
inquired.

"Unfortunately, I fear my gaming days are behind
me. I'm a married man now. Cannot spend all night
playing cards anymore."

Merivale chuckled. "I expect Lady Stonevale would
have a few words to say about that, wouldn't she?"

"My wife is rarely at a loss for words," Lucas agreed.
"Any news of interest?"

"That's right, you have been spending the last few
weeks rusticating in the country, haven't you? Since
you had that bit of a scene with Edgeworth shortly
before you left Town, you might be interested to know
that he is rarely seen in the clubs these days. He was
obliged to resign from this one, in fact."

"I cannot imagine Edgeworth giving up his gaming."

"Oh, don't think he has. But word has it he's carrying

on his business in somewhat less respectable surroundings. Heard he was seen in that same gaming hell you
rescued me from a while back. The Green Pig. Nasty
place. Rather suits him, though, don't you think?"

"I am sure he will feel very much at home there,"
Lucas agreed.

It was another two hours before Lucas walked into
the Green Pig. Nothing had changed since the night he
had brought Victoria here. It was still the same oppres-
sive, noisy place it had been when he'd deliberately
chosen it with a view to shocking Victoria into realizing
she did not really want to frequent gaming hells. Not
that it had achieved its purpose, Lucas thought with an
inner grin. Victoria had had a great time that night.

Edgeworth was sitting at a card table with a group of
well-dressed young dandies who were clearly deeply
into their cups. They had apparently set out to spend an
evening savoring the dregs of town life. Lucas got a pint
of beer from a passing barmaid and walked over to the
group of card players.

"Gentlemen," he said calmly, "I wonder if you would
all be so good as to allow Edgeworth and myself a word
in private."

One of the young pups looked up, scowling. "Here,
now, we were just getting into some deep play. You've
got no right to barge in like this."

But another young man was already on his feet, eyes
widening in belated recognition. "Your pardon, Stonevale.
Take your time. I believe we can all wait to continue
this particular game. Perhaps our luck will turn in the
meantime."

Lucas glanced at the man and smiled faintly. "The
only way your luck will come about is to find another
game. As long as you play with Edgeworth, you will no
doubt continue to lose."

"I'll have you know I won several hundred pounds
not more 'n an hour ago," the first man declared.

"Did you really? And how far down are you now?"

The man glared at Lucas. "That's none of your
business."

"I agree. But you may do as you wish. I assure you I

have no great interest in your losses. Now, if you will excuse me?"

"Come on, Harry," the second man muttered, dragging his friend away from the table. "You don't want to get into a brawl with Stonevale. Take my word for it. Friend of mine served under him on the Peninsula. Says he knows how to take care of himself."

Edgeworth watched the two young men disappear and then he turned to face Lucas. "I don't much appreciate your scaring off my lambs before they have been properly fleeced, Stonevale. Just because you have had the good fortune to marry money does not mean the rest of us must not continue to make a living."

"I am certain you will find other sources of income before dawn. You have always been quite adept at relieving the unwary of whatever they happened to have in their pockets. Tell me, Edgeworth, is there a bit more sport to be had in cheating foolish young men who have merely had too much to drink than there is in stealing from young men who are dead or dying?"

Edgeworth ruffled the cards on the table. "So you did see me that day. I wondered about it at the time. I should have slit your throat while I had the chance and made quite certain you were dead."

"Why didn't you?"

Edgeworth shrugged. "To be honest, I did not think you would live until sundown with that hole in your leg. Who could have guessed you'd make it, Stonevale? You do seem to have the most amazing luck."

"Lately someone has been trying to change my luck. I decided to consult with you to see if you might have any notion of who would want to do that."

Edgeworth smiled, his eyes glittering behind half-closed lids. "Someone who has lost a great deal of money to you at some point in the past, perhaps?"

"That list would include yourself."

"So it would."

Lucas paused. "Are you going to force me to kill you, after all, Edgeworth?"

"Rest assured, I have no intention of letting you call me out. Just how do you perceive your luck to have changed? It seems to me you have done very well for yourself lately."

"There have been one or two minor incidents. There is no need to detail them. If you truly know nothing about them, then the less said, the better. If you do have some knowledge of them, however, then you may want to see that they cease."

"Why should I care what happens to you? You have been a great nuisance to me, Stonevale."

"Let me put it this way. If there is another incident of any sort that I find, shall we say, disturbing, I shall come looking for you and we will discuss the matter in more depth. Perhaps at Clery Field? At dawn?"

Edgeworth's hand stilled on the cards. "Hardly fair if I am not the perpetrator of these incidents."

"Yes, but very little in life is fair, is it? I found that out for certain the day I watched you walk among the dead and wounded and take whatever you could find in their pockets."

Lucas got to his feet, turned, and walked away from the card table without a backward glance.

Victoria was standing at the window clad in her nightgown when she heard the connecting door open behind her. She whirled around. Lucas had changed into his dressing gown.

"There you are. Thank heavens. I have been so worried." She flew to him on bare feet and threw herself into his arms.

Lucas staggered a bit as his bad leg gave slightly under the impact, but he caught his balance quickly. His arms closed tightly around her. "I shall have to see to it that you get worried more often if this is the greeting I can expect."

"Pray do not tease me." She raised her head from his shoulder and frowned severely. "Where have you been? What have you been doing? Did you discover anything useful?"

Lucas caught her chin in his hand. "One question at a time, sweetheart. I have had a long night."

"Well, so have I. And I must tell you, Lucas, that I

will not allow you to order me to stay home again while you are out larking about in search of information. Sitting around waiting is very hard on the nerves. Now, just what did you do? Did you find Edgeworth?"

He released her and dropped into a chair. "I found him, for all the good it will do. I cannot tell if he knows anything about what is going on or not. But he does have some motive for wanting to cause trouble for me."

She nodded quickly, sitting down across from him. "Because you are more or less responsible for making him unwelcome in the clubs."

Lucas rubbed his leg. "Actually, it all goes back a bit farther than that."

She studied him intently. "Just what does it all go back to, Lucas?"

"To the day I got this damned hole in my leg. Edgeworth was there."

"You mean he also fought that day?"

"Not exactly," Lucas said. "Let us say he chose to watch the battle from a safe distance."

Victoria finally understood. "He broke and ran?"

"It happens in battle. Edgeworth was not the first, nor will he be the last. Who knows? If more men had the sense not to stand their ground and shoot at each other until there was no one left standing, we might have less warfare."

Victoria was astonished. "Lucas, you are not condemning him for his cowardice?"

"Not particularly. Cowardice under fire may not be considered an admirable trait—"

"I should think not."

"But I can understand it." He slid her a cool glance. "And forgive it. Fear is not easy to deal with and warfare is a remarkably unintelligent way to resolve problems. If I learned nothing else during my career in the army, I learned that much. The idea of a man choosing to flee from the scene of battle is not so difficult to accept. It almost seems rather logical when you think about it."

Victoria recovered from her initial shock and gave that notion some close thought. "You may have a point.

Never let your friends in the clubs hear you say such things, though."

He smiled. "I am not a complete fool. I only say such things to you, Vicky. You are the one person I know with whom I can talk freely."

She smiled at him, aware of a sweet warmth welling up inside. "That is the nicest thing you have ever said to me. I am very glad you feel that way, Lucas, because I have discovered I feel exactly the same toward you. I have told you things I have never even told Aunt Cleo."

"I am glad," he said simply.

Victoria smiled warmly. "But no matter how you feel intellectually on the subject of cowardice under fire, I know you would be incapable of behaving like a coward yourself. Edgeworth undoubtedly knows that, too. Is that why he holds a grudge against you? He knows you saw him flee?"

"That is partly it. The other part is that I saw what he did after the battle. He walked through the field and robbed the dead."

Victoria stared at him. "Good God, I can hardly credit it." Then another thought shook her. "Did he know you were lying on that field? Did he see you?"

"He saw me."

"And he did nothing to help you?"

"He assumed I wouldn't last long anyway and he was rather busy collecting jewelry, watches, and other souvenirs," Lucas explained.

Victoria leapt to her feet and raged back and forth across the room. She had never been so shaken with fury. "I will shoot the man the next time I see him, I swear I will. How dare he sink so low? How could he act in such a despicable fashion? To leave you lying there like that. It is absolutely unforgivable."

"I tend to agree with you that he sank to the depths that day. Nor has he conducted himself with much honor since," Lucas said grimly.

"No, he certainly has not. I wonder if Isabel Rycott found out about his habit of cheating at cards. Perhaps that is why she dropped him. She likes weak men, but she may draw the line at that sort of weakness."

"Perhaps."

Victoria whirled around and paced back the other way. "So you believe Edgeworth really is behind the incidents? That he holds a grudge against you because you know the truth about him?"

"It is possible. I cannot escape a certain feeling that he knew more than he was willing to say tonight. I warned him that if anything else happens, I will look to him first for an explanation, but . . ."

She eyed him carefully. "But you are not one hundred percent convinced he is to blame for what has happened to us?"

"I think there is more to the story."

"Because I was the target of some of the incidents?"

" 'Tis entirely possible Edgeworth selected you as a target because he knew it would annoy me," Lucas said.

Victoria sat down on the edge of the bed. "This is very frustrating. We are no better off than we were before you sought him out."

"That remains to be seen. If there are no more incidents, I will be able to assume I warned off the right man."

"True." She frowned, thinking about it. "But if the incidents continue, we must also consider the fact that my stepfather is alive."

"Regardless of the outcome in that quarter, I, personally, feel that I made tremendous progress in another area this evening," Lucas continued smoothly.

She looked over at him, intrigued. "How is that?"

"I was referring to your admission that I have the power to seduce you anytime I please."

"Oh, that." She felt the heat flood her cheeks.

Lucas got to his feet and came toward her. "Yes, that. A minor issue to you, perhaps, my dear, but a matter of overwhelming import to me. It gives me great hope, you see. One of these days you are going to take the last step and admit you love me."

She rose and backed away from him. "You probably should not read too much into what I said as we got out of the carriage, Lucas. I was very annoyed with you at the time and spoke without thinking."

He smiled. "Are you going to retract your words now? You cannot possibly deny them. I will not allow it."

She groaned and took another step backward. "You are going to assume far too much from this. You will see it as a form of surrender. I just know you will."

"Would surrender be so bad, Vicky?"

"Intolerable." She took one more step backward and found herself up against the wall. Her eyes widened as he stalked toward her.

Lucas's eyes were gleaming as he closed the distance between them. Very deliberately he caged her, flattening his palms against the wall on either side of her head. His mouth hovered bare inches above hers.

"Intolerable, hmmm? Very well, madam, why don't we call it a step toward a negotiated truce rather than a step toward surrender?"

She caught her breath. "In order for it to be a step toward a negotiated truce, we would both have to give up an equal amount of ground, my lord. You would have to admit I have the same power over you."

"Yes, I would, wouldn't I?"

Her tongue touched the corner of her mouth. "Are you admitting I can seduce you at will?"

"Madam, you can seduce me by merely walking across the drawing room or serving me a cup of tea. Every time I look at my picture of *Strelitzia reginae*, I am seduced."

"Oh." Then she smiled slowly. "Is this another example of your skill at strategy, Lucas?"

He did not answer that with words. Instead, his mouth closed over hers, hot, exciting and intoxicating. Victoria put her arms around his neck, glorying in the heat and strength of him.

He slid his hand down her side to her thigh and lifted the thin stuff of her night clothes up to her waist.

"Lucas?"

"Part your legs, sweetheart."

She moaned softly and, shivering delightfully, did as

he directed. His hand slipped between her thighs.

"*Lucas.*"

"Yes, sweetheart. That's it. That is what I want from you. Call it a truce or call it surrender. It does not signify."

She clutched at him as his tongue eased into her mouth just as he eased a finger into her moist heat. He began moving both tongue and finger in and out of her in a simultaneous rhythm. Victoria thought her legs would collapse.

She retained just enough self mastery to fumble with the opening of his dressing gown. She found him hard and heavy with his arousal. Her fingers circled him gently.

"Oh, God, Vicky."

He pulled her back toward the bed, dragging her down onto it. Then he was on top of her, kissing her breasts, her silky stomach, and the soft skin of her thighs. Without warning, his kiss became even more intimate. Victoria gasped, first in shock and then in wonder, as she felt his mouth on the most secret part of her.

"Lucas, this is outrageous. You cannot mean to . . ." Her fingers clenched in his dark hair and her whole body tightened unbearably. "*Lucas.*"

She was still in the midst of her searing climax when she felt him glide up the length of her and surge deeply, heavily into her body. Victoria's teeth sank into the skin of his bare shoulder. She clung to him as if she would never let him go as his hoarse, exultant shout echoed in her ears.

18

"I must say, you and Lucas have certainly contrived to brush through the entire incident quite nicely." Cleo raised her watering pot to reach a fuchsia plant that hung from a beam. "You were a great success at the Foxtons' last night. It is obvious you do not even need Jessica Atherton's public approval. The ton has decided you are their favorite couple, and the Season, one hopes, will be over before you can do anything to ruin that status."

"One hopes." Victoria grinned. "I believe Lucas is harboring the same sentiments. You and he must get together and share your concerns over my behavior."

"We would no doubt have a great deal to talk about, would we not?" Cleo smiled. "I did tell him once that one is seldom bored around you."

"Well, as far as I am concerned, it is not Lucas and I who contrived to escape the potential scandal, Aunt Cleo. You are the one who accomplished that. With a little help from Jessica Atherton, of course," she added in regretful honesty as she studied the half-finished painting of a cactus on the easel before her. Cacti were a nuisance to paint. All the little spines were something of a bother.

Cleo moved on to the next pot but she searched Victoria's face with concerned eyes. "I worried a great deal at first after Lucas took you away to Yorkshire. I could have strangled Jessica Atherton for showing up the morning of your marriage and causing such a stir."

"I had a few thoughts along that line myself. Lucas did, too."

"Not surprising. I am certain he could have done without her interference. The whole situation bordered on disaster, but I told myself that there was only one man of your acquaintance who could deal with such an imbroglio and you were with him. When I got your first letter requesting plants for his gardens, I knew the worst was over," Cleo explained.

" 'Tis true we have arrived at an understanding of sorts, Lucas and I."

Cleo's head came up sharply. Her eyes sparkled with laughter. "An understanding? Is that what you call it? You should see yourself when you are anywhere near him, my dear. You practically glow. I trust you are no longer worrying about following in your mother's sad footsteps?"

Victoria carefully mixed yellow with a touch of blue to create just the right shade of green she was seeking. "Lucas is no Samuel Whitlock."

"Good heavens, I should say not. Just as you are nothing like your mother, dear Caroline, rest her soul. She truly loved your father, you know. If he had lived, everything would have been much different. She would never have become an easy target for Whitlock's charms. But she was so hungry for love after your father died that she fell immediately for the illusion Whitlock was quick to offer."

"Love is a dangerous thing, rather like electricity, I believe. I think it is better to form a solid, working partnership with a man. That is what I am doing with Lucas, you know. We are making progress."

Cleo gave a start. "I beg your pardon? You are forming a business alliance with Stonevale?"

"It is the logical thing to do, given the circumstances under which we were married. There is no denying that Stonevale itself is an excellent investment. It is good land."

"I see." Cleo looked dazed. "How very fascinating."

"The arrangement works well, for the most part, although Lucas does have the lamentable habit of giving orders when he cannot get his way through reason and logic."

"Vicky, dear, this is quite interesting. Stonevale is going along with this partnership notion?"

"On the whole. I am meeting with some resistance in certain areas."

Cleo's eyes widened. "I can imagine. What areas?"

"He would still very much like to believe that I am in love with him and he never loses an opportunity to try to coax me into admitting it."

Cleo put down the watering pot with a small thud and stared at her niece. "Are you not in love with him? Vicky, I assumed from the start that your heart was charting your course in all this. Otherwise, I would never have insisted—"

"Of course I am in love with him. I would never have gone to the inn that first night with him if I hadn't been. But I am not about to give him the satisfaction of admitting it to him," Victoria declared.

"Why ever not?"

Victoria looked up from the painting. "Because, to be blunt, he is not in love with me."

"Good heavens, Vicky, are you certain? He seems inordinately fond of you."

"He is fond of me. That is one of the reasons the marriage is working. But he feels he cannot allow-himself to love me because if he does, I will use the knowledge to run roughshod over him. He thinks I am something of a shrew, you see. Too independent and headstrong by half. Give me an inch and I will surely take a mile."

"Perhaps he is merely uncertain of you and cannot admit his love until he knows you love him," Cleo suggested.

"Why should he be uncertain of me? The man is married to me."

"What does that signify? How many married women of our acquaintance are head over heels in love with their husbands? More than one has resorted to a discreet affair, as you well know. And women such as Jessica Atherton, who would almost certainly never indulge in an affair, are testimonials to womanly duty, not womanly love. The thought of being married out of a sense of duty must give a man a few chills."

"Why should it? Lucas certainly had no qualms about marrying me out of a sense of duty. His goal from the start was to save Stonevale, not find a deep and abiding love for himself." Victoria dashed the brush fiercely across the paper and immediately had to blot up a long smear of green.

"Just because a man is forced to marry for the sake of his responsibilities does not mean he is not human enough to want to be loved. Lucas told me the morning of your marriage that he truly wished things had progressed in a far different fashion. He knows that because of that debacle at the inn, he never had a chance to finish the courtship properly."

"He finished it, all right. He concluded the matter with a special license, if you will recall." Another smear of green appeared on the paper.

"My point is that he is only too well aware of the fact that he did not have a chance to win your love. You did not marry him entirely of your own free will and he knows that. Later, when you found out he had begun his pursuit of you because you were an heiress, his position was further weakened. How can he possibly be all that certain of you unless you have assured him of your love?"

Victoria looked up, feeling pressed. "Just whose side are you on, Aunt Cleo?"

Cleo sighed. "I am not on anyone's side. I just want to see you happy, Vicky."

"You think I would be happy if I simply surrender completely to my husband?"

"Surrender? What an odd term."

" 'Tis the one he uses," Victoria muttered. "Except when he's trying to find euphemisms such as 'negotiated truce.' "

"Does he really? I expect 'tis because he spent so much time in the military and then devoted himself to gaming. Military men and gamesters have a somewhat similar vocabulary, you know. They are always thinking in terms of strategy and winning and losing. There is very little middle ground for them."

"Yes, I have discovered that for myself."

"Women, on the other hand, are capable of more flexibility in their thinking," Cleo continued.

"That is undoubtedly a weakness when it comes to dealing with men. It gives them a license to indulge their own inflexibility. No, I am married to a man who thinks like a soldier, and I must either break him of the habit or teach him to be content with the partnership we have managed to establish. The one thing I will not do is risk everything by giving him the surrender he wants."

Cleo considered her thoughtfully for a long moment. "What is it, precisely, that you would be risking?"

"My pride, for one thing."

"Is that so very important?"

"Of course it is."

"Well, he is your husband, my dear. You must do as you think best."

Relieved to be through with that topic of conversation, Victoria hurriedly switched to another. "Perhaps you would care to go shopping today? I mean to purchase some books on gardening and horticulture to take back to Yorkshire."

"I would be delighted. Are these for your library at Stonevale?"

"Some of them will go into the library but the rest are to serve as a gift to our local vicar and his wife. They have been most helpful. The vicar is writing a book on gardening." Victoria hesitated and then added in a rush, "And I am to the plates."

Cleo beamed. "Vicky, how marvelous. You are going to get your lovely botanical work published. I am so pleased. How did that arrangement come about?"

"Lucas arranged it," Victoria admitted softly.

Cleo's gaze sharpened. "How did he do that?"

Victoria flushed. "He showed one of my paintings to the vicar, who instantly asked to meet the artist to see if she would be interested in doing the plates for his book. Lucas swears he did not influence the vicar by telling him who the artist was until after Reverend Worth admired the picture. The vicar seems genuinely delighted to have me do the plates. I must confess, I am very excited about it."

Cleo leaned forward and admired Victoria's painting, musing thoughtfully. "Trust Stonevale to find a way to give his heiress the one gift she could not have bought for herself."

The amber yellow silk gown was stunning in its elegant simplicity. Victoria was pleased with the effect. The skirt fell in a narrow, graceful column to her ankles. The high waistline, topped with a small, artfully draped bodice, displayed a wide expanse of white skin and emphasized the gentle curves of her breasts. Her slippers were embroidered in gold thread and matched her long, elegant gloves.

The amber pendant hung in solitary splendor around her throat. With a last glance in the mirror, Victoria decided she was as ready as she would ever be for Jessica Atherton's reception. She picked up her gilded fan.

"I will take the black cloak, the one with the hood lined in gold satin, Nan."

"Ye do look wonderful tonight, ma'am," Nan breathed reverently as she carefully draped the long, flowing cloak around her mistress's shoulders. "His lordship will be ever so proud." She adjusted the hood so that the gold satin formed a deep, rich collar around Victoria's throat. "Wonderful."

"Thank you, Nan. I must be off. His lordship will be

waiting in the hall. Pray do not wait up for me. I will wake you when I return if I need any help."

"Yes, ma'am."

Lucas was pacing impatiently at the foot of the stairs, but when he saw Victoria draped in black velvet and gold, he halted abruptly. His eyes were full of gleaming, sensual admiration as he watched her come slowly down the staircase.

"Ready for battle, are we?" he murmured as he took her arm.

"Let's just say I do not want Jessica Atherton feeling sorry for me."

He laughed as Griggs opened the door. "She is far more likely to feel sorry for me."

"Oh, really? And why is that, my lord?"

Lucas tightened his hold on Victoria's arm. "She will know I must be helpless to resist my Amber Lady. She will undoubtedly worry that you are already in command of this marriage."

Victoria slid a sidelong glance at him as he assisted her into the carriage. "And are you helpless to resist me?"

"What do you think?" He climbed in beside her.

"I think you are teasing me again."

He reached for her hand and inclined his head gallantly over her gloved fingers. "Madam, I assure you that I find you utterly irresistible."

"I shall bear that in mind."

The streets near the large Atherton home were filled with carriages. Dozens of elegantly dressed people clogged the front steps. But Lucas and Victoria, as guests of honor, were quickly ushered past the crowds.

When Victoria handed over her cloak in the wide, brilliantly lit hall, the amber yellow gown was revealed in all its glory. Lucas took one look at the graceful expanse of his wife's throat, shoulders, and bosom revealed by the small bodice and he set his teeth.

"No wonder you kept that cloak wrapped around you until we got here," he growled. "This will teach me to examine your attire far more carefully before I take you anywhere in the future."

"Trust me, Lucas. This gown is in the height of fashion."

"It reveals more than a tavern maid's dress. You are practically falling out of it. If I had seen it before we left the house, I would have sent you straight upstairs to change."

"Too late for that now," she told him cheerfully. "Now do stop frowning so. We are about to be announced and you surely would not want Lady Atherton and her guests to think we are quarreling."

"You have won for now, madam, but rest assured, this discussion will continue at a later time." He led her toward the top of the stairs that descended into the glittering, crowded ballroom.

A hush fell over the throng of beautifully dressed people as the Earl of Stonevale and his lady were announced. And then a ringing cheer went up and glasses were raised in a salute as Lucas and Victoria went down the staircase to greet their host and hostess.

Lady Atherton's gaze held a trace of wistfulness as she smiled at Lucas. Lord Atherton, an austere man who was active in politics, inclined his balding head over Victoria's hand.

"So kind of you both to honor us with this reception tonight," Victoria forced herself to say as sincerely as possible.

"You look lovely, my dear," Jessica said to Victoria. "That gown is simply exquisite. And such an unusual style for a new bride. But, then, you have always been something of an Original, have you not?"

"I do my best," Victoria assured her. "After all, I would not want to bore my husband."

Lucas shot her a warning glance. His smile was full of menacing charm. "Boredom is not something I have suffered from much since the night I met you, my dear."

Lord Atherton smiled briefly. "And as I understand it, that momentous occurrence took place right here in this ballroom, did it not?"

"Lady Atherton was kind enough to introduce us," Victoria said politely.

"So I heard." Lord Atherton extended his arm. "Would you be so gracious as to honor me with the first dance, madam?"

"It would be my pleasure."

As she was led out onto the floor, Victoria glanced back over her shoulder in time to see a crowd of people close in around Lucas. He caught her eye over the heads of the throng and smiled faintly, a smile of possession, admiration, and sensual promise; a lover's smile.

Warmed by that smile, Victoria turned to give her attention to Lord Atherton, who was already starting to talk about politics.

Lucas kept an eye on his Amber Lady as the evening passed, but he had very little opportunity to speak to her. Just as well, he told himself. If he did get close to her, he would probably be unable to avoid bringing up the topic of the dress again, and since the damage was already done, it would be pointless to continue the argument.

A husband had to learn which battles were worth fighting, and he could not deny that the military strategist in him could not help but sympathize with Victoria's need to make a brilliant splash tonight in front of Jessica Atherton.

Nevertheless, he vowed as he caught sight of Victoria being led out onto the floor again, he would pay much closer attention to her clothes in the future.

"Your wife is cutting quite a swath through my male guests tonight," Jessica Atherton murmured as she glided up to stand beside Lucas. "I am gratified that she is enjoying herself."

"She deserves to enjoy herself."

"Yes. It cannot have been easy for her to come here tonight."

Lucas raised a brow at that bit of unexpected insight. "No, it was not."

"I know she must have been feeling somewhat battered by all that happened at the time of her marriage to you. And I did not aid matters by calling on her that morning before you left for Yorkshire. I am sorry about that, Lucas. I have wanted to apologize for it. My only excuse is that I was desperately anxious to know if you were going to be happy with her," Jessica said weakly.

"Forget it, Jessica. It is all in the past."

"Yes, you are quite right. It is just that I know you were angry with me that day and I expect I am trying to find out if you have forgiven me."

"As I said, it is over and done. Don't fret about it. Victoria and I have arrived at an understanding and we are both content with the marriage."

Jessica nodded. "I rather thought that is what would happen. She is, after all, an intelligent woman. She may be rather outrageous at times, but she is also a woman of honor and integrity. I would not have introduced you to her if I had thought otherwise. I was certain that when all was said and done, she would learn to accept her fate and fulfill her duty, just as you must."

Lucas realized he was starting to grit his teeth. He reached for a glass of champagne and took a large swallow. "Tell me, Jessica, have you had much pleasure in your marriage?"

"Atherton is a tolerable husband. That is as much as a woman can hope for from her marriage. I take satisfaction in knowing I am a good wife to him. One does what one must."

A tolerable husband. Victoria had called him that once or twice, Lucas reflected. He suddenly felt slightly savage. Was that all he was to her he wondered? *A tolerable husband?*

"Excuse me, Jessica. I think I just saw Potbury in the crowd by the window. I wanted to ask him a question."

"Of course."

Lucas escaped his hostess, but he knew he could not escape her words. As was frequently the case with Jessica Atherton, she might grate a bit, but she was not altogether wrong in her observations. She was right about Victoria being a woman of honor and integrity.

But Lucas did not want to think she was also right when she claimed that Victoria had no doubt accepted the marriage because it was the reasonable thing to do. He did not want to be merely a tolerable husband.

He could not bring himself to believe that when Victoria shivered and cried out in his arms, she was merely performing her wifely duty. She cared for him, he told himself. He was almost positive she could learn to love him again if she would just stop erecting defenses to protect her pride. Her damned female pride was all that kept her from the final surrender.

Lord Potbury smiled in genial welcome when he saw Lucas coming toward him. "Good to see you again, Stonevale. Must say your bride is looking positively radiant this evening. How are things in Yorkshire?"

"Very well, thank you. But I miss our weekly meetings of the society. Wanted to ask how the electricity experiments were proceeding. Heard of any more interesting work in that area?"

Lord Potbury brightened. "Grimshaw had a bit of an accident last week. Gave himself a terrible jolt. Thought he was done for at the time, but he is quite recovered now."

"I'm relieved to hear that. What was he working on?"

"Thinks he's got an idea for creating a smaller, more compact system for storing electrical energy. Have to hope he doesn't kill himself with the stuff before he finishes his work on the invention."

"I read something recently about more work on reanimation of the dead," Lucas said casually.

"Yes, yes, saw that bit myself. Quite interesting, but so far no one's seen any reanimated corpses walking about." Potbury chuckled.

"You don't believe that line of experimentation will prove fruitful?"

"Who can say for certain? But personally I'm highly doubtful."

"Yes," said Lucas. "So am I. Which means that we must look to the living for answers."

"Beg pardon?"

"Never mind, sir. Just making an observation to myself. If you will excuse me, I think I shall try and forge a path over to where my wife is standing."

"Good luck. Quite a crush here tonight, ain't there? And getting worse. More people arriving by the minute. Probably going to be the rout of the Season. There's Lady Nettleship. Looks quite lovely tonight, doesn't she? Believe I'll try to make my way over to her."

Lucas nodded politely and started off through the crowd. Progress was difficult because nearly everyone he passed insisted on stopping him long enough to congratulate him.

He was midway in his journey across the ballroom when one of the liveried footmen stepped into his path. He held out a small silver tray on which lay a sealed note.

"A man appeared at the door and asked that this be given to you, my lord," the footman said politely. "I am sorry for the delay. It took me a while to find you in the crowd."

Lucas frowned and picked up the note, nodding abruptly in appreciation of the service. He put a few coins on the tray and the footman disappeared into the sea of guests.

> Have information that
> should interest you concerning
> certain incidents. Very
> urgent. Am waiting outside in
> black carriage near corner.

Lucas crumpled the note and looked across the room to where Victoria was standing in a group of chattering, laughing people. He started toward her again, this time not pausing politely when he was greeted by well-wishers.

"I wonder if I might steal my wife for a moment or two," he said as he moved through the small crowd around Victoria. It was a command, not a request, and everyone stepped back immediately.

Victoria looked up in surprise and then smiled knowingly at the women in the group. "Men go through such a change after marriage, do they not?" she murmured by way of apology. "Why is it they are always so accommodating and gallant before the wedding and so dreadfully dictatorial afterward?"

Lucas took her arm and led her a short distance away, aware of the laughter and giggles behind him. "I shall only keep you a minute, madam, and then you may return to your observations on husbands."

"Lucas, I was only joking, for heaven's sake. What is it? Is something wrong?"

"I don't know. I just got this." He showed her the note.

She read it with widening eyes. "Edgeworth?"

"It must be him. He probably does not have an invitation and could not get inside to talk to me. I am going outside to see what he wants. I came to warn you I would be missing for a while. I did not want you calling attention to the fact that I'm gone. I don't know how long this will take."

Victoria glanced around assessingly. "I think it will be perfectly possible for you to slip away unnoticed. Do you know, I believe we could both slip out. This crowd has gotten so huge no one would guess we had left. Anyone looking for us would just assume we were at the other end of the room or on the balcony or in the card room or even outside in the gardens."

"Victoria . . ."

Her expression brightened with anticipation. "Yes, I am certain we could both slip out. You go first and I will just sort of casually move out into the gardens, hop over the wall, and pop around the corner. You can meet me there."

"Are you out of your mind?" He was thunderstruck even though he supposed he should have been expecting something along this line. "You will do no such thing. I absolutely forbid it. You are to stay right here, Vicky. That is a direct order. Under no circumstances are you to leave this ballroom. Do not even go out into the gardens for fresh air. Do you hear me?"

"Very clearly, my lord. I assure you, you have made

your point. Honestly, Lucas, sometimes you have the most annoying tendency of putting a damper on something that particularly interests me."

"Forgive me, my dear, but sometimes you have the most annoying tendency of coming up with the most idiotic notions I have ever heard. Now go back to your friends. I shall return as soon as possible."

"I will require a full report as soon as you get back inside the ballroom."

"Yes, madam."

She put her hand on his arm and her eyes were suddenly very intent. "Lucas, promise me you will be careful."

"I am sure there is no danger in this," he said soothingly. "But I give you my promise." Then he scowled briefly at the décolletage of her gown. "The only real danger around here tonight is that you might catch a severe chest cold."

She grinned. "I shall try to keep warm by dancing. On your way, Lucas. Hurry back."

He wanted to kiss her full on her lovely mouth but knew that was impossible. Such a public display of affection would be quite scandalous. Absolutely unthinkable. Except that he could not seem to stop thinking about it.

"Vicky?"

"Yes, Lucas?"

"Do you still find me merely a tolerable husband?"

"Quite tolerable, my lord," she said cheerfully.

He turned and pushed through the crowd toward the windows. He took his time, not wanting to call attention to himself now. When he was satisfied no one would think it amiss if he stepped outside for a breath of fresh air, he did so.

And kept on going.

The Athertons' garden wall was no more difficult to climb than Lady Nettleship's. Lucas found a few chinks in the bricks, a handful of ivy, and a moment later he was over the top and safely down on the other side.

He found himself in a narrow alley that was nearly

pitch dark. It stank, as all London alleys seemed to do, but other than that presented no great difficulty. He walked around to the front of the house and moved through a group of lounging coachmen and grooms who were throwing dice.

He paused in the shadow of a team of horses and scanned the line of carriages. Near the corner, a little removed from the others, was a small, black vehicle of undistinguished lines. The coachman was on his box, apparently waiting.

Lucas circled around two other coaches that stood between him and the small, black one and came up on the far side of the vehicle.

"Were you by any chance expecting someone?"

The coachman turned around with a start and peered down at Lucas. "Yes, sir."

"Perhaps I am he."

"Never even saw you come out of the house," the coachman said with a touch of admiration. "Got a passenger inside who wants to have a word wi' ye."

Lucas glanced speculatively into the dark carriage and saw a man lounging in the corner. He reflected that being obliged to leave the party unobtrusively as he had, he had not been able to collect his greatcoat. There was, of course, no way to secret a pistol in his close-fitting evening clothes. Pity.

"Good evening, Edgeworth. Waiting for me, I presume?"

"I have something that I think will interest you, Stonevale. Do step inside for a moment, won't you?"

Lucas considered the possibilities and decided the prospect of getting some answers outweighed the risks. He opened the door and got into the carriage with some awkwardness, deliberately favoring his left leg more than was absolutely necessary.

He was not particularly surprised to see Edgeworth pull a pistol out of his heavy coat.

"I imagine you recall that day you should have died every time that leg of yours fails you, don't you Stonevale?"

"I do hope you will at least do me the courtesy of explaining what is going on before you pull the trigger," Lucas remarked, massaging his thigh as he sat down across from the other man.

"You may relax, Stonevale. I will not be pulling the trigger for some time yet. My associate has a few plans that must be carried out before I shall have that pleasure."

"Would the name of your associate be Samuel Whitlock, by any chance?"

"Whitlock? What an amusing notion." Edgeworth rapped twice on the roof of the carriage and the vehicle moved off. Then he looked at Lucas and broke into outright laughter. "Imagine forming a partnership with the dead. Most amusing."

19

The message reached Victoria on a silver salver just as she came off the dance floor with Lord Potbury. "Please excuse me." She smiled quickly at her escort as she opened the note.

"Of course. Nothing serious, I trust?"

Victoria scanned the brief message and hoped Potbury would not notice that her fingers were shaking inside her beautiful gloves.

> Come at once if you value
> your husband's life and honor.
> A carriage waits at the corner
> with the garments you will
> need. The driver will give you
> instructions when you arrive.
> Time is of the essence.

"No," Victoria said, smiling very brightly at Potbury. "Nothing is wrong. Just a short note from a friend to tell me she is going to take some air in the gardens. She invites me to join her. I suppose she felt it would be easier for one of the footmen to get the message to me in this crowd than for her to get through the crush. Will you excuse me?"

"Certainly." Potbury bent gracefully over her hand. "Enjoy yourself. Lady Atherton's gardens are quite extensive. Once again, my congratulations on your marriage. Good man, Stonevale."

"Yes, he is, is he not?"

Victoria unobtrusively collected her cloak from one of the footmen, explaining that she was going out into the gardens for a few minutes and found it cool outdoors. Then she made her way discreetly toward one of the windows.

A moment later she was deep in the unlit portion of Jessica Atherton's precisely manicured gardens. Several rows of clipped hedges and elaborately designed topiary shielded her from the ballroom windows. Jessica Atherton's gardens were rather like Jessica herself, Victoria concluded: beautiful, perfect, untouchable.

Climbing the wall took a bit of doing. She was obliged to hitch her gown up to her thighs in order to accomplish the feat and she thought fleetingly of what Lucas would have said had he seen her expose so much leg. The thought brought tears to her eyes and she dashed them away immediately. She would do something violent to Edgeworth as soon as she found him if Lucas had not already done so.

Victoria wrinkled her nose at the stench in the alley as she put on the cloak and pulled the hood up over her head. Then she walked swiftly to the corner.

A public coach was waiting. An obviously half-drunk coachman tipped his hat with mocking respect. "Expect you be the *lady* I been waitin' for."

Realizing he probably thought he was taking her to meet a lover at a secret rendezvous, Victoria said nothing. She shrank deeper into the cloak and climbed quickly into the coach. The vehicle jolted forward before she was properly seated and she nearly lost her balance.

When she reached out to brace herself, her hand touched a sack. She knew immediately it contained the clothes she had been told to wear.

Even as she pulled the breeches, shirt, and boots from the bag her stomach turned over with a sickening realization. This was no coincidence. Whoever had sent the note must know that she was in the habit of wearing men's clothes at night. If that same person knew that dark secret, he might know others.

A ghost would know such things, she reflected, or a man who trailed her like a ghost the way she had once trailed Samuel Whitlock through the corridors of his own home. Victoria shuddered.

But she could not think about that now, she told herself as she changed quickly into the male garb. Indeed, she must not think about it. The only thing that mattered was rescuing Lucas.

Her stomach felt distinctly queasy again as the coach pulled up outside the Green Pig. The choice of destination could not be a coincidence either. Someone knew everything.

With shaking hands, she put her cloak back on over the masculine clothing and pulled up the hood. Then she quickly rolled up her gown and the rest of her discarded clothes and stuffed them into the sack.

"Third room at the top o' the stairs," the coachman muttered as she stepped down from the cab. "Trust you'll 'ave fun. Quality usually does, unlike the rest o' us that's got to work for a livin'." He did not even bother to look at her as he took another sip from his flask, flicked the reins, and drove off.

Victoria watched the carriage roll out of sight and then she removed the cloak and put on the high crowned hat that had been provided. Taking a deep breath and squaring her shoulders, she walked boldly through the front door of the gaming hell.

Everything was different this time, she thought nervously, and she knew that was because she did not have Lucas by her side to make it all seem a grand adventure. The red glare from the hearth illuminated the rough crowd of Green Pig patrons, making them look like demons from the underworld. The coarse, drunken laughter was unnerving. She had the feeling a violent brawl could break out at any moment. As she started toward the stairs one of the barmaids sidled up to her.

"You don't want to be goin' up there alone, now do ye, sir? You'll be wantin' a lady friend and it just so 'appens I'm free at the moment."

Victoria thought frantically. "Thank you, but there is someone waiting for me."

"Ah, so that's the way of it, eh?" The barmaid winked. "I saw your *friend* go up earlier and I ain't one to pass judgment on that sort o' thing. Besides, the bloke already paid for the room. Good luck to ye, I say. But if ye decide you'd rather have a woman, ye just give old Betsy a shout, hear?"

Victoria stared at her in confusion. "Yes, thank you very much, I'll do that."

Betsy roared with laughter. "Ye can always tell the well-bred coves. They remember their manners even in a place like this." She sallied off into the crowd, still chuckling.

Victoria went grimly up the stairs, the sack containing her dress still clutched in one hand, the cloak draped over her arm.

At the top of the stairs she found herself in a dark hall. She could hear obscene laughter and groans coming from the rooms as she passed two doors and stopped at the third.

She hesitated a moment at her goal and then tapped cautiously on the third door. It opened immediately.

Isabel Rycott stood framed in the doorway, looking even more exotic in men's clothes than she did in a ball gown.

"Lady Rycott. What a surprise." Victoria struggled to sound calm and cool and almost detached, the way Lucas always managed to do when he was facing a startling situation. At least she was not dealing with the reanimated corpse of Samuel Whitlock, Victoria told herself. "Where is my husband?"

Isabel Rycott smiled with a terrible satisfaction and revealed the pistol in her hand. "Won't you come in, Lady Stonevale? I have been waiting for you."

Now that she was over her initial shock, Victoria told herself she must stay calm. She would be no help to

Lucas if she had hysterics. "Is Edgeworth with you?"
she asked as she stepped into the room. "I cannot
imagine you have managed this entire business by yourself. You are accustomed to using your male acquaintances, are you not?"

"How very astute of you." Isabel backed away from
her. Her eyes were feverishly bright. "But, then, you
always were a very clever girl, weren't you? Too clever
by half. And now you are going to pay for it."

Still clutching the sack of clothing and the cloak,
Victoria wandered over to the fireplace to lean negligently against the mantel. The blaze on the hearth cast
a sordid glare over the small, shabby room. "You don't
mean to tell me that all this is because you hold some
sort of grudge against me, madam? What on earth have
I ever done to you?"

"You killed him. That's what you did," Isabel hissed.
"You killed Samuel Whitlock and ruined everything."

Victoria went still. "Perhaps you will be good enough
to tell me just what it was I ruined for you?"

"I had it all planned, you stupid little bitch. Whitlock
was going to marry me after he killed your mother. It
took me months to work him up to the point where he
had sufficient nerve to see to the business of murdering
Caroline. *Months.*"

Victoria almost collapsed against the mantel. "You
prodded him into murdering my mother?"

"Do you think he'd have done it on his own? He
hadn't the guts to do it without being pushed into it.
He saw no need. Kept saying he had the use of her
fortune anyway, so what did it matter if she was alive.
But I did not have the use of that fortune. So I made it
clear to Samuel that he could not have me unless he got
rid of her, and he wanted me very badly, Victoria. Very
badly, indeed. He finally arranged the riding accident."

"I *knew* it was murder, even before he confessed."

"Yes, you guessed that immediately, didn't you? Less
than two months later he started acting very strange.
Kept saying he was seeing your mother's ghost. I was
afraid he was losing his mind, that he would get himself
sent to Bedlam before he could marry me. So I decided

to see for myself what was going on at his house at night."

Victoria's fingers tightened on the sack. "You were there that last night when he came at me with a knife, weren't you?"

"Who do you think put the knife in his hand? I told him he must kill Caroline again and this time she would stay dead. He was so crazed with drink and the notion that Caroline had come back to haunt him that he did as I told him."

Victoria's pulse was racing, driven by savage anger and a terrible fear. "Where is my husband? What has he to do with any of this?"

"All in good time, Victoria. All in good time. He will be here, never fear. Edgeworth is going to bring him."

"So Edgeworth is involved."

Isabel tightened her grip on the pistol and laughed softly. "Oh, yes. It was Edgeworth's idea to finish the matter in this particular fashion. He has a score of his own to settle with Stonevale, you see. I agreed to do it his way so long as I could be certain of your death."

"You cared so much for my drunken sot of a stepfather that you wish vengeance on me? I am appalled by your taste in men, Lady Rycott. But, then, I suppose I should not be so astonished. After all, you took up with Edgeworth and he certainly is not an admirable specimen of manhood, either, is he? Perhaps you like men who are as low as you yourself?"

"I told you once I like men who can be controlled. Men who are weak and therefore easily manipulated. It makes everything so much easier, you see. Whitlock was completely in my power. Edgeworth is now, too."

"How did you happen to select Edgeworth as your assistant?"

"I heard the talk that there was ill feeling between him and Stonevale. When Stonevale began pursuing you, I decided a man who disliked him as much as Edgeworth did could be of use to me."

" 'Tis a bit late to murder me," Victoria pointed out. "My husband has legal control of my money now. In the event of his death, the inheritance goes to our remaining relatives, including my aunt. You will never see a penny of it."

Isabel's eyes sparked in anger. "Don't you think I know that? You deprived me of any chance of getting hold of your fortune the night you caused poor, stupid Samuel to fall down those stairs. You ruined all my plans and now you will pay."

"Why have you waited so long to take your vengeance? Why did you go to the continent after Whitlock's death?"

"Because I was afraid you would realize I had been involved. You were so damn clever that I could take no chances. I had no way of knowing how much you knew or how much Samuel told you that night he tried to kill you. I fled the night of his death because I feared you would put the entire tale together. But you never did."

"No. But for the past few months I have had the oddest feeling that there was something left unfinished." The nightmares had begun shortly after she had been introduced to Isabel Rycott, Victoria realized with a chill.

"I did not care for life on the continent," Isabel continued coldly. "Oh, it suited me well enough at first, but there were problems after I became involved with a young Italian count. His mother, you know. She was afraid her precious son would marry me and she could not bear the notion of the family fortune falling into my hands. She contrived to have me cast out of the higher circles of society, ruining all my opportunities. Most unpleasant."

"So you decided to return to England."

"It is here I have the best chance of securing another fortune. And mark my words, I will find another Samuel Whitlock, and soon. I have gone through my first husband's money and I find myself in need of more. Quickly. While on the continent, I had kept track of you through friends. After several months I realized I was safe, so I returned to London."

"And decided to make me pay for ruining everything for you?"

"Precisely. But I also wanted you out of the way

because it was simply good policy to tidy up after oneself. There was always the chance that you would put it all together, you see. Since I must be free to stay in England, I could not take the risk that you would eventually figure out that I had been involved in your mother's death."

"It was you who put the scarf and the snuffbox where you knew I would find them," Victoria said evenly.

Isabel glanced down at her breeches and boots and smiled strangely. "You are not the only one who has learned to enjoy the freedom of men's clothing. I owe you for that, by the by. Do you think there will ever come a time when women will be free to wear breeches in public?"

Victoria ignored that. "You followed me about at night."

"Oh, yes. I kept very close watch on you for weeks before I made my plans, learning your habits and your ways. When you took up with Stonevale, it all became vastly easier. You began taking so many risks, you see."

"Yes." Greater risks than even Lucas had imagined, Victoria thought. "Who was it who nearly ran me down that night outside this tavern?"

"That was Edgeworth. I told him I only wanted you frightened, but I do believe the fool saw his chance to get rid of Stonevale in the process. I was very angry with him afterward."

"And the footpad who attacked my husband?"

"Edgeworth hired him for me. Again, you were supposed to be frightened, perhaps nicked a bit with the knife, but that was all. Something went wrong, however. You did not follow your usual pattern that night. Stonevale went to fetch you from the garden as usual, but you did not return to the carriage with him. The dolt of a footpad attacked him anyway, figuring he had to earn his money somehow," Isabel said.

Victoria remembered that had been the night when she had summoned Lucas to the garden to tell him she wanted to begin a love affair with him. She had not planned to go adventuring that evening, so she had not gone back to the carriage with him.

"Why the haunting tactics, Isabel? Why the business with the scarf and the snuffbox and the pamphlet on reanimating the dead?"

Isabel's eyes brightened noticeably. "I got the notion from you, of course. Don't you appreciate the irony? I wanted you to be scared out of your wits and to know there was no one you could turn to. After all, who would believe Whitlock had come back from the grave to kill you? My original plan was to terrify you into believing you had lost your wits. Everything would have been so simple if you had gotten yourself committed to a madhouse. Imagine yourself chained to a wall to rot for the rest of your life. A sane woman trapped in a world of madmen. It would have been a most piquant ending. And a safe one for me."

Victoria nodded. "You would not have had to risk your own neck by resorting to murder."

Isabel paused, considering Victoria's words. "True. I do not like this business of having to do one's own killing. However, once you married Stonevale and left Town so abruptly, it all got very complicated. There was always the chance that if you confided in Stonevale he might decide to make an investigation. That was when I began to agree with Edgeworth that you both must die."

"You still have not answered my first question, Isabel. Where is my husband?"

"Edgeworth is bringing him here so that you both may die together in this room. It will all be excessively tragic and very romantic, I assure you. We should not have much longer to wait."

Victoria smiled coolly. "I fear you have made a mistake in sending Edgeworth to fetch my husband. Stonevale will be here soon, of that I have no doubt. But it is my guess that Edgeworth will not survive to accompany him."

Isabel walked over to the window, gazing at the dingy alley that ran alongside the Green Pig. "I fear you have a great deal of misplaced faith in your husband's abilities, Victoria."

"I have a great deal of faith in his knowledge of strategy, madam."

*   *   *

From the dark confines of Edgeworth's carriage, which was parked in a lane near the Green Pig, Lucas watched Victoria alight from the coach and go into the gaming hell. His hand tightened into a fist.

"You have just sealed your own death, Edgeworth. You should never have involved my wife in this business," he said icily.

"Your wife was involved before I was," Edgeworth said with a thin chuckle of satisfaction. "Her death is as important to Isabel as yours is to me."

"What is your plan?"

"I suppose there is no harm in telling you now. You are known for your ability to plot tactics and strategy, Stonevale, so you should be able to perceive the cleverness of my scheme."

Lucas did not take his eyes off the front door of the Green Pig. He could feel Edgeworth's tension filling the coach. The man smelled of it. "You are a coward and a fool, Edgeworth. The combination means that whatever you have planned is bound to end in failure."

Edgeworth raised the pistol slightly, his smile of satisfaction turning to a snarl. "You will see, Stonevale. This time your luck has finally run out. It is not only your life you will lose tonight, but your precious honor. Tomorrow morning all London will be talking about how the Countess of Stonevale left Lady Atherton's reception to carry out a secret rendezvous with an unknown lover in the upstairs room of a gaming hell. They will delight in saying how you followed her and discovered her in bed with another man."

"Who is this other man?"

"No one will ever know because he will have mysteriously escaped while you were busy killing your wife."

"And my own death? How will it be explained?"

"Very easily. What else could a man in your situation do except put a pistol to his own head?"

"Tell me, Edgeworth, was it you who notified Lady Nettleship of Victoria's whereabouts on a certain evening?"

Edgeworth smiled dryly. "I followed her from the ballroom that night, as usual. When I realized you were taking her to that inn in order to seduce her, I thought I saw my chance to enjoy a most agreeable vengeance against you. I was certain that when you were discovered, your reputation would be in shreds. I thought you would be shunned by Society afterward and cast out of the clubs. But you moved too quickly and married the lady within hours. And once Lady Nettleship and Jessica Atherton made it clear they approved the marriage, there was nothing to be done."

Edgeworth motioned with the weapon in his hand. The movement was jerky, betraying the man's anxiety. "I think we've given my associate enough time alone with your wife. Isabel has the instincts of a cat, you see. She wanted to toy with her victim a few minutes before she delivered the deathblow."

Lucas started to step out of the carriage. He stumbled in the process and grabbed at the edge of the door, stifling a groan.

"Damn you, Stonevale." Edgeworth moved back hurriedly, the pistol coming up sharply as he made a grab for his own balance.

"Sorry. My leg, of course. It has a habit of giving way at inappropriate moments."

"Shut up and get out of the carriage," Edgeworth said nervously.

Lucas obliged, moving cautiously. He watched Edgeworth alight behind him.

"There is a flight of stairs at the back. We will use those," Edgeworth said. "I don't intend to have you try to escape in the tavern, where there would be witnesses if I was forced to shoot you."

"Very farsighted of you." Lucas started into the dark alley that led to the back of the building that housed the Green Pig. The shadows suited him well. All that running around at odd hours with Victoria had paid off, he thought wryly. He had become quite accustomed to moving about in the deepest part of the night.

He did not make his move until they reached the stairs. Then, in obedience to Edgeworth's command, he started up the steps ahead of his captor.

"Hurry," Edgeworth muttered, his voice quavering and anxious now.

"This must be exceedingly difficult for you, Edgeworth. Your nerve was always somewhat weak, was it not? I can just imagine what a strain this must be on you."

"God damn you, Stonevale. You will soon pay for that, I swear it. *Hurry.*"

Lucas waited until he was on the third step before he deliberately let his bad leg go out from under him again. He started to reel backward, flailing wildly.

"What in hell's name are you . . . ?" Edgeworth instinctively tried to get out of the way, but the stairs were narrow and he wound up having to grab at the shaky railing as Lucas's full weight hit him. He fought to get the pistol back in line to fire but it was too late.

The struggle was brief. Both men rolled together down the three steps. Lucas paid attention only to the pistol in Edgeworth's hand. Edgeworth's finger began to tighten and Lucas used both hands to force the man's arm across his body.

Edgeworth heaved frantically, just as the pistol exploded. He cried out as the bullet went into his own chest at point-blank range.

Lucas felt the shock and the sudden, terrible limpness that went through the other man. He was vaguely aware of a ringing in his ears caused by the noise of the pistol. Then he felt the unmistakable sensation of warm blood pumping over his fingers.

"God damn you to hell, Edgeworth." He levered himself away from the dying man.

"He did that a long time ago. The day I turned and ran on the field of battle." Edgeworth's eyes were already closing. "You never told anyone about that."

"Each man must see to his own honor."

"You and your bloody damn sense of honor," Edgeworth said, his voice strained and not much above a whisper.

"Which room is my wife in, Edgeworth? Do not go to your maker with murder on your conscience along with everything else."

Edgeworth coughed and choked on blood. "Find her yourself, Stonevale." He fell silent.

Lucas got to his feet, certain the man was already unconscious. He dried his hands on Edgeworth's coat and picked up the pistol.

He had just turned to start back up the steps when Edgeworth spoke one last time.

"Should have slit your throat that day when I saw you lying on that goddamned battlefield, Stonevale. Should have killed you when I had the chance. You have haunted me ever since like some damned ghost. And now you have had your vengeance."

Lucas said nothing. There was nothing left to say. He bounded up the stairs as fast as he could without jeopardizing his balance.

At the top he found himself on a narrow landing. There was a door at one end which opened onto a dingy hallway. The grunts and groans and laughter that came from behind the closed doors told him where he was.

He could start throwing open each door as he came to it, but that would cause alarm and give Isabel Rycott too much time and warning. Lucas reluctantly stepped back out onto the outside landing and eyed the narrow ledge that ran beneath the windows. It was a lucky thing he had a head for heights, he decided.

Victoria was still leaning against the mantel when she caught the trace of movement outside on the window ledge. She knew immediately who was out there. Relief soared through her. Lucas was here and everything was going to be all right. She redoubled her efforts to keep Isabel talking and to make certain the other woman's attention did not stray to the window.

"Tell me, Isabel, do you think you will be able to give up the habit of going about in men's clothing now that you have discovered the freedom associated with it? I vow, I will have a hard time resisting the temptation. It is a marvelous sensation, is it not? Think how much better off the world would be if all women felt free to wear breeches when it suited them."

Isabel shook the pistol menacingly. "Shut up, Victoria. You will not have to worry about that particular temptation after tonight."

Victoria smiled and used the toe of her boot to poke a small stick back into the fire. "Edgeworth will let you down, you know. Weak men may be useful on occasion, but I fear they cannot be counted upon in a crisis. I shall be the first to admit there are difficulties in dealing with a strong man, but I have learned that at least one can depend upon them. Have you ever met a man you could depend upon, Isabel? I have come to the conclusion that they are a rare and valuable commodity."

"I told you to shut up, damn you. Edgeworth will be here any minute and then you will not be feeling so talkative," Isabel hissed.

Out of the corner of her eye, Victoria saw a booted foot slide along the ledge. She put down the sack of clothing and absently fiddled with the cloak that was still draped over her arm. "The thing about talking is that it will help to pass the time until Stonevale gets here."

"Your husband is not going to rescue you, Victoria. You might as well get that notion out of your head."

"Nonsense. Lucas is the most amazing man, you know." She smiled very brilliantly and in that second Lucas came through the window in a shower of glass and shattered wood.

"No." Isabel Rycott screamed in fury and swung her pistol toward the window.

But Victoria was already whipping the cloak out in an arc that caused it to settle over Isabel's head. Isabel screamed again. There was a shriek from under the cloak and then the pistol skittered along the wooden floor.

Lucas looked at Victoria as he straightened and brushed off his clothes. "Are you all right?" he asked quite calmly.

"Amazing." Victoria ran into his arms. "I knew you would get here. Where is Edgeworth?"

"In the alley. Dead."

Victoria swallowed. "Somehow that does not suprise me. What will we do with Lady Rycott?"

"A good question." Lucas released her and picked up Isabel's pistol. Then he yanked the cloak off his victim, who glared at him with her glittering, gemlike eyes. "We don't have a great deal of time to make the decision. We must get back to the ball before we are missed. I suppose the easiest thing to do is simply kill Lady Rycott here and now. The proprietor of the Green Pig is already fated to discover one body in the morning. He might as well discover two."

Victoria was horrified. "Lucas, wait. You cannot simply shoot her dead."

"I told you, we cannot afford any time to think about alternatives. We must be gone from here as quickly as possible."

Isabel stared at him, her eyes full of fear. "You cannot just shoot me in cold blood."

"I fail to see why not. The proprietor will no doubt see to it that both your body and Edgeworth's are removed from his premises and dumped into the river. There will be no questions asked."

"No," Isabel choked on a scream. "You cannot do such a thing."

"Lucas, she's right," Victoria said.

"You care what happens to her?" Lucas asked.

"Of course not. But I cannot allow you to shoot her down like this. Not only will it go against your sense of honor, but I do not want you to have to endure yet another act of violence. You have had far too much of killing in your life as it is."

"You are, as usual, much too softhearted, my dear. I assure you my honor is not offended by the thought of killing the woman who was going to kill you, and one more death on my conscience will not make much difference."

"It will to me," Victoria said quietly. "I will not allow it."

"Then have you any other ideas?" Lucas asked a bit too casually.

Isabel's eyes widened in horror.

"Well," said Victoria, thinking quickly. "I don't see why we could not just leave her here and let her find her own way home tonight. In the morning, she can begin making arrangements to return to the continent."

"The continent?" Isabel looked momentarily startled.

"But I cannot go back there. I will be penniless. I will starve."

"I doubt it," Victoria murmured. "Lucas, make her leave the country. It will serve our purposes just as well as killing her."

"Yes," Isabel said slowly, taking another look at the pistol Lucas was idly pointing at her. "Yes, I will go back to the continent. I give you my word I will leave the country at once."

Lucas considered that. "I suppose it is a possibility."

"*Yes.*" Victoria spoke at the same time Isabel did.

"You will naturally want to leave Town at the earliest possible time," Lucas remarked. "And you will not return for a very long while, if ever."

"No, no, I won't come back at all, I give you my word."

"Because if you do decide to return, you would very likely find yourself tried for murder."

Isabel's mouth fell open. "But I have killed no one."

"I fear you are wrong, Lady Rycott." Lucas smiled. "You see, in a fit of jealousy, you followed Edgeworth to this tavern tonight, where you suspected he was meeting another woman, and you shot him."

"But I did no such thing."

"Unfortunately for you, madam, there will be a signed confession saying you did precisely that. That confession will be produced under appropriately dramatic circumstances should you ever return to England."

Victoria looked at Lucas with fresh admiration. "How very clever of you, Lucas. What an excellent notion. It is the perfect answer. We shall keep the confession and have it handy in case Isabel returns."

Isabel's gaze swung from Lucas's calm, implacable face to Victoria's delighted expression. "But I have signed no such confession."

"You will before you leave this room, Lady Rycott," Lucas said.

20

‍

"**H**urry and get those damned breeches off. We have no time to waste if we are to salvage both our reputations." Lucas opened the sack that contained the amber yellow ball gown. He tugged out the rolled-up silk as the public coach he had hailed a few minutes earlier worked its way through the crowded streets.

"I am doing the best I can, Lucas. There is no use snapping at me. It is not my fault men's breeches are difficult to get off."

"If you think I am snapping at you now, you may rest assured it is nothing compared to what I am going to do to you when we get home tonight."

Victoria stopped working at the breeches, her head jerking upward in consternation. It took her a few seconds to realize he was furious. "Lucas, what's wrong?"

"You have the nerve to ask me that? After what has happened tonight?" He peeled off her waistcoat and shirt, seeming not to notice her bare breasts in the shadows. He was too busy trying to stuff her into her gown.

"Be careful or you'll tear my gown." She thrust her

698

arms through the small sleeves. "I really wish you wouldn't yell at me just now. I have had a most upsetting evening."

"Your evening has not been any more upsetting than mine, and I would like to point out that I am not yelling at you now. I will save that for when we are in the privacy of our own home. Good God, we forgot your petticoat."

"Never mind. No one will know I am not wearing it."

"I will know it. I am not about to let you go back into Lady Atherton's ballroom without a petticoat."

"Yes, dear." She struggled obligingly with the petticoat. "Lucas, I was so worried about you tonight."

"How do you think I felt when I saw you get out of the carriage in front of the Green Pig. You would have been in no danger if you had done as you were told. Here we are. Put on your cloak."

She slid her feet into her slippers and pulled the hood of the cloak over her head. The next thing she knew, Lucas was opening the carriage door and hurrying her out onto the street.

A few minutes later he led her back into the alley outside the Athertons' garden wall.

"I will go first." Lucas found a toehold and hauled himself up to the top of the wall. Then he leaned down to pull Victoria up beside him. "I think breeches are a better idea for climbing walls," he muttered as her skirt hiked up above her knees.

They dropped down onto the graveled walk on the other side. Lucas rubbed his leg and glanced around the dark, empty corner of the gardens.

"The worst is over," he announced. "If we are seen now, the most anyone can say is that the Earl of Stonevale was dallying with his bride in the darkest section of the garden. Not exactly proper, but hardly scandalous. Let's get back into the house."

Victoria ran a hand through her short curls, brushed a few creases out of her skirts, and put her gloved fingertips on her husband's proffered arm in a graceful gesture. She could not repress a small grin as he walked her back toward the lights and laughter of the crowded ballroom.

"There is nothing funny about this, Vicky."

"Yes, my lord."

"I ought to paddle your backside," he said.

"Yes, my lord."

"You have implied before now that I have turned into a conservative prig of a husband, but by God, madam, you have not seen anything yet. Henceforth I intend to show you just what a conservative prig I can be."

"Yes, my lord."

Before Lucas could utter further threats, a familiar figure caught sight of them from the terrace.

"Oh, there you are, Vicky," Annabella Lyndwood called cheerfully. "Enjoying the gardens, I see. I want you to meet Lord Shipton. Bertie says there's a chance he will be offering for me one of these days and naturally I wanted to get your opinion on the man."

"My wife is no longer in the business of hiring runners to investigate her friends' marriage prospects," Lucas said. "She has decided that the time has come for her to start acting in a more refined, conventional fashion."

"Oh, dear," said Annabella. "Are you hoping to turn her into another Jessica Atherton or a Perfect Miss Pilkington? How depressing."

"Yes, Lucas," Victoria asked, turning innocent eyes up to meet his grim expression. "Would you like me to model my behavior after that of Lady Atherton or Miss Pilkington?"

"I don't believe we need go quite that far," Lucas muttered. "If you two ladies will please excuse me, I believe I see Tottingham standing with Lady Nettleship. I want to see if he has read anything interesting lately on manure. For some reason the subject is uppermost in my mind tonight."

Victoria watched Lucas saunter into the ballroom and then she turned to smile at Annabella.

"Lovely party, isn't it?" Victoria remarked as she removed her cloak and started toward the open windows.

Annabella grinned. "Lovely. But, then, one can always depend upon Lady Atherton to give the perfect soirée. And I think if we are very careful to stay close together once we are inside, I can arrange for the skirts of my gown to hide the dirt stains on yours."

Three hours later Victoria sat on her dressing-table chair and watched her husband pace back and forth in front of her. She had never seen him this angry. His voice was low and dangerous and his mood was precarious. It was clear that he had been pushed as far as he intended to be pushed tonight.

"Why in God's name did you fail to follow orders, Vicky? Answer me that, if you can. I told you not to leave the ballroom under any conditions. But no, you could not be bothered to obey a few simple instructions designed to protect you. You must go gallivanting off into the night at the first opportunity."

Victoria frowned. "What could I do after I got that note saying you were in danger?"

"You could have done as you had been told, that's what you could have done."

"Would you have stayed behind in the ballroom after getting such a note?" Victoria said in an effort to defuse his anger.

"That is beside the point. You should never have left Jessica Atherton's house alone and you know it."

"I am sorry, Lucas, but I must tell you in all honesty that if I had it to do over again, I would do it exactly the same way."

"And that's another point. For a supposedly intelligent woman, you do not seem to learn much from your mistakes. As soon as one adventure is concluded nothing will do but for you to start looking forward to the next. Well, I have news for you, Vicky. You have climbed your last garden wall."

"Please, do not make rash statements now in the heat of anger, sir. Give yourself a chance to cool down. By tomorrow I am certain you will see that I acted in a reasonable manner, given the circumstances."

"Your idea of a reasonable manner is totally opposite from my own."

"I do not believe that, Lucas, not entirely. I know I

am too headstrong as far as you are concerned and that
you think me rash on occasion, but—"

"On occasion?" He rounded on her with an incredulous glance. "More like ninety percent of the time,
madam."

"Really, my lord. Surely I am not such a bad wife?"

He stalked past her. "I did not say you were a bad
wife. You are a disobedient, wayward, reckless wife
who will almost certainly wear me out before my time if
I do not teach you some respect for your poor, harried
husband."

"I do respect you, Lucas," she said very earnestly. "I
have always respected you. I do not always approve of
your actions and sometimes you annoy me no end, but
be assured I have the greatest respect for you."

"Yes, you find me *tolerable*, do you not?"

"For the most part."

"That is, of course, vastly reassuring," Lucas said
through his teeth as he turned and stalked back across
the room. "I shall remind myself that you have the
greatest respect for me and that you find me tolerable
the next time you willfully defy me."

"I have never actually willfully defied you, my lord."

"Is that right?" He swung around and came back to
her, stopping directly in front of her. "What about what
you did tonight? Was not that an act of defiance? Of
disobedience?"

Victoria straightened in her chair. "Well, I suppose it
could be viewed as such if one were to put the worst
possible construction on my behavior, but I never
meant—"

*At least have the grace to admit you did it because
you loved me."*

Victoria's eyes flew to his and a great stillness descended on the bedchamber. She hesitated a moment,
cleared her throat delicately, and nodded. "You are
quite right, my lord. That is, of course, precisely why I
did it."

"My God, I don't believe it." Lucas looked stunned
for a moment and then he reached down and hauled

her to her feet. "Say it, Vicky. After all I have been through tonight, I deserve to have the words at last."

She smiled tremulously. "I love you. I have loved you since the beginning. Probably since the night we met at Jessica Atherton's party."

"That was the real reason you rushed off to rescue me tonight, the real reason you would not allow me to kill Lady Rycott as she deserved. You love me." He tightened his arms around her, crushing her close. "My dearest wife. I have waited so long to hear you say that. I thought I would go out of my mind waiting."

"Do you think there will ever come a time when you will be able to say those words to me, Lucas?" Her voice was muffled against his dressing gown.

"Dear God, I love you, Vicky. I think I knew it the night I took you to that inn and made love to you. I certainly knew then I would never desire another woman the way I desired you. But everything went to hell the next day when I walked into the conservatory and realized Jessica Atherton had told you why she had introduced us. All I could think of was that she had cost me far more than she would ever realize. I wanted to lash out at anyone and everyone. I knew you would never believe I loved you after that."

"I was not in a mood to hear a declaration of love just then. But you could have told me later, Lucas."

"Later you were too busy telling me that you would graciously condescend to form a business association with me. You made such a point of painting our relationship as a partnership that I grew desperate. The only thing that gave me hope in my darkest moments was the fact that you never removed the amber pendant."

She looked briefly startled. "The pendant? I never removed it because there were times when it was the only thing that gave me hope."

" 'Tis your own fault for being so stubborn," Lucas said.

Victoria fingered the pendant around her neck. "You could hardly expect me to tell you I was in love with you after learning you had married me for my money. Besides, you were very busy letting me know that you were not about to give an inch lest I take advantage of your good nature and try to manipulate and control you. You wanted my surrender, Lucas."

"I may love you to distraction, my dear, but I also understand you, at least somewhat. You would not have been above using any leverage you could get in our small war and I could hardly have blamed you for doing so. You have my utmost respect as an opponent, but I would much rather have you as a loving wife, Vicky."

"Very nicely put, my lord." She hugged him fiercely. "Oh, Lucas, I do love you so."

Lucas kissed her warmly. "And while we are on the subject, there is another point I would like to clear up. I did not marry you for your money. I started courting you for it, I'll admit, but I wound up marrying you because I could not imagine being wedded to anyone else. Good God, woman, I had to be in love with you. Why else would I have gotten myself leg-shackled to a female who was almost certain to turn my life into a series of near disasters?"

"I suppose that's true enough. Let us not forget you did have a choice. There was always the Perfect Miss Pilkington to whom you could have turned in a pinch."

He shook her gently. "Are you laughing at me, wench?"

"Never. I would not dream of laughing at my husband. I have nothing but the highest respect for him." She lifted her head from his shoulder, her eyes sparkling. "Does this mean you are going to cease reproaching me for my actions tonight?"

"Do not look so pleased with yourself, madam. I have not finished with you yet."

"Really? What is next? Will you have me hauled before a court-martial? Shall I be stripped of my rank and privileges?"

"I think," Lucas said, "I will simply take you to bed and strip you of your nightclothes. Then I shall make love to you until you have been brought to a full realization of your erring ways."

Victoria put her arms around his neck as he picked

her up and carried her to the bed. She smiled up at him through her lashes. "That sounds delightful."

His laugh was husky with passion as he settled her down onto the turned-back bed. "As usual, we are very much in accord in this area of our marriage."

He removed his dressing gown and came down beside her, already fully aroused. He fumbled briefly with her nightclothes and then he tugged her down across his body. The amber pendant dangled from her throat, brushing the crisp hair of his chest.

"Tell me again that you love me, Vicky."

"I love you. I shall love you always." She cradled his head between her palms and kissed him with all the emotion that was in her heart. "You are the only man on this earth I could have married. What other man would discuss the merits of manure with me during the day and climb my garden wall at midnight to take me to a gaming hell? You are unique, Lucas. Now tell me again that you did not marry me entirely for my fortune."

His hands tightened on the back of her head as he brought her mouth close to his once more. "It does not really matter why I married you, my Amber Lady. I am so deeply enmeshed in your coils now that I will never be free. I love you, Vicky. I will put up with any amount of wall climbing, ledge crawling, or midnight adventuring if you will just give me your word that you will love me for the rest of your life."

"You have my most solemn vow, my lord."

She no longer saw ghosts in his eyes, Victoria realized as she gave herself up to his kiss, only moonlight and love, and a passion that would last a lifetime.

Lucas woke once during the night, aware of a familiar ache in his leg. He thought about getting up for a glass of port, but before he could slide out of bed Victoria put her hand on his thigh and began to massage it gently. Lucas closed his eyes again and a moment later he was asleep.

The following spring Lucas went in search of his wife. He found her, as usual, in the conservatory, where she

was working on a painting of an odd little lily she had
just recently received from America.

She had returned to her watercolors immediately
upon rising from childbed the previous month. She had
been greatly inspired, she said, by the news that Reverend Worth's *Instruction in Methods Guaranteed to Create a Beautiful Flower Garden* had sold out the first
edition and gone into a second printing.

The vicar had been adamant that the plates, etched
and hand-colored from original paintings by Lady Victoria Stonevale, had ensured the book's overwhelming
success. He was most anxious to get on with a sequel,
this time on the subject of exotic plants for private
gardens.

A baby's happy gurgle greeted Lucas as he made his
way down the aisle of luxuriantly blooming exotic plants.
He paused by the cradle which had been set next to the
easel and grinned at his healthy baby son. The babe
seemed symbolic somehow of the now-thriving lands
that surrounded the great house.

The gardens outside the windows were lush with
blossoms and the fields beyond were rich and green
with the promise of excellent crops. It was going to be a
good year for Stonevale, the first of many, Lucas vowed
to himself.

He leaned down to kiss his wife, who was busy
mixing colors with her brush, and noticed a spot of
orange on her nose.

"What have you got there, Lucas?" she asked, glancing at the leather-bound volume in his hand.

"A small gift, madam. I had a copy of your book
bound for you."

She blushed with delight as she reached for it. " 'Tis
not precisely my book, you know. It is Reverend Worth's
book."

"I shall let you in on a little secret, my dear. Your
aunt Cleo says people are buying the book as much for
the lovely plates as they are for the vicar's excellent
treatise on gardening."

Victoria examined the book, running her hand over
the leather.

"Oh, I doubt that."

"It is quite true."

"Thank you, Lucas." She looked up at him, her love in her eyes. "Aunt Cleo was right about one thing. You do have a knack for being able to give me gifts I could never buy for myself."

He smiled his slow smile. "And you, my love, have given me far more than I ever bargained for when I went hunting for an heiress."

"Do you know," she murmured, idly touching the pendant at her throat, "I think it is about time for the Amber Knight and his lady to make another midnight appearance on the grounds of Stonevale."

Lucas groaned. "And you only a month out of childbed. Forget it, my love." He glanced significantly at his son. "Besides, you have other things to do at midnight these days."

"Well, perhaps not tonight, I grant you. And mayhap not tomorrow night, either. But soon." She laughed up at him, her eyes brilliant. "You know how you like to indulge me, Lucas."

"Why is it," he asked as he brushed his mouth lightly, lovingly across her own, "that I still ask myself which of us did the surrendering?"

Victoria's answer was lost in the kiss, a kiss that held the promise of a lifetime of glorious midnights.

From *New York Times* bestselling author

Amanda Quick

Stories of passion and romance that will stir your heart

___28354-5	*Seduction*	$7.50/$10.99 in Canada
___28594-7	*Surrender*	$7.50/$10.99
___28932-2	*Scandal*	$7.50/$10.99
___29325-7	*Rendezvous*	$7.50/$10.99
___29316-8	*Ravished*	$7.50/$9.99
___29315-X	*Reckless*	$7.50/$9.99
___29317-6	*Dangerous*	$7.50/$10.99
___56506-0	*Deception*	$7.50/$10.99
___56153-7	*Desire*	$7.50/$10.99
___56940-6	*Mistress*	$7.50/$10.99
___57159-1	*Mystique*	$7.50/$10.99
___57190-7	*Mischief*	$7.50/$10.99
___57407-8	*Affair*	$7.50/$10.99
___57409-4	*With This Ring*	$7.50/$10.99
___57410-8	*I Thee Wed*	$7.50/$9.99
___57411-6	*The Wicked Widow*	$7.50/$10.99
___58336-0	*Slightly Shady*	$7.50/$10.99
___58339-5	*Don't Look Back*	$7.50/$10.99

Please enclose check or money order only, no cash or CODs. Shipping & handling costs: $5.50 U.S. mail, $7.50 UPS. New York and Tennessee residents must remit applicable sales tax. Canadian residents must remit applicable GST and provincial taxes. Please allow 4 - 6 weeks for delivery. All orders are subject to availability. This offer subject to change without notice. Please call 1-800-726-0600 for further information.

Bantam Dell Publishing Group, Inc.
Attn: Customer Service
400 Hahn Road
Westminster, MD 21157

TOTAL AMT	$_____
SHIPPING & HANDLING	$_____
SALES TAX (NY, TN)	$_____
TOTAL ENCLOSED	$_____

Name _____

Address _____

City/State/Zip _____

Daytime Phone (___) _____

ENJOY THESE OTHER ENGAGING AMANDA QUICK NOVELS AVAILABLE ON CASSETTE FROM RANDOM HOUSE AUDIO

WICKED WIDOW

She's known as the Wicked Widow, for rumors abound that she had dispatched her husband to the next world. But Madeline Deveridge has a more vexing problem than her scandalous reputation. Her husband's ghost is haunting her!

Cassette: 0-553-52682-0, $18.00
Performed by Katherine Kellgren

SLIGHTLY SHADY

Antiquities dealer Lavinia Lake's first encounter with investigator Tobias March had been anything but pleasurable. March had ransacked her shop and claimed that she was in cahoots with an underground criminal organization. However, Lavinia soon finds herself partnering with March in his pursuit of a killer, neither of them anticipating the growing desire that arises between them.

Cassette: 0-553-52795-9, $25.95
Performed by Elizabeth Sastre

DON'T LOOK BACK

In this most entrancing tale of mystery and romance, lovers and partners-in-crime investigators Lavinia Lake and Tobias March continue their exciting newfound relationship, with its delicious mix of risky business, rising passion, and now...murder.

Cassette: 0-553-75611-7, $25.00
Performed by Jennifer Wiltsie

LATE FOR THE WEDDING

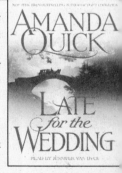

An invitation to a country house party at Beaumont Castle provides a perfect solution to Tobias and Lavinia's most exasperating challenge: how to escape the chaos of London for a retreat from prying eyes and wagging tongues. But the lovers' plans are foiled by the appearance of a stunning woman from Tobias's past.

Cassette: 0-553-75612-5, $25.00
Performed by Jennifer Van Dyck

RANDOM HOUSE AUDIO

Also available as a Random House Large Print hardcover:
0-375-43206-X, $26.95

RANDOM HOUSE LARGE PRINT